# Table of King-tents

# ҺΣ King of ΣⓇotic@™

# ҺΣ Kingdom

Award-winning, Bestselling author
Dapharoah69's
Kingology/Autobiography
Pharoah and Lord Jennings

If you don't love yourself...
How can you truly love anyone else?

## Book 1 of 2

K. Є. PUBLICATIONS

PUBLISHED BY LARRY WILSON, JR
DAPHAROAH69)
**EYE'M FROM GOULDS, FLORIDA**



IN THE EVENT OF MY DEATH: UPDATED AS OF DECEMBER 26, 2011 **JOHN WILSON, TREVOR ALFRED AND KELVIN BROWN** oversees and jointly, with my nieces—with Aliyaih, Sunjaraih, Kamilaih and Latahvia having overruling authority—own all my books, short stories, poems and images for the sake and well being of my above-mentioned nieces ONLY; unless otherwise directed by me in writing, this decision stands.

LIBRARY OF CONGRESS CATALOGING-IN-PUBLICATION DATA HAS BEEN APPLIED FOR.

Edited by Dapharoah69, The King of Erotica®
MEAK PRODUCTIONS AGENCY represents
Dapharoah69, The King of Erotica ™
**Fran Briggs, Cyrus Webb—Publicist**

# S
# O
# U
# L

*By Dapharoah♋*

FOR YEARS Eye WAS AN OMEN THE BIBLE FAILED TO MENTION
Eye TOSSED MY CRAYONS WHEN A SICK MAN SHOWED ME
ON THE SMALL OF MY BACK: 666
LIBERALS TASTED MY ELEGANT EXPLOSIONS
AND FOUND THE DISGRUNTLED WATER

F
A
L
L

ETCHED INSIDE BIASED AND UNFOCUSED INTRUSIONS.
FOR YEARS Eye WAS THE MISPLACED INCISION
IMPROVISED AND PROHIBITED COLLISIONS.
THE ARCHEOLOGIST DUG INTO MY LIPS
AND FOUND THE SUNKEN SHIPS:
HIS FATHER'S BOXERS AND HIS MOTHER'S PANTIES!
THEY LAY ON MY DRESSER HAPHAZARDLY
NEXT TO TWO WEDDING RINGS
AS THEY SNORED AWAY ON MY SHEETS
HE WAS ABOUT TWENTY-THREE
SHE WAS ABOUT TWENTY-TWO
Eye WAS ABOUT THIRTEEN
IN THE DARKNESS SMILING, EATING STRAWBERRIES

WHILE MAMA WAS WORKING...
FOR YEARS Eye WAS THE BLACK SHEEP
THAT LEFT THE TIMID WHITES A FIELD
DESTROYED BY LUSTFUL FIRE
Eye GAVE THEM MY ROD TO COMFORT THEE WRATH:
AND MY SHAFT WAS THE REVERSE OF SYLVIA PLATH
Eye LIVED A LIE WHEN Eye DIED EXCEPTIONALLY WELL
Eye WORE A MASK
TO HIDE HOW Eye TRULY FELT INSIDE
FOR YEARS Eye TRIED TO HIDE MY PRIDE
Eye HURT A LOT OF PEOPLE
AND MISUSED MY RESURRECTED TEMPLE
THE STROKE OF MY WRIST
ERASING MY NEXT OF KIN
WAS IT AN UNTIMELY SIN
TO HAVE TWO FACES
THAT KEPT MY SELF-HATRED UNABASHED?
FOR YEARS Eye MISGUIDED SOULS
FED HORSES THY APPLE
OVERTURNED CHURCHES
DUG MY HANDS INSIDE AN EARTH
WITH NO TURF...
FOR YEARS Eye COVERED MY DIRT
AND STAINED MY SHEETS
EVERY NIGHT WHEN Eye LAY AND CRIED
LAST YEAR Eye ATTEMPTED SUICIDE
Eye HAD GIVEN UP ON MY LIFE
THIS YEAR Eye GAVE MYSELF THE GIFT OF CHEER
AS INSIDE OF ME THE DARKNESS
HAS FINALLY BEEN EXPOSED TO THE LIGHT
PERSONAL STRIFE HAS BEEN GIVEN THE BOOT
Eye NO LONGER CLOSE MY EYES WHEN Eye LOOK INSIDE
THE MASK THAT BURNED MY FACE
HAS LEFT IN YOUR MOUTH A BITTER TASTE.
SO SWALLOW MY SEEDS
TO BURN IN THE BELLY OF THE WHORE
FOR YEARS TO COME Eye WILL LIVE THE TRUTH
Eye'M A PHENOMENAL MAN
WHO NO LONGER HAS TO PIERCE A PIECE OF MY NECK
TO DISCOVER THE TRUTH
ABOUT MY ROOTS, ARCHEOLOGISTS,
LIBERALS—ThE CHURCH—AND THE MASK
THAT BURNS FROM TRUTH.

# LUKE 21: 8-13

8 *And He said, "See to it that you are not misled; for many*
*will come in My name, saying, 'I am He,' and, 'The time is*
*near ' Do not go after them.*

9 *"When you hear of wars and disturbances, do not be*
*terrified; for these things must take place first, but the end does*
*not follow immediately."*

10 *Then He continued by saying to them, "Nation will rise*
*against nation and kingdom against kingdom,*

11 *and there will be great earthquakes, and in various places*
*plagues and famines; and there will be terrors and great signs*
*from heaven.*

12 *"But before all these things, they will lay their hands on you*
*and will persecute you, delivering you to the synagogues and*
*prisons, bringing you before kings and governors for My*
*name's sake.*

*It will lead to an opportunity for your testimony.*

*Growing up in* GOULDS, FLORIDA, *Eye wasn't exposed to successful blacks living amongst bloodshed, rape and poverty. Eye worked hard on myself—against the world—to redeem myself. And eye will work twice as hard to continue writing the books that inspire, entertain, and offer a problem, conflict then a solution. Thank you Jesus for the gift of words. Despite my darkened past, Eye stood up, took accountability, responsibility and made a success out of myself. Eye can now say Eye'm award-winning, best-selling author Dapharoah69—and Eye Am from* GOULDS, FLORIDA.

*And proud of it.*

# My Legacy

EYE WAS HOMELESS WHEN I STARTED WRITING MY FIRST BOOK…

# SUMMARY: THE KINGDOM

*The Kingdom was the hardest book Dapharoah69 has ever written. Going through 9 months of Hell, three alter egos and a deep, dark depression, he has dug deeply into his subconscious and re-created the very sinister past life that would make or break your everyday person.* **HE IS A SURVIVOR!** *And has inspired thousands upon thousands of fans extending all races, sexual orientations and creeds. Before he helped inspire 14,000 + fans to get tested for HIV and other STD's through his publicly spoken struggles via his social network status updates and interviews, he was doing one other thing: suffering, for 20 + years, in silence. He has written memorable characters...now for the first time he gives his powerful testimony. Pharoah has survived:*

LIFE WITHOUT LARRY C WILSON, SR.
THE HELL OF GOULDS, FLORIDA.
A GENERATIONAL CURSE.
FOUR YEARS OF CHILDHOOD RAPE.
FOUR YEARS OF PRISON.
TWO YEARS OF STRIPPING.
THE UNITED STATES ARMY.

*All of his young life everyone had everything to say about the shy introvert who was scared of his own shadow. After 27 years of forced silence...FINALLY the SILENCE is BROKEN! To a therapist named Lord Jennings...*

THIS VERSION OF MY 11TH BOOK, THE KINGDOM
WAS UNIQUELY MADE FOR MY HOMEBOY
AND GOOD FRIEND

# *Felix Soto.*

I LOVE YOU, BRUH.
I'M SORRY ABOUT YOUR LOSS, AND I KNOW THE FEELING.
I LOST MY BROTHER/BEST-FRIEND CHAD TO GUN VIOLENCE
7/27/1997, A DAY I WILL NEVER FORGET.
I OFTEN PRAY FOR YOU, AND I'M HERE IF YOU EVER NEED ME.
TURN THE NEXT PAGE,
SOMETHING SPECIAL AWAITS.
NO OTHER VERSION OF THIS BOOK EXISTS,
IT'S RESERVED FOR YOU, BRUH BRUH.
PHAROAH.

*In Loving Memory of:*

# Angel Soto

November 1987 - January 2012

Felix Soto, my friend
just know that you have family and friends that
both love and will be there for you
when you need them the most...
Eye'm one of them.
Your brother will be missed,
but never, ever forgotten.
Touch your heart and know
he's always there...

The Kingdom was written for my fans and my fans only. But eye must say this, and listen carefully because Eye'm not kidding around. Eye'm trying to save lives through my testimony. For 27 + years Eye've sat back in silence while you all ran your mouths about Pharoah C. Wilson, Jr. The more you spread misconstrued information, never getting your facts straight, the angrier Eye became...Now it's my turn to talk! The difference between you and Eye was simple—thousands of people listened to your rumors about the king and found it all amusing and funny. Check this—thousands of folks around the world have their wallets and debit cards on *standby*...waiting to purchase my response, finding inspiration in my testimony, *Suckah*!

Shalom,

Pharoah

Call Her Queen
Hatshepsut

PHARAOH

The King of
Erotica 4

# The Kingdom

Is dedicated to my sister Chandra McCray and her daughter Kamilaih (my niece).

The Kingdom means one thing, really—Survival. I could not have made it this far without a collection of people that keep me grounded and whole. **Mama**: Good or bad I love you, and I only have one. Thank you for loving me, and for *finally* accepting me for my faults and flaws. **John Wilson**: I love you with all my heart and soul. Thank you for being there for me when no one else was there. Thank you for investing in me, and for offering me sound advice. I love you till my dying breath. **Trevor Alfred:** I love you very much and I will always be there when you need me. **Demetrius Mozell**: My brother where would I be without you? Thank you for everything you've done for me. **Eric Bryant**: Bruh I really, truly appreciate you. You mean a lot to me. I thank you for everything you've done for me. I love you with all my heart. **Luther Evans:** I am so very proud of you Mr. Army Man. I believe in you, and the sky is the limit. **Jhamelia Harvey** and **Sean timberlake**: Thank you for letting me use your computer Jhamelia when mine choked out. Thank you from the heart. I love you. Sean, I love you, Ying! **LaQuandra "Nee Nee" Harvey**: I both love and believe in you. You are a very talented young woman and I am proud to call you my blood cousin. You are the definition of a Queen. **Deborah Fields**: I love you. You are my big cousin, but in some ways you have always been a mother figure to me as well. Thank you for opening your heart and your home to me. **Khambrell Harvey**: you have always been good to me and had my back and for that I thank you. **Tamika Newhouse**, my favorite female author and dear friend, I love you. Check out "The Ultimate No No!" **Cyrus Webb**; **Lee Hayes**, thank you for writing the Forward my brothah. My **Outback Steakhouse Crew (Pierre, Ken Williams, Kelvin Brown [Scooby], Dave, Ben, Elton, Linda, and David)**. You guys get me through my day, especially you, **Scooby** with your non singing ass! **Auntie Debra Brown**. I love you so much! For years you stood by my side. I love you. My sisters **Carissa and Jaime**, and my nieces and nephews. **Shavette**, keep your head up, boo! **Jhonathan Pierre**, love you boo (Honk, Honk!). **Michaela**, you're still my baby lol. My **Grand Daddy**, love you and **Grandma**! Thanks **Tangie** for the love and for treating me like a brother. My immediate siblings, **Christopher Lee** I love you bruh bruh, always. My brother and my hero, **Phillip Michael and Lisa Jo Sorro** (love you Mom!). **Jackie Wilson** (my Mama-in-Law) I love you and thanks for accepting me for who I am. **Jalunda**, I love you sis! **Pamela Edwards, Rhea, Gloria Bronson and Brenda Williams**, I love you both so much, and I will always be there for you both. **Mike Devine**, I love you my Brothah always and forever. **Angel Miller**, I love you boo! **Tara (Red Pepper),** the best Chef in town, and my sister at heart. **Alicia Eaddy,** thanks for understanding me. **Kalvin,** love you dude! **Marco and Sean**, the cutest couple alive. I love you both. **Jay Jay and Uneeik (Unique)**, I love you both, keep your head up! **Miss Bling Diva, Arica Campbell, Damian Campbell**, you keep me on my toes with your lyrical skill. My sister **Danielle Mainor**; my big sister **Attica Lundy**; **Janice Combs** (I love you my queen); **Ethan Ogden**, love you Bro **Antonio (Romel Cee),** keep making those amazing songs. My sister **Ty'Ann Payne** (with her cute self!), and my little brothers **Aaron "L.A." and AnWahn Gates.** The future #1 Boxing Champ in the World, and you heard it here first! And **Janet Jackson**…thanks for inspiring me for 27 years. Rest In Peace to the **Trailblazers and Icons**: MICHAEL JACKSON, RICK JAMES, TEENA MARIE, VESTA, HEAVY D, ETTA JAMES, DON CORNELIUS, NATE DOGG, AND WHITNEY HOUSTON.

# GRAND OPENING

WITHOUT FURTHER ADO, WELCOME.
EYE'M SO GLAD YOU COULD
MAKE IT TO THE GRAND OPENING OF

**ҔΣ KING:DOM**

MY TWO BOOK AUTOBIOGRAPHY.
SPENDING SOME TIME WITH ME
MEANS THE WORLD.

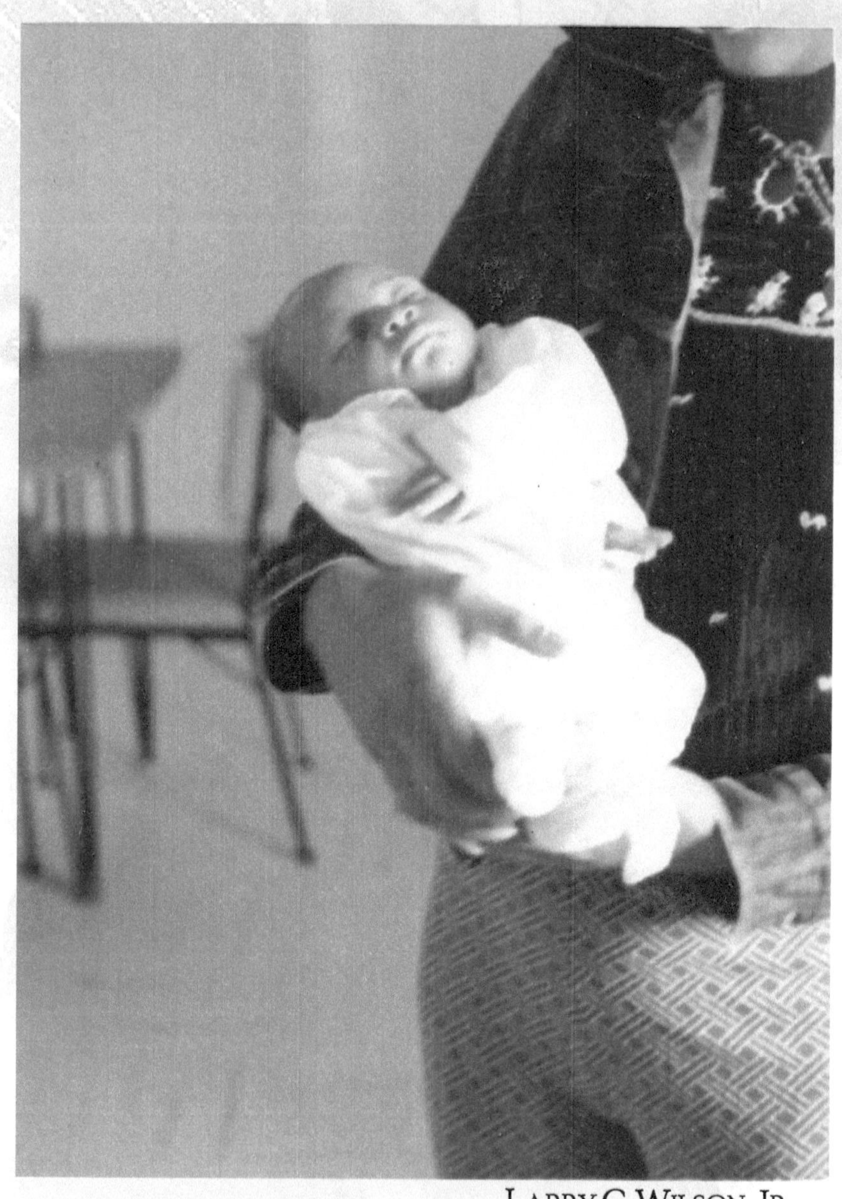

LARRY C. WILSON, JR.
**PHAROAH**
**The KING of EROTICA**
JUNE 26, 1977
BIRTHPLACE: SALINAS, CALIFORNIA

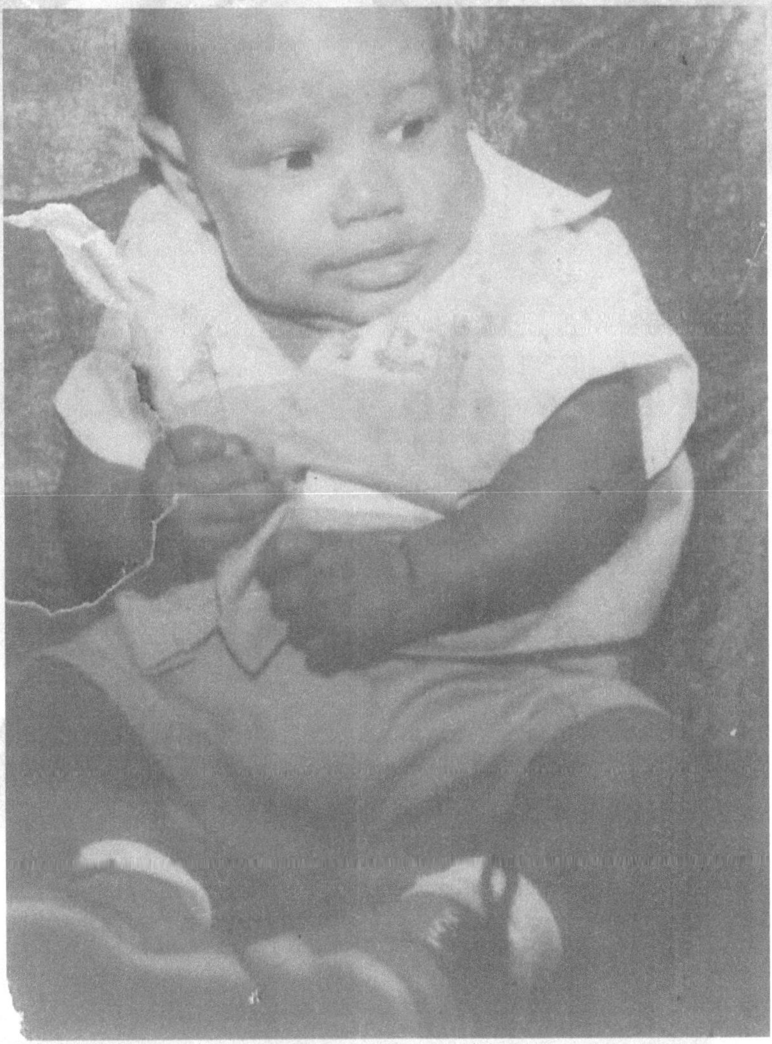

PINE-VILLA ELEMENTARY (KINDERGARTEN THROUGH THE 3RD GRADE)—TWO LOWER PHOTOS—AND CUTLER RIDGE MIDDLE SCHOOL, 6TH GRADE.

Southwood Middle School
Home of the Stars
7th Grade and 8th Grade

Southridge Senior High (Mighty Spartans!!)
9th Grade, 11th and 12th Grade

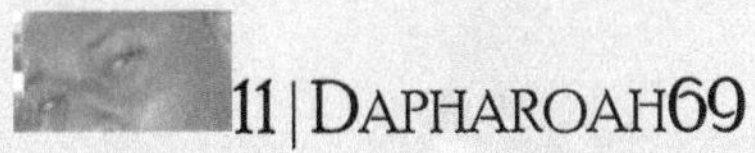

BOYD ANDERSON SENIOR HIGH
THE HOME OF THE COBRAS
10TH GRADE, 1993

SOUTHRIDGE PROM, AGE 17
WON PIROUETTE AWARD. THE HIGHEST HONOR
TEACHER, MRS. CUETO
WON HONOR'S PRODUCTION AWARD, MR. STONE. TV PRODUCTION

MIAMI SOUTHRIDGE
SENIOR HIGH

**SPARTANS**

CLASS OF
1995

*1995*

Age 19-21:
The $tripper Years

Photo copyright Steve Shires, Ft Lauderdale

Thank you Barbara!!! *For buying the very first copy of the king of erotica 1 the throne 5 years ago; 5 years later...it's a barnes and noble.com top 100 bestseller.*

## THE KING OF EROTICA 1

WRITTEN IN 5 DAYS
HOMESTEAD AIR RESERVE PARK
687 PAGES. THE FIRST PROOF COPY.

*Naranja, Florida. The first printed copy of The king of erotica 1, 2006. In the photo I was homeless (and kept it hidden) and was homeless while writing it. Family didn't believe in me. Only a handful of people believed in my dream—*

## LITERARY ACHIEVE MENTS:

—The king of erotica 1, #100, The king of erotica 2 #99 and The king of erotica 3 vip, #71—THREE BOOKS ON THE BARNES AND NOBLE.COM TOP 100 BESTSELLER LIST AT THE SAME TIME. Dapharoah69 shared the list with President Obama, Steve Harvey, John Grisham and The Twilight Series.

—FEATURED IN E LYNN HARRIS'S THE BASKETBALL JONES LITERARY CAFÉ, MAY OF 2009, SIZZLE MIAMI.

—CLIK MAGAZINE TOP 25 SEXIEST, MOST ELIGIBLE BACHELORS;

—Splash Hall Poetry Poet of the Week

—Trimaxx Publishers Poet of the Month (twice in a row), And Erotic Author of the Month.

—500 #1 Blogs, MySpace writing and Poetry category;

—#7 Most Popular Blog, 30th Birthday;

—AAMBC Male Author of the Year Winner, June 2010

—AAMBC Book of the Month May of 2010

—Cyrus Webb's Top 25 Summer Must Reads, Pharoah

—AAMBC Book of the Year Winner:
Call Her Queen Hatshepsut.

—Meak Productions Talent

OF THE YEAR 2010

—Sexiest Male Author of the Year Nominee 2011
—AAMBC Author of the Year Nominee 2011;

—MEAK PRODUCTIONS TALENT AGENCY TRANSPARENCY AWARDS 2011: THREE NOMINATIONS: —ENTREPRENEUR OF THE YEAR —BEST CAMPAIGN,—LITERARY TALENT OF THE YEAR

—COVER FEATURE FOR CONVERSATIONS MAGAZINE JUNE/JULY 2011

—CYRUS WEBB'S SUMMER MUST READS PHAROAH AND LORD JENNINGS, BOOK 2 OF MEMOIRS

**—BUZZILLION'S READERS CHOICE AWARDS FINALIST:**

—The King of Erotica 1 The Throne
—The King of Erotica 3 Vip

—The King of Erotica 4: DeThronment
—The King of Erotica 7: Pharoah

## Buzzillion's Reader's Choice Awards Winner:

—Call Her Queen Hatshepsut
—Some Men Wear Panties

- Author of 11 books

- CEO TKOE Publications

- Editor

- book format artist
- cover designer
- Model
- HIV Spokesperson
- Spoken Word Artist
- Poet

# Freward:

## LEE HAYES, MPA

Author of *Passion Marks, A Deeper Blue: Passion Marks II, The Messiah* and editor of *Flesh to Flesh – An Erotic Anthology.*

WWW.LEEHAYES.INFO

WWW.MYSPACE.COM/LEETHEWRITER

∞

**WHEN LARRY WILSON(PHAROAH)—THE KING OF EROTICA™—asked me to write the foreword for his autobiography, I leapt at the opportunity to become a permanent part of a work of art that will long out live any of us. As I sat to put pen to paper, I wondered what I could say** about a prolific author whose previous work has already garnered over two hundred (5) Star Reviews. What do I say about a literary force who has sold thousands of books and has been a featured novelist in numerous national book clubs? What do I say about a writer who has taken the literary world by storm after being told that his work was good but not **"RIGHT FOR US"** by traditional publishing enterprises? Even further, **what do I say about a man who has overcome many obstacles, including childhood abuse, suicidal thoughts, prison and poverty, who continues to stand?**

I could say a lot, but mainly I'll say that through it all, he continues to stand and push forward.

Bucking the traditional publishing process, Larry has shown us that well-written, salient and unapologetically raw stories that speak of real life issues, including pleasure and pain, will sell, regardless of the **"PROCESS"** that is chosen to distribute the work.

**Through Larry's hard work and dedication to the craft, he has etched out for himself and his works an enduring place in the upper echelons of literature.** Transcending demographic classifications such as gender, sexual orientation, socio-economic conditions, Larry carefully crafts characters and stories that resonate within the human spirit and uplift the human condition. His words are masterful and his stories are powerful.

He is a giant among mortals.

This autobiography will show a complex man, full of doubt and confidence, belief and incredulity, passion and pain. Larry's honesty regarding his sometimes turbulent life is refreshing and courageous. From his own words and his personal experiences, we bear witness to the phoenix rising from the ashes to claim glory. The lessons of Larry's life are universal and we all stand to gain wisdom from his hard-fought years. If the adage that life is not measured by the breaths we take, but by the moments that take our breath away is true, then Larry has led a truly breathtaking life. And, through it all, he continues to stand and push forward.

Once the tapestry of his life is complete, it will illustrate a bold and colorful life that will serve as a unique model for perseverance and it will celebrate the triumphant human spirit.

**Through it all—the pain, the grief, the drama, the sorrow—LARRY NEVER SURRENDERED.** And, through it all, he continues to stand and **PUSH** forward. Through his writings, Larry continues to challenge mainstream conventions while defining life on his own terms, just as we all should. I tip my hat to you, sir. Onward and upward, my brother. Onward and upward.

PHOTO COPYRIGHT RORI-TAI
Dapharoah69 holding Ђe King of Erotica 4 (Atlanta, Georgia) in September of 2009. Tribute to E. Lynn Harris poem, called "Ђe Greatest."

†

EYE HOPE YOU REACHED ЂE DOORWAY TO ЂE KINGDOM in the best of health because Eye wrote this in the best of health. Eye'm from GOULDS, FLORIDA, and Eye both love and cherish my hometown, G-TOWN. But Goulds has also been the source of some of the gravest pains Eye would ever encounter. It nearly destroyed me as a child…Eye wasn't going to release this book, but the outcry of my fans prompted me to do so. Eye may never win an award for this, or get any recognition, but Eye don't care. The release of Ђe Kingdom symbolizes where Eye've come from, where Eye've been and where Eye'm going.

As you may or may not know…Eye replaced "I" with "Eye" as a way of watching my words as Eye write them. So please don't be distracted. Eye wrote this from my heart. In the beginning there was the Word, and the Word was with God and the Word was God and ever since eye was 6 years old Eye've been fascinated with words and dictionaries. With that being said, Eye don't care who does and doesn't like my writings or my books. As long as you get something from them then my job is done. Eye "StimYOUlate then EdYOUcate."

Ŧat's my theme; my motto and what Eye stand for. My autobiography, both parts, is in no way designed to hurt my Mother or my family. Eye love and cherish my Mama with every fiber of my being, but at this stage in my life Eye must take care of myself. Yes, Eye'm a struggling writer, but Eye enjoy each and every obstacle Eye overcome. Because it reminds me that Eye Am alive and Eye Am a Work in Progress.

Eye must depend on me.

My intentions for writing a book that houses a huge part of my soul is to show my fans how Eye survived traumatizing times, and why Eye keep my faith in God, even after the ashes of disaster fumigated the very air Eye breathe.

Ŧe Kingdom is my open love letter to my friends and fans. Eye've scaled it down so that young adults that are going through any type of hell on Earth can pick up my book and see how Eye survived the nasty onslaughts Nature and Destructive People threw my way. Eye write to express myself. And in that Eye have eliminated 98% of the cursing Eye am known for and in its place are words Eye would hope carries the strength of my spirit. But if you want the explicit versions they are available online or to order at your nearest book store.

Ѣe Kingdom represents how one can overcome emotional, sexual, family and financial hardships by embracing God (if you believe in Him—Eye do!), loving the Inner You, becoming a stronger person and moving forward…Taking with you education you can pass on to someone else.

Despite differences with my family, Eye love them very much and Eye always will. Eye used to have a lot of anger towards some of them, but as of today that's no longer my reality because Eye've forgiven myself.

Eye let it all go. Gave it to God. Ѣe Kingdom wholeheartedly reflects how Eye felt during those trying times in my past that used to hinder my growth and maturity as a human being. Eye changed names to protect my family. So the focus remains on my art, and my life.

Eye have no desire to punish those who have wronged, brutally raped, molested or verbally and sexually abused me and that is my choice and MY CHOICE alone. Eye am an adult now, and after years of rage, embarrassment and suffering in silence, Eye have forgiven them and forgiven myself. Forgiving those that wronged or hurt me releases the hold and the power they still held over my life.

No more chains.

Present day, Eye am blessed and Eye love and adore my mother. In a lot of ways she's my Hero and always will be. But my story, my testimony and my life must be told and Eye will tell it in pure, blunt, blood-raw fashion.

My voice, after 20 + years of silence, will finally be heard.

Mama, Eye hope you understand that your son, your first born, is now an award-winning, best-selling author whose life is influencing not only thousands of fans around the world, but Eye've become The Voice of the very fans that buy my work, the very fans that have been abused, the very fans that have been falsely accused of heinous crimes and are too afraid to talk about it. They live through me. Most of all Eye have learned to live, like, appreciate and love me, myself and Eye.

*Sincerely Yours,*

In The beginning There was The Word.
The Word was with God; The Word Was:

**GOD**

*Adam and Eve*

Eye was Made in his Image † His breath is in My Lungs

J E **S** U S

He Never Forsakes You

U N I V E R S A L

JUDAS CRUCIFIXION THE CROSS
DEATH
RESURRECTION

*C o n f i d e n c e*

TH E HOLY GHOST

Beauty/Anger Potentiality/ Abundance

The Boston Tea Party † Taxes and Levies

Angels and Demons

Rent D e b t BLACK

GENERATIONAL CURSE...

W R I T I N G IS MY PASS I O N

# EYE AM...

*Something—Anything, but nothing...*

## BE WHO YOU ARE:

For my fans. If you're straight, homosexual, bisexual, on the Down Low, transsexual, tri-sexual, metro sexual, a single parent, a widow...living with a terminal disease or the Black Sheep of your family: **BE WHO YOU ARE**. Stop bashing each other. We share this earth, yet we die alone and can't take earthly possessions with us. The breath of Jesus is in us all via God breathing Life into Man and naming him Adam. Don't let anyone change you if you're not willing to change yourself, for yourself, by yourself. Don't let oppressors depress you. Embrace YOU. Educate yourselves. Guns are not the way. Murdering each other is not the way. Abuse is not the way. Spreading HIV is not the way. Show your fellow man love. My homeboys in prison, Eye love you all. Keep your head up. We are no better than anyone. No one is good—no one! Everyone is a Sinner—we are all without flaw. Love God, Yourselves—*then* your neighbors. Forgive yourselves—forgive others. Eye haven't always been humble. Eye faced hell on earth and made many bad decisions leading to this point. But eventually, inevitably, Eye matured into the man Eye Am today. Determined to change lives through my testimony. And for those who were abused and silenced...help is out there. Tell someone.

Eye love God more than anything in this world, even more than Eye love myself. Eye love me.

Eye embrace ME.

Eye am the Master of my Thoughts...

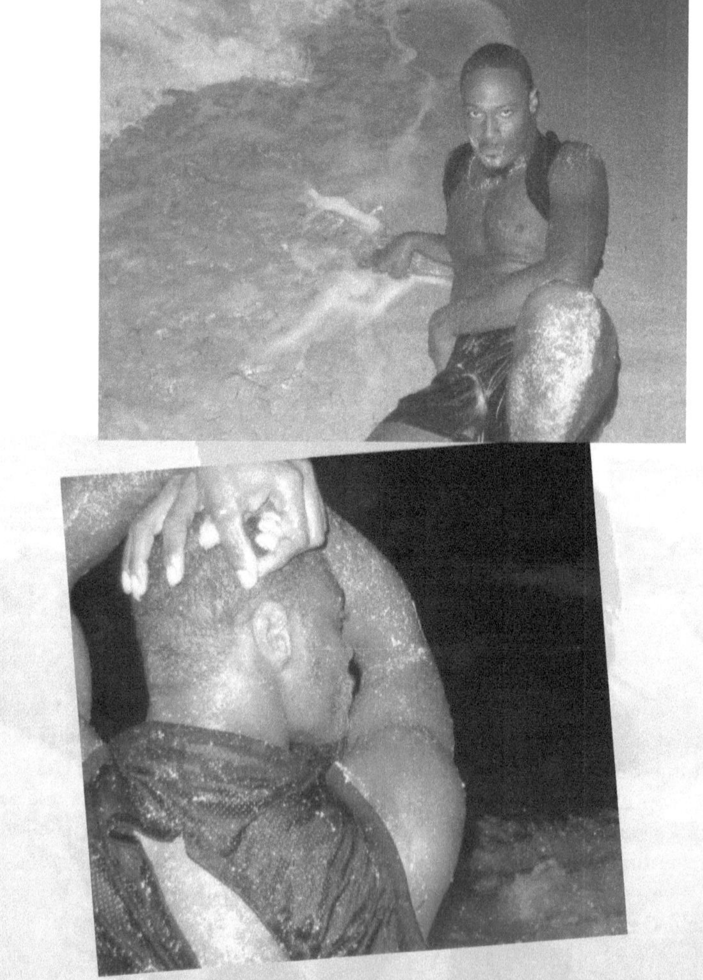

# Dapharoah69 Presents. . .

Eye knew Eye was different from my classmates when Eye was much younger than Eye was now...typing this as an adult male, my fingers trembling across the keyboard...as Eye type the first glimpse into my battered soul. Eye knew Eye was different because, when my classmates acted up in class, my 10th grade teacher—at Boyd Anderson High School (Ft. Lauderdale, Florida)—called their parents, sent them to the principal's office or scheduled teacher/parent conferences. Parents hardly showed up to those scheduled engagements. But when Eye acted up the teacher simply looked up and said, "Pharoah. Stop!" And quietly went back to his lesson. And Eye grinned. Eye grinned so big my heart smiled with me. Eye grinned because he knew that deep down if he called my mother and told her anything about me Eye would make a phone call, too. And it wasn't to his parents— 911 were only three numbers. Three numbers that would destroy everything he ever worked hard on.

So we had an agreement.

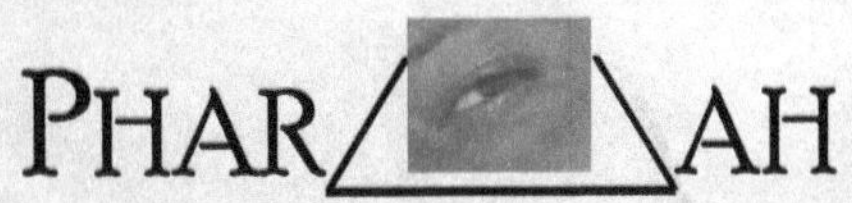

*Eye get thousands of letters and emails from fans. But Nikki's story is different. Part of me can't accept that Eye affect people. Maybe it's because Eye'm from Goulds and Goulds natives don't always get love. Eye met Nikki at the ITLA Pride in Atlanta September of 2009. She was tall, beautiful, well proportioned. For a minute Eye wanted to ask her on a date. Not to get with her, but to bask in her smile. Something about her smile made me give her The King of Erotica 4 free of charge, and her eyes were wide with happiness. The next day she saw me and hugged me and slipped a letter in my hand. Before Eye read it she told me her ex boyfriend killed her two beautiful children some time ago, and then turned the gun on himself and Eye just hugged her. Her kids are tattooed on her arm. Eye share her letter with you.*

# To The King of Erotica From Nikki

*It is not often that I am taken aback by someone or at a loss for words, but meeting you and reading your book has done that to me. Everyday I laugh and joke and carry on as though I don't have a care in the world...but a smile is not always a smile. Sometimes it*

*is a disguise or a defense mechanism that is used to cover up how I really feel inside. I walk around each day with hurt, with guilt, with hate for the world, with hate for God...with self-hate. I walk around loving a man 100% with my heart that took everything I have ever loved and left me with zero. I feel like giving up all the time, like I am in an ocean with one paddle and no compass.*

*Lost with no direction. Should I row on or should I stop and sink? It changes day to day but when I met YOU and FELT YOUR ENERGY, your SPIRIT and to HEAR YOUR STORY for the FIRST TIME I felt HOPE! I gained CONFIDENCE! I felt the URGE to row on.*

*This morning as I write this my SMILE is a SMILE!!!! My laugh is a LAUGH!!! And my world is a little brighter. I would like to thank you because in doing so little, you have done SO MUCH!! And I know it's not only to me but to so many more. Enjoy your day because I am NOW going to enjoy mine.*

MY FATHER MARRIED MY MOTHER
DURING A SNOW STORM IN CALIFORNIA...
*Eye'm ♀♂ and ♀♀*

# Goulds—

. . . ***is a census-designated place*** (CDP) in Miami-Dade County, Florida, United States. The area developed originally as a stop on the Florida East Coast Railroad. The railroad depot was located near today's Southwest 216th Street. The community was named after its operator, Lyman Gould, who cut trees for railroad ties. The downtown area had a post office, a grocery store and an apartment building. Most of this former downtown area is now a part of the Cauley Square shops. The area that became Goulds was settled in 1900 by homesteaders. It received its name when the Florida East Coast Railway built a siding in 1903, operated by an employee of the railroad named Goulds. It was first known as Gould's Siding, and later shortened to Goulds. Many packing houses were built along Old Dixie Highway. Early on Goulds had a reputation as a rough town, with several saloons serving itinerant field workers. Most of the packing houses were destroyed by a tornado in 1919, or the 1926 Miami Hurricane, but were rebuilt.

***If they show that Everest College*** commercial *one* more time with that Oreo cookie-acting Negro barking "Call us now!—Eye did!" every five freaking seconds Eye think Eye was going to scream! If Eye had a dime for every time *that* commercial came on, *ruining* my day, Eye wouldn't *need* to write a book about my life. Because Eye'd be beautiful and dirty rich!—Sigh. Eye'm dreading it, too—*editing* Ђe Kingdom. Using a commercial to mask my unease. Eye couldn't focus. Eye was *tired* from 10 hours of Prep work at the Outback Steakhouse in Islamorada, Florida. On December 25, 2011, my three year anniversary with John, my fiancé, was spent making 75 veggie bags, 50 broccoli bags, carving an x on the ribs after brining them for two whole hours, switching from Prep Cook to *dishwasher* for a few hours—Eye pulled a double—taking a hit on my hourly pay…my brother and my baby had to come get me from work in a light blue PT Cruiser when my shift was over. My feet hurt so badly Eye could barely walk to the car. And Eye still had a book to edit, interviews to set up and promotional books to send out. E. Lynn Harris' death still toys with my mind; the fact that he was found dead of cardiac arrest in his hotel room two months after Eye met him still has me baffled. He was my mentor, and someone Eye visually thought about when it came to success. Eye wanted the same thing—success. But Eye wanted it on an even *greater* scale. E. Lynn once prophesized that some day soon Eye was going to be a superstar.

Looks like it has already happened. So Eye worked in secret to *make* that happen. And now Eye sit back and let things do what they do. Who dies on the way to talk to Tracy Edmonds about *adapting* one of his books into a feature film? Eye didn't know. And Eye didn't think Eye wanted to know the answer. But Eye would get it *anyway!*

When Eye least expected…

*It was bad enough Eye had* to relive the abuse Eye suffered as a child for my memoirs; simply calling it a memoirs sets limitations on my book and Eye couldn't be boxed commercially, so Eye will label it a "testimony." Abuse that was physical, sexual and emotional sets me on auto pilot when Eye re-create my past. It was even worse writing *Pharoah* and *Lord Jennings*, remembering the circumstances that nearly ended my life. Eye will never trust a "therapist—The.Rapist." again.

What you put into the Universe always comes back to the source—and that's energy, the ability to do work. Maybe that's why those Everest College commercials keep coming on my Samsung flat screen TV —Eye bought from Mama for $300. They were *reminding* me of something. One thing was for sure. They were driving me crazy! And that's what Eye took from them—pushing out of my mind the negative.

When going after your dreams *Shut up and Drive!*

*Always f⟷o↓ll⟶o↑w your* ♥. Eye placed a phone call the other day when boarding the JGT Dade-Monroe Connection bus, going to work. After fighting folks (more Haitians than anybody) for a seat on the bus—an every day thing—Eye nearly called out from work and wanted to go back home, but Eye had rent to pay now so there goes that notion. If you didn't get a seat before the bus filled to capacity you had to get off and catch the 8:30 bus. And Eye couldn't be late for work. Eye always got a seat.

While staring out of the Plexiglas window at people pushing and stampeding on the bus, Eye smiled when the lady said, "Thank you for calling Everest College!" through the phone' receiver. Eye shook my head, pulling out Stephanie Meyer's *Breaking Dawn* novel. A 700 page book and Eye was 15 pages from the ending. "Hold for a few minutes."Eye waited till they were all settled in their seats, and the bus driver walked along the aisle, making sure all the seats were filled before he pulled off and gunned it into The Keys. Eye was glad the buses couldn't go over 69 miles per hour.

"Okay, Eye'm back," Eye told the lady. "And you're welcome! Could you do me *one* small favor?"

Eye put the phone on speaker, and she said, "Yes, Eye can! What is it? Are you interested in attending our school?"

Some folks had to get off the bus because they were standing. They left quietly—after paying their money.

Eye shot my cuffs. "Can you pull those *tired* Everest commercials *off* TV?" Eye meant it. "Ya'll *killing* me!"

And the bus roared to life, laughing. Eye didn't even realize they were all in my grill. All Eye could do was smile.

*"Amen!"*

*"They play that commercial 90 times an hour!"*

Eye smiled again and said, "Majority rules!"

And Eye hung up. Eye was happy now. Surprisingly, every happy personality on the bus was attracted to me. *Like attracts like. It works! Start small, Pharoah!*

We talked all the way to work, my friend Brenda Williams and Eye. She was sipping McDonald's coffee, and Eye was reading one other book.

It had an S on the cover…

☯

***When Eye looked in the mirror*** the other morning, after surviving another bout of nightmares, dreaming of the same thing *every* time—a black hole in my heart—what reflected back weren't images of Langston Hughes or the harsh whispers of his renowned poetry.

When Eye smiled to mask an abundance of internal pain…what reflected back *wasn't* the gift of Alice Walker *nor* the heart-pounding cry of Celie reaching out for Nettie when Mr. ______ (Albert)—Celie's husband—viciously snatched her from Nettie's life. After years of abuse. No matter how hard we reach and stretch and grab something, trying with all our hearts and souls to hold on...*sometimes* people, places, settings and *things* become the deciding factor in our lives when we don't have control of our thoughts…

And in *my* case there was only one person that hurt and abused Pharoah for *years*…There was only *one* person that attracted all the negative, bad things Eye encountered in this quantum state called Life: And that was Pharoah *himself.*

And the decisions Eye made. Even before Eye started the 2nd grade…Eye'm silent long enough—when Eye'm writing— to notice lurking ghouls tending the epiphany of timid fields whenever Eye inhale; causing me to gasp from what is revealed from the *source* of my conscious. When others try to destroy me after inviting them over for a cup of tea, Eye scarcely acknowledged *The Color Purple*, but *The Color Black* called the epidermis protecting flesh and bone has been cursed, shamed and tortured. Eye am *plagued* with a Generational Curse. From my Mother *and* my Father's side.

*Combined.* And that was confirmed in Atlanta, from the mouth of two Pastors a couple years ago. One of those Pastors, at a Baptist Church my big sister Attica took me to when Eye was visiting her in 2009, told me Eye was under a Generational Curse from my father's side. It was like Eye was hit in the gut with a wrecking ball. The breath left my body. Eye was stunned—standing before my sister, nephews, niece and strangers, never before hearing this from a Pastor that singled me out the instant he saw me sitting in his church. Eye felt naked. *Exposed.* Caught out there.

He said a lot without saying much at all. He summed up my life and everything Eye went through in one statement, and Eye didn't know how to take it. How do you receive the truth so vividly? Like Eye was caught masturbating by a group of nuns.

His revelation kept me up all night. It played over and over in my mind. The *Revelation* was the interruption of e*verything.* Eye meditated for hours. Images of my past combing through his words immaculately. Eye came to one conclusion while Eye bounced, flew and floated around inside the darkness of self.

*Get a second opinion from another Pastor.*

The next Sunday Eye caught public transportation behind everybody's back and went to another church for a second opinion. Eye followed my gut—my heart Eye ignored. We're never rational beings when we're deep in our feelings. Because that opens the door to real emotion, and emotional attachments has hindered me enough in life, especially when it came to the drama in my family. And that has influenced my thoughts. But not anymore.

Where Eye'm from it reminds me of a 40 year old soap opera. Everybody knows everybody's business.

Eye was handsome in a black suit with cream colored tie—but Eye felt like crap. Eye was having thoughts of giving the gift of writing back to God, because Eye wasn't sure if Eye wanted it any more. Too much came with it. Too much is required to maintain and maintenance it.

Eye've been writing since Eye was 6 years old because Eye had a lot on my mind, and was fighting to survive—over 490,000 + hours of writing Eye have performed in 34 years. Because of the therapy of writing, Eye remained strong and humble enough to *still* be of sound mind, even after the brutal dealings of abuse on every level imaginable implicated on my young life from those Eye used to love and trust the *most* in the world—even the abuse Eye inflicted on myself.

Man wasn't created with trust in mind. God knew Adam was going to deceive him using his own Free Will when he breathed life into his lungs—that's how Thee Holy Ghost took form from the Word, and began to inhabit our bodies. So "trust" wasn't a factor. Those that hurt or abused me Eye truly forgave—and Eye forgave myself. But those are the very ones Eye will never speak to again.

Because Eye will never forget...Mariah Carey's "One Sweet Day" flowed into my ears—on repeat— via my walk man, thinking of and missing my best-friend Chad. It's been 11 years since he was murdered—and Eye am still not over it. It hurts every time Eye think about it. Eye won't be able to talk to him, laugh with him, or lay my eyes on him again. Our faces used to light up Times Square every time we saw each other. Now my face was permanently dark.

Tears fell down my face, my heart in shambles. Before Eye arrived at the Baptist Church, nine Down Low brothahs asked for my number and Eye respectfully declined. A few of them were offended by rejection, and said Eye wasn't all that anyway.

Eye smiled at each of them and said, "And you're not *half* of that, *that's* why Eye didn't *give* you my number!" Enough said.

In contrast, a plethora of feminine men didn't hide their admiration for the stranger on the bus obviously from another city.

My sterling silver earrings caught the rays of the sun and threw beams every time Eye turned my face while observing.

Being a foreigner *oozed* from me, even in my body movement. The fem dudes were respectable, and a couple of them asked did Eye write books and Eye hesitated before

Eye answered. Eye loved that *nobody* knew who Eye was. So Eye decided to be truthful, and Eye said, *"Yes."*

There goes being just another face on the bus.

Shades were raised from ten pairs of eyes. When it *dawned* on them that THE KING OF EROTICA was on their bus in their city *suddenly* Eye was being bombarded for autographs and books, and a few of them made threads about me on BGCLive.com in the Forums, Drama Central. Even those that never heard of me whipped out their cell phones and Google.com'd my tail, pulling back every layer that Eye, the stranger, was. Bestselling Author. My mind was still on the Pastor's revelation. *You are under a Generational Curse from your father's side!* But my heart was on my career.

And my future…

*When Eye arrived at the breathtaking* church, bigger and more elaborate than the one in the 'Hood, Eye was greeted at the door by a tall woman. She had on a long black dress and a huge black hat with white orchids in the front. A floral shop in heels. Before we could get acquainted with each other, one of the feminine dudes from the bus bumped into me and said, "Oops, Eye'm sorry, King! Eye love your books! You keep it real!" And raced up the ante chamber to what looked like the Pastor's Office.

A huge oil painting of him and his wife hung above the door. *Pastors got offices? Eye'm not putting ten percent of anything in this church!*

"Never mind him," said the Sister. She shook my hand and said, "Are you Pharoah?"

Eye gave her pupils hell with my piercing gaze. "Yes Eye Am. And you are?"

She held her pearls, blushing. Eye smelled her wetness in the air. Eye nodded, but remained quiet. "Sister Florence! Eye hear you're from Miami, Florida!"

"Eye'm from Goulds—The Forgotten City—but Eye *currently* live in Naranja—Homestead in other words."

"Eye have family in Homestead. Never been a fan of Goulds. Eye used to live there for 20 years. Eye've been living here for the past 10 years. And Eye *love* it. Eye never tell anybody Eye'm from Goulds. Eye'm amazed that *you* acknowledge that."

"Well Eye *love* Goulds. G-Town holds a special place in my heart." Eye was uneasy.

She ignored me. "Right this way. The Pastor wants to talk to you. He told me to bring you to his office the instant you arrive."

She put her hand on the small of my back, the bottom of her hand resting on the start of my ass. "After you," she said.

And she walked behind me the entire time. And didn't utter another word…

Eye wondered was she going to change her panties before service.

Because they were wet.

*"Mr. Wilson!" said the Pastor,* standing up from behind his desk with a Cheshire cat smile. Eye didn't like cats. And Eye *never* trusted the smile of a Pastor.

The office looked nice; it was nothing over the top. Eye actually thought it fit him rather well. All his doctorates were neatly framed in gold and strategically hanging on four walls. There was a bathroom with light blue tiled everything off to my right—his left.

Photos of his family—his wife was beautiful, his teenage sons (4 of them) clinging to their dad with huge smiles in every picture.

You could tell they were close. My Daddy could go to Hell with a dildo drenched in gas stuck in his…

There wasn't a speck of dust or lint anywhere. Smelled of something chocolate. Eye sniffed again…*this* time Eye smiled and so did he, rubbing his chin. *Caramel*, possibly. Chocolate was an aphrodisiac of mine, and that was the Pastor's complexion.

"How are you Pastor Thomas? Pleasure to meet you."

He refused to break away from my gaze. "The pleasure's all mine," he responded. "Have a seat, Pharoah…so what brings you to my church? How did you hear about us?"

Eye thought to myself for a minute, and Eye said, "Eye looked you up on line."

"Did someone tell you about our church, or give our website?"

*Is this a questionnaire?* "Nah, Eye Googled Baptist churches in Atlanta and randomly picked this one."

He nodded, sipping coffee. "Are you looking for a church home?" he asked, studying me.

Damn! "No. Eye'm looking for a second opinion."

He sat up, setting the coffee mug down. His reaction startled me, but Eye kept my composure. A different tone befell the room. Eye was more relaxed, and Eye felt myself growing *snug* in the cushioned chair resting on Oriental carpeting. Pastor Thomas, on the other hand, leaned back in his chair with his hands crossed.

Something disturbed him.

*He said, "Eye don't know you* from Adam, but something troubles you."

*Who couldn't guess that from looking at me?*

He went on, his voice stern, on the border of barbaric. It took me by surprise, but Eye listened to every word.

"Something deep and dark troubles you. Satan wants you, Son."

Eye grew quiet.

"And he wants you badly! Pharoah Wilson…Eye don't know if you're aware of this or not, you probably are—something tells me you know half of it."

"Half of it?" Eye asked, confused. Eye was lost.

He crossed his hands in front of him. "Yes. *Half* of it. You think you're under a Generational Curse from your father's side, *don't* you?"

Eye was stunned. Eye never told him my intentions for coming to this church, until a few minutes ago, and when Eye called ahead of time and spoke to him Eye never told him two things. One, Eye never told him my last name, but he greeted me as Mr. Wilson when Eye walked through the door and secondly, Eye never told him what the first pastor told me, nor did Eye tell him the church Eye heard it from. His church was 30 minutes away from the other one.

And he knew why Eye was there.

My lips refused to move. He opened his Bible and leaned closer to me. Eye dug my nails in my lap, and hid the pain from my face. Eye had a feeling Eye wasn't going to like what Eye was about to hear. Eye knew that once Eye heard it…it would *change* my life forever.

For some reason we connected. "Mr. Wilson. You are under a Generational Curse from both sides of your family. Your mother *and* your father."

The blood left my face.

*Eye was stone in his chair.*

"There is a *reason* both of your grandmothers died before you could meet them. There is a *reason* your mother took you from your father. There is a *reason* your father pulled a gun on her and threatened to kill her if she left him. There is a *reason* his family didn't think you were his child in the beginning, though you *are.* There is a *reason* you were abused on the grand scale that you have, and Eye apologize for that. Eye wish Eye could be the father you have always been searching for."

"*What* are those reasons?" Eye asked, my voice cracking. Eye didn't realize tears were falling from my eyes. "And Eye don't *need* a father. God is all the Father Eye need."

"Your mother has done something that only God knows about, your father has done something that only God knows about, and you are paying for their ultimate sin. You will pay for the rest of your life, if you don't change your thoughts…"

That was all the confirmation Eye needed.

That, and the fact he had all my books on his computer screen, and the last text interview Eye did a few weeks before Eye arrived at his church. He already knew who Eye was. He did his research on me before Eye showed up.

"Son…you are going to start receiving things in the mail disguised as junk mail, so get ready. The envelope will have a distinct layout along the perimeter with pertinent instructions. Jesus touched my heart. He wants me to tell you to *never* submit. You are making a difference in your life, but the battle between you and the devil is not over."

"And how do you know its not?"

"Easy. When you were a child, he tried to destroy you with things too advanced for your age. And now that you survived it with books to your credit you are on the next level, and that level has a nemesis on *your* level…waiting for you while you go after success."

Eye closed my eyes and pondered his words.

He knew all about Dapharoah♋. The question was…how long did he know…?

Eye would never find out…

*Yin Yang flows from my fingertips* as Eye edit a book Eye like to think of more as a Presentation. My skin tone has become an endangered species, because my kind lived and died the instant Eye took a deep breath outside of Mama's Womb. Experiencing information Overload. Eye was overwhelmed, only recognizing the scent of my mother, and it faded every time Eye wasn't near her. It was a *culture* shock to be outside the womb, brought through a portal called a "coochie."

To grow and find out there was life outside of Mama's Womb still amazes me till this day. Many view pregnancy as a beautiful thing. Bringing a child into the world was a precious gift. There's always a downside to everything, The Law of Polarization never changes. Everything has an opposite, even pregnancy. Eye view it as a form of control and conditioning. Most babies are made because the sex was good. Saying things you don't mean because he's knee deep in it. Slap it up, flip it up, rub it down…take it to the tonsils, arch that back—take that!

Eye think Eye wanna have your baby! And he spits the seed of his intention deep inside you—from the flaming hole of perversion; deep inside something that materialized at the height of pleasure, and died the instant you lay, spent.

And to bring a child into this sick, ailing world wrought with government cover-ups, social conditioning and two selfish, horny parents that didn't love each other (one night stands) saddens me.

Eye didn't believe in *abortion*—but in some instances Eye think its necessary. But the choice belongs with the woman carrying the child. *Not* me. Eye know of some women who only had a baby because the father was cute, or because he had a golden penis, or because he made over $70,000 annually; and he hasn't had that *good, good* (good coochie) until he experienced yours. Ain't that right, Sue?

She had a baby intentionally. The man in question was a certain Draft Pick in the NFL—Eye won't say what number he was in the draft, nor the year for *his* protection. He's a very dear friend of mine. She was a dirt poor hood rat trying to escape the misery of her mother's HUD housing at the time she met him, when he was in the 11$^{th}$ grade.

She once admitted to him, with me present, that she was putting holes in condoms and using a turkey baser to thrash the inner sanctuary of her coochie when he threatened to divorce her when she found out he was gay and liked it in the butt. She let *every* cat out of *every* bag in her closet, nearly crippling him. It hurt to watch.

All Eye could do was shake my head. You trap a man in an unwanted marriage using an unborn baby (when they were in high school), he was forced to make rash decisions.

She was jealous that colleges were fighting to lure him to their school—and any girl that spoke to him walked away with a black eye after she stomped them with her heels.

Colleges were offering him *thousands* of dollars in under the table cash. So she listened to her mother (she didn't graduate school), her father (he has a GED and hasn't worked in 11 years) and her dope dealing brothers (been in and out of prison for years) and put holes in Mr. Draft's condoms, and used a turkey baser to suck the rest of his cum out of the rubber, and inserted the nozzle deep inside her and impregnated herself behind his back.

Now they have a beautiful 7 year old son.

And the *ugliest* marriage in America. But when you see them on TV, they are happy go lucky—with no signs of the earthquakes in their private lives. But Eye saw things with my own eyes Eye could never type in this book, and it changed my view of the world and entertainers.

That's why the media wasn't to be trusted.

Eye know a few women, *personally*, that cared more for the man than the welfare of their kids. Spending child support money on his gold teeth, sneakers and weed.

Joyce Sharps received about $300 a month in child support. And those children had yet to see 5% of it.

Her man saw 80% of it; another 10% for her outfits for the club, her hair and her acrylic nails with Skittles candy glued to each individual fingernail; the other 10% was used for Swisher Sweets, blunt wraps and weed and coke.

My thing was simple: Why didn't the courts assign social workers to women who received child support to ensure they are doing with the money what they are supposed to be doing? Why?

FEMA—for victims of natural disasters—requires you to present receipts to prove you used the money for the *means* of your family, yet the government couldn't require "receipts" when it came to child support?

A man *barely* makes enough to live, eat or survive, yet what he has left she's trying to take him back to court to get.

You didn't know *what* this man had to do for money. He does construction work—two types of construction jobs for two different companies—porn on the side (wearing a mask in straight and gay films), and stripping thirty miles from his home just so he can survive.

Why Joyce Sharps needed all that money when she made more than him? Why did she punish him for her guilty sin? She cheated on him with three of his brothers and he left her ass after walking in on his oldest brother banging her in the booty; and the baby brother was under her, deeply inside her—*double* dong.

After they came in both holes and rubbed nut all on her heavily made up face (without rubbers, and she was banging him without rubbers as well), all of them wound up with HIV, including my friend and he was the innocent bystander in his own relationship.

He adored her, treated her like the Queen he thought she was, worked to help provide for his family—his job got him off the streets, and away from that Thug Life bull. He gave her whatever she wanted, bought her a Nissan Maxima (she was sucking a different penis in it as well, behind his back). And in the end she cheated on him because his sex game was whack. She chose his brothers' gargantuan penises over *love.* Who does that? And now they have a set of twin girls caught in the middle.

Of *emotional* abuse…

## Joyce.

**You turned a good man** into a bitter shell. Now he wasn't *open* to love with a woman. *Currently,* he has a dude on the side—he plays for the *other* team, The Swinging *Cocks* League. Now he takes out on dude's chocolate opening what he could never do to his ex-girlfriend. The woman he wanted to be his wife; now he was about to marry the man of his dreams. They love each other deeply—but they are on the Down Low with it. And that makes me smile.

And like Eye told him. That couldn't have been *me.* The bitch wouldn't have seen the sun rise if she fucked me, my kids and my money over like that to give to my brothers in the end after a good nut. All his child support money she spends on his low life, never-had-a-job brothers.

And Eye'm even madder at his brothers for picking a juicy twat over blood. And trust Eye told them all in their faces exactly how Eye felt, because the children suffered in the end. They were in the middle of all the drama.

YOU PUT NOTHING OVER YOUR BROTHERS—ESPECIALLY NOT ANOTHER WASTED TRICK! Child support money WASN'T THE MOTHER'S MONEY, or your no good ass ex-convict's money…

IT BELONGS TO THE CHILDREN!

**To show how grateful he was** about spending Joyce Sharps' money, he became the object of her sexual desires, fulfilled every single fantasy and once he was done using her body as a urinal he slid back up in it, raw, and they slept the night away. Whenever he was out and about, sometimes spending his nights at his other Hoe's house without giving her a second thought, she had recurring nightmares and could hardly breathe without Daddy's penis deep inside her.

Her kids were thankful when he stayed away. They got tired of listening to her sexual chants on the other side of the wall. Presently, 2012, Joyce's *oldest* daughter was 16, and just had her third child; her first when she was 12—and it was a big cover up in her family; Joyce Sharps had her first daughter when she was 14—and that was a cover up as well. They had a huge family, and only 3% *knew* of it.

Joyce brought man after man around her children when they were growing up, having sex *without* discretion. And eventually her youngest kids, a beautiful 7 year old and a handsome 11 year old are now in the system. The Department of Children and Families removed them from her promiscuous world. But the damage has been done. The seeds of disaster: planted. Lying dormant until the time was right.

There were innocent kids in various systems *globally*—the parents didn't want them; once they reach the age of 18 they are released from systematic prison. A few of them, Eye know personally, told me they were being abused and forced to remain quiet about it by faceless authority figures. They were warned that if they told anyone...they would suffer the repercussions.

Some of those kids are now *adults*, and they have bought my books and reached out to me, giving me their testimonies over the past year, 2011. Suddenly my abusive past didn't matter. There was always someone going through something worse than you. Hearing their stories showed me one thing, and Eye acknowledged it, and accepted it.

Eye can no longer let my past dictate my future.

What's done has come to pass.

*Over the past year—2011—thousands* upon thousands of people from around the world wrote me private messages, admitting to me what they would never tell their families—*ever*. To be burdened with their blood-curdling, soul-lacerating truths makes me uneasy when Eye sleep next to my fiancé at night. Sometimes it brings tears to my eyes because Eye never imagined my gift for writing would open portals to the human experience—and bring about skeletons that scared me half to death. A couple of those testimonies shocked me into silence; others made me fall on my knees in prayer, asking God what it was about my writing that attracts such candid, vivid dialogue.

The last conversation Eye had with a man from New Zealand told me his military father used to wrap him in barb wire when he was ten, beat him with spiked leaves, and left him out there all night to think about ever worshiping Jesus Christ again. He was forced to be a Buddhist. Eye cried for three weeks straight. Eye couldn't even finish writing the opening to THEKINGDOM.

The answer was simple: Like attracts like.

*Eye'm a firm believer of that*. Eye almost feel *guilty* for possessing such a gift. People from all walks of life, folks from different countries, cultures, races and creeds has befriended me on 9 social networks and opened their souls to me on the streets. Eye am always approached by different people with a different darkened past; those that catch the 7:40 a.m. JGT bus would often times tell me their abusive pasts, even when Eye didn't ask. And the looks on their faces is one of relief. To finally open up to someone and tell that person something you held in since you was a child was *invigorating*. And now as adults…to share a part of their lives with me, a regular dude that happens to write books, brings two things to their faces—tears and a smile of forgiveness.

Eye met incredible friends on the JGT because of it.

Gloria Bronson and Brenda Williams (Hampton Inn employees) are my babies. Those two are my world! And have been for years!

Cody, Mike Devine (the best looking 40 year old Eye ever seen, and my brother at heart), Ken Williams (my inspiration), Pierre (my buddy for life) Dave, Kelvin (Scooby, my boy! Always singing at work, getting me through the day), Angel and Bertha; Shavette, Miss Thicky thick. With her cute self (hey, boo!) and a few others.

Eye've given my testimony on that very same bus before half of them even knew Eye wrote books; nearly half the bus didn't realize Ђe King of Erotica rode their bus to work everyday, and a few of them read my books already.

There was hardly a dry Eye around me when Eye gave them my life story in a nutshell, without saying too much. Everyone listened, intently. My boy *Scooby*, with a black skull cap on his head, prison tats on his muscular arms and ear phones in his ears, glanced at me with a smile of both shock and intrigue and said, "Pharoah, *come* on dude! Don't tell us the entire book! We won't have anything to read when we get it!"

By the time Eye was done talking, with Gloria sitting in my lap all the way to The Keys, over half the bus wanted Ђe Kingdom when Eye was done editing. Eye was being Googled and Amazon and Barnes and Noble searched the more Eye talked.

When it came to others…Eye was always there to listen to their testimony without passing judgment. In the past 8 years…4 million plus people have read my blogs, poetry, books, blurbs, online stories and my personal notes. My photos were combed over and seen by 3 million + people.

But they didn't know the source of my pain. Eye never revealed it. Until now. Eye didn't watch the news. You all are going to learn to *never* trust the media. Child trafficking sickens me. To inflict such a punishment on innocence reminds me of the first time Eye was raped. And for the next four years Eye was thought of as a sex slave. Beaten with extension cords. Shattered. Bloody. *Torn* down to shreds. Spat on. Swept under the rug. Forgotten. *Brainwashed.*

In the beginning, that's what got me *through* the abuse.

My writing—the *word—My* words. The words Eye studied in dictionaries and thesauruses since the age of 6, reciting Robert Frost and Sara Teasdale poetry. Writing my life in my journals like my teacher Miss Mike once told me when Eye was 8. She saw it in me *then.* That Eye was to be something great in this life. Eye was winning poetry slams.

Eye was easily beating out high school students because of her faith in me. Eye remember walking up to the microphone in a light blue pin stripe suit at age 8 during my first poetry slam on the Pine-Villa Elementary stage in the auditorium, before it was a magnet school.

Eye was shaking. Eye was n*ervous!* Eye had stage fright. Images of the demon raping me in my home while Mama was at work flashed before my eyes as Eye looked out at the eager crowd.

From the first word of my breath, Eye annihilated the competition one by one because Eye told myself, before Eye uttered started, that Eye was going to *win.* Because Eye wanted something to call my own. Something that couldn't be fondled and beaten.

Something the demon couldn't control.

*Winning was imperative. Anything* outside of that *wasn't* an option. And once Eye came, saw, and conquered…Eye threw my 1st place ribbons in the trash because Eye didn't want my mother knowing anything about it. And Eye didn't want the demon living amongst us to know either. Eye didn't like how empowered Eye was when Eye recited poetry. Eye didn't know how to handle that kind of power.

All Eye wanted to do when Eye awakened every morning when Eye was a child was write and *die.* At age 6 Eye knew in my heart Eye'd seen enough of what life had to offer—so Eye wrote about it every now and then. Eye didn't take writing seriously until Eye met Miss Mike and she introduced me to writing in a Journal. Eye took it a step further. Eye gave each journal a name—my journals were my imaginary friends. Eye didn't care to see anything else life had to offer. Eye didn't care what was on the other side of a sun rise. Eye didn't care what lies behind the sun set. Who cared what secrets lines the crater of the moon? Even the glow was disturbing to me at times.

Eye never dreamed to be older than the age Eye was, being touched and pleasured against my will.

Eye went to bed often times with a sore romp. And the painful throbbing Eye had to nurse with silent tears was unbearable at times. Eye rubbed my booty half the night, crying so hard Eye couldn't breathe. Eye rarely rested on my stomach—not with the pervert in the house. It hurts to lie on my back, but Eye did! With the sheets wrapped around me and my face turned towards the door at all times. And Eye couldn't even tell Mama because the demon said and promised—after once beating me for 15 minutes straight with an extension cord (Eye could *still* smell my own blood years later)—that he would kill my mother in front of me, and then kill me in front of her dead body.

That type of pain no 6 year old should ever have to *experience.* But it was one Eye inevitably (and with great struggle) survived. Eye remember thinking Eye was worthless, staring at the moon in different phases every night. Some nights the blackened sky didn't have a moon at all. The stars didn't compliment any of the purplish clouds either. Just pitch blackness, and Eye stared on for miles. Dreaming. Thinking. Writing in my journals.

*Becoming...*

And that's when Eye was the happiest.

Death never looked so sweet.

*Eye could never bring a kid* into the world. Because the one Eye lost was the child Eye always *wanted.* Eye wasn't going to say anything further about that. The story behind that comes later in this book. Eye couldn't imagine cringing *every* time the telephone rang, *wondering* was that going to be the day Eye find out my child was kidnapped, or shot with a stray bullet, or hit by a drunk driver. Somebody hurt my child the price was death. To Hell with a 911 call! Eye would call them *after* Eye handled the problem. Eye'll be sitting on my front porch with a gun on my lap, blood on my hands, a dead body in front of me and my child's respect.

To hurt my child, if Eye had one, would cause me to remember the shell of my childhood, the one Michael Jackson sings about in one of my favorite songs of all time. "Childhood." *Have you seen it?* Till this day Eye feel in my heart Michael wrote that song for me. And we never even met. Eye wouldn't have the strength to enter a church and pay respects to the most innocent thing in earth's history—a child's life. The *innocence* of a child. Eye couldn't bare it. Eye'd burn the church to the ground before Eye enter and capture the last burning image of a life that was no more surrounded by mourners and flowers.

Eye couldn't *do* it. Eye couldn't handle reading over my child's life immortalized on folded sheets of paper labeled OBITUARY. Who wanted to see their child in a casket and know there wasn't a thing you could do to stop it; there was nothing you could do to erase the pain, you have bouts of suicide; some people turn from Jesus and turn their backs on years of dedicated church service when their child was killed. But the gravest pain of them all: knowing there wasn't a thing you could do to bring him or her back.

That has to be the most helpless feeling of them all. Eye would sulk into the trenches of death. If something happened to my child Eye would slit my wrists because Eye wasn't there to serve and protect.

So NO Eye Am *not* a supporter of procreation—it has too many side affects. Eye think of my own beginning. The Alpha of my life. For 9 months Eye was set on idle inside the addictive warmth of Mama's womb. The cusp of my parents' sin brought me into the realm of procreation—finalized through conception. The dawn of my existence sprouted from the gentle folds of Daddy's deepest pleasure—Mama's *Nookie.*

Who knows what was on Mama's mind when she gave it up to my father, who was an ex-convict at the time with thoughts of the Blood gang and the streets. Who knows what was on my father's mind when he buried the treasure between Mama's legs. Who was to say that Mama wanted a marriage, but Daddy only wanted good sex?

Her coochie becomes Pandora's Box, and Daddy's fiery seed created me. Pharoah C. Eye'm named after a man Eye haven't seen in 32 years.

Eye had no knowledge of a world outside of her stomach as Eye went through trimester after trimester. But Eye knew

Eye had life, but no memory of what the inside of Mama's body looked like. There are things Eye will never stand for.

And it's simple.

Eye won't ever be set on idle ever again.

*Eye may not have Oprah Winfrey's* money nor have an estate built next door to Bill Gates. Eye may still catch the Metro Bus and walk around sometimes broke, but my bills are paid; Eye may not be the heir to the Hiltons or the Lucas's or phone E.T. after the war in Vietnam left me a schizophrenic mess and now Star Wars are in VA Hospitals silenced and brainwashed through various psyche meds. Eye may not be what you expected me to be.

After the storms, after the abuse, after the suicide attempts, after the ups and downs of the ghetto…Eye still became something great in this life. Beyonce, you aren't the only one that was "here." Eye lived, and Eye loved, too.

Eye'm an award-winning, bestselling author. Eye was here. And Eye'm blessed with that. You see, *God*, Eye didn't ask for much and what Eye did ask for Eye *couldn't* live without. Writing was my passion and Eye loved it. Eye may have gone to prison 14 years ago. Eye may have a past. Eye may not be what Mama *preferred.* Eye may not drive a flashy car and on my fingers the brilliance of materialistic jewelry doesn't gleam, shine, tinkle or bling.

Eye may be a lot of things in your mind and Eye may *not* live up to your expectations. Eye may have done some things that disappointed you. And half of the people Eye know say Eye'm out of control because Eye'm out of THEIR control. Eye may sleep late into the day and bump Janet Jackson from my iPod at night writing these books, incarcerating my soul behind an eclectic blend of words. Eye may *not* be perfect. My crap *may* stink. But there's one thing no one can take from me. Eye'm the first one in my generation of people to be a successful multi-*published author.* THE KINGDOM marks my 11th published book, and my 16th published work to date. My other submissions were in SHANI MCDOWELL'S MOCHA CHOCOLATE (CHECK HER OUT), VOICES FROM

WITHIN (A BODY POSITIVE MAGAZINE BOOK CLUB FEATURE, MAY 2001), AND THE WSN NETWORK ANTHOLOGY.

To say Eye arrived as an author/poet on crystal stairs would be to deny all the Hell Eye endured to make it there. The road less taken was a fabled one. Traveling down *that* road left me mentally baffled, soulfully constipated and crazily different.

So Eye never traveled that road again.

*Some members of my family* stood in my way. Some of my cousins bashed and talked about me so badly Eye *distanced* myself and haven't lost any sleep. Eye never verbally let them know of the things that were whispered about me. A few of my friends turned on me because Eye don't talk or act the way they want me to; and Eye had to cut a 16 year friendship with one of my female friends because it wasn't worth saving.

Others cling to me hoping my books take off. Little do they know Eye am aware of the sharks in my waters. Eye didn't let that stop me.

Before my books were published the fellahs on the block denounced me.

*"Boy pick up a basketball or slang some weed. Niggahs in the 'Hood don't write. We survive."*

Unfortunately, Eye took a look at his living situation and shook my head at his small bedroom in his sister's house and she wasn't even his half sister. She was a good friend turned sister, the Negro didn't even have goals and his dreams died before he turned 13, so he never fully matured into a man. He was a freeloader.

Grudgingly, Eye looked at ole boy and said, "You survive?"

He grunted with pride. "*Eye* survive."

Eye laughed, holding my stomach. "*Barely.* You are not Pauline's brother, boy, and we all know it."

He fell dangerously quiet, raising the bottom of his shirt and revealed his dusty, dry Smith and Wesson. Was Eye supposed to be scared? Eye'm from G-Town! The sight of a gun didn't make me stutter, not like it used to when Eye was much younger with no sense of direction.

His eyes were narrow slits of anger. Eye guess Eye offended him. *Yawn.* "Dude don't *press. Don't* press forward! You're walking in dangerous territory."

"Did you pay your rent yet, since we survive? Dissing me because Eye wanna be a writer?"

He snapped. "You live with your Mama and you don't even have a book out!"

Eye smirked. "At least she's *blood.* Pauline and you, blood? Naw, dude. If you and Pauline have the same Mama she must be a transsexual because there's no way you and Pauline are related. Yet *you* live with a stranger. Where did you *meet* her? Yea, that's right: on a Hook up site on the Internet."

He was shaking his head, contemplating pulling his gun.

"Pressed?" Eye asked. "…You *mad*? Daddy skeet dog water because you're blacker than tar, Pauline is white as snow, full blooded German at that and you're *telling* people she's your biological sister? Can your dumb ass *spell* German? Can you spell dumb ass *in* German? Eye'll spell it: N-O-T- Y-O-U! She doesn't even wash your dirty draws. All over the floor. Now that's just nasty, Niggah and you're trying to chin check me?"

He grabbed his crotch, looking around making sure his "dope-dealing Niggahs" were out of ear shot; and they were over on the court sweating, playing their version of basketball, or was it *screamball* because that's all you heard. "You ain't *anybody*, dawg," he managed to say.

Eye had him. Eye had thug boy publicly drowning in his emotions, something all thugs chanted they didn't have and to have that feeling was an emotion itself, or have they forgotten. "Not to be *is* to be!" was the *real* answer to the question, but stick with that Shakespeare stuff if you chose to.

Eye said, "At least my Mama washes my dirty drawers and cusses me out about it, won't let me hear the last of it. No wonder roaches are starting to pile in your kitchen."

"And why is that?" he asked, setting himself up.

Eye shot my cuffs. "They said you keep a dirty house. That's why a lot of people won't let you live with them. And for your info Eye don't have a roach infested kitchen. You couldn't go to *Joe's Apartment* because a crackah eating with roaches wasn't your idea of the Last Supper so you're over here in my face trying to get into my properly sealed stuff. Eye don't keep it in the closet. Eye like it on the living room couch, Niggah; beat it up to the bedroom! Then once you're done leave and go back to your German Hoe."

He was offended. "You will *never* get published!" he promised. "Ain't nobody reading that sappy gay shit. Don't come at me like that, disrespecting me!"

Eye tucked my chin back. "Gay? Did you just *go* there? Gay?" Eye asked and everybody was listening.

"Shh, shh…shut up!" one of them said, observing us.

"Eye'm trying hear what Pharoah 'bout to say!" another one of our friends harshly whispered.

Eye didn't hold back. "Did you say that when Eye sucked you up?"

People were in an uproar of laughter and Eye held my head high, chest out and dared his uneducated ass to mess with me today. Eye had a razor under my tongue, a pocket knife in my sock and a small can of mace on my keychain. Bring the funk, Sucker!

He didn't know what to do—run, or face his demons. "Shut up, Pharoah!" he stammered. "What the hell, yo! You're character assassinating me like *that*?" His hand was on his gun.

Eye kept my cool. "You don't remember? Lemme remind you...You've been begging to toss my salad a while back and Eye told you Eye wasn't a woman. Eye didn't have a vagina. Eye had a penis. And it varies. A booty hole is coochie's alter ego. Yes, they're *both* holes. But two *different* feelings. Some like the booty more; most like the coochie better. Win, win. Who gives a f? We like what we like."

His eyes bulged out of his head. Eye wanted to laugh, but Eye didn't because this scene could turn bloody and deadly in a millisecond, so Eye was on guard, my hand already by my backup plan—mace.

He scowled. "What m*e* and you did together was private!"

*Oh, boy! Here we go! The Song of the Trade. Spare me. You got all that mouth in public but can't handle what Eye have to say in your face in public.*

*And you call yourself a man.*

*Yea, Okay.* "Yet you just confirmed the union between us with *that* statement; you don't do well under pressure do you?"

He looked around wildly, wanting to run. People were pointing and laughing at him. A few of my friends told me to go easy on him. Um, when Pee Wee Herman lick a pig's butt then *maybe* Eye'll think about it. "Eye never did anything with you!" he stammered, stuttering as he spoke.

*The Judge can tell the jury to disregard, but the damage has already been done.*

"Yes you did!" somebody yelled jubilantly, and more laughter rose from the crowd like a whale coming up for air; a roar of a sound that rendered me speechless for a brief second, and actually made me inwardly smile.

Eye said, watching him quiver against the world, the way you're going to be in the end, when you are judged for judging others, "You beat it up and spanked it, tooted it up to those chapped lips in dire need of Chap Stick and Eye slapped my cakes up and down your tongue, having a bout with your nostrils. Your lips are *sweating* trying to keep up. Remember Eye said, 'Eat it, smell it and tongue it good? You say you keeps it one hundred percent real—okay, *let's* keep it 100! *Be* about it, Niggah! Eye *told* you to talk hit to dirty to my buttocks and you *did.* Telling me Eye taste like cotton candy—Foxy Brown doesn't have *anything* on me! If you're a thug you don't need a fifteen minute break…you got fifteen minutes to convince me *your* undercover-Bottom-ass is a thug!"

His erection contradicted his words and he's caught out there, images of him knee deep *in* it sending his pulse to the state senate.

Looking like Kelis and Nas in court.

Forty something thousand a month for child support payments?

Chile.

This baby better look like Brangelina!

Kelis ain't no Janet Jackson.

That's a lot of money for a 'hood looking chick. And that's what Thug Boy was looking like.

A Hood Rat. Ugh—what did Eye ever *see* in him anyway?

Easy.

A Good Time.

And *nothing* more.

He had enough.

***He ran at me, swinging perfectly*** executed blows at my face... He's 5 feet 7 and Eye was 6 feet 2. Eye mean, *dude*, you're a little Chihuahua; Eye'm a Pitt Bull.

Impulsively, Eye stepped to the side and pushed him in the back and he flew into awaiting chairs and a few tables in his friend's front yard. From the corner of my Eye a few dudes from the basket ball court (across the street) were rushing over to where the action was, watching Thug Boy get embarrassed.

He jumped up like jack out the box and Eye shook my head. "Eye don't wanna fight you, *dude*. Eye'm a writer. You're a thug—um, yea—ok...we got differences; so mind your own and stay outta mine and we're good."

Eye walked off and left him to his fans; he was calling me every name in the book.

Say what you want, but at least my draws were clean.

***Eye nearly listened to everyone*** about turning my back on writing when Eye first started taking it seriously. You couldn't expect those with nightmares to kiss you good night and say Sweet Dreams. There's nothing *beautiful* about a nightmare. Don't listen to Beyonce. Follow the sound of your own heart, and stop worshipping those entertainers. They'll lead your ass straight to the sulfuric lake of fire if you're not aware of the lyrics you utter from your lips. Write your own lyrics, follow your *own* heart.

Writing, for me, was therapeutic. But during that time Eye whole-heartedly cared about what people had to say about me. Eye would throw my manuscripts away just to—days later—dig them out because my heart told me to.

Satan knew what Eye was to become as an adult, that's why he tried to destroy me as a child…

And when he failed, when Eye survived his full aerial assaults, he wore my family members like dark cloaks and tried to destroy and dismantle me emotionally, spiritually and physically. Eye've become a little bitter because of it.

Around me are walls made of steel…*reinforced* to trigger the warrior in me whenever battle rams rummage my terrain. Eye worked really hard and sacrificed a lot for my books, my art, my craft and my legacy.

Because of self-loathing and self-induced hatred and pain, Eye went though suicide attempts, jail, porn, scandal and scorn to arrive at the point Eye'm at in my life. Eye'm not proud of some of the things that Eye've done; but bet your tail Eye didn't regret a thing, and Eye never will.

Before all of the book writing, Eye was a normal Negro from Goulds, Florida. No particular direction in my life. *Never* thought of writing a book, but Eye *did* write for leisure and to free my mind of the ghetto's slavish chains that kept me shackled. Eye've been through a lot of abuse as a kid, which fuels nearly *every* character that Eye ever created. My talent comes from the source of my pain.

My father—Daddy, whatever—had never been there for me. He has some *splannin'* to do. For years Eye wrote down the thoughts my anger so masterfully created about him. How Eye wanted him dead. How Eye wanted him to suffer for abandoning me. How Eye wanted to beat him till he couldn't move. *Any* man that abandons his child doesn't deserve to live, and that is how Eye thought back then. As a mature male, Eye have *no* right to dictate who lives and who doesn't.

Eye have taken control of my writing and honed my skill. Eye have been poet of the month on so many online forums Eye lost count after twenty. Eye have written my life and my soul in my Myspace Blogs that have reached #1 over 500 times in the WRITING AND POETRY category. Eye have *amassed* a following that come to me because, no matter if it makes me look good or bad, Eye write from the soul.

Because of my sexuality doors were slammed in my face. Eye sent query letter after query letter to publishing houses, more doors slammed. One publisher said Eye was very talented, but there was no room for gay fiction. And my book wasn't mainly about that at all.

My stories were for *everybody*. Eye write from every point of view. If you could withstand the lies on the local news and CNN you can read my books. Another publisher rejected me without a second thought. So Eye took charge and did it myself. Eye told myself what could Pharoah Wilson *do* that's different from all the other authors out there—and separates me from Zane because in my eyes Eye Am just as powerful?

Eye created ҔE KING OF EROTICA 1: ҔE ҔRONE (while Eye was homeless), which was intended to be a promotional book Eye was going to give away for free; to show people who Eye was and what Eye represented. Half of the book was erotic sexual short stories exploring why people have the type of sex the way they do. And the other half showcased my knack for poetry.

To make a long story short, in four plus years Eye sold over 100,000 + copies of my work, was featured in the Express Newspaper, featured in E. Lynn Harris Literary Café, been featured in over 600 book clubs worldwide; worked with J.L. King on my book *Some Men Wear Panties* (only to get burned by him as well), was picked by CLIK magazine as one of the *Top 20 Most Eligible Bachelors in America*, beating out thousands of men, made the front cover of *Conversations Magazine* (June/July summer issue) and a ton of other achievements Eye'll leave to myself.

All thanks goes to God.

*Shalom*

The Kingdom
Begins now

# PrΣludΣ

## Hanging Like Janet's Breast

*Eye'm blessed. Blessed to* be writing the books Eye wanna write with full creative control. Hell, Eye own everything. Eye use these books to elevate myself. Who would have thought the tall, bony Niggah who broke it down dancing all over Naranja, a Brothah that was raised in Goulds, Florida, coming from the beautiful ROLLE family would be writing books that got wives, sisters, aunts, mama's and grandma's reading, and burning the midnight oil like crack pipes to a baser's lips till their eyes slide past the last word on the last page.

And DL men, too. Pa$torS. Elders. Military personnel. Police officers. Men who were cocky sonofabitches with Operation Overload Testicles. *Scary*, isn't it? That a few of the well-seasoned men talking amongst your circle of friends or in your family Eye probably slept with back when Eye was a confused, battered teenager. And *yes* they knew Eye was a minor when they sexed me, leaving my spent, exhausted, worn body the image of wet cocaine—won't sell nowhere.

When Eye was in my late 20's, Eye used to wonder how their wives would feel if Eye told them what their police husbands were *doing* to me with their hardened swords behind their slacks and batons. Those cops told me they were married *after* we had sex, so you must not have been *that* important if he failed to mention that when he got at me for the first time online on a gay hook up site when Eye turned 27 years old, begging me to replace the burnt out fires of a defunct marriage held together ONLY by your kids. And like a fool Eye gave in to the attention, and it nearly cost me my own soul. Eye had a public display picture and my literary achievements posted to inspire. One man in question had hit me up, hiding behind a question mark default picture saying he read my book online; some married women were talking about it in the hair salon his oldest son worked. Could he take me out to eat? Eye said Eye didn't *date* question mark Niggahs and Eye wasn't looking for a Keeper. Eye got to talk to you at a distance. He sent me a picture of him to my email. Wow. He had a crisp police outfit on. Handsome. Masculine. Looking at him you couldn't tell. Eye liked him. Eye always wanted to get sexually roughed up by a cop. It used to be a secret fantasy of mine, only because Eye detested authority. All that pent up aggression turned me on.

My immaturity getting the best of me, we hooked up and he couldn't keep his hands off me. We were in a thirty dollar a night motel he paid for with cash. Eye lay down with my misery playing symphonies all over the bed and his scrumptious Station 4 body and when he was inside me wearing an expired condom, he groaned seductively in my ear, telling me Eye had some good booty, that Eye felt better than half the niggahs that gave him some good head and good sex to get out of a ticket or to stay out of jail. Eye rolled my eyes, knowing he was full of it. He grunted a final time, thrust deep inside me, kissing my shoulder blades. His saliva cold against my skin from the roar of the AC.

Eye felt him jerk and his toes curled. Abruptly, he pulled out and the condom burst and cum spilt all over the place.

Eye was angry. "You used an expired condom?"

He looked delirious. "Shit, Eye am married you know."

*As if that explained it. What did your marriage have to do with a grown ass Cop wearing expired rubbers?* "YOU ARE?" Eye asked in shock. He avoided my eyes. "Yes. When Eye got married the condoms Eye bought Eye didn't need anymore; so Eye put them up on the top shelf of my closet. So when Eye hit you up and agreed to hook up Eye wanted you so badly, Niggah. B*adly!* So Eye had condoms on the top shelf of my closet and Eye used one of *them*."

Disgruntled, Eye walked past him.

He was alarmed. "Where are you going?"

*As if you care!* "Home," Eye said.

"Pharoah!" he called out, yet Eye ignored him. Didn't want any more dealings with him.

"Pharoah!" His voice was darker.

Eye spun on my heel and barked, "*What*, cop? Eye got a bench warrant or something, Sergeant?"

He showed some sympathy. Not much. Just enough to keep his erection. He wanted more of me. Eye saw it in his eyes. *What about your unsuspecting wife*, Eye thought gravely.

He said, "Eye know you're mad."

His cologne lingered in the air. A faint smell. "Yea, Eye'm pretty pissed. But Eye gotta blame me. Eye should have known better. Eye lay with cops Eye get undercover prostitutes with a mental problem."

He was offended. "Go to hell!"

My eyes were wide. "*You* go to hell! You the one banging Niggahs so they don't get tickets and jail time dummy! Not me. And you got a wife. Eye swear!" Eye started humming the theme song to *Looney toons*.

He clapped, nodding his head, mocking me. "You ain't no perfect Niggah!"

"Go file a report, cop."

Eye opened the door.

He started plea bargaining. The tough guy exterior turned into a puddle of sand instantly. He fantasized about sandy beaches—making love to me. Fantasy Island projects only fear. The only sand Eye ascertained was incarcerated in an hour glass—the sands of time, moving like the prince of tides to escape the death of my flesh. And that's where Eye build my sand castles. Eye'll furnish them later—The Law of Time deeply embedded inside my cranium for safe keeping, like a good book hiding amongst the dismal in the public library.

"Pharoah. *Don't* leave. Eye am addicted to that booty, baby." He was rubbing himself, getting hard again, narrowing his eyes and licking his lips, his nipples hard as hell.

Eye protested. "You brought me to a cheap, pissy motel. Goes to show how much you think of me. Tell your wife Eye said *hi*."

"*Pharoah.*" Jumping out of bed, naked, he grabbed my arm. "Come to my house. Eye will show you where Eye live. If my wife comes home early tell her you're my officer in training. Eye got a spare uniform in my closet. But Eye must get another shot of the booty. Damn, baby! Where have you been all my life Niggah?"

Eye didn't know about that.

"Ok," Eye said, the side of me that needed to validate becoming my Scarlet Letter.

*Sincerely Yours, Dummy,*
*The Weakness of Your Flesh...*

*So we get there*—to his expensive home. Eye was having second thoughts, but his possessive hand on my upper thigh convinced me to go further—*deeper* into a vortex. He lived large: big house, Cuban wife and Cuban parent-n-laws. His black ass need to remember his roots—ass kisser; brown noser! We go inside paradise and everything was inspired by the Spaniards. Nothing in his crib reminded me Eye was with a black man. Gloria Estefan old song CONGO playing at a moderate tone. Eye cringed. Eye felt like Eye was on a space ship with an alien that forgot he was an alien—Eye was a foreigner, Bahamian illegal alien in his home, though Eye was born in California—and didn't know what the hell a spaceship looked like. He was pointing at a Frisbee. Eye *never* liked Gloria's music anyway. Those fake lion fur pillows weren't fooling me. There were *too* thick to be real. Lions have sophisticated manes and fur. The fake stuff on those pillows. Nah. FLEE MARKET! There was more Big Lots and Family Dollar *crap* all over the place than anything. Paradise got some discrepancies. Looks were deceiving the hell out of my senses. I was tasting the smell and hearing the vision. Confused, in other words…

We get in the well-furnished den and a home tutor, a short, chubby white woman with thick dusty glasses, was frustrated because The Cop's 7 year old black son (from a ghetto black chick filing for Section 8) couldn't learn Spanish at his father's pace. He was struggling with it, and everything in his eyes told me he didn't wanna learn about Cubans or learn their language. Get this. The Cop didn't know Spanish either. So why he making his son learn it? The rebellious look in his son's eyes went over his head.

He kept saying *Rojo* was the color for white and *Blanco* was the color for red when it was the other way around. *Rojo* was red. Eye knew that. *Reciprocate it, young man!* Eye wanted to say, but Eye refrained. It wasn't my place to pry.

Deeply offended by his son's insolence, The Cop *angrily* stormed over to his son and snatched him up like Raggedy Ann and Andy. He meant business. "*Learn Spanish, boy!* DO YOU HEAR ME? Your step Mama ain't here! Cubans are taking over Miami! They even got Cuban bitches in the black neighborhoods giving out housing applications! Blacks in high positions are being set up and fired and in their places are Cubans with no experience with fake resumes and doctored applications. *You will learn Spanish!* You *will* marry a Cuban woman and give me Cuban grandkids! Do Eye make myself clear?"

Eye was appalled. Eye couldn't believe what Eye was hearing. Social conditioning. If you can't beat 'em, join 'em, 'ey shit head? Wrong. *Granted*, some of the things he said about Cubans were true, especially the firing of blacks and the hiring of ineligible Cubans. Eye loved Cubans, personally, but a lot of them Eye couldn't stand for the life in me. The boy seemed to cringe under his father's stern hands and demands. A split second decision compelled me to snatch the boy from his no-good father. Eye put him behind me, like a lion protecting its cub. And Eye pointed at the dumb ass cop.

Eye had fire in my eyes. Abuse is abuse. "Don't you DARE try to brainwash this innocent child in your retorted racist bull!" Eye turned to the child and got on my knees while his father looked on in mock horror. "Look, lil dude. You are BLACK AND PROUD! SAY IT LOUD LIKE JAMES BROWN!"

"Eye'm black and Eye'm proud!" the kid chided happily, clapping. "Daddy! Eye *like* him! Who's he? What's your name, Sir?"

Eye grinned, patting his head. "My name is Pharoah. Eye'm a writer."

Out of the blue, The Cop pulled me to my feet, brutally slapped me, pushing me into the wall—**BOOM!** The framed photos shook.

The pain rocked me silent.

Eye had to gather myself.

The boy was scared.

He ran over to the couch and sat on it, covering his face.

*Emotional abuse…*

***He started punching me***, and the boy looked up, stunned, then he rushed up to his father and said, "DADDY STOP DADDY DON'T HIT THE NICE MAN!"

Brutally, he punched me in the jaw, opening the door and pushing me out into the front yard. Before Eye could recover, The Cops whistled—**WHEEEEEE**—a piercing sound that reverberated my ear drums and four pit bulls, salivating at the jaws, were rushing towards me, in the distance. Eye was so scared. Eye didn't know *what* to do. My eyes were wide with fear. "PLEASE!"

The King of his domain, he stood in the door way, with his son at his side, gripping him—like a puppy—by the back of the neck like he was going to shove his nose in dog poop. He forced his disheartened son to look down at me. "Tell my son you were playing a joke. He's black/Cuban and proud."

*Over my dead body! So help me Jesus! Eye'd rather get eaten alive by those* dogs *before Eye help brainwash your procreated seed.* "PLEASE!"

*Had to think fast!!*—the dogs were almost ten feet away from me. Spit falling from their sharp teeth. Eye could smell them—a terrible stench. This told me they hadn't been properly bathed. Eye ran towards a loose pipe Eye saw, over by a small bush of sorts. Those dogs were grunting, determined to tear me a new existence. When Eye turned—two dogs jumped for me and Eye beat them like Eye was Barry Bonds on steroids. The smile stayed frozen on The Cop's face, his son crying. Eye was so afraid an unknown life-force took over me and Eye felt myself getting stronger and Eye beat the third dog till he wasn't moving. The smile slowly died from The Cops face. Eye had to relieve those lips and teeth of their duties—and it took a pole to do it.

The fourth dog retreated, running off in the opposite direction.

Eye looked up at the sky. Trying to calm my nerves.

The cop smiled at me evilly, and then slammed his door closed.

Not before catching the smile on his son's face.

That no harm came to me…

**Exhausted, Eye walked towards** the bus stop. It was a few minutes up the road from THE WANNA BE CUBANIGGA'S home. Eye dragged the pole like wasted dick, nah more like Linus van Pelt and his blanket on Charlie Brown. Eye was tired. Mentally drained. Embarrassed. Breathing so hard it felt like my alter ego was breathing too.

Maybe Eye should believe in the Great Pumpkin and see if the outcome was all the same, since Linus was the only one that believed it was real. Felt like it was Halloween, even though there was nothing *sincere* about the situation Eye was in, and, looking around the unfamiliar neighborhood, some folks giving me off handed glances, Eye didn't see any pumpkin patches.

My clothes were stained with dirt.

Eye was sad because a prejudiced man was trying to raise his black son into a Cuban.

Eye said a prayer for him. Jesus, protect him.

Amen.

So be it.

*Detachment.*

**Eye reached the bus stop,** and wiped sweat from my face. Dropping the pole, Eye covered my face, sat on the green bench and balled.

Eye cried so hard Eye couldn't stand it.

Jeez, Eye did it again—*slept* with someone to validate myself. Eye thought Eye matured.

Eye thought Eye grew up. Eye thought Eye changed.

That's what Eye been telling everybody to save face. And Best Face goes to—" (drum roll) "—*Another* bitch—*not* you!" And now Eye was abandoned.

Abandoned by The Holy Ghost.

That nut certainly wasn't worth the *recall* Eye put on repentance.

*Some straight dudes read my books in secret*; DL men read my books online; a few gay men openly discuss my books; and in the last forum Eye attended a straight man showed up to a gay meeting because he said he wanted to understand his gay brother better because, reading my books and my life, he realized and remembered we all fall short of God's grace.

And to you fake, *judgmental* Catholics! Just because you tote and quote The Bible didn't mean your *twats* spit fire and it dang sure didn't mean you can split the Red Sea with your clits.

The biggest freaks are in the *church.* And the real church is the human body, *damn* it—The *real* Temple. *Not* a freaking building! So if Eye wanna chew gum then *damn it* stop me from opening the wrapper.

Don't get me wrong, true Christians Eye love and respect and they have the right to feel what they feel for *any* reason. But you fake Catholics could *Suck* It! For real.

Save your bias because Eye didn't give a damn!

Just know that when Jesus comes back *He's* starting with the church, ha, ha! Because He knows of the phoniness within his organization. The last catholic that told me Eye was going to hell for being bisexual wound up eating me out in his sister's bed (she was out of town) with his baby mama and his son's pictures turned face down on the dresser.

A few months later, after being there for him and actually growing close, he bought me a ring from Kay Jewelers (worth $5,500) and asked me to marry him. Negro, *please.* Eye'm sorry.

Niggah, please!

*But Eye did keep the ring;* Eye pawned it and used the money for promoting and advertising The King of Erotica Empire, took my nieces out to eat at Applebee's, bought them some toys and gave them $25 each and taught them how to properly spend money. That was my thing. Eye would buy stuff and give the money to my nieces and teach them how to say "Hello" to the cashier with a smile; never let the cashier see how much money you working with and always be aware of who's behind you or watching you without making it obvious. Pretend you're getting a candy bar and change your mind after a quick sweep of your surroundings with your eyes. They were quick learners. And always ask for a receipt.

As far as Mr. Catholic, he turned on me when Eye rejected the idea of *marrying* another man. Eye didn't even want to marry a woman. Eye didn't believe in marriage, not with half the friends Eye had cheating on their spouses, so why would Eye throw myself in the Lion's Den of Commitment? [Presently, as of January 21, 2012 Eye am getting married to my fiancé on my 35th Birthday in new York].

He called me all sorts of names. Throwing God in my face, damning me to Hell.

Whatever.

All around the world same song, dude. And he tries to judge me? Because he publicly prayed about something he secretly did, did that automatically give him leniency or a sexual pardon to be publicly forgiven for the very dark things the public didn't quite understand?

And Eye was left like Janet's tit to defend my honor? Eye think back to when Eye was 15.

When Eye wasn't writing a book, but creating journals.

When Eye didn't love myself until *after* Eye made a journal entry. Eye wrote my life at such a young age and when you can write an autobiography on just your childhood alone you KNEW you've been through a lot. But we didn't celebrate those kinds of events, like a normal person, that wasn't a celebrity, surviving. We praise Hollywood and fake bitches with fake tits, fate noses and bleached skin. That's what we celebrate.

But *not* today.

# Kari Morrison interviews The King of Erotica:

*We're you sexually abused as a child?*

Yes. Eye went through four years of rape, from age 6 through 10. And was raped again when Eye was 10 by my older female cousin, and she was pregnant with my child when Eye was 11.

*Have you lived life with feelings of shame because of the abuse you suffered as a child?*

Yes, Eye did. Throughout my teenage experience, Eye slept with people twice my age out of resentment and anger. Eye hated life and Eye hated me. Eye tried to commit suicide over 100 + times before Eye turned 15 years old. Eye hated even being black.

*Have you felt that the sexual abuse was somehow your fault?*

*Yes*, initially Eye did think it was my fault. Eye thought it was my fault because Eye had given in to the rape and started to enjoy the pleasure and Eye hated me for it for a very long time. When my older cousin was doing what she did, Eye didn't know at the time sex with a cousin was wrong and she kept telling me it was right.

*Did you feel "groomed" by your abuser at the time of the sexual abuse—or did it take you years to realize you had been "groomed" by your abuser?*

Yes, it took years. He was my step father at the time, and he abused drugs and alcohol when he did what he did. He was never sober when he raped me, always under the influence of something. With my female cousin, she always said Eye was handsome, that Eye was her favorite cousin and that she was teaching me how to treat my wife if Eye ever got married by using her body as a tool.

*What kind of emotional damage did the abuse do to you as a child and as an adult?*

Eye suffered internally. Eye suffered in silence. Being that Eye did go to a couple of my mom's cousins for help when Eye was a kid and they turned me away, didn't believe me and called me every gay name in the book so Eye grew quiet and even as an adult. Eye was accused of molestation when Eye was 19, a crime Eye never committed so Eye was also on the opposite end of it. But Eye remained strong and knew in my heart Eye would still remain humble and giving, but Eye was insecure with me. Eye hate a crowd, don't like strangers around me and now 13 years later Eye'm 32 and Eye'm bestselling author Daphroah69. Eye use the abuse to help others through my books.

*In what ways has the abuse affected the rest of your life?*

The abuse brought me *closer* to God. It brought me closer to self-love and endurance. It made me a very strong man. Eye live with HIV, and that caused me to stop making excuses and take accountability for my actions. Eye learned to work through adversity. Eye learned to depend on myself. Now, being one of the most popular authors on Facebook, Eye use my past and experiences, good or bad, to help my fans and they have written me about how my testimony have changed them. The fact that the abuse didn't break me, it has affected how Eye view things. Eye forgave myself for the abuse.

And Eye moved on to help others who may not have a voice...

# SupΣr bowl Sund@y

# 2010

**Love. Eye have a problem with** you, Love. You see, Love doesn't *love* LOVE, but love has blinded me beyond measure. Sometimes, what does love truly have to do with it when so many people Eye've encountered were some of the most demonic beings Eye have ever met and don't care to see ever again in this life, the afterlife, the next life, nothingness or whatever followed death? Where's the love within themselves? Maybe they love being corrupted, envious, jealous and menacing. It has come to the point where *sometimes*, for *others* Eye simply *don't* care—truly. Most don't even care about themselves. Do Eye love myself? No, Eye don't. Not fully, at least. And it may shock a lot of you, but Eye haven't loved myself for a very long time. Eye used to stand naked in a mirror and tear myself down, finding things to hate and letting it fester inside, withering confidence. They say you can't love anyone else if you don't love yourself and you know how Eye feel about someone's opinion of anything. Eye could care less. Eye love *writing*, yes, but my soul was intricately lost somewhere in the mountains of text Eye've penned for 28 years. My soul roams and breathes in the books and short stories and poetry Eye've written. No one knows of the mountain of work Eye've created from my source of pain, which stems from my childhood and was fueled by the grotesque things Eye had to endure as Eye matured in age. Eye'm whole and complete when Eye am creating—full circle, Eye don't know it begins nor where it ends no matter how you stare at it. A part of me colors every emotion, tickles every character into the memorable beings they have become to the point Eye sometimes can't separate fact from nonfiction and those characters feel so real, like they are people Eye know and trust, people Eye see and speak to daily.

A piece of you, and you and you, and yes you may be an immaculate part of my characters DNA. Maybe that's why they feel so real. If you've ever hurt me, chances are Eye've written about you in my books.

Eye've tried to force myself to love myself, but to no avail. You can't force love. Some of my family didn't even like or love me. And that was fine. Eye could survive on my own. Eye got two balls. Eye've stopped living for others a long time ago.

Eye'm just learning how to live for myself, finding ways Eye can become a productive young man despite the checkers of my past. If that means Eye have to take myself out on a date, treat myself to a movie clad in a nice suit and neatly barbered, if that means take a walk around the park or doing some pushups in my room after treating myself to some ice cream then so be it.

*Now*, looking back a year plus ago when writing this account, Eye didn't just live for *Pharoah* anymore. Eye live for my family and my nieces Aliyaih, Sunaraih, Kamalaih, Khia, Kayla, Latavia (Latoya Hush, the love of my brother's life, is going to have her labor induced Tuesday, January 24, 2012, and Eye am excited to meet Latavia!) Trinity, Legacy, Alana Shay, and a few others. And Eye live for the man that now takes me out, treats me like a King and was building a home with me. He's 280 pounds of intellect, graciousness and love. Eye *never* loved anybody as much and as hard as Eye love John Wilson and Eye never will. Eye am by his side in sickness and in health and we haven't said I Do quite yet.

He was my earth, the air Eye breathe…For three years Eye was unemployed, and he carried me, even when Eye was too weak to care for myself. The times Eye hurt him by being lippy and selfish wasn't fair to him, and through his patience and abrupt flashes of anger Eye have been redefined.

Reaching out to another dude because John and Eye couldn't communicate was something Eye will regret. Eye cheated on him at heart, when it wasn't even my intention and Eye made excuses for it. He packed his shit and left me dry. Gave me something to think about, and eye couldn't make it through the night without wanting to die, going through withdrawal, making the transition…from committed relationship to single man, cold turkey.

But the next day, after he took my brother Demetrius Mozell—*yes*, you're still my brother—you always were, even when Eye called myself cutting you off—and my sister Starling out to eat at the Olive Garden on their wedding anniversary he came inside a room we shared, a room he abandoned when he left me and changed his number, and within minutes we were a couple again.

Eye am truly sorry for ever hurting my baby, and Eye am so thankful he wanted to be my husband. And Eye was looking forward to that which will be the happiest day of my life—to take vows and mean them, and to have his Mama (and my boo) Jacqueline Wilson stand in for us. Eye love her with everything in me, always. She's my mother, too.

Eye've even tried to buy myself some love. Sex toys. Females. Men. Janet Jackson stuff off Amazon.com. Strawberry daiquiris. Clothes. Shoes. You name it Eye tried to buy it for some form of happiness. Material possessions were created to keep you preoccupied from reality. And just like a brand new shirt you've worn over the next 5 months, everything purchased grows old and tired; then again you're bored with yourself trying to find new entertainment. Eye've taught myself to search deep inside myself for the guiding light Eye need to grow as a person, as a son, as a grandson, as a lover, as a best friend, as a companion, as an author and as a friend. Sometimes that search comes up empty, especially when Eye'm feeling down and out. But as of lately Eye've been somewhat happy, but truly not at peace.

As a Cancer, Eye was very sensitive and very insecure with my body and looks. People say Eye'm sexy, but Eye didn't *feel* sexy. Eye was told Eye was one of the sexiest male authors in the world [and that was complimented by being nominated Sexiest Male Author of the Year], Eye was also told that Eye have become a Gay Icon, my face being a recognizable force throughout the gay experience…but Eye didn't feel it when people told me that every day. Beat it in my head so much Eye scream when Eye hear it. OH MY GOD! There was more to me than *looks*. Beauty was skin deep. Eye never think too much or myself or think Eye'm just the Mecca for good looking men. Nah. Honestly, as long as Eye look good to my significant other, as long as Eye look good to me then it's all good. Eye was made in God's image. That in itself gives me a very fine arsenal Eye can take with me through the darkest of times, and the brightest of days as well. Sexy, sexy, sexy Pharoah…What about my heart, because *that* part of my being was suffering and haven't fully recovered from the arsenals of life. Eye come in contact with people from all walks of life, even entertainers, on a daily basis, and only 40% ever ask me how Eye'm doing, or how was my day. The others couldn't look past my face, seductive eyes or my toned body and scrumptious tush.

Eye don't *think* Eye'm sexy. Eye hardly look in a mirror and when Eye do Eye am tearing myself down to shreds relentlessly. Look at those buck teeth, Pharoah. Change it. Look at those Dr. Spock ears. Chi…cosmetic surgery perhaps? Look at those big ass feet. But my ex lovers used to suck my toes and tell me Eye had gorgeous feet to be a man; whatever that meant. Look at that lazy Eye. Squint a little more when Eye am being photographed so it doesn't show. That cone ass head you could do without; but you're stuck with it. And my penis. My package. Could be a little more…but Eye've never had any complaints.

FLAWS, FLAWS, FLAWS!

That's what Eye see when Eye examine myself.

Writing as *Ђe King of Erotica*™, the part of me that protects Pharoah Wilson, Ђe Human, and Dapharoah69, Ђe Robot—Ђe Author and problem solver, wasn't enough for the things Eye had to dig up. Eye didn't look forward to reliving anything from the past, but Eye had to…so Eye could complete the project.

Going through old photographs and letters was a bit awkward; some of those letters and photos Eye hadn't touched in years, worn from the sands of time, photos yellowing at the edges…so imagine going through my feelings for an autobiography. Some of those feelings Eye hadn't explored in years, other feelings Eye've tried to push out of my mind and pretend Eye never felt them. But man wasn't designed to control his emotions. It's like discovering a trunk you long ago put on a shelf and now years later you open it, choking from thick black dust and you remember this and *oh my God*! Eye remember *that* and the smell of the old mixing with the atmosphere of the new totally blindsides you and gives you a different perception of the very things you've survived.

Never did Eye think my life was worth documenting or talking about. But much have been said about me and bitches *weren't* me so why was my name in their mouths?

Those gruesome years Eye suffered in silence hindered me once upon a time, when Eye didn't have a backbone; back when people hurt me and hung me out to dry in the blistering sun and Eye would keep a still tongue and reddish, painful eyes. All the times Eye was forced, as a child, to never utter a word has gotten the best of me. To break it Eye started writing my life story, to face my demons.

All the nights Eye've begged God to kill me in my sleep went ignored. God has his own plans for my life, and Eye was glad Eye knew those plans now.

Bestselling author.

Eye used to go to my cold, empty bed *begging* God to kill me. Please don't let me wake up the next day, Eye begged and begged and BEGGED with everything in the core of my soul and Eye fell into complete darkness after a sweaty masturbation session. When the sun rose on my face Eye awakened another day, facing another fight, barely making it through another struggle and taking yet another shower to wash away the dried productivity of my palms, wrist and torso. Eye stood on my own when Eye battled perverted adults while growing up. Pharoah had to fend and fight for himself. Stand on my own two feet.

Eye never understood why. When Eye published my first book, it all made sense. Reliving the past was a demon of its own design, and it was one Jordan River Eye had to cross. Thank God Eye made it across without drowning or being swept away by its ravenous waters. Eye've written notes, jotted down ideas, and rewrote this opening a gazillion times.

Because Eye had so much to say, but nowhere to start. If you thought a ghostwriter wrote my books then Eye hate to burst your bubble. Eye write my OWN books, slap my own self on the cover, and edit them too.

Yea, Eye talk a lot of noise. Because Eye could back it up. Don't you think Eye *know* Eye spelled

**/P\H/A\R/O\A/H**

wrong? Eye know its spelled P-H-A-R-A-O-H, *duh*!

Eye spelled it wrong for a reason.

It was a reminder of something.

2

In 1983, The Year of Michael Jackson's *Thriller*, my first grade teacher, Miss Left, at Pine Villa Elementary, now a magnet school, said we were slaves. Problem was she was a skinny white bitch throwing slavery in my face, and the other black faces as well, making us inferior to ourselves. My friends believed everything she said. But for some reason Eye begged to differ. Because everything Eye learned was contradicted at home.

"Were we Kings and Queens?" one of my friends asked her, looking at a picture of Queen Elizabeth hanging on the wall.

In fact everyone from Christopher Columbus to Napoleon and white rulers were hanging everywhere. Not a black face in sight—except for the faces of me and my classmates. White folks loved using the out of sight, out of mind trick when it came to our history like Eye wasn't going to ask questions; and when they meet me they suddenly viewed me as a threat, because not only was Eye going to ask questions that my classmates would want to know the answers to, but Eye would research it on my own for clarity and when Eye started doing that the lies were uncovered. My grandfather always taught me to research things for myself.

She gave me an off look. "No," she said. "You used to be *slaves.*" She turned away from me rather quickly and my heart burst with disappointment.

"Can Eye use the bathroom?" Eye asked, upset. Eye just wanted to run and keep running till Eye got tired. *You were only slaves! You were not Kings and Queens!*

She didn't look up at me. "Sure, go ahead."

With a sense of purpose, Eye walked out the class, and made my way down to the library.

Eye was on a mission and Eye didn't really know what Eye was going there for. But a library had all those beautiful books and Eye loved books.

Eye loved books because my Granddaddy was an avid reader and had shelves and shelves of books and tons of *National Geographic* magazines and Eye LOVED those maps.

Eye collects *all* of them. Eye tried to read all the books at the same time, many different worlds uncovered and leaving me enlightened and entertained. My grandfather Burke was the most important man in my life at the time. A seasoned Air Force Vet, he did 28 years and retired a Master Sergeant. He spoke seven languages, was always easy going and knew about the type of things you never knew existed.

Once Eye walked inside the elementary school library, having lied about having to pee, Eye looked around, for a book. Eye saw it before, but Eye couldn't remember what it looked like. The library seemed the size of four classrooms, and the wooden shelves were intricately organized with books and books and BOOKS AND BOOKS OH MY GOD EYE LOVED BOOKS! Eye wanted to take them all home. Eye wanted them all to be mine, all this knowledge and education here at my grasp and Eye wanted to soak it all up immediately. My hands shook in anticipation. My heart was about to burst!

The librarian was a white woman. Hardly any white kids in my class, but a few were teachers, keeping up the white man's lie.

The Librarian, dressed oddly in a loose black dress and low heels, came up to me. "What are you looking for?"

*You were only slaves. You were not Kings and Queens!* Eye smiled. She was a sucker for it. "A book on us being kings and queens," Eye said, my chest puffed up with heart.

She wanted to laugh. Did *Eye* say a joke? "Blacks were *never* Kings. Who told you that?" she asked, getting down on one knee. Staring deeply into my eyes.

Huge tears fell down my face. Eye hated myself. Were my people only beaten and abused?

Eye wasn't being raped in my home as of yet, but that would cloud my judgment in the days to come.

Eye decided to believe we were Kings and Queens, why Eye didn't know. Maybe Eye was making a fool of myself. "Are you sure? Because Eye saw a book in here last week with a black face on the front. And a head rest on his head. Eye think it said we were Kings inside the book."

She rolled her eyes. "That was a fiction novel. Make believe," she said rather quickly.

*Defeated! Maybe she's right!* "Oh, ok." Oh, well. Eye tried.

She went about her business, shuffling through some folders on her small, cluttered desk. The sunlight poured through the huge dirty windows, glowing on my perspiring skin.

Eye looked at her a second.

*That was a fiction novel. Make believe.*

*So a fiction novel means make believe, but then again you can't believe a thing some white people say.*

Eye still went looking for the book, Eye was one determined kid. Eye couldn't shake the feeling. Eye wanted to find and read the book anyway. That way Eye could pretend to be a *King.* When Eye wanted something Eye went after it.

Eye looked around and the Librarian said, "Ok, go back to *class.*"

Eye looked at her. "But Eye wanna find the fiction book of the black King."

She glared at me with contempt.

"No such book exists."

With my head hanging low, felt like my dog died.

Eye was deeply depressed. Eye hadn't known such depression at that particular time in my life and it was all over the white bitch telling me we were never Kings.

Maybe she was right. After all, Mama and Step daddy never taught me anything about being a King.

So Eye never asked them.

**Eye made my way out of the** library. Eye cried really hard.

*So we were only slaves. We had Masters and had to clean dirty toilets!*

A male janitor saw me. He smiled, and said, "Lil' niggah, what's saddens you?"

Eye looked at him with deeply saddened eyes. Not understanding life or why Eye was here. Eye was too young. Eye just felt like a complete fool for thinking blacks were Kings. "We were never Kings," Eye said. "We were only slaves."

His eyes bulged out his head. "*Who* told you that lie?"

Eye looked up at him, my tears drying. Eye saw some hope beaming through, but it was short lived. What if he's lying?

Eye played footsy with my sneakers, looking at the shoe laces. "The librarian and my teacher Miss Left. The library lady said us being kings was a fiction novel."

Anger befell his face. "She said that?"

*Come on man, what can you do? Nothing!* "Yea."

"Two white bitches. That explains it. Come with me."

Eye looked up into his eyes. They were both inviting and scorned. "But Eye gotta go back to class. Eye told the teacher Eye was going to the bathroom."

"Just tell her you had diarrhea, something you ate." He put his arm around me like a big brother. "Come on."

Eye followed him.

## 3

***When we went in the library*** he held my hand, taking me to the back book shelf. There were a lot of books, mainly with white faces on them. They were laughing, playing or doing something *heavenly* on those book covers. When we got to the back shelf he thumbed through some books, wrinkles forming on his forehead. "Where is it?" he asked, as if he knew exactly what he was looking for.

"Where's what?" Eye asked, confused. You brought me back here; you're supposed to know what you're looking for.

He frowned. "There is a book in here on Africa. A King was considered a Pharaoh and he had a Queen or many wives."

My face lit up brightly. But what if he's jiving? Then Eye'll be back to Square 1. "Wow. You're *lying*, Mister. Eye heard that's a *fiction* novel."

Eye told him she said it with a straight face and the brothah was about to beat her white tail. He looked at me in silence. Hardened eyes vs. my wet eyes.

His look turned into a frown. He snatched me by the shirt. He meant business. "It's a non fiction novel. Non fiction means real, factual. Don't let those crackers tell you that *you* were only a slave. Don't ever let them program you, young man. Always search for truth amongst the wolves."

*Always search for the truth amongst the Wolves.* "Ok."

He lightened up a tad. "Eye never encountered a youngster that asked were black men Kings. You're different and all together special."

Eye *felt* special.

He released me. Eye sat down on the floor, playing with my shoe laces. "Where is that book on Africa?" he asked rhetorically, thumbing through another row of books, cursing under his breath.

Eye was confused. "What is Africa?"

"That's where our ancestors are from. We were sold into slavery by our own kind. We were brought over here on huge slave ships as the white man's property and once our people got here they handed them the United States Manual."

"A manual, sir?" Eye asked at this burst of information Eye felt myself opening up in ways Eye never imagined in my life and Eye felt good about myself, a whole new world beckoning to understand the simplicity of my life.

"Yes. A manual. It's called *The Holy Bible*. Religion was forced on us. We couldn't read, and we were dumbed down. We couldn't go to school or college, my boy. What you are doing now, going to school and learning to spell your name, was because of folks like Sojourner Truth, Harriet Tubman and Martin Luther King."

My eyes were wide with jubilancy. "Wow, who are those people? Please don't tell me they are crackers!"

He laughed. "*No*, son. They were African Americans."

Eye held my head high. "Am Eye a African American?"

He corrected me, just like a big brother. "Are you *an* African American? Yes. And talk correctly. Any vowels, a, e, Eye, o, u and sometimes y you say *an* before it. Like this. Eye want *an* apple. *Apple* starts with *A*. Eye want *an* omelet for breakfast. *Omelet* is spelled O-M-E-L-E-T."

Eye soaked it up like a sponge.

"Ok. Eye will remember that." Eye was looking ahead, under the shelf.

Eye saw a book.

"What are you looking at?" he asked, baffled.

It took a moment for me to say it. Maybe Eye was seeing things. "There's a book under the shelf."

He tried to bend over to look, but he was too tall and he didn't feel like getting on his knees. "Can you get it?"

Eye was determined. "Yes." *Why a book would be hiding beats me.*

Eye pulled it out and the breath caught in my throat.

It was the "fiction novel."

With the *Pharaoh* on the front.

Eye held it up at him.

"Oh my God. Somebody hid the book under the shelf." He glanced at the Librarian. She was cackling on the telephone.

"But its make believe," Eye said, remembering what the Librarian told me.

"Son. This is a non fiction book on Africa."

My mouth fell open in shock.

*He hid the book in his pants*. He looked guilty as hell, but he didn't care. He zipped a thin jacket over his work shirt.

"Let's get out of here," he said.

"But you're stealing that book, Sir."

"Eye'll explain why. Follow me," he said, ushering me out the door. "And what's your name?"

"Pharoah."

"Excuse me," said the Librarian and he kept walking. "Yo. Eye know you hear me," she said. Eye didn't look back.

We were gone. Eye *didn't* go back to class.

And my teacher didn't seem to care.

## 4

*We sat in his Cadillac*. He put on some Grandmaster Flash. "Where do you live?" he asked me.

"Right there across the street in that wooden house with the broom on the roof."

"Ok, Eye'll take you home. But let me show you something."

He opened the book and pictures were in there of Pharaohs. And words couldn't describe the look of victory on my face. He pointed to one. "That is Akhenaton. Nefertiti was his wife."

"Wow! He was a king?"

"Yes!"

"Wow, man! Can Eye keep this book? Eye'm gonna try to read it!"

"Yes. Keep it. Put it in your book bag."

"Ok. But you don't have to take me home. Eye'm going back to class. Eye come home early my parents will kill me!"

"Ok, lil niggah. Read that book. Reading is fundamental, lil niggah."

"Ok."

"Do good in class."

"Bye!" Eye rushed back to Miss Left's class.

My robotic eyes, shaded—activate…

***"Where have you been?" she quipped***, looking a mess in that ugly blouse.

"Eye was on the toilet."

People were laughing.

"Sit down. Class almost over," she said sternly. Eye could care less. Eye felt myself getting an attitude over her obvious lie.

"Eye have a question," Eye said, because when Eye knew something Eye had a problem keeping my mouth closed, but that would soon change.

"What?" she snapped back.

"Why you lied?" Eye asked her.

Everyone grew quiet.

*"Oooh you called the teacher a liar."*

*"You can't be calling that white woman a liar!"*

*"The principal gonna paddle you."*

"This cracker ain't gonna do nothing to me!" Eye stammered, anger surging along with my quickened pulse.

"WHAT?" she screamed, standing up in her cute pressed skirt and her dingy white blouse and her blonde hair. "What did you call me?"

"You heard me. Eye called you a cracker!"

"He's trying to die today," said one of my friends.

"Pharoah, man you're in *trouble*."

"What has gotten into you?" she asked, appalled.

Eye stood up, holding the book. "You lied. About us only being slaves."

"Eye didn't lie. You were only slaves. Slavery has been abolished by the Emancipation Proclamation created by Abraham Lincoln."

"Was he black?" Eye asked?

She stuttered and then fell silent. After getting her wits in check, she decided to challenge me. "Is everything a black and white issue with you?"

"Yes. Eye'm black, ain't Eye? Don't you got white people hanging up all over class? Was Abraham *black*?"

"No."

"So the hell with *an* Abraham Lincoln then!" Eye thought of the janitor, saying "an" in front of A, Abraham. "You said we were slaves. But you lied."

"Go to the Principal's office!" she said, trying to get me out the class before Eye informed every black child in there that we were kings and queens and not just Queen Stupid Elizabeth!

"With pleasure! But not before Eye say we were Kings!" My cousin Cyn used to say "With pleasure," and Eye picked up on it and started using it.

Eye held up the book.

Eye walked to the chalk board. Eye wrote 'Eye am a Pharoah' on the board.

"You spelled it wrong!" she announced, pleased at my ignorance. But it was a big word for a first grader like me, but it was worth gold! It was worth more than any word the dumb ass teacher funneled from her thin pink over made up lips. Eye swelled with anger, frustration and aggravation. Eye was about to explode. "So what! We are Kings. Those Kings had Queens. Akhenason and Neferwihi were king and queen in a place called Afrika." Eye said it wrong but Eye knew what Eye was trying to say.

Everyone was laughing. But they thought Eye was joking and this upset me more. Presenting the truth to their late asses and all they could do was laugh?

*"We weren't kings and queens."*

*"You heard that white lady. We were only slaves."*

*"Pharoah you're crazy."*

Eye slammed the book on the ground and said, "FUCK ALL OF YOU!"

And they all fell quiet.

"ALL OF YOU. GO TO HELL!"

*Eye marched my ass right* to the Principal's office.

He was sitting at his desk, an Uncle Tom raised in Uncle Tom's cabin, or so Eye assumed. Trying to calm down, Eye walked inside and closed the door.

"Eye am *not* going back to that cracker's class."

His head snapped up. "What did you say young man?"

"You heard me. She's a liar!"

"What did she do to you?"

"She said we were only slaves in a place called Africa and Eye just saw in a book, black men in Africa with diamonds and gold and jewelry on and they are called Pharaohs!"

Eye could have said an elephant licked a dog's butt crack and he wouldn't have cared. "Son, *have* a seat."

"Paddle me so Eye can go home. Call my Mama Eye don't care. Why you let a teacher lie so much? Ain't it wrong to lie?"

"Son you're six years old. And you talk ahead of your years."

"Eye'm not dumb!"

The pressures of managing an elementary school was getting to him, judging by those deep dark rings around his eyes, like he barely slept. "*Clearly* you're not. But you're in school and you will follow the rules."

"Eye don't wanna learn the lies that white woman teaching."

"She has a college degree, something you may not ever get in your life time."

Those words stung me. Eye looked like a cow gazing at a new fence. He was no better than Miss Left telling us we were only slaves. *We sold ourselves to slavery,* Eye remembered the janitor telling me. Maybe he's right, judging by the reaction of the very black principal. "Eye wanna go home to my Mama! At least she doesn't lie!"

He'd had enough. "Son, come over here now. Pull your pants down!"

Reluctantly, Eye pulled them down and walked over to him. He stood up, picking up his wooden paddle. Wrapped with duct tape. Eye held the desk. This was the first time Eye was paddled.

He hit my naked ass three times.

*Eye went back to class with* sore booty cheeks. The tears fell. But Eye didn't utter a sound…"Are you gonna apologize?" Miss Left said, and Eye glared at her.

"Eye'm *sorry,* lady. But Eye'm *not* sorry for finding out we weren't just no slave. And we didn't just clean no shitty toilets."

"You're rebellious. And Eye mean no harm, but you will *not* disrespect me."

"And you won't call me no slave! My name is Pharoah. And Eye am a King."

"Learn to spell it right!"

"No. Eye will spell it Pharoah (meaning the 'o' before the 'a' to remind me of that day in class). Eye will never forget this for as long as Eye live."

*Bwahahahaha*, she laughed. "Sit down, Pharoah. So Eye can assign your homework."

Eye sat down. Eye had nothing else to say.

Eye was looking around for my book and Eye suddenly sat paralyzed with fear. Where was it? It was gone! "Where is my book?" Eye asked.

"*In* the trash," she said absent-mindedly, oozing with deceit.

"What?" Eye got up and walked over to the small green iron trash can.

"Sit down!"

*Eye want the book!* "Why you throwing the school library book away?'"

"Eye thought it was yours," she said, my friends laughing at me.

"So if it was *mine* you will throw it away?"

She barely looked at me. "Yes. Don't want trash in my class on the floor."

Eye was offended. "But my ancestors aren't trash, lady!"

She smiled, finding it all funny. "Eye never said they were. Eye said the *book* is trash."

"Isn't that saying the *same* thing?"

"Eye'm calling your mother."

"Eye don't give a damn!"

"Mr. Wilson!"

"Eye don't *like* you. Eye don't want you being my teacher. Why would Eye want a liar teaching me anything?"

She was on her heeled feet, pointing at me, her face flushed beet red. "GO BACK TO THE PRINCIPAL'S OFFICE DAMN, IT!"

"With pleasure. Eye will happily take that paddle. Eye don't *like* you. And bad enough somebody hid this book under the shelf in the library."

"When you get back Eye will be on the phone with your mother."

And Eye walked up to her. "And when you do Eye will tell my uncles to beat you up, *bitch,* for lying that all we did was clean shitty toilets."

"Eye am disgusted."

"Funny, so am Eye."

And Eye took the book with me, and walked all the way home. Right past the Principal's office.

He might donate me to slavery.

*Across The Tracks*
*Goulds, December 2011*

# 5

*Independence was a very hard* thing to maintain, especially when you lived your entire life pleasing others. Eye used to look for happiness to come from others and Eye wound up hurting me. Eye lost me in search of acceptance. Eye started to hate myself when Eye searched for a place to belong. Eye used to think being bisexual was my Scarlet Letter because Pa$tor$ who tried to suck and sex me (and a few succeeded) told me it was. *But* Eye *know* better now. Being bisexual was PHAROAH'S BUSINESS. The purpose of church was to keep us conditioned and set on idle, in my opinion. Home was where the heart was, not the Pa$tor'$ Pulpit. As you can see, the buck stopped with me. Eye love God to death, but to HELL with church! The thought of congregating with a bunch of nosey strangers made me queasy. The day my old Pa$tor slid up inside me without a rubber, when Eye was 14, was the day Eye told the church to go to hell. And take those Caucasian, face-lift Bibles with you. And those *white* pictures of Jesus, burn those too! Nowhere in those photos did Jesus have hair of wool and feet of bronze, so that contradicted your entire sermon, tarnished what you stood for. Eye was just bold enough to tell the Pa$tor in his face. Eye used to love people and wished they loved me back because LOVE was a four letter word short of HATE and my life has become the mighty thin line separating them both. Eye used to try to buy my lovers' love. Eye failed. They took the money and

ran. Then Eye tried to make them love me. Failed. They called me crazy and vanished. Then Eye opened up about my past too soon to keep a lover. They left, saying Eye needed help. So Eye got help by turning to one person: GOD. And Eye've been stronger since.

When your family holds you in bondage, every move you make becomes microscopic, dissected and family chatter at the dinner table. My life has never been a crystal stair. My life wasn't supposed to succeed my failures. Eye wasn't perfect; *yes* Eye've hurt people out of my need to feed my anger; *yes* Eye have done questionable things; *yes* Eye am *not* a saint; *yes* Eye swear day in and day out, smoke pot and sometimes Eye drink Old English to drown my past. But until this year Eye had to face it. And Eye have. Bitterly. Aggressively. Yes, Eye write and sell books; yes Eye'm on sale on Amazon.com from here to Canada, Europe, Germany, France, Japan and the United Kingdom. Eye'm no better than the person reading this book. Eye know ME better than they know ME; Eye know myself better than Eye know anybody so Eye will tell my story MY way on my terms. Eye'm leaving NO STONE unturned. Some say Eye took a chance writing this, but those were the very *same* people who trembled with the book's release. My mission was to show ALL MY PITFALLS and hoped it inspired those who were going through some things Eye've gone through. It's written to inspire. So if Eye'm making anybody look or feel bad it's myself. Eye will change the names throughout, so the focus stays on the ups and downs of making my own decisions. It will show the distorted thinking Eye suffered, the bad decisions Eye made, the justifications, the stark contradictions. Eye love God with all my heart. And he loves me, good or bad. Eye'm telling you now, don't gun for me and my love for God because Eye will curse you out. *Simple.* God knows my heart; you won't ever know what's in mine. And don't go there about church. Churches are filled with sluts, whores, fags, crooked Pastor$ and those who think they are better than me. You aren't *better* than me, and you are going to be judged, *too.* Eye'm always falling out with sanctified bitches, shaking my head. Sophia, this was for you. Eye've been wanting to address you since Eye was 25 years old. How were you going to tell me about God and damning me to hell—and calling me an Abomination—*Yawn...* When the drug dealer you're sucking behind your husband's back pounds you in the booty eight times a week. He resuscitates your booty because your coochie reminded him of ant marching down the hall way. Space all *around* that muthafugger. Nookie was *looser* than a bitch.

The word FAMILY makes me cringe inside, because Eye know where Eye've gone and where Eye've been dealing with them. GOD knows of the hell Eye've been through. Some of that hell Eye brought on myself. Before you start reading THE SESSIONS, just know this will be a very *blunt* testimony. Blood raw. The purpose was simple: to show what Eye was before and after Eye became bestselling author Dapharoah69. The first "King of Erotica" and the most *successful* King of Erotica ever. There are a lot of people silenced from childhood abuse. Eye was one of them. We were written off like bad checks.

Sapphire told *Precious* told her story.

*Pharoah* was about to tell *his.*

# 6

OCTOBER 14, 2009
5 P.M.

*The cell phone wails. Ugh!*

Eye'm sleep! Eye reached over and snatched it up without opening my eyes. Eye answered it. Through the receiver came, "Pharoah."

Eye was rolling over in my bed, trying to suck in the atmosphere. Eye was groggy, and Eye hated being awakened from slumber.

"What?" Eye asked, trying to open my eyes.

"Pharoah, this you?"

"Yes, it is. Who is this?" Eye yawned. Felt good taking a nap, been writing for the past 17 hours. Needed that two hour nap.

"Your cousin. Eye heard you're writing an autobiography."

Eye was trying to figure out which cousin this was. Didn't have this number saved in my phone, so it's probably one of those yuck mouth bitches Eye cut off. "Yea, Eye am. Why?"

"What you gonna write about?"

Eye rolled my eyes, bursting open instantly. Eye said, "Don't worry about it, and why the hell are *you* calling me *anyway*? You ain't talked to me in years!"

"Why are you doing this, Pharoah? Revenge? Nobody listened to you? Payback?"

Eye was wide awake now. "Nah. Eye wouldn't flatter yourself if Eye were you."

"Eye know Eye shoulda did something. Eye knew that man was doing that to you as a kid."

"My book isn't all about that. That's one part of it, but not my entire book."

"Is my name gonna be in it?"

"Nope, but Eye will give you another name, but not your government so a bitch can't try to sue me, even though a lawyer said Eye can't be sued anyway for writing about MY life and the people that burned me. Freedom of Speech!"

"Why are you writing this book…?"

"Because Eye'ma grown ass man. *That's* why!"

"Leave the past alone, Pharoah. Baby…"

"Eye'm not your baby. A few years ago you called me every faggot in the book. And a couple of your big ass sisters had a lot to say, too."

"Pharoah, they talked about Jesus."

"Am Eye Jesus, goddamn it? If Eye was sent here to die for your sins ya'll fat asses will turn up like beached whales."

"Go to hell!"

"*Trick*, talking to you *is* hell."

"You *used* to be so fun and loving."

*Reverse Psychology don't work on me!* "Until your family destroyed it. As long as Eye marched to your drum major life was cool."

"Ok, you're gay. Big deal."

"Bitch Eye'm bi. Eye eat coochie just as much as Eye suck popsicles, since you're trying to be funny."

"You're too blunt. Eye can't take this, Pharoah. Don't write the book."

*And who the hell are you?* "Too late. Book almost done."

"And it's still coming out? Am Eye gonna get a copy?"

Eye was getting real tired of the back and forth. "Hell. Fuck. No."

"Pharoah!"

"Bye!" Eye was about to CLICK in her face.

"Don't hang up. Just listen to me. Please."

Eye thought about it, my patience worn thin. "Listen to *what*?"

"Eye know you are angry. Eye know you have a lot of hatred in your heart. Eye know this."

"If you *know* that then *why* are you telling me what the hell Eye already know?"

"Don't turn into your Mama."

"What does that mean and why is everybody saying that?"

"Life turned her into a very opinionated, bitter woman. You're headed in that direction."

"You know what? Maybe Eye should be a bitter bitch. Then maybe, just maybe, people will leave me the fuck alone."

"Will you *please* reconsider releasing this book?"

"NO *DAMMIT*!"

Eye hung up the phone. No time for that nonsense. She never talked to me and *now* she has a lot to say? Who said Eye wanted to hear all that blah blah? Did Eye look like Charlie Brown? She got demons herself. Think Eye didn't know? The men she had sex with, the promiscuity around Goulds before Eye was born and she wasn't even married. And she's judging me? She called back. Eye didn't pick up. Went to voice mail. Eye got the beep. She left one. Eye checked it. She said, "MAKE SURE YOU WRITE THAT YOUR GRANDMA KILLED MY DADDY!"

Eye didn't say anything. Eye politely walked out the house, with my book bag. Eye text her back. Eye DON'T GIVE A DAMN! And caught the bus to Miami-Dade

Homestead Campus to do some writing. *Make sure you write that your grandma killed my daddy. Ask* me do Eye give a damn!

**J**

*My Great Aunt Rozella told me* about each and every last one of her kids and their flaws, ups and downs and everything in between when Eye used to go visit her in the hospital, on 8th street, and Eye never told a soul.

Eye kept those meetings (3 of them) between me and her. Whoever did her wrong Pharoah knew about it. And it wasn't just about what they did wrong to her.

She was a noble woman. She also told me her flaws, and things she did wrong.

A few of those things had me in shock, but Eye didn't love her any less. And Eye would NEVER repeat what she told me, not even in this book. That was told to me in the strictest of confidence. Eye took her hurt to heart, even though she told me not to. She said her battle wasn't mine to fight, but Eye begged to differ. She was the Oldest living member of our family. The Rolle Family.

The things she told me had me so angry Eye wanted to kill them all! And as she went down the line Eye grew even more pensive, because some of those things Eye never knew.

And *Eye* was the promiscuous man, Eye thought to myself. And they talked about me like a dog? The things Roe told me made me look like the Virgin Mary.

*Damn Eye wanna go yell it in their faces!* Eye thought gruesomely. *But Eye won't. Eye'll keep my little ole mouth closed. For now.*

Eye shook on the chair sitting next to her stroking her face and kissing her lips.

She was going deaf and blind, and it killed me to see her there. She just wanted to go home in her house and be to herself. Eye hurt so badly. Eye wanted to switch places with her, so she could live a longer life than Eye.

Eye remember my tears fell on her cheek and Eye shook and she raised her arm to hug me close to her face.

A huge cloud of heat befell my body. "EYE HATE YOUR FAMILY, ROE! OH MY GOD! EYE HATE THEM SO MUCH!"

"Don't hate, Pharoah. It's not pleasing to God. Just be strong. Life is a mystery. We play our part and we go to God."

"Eye don't care. Eye hate them so much! Eye have never hated so deeply. Eye am black inside. HOW CAN THEY DO YOU LIKE THIS?"

She remained calm. It always fascinated me how she remained cool, calm and collected through anything. "Pharoah it'll be ok!"

"Let's get it straight, Roe. Eye don't hate all my cousins, no. Koont, Meka, Jr, Tara, Keyshala, Lala, Marah (that's my baby!), Lil George, Smoo, Koemba…cousins like that Eye love to death. We never really had any problems, except growing up we fought a lot."

"Eye know," she said. "You and Koemba used to have your birthday parties together."

"Damn that seems like an entire different life time ago."

"And now you all love each other."

Eye actually smiled, faintly. "Very much. We don't talk day in and day out, but when we do meet up the love is always there. But your grown ass so called children? Those are the ones Eye hate."

"Pharoah just let it be. To hate is to give them control over you. Kill 'em with kindness."

"If Eye had a gun Eye'd kill 'em with that!"

"You don't mean that."

"No, Eye don't. But Eye still hate them. And they can leave my Grandma name out of their fucking mouths. That is slowly pissing me the hell off!"

"Pharoah, again, it'll be ok. Your Grandma Alice was a very good woman. She didn't take any mess, Eye won't even go there but Eye know deep down in my heart she didn't kill my late husband."

"Tell your bitter children that. They're older than me and carrying grudges over into the next day—40 years worth.."

"It'll be ok, son. Just let it go, and let God."

Eye jumped up to my feet, my hands fists. "It won't be ok! EYE HATE THEM! Eye will *never* forgive them!"

"Pharoah, come closer to me. Eye can hardly see you."

*"NO! EYE HATE THEM SO MUCH!"*

"Hate is a very strong word."

"Look at you, Roe. Look at how they leave you. In this cold hospital. Every time Eye visit you no one is here."

"They come when they can."

"Even before you came here. When Koody Kat used to look after you. A couple of your *own* kids bitched over you taking your breathing treatments. Eye used to sit and watch how a few of them talked to you. Like they gave birth to you. With no respect."

"They meant no harm."

"Bullshit! You had to beg just for your breathing treatment. It broke my heart. That's why Eye stopped coming over there as much. Eye wanted to stab them in the fucking mouth."

"You're very protective of me."

"*Yes* Eye am! And one of them swore she pays your bills when Eye know your checks pay your damn bills. She think Eye'm stupid. Does she show you a receipt for your money she spending? Is all your money accounted for, Roe? You can't be trusting people with your checks, not even your children!"

"Her heart's in the right place."

"If you say so," Eye steamed. "But Eye know better. They ain't fooling me. And Eye won't let them hurt you, Roe. Eye swear Eye won't."

"Eye have the full armor of God, baby. Promise me you will *never* let *anything* come between you and God."

"Your faith always amazed me, Roe. You have been through so much."

"And my faith never waivered. Satan will never have me."

"Eye promise. Eye won't let nothing and no one come between me and God. Eye will think of you if someone tries."

"Eye'm pleased to hear that…could you put me some water in that cup with the straw and hold it up to me?"

"You don't gotta ask me twice, Roe." Eye fixed her some water, put a straw in the small cup and put the straw in her mouth.

She sipped till it was gone.

"That hit the spot."

We both shared a laugh. Eye loved how her belly shook and her face lit up with the brilliance of a child when she smiled. If Eye could frame her smile Eye'd hang it on my wall forever.

"Eye wish you were my Mama. My own Mama hates my guts, Roe. She doesn't freaking love me. If Eye woulda played basketball and been her Hebrew slave Eye would be her shining apple. She is calling me all those names when her ex husband was the one who first introduced me to this gay shit. And she throws stones at me?"

Her beautiful eyes lights up. Eye feel all warm and fuzzy inside. Ugh, Roe! "Clara loves you. And good or bad always respect her."

"Bullshit, Roe! The bible says 'Parents, don't provoke your children to wrath,' does it not?"

"Yes, it does say that. That's why you should continue to respect and love her for your days will be long. Let her provoke you all she wants. Clara gotta answer to God. So do you. So do Eye."

"She doesn't love me. Her actions speak louder than words. She loves Kells, the college boy and Eye taught him half the shit he knew before he even started pre-school. He was counting to 100 and saying his ABC's before he learned to spell his name. Eye taught him. Eye used to take him to school on that small bike, being chased by dogs when we lived in Perrine. Eye took him to RR Moton. He better be careful. The minute he starts thinking for himself she is gonna cut him off just like she did to me. And she loves Laron more than any of us and he uses his illness to stay in her good graces. He plays that shit like a fiddle and her blind ass don't see it."

"Sit by me, Pharoah."

"No. Eye'm leaving!" Eye started for the door so Eye could take my homeboy back his car.

“Pharoah. Bring that ass here. Sit down. That wasn’t a request.”

Eye paused, conflicted.

Eye loved her so much. Eye loved Roe more than the very air Eye breathed. If life was love then she was endurance.

My respect for her knew no bounds. If Mama told me to cut the grass and Roe told me to clean the house Eye would clean the house first then cut the grass.

Reluctantly, Eye sat down.

“Squeeze my hand.”

Eye squeezed her hand.

“Listen, baby. Eye always loved you. Do you know that? Eye always held you in the highest regard. Eye will love you until my dying day.”

Eye kissed her hands. “But you’re leaving me, Roe. Don’t leave me here by myself, please!”

“Eye won’t leave you, but we all gotta go. And when Eye go you gotta go on living, Pharoah. You are a writer. That’s your purpose in life. You gotta do God’s will.”

“Sweet left me already. He is my cousin and the only father Eye ever knew.” Sweet [Alfred] was her oldest son and the biggest father figure Eye would ever have in life, besides my Grandfather.

“Pharoah, we *all* have to go. Sweet was my son; of course his death greatly pained me. He was the rock of the family, held what little family we had left. We will all surely die.”

“But why? God hate us so much he kills us off?”

“Jesus bought our lives at a price. God collects taxes, a life or lives every minute on the hour, son.”

Eye shuddered with fear. Eye put my chin on her forehead and Eye broke apart. Eye have never cried so hard in my life, not even when Eye was raped as a child.

“Don’t leave me! Sweet is gone. You’re leaving. Don’t leave me here by myself.”

“You have your Mom.”

“We ain’t talking right now! She threw me out of the house over some petty shit.”

"Make it right. Eye could live another ten years, Pharoah. It looks like the end but trust me Eye got a lot of fight in me."

"Eye love you Roe." Eye kissed her lips.

*Super bowl Sunday. Yay! The day the* world was waiting on. The Saints made it to the Super bowl. Eye had a few homeboys (Kalvin, Rico, and Zoe) that lived in Louisiana, so in that Eye would root for the Saints, even though Eye was and always will be a die hard DolFAN. While the country was hosting Super bowl parties and half of Miami treating the Colts and Saints fans like royalty, Eye was doing one thing: Moving out of Mama's house. And this time Eye wasn't messing around.

Oh my God! Family was so overrated. Why claim to have a family when half of them called me every gay and faggot name in the book every time they get mad? Shit has gotten old. Eye have an extended family. Attica Lundy, was my big sister out of Atlanta. Her sons were my nephews, Trinity was my niece. Cam (Durrty Byrd) was my brother. Kim Jordan was my sister, and my good friend, though we didn't talk much because Eye was always busy. My Aunt Debra lived in the projects, her daughters Jaime and Cole were my sisters and Eye loved them to death and they adored me, with all my flaws. Never called me a faggot when they got mad and never would. Cole's kids are my nephews and niece, Doo Doo, the baby (Eye love him so much and he loves his Uncle), T-Man (gotta be Uncle Pharoah on him when he gets outta line) and Pooh Pooh, my niece. But right now, the word "family" has gone with the wind. People are in your life for a reason or a season. Knowing when the season ended depended on you. Whoever said that didn't pertain to family was sadly mistaken. Eye was tired of being hurt by the "family." Eye loved them to death, but Eye could NOT do this anymore. Eye have cried for the last time. Yes, Ma'am. THE LAST TIME!

At this point if Eye lost them all Eye wouldn't shed a tear. If you asked me, Eye lost them already.

When a man cried uncontrollably he's reached the boiling point. The breaking point, the point of no return. He wasn't crying because he's weak. We all shed tears, everyone, even Jesus wept. That passage alone was the only two words in that verse. Jesus wept. Nuff said. And we'll never be on the same level as Jesus, so if he did it, why shouldn't we? The more strengthened a man tried to make himself look the softer he appeared, Eye just never say anything and in this case Eye did that when Eye put up a front. Like nothing bothered me when in fact it did. But Eye was never one for charity or sympathy, especially over things out of my control or things Eye couldn't change or control. Eye was a glass. Life was a sink. Mama was the faucet. My buttons were the hot and cold knobs. And she turned them; *boy* did she turn them with the evil things she said to me. Things a Mama should NEVER say to her son.

The water (bitterness) filled my glass and it started to overflow into the drain making suction sounds. Those suction sounds were my voice, talking back but never cursing her. Eye may yell, rant and throw a fit but Eye never called her a "hoe" or a "bitch," despite what Eye called her in my head. Eye never verbalized it, no matter how it fell on the tip of my tongue.

A man crying represented that glass overflowing. At least that's what it was to me. Eye was filled with so much hate, inferiority and emptiness, vulnerability that it overflows. Too much of anything wasn't good for you.

In fact, a couple hours after the sun set and took her brilliant rays with her, Eye was battling the cool air, walking and carrying bikes, the lawn mower, and old blankets and Tupperware containers out of the shed, and neatly setting them along the wooden gate in the back yard. Eye was crushed inside. That a woman that gave me life continuously tried to make my life a living hell, and Eye had had enough. She was determined to control me, and Eye was UNCONTROLLABLE. How did she try to control me? Easily, by making life for me unbearable while living in her house. It was like Eye was in prison again!

In my opinion, she didn't love me or respect me, and that was fine because Eye haven't sought her approval in years. How her father treated her was how she was starting to treat me. The things he used to do to her, according to

Mama, were the things she was starting to do to me. She alienated me. Eye used to dread coming home to that house. No matter how good my day was, when it ended and Eye had to go home great depression and sadness befell my heart and soul, and Eye was like a zombie.

The house that snatched your soul and was controlled by Mama. The house that Eye hated to sleep in. The house Eye suffered so much emotional abuse from a woman who used to be my hero. Now Eye didn't know what she meant to me anymore, and Eye wasn't going to be quiet about it. She walked around that house like a tyrant, yelling, cursing and screaming. Life for her were parties (all of a sudden), bags of weave (when she didn't need it) and buying expensive gadgets, rubbing all that shit in my face. [Update, Mom and Eye have a closer relationship and Eye no longer have those feelings towards her. Eye love her with all my heart and soul, April 12, 2011]. The harsh whispers about me (she thought Eye didn't hear, but trust me Eye heard every word), how she throws her money around to keep me insolent nearly pushed me away forever.

If there ever was a term kick a dog when he's down, Eye was stomped over and made out to be the crazy one. Pharoah's the black sheep because Eye stopped her from controlling me years ago. But being in her house, she purposely called me to do unnecessary things. Eye painted that entire house and held a job. That wasn't good enough. Barely got a thank you. Eye got crap rubbed in my face.

Some dumb dude was hired to put in the doors in her house a few years ago, a boyfriend of one of my older cousins who Eye didn't talk to because the bitch always got something negative to say and Eye wasn't gonna argue with a ghetto bitch. Sorry. Not Pharoah. As a matter of fact he dated the "cousin" that called my phone harassing me about releasing my autobiography, and telling me to make sure Eye put that my grandma killed her father.

Forty dollars come up missing out of Mama's purse, that this man been around and Eye was nowhere around. Eye was on my computer writing books about 8 hours out the day because Eye had a job with my own money and talking to three brothahs getting their money, *too*, so trust Pharoah was *never* hurting for cash. Eye just acted like Eye was broke; my sister does the same thing. Pocket full of money and spent your money with the same Eye'm broke song that you always fell for.

Mama said, "Eye had forty dollars in my wallet. It's gone."

Eye was frustrated big time. "Ok. And you're telling me because…" Eye was shaking my head.

Her eyes flashed deadly. "*You* took it!"

Eye was appalled. "No the hell Eye didn't. Why are you always picking fights with me? You probably didn't have no damn forty dollars."

She wasn't hearing it. *"Eye want my money!"*

"Eye don't have your money! You got your purse lying around that man and you in my face?"

She glared at me. "All Eye know is that Eye had forty dollars in my purse and it's gone and if you don't give me my freaking money pack your shit and get your thieving ass out my house."

Eye was in shock now. You couldn't win from losing at Camp Clara. Eye saw why NO ONE came to our house. Nobody. Mama ran *everyone* away. We didn't get any visitors. And when Eye asked my other cousins why they didn't come over it was the same response.

"You're Mama is crazy! Hell naw! We cool! You can come see us but we ain't stepping one foot in Clara's front yard."

And Eye could see why, as much as Eye tried to deny the fact. Eye hated stepping foot in her front yard sometimes and Eye was her first born and her most *HATED* son.

Eye didn't take money from her. Was she serious? Did she forget her Meds today? Yes, once, a couple years ago, when Eye was on parole, Eye used her debit card without asking her to pay my parole because Eye was behind, and Eye was going to pay her back by giving her $140 instead of the $100 Eye gave her out my check.

Eye was desperate, and instead of robbing a bank Eye chose the littlest of all evils. When she called me and asked did Eye use her debit card Eye didn't lie. "Yea, Eye did. Eye had to pay my parole."

"Did you ask me?"

Eye took a deep breath. "Well, yea Eye did. But you forgot, so Eye used your debit card and did it myself."

"Don't do that again, Pharoah. Ask me."

"No problem."

"Where's the receipt. Show me that's what you did with it."

When Eye got the receipt Eye showed her and case was closed. But Eye never did that again out of respect. It was wrong of me to even get the money myself, that Eye must admit, and did Eye feel sorry for that? No. Eye didn't wanna violate parole over money, and if that's what Eye had to do to keep up with my payments then God forgive me.

Anyways. Eye guess that's why she thought Eye took $40 out her wallet.

Eye had ninety dollars in my wallet. Eye gave her forty of that and called it a day. Eye wasn't even gonna feed into her bullshit.

But bet your ass that man got confronted.

Eye overheard a conversation Mama had with him. He said he didn't have any money, and asked could he get a few dollars, since she had to pay him for the house work he was doing.

But Mama was air sealed tight 'bout her cash. She'd pay you something, but you aren't getting it all till the job was done and she inspected it on her terms. And she had a way of talking to you like you're stupid.

The $40 Eye gave her she wasn't gonna give him. So she went to the bank because she had to go by the bank anyways.

*He was putting up a closet door* with hints of victory on his face. In is mind played the local news, and on it he committed the crime of the century, but he inwardly smiled when cops said they had no leads—he got away Scott Free; um, no he didn't because Eye was on to his ass. Eye quietly walked in the room. It was just me and him. Eye observed him for a minute. Older man. *Much* older. Focused on his work.

"How are you?" Eye asked with an attitude. Eye was mad about my money. Eye needed my cash.

Sweat on his forehead, he glanced at me, "Eye'm ok, just trying to put this door up."

Butter him up Pharoah. "Looks good, the work you already did."

He beamed. "Thanks."

"Want something to drink?" Eye asked, thinking about spitting in it like Whoopee did in *The Color Purple* and sticking my finger in my colon and stirring his water with that, see how that taste in his mouth.

"A glass of water."

He barely looked me in the eyes.

*Eye never took my eyes off him*. "Eye'm going to the store across the street," Eye said, baiting his ass and he didn't even know it. "Do you drink beer or anything?"

"Yea, you can bring me something."

"What kind? Eye drink Old E."

"Eye don't drink that. As a matter of fact bring me a bottled water."

*Bottled water? He looked like a drunk*. "Ok, Eye got you."

"How much are they?" he asked off handedly.

"A dollar. But Eye got you."

"Naw," he said, pausing. He pulled some money out of his pocket and shuffled through his bills. "Damn, don't have a dollar. All Eye got is two 20's."

BINGO!

Eye was so upset Eye could have screamed! "Eye got you," Eye said. "It's no problem."

"Thanks, 'ppreciate it, Pharoah."

"For real," Eye said, edge on my voice. It took everything in me not to snatch his head off. Stealing from my Mama and she's taking up for his old ass, over her own SON!

Eye cursed all the way to the store. Thieving grease monkey!

He told Mama he didn't have any money but the bitch pulled two 20's out his pants pocket.

UGH!

He never got that water, either.

*If Mama wasn't happy* NOBODY was gonna be happy in that house. She made sure everyone was just as miserable as she was; at least that's how Eye saw it at the time. Pesently 2012, Mama and Eye got along and things were much better between us now that Eye had my own apartment with my baby and a good job and writing books on the side. But back then, the time Eye spoke of was hell. Sometimes she picked fights with us just because she knew what buttons to push. And don't ask Uncle Siegal for his opinion. That's his sister. She buys his cigarettes and his case of Natural Ice beer. He'd be her sideline Hoe till the wheels fell off. Eye should buy him some pom poms for Christmas.

My heart was sore, but my pride shielded it from my face. If Eye didn't move out her house Eye was seriously gonna hurt somebody. Eye've been studying things, reading up on an organization and suddenly, when my popularity boosted through the roof Eye was getting things in the mail from that organization, a secret society Eye will leave nameless; Eye was studying stuff and eating less, writing even more, and making sure Eye took my Meds on time and my entire thought process shifted.

Eye didn't argue with people anymore. In fact Eye was standoffish and quiet, to myself a lot. If people came around me arguing Eye kept my mouth closed. Let them argue with themselves. The Old Pharoah would curse you down into the ground and had to have the last word. Eye didn't *like* that Pharoah. So Eye changed it. Gradually, but eventually Eye did and Eye loved the new Pharoah. The Keep your Mouth closed Pharoah.

And Mama, nobody for that matter, ain't worth my freedom.

Eye was determined to move out, since Mama was doing her regular shift in the Control center at FCI Miami Federal Correctional Institution, and from there she was going to Larkin's hospital to do overtime.

She was the overtime queen, one of the hardest working people Eye know. Eye did love that about her. Her determination to succeed.

But that's just it. She has become her work. She talked down to me like a dog and Eye was supposed to greet her with a smile.

My brothers have cursed her out, talked all kinds of mess, put their girlfriends over her, and got all up in her face yelling and screaming and she had them on pedestals.

Hogwash! Eye didn't yell or scream half the things they said to her face.

But Eye was the Black Sheep?

*Jesus*! Eye was TIRED of people saying, "Oh she's your Mama. Respect her!" Bull! Just because she's "Mama" didn't *give* her the right to belittle me, stomp on my manhood and treat me like a dog regurgitating yesterday's newspaper. Enough was enough, sorry. Eye wasn't with the program anymore. Eye loved AND respected her—yes. But that didn't mean she treat me like trash. And Eye DAMN SURE wasn't going to stand for it any longer.

Pharoah had it UP TO HERE!

She's *always* bringing me down, telling me to let go of the past, forgive and forget. But she wouldn't do it herself. She talk about stuff that happened to her thirty years ago, wouldn't let it go. Especially on the subject of her father and how he treated her mother when she was alive.

She walked around that house saying, "Oh, he gonna go before God for that!" And, "Michael Jackson this!"

She got an opinion about *everyone's* mishaps but her own. And people in that house too scared to tell her.

But not me. And Eye *have* told her. To no avail, but at least she knew exactly what Eye thought.

When was she going to let that go? But *Eye* was bitter? Eye was uncontrollable? Eye had mental problems?

If Eye had mental problems, then the nuthouse would love to cross examine her brain. Two failed marriages forever ruined her ability to think with a clear head. She once told me she hardly made a mistake in her life and Eye rolled my eyes. Eye was her oldest son. Eye knew half her dirt and didn't open my mouth about it. Eye kept on watching her lie in my face like Yea, right, Mama. Ok. Whatever.

And throwing yourself into work with the FEDS ain't what Eye called healing when you get paid to tell grown men what to do. That job fit her perfectly.

After everything Eye been through in my life, Eye didn't need this. If Eye wanted to be a Hebrew slave Eye'd write the screenplay myself and dress the part.

Sometimes Eye thought her name was FCI Miami. The woman who was my mother now has become a complete stranger in my life; or so Eye thought. You couldn't exactly turn on your mother and Eye never would. Eye just got tired of the arguments and the back and forth. Eye looked at her and Eye didn't know who she was sometimes. Nowhere on her face was that loving woman Eye used to know, the woman who would give her last and her all. So many people have hurt my mother she has become bitter and was now taking it out on me.

Part of me knew the reason why she treated me the way she did. The only thing she did for me was allow me to live with her when Eye was down and out, and Eye thank GOD for that, but it has gotten to the point that she uses the THIS IS MY HOUSE! line a little *too* much.

Do Eye follow her rules? Of course. It's *her* house. But things in my life that didn't APPLY to her house she tried to control.

Like whom Eye could talk to. And whom Eye could date. If she didn't like the people Eye talked to there she was, talking down to me because of it.

If Eye wore something she didn't approve of, there she goes with the side remarks. She would whisper things to anybody who would listen (LOOK AT THAT RING PHAROAH GOT, THAT'S A GIRL'S ENGAGEMENT RING…) and it wasn't an engagement ring at all.

It was a gift from a friend, and she took that and ran with it, telling her bum brother who hasn't worked in God knows when, and Eye was tired of him and his big mouth. He reported to her like a good little boy, telling her everything we do in the house, excluding the stuff he does. Like doing drugs across the street in the projects, tell that.

Eye didn't understand my dysfunctional family. Eye guess everybody's family has a bit of dysfunction in it.

She loved her brother, and treated him better than me and Eye cleaned and ran that house for 20 plus years so she COULD have a federal career.

Eye hoped she didn't think she got to her level of success by herself, because Eye sacrificed my teenage life to run Camp Clara.

She has two cars, a few bank accounts, plasma this and that, everything she ever wanted, awards from the FEDS, fantastic evaluations. Congrats, Mama.

But when was she going to *thank* me for all that?

When was she going to remember Eye was staying home cooking and cleaning her house and rearing my brothers and sister for her so she could have a career? Eye was a minor that had to grow up FAST. Mama laid down the iron law when she had to work. Eye couldn't answer the phone. If she had a feeling Eye did she would whip my ass.

Eye couldn't use the stove. She cooked what she wanted us to eat. My brothers had to be in the bed by 8 p.m. And not a minute later. Don't let anybody in the house while she was gone, or that was my ass. Don't go outside when she was at work. She had other trusting adults watching us and their nosey asses always reported to General Clara.

Eye was proud of her for getting us out of the ghettos and projects and HUD housing when she got her seedy career. So Eye did anything for her. Did Eye get a thank you when she made it to the top? If Eye could make the entire situation a quote it'd be:

*You're just a nigger now that Eye got everything Eye ever wanted. Bye, don't need you.*

*Eye* was the nigger. Now that she got the world, the hell with Pharoah. Don't care about him. He's a faggot. Gay ass.

And Eye was tired of it.

What got to me was as long as Eye kept quiet Pharoah was in heaven. Don't question her, when she's not God. Eye was 32, and true enough Eye was too old to be at home. That ate away at me day in and day out.

She claimed she would never talk to her own father till he apologized for saying he wasn't her real father, when he truly was. And she said she wasn't going to change her mind.

Yet her hypocritical butt said a LOT OF THINGS to me she hasn't apologized for.

A), she got mad at me once, over something so trivial. Small. She looked me dead in the eyes and said, "Don't say Eye'm your mother. Eye'm *not* your mother." And that cut me deeply, but Eye didn't lose any sleep.

Then when Eye contracted HIV, she showed concern. But that was short lived. Piss her off about ANYTHING she would use your weakness as her weapon.

Eye remember my nieces were over, and so was their mother. They were out in the living room, and she was dressed for work. That federal uniform was her brass ring, her biggest accomplishment.

Eye was in **"The Room,"** minding my own business. She came in the room and said, "When are you cooking dinner?"

Eye did my best to keep from getting smart. "Eye don't wanna cook. All those grown people out there." It came out blood raw anyway.

Fire was gradually dancing along her corneas. "Eye don't care! You need to go cook. My daughter's hungry."

My eyes transitioned to accommodate hers. "Your daughter is a grown woman."

Hardened eyes, she narrowed. "Don't cuss in my house."

Eye was swelling with anger. "Eye don't *wanna* cook."

She tilted her head. "Eye don't *wanna* take *care* of your ass. Eye don't *want* you in my *house*, but you're here."

"Eye'll leave!"

Now she wanted to put on a show, make an example out of me. "Leave now! Pack your things!"

Eye was clearly embarrassed. "Eye don't wanna leave now." One Flew Over the Coo coo's nest my ass. Eye wasn't ready to fly yet. Eye played jumping jacks with the umbilical cord that attaches Mama and Eye together.

"Get out!"

*You took me from my father and now you want to throw me out. Eye wondered what my life would have been like if my father took me from Mama, moved 3,000 miles away to California and raised me. Would Eye have turned out a straight man about to marry a fine ass woman with some good coochie? Eye will never know.* "*Make* me get out," Eye said, stalling for more time; time to think and gather my thoughts.

The disgust in her eyes hit me like a ton of sand, stinging me all over. "With your punk ass. Letting men sleep with you."

"That doesn't bother me."

My nieces and their mother heard. Eye was clearly embarrassed, but Eye didn't show it on my face. Eye had so much hate in my heart for her, but Eye held it inside.

"Whatever, you ain't perfect either."

"At least Eye didn't get AIDS from letting a man pound me in the butt!"

My nieces heard that. Eye got really quiet. And Eye said, "That was a low blow." Eye resented her for stripping e down to the bare essentials with her systematic rule.

She grinned in victory. "Go cook the food. Or get out my house."

And she left me standing there. Shaking with rage. *Eye hate you!* Has SHE apologized for saying that to me? Saying something a mother should never say to her child? Nope. She hasn't. Yet she wants my granddaddy to apologize to her. You want some Parmesan cheese on that Contradiction Much salad?

Eye tell you.

*Shaking all those thoughts away*, Eye thought about an earlier conversation while locating my stuff in the shed. Yup. That's where my stuff was put. Everyone else's stuff, including my Uncle's, who had no damn job, and lived with us for nearly two years, was sitting cozy inside. But my stuff was ordered to go into the shed by General Clara and of course when the General speaks, everyone snapped to attention. But not me. Eye stopped snapping to attention years ago, because Eye started to see through the institutional crap. The Saints must be on a roll because Eye could hear people from the Super bowl Parties in Hartford Square roaring with cheer. Yay! Yea! Together their voices put a smile on my face, despite the tears rolling past my chapped lips. Eye found one of my suit cases with my manuscripts in it. Books Eye wrote when Eye was institutionalized in Oregon nearly eleven years ago—if not eleven years ago. Back during a time when Eye hated life and wanted to die. Eye continued moving my stuff out of the shed, neatly setting it and an old trunk on the glass topped table by the back grill and sliding glass door.

My sister's dog Gizmo wasn't wagging his tail happily like he usually did when he saw me. Because he was sitting on his back legs, watching me cry and he whimpered a few times.

Eye have been going through it with Mama. Yes, Eye loved. Her. Yes. Eye. Respected her. But no, Eye would not be her punching bag, her puppet and her remote control any longer. Eye was 32— [34 years old as of January 23, 2012]. *Why* was Eye still living with Mama, and called myself being a bestselling author. Three books on the Barnes and Noble Bestseller's list at the same time (In Feb 2009). The enigmatic pioneer E Lynn Harris, who sold millions of books, picked me for his Literary Café last year. Stopped my heart when he held up my books in a photograph for his generous endorsement. He told me that's something he doesn't do. So doing that for my work was his pleasure.

Oh my God! Eye remember that day, but Eye didn't remember it deeply right now. Because the love Eye had for Mama was slowly vanishing. You think my Mama cared about my success? Nope. Why? Because Eye wasn't rich, maybe, and Eye was still struggling. Mama loved money, even though she claimed she didn't. She spent extravagantly and everything in her house had to match: from her panties and bras to the appliances. She didn't care about my success because a) she couldn't "control" it like her federal inmates and b) she was one of the few people, in the beginning, that actually tried to deter me from writing. She never believed in my books, even while Eye was writing them in prison.

That's why Eye used to send them to Sweet or my Grand Pa because Eye knew they'd protect them. While sorting through my stuff in the shed (a shed Eye personally cleaned out a few times last year, and Eye'll be damned lazy people didn't come behind me and mess it back up!), Eye thought back to an episode with Mama. It was over a computer. Now everyone in the house had laptops, but she told me Eye couldn't bring one in her house. "Why?" Eye asked, annoyed.

"Because Eye don't have the room for a computer."

"But everyone else got one! *And* Eye can't write the way Eye want to *without* one."

"Eye don't care!"

"What do you mean? Eye wanna write and Eye can't do it without a computer."

"Eye ain't changing my mind. No computer, Pharoah."

"But that's not fair! Why can everyone else have one?"

"MY HOUSE!"

"Duh, you are always reminding me of that. Wasn't saying that when Eye was cleaning this damn house since Eye was 13."

"That ain't gonna work on me."

"Don't have to work. Eye stayed here cleaning this house, mopping and sweeping, looking after my brothers and sister for you to have your federal career. Eye kept this house in order, not you. You just kept the bills paid."

"So what! You were supposed to do that. What are you saying, that you didn't wanna look after your brothers and sister?"

"Your manipulation ain't working."

"You have a smart mouth," she said.

"My mouth ain't smart. But you're going to hear what Eye gotta say."

She pointed at me. "You're a very rude, disrespectful child."

"And you're a very rude, *bitter*, disrespectful mother."

She slapped me so hard my teeth clamped on my tongue. Eye tasted blood. We stared each other down as she provoked me to wrath. We were too much alike; at least that's what those close to us say. Some even call me Clara Junior and it pisses me totally off!

"Don't bring a computer in my house!"

Eye brought one in *anyway*. Eye actually set it up without telling her. It was a slow, older model Eye got from one of my white friends who was going to throw it away. Eye loved that computer. It was a PC. After setting it up Eye started to write. Day in and day out when she went to work.

Eye was happy to be writing with the computer. Until she found out. One day she came home early and came to my room (wasn't really my room, everyone but me had a room at Camp Clara), she opened the door and saw me typing away. The Demon surfaced. "What is that crap doing in my house?"

"It's not *crap*! It's called a *computer*! And Eye'm *trying* to write."

"But Eye told you not to bring a computer in here."

"Well, if the rule applies to me it should apply to everybody. Everybody in here shouldn't be able to have a computer and as long as they got one Eye'm keeping mine."

She snatched the keyboard from me and threw it. "Get it out of here, now!" She had fire in her eyes and she meant business.

"NO!"

"Eye'ma break it! Get it out of here! You're very disobedient. Eye want it out of my house now!"

"No, Mama!"

"NOW, PHAROAH!"

My sister and other two brothers heard, and of course they aren't going against what *Mama* say. Not willing to lose that roof over their heads. Eye started unhooking the computer, tears falling down my face. Luckily Eye saved what Eye typed on a disk, so Eye was good. Eye took the monitor, hard drive and keyboard and set it by the garbage can outside. Eye went back in the house and she pointed at me again. "Eye don't like the way you treat me in front of my kids. They are getting tired of watching you disrespect me."

"*Bull!*"

"Don't curse in my house!"

"*You* curse in your house!"

"My house!"

"God gonna take your house one day," Eye huffed. "You watch."

"At least Eye'm not gay. Eye didn't raise you that way."

"You're right. Your ex *husband* did."

She slapped me again and Eye exploded. "For one your slaps don't mean *anything*! They don't hurt! You brought that sick, perverted dude in here when Eye was little and he turned me into the very thing you hate."

Her boulders set formation around her spirit. Her eyes were as dangerous as they'd ever been. She's in defensive mode. "You shoulda told me! It ain't my fault!"

"It ain't your fault, but damn it nobody helped me. Eye told a couple of your cousins—" Eye went on, cracking open. My lungs felt like the atmosphere. My body felt like waves in an ocean.

Her eyes were empty…but Eye saw, just for a brief moment, a flicker of empathy, Eye saw a mother that wanted to hug her son but it quickly died when she said, "Grow up."

Eye was depressed. "And you act like you don't care."

"Eye don't! Eye don't *care* about it! You shoulda told me."

"So because Eye didn't tell you it made it right?"

"Eye don't care. The tears ain't working on me."

Eye was dumbfounded. Why did she hate me so much? "Show some love. All you care about is that federal prison and your awards and your career."

She laughed in my face, with my other brothers laughing too. Except Kells, and Diva. "Look at him ya'll. Boo hoo. Always crying. Grow up." She turned my feelings into a circus. STEP RIGHT UP STEP RIGHT UP AND WITNESS THE TALL GAY BITCH WITH THE WORLD'S BIGGEST FEET! That was the last day Eye would cry over being raped as a child. And having a heartless mother who didn't care if Eye lived or died. Because Eye was bisexual. Something else she couldn't control…

*The Internet Eye didn't like.* It's nothing but an adult virtual video game with you as the Main character. Internet so powerful could hold a billion of you on it for more than an hour. Some of you couldn't live or function without this Web. And the Internet was designed for future tracking purposes, but the government thinks people are stupid—speaking for myself. Eye spend more time writing than getting on the Internet and when Eye do Eye speak to all my fans, whoever sends a kind word or encourages me to write. Once Eye'm done with that Eye log off and cut my phone off and Eye write and write till Eye fall asleep. Now young adults were on the internet with stolen Adult pictures as their current default telling somebody how you mistreated them or abused them as their parents. And they were young adults talking with a child's mentality through the representation of the Celebrity Default picture they feel represents them and their Era. For me it was Janet Jackson. Every album she's put out has songs that were soundtracks of my life. When Eye was being raped Eye was listening to the *Control* album on vinyl record on my friend's Mama's record player. *Rhythm Nation* when Eye was a teenager living amongst drugs, prejudice and bigotry watching men with darkened souls hustle drugs and sell the lower part of the female's body like the stock exchange was near distinction. And Eye stop with RN1814 because to me this was the BEST album ever made on planet earth. RN1814 changed my life. When Eye was suffering emotional and sexual abuse Eye had her songs of hope. *Living in a World we didn't Make* was my favorite song off the album. She felt my pain and it felt like she was singing for me. Eye actually did this song in my TV Production video, with me in it sitting on a drum stool lip-synching and crying, in the 8th grade and it was shown to the entire school. The songs reconstructed my thoughts to an 1814 symbol. Eye practiced and practiced and practiced all her videos all night knowing Eye had to get up for school. Recorded all over Mama's *Imitation of Life* movie because my life was more of an invitation than that. If Eye got a move wrong Eye did it again. Eye cursed myself, disciplined myself and those hard moves took me about two weeks to learn and now Eye have it all mastered.

Eye was cocky. Eye went from ignoring and sucking my teeth at talent shows to entering with a clause that stated Eye perform LAST and winning first place 15 times before Eye graduated high school was the end result.

Dancing became my Plan B, if my writing doesn't excel. Eye would have that to fall back on and baby Eye was a beast with dance. When Eye dance it feels like Eye'm having an out of body experience, where anything goes. It's my code language, like Eye'm having a conversation with Jesus.

Eye was even beating dance groups and Eye was dancing by myself, doing nothing but Janet moves mixed with some urban booty shake, baby and it was a wrap. Eye came out the victor. The #1 Stunna. Eye could honestly say that practicing Janet's videos all night long and still making it to school on time (and doing Janet moves for all my friends in class and they were wide eyed because Eye wasn't doing no Madonna *Vogue* crap!) was truly the Highlight of my Teenage Experience. Practicing Janet's videos like Eye was on tour with her and Eye was an adolescent niggah in the ghetto going through abuse of all kinds, and Eye still didn't care. That's when Eye started writing her letters, and no matter how Eye mailed them to her they never came back and there was never a response. So Eye gave up, loved Janet anyway and made it right with God. Eye knew then that Eye love Janet but Eye wasn't going to model my life after a recording star who didn't even know Eye existed. Eye had to love myself and God more than myself. So Eye looked to Janet for encouragement. What jolted in me that forever keeps me as a fan was when Eye realized that the woman Eye listened to on the *Control* album and the woman in the Rhythm Nation get up was really Lil Penny (remember the one episode Penny's mother burned her with an iron? Eye cried for weeks after seeing that episode and Eye was just a kid) Michael Jackson's little sister. Eye didn't even know she was Michael's sister. Wouldn't have thought it because Eye wasn't on Michael's music at all like that back then, Janet was IT for me! So when people say she escaped Michael's shadow Eye'm like shit, never knew she was in his shadow. Didn't know they were related, so Eye bought Janet's albums based on her talent, singing and entertainment. Not because she was Michael's little sister. And for that Eye would always spend my cash on her stuff. And no bootleg version either. To me Miss. Damita Jo (JANET) surviving in the *Good Times* episode she played an abused kid and becoming Janet, the Global superstar with videos Eye stay up all night trying to master inspired me to always work through adversity. Eye didn't care who didn't like me giving Janet props in this book; it's my damn book. Eye thank God for answering my prayers throughout my teenage experience. Thinking he ignored me. And he was really answering me through *Janet Jackson's Rhythm Nation 1814.*

Eye have been pulling away from everyone the past few weeks. Eye have stopped arguing with people. Eye've been reading stuff in private, and taking all the information in. Eye have stopped explaining myself. Eye have stopped depending on people. Eye have stopped worrying about others and focusing on myself. Eye've become selfish when it came to my career. Eye was still in prison at Mama's house. Camp Clara Eye called it. Her way or no way. If she couldn't control you or your decisions you had to get out her house, and that's just how she talked to me. As long as Pharoah sat there and shut up and smile and be like "Sure Mama ok whatever you say! You are right, okay! Eye will stop writing my books and miss a dead line to get a mattress out the car! Yes, Mama, Eye will love to do whatever you say because Eye have no life and its all about yours."

Eye stopped doing that a long time ago. The day Eye discovered she no longer put the fear of God in my heart.

The Saints must have scored again. People were going crazy, but not me. Eye cracked a smile, wondering were my homeboys from Louisiana watching the game. Eye certainly wasn't invited to any Super bowl Parties, but then again my friends know Eye didn't watch TV and hadn't for years because Eye'm always writing 24/7. If Eye do watch TV there's something about Janet Jackson on. Eye love her. Twenty seven years now. Eye sat down to cool off, sweating profusely emptying the shed. So much stuff Eye had to maneuver through just to find my things, almost like looking for needles in a haystack. Eye thought back to the phone conversation an hour ago. The one Eye eavesdropped on, with the cordless phone on *Mute.* The call that made me pack my stuff and leave my family.

Once and for all.

Eye was writing on the family computer. Eye write 14 hours a day, and hardly come out the room. This already irked Mama, Eye didn't know why she didn't like when Eye was writing. Eye guess she would be happy if Eye was out robbing people or something. Everybody, even the crack heads and prostitutes loved my books, but not Mama.

Eye decided to go dance around THE HOMESTEAD AIR RESERVE PARK. Get my dancing on to some Janet tunes. Eye was a flawless dancer as well; many people who just met me didn't have a clue. Eye always went to the park as the sun set and got my workout on, doing all out choreography, not giving a crap who saw me nor did Eye care what they had to say. Eye was talented, why hide it? People around the 'Hood lived for my dancing. They would sit out in lawn chairs behind the Pine Island Projects (Whore Central) and watch me throw down without a care in the world. Eye wasn't entertaining them; Eye was talking to God with my body, working the track like Eye was in concert.

When Eye was done, Eye came home, and my brother was in the passenger seat of his girlfriend Toya's car.

"Help uncle…" Eye couldn't hear him.

Holding my touch screen iPod, in sweats and a white skull cap Eye said, "What?"

"Help uncle…"

Eye took off the headphones. "What?"

"Help Uncle Siegal put the mattress on the bunk bed in the computer room. Eye was coming to do it 'cause Mama been calling you and you don't answer."

"Eye hardly answer when she call because Eye don't like being talked to like Eye'm a dog."

But Eye agreed to help my uncle. But Eye couldn't find him. Where was the mattress? Eye was already mad she threw the bedroom suit away and replaced it with a fresh coat of paint on the wall and bought oversized bunk beds that really couldn't fit in the room.

And she was going to give me the top bunk. Eye was steamed. Eye gotta sleep in the room with my 50 plus year old uncle. Eye didn't think so. Eye did four years in prison sleeping on a top bunk. When Eye realized this was her institutionalized way of showing me whose boss, Eye decided to move out then. Eye just didn't say anything.

Eye noticed the mattress in the back of her SUV. Eye got the keys and fetched it like a good boy for General Clara.

Eye took it inside, put it on the bunk bed (what was so hard about that?) and put fresh sheets on it.

After Eye was done, Eye then sat down behind the PC and started writing some of my autobiography. Eye wasn't 30 minutes into creation when the house phone rang and Eye didn't answer it. My uncle got it. Where he come from? Eye've been looking for him.

Mama's secretary, Uncle Siegel, comes to the door and said, "Your Mama want you."

Eye rolled my eyes because Eye was trying to write and focus and every time Eye do somebody toying with me. He handed me the cordless phone. Eye looked at it a second, my heart pounding. Eye put it to my ear and released a large gush of air. "*Yes*, Ma."

"Where were you?" she asked with an attitude. Figures.

"Out, minding my business, why?"

"You left and you knew you had to get the mattress and put it on the bed."

"That's what your brother is for. And Eye did put the mattress on the bunk bed."

"No you didn't!" she steamed from the Control center at FCI Miami. "Jarshawn did."

"No he didn't. Eye did! Eye told him Eye'll do it when he came."

"Who you're getting an attitude with?"

"Eye don't have an attitude, but don't insinuate Eye'm lying over no dang mattress when Eye was the one who brought it in here."

"All righty then. Where…is…Uncle Siegel?"

Why does she call her brother Uncle Siegel? "UNCLE SIEGAL, MAMA WANTS YOU!"

Eye set the phone down, upset because people keep interrupting me from writing. Eye couldn't write like this.

"She's getting on my nerves about this mattress!"

Uncle picked up the other phone. "Yea."

Eye pressed the *mute* button and listened. Eye knew her like the back of my hand.

"Did Pharoah put the mattress on the bed?"

"Yea, he did."

"Eye got something for his ass when Eye get home. Disrespecting me."

Eye stopped typing, turned the volume down on the phone and closed and locked the room door. Eye leaned against it, narrowing my eyes, my heart pounding.

"He did?" my Uncle asked, as if he really cared.

"Yea. He said Eye'm getting on his nerves. Eye told him if Eye'm getting on his nerves he can pack his things and get out my house."

"Eye know that's right."

*Listen to the side line Hoe*, Eye thought. He does drugs across the street in the projects in a woman's room Eye know be dealing crack and he instigating?

"Eye gotta trick for his ass. Eye'ma screw him up!" she promised.

"Yea…"

"And you can sleep on the bottom bunk. It's bigger anyway. Let his butt curl up on that small top bunk. Talking crap to me."

"Naw, leave him alone. He be writing."

"That's just it. Eye moved the TV you been watching for months outta my living room and into that room. He doesn't have a room. So you can get out my living room. Watch TV all you want in that room."

"Ok."

"Yea. Eye'ma fix him. He doesn't get it. Eye moved the bedroom suit out [of the room he sleeps in] and put bunk beds in there hoping he got the hint. Eye want him out of my house. But he ain't getting it."

*Eye got it now,* Eye thought, shaking my head, betrayed.

"Well, Eye have no problem sleeping in the top bunk. Eye'ma be watching TV." He threw indirect shade. "Gonna be kinda hard seeing the TV from the top bunk."

"That's what Eye'm saying. Put him on the top bunk, and you can chill out on the bottom bunk, watch TV and your movies all day and he can't write or do nothing. In fact Eye'm gonna have Jarshawn change the password on the family computer and delete his stuff off. Eye'm gonna mess him up. He ain't gonna know."

"Yep. *That's* a good idea."

*Devastated, it took me a long* minute to calm down. Rage bit me so sharply Eye had to scream in a pillow to keep from snapping my uncle's neck. Eye had trouble breathing, a burning in my chest made its way to my gut.

Eye sat down and put my USB drive in the proper slot of the hard drive on the Family PC. Eye started saving and transferring all my stuff off the hard drive, the red light flashing violently. It took me 15 minutes. Once Eye was done Eye deleted it myself. "Wow," Eye said. "She was going to delete my books and not tell me. Evil."

Eye put the phone on speaker, and left it muted.

"Hold on," she said. "Eye guess Noriega coming out."

"What you mean?" he asked.

Mama was talking to somebody in the Control Room of the Institution. "Yea, he is coming out. Eye think he going to walk around the lake."

She came back on the phone. "Eye'm bored! Eye'm doing overtime at the hospital when Eye leave here."

He could care less. Just buy my Natural Ice and cigarettes so Eye can go behind your back across the street and smoke crack. "Oh, yea?"

"Yea. Did Pharoah clean out the refrigerator?"

"Eye don't know."

"Go and see."

Eye set the phone on the bed, and unlocked the door, playing it cool, whistling. Eye took the phone off speaker.

He opened the door.

"Your Mama said you cleaned out the fridge?"

*You can't knock?* "Eye'll do it in a minute," Eye lied, crushed and deeply hurt in my heart. Eye hid it from my face. He closed the door and Eye picked up the phone.

"He said he's gonna do it in a minute."

"Good, then Eye can go grocery shopping

Eye hung up the phone on that part.

And been in this shed moving my stuff out.

Eye was empty inside, feeling myself let go. Eye been posting my status updates on Facebook, and lately they have been dark. A lot of people follow me on there and Eye just stopped doing updates as of today.

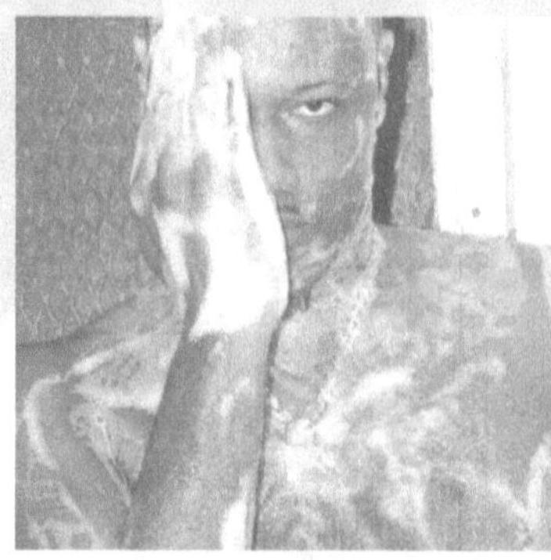

Mama hated me and that was fine. She hated my sexuality, which was the catalyst, because Eye wasn't making her a grandma. Jarshawn and Laron did that already, and Eye'm allergic to child support. Once Eye had all my stuff packed from the shed, Eye locked it, went inside and put my clothes in garbage bags. Eye put all my books and writing in a suit case. Eye marched it out to the front door. Dead inside. With no where to go. Eye did it again.

And this time.

Eye wasn't *coming* back.

*Be who you are. Follow your heart. Love God, love you, love your family. At age 34 Eye am in a different space now, and Eye love and adore my family. As of January 2012, Eye no longer have hate or anger. Tomorrow, Tuesday, my fourth niece will be born. Thank you Tay and Latoya Hush for such a precious gift. Now Latavia is a part of my legacy...*

SATAN KNEW OF THE MAN EYE WAS TO BECOME. THAT'S WHY HE TRIED TO DESTROY ME AS A CHILD.

PHAROAH™
The King of Erotica™

**Eye knew Eye was born special** before Eye even learned how to spell the word *special.* God knew the reason for my life before Eye found out it was pre-destined, plotted and executed. Unfortunately, Satan knew that too.

When Eye was learning the word Eye grabbed my crotch in front of the class and said proudly, "S-P-E-C-I-E-L!"

"No, no, Pharoah!" Miss George, thicky thick bone with an afro, said sternly, looking me deeply in the eyes. She then snatched me by the top of my shirt. She had on those thick glasses today we called Coke bottles.

She was leaning down towards me, her camel's toe all up in my face and Eye could smell her essence.

"Ok, Lady, damn," Eye said, using a word Mama used on my step daddy whenever he aggravated her.

She jerked my shirt, the sweetness of her breath making me dizzy as she pulled me closer to her face, her eyes latching onto my pupils, *bluntly* giving me her version of life. Coaching and coaxing me into her way of thinking as Eye learned a word Caucasians created and printed in dictionaries.

"Don't curse!"

"Ok!"

She smacked me upside the head.

"Lady Eye just got a hair cut. Licking your hand and smacking the back of my head. All because Eye spelled a word wrong?"

"Yes. It's S-P-E-C-I-A-L! 'A.L.'"

Eye was enlightened. "Oh, oh okay!"

Eye spelled the word correctly but it didn't feel like Eye accomplished anything because she taught me how to spell the word only *after* Eye spelled it wrong. Yea, she wrote it on my ditto sheet with a marker but that wasn't teaching me; that was the *push* in the push-and-pull factor.

So Eye went home and picked up the dictionary and looked up the word following how she wrote it on my ditto sheet and Eye smiled at the definition, coaxing me into a certain type of thought process Webster style then Eye went back to school with a new attitude, thinking what a wonderful world and got in front of the class with my hands on my little hips and said, "My name is Pharoah Wilson! And Eye am special. Why? My teacher said its spelled S-P-E-C-I-A-L, not S-P-E-C-I-E-L!"

My friends were haters.

*"So what!"*

*"Who cares!"*

*"Who saw the Jackson 5 cartoons on Sunday?"*

*"Eye did!"*

And Eye was disappointed. The cruel way they mocked me, tore down the glory Eye thought Eye was rewarded for spelling the word right, didn't grant me any type of popularity. Eye lowered my head and my teacher put me on blast.

"Very good, Pharoah. Now spell your *name,*" she said, eyeing me suspiciously.

Eye was stuck. Eye was only in this class for 6 days and she already asking me to spell my name. Eye'm only in Kindergarten.

"Eye don't know how to spell my name," Eye said quietly and everyone started laughing, further pushing me into the failing trenches of life and forever leaving me pressed with pressure.

They were pointing, coughing, choking and crying.

"Spell your name!" Miss George said more sternly.

"He can't spell his name!" somebody said aloud.

Eye had enough. Eye hated to be embarrassed. "SHUT UP MUTHA*UCKAHS!" Eye yelled so loud everyone was quiet.

Eye pointed at the fat one. "Spell your name, wench!"

She was quiet, covering her mouth in shock at my outburst. Stunned by my choice of words, my teacher jumped up to her feet in a fit of rage, pointing. "Watch your mouth." Her cheeks jumped.

"Watch my mouth for what? You ain't my Mama!"

And Eye rolled my eyes and twirled my head at the short little Niggah, 5 and a half years old—and Eye said, "Spell your name, Dwight?"

"Eye don't know how to!"

Eye laughed at my teacher. "They can't spell their name, so why you put me on the spot?"

She was studying me, holding the Bible in her hands. Looking me over. Nose flaring. Eyes wide with something soft on my skin. Back straight, ass out, legs popped into the upright position. She said, "Pharoah, what was the first word Eye taught you to spell?"

The class was still laughing, so Eye really didn't hear her question. "What?" Eye asked, wanting to run.

"QUIET!" Miss George stammered.

Oh. Their laughs were ghost towns now set up amongst the rolling tumbleweeds of their brainwaves.

Eye had their attention.

All eyes on me.

She patted her afro, pep in her step as the heels clicked, clicked, clamped up the concrete-type, cheap flooring.

"What was the first word Eye taught you to spell?"

"Special," Eye said faintly.

"With your head high and back straight, lose the attitude and using no curse words, how do you spell it?"

"I-T!" Eye said smartly.

Everyone laughs. Dies. Ha, ha. Bwahahaha! Eye had fans now. She shut 'em up long enough for me to make an impact.

"That's right! I-T. That's how you spell 'IT!'"

My friends were clapping. She took my hand, and pulled me to her desk. Looking over her shoulder, those tight brown spandex type pants with an earth-toned, light brown blouse was unflattering and so not her. "So *not* cute!" one of my favorite cousins always says, but who was Eye? Eye was just a 5 and a half year old raised thinking my opinion didn't matter because Eye wasn't old enough to pay bills Mama had to screw her husband to have paid. Eye had to stay in a child's place and stay out of A, B and C conversations with adults, yet adults talked about intriguing things.

"Eye taught you to spell *special* because you *are special!* Eye see it in your eyes, *Pharaoh*."

This time she let the class laugh, scream and talk loud; kids running around tearing things up, swinging off the walls and opening little kids books, ripping out the pages. A few of them were putting Winnie the Poo and Big Bird and The Grouch and Count Dracula 1, 2, 3, 4, 5, 6 and Snuffleluffogus and the Cat in the Hat and Curious George and the Gnomes pictures over their happy faces, not at all concerned with the words and stories on the pages. Eye died inside at the death of so many amazing books, and Miss George had a problem getting the classroom back in order. She seemed about to have an anxiety attack.

With masks on their faces, my classmates played the role, the role that would transition their lives onto whatever path they decided to choose.

My teacher raised her index finger mid air, and Eye came to her. At that point she was no longer concerned with my classmates. She let them be, because nap time was soon anyway.

She had big breasts mashed together with a black bra. Eye knew the bra was black, Eye saw the straps. Eye *knew* my colors, wasn't Eye black and proud?

Mama was always playing that song. Eye'm black and Eye'm proud.

"Eye'm gonna teach you how to spell your name, now. Are you ready, young man?"

My eyes lit up! And then Eye can learn how to write my name! "YES!"

Now Eye felt special.

She gave me her undivided attention and Eye gave her mine, submissive to her teaching, alert to her sense of education.

It would take me through my entire school experience.

She said, "You spell your name P (L)…" She wrote it on the paper, a big:

*P (L)*

"H (A)…"

She wrote:

*H (A)*

"…A (R)…"

She wrote:

*A (R)*

"R(R)…"

*R (R)*

"O (Y)…"

She wrote:

*O (Y)*

"A…"

She wrote:

*A*

"H…"

She wrote:

*H*

*Eye smiled because she helped me* out a little spelling it, pronouncing it and writing it. *Before*, she haphazardly gave me the ditto paper and expected me to learn words on my own. Never bothered to sit with me and patiently show me the dimensions of learning a word.

"Thanks," Eye said.

"Spell it!"

Eye looked over the paper a few times, balled it up and said, "P-H-A-R-O-A-H!"

She set the Bible down, clapping. She stopped activity when she embraced me with a motherly hug! Her arms felt like angel wings.

Now everyone wanna stop playing and laughing and looked over at me and her celebrating the speed Eye learned to spell my name.

"Very good!" She handed me two books.

"These are the two most important books you will ever know. Gifts to you, Pharoah."

"Ok."

"The Holy Bible. And the laments term version: The Dictionary."

"Thanks!" Eye looked them over, not knowing what they were really used for.

"You can learn to spell lots and lots of words using the dictionary!" she said. "And you're special and bright. Always read the dictionary. Understanding it opens the gateway to books and encyclopedias!"

"Yay! Eye can't wait!" Eye looked over the books, my Lancelot swords of the Era. And Eye will store them in my mouth, my lyrical and biblical swords for safe keeping by practicing my reading day in and day out of the edited inner contents and numbered pages of the books, teaching myself math and how to say my 1,2,3's. All that knowledge shielded by a front and back cover.

"Eye'm looking forward to your vocabulary expanding! Read your dictionary every day."

*But what about the Bible?* "When Eye go home Eye'm gonna find the first word to learn!"

"Eye know where you can start," she said, patting my big head. "Read *Genesis* in the Bible. In the beginning there was the Word. The Word was with God and the Word was God. Then study the dictionary and find your own understanding."

"Eye surely will."

"Remember, libraries will always be your friend. A library is an *Author's* bedroom. In the beginning God said let there be light, Son. And he separated it from the darkness. Night and day. Ying and yang."

Eye soaked up the information like a sponge. Never breaking away from her eyes, only to look at the two most important books Eye would ever own.

She pats my head again.

"Always think with the *big* head—" She laid her open palm on the top of my head "—in any situation. Life is going to get tough for you on your journey, but remember your Kindergarten teacher, Miss George, told you first. The key to adversity is to work your tail off. Understand?" she said, tucking my chin in her hand and shaking it up a little bit.

Why did tears form in my eyes? Like she was doing some sort of secret ritual, telling me of future sacrifice. Nothing could have prepared me for what was coming in a few weeks.

But Eye would write it in my journal when Eye turned 8 years old, at the behest of Miss Mike.

In the coming weeks Eye would read one book *more* than the other.

Making up my mind to do so, the Bible does say we were "Born" with Free Will. At what point we started using it didn't depend on age, but rather depended on awareness.

Acknowledging life and understanding we had two parents or a parent or an adoptive parent teaching us their values, goals, pushing religion (not God) in our faces. Making us believe what they believe and whipping our asses to set it in stone. Making us live out their dreams and the instant, the very instant Eye started voicing what Eye liked and loved and what Eye hated Mama whipped my ass for being defiant. She told me to the rhythm of a thick belt falling on my hind part, "You ain't old enough to tell me what you will and won't do now go do what the hell Eye told you!"

At that point Eye rebelled against anything she or my stepfather demanded of me.

In place of my right to Free Will.

But Eye did it in silence.

***Then Satan came to me in a dream*** one sound night before Eye turned 7 years old; and he spread his arms with many nipples on the tongue of his lips and with sad/happy oxymoronic eyes he said, “Greetings! Seed of *Babylon*; the one born out of wed lock by two parents who doesn’t particularly go to church for the Son of God.”

So distorted was my thought process Eye fell into the sea of darkness, with no trace of light. Where was he? Eye was too young to understand his breath on the nape of my neck.

Eye tried with all my might to see Satan, but it was so dark.

Eye activated one of my senses to raise my hand in front of my face, Eye know Eye raised my hand in front of my face because it was RIGHT THERE! Yet Eye couldn’t see it, focus on it or touch it unless Eye raised the left hand and touched it. Then Eye would truly know it’s there.

Eye was uncontrollable; my loose thought reminiscent of my swinging fists and kicking feet and Eye was being swallowed into deeper blackness; darker in sobriety and longer in latitude; Eye was crying out for Mama and no one came to my aide.

Eye was bobbing and weaving on warm waves. Didn’t feel like water, thicker than water and smelled like my blood stream.

My heart appeared, the left ventricle covered with piercing eyes and the right ventricle covered with leeches. Sucking and drinking, swallowing blood. Every time the leeches swallowed blood they thumped with the *poom boom!* of my heart and the eyes blink in sync with mine.

Cliffs morphing into things my young eyes didn’t understand rendered me speechless. Eye held my breath. Eye was high and intoxicated and didn’t understand the feeling of nausea.

Had never been drunk or high. Didn’t know what pot was, but Eye smelled it. Filled my nose, raising me to his royal highness.

Or so he said he was.

Eye said, finally, "Huh?" He flew with huge bat wings from behind my coronary artery, shining in my eyes with diamonds from the necklace of the rich.

"Huh, what young one?"

He didn't have black horns arched towards a place he was banned and cast from (Heaven, just in case you forgot) or red skin the color of blood's bitter enemy, but the huge anaconda hanging between his legs with one hole being his one Eye and mouth was his definition of a Black Horn and his red eyes was the color of blood. He batted them like a girl.

His curled lashes longer than my fingers and toes. His tears the color on my skin and ran like intersections all over his erection.

"Who are you?" Eye asked breathlessly, searching for an understanding and never finding it.

"Eye said greetings seed of Babylon! You are such a gay child!"

"Gay? What is that?" Eye asked, confused as ever.

Under my left foot was the Bible.

Under my right foot was the dictionary my teacher gave me.

Between my legs, my penis hung, still waters in my testicles, calamity in my eyes.

He laughed wickedly and my penis was hard. Eye didn't understand the sudden pressure in my testicles. Calamity destroyed in my eyes, replaced with the sensations of my big head, brain waves moving a mile a minute; traveling my body at warp speed.

His endowment pointed towards me, dangling along the way, stopped just before thy lips. The one eyed Cyclops awakened. It bobbed side to side like Eye had on the blackened waves of the abyss. Sound entered my ears and deciphered logic into a ball of crap.

Nothing made sense.

"Touch thy rod, Youngin! Understand this erection of mine will separate nations into lustful fires of nothingness. The way the Jezebel had in one of the seven churches. One day, Pharoah, ha ha ha ha, this very hardened vessel will be your down fall and cause havoc in your life."

Eye gripped it, hypnotized. Couldn't break free. Warm in my warm hands, the transference of heat into my nipples electrifying.

Suddenly, out of nowhere the ground shook, my heart vanished and the light was swallowed by the glow of Satan's eyes, all eyes on me as it turned into a juicy strawberry lollipop!

Wow!

Oh, my!

And Eye laughed, jumped up and down with closed palms under my chin, my head turned like so with HERO in my eyes.

Eye loved the magic trick. Satan, turning his hardened member into the object of my fancy. Eye loved lollipops!

"Do you want to taste it?" he asked.

He didn't have to ask me twice. Eye gripped it, taking it to the throat and the head of his passion pushed too much air into my throat and Eye gagged but didn't choke and gripped tighter.

A black hole opened up behind me, the backs of my feet directly on the threshold and Eye didn't look back out of fear.

Eye slurped and sucked, jacking and gripping…trying to lick up the liquid strawberry mixed with my spit and his snake was so sweet and big in diameter Eye choked up the bad dream and his eyes were wide and he grabbed the back of my head and said he was cumming the juice of the forbidden fruit down my throat and Eye jumped up out of my sleep, profusely sweating in this darkened room.

No lights, curtains closed over the windows and Eye was gasping and panting it was so hot!

"Oh, God!" Eye said, getting out of bed, flinging my arms in a dream state, fumbling for the light switch.

Eye turned it on and realized dried cum was on my black underwear, my dick was hard and Eye held my face, having a few hot flashes.

Eye turned to the mirror at the tender age of 32.

My eyes filled with tears.

"That's the 6th time Eye had that dream," Eye said, closing my eyes.

Eye gotta finish writing this autobiography.

"Oh, God. Why do you want me to give this testimony?"

A whisper filled my head just as quickly as an easterly wind.

All men think with a little…head.

All it takes is a tongue to destroy a happy home.
Eye closed my eyes again.
*And Lord knows my tongue have broken up marriages.*
*And ended relationships.*
*Before Eye turned 15 years old…*

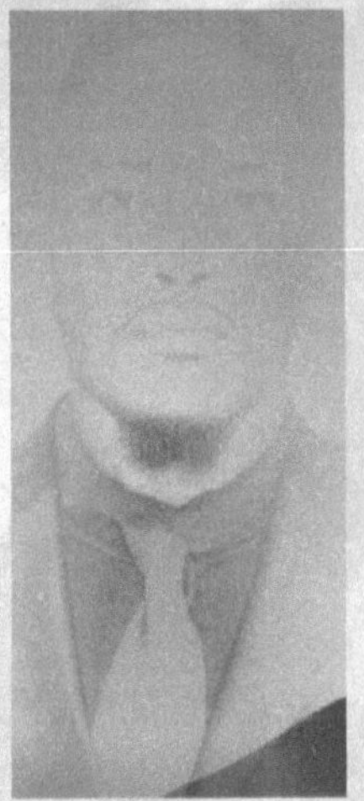

# BOOk 2

# The Abyss

# *Mama's Womb*

By dapharoah♋

Sometimes:
The butterfly
finds the cocoon
it left behind
several seasons ago
desperately trying to recover
the serenity and security
it once had.
If only I could
shrink in size

return to my
Mama's Womb,
go through
a rebirth.
back to
a seed.
give daddy
back his ballot
labeled "absentee."
and let Mama's body
shed me in the form
of her monthly period.

# ҔΣ

# ✦ SESSI☯NS ✦

*This book will feature chapters from therapy sessions Eye received free of charge back in January of 2009 with Lord Jennings. Eye changed his name. Eye met him on Facebook. We did those sessions at his condo 56 stories above the Atlantic Ocean, Downtown Miami. You could see the ocean and the sandy shore from his windows at night. Such a beautiful sight. Eye tell my story in no particular order. He wrote a subject on a piece of paper and Eye revealed my soul. Things Eye talked about, events that unfolded after Eye published my books, and my relationship with the shrink will be unfolded. So the chapters wouldn't be from age 4 to 32. Nah, Eye would talk about things as they were asked. Things Eye had to look back on, things Eye had to come to terms with and things that strengthened me to persevere and to endure line this book. But everything doesn't come free, and Eye should have known that. The sessions came with a price. Nearly taking my life...*

*My nieces Aliyaih and Sunjaraih—My Angels! Eye wrote for their future. They own everything with my name on it when Eye perish...*

PHAR☯AH...

# DAY

# 1

# Kitty J. Johnson

THANK YOU KITTY—RESIDENT OF NEW YORK—FOR YOUR UNDYING LOVE AND CONTINUOUS SUPPORT. YOU PURCHASED EVERY BOOK WITH MY NAME ON IT, AND FOR THAT EYE AM ETERNALLY GRATEFUL. THANK YOU FOR BEING NOT ONLY MY BIGGEST FAN, BUT MY VERY DEAR FRIEND FORLIFE AS WELL. STAY ENCOURAGED IN ALL YOU DO.

I LOVE YOU WITH ALL MY HEART.

*Pharoah*

## *Why are you writing an Autobiography?*

LORD JENNINGS

*Your soul will dwell in the stars.* You can't hold on to your physical appearance forever. We get old and die over the changes we encounter in this quantum state. You were made to believe your entire life one thing about heaven and hell out of fear to do what's right—thanks to the brainwashing of some darkly inhumane atheists clad as Christians; and a love for what you *don't* do wrong. But those are limitations put in your mind for you to haphazardly grow and get set in your ways. We are *all* powerful. We are angels/demons because some people might not see you in the same light as Eye see myself. Some people do not see me in the same light as my friends and family do.

Eye shower, pray and write. Eye write more than Eye eat. That's my life for the past three years. Eye don't really go out, but when Eye do it is to promote and sell and sign books, to stand behind the man on the book cover, the sexy dude in the photographs. To the world he's Dapharoah69, Þe KING OF EROTICA. For *myself,* Eye'm just Pharoah. A regular guy that enjoy simple things like watching Janet on You Tube and daily checking in on www.janet-xone.com or www.janetjackson.com, playing games with my nieces, being Uncle Pharoah or going to Club Rumors on Old Cutler Road with my cousins and friends Bread, Jhamelia, Eboni Honey Jackson, Shakira, Jay, Polar Bear and Khambrell; or working beside my three favorite people at the Outback Steakhouse—Ken Williams, Pierre, Dave, Kelvin and Ben. It gives me joy to play with my nieces and talk to them and be with my real friends like Demetrius and Trevor and Landis. Most of my friends were straight men. We had a deep bond. Eye didn't have very many gay friends.

These days some people were dumb. A complete turn off. Crucify me for what Eye do wrong, yet turn a blind Eye when they make a bad decision. Eye used to do dumb things also, so Eye'm not judging anybody. For real. Eye mean, seriously, when you're a dummy there were books you can read, Computers for Dummies and Typing for Dummies but who will write the Family for Dummies book because some of your family were jealous, egotistical and jealously wound up individuals who messed up in life and had the gall to keep reminding you of your faults. Chile, puleaze. Miss me with the B.S. That's another reason for this book. They have been talking about me for twenty plus years. Now it's my turn.

It's funny, really. When Eye came to a lot of them when Eye was being raped and humiliated and stripped down to the core of my soul and made a complete fool of when Eye was a child—they had nothing to say. They had nothing nice to say either. Fast forward 26 years later, and Eye posted on FaceBook Eye started writing my autobiography, the title The King of Erotica 7 Weapons of M(ass) Destruction (It's been changed to PHAROAH). *Oh* snap, folks! **FAMILY HAD SOMETHING TO SAY!** Now they wanna run their mouths. Now they wanna call me. Eye got over 184 phone calls from various family members calling to check on me and 99% of their butts *never* checked on me and *never* called my phone a day in their lives. The messages on my voice mail were endless, a sea of pleas that fueled my anger.

*"Pharoah, please let the past go."*

*"Pharoah, Eye know Eye should have stopped the man from raping you. Believe me, Eye live with it daily,"* said one of Sweet's siblings. *"But, Pharoah, you're grown. Let it go."*

*"You make sure you put in that book that your grandma killed my daddy."*

And Eye'm supposed to let the past go but her big ass still *lying* about my Grandma killing her daddy (her own brother, mind you), what, four, maybe five years before Eye was born? And now that Eye'm 33 (34 years old now you're reading this in 2012), that Urban Legend was nearly forty years old. Hell it might be 40 years old. Saying the same lies for nearly 40 years. Keep my grandma name out your fat mouth.

Well Eye've been silent for too long. And now Eye have a lot to say. Its gonna be a lot of revelations in this book.

For years, since Eye was small, people had something to say. Half of those things were falsified, fabricated and embellished, but Eye kept a still tongue.

All the anger and bitterness was contained inside. My ups and downs; the good, the bad, the sick and the evil line the upcoming pages. Eye was ALL OF THOSE THINGS at one point in my life, let's put it bluntly. Pharoah wasn't a saint and using my rape as an excuse didn't make it better. A lot of things Eye decided to do in life Eye made the conscious decision to do. So in a sense Eye'm bashing myself in this book, and Eye need to bash myself, because a lot of things Eye was and have become and transitioned from in life wasn't the Rosa Parks story. If you told me not to do it Eye did it, back in the day. Eye hated being controlled, and part of that came from being controlled as a kid with a grown man's penis deep in my rectum and his hand tightly covering my mouth. When Eye was down and out Eye never imagined crawling back to the top. Situations became mountains and by the time Eye kept climbing, slipping and praying there seemed to be no end. When Eye did reach the top, after beating adversity, Eye found myself faced with another obstacle. Eye guess that was Life's test, letting me know that there would never be just one question.

Eye remember logging onto the *Yahoo* instant messenger and getting an off line message from someone Eye hadn't heard from in ions. Eye think cavemen were roaming the earth when we last corresponded.

The message read:

Eye remember a few years back when Eye was in church, Bishop _____ told me to sit down and the next time Eye praise Eye better have some power. Well, Eye didn't understand it then but Eye understand now. Those who know me know these past few months have been hell but Eye just praised my way into 3 job prospects in a matter of 15 minutes, back to back calls. Eye'm saying that to tell you that no matter how things may be, if you can dance through despair, praise through pressure and worship through war, a turnaround is mandated by God to occur. Believe it!

*To put it bluntly, his message* struck a chord with me. One, because it was the God awful truth and secondly, it let me know that Eye'm not the only one in the world with the problem of climbing a mountain only to get to the top and remember that GOD said pray to him, and he would move mountains. But because Eye was hard-headed and thinking Eye was in control, Eye climbed the mountain…slipping, climbing and falling, holding onto the edge and scrapping my knees and God was on standby waiting to move it for you if only you ASKED. A closed mouth doesn't get fed, and your pride could ultimately hinder or destroy you.

So my life was Mountains of Pride that Eye'd climbed unnecessarily. Eye wasn't equipped or properly trained to climb mountains, but some mountains required you to act fast, no time for thinking. So when my life became a series of obstacles, some mountains crumpling to winding roads criss-crossing into each other, confusing the Good Path with the Bad Path, Eye felt truly alone. Going north was south and east was west. Eye had *no* sense of hope, no sense of direction and it started affecting my dealings with everyday people Eye'd grown to love.

We may have a legion of friends, bad times and family. But we always go to sleep alone, you die alone. You were born alone. But you were created with Alpha, your mother and Omega, your daddy. When you need help just ask.

Life is a strange entity. Sometimes she wants to wear pumps and crotchless panties dealing in caviar and other times she wanna be a ghetto trick loving her weave more than the safety of mankind. But who said Life was a woman?

Mother Nature this and Mother Nature that. As a child growing up that's all Eye heard in Goulds, Florida, when Eye was educated by potty-mouthed teachers at Pine-Villa Elementary. Life for me back then was no bigger than He-Man and Battle cat, *the Thundercats*, the *Jackson 5* cartoons. But even Eye knew that Mother Nature wouldn't be anything without a man to stimulate it. Man was made first. Women seem to forget that they supposedly came from a man's rib cage. Women gave birth to life, but man had sex with woman to procreate, and men chose the *sex* of the child; so who was truly the weaker sex? It wasn't woman. If men determined the sex of the child they were the weaker sex because a victim always has options but the dominant one has a choice. The dominant one chooses his victim, the weakest in the bunch. So when Eye was chosen Eye was thrown into something so wickedly dark Eye lost myself before Eye was a teenager. These days all you heard on the radio were the same things, non-singing ass Rhianna being shoved down our throats and Beyonce making my damn eyes hurt. Independent women this, throw your hands up that, Eye buy my own rings this, and men claiming they love her 'cause she got her own. Bull. Radio and today's commercialized pop, hip-hop slop crap was brainwashing folks and keeping us programmed. The world praised music videos, but Eye'm looking deeper.

Eye'm noticing the hand gestures Lady Gaga and Jay Z make, the all-seeing Eye matching that on the back of a dollar bill…the devil horn symbols everyone from 50 Cent to Lil' Wayne makes and the song lyrics never matching the images of music videos. If the song is about self love why is a half naked bitch popping her coochie and booty cheeks in your face? But no one pays it any attention. Because it's the rapper of the moment. And it's alright to rap about smoking weed everyday and being the "snowman," and you never sold drugs a day in your life. But this was how you program young black men who were down and out; these were the very images flashing in the homes of the inner city reinforcing stereotypes. Poor folks don't have anything coming. When you have a criminal record you don't have anything coming, but Cubans can come over on a boat, some of them with rapes and molestations on their name from Cuba and get a better paying job than your parents who been here all their lives slaving to survive. And now those felony-banded Cubans are in high positions and are the Hiring Managers at some of the corporations Eye applied for and had the *gall* to deny me employment because of what came back on a consumer report but failed to realize their own past sexual crimes, and yea Eye said it. Didn't know ya'll turned away an author, did you? Surprise, surprise! Their background checks are falsified, erased or "lost."

Eye remember back in the day you called for housing, school or church in Goulds, Florida, blacks answered the phone. Today, you called for housing, school and church…A Cuban or person of Latin descent answered the phone. So we're left to go out robbing folks to feed our families, or to give our children a good Christmas.

Eye was raised with this influencing me.

*You don't give a black man* something he will take it. At least that's what a crack head once told me when Eye was walking home from Whipple Store. Eye was 5 years old, sipping my little grape juice and glared at him like he was a three headed dragon. Just like my life, Eye come to the conclusion that music, movies and million dollar performers weren't paid to entertain, but to keep us programmed. Eye knew it because Eye've been programmed since Eye was 6 years old. Before Eye knew what my penis was for a grown man was pushing his pipe so deep in my rectum Eye felt like a prostate gland. Before Eye found out Jesus died for our sins and that there was a God Eye had a grown ass man telling me "You are my bitch! Take this pipe, faggot," and Eye wasn't even 8 years old and Martin Luther King was preaching his EYE HAVE DREAM speech from the black and white TV all in our faces, and all Eye could think about was dying. Eye mean *who* wanted a dream when Eye wanted to die from living a *nightmare*? Eye wanted to die to escape the pain, the pain of seeing my own blood. Frequently, Mr. Grown Man had sex with me raw. HIV and AIDS wasn't that big a deal during this time, the early 80s. So Eye didn't even know of condoms back then. Eye would take a bath sobbing in silence with blood tainting the bath water.

But Eye owned the pain and didn't utter a word because he said he would kill me, and Mama seemed so happy to be married to him Eye didn't open my mouth because back in the so-called glamorous 80's, music continued to program us as a nation and rapes and molestations were suppressed within the family. Because it was your uncle, brother or close friend of the family who was raping people and nobody wanted to talk about it. When emotions are involved, and you find out that it's your family member or close friend or Pastor that is harming your child, back then all you cared about was saving the perpetrator to duck public scrutiny and you brainwashed the victim and told him or her it really didn't happen or you just flat out say, "You're lying! Eye don't believe you." So all you have left is silence, and losing yourself to depression. In my case…when Eye was rejected, when Eye was turned down and turned away it did something to me. Eye learned to keep things bottled up. So when my own cousins didn't believe me Eye remained silent.

Till the creation of this book. Pull up a chair, Lord Jennings.

It's time for me to talk.

☯

*Talk about your autobiography and yourself. How did you feel about Me being your shrink?*

Lord Jennings

## The Huxtables

***Eye didn't care who Eye lose*** with the release of this book. If you didn't wanna talk to me again bye, bye and keep your post cards! For real. Eye have God so deep in my heart Eye didn't care if you wrote an essay about my book. Ain't gonna change me. Do Eye have hatred in my heart? *No* Eye didn't. To have hate means my perpetrators still have control of me and my mind. Don't tell me about me. *Nobody* knows me. Let me say it again. NOBODY KNOWS ME; *NOT* EVEN MY MOTHER!

If my family stopped talking to me because of this book Eye *wouldn't* care. Eye already accepted my imposing death through God, so Eye already released all earthly things and relationships. Eye was at the point in my life Eye could be me or be an image. As long as *Eye* did what some of my family and friends wanted Eye remained in their good graces; as long as their decisions for my life was my reality, they were very close to me, controlling me, telling me what Eye can and can't do. Talked about me, bashed me into the ground, kicked me like a dog when Eye was down and out, turned me away hungry, but fixed plates at the parties for their FRIENDS. The anger and resentment for certain members of my family was years in the making.

Thing with my family was simple. If you *didn't* challenge them then you were ok. If they could say *what* they wanted then life was *good.* They could talk about you and air out your laundry, and keep the focus off theirs. Eye used to live this way. Going around them with a mask on, being what they wanted.

Well, Pharoah got tired. Whoever said family was the best thing since sliced bread must have never had food poisoning. Believe that if you want to. FAMILY WILL HURT YOU BEFORE YOUR FRIENDS WILL! Despite *that*, family would tell you about your ass and hand it to you on a silver platter. Mine tried that, and Eye looked at the platter like Bitch, please, flipped the bird, grabbed my sack, wrote a book, and handed MY PLATTER to my fans. Oh, they wanted an autograph, too. Take a picture with you, fan? Sure. Give 'em ɄE KING OF EROTICA stare…forehead down and eyes up. Back straight. Legs shoulder length apart, hip swayed to the left, slightly.

My family was far from Ʉe Huxtables, really. Eye've been stabbed, hurt, spat on, talked about, broken, savaged and slain by different members of my family.

Eye wasn't that close with my immediate family, with the exception of my Brother Kells and my sister Diva, but Eye loved them unconditionally. As of April 2011 Eye even found myself getting closer to my brother Jarshawn. But the family Eye spoke of, the family that has hurt me the most, wasn't my Mom or brothers or sisters or uncles.

No. It was my 2$^{nd}$ and 3$^{rd}$ cousins, Ʉe Rolle family, my family, *that* family. Yea, *them.*

Granted, not all of them were bad. Eye loved them all, yes, but Eye couldn't *stand* some of them. Mainly some of the older ones.

This wasn't about any of my cousins within my age group. PHAROAH wasn't about *them.* It wasn't designed to hurt them, but it was designed to leave a recorded document of my journey from nappy headed Niggah to a bestselling author and unravel the trials Eye faced along the way that nearly made or broke me.

This wasn't about my little cousins Smoo or Lil George. Eye loved them beyond reproach and we never had a falling out. This was about a few of my OLDER cousins. The same ones who Eye went to for help and they turned me away. Did Eye go to all of them? No. Surely didn't. Eye went to three of them. Two were dead. One was still alive and Eye hardly said two words to her. Every time Eye lay eyes on her Eye just wanna throw up. Let's get this off my brain right now. Eye was a bisexual male, but Eye didn't live by labels. Eye was a contradicting sonofabitch because Eye didn't want anybody figuring me out. You get too close to me and Eye wasn't ready Eye will be the gentle, quiet chameleon and switch on your ass, say something foul to ruin a friendship and change my cell phone number.

Eye was very insecure in a friendship. Been hurt too much and don't tell me that's life. No. Life was one way every day. God made life and life was made through the genius of Genesis.

A few people in my life were the deranged ones, not Mother Nature. Always wanted me to change, but they were the perfect ones. Don't curse, don't do this and that and when Eye tell you to go make you some babies and tell those nappy headed little things what to do you throw an attitude.

At this stage in my life Eye was blunt and blood raw.

Twenty, twenty-five years ago Eye never dreamed of being so raw. Eye was guarded, quiet and meek. Being raped in my own home and forced to be quiet about it made me feel worthless. Being annihilated within my family and brushed off as a failure made me curl up and die. Mom never sexually hurt me [Overall, and despite how Eye feel about her now she was a very GOOD MOTHER and, presently, Eye love and adore her], but people around her tried to destroy me for mistakes Eye never made, but for mistakes and bad decisions of those in my immediate blood line.

When Eye did something Eye didn't explain myself to nobody. You didn't like something Eye did go pray about it and leave me the hell alone because you won't get any tears. This is my life. Let me live it accordingly.

Eye was 6 feet 5 inches above the ones buried 6 feet under, 223 pounds of guts, glory and inner beauty. Eye hated some days, loved other days and Eye hated my temper. Sometimes Eye read the Bible, sometimes Eye didn't, but Eye did talk to God, the God in me and my own inner self as well. Eye knew all three really well.

One friend of mine once asked me, "How can you love God, but you're bisexual?"

Eye looked him in the face, sucked my Blow Pop and said, "How can you be a Pastor and you get poked in the butt by the drummer and you barely even kiss your fat ass wife?"

He deleted my phone number, and Eye never put any more of my hard earned money in his fake ass tithe plate.

Talk about hypocrite. Jesus died for my sins, that meant he died for my sexuality too, uptight buttholes.

Eye was a Cancer, sensitive, loved Alaskan Crab Legs, loved Janet Jackson for 27 years and believed in God in my own way; not the church way. Eye didn't let an organized church full of secret sluts and whores run my life and Eye loved writing and reading and researching.

Eye loved sex, masturbation and lotion bottles. But if Eye didn't like you or love you Eye didn't sleep with you.

Eye masturbated more than Eye slept with anybody. To me, that was the highest compliment of self love Eye could display.

In fact no one has touched, scratched or sniffed my body sexually in a very long time because Eye wanted it that way. Men and women hit me up online, bring up my books as an ice breaker and always resulted in, *"Can Eye have sex with you? You're so fine!"*

One man from Switzerland hit me up and said, *"Let me freak you, King. Let me grind in that intelligent booty and make you cum another book on my stick."* An Australian fan said, *"Eye wanna eat snake off your buttocks."* A man from Germany said, *"Eye wanna marry you. Let me buy you what your heart desires."* A famous actor in New York said, *"Be with me. Eye have your work. Phenomenal. Eye will set you up for life, King."*

So many NFL and NBA stars have hit me up its crazy. Two of them, very high profile millionaires, made me cum all night in an expensive condo on Miami Beach. When Eye worked at Dolphin Stadium, as one of the Retail Warehouse Supervisors, one of the Marlins came up to me and said, "Eye saw your books online. Eye ordered the first two. Eye read them. Here's my number." He handed it to me in a Marlins' souvenir cup. "Call me. Let me dig in that ass."

He winked and walked off.

A certain NBA player came up to me on South Beach, when my first book came out, and he said, "Eye think you're on my Myspace page." People were looking at him from Wet Willy's, calling his name over and over, snapping pictures and he was all in my face, whispering.

"Walk with me," he said. We talked all the way to an awaiting limo. Once Eye got inside, we would have a two week affair. But when it got to the point of possessing me, telling me where Eye can go and what Eye can do, telling me he had other men set up in condos all over the country, no matter where they played a game a piece of male ass was a pit stop away, Eye couldn't do it. He wanted to set me up in a condo on South Beach, but the fine lining was simple; nobody can come there, Eye can't tell anybody. "Don't post anything on social networks that can cause me to lose my career and be readily available for me to fuck at my leisure."

Basically, prison. Eye kissed him, gave him a hug, said "Sure, dude," walked out of his high rise on South Beach and never contacted him again. And the women were equally forthcoming. The more Eye said Eye was bisexual the more a bitch threw her panties at me. Eye begin engaging in foreplay with beautiful women. Eye pulled more females as a bisexual male than Eye got as a so-called straight man.

Eye got lost in it. Eye thrived on it, making them nut and having sex with nameless women with different types of coochie out of the same anger Eye had when Eye was sleeping with men and women twice my age when Eye was a teenager.

But that's all sex was when Eye became an author: an image. A nut. A feeling. Eye didn't love any of them. Eye wanted my nut, make them nut and kapow, Eye was out the door. Eye never looked back and didn't call your phone. You got what you wanted, Eye got what Eye thought Eye needed and we were happy.

First one cum, wins became my drug of choice.

Eye get horny just like you and Eye didn't apologize for it. If you got a *negative* opinion or something bad to say about my autobiography close it and go jump off a cliff. Eye was telling you up front, keeping it one hundred percent with you. Eye'm all for *constructive* criticism, and will listen to your point of view. But remember that's all it is. Your point of view. *Not* the gospel. This book was for my fans, they requested it and they wanted it. Eye got over 56,000 emails, letters and requests for my life story, for the book about the man who was and is ƂE KING OF EROTICA, the first in literary history was me. Google ƂE KING OF EROTICA, Eye popped up FIRST. Put ƂE KING OF EROTICA in Barnes and Noble or Amazon.com's search box, Eye came up first and only Eye come up, period. If you *think* Eye was gay then, trick, *you're* gay. Niggah, if you think Eye'm gay then trick, *you're* gay. Eye'm your mirror. When you look at me you see yourself with a hard on, secretly wanting to bang me and you wanna talk a bunch of noise because you think Eye was a quiet Niggah.

Nah, Eye wasn't quiet. Eye was cautiously writing about you in my book and once Eye published it Eye gave it to your bitch as a Christmas gift.

That's how Eye've slain Niggahs in the game. It's to the point they are too afraid to even tell me *Hello* in the neighborhood. Talk crap about me Eye will tell your clueless, baldhead girlfriend our rendezvous in my book in the form of a character.

For as long as Eye could remember Eye was a blotch mark. Being whatever people wanted to see. My biological father didn't love me. Eye haven't seen him since Eye was 14 (or 15) months old and Eye have no recollection.

His name was Pharoah Curtis Wilson, Sr. He's from California. His Mama used to live on West Vine Street or something like that (in San Bernardino). Eye *never* met her, but Eye spoke to her a few times before she died around the time Eye was in high school. Eye remembered how Eye found out she died. Mama, back then, was driving a rusty two door Mustang that was slow on the take off. So coming to terms with losing both grandmas, on Mom and Dad's side, was next to impossible. Eye hated life. Eye hated my existence. Eye had so much hate Eye became blind to rationalizations. *Learning* to cope with never hearing Grandma Alice's voice or hugging her and smelling her scent and listening to her talk forever plagued me.

Hate burned me inside and out, because, even dealing with that, Eye had a lot of things plowing through my mind. YOUR GRANDMA KILLED MY DADDY! Those words would shape the beginnings of my life; Eye would take the words to heart and hate myself because of it for years to come. That was, until Mom sat me down and told me the REAL story and Eye concluded that my Grandma didn't kill anybody. She was never charged, jailed or anything. Eye let it go then. But not the anger. Eye'll get into that urban legend later. Eye wrote books but Eye wasn't a book. Eye have been writing ever since Eye was a small child, age 6 to be exact. When Eye was 8 years old my teacher beat my ass and made me write in a journal, gave me a Sara Teasdale's poem "The Falling Star." Eye won my first poetry open mic night in the third grade reciting this poem in front of teachers, a panel and parents. Eye had on a light blue pinstriped suit, long sleeved white shirt without a tie and buck teeth.

Eye was so nervous, walking up the microphone and opening my mouth to recite the poem from memory.

"Eye'm Pharoah Wilson. And Eye am gonna recite The Falling Star," Eye said, my nerves sending me into hysteria. Eye shook so hard Eye had to put my hands in my pockets.

Everyone looked at me, saying nothing. Eye looked at them, saying nothing. My teacher looked at me, urging me on. Smiling, Miss Mike nodded.

"Eye saw a star…"

And Eye received a thunderous standing ovation when Eye was done, shocking the hell out of me. eye wasn't even that good, and y voice cracked before Eye uttered the first word! When Eye won the first place ribbon—again, Eye was *shocked.* Were the judges playing a trick on me?—Eye did one thing with it as Eye exited the building. Eye trashed it. Eye didn't want Mama knowing Eye won anything. And Eye didn't want my ex step father knowing either.

He was the devil.

*As Eye got older and into* writing books, Eye wrote short stories, but Eye *wasn't* the characters. It wasn't until Eye went to prison that Eye decided to take writing seriously, because Eye didn't want prison being a rotating door in my life. Eye never made excuses for being there, and Eye hardly shed a tear. Prison taught me to man up, and Eye stopped sucking my thumb in jail, especially with men chasing my ass like a Frisbee.

Eye was *never* raped in prison. Eye nearly was, though…

But that would be explained later on in this book.

Eye was bisexual, but Eye haven't really touched a woman in a very long time.

Come to think of it Eye haven't really slept with a man, either. Since contracting HIV, Eye have been standoffish, afraid to touch anyone. Eye grew pensive, hating myself, the little love Eye had for myself was swallowed whole and Eye felt empty, like a void searching for fulfillment and finding another abyss and falling into the darkness and no matter how Eye flung my arms or screamed for help Eye still fell.

Deeper into the abyss of my subconscious, to the point it became my reality. Eye opened the door for all women, young and old, fat or skinny and Eye always nodded my head with a smile. Didn't matter if they thought Eye was gay or not. What mattered was that, despite the ups and downs with my mother, Eye never let Mom open the door if Eye was with her, or pump the gas. Just encoded in me. The *purpose* of this book was *not* to expose people. That's why Eye changed their names And it won't be exposing anybody, really. This book was to mark my journey, from abused, rape victim to bestselling author. From confused, angry kid without a voice to becoming the voice of thousands who didn't have a voice. Some things Eye left for myself and some names Eye changed to protect whoever needed protecting.

Despite what Eye wrote, some things Eye won't ever talk about. It was just too painful for me. One thing bothered me, though. A recent conversation with one of my favorite female cousins.

## THE PHONE CALL

*Eye called her, late January of 2010*, and she told me a couple of her aunts claimed Eye never came to them and told them Eye was being raped.

Eye laughed so hard Eye nearly choked.

"What?"

"Yea, Pharoah. That's what they said. Eye know what you went through, but my Mom said you never came to her…"

"Um, she wasn't the one Eye went to. Eye don't talk to your Mama because she calls me all kinds of names behind my back and people kept coming back to me with it. But, baby, one of your aunts and two of your uncles damn sure knew Eye was being raped. Eye told them."

"Pharoah, calm down."

"Calm down? For *what*? They banding together huh? Let them, Eye will tear their asses down."

"It's not about that, Pharoah. You should let it go."

"And Eye did, that was until they claim Eye never came to them? Are you serious? Then why are they calling my cell phone begging me not to write the book? One of your aunts called and apologized for not helping me, yet sitting around her sisters and brother and claiming Eye never told anybody?"

"Pharoah…"

"Don't worry, Eye won't name her. But Eye will talk about it."

"Ok, you gotta do what you gotta do."

"Eye have been doing that. For four years now. Anyway, Eye have to go." Eye hung up.

*Eye was introduced to Lord Jennings* by one of my homeboys Eye went to school with. We only spoke on Facebook.

A very seasoned 29 year old, he had it all. House, car, money and a good career. He was handsome, tall and a bit hard-edged.

At first, Eye told him Eye didn't need counsel, but he hit me up on Facebook and he said he read about my life and was bewildered, that if Eye wanted to get some professional help about my past he was the man.

Eye laughed, deleting him off my friend list but he was consistent. He started emailing me and telling me, "Pharoah, Eye wanna pick your brain. Eye wanna do this," but Eye ignored him.

Then it all changed. It was a few days into September, and Eye had just returned home from the ITLA Atlanta Pride.

He sent me another friend request right after Eye posted on Facebook that Eye was depressed, that Eye was tired of being the author everyone wanted me to be. That Eye was tired of my backstabbing family, and just tired of everybody making me out to be Pharoah the Robot.

Eye was even more obsessed with writing. Eye was spending less time with my significant other and more time behind the keyboard creating. Eye was losing myself and slowly turning my back on writing.

Eye used to cry myself to sleep from the loneliness.

When Eye logged on Facebook and noticed there were 140 Friend Requests waiting, even though my list was maxed out at 5,000 and they didn't wanna join the Fan Page, they wanted to be on my Main Page; Eye deleted a book club off my friend list and accepted his request.

When Eye did, he hit me up on the IM.

"Pharoah. Come to Downtown Miami. Eye wanna counsel you. Eye'll do it for free."

Eye wrote him back, "No, man. Eye don't *need* a shrink."

"But you need a friend. Someone who sees Pharoah as Pharoah, not Ҍe King of Erotica. Talk to me. Let me counsel you. Come tonight."

"Eye can't. It's after 6 p.m. and Eye don't feel like coming way up there."

"Eye'll come get you."

*Damn he's consistent! He doesn't give up!* "Yea, right. All the way down in Homestead?"

"Eye'm heading for my Jag right now. Text me your address and Eye'll Map Quest it."

Eye hung up, putting my phone on the dresser.

Crazy, Eye tell you. Eye was not letting a stranger pick my brain. All the freaks online, prying on your vulnerability, and being that Eye had some celebrity, Eye had to be careful.

Eye text him my address.

John, Eye love you with everything in my soul...
At my lowest point...you were there to
lift me up with your humbleness, loyalty and love.
Thank you. Eye see Jesus every time you smile.

# Part 1

EYE'M NOT WORTH THE WOMB
EYE CAME OUT OF.

## Sessi☯n ☯nΣ

*"Pharoah, how do you feel?" Lord Jennings* asked with an air of professionalism Eye've never really experienced with anyone else, and that in itself gave me some hope that these sessions would work. But it was too soon to talk.

Eye didn't know how Eye felt. *Truly* did not. The things Eye've seen and endured in my life has changed me for the better or for the worse, depends on my mood that day to challenge either side.

Eye was 32 years old—at the time. Still in my Mama's house, and calling myself a bestseller. When was Eye going to fly away from the bird's nest?

"Pharoah?" he called out, brows rose.

Eye barely looked at him. Eye hated talking about me with a passion. Eye'd rather you talk about you. "Yes."

"Talk to me."

"Eye just have a lot on my mind."

"Isn't that the point of this therapy session?"

"Yes, it is…but, you know. Eye just don't like accepting free things from people."

He grinned, small lines forming around his gorgeous eyes. Soft eyes. Piercing eyes. "Are you apprehensive about this?"

Eye looked at him. "Yes. Eye am."

"Eye offered these sessions to you, free of charge."

"Yes, you did. And at first Eye nearly bit your head off."

"Because you thought Eye had motives."

"Yes, Eye did. Eye'm from Goulds. Rule number one. Nobody does *anything* for free."

"And *now*?"

Eye thought about it. "Eye see you genuinely want to help me deal with the past."

"And you're still uneasy?"

This time Eye looked deep in his eyes, see the actual man Eye'm speaking with. "Easy things have blown up in my face."

"So yes, you're uneasy."

"Very. Telling my business to a complete stranger was never my cup of tea."

He crossed his legs, his loafers shining from the expensive ceiling fan lights. "Do you wanna move forward? No pressure."

"Yes, Eye do. Good thing these sessions are free."

He stopped smiling a bit, more alert. "Why you say that?"

Eye waved my hands. "Off the record, you feel me?"

He smiled again, his eyes sparkling. "Big author, huh. Scared Eye'm gonna sell your secrets?"

Um. "Yes."

He sat up, uncrossing his legs. "Eye won't, trust me. My wife already didn't want me to do this and Eye told her Eye wouldn't."

*So this one is married. Well, he's fine as hell; Eye can't say Eye'm surprised.* "Oh…"

"Yea. Thing is, she knows who you are. She has your books, and she's a huge fan."

*Why was he stuttering?* "So the problem is…?"

His face lit up. "You're gorgeous, she says that of course."

Um, ok. "And you think…?"

He got dark. "Eye don't judge men."

Um, yea, ok. *Then why does he have a hard on? Eye won't burst his bubble.* "Right, yet your wife is threatened why? If you don't judge men why lie to her and say you're not gonna counsel me?"

"Eye find you intriguing. You gotta understand, from a straight man's perspective, you are a dream. Not to sleep with you, no sir. Eye want to understand you. You are so free. You come as go as you please. You walk in a room and people look at you. Eye don't know thugs or gangsters who are that free."

"That's not true."

"Yes it is. When we grabbed a bite to eat at the diner, people stared at you. Women did as well as so-called straight men. That fascinated me."

"Well, Eye heard that before but Eye don't stop long enough to be engrossed in trivial things like that."

"Trivial how?"

"Eye am not stuck on myself."

"Come on, Pharoah," he said, taking off his jacket. "You're not?"

"Eye used to be, back when Eye was an angry high school teenager. Had a lot going on."

"That's what Eye wanna get into. That aspect."

"Ok, it's a start."

"Are you still feeling uneasy?"

"No, Eye'm not."

He looked at his watch. "Well, this session is almost over. But Eye tell you what, the office is about to close but Eye don't want the session to end. After all Eye drove all the way to Homestead to pick you up. Don't feel like driving back down there, Pharoah."

"But you gotta get home to your wife."

"True, but there is something Eye didn't tell you."

"What?"

"She thinks Eye'm out of town."

Eye narrowed my eyes, my guard going up. *Emotional walls, Tasha Mack. Emotional walls.* "Why does she think that?"

"Eye couldn't pass up the opportunity to get in your head. You write books, people love you on Myspace and Facebook. People adore you. Eye wanna get to know Pharoah. The man behind the books."

"Oh, God. You make me out to be JL Queen or James Baldwin or something."

"Pharoah. JL Queen could never match your artistry. In fact he got backlash for that On the Down Low book. James Baldwin is deceased, yes and certainly a pioneer. And so are you. You're doing what no other male author has done. You've packaged yourself, made you and your photographs a brand people look at and wanna buy. Men don't know whether to buy your book or jack off to your picture on the cover."

Eye turned beet red. "Oh, stop." But he was right.

Eye logged onto the different social networks and let him read all the fantasies Pa$tor$ (Eye spelled Pastor with a $—dollar—sign), married men, straight men, gay men, feminine men, women, married women and sisters, brothers and uncles and aunts send me every day.

His mouth fell open clicking through the messages, reading. Eye looked down. He *still* had a hard-on.

He went on. "White women, black women, gay and straight men read your work. Eye was on your Facebook page last year and E Lynn Harris even spoke to you. Publicly said hello."

"That is pretty cool. Eye look up to him. He said he wants to mentor me."

"That's a huge accomplishment."

"Eye keep hearing that."

"See there. A Negro from Goulds? Eye mean, outside of Florida who has heard of Goulds?"

"Eye know, right."

"Now people wanna know more about you, your life and Goulds. What is it that makes you smile, mad or tick? We are getting into that tonight."

"How?"

"Eye have a condo in one of the high rises, Downtown Miami. About fifty six floors above the Ocean. You should see the sunset from up there."

"Ok, but Eye don't know about this."

"Pharoah." He took my hands and gazed deep into my eyes. "My wife doesn't know everything Eye buy. Plus the condo Eye bought is in my brother's name."

"Wow, ok."

"My brother is dead, Pharoah. So don't worry. Let's go. We got a long night."

Eye stood up, grabbing my book bag. Out the corner of my Eye he took a huge swig of liquor. It was in a shiny, silver, flask. Eye swallowed hard. My mind told me to go with him.

But my heart said *Danger, Danger, Danger!*

*When we arrived at his pricey* condo, Eye had heart failure going up the elevator. Eye had a phobia for them, and Eye didn't like them. Eye was nauseated, and wanted to puke, holding on to the side like it was about to tip over. For some reason every time Eye got in one Eye thought it'd snap and kill me or it'd stop working and Eye'd die from lack of oxygen.

He looked at me, ill at ease, like he was used to it.

"Scared, Pharoah?"

Eye held my forehead, about to pass out. "Eye don't like this thing. Why is it going so fast?"

"It's an elevator, designed to get you to where you're going…"

It jerked a tad and Eye jumped out of my skin, covering my face.

He reached over and took my right hand and squeezed.

"You're safe. You're with me. In my environment. Eye won't let anything hurt you."

He hugged me, a brotherly hug. No homo, as the in-the-closet rappers say these days.

"Calm down, all right, dude?"

Eye didn't say anything.

Eye followed behind him to his condo.

*Inside his condo was breathtaking*. A very eclectic man, he had some of everything. Books from every author you could imagine, but he didn't have mine Eye thought to myself.

The living room looked more like something ripped from *Architectural Digest.* Thin carpets, amazing busts, and a dining room table that mimicked something from Michael Jackson's house.

Stuffed animal heads on the walls, pictures of his mother and father, married, hung in the middle of the wall. His father looked strangely familiar, but maybe it was my nervousness getting the best of me. On the low table were silver framed pictures of his son, from age 1 thru 5, his wife, and of him, in his football uniform in high school.

His graduation picture from high school and college, and a picture with actress Vivica A. Fox.

"You met her?" Eye asked. Eye had it bad for Vivica.

"Yes," he said. "Eye did."

"Wow. Impressive house."

Eye was walking through the high tech kitchen. Simple yet bold. Black walls. Platinum stove and fridge.

Eye opened the fridge. Bottled water on the top shelf. Heinekens on the bottom shelf, about twenty of them. Fridge looked like it was stocked by a Publix stock man.

Cream colored counters, marble topped island counter.

Eye walked to his bedroom, and opened the double doors.

Oh my God. Paradise. He sat on the couch; crossed his legs, watching me with a smile. "You like it, huh?"

"Man Eye could never own something this exquisite."

"Why do you say that? You have books out. You're well on your way. When God *says* its time."

Eye turned to face him. Eye was a little confused. "You almost stuttered when you said God."

"Yea, Eye'ma little tired. But come on, man," he said, standing up, taking off his suit coat. "We got a week to do this. Eye'll get my tape recorder and memo pads and we can start tonight."

"Ok." Eye closed his bedroom doors, setting my book bag by the couch. Eye brought my HIV medicine with me so Eye was straight. Eye didn't tell anyone about this meeting because Eye didn't need praise for wanting to help myself. Eye put my phone on silcnt.

Eye sat down, leaning back on the comfy sofa. It seemed to swallow me, but it was very relaxing.

He turned on soft jazz.

"Eye know this may seem weird, but do you have candles?" Eye asked politely, wondering did Eye overstep my boundaries.

"Eye have a gazillion of them."

"Mind lighting a few? Eye sometimes light candles when Eye write. Helps free me."

He thought about it. "Sure. Anything to make you comfortable."

It took him about fifteen minutes to set them all up. About forty of them, different sizes. This felt like a fantasy. He didn't have to pull out that many of them. Three would have sufficed.

He offered me some Moet and Eye said yes because Eye never tasted it before. Eye wasn't much of a drinker outside of strawberry daiquiris and B&J wine coolers. And like damn who drinks Moet anymore?

Eye was sipping Moet, *hey*! And looking around at the massive book shelves. Polished to a shine. You could see your reflection in the wood. Eye loved books, made me horny seeing them all. Not towards him, even though he was handsome, but Eye wasn't there for that so that never crept into my mind.

Eye was thumbing through books. James Patterson. He had them all. He had over 30 Stephen King books, Dean Koontz, all in hardback. He didn't have one soft back book.

Interesting. He had Jackie Collins, one of my favorite authors, he had every Sidney Sheldon book. Oh my God, *Master of the Game* was my favorite book, next to Sistah Souljah's *The Coldest Winter Ever* and he had that and *No Disrespect.*

He had autobiographies by Janet Jackson (*Out of the Madness*, Eye had that one), Michael Jackson, Diana Ross, and a host of other entertainers.

"Eye read every book on that shelf," he said. "Eye love to read."

After lighting the candles, he turned off the lights, the soft warm glow cast on my naked arms. Cackling flames filled my ears, relaxing me. Eye had on sweats and a wife beater and black socks smelling of Johnson and Johnson lavender powder. An easy smell, couldn't have funky ass feet and Eye wore a size 14.

The Moet was loosening me up.

He walked over to me, paused beside me and said, "Keep looking, tell me what you see."

"Duh. Eye see books."

He pulled my first one, in hard cover, from the shelf. My mouth fell open.

"You got my book?"

"Eye have them all, in hard cover. Unfortunately Eye'm a little mad because your third book, The King 3, was only in paperback and Eye hate paperback books but Eye bought it anyway to support you."

"Wow, dude." He had them all, all 7 of them. Even *Call Her Queen Hatshepsut.*

"Have you read book 1?"

"Pharoah, Eye read the all. You are a literary genius, you know that?"

Eye looked away. No Eye wasn't. He replaced the book and said, "Come, let's get started. We got a lot of work to do."

He handed me something.

Eye looked at him. "You smoke pot?"

"No, but you do. Eye read that you smoke weed when you read important books. Eye want you free, so we can do this right. Do what you do. Eye'll be in the kitchen, and when you're ready to start the session let me know."

He handed me a lighter.

*Once Eye was on Saturn,* Eye felt like Eye was out of my body, watching myself roam around. Eye sat on the couch.

"Are you relaxed, Pharoah?"

"Yes, Eye am," Eye said, the flicker of the flames igniting something deep inside me.

"Are you ready to start?"

"Yes, Eye am."

"What did you bring with you?"

"A couple old journals of mine, some letters, a few things Eye have written over the years, like poems and stuff, photos and my HIV medicine."

He smiled, crossing his legs, jotting down some notes.

"Pharoah, why do you wanna deal with your past?"

Eye looked at him. "Because tomorrow isn't promised."

He closed his eyes.

"Damn, you're deep," he said easily.

"Eye know."

"State your full name."

"Pharoah Curtis Wilson, Jr."

"Do you *like* your name?"

"Um, no."

"Eye'm surprised. Why don't you like your name?"

"Because Eye'm named after a man who didn't lift a finger to raise me."

"And this man was…?"

"My biological father."

"And his name?"

"Sperm. Donor."

"Pharoah."

"Pharoah Curtis Wilson, Sr."

"How do you feel about him? Do you love him?"

"How can you love someone you never really met?"

"Didn't you write a letter to your father in your book?"

"Yes and Eye regret it."

"Regret it why?"

"Eye just do. Eye wish Eye could go back in time and delete it."

"Will you ever write a letter to your mother?"

"Eye plan on it. So much Eye wanna tell her. Eye am both proud and angry with her. It's like Mama is two different people. Maybe in my autobiography Eye'll open it with a letter to her."

"Smart move."

"Gee, thanks."

"Was he ever in your life, your sperm donor?"

"Yes, he was. Mom was married to him. She left him when Eye was 16 months old or so she says."

"Do you believe her?"

"Yes, Eye do. Eye just don't know why, really."

"Do you think you know why?"

"*Kinda.* Eye *heard* he kept running the streets and going to jail. Eye heard his family denounced Eye was his child. Eye heard my grandma, his mother, didn't like me very much, because she said Eye wasn't her son's child. Eye also heard one of my aunts bit me on the ear. Eye heard he pulled a gun on mom and Eye…"

"How did that make you feel?"

"Lost. To hear this made me cut him off completely, any feeling or any wish for him to be in my life."

"At what age did you cut him off?"

"When Eye was about 18. Eye was in the United States Army, and he had already stood me up by not coming to my high school graduation like he told me over the phone he would. Eye was devastated, but Eye got over it. When Eye was in the Army Eye sent him a letter, telling him where Eye was. He wrote back, sent me pictures of my siblings and *Eye* wanted to meet them."

"And did you?"

The tears fell. "It was the last Eye ever heard from him."

"And now, how do you feel about Pharoah Wilson Sr?"

Eye looked up into his eyes. "He can croak for all Eye care."

"Do you love him?"

*Yes Eye do!* "No, Eye don't."

"Do you wanna meet him?"

*No Eye don't.* "Yes, Eye do."

He looked at me a moment. Thinking. "If you hope he croaks, why bother?"

*Here we go. Psychoanalyzing me.* "He needs to know how Eye feel."

"He should already. Didn't you write a letter to him in your first book, ҔE KING OF EROTICA 1?"

"Yes, and you already brought that up. But how do Eye know he read it? How do Eye know he even KNOWS *Eye'm* a published author?"

"Your books are slowly becoming a household name."

"That's all good, but my *father*...Eye *need* to see him face to face. Just to talk. Do Eye hate him, no?"

"But you do have some sort of resentment?"

"Of course, yes. Eye need closure."

"This is how we're going to do this session, and all the others for the next week, before Eye go back to my life and wife...Eye will bring up something and Eye will have you talk about it. It doesn't have to be in order, from age so and so up to age 32. In fact, you can bring up bad things that happened to you in your life and tell me exactly what happened. Eye want the naked truth, the fine print, the underlining tone."

Eye was hesitant. Eye smoked the entire blunt, so Eye was deep within myself like Eye was meditating with my eye wide open. The music sounded different, and it *relaxed* me more. Eye felt myself letting go.

"Ok, we can do that."

He smiled. "Where do you wanna start first?"

"When Eye was raped..."

He rubbed his palms together. "Ok, let's begin."

Eye was suddenly choked up. "It's hard, man."

He reached over and squeezed my shoulder. "Pharoah *Eye* know. But remember Eye am *not* going to pressure you."

"Eye have dealt with it."

"Have you really?"

"Yes."

"Pharoah, say the words. Say you are about to talk about being raped."

Eye hesitated. It was hard to say, to a stranger at least. How…"Eye can't just do that."

"But you've dealt with it?"

"Yes."

"Say the words."

"No, Eye'm not ready to say the words."

"Its simple, if you've dealt with it. Just form the words and make sounds. Say it, like this, 'Eye am going to talk about being raped.'"

"You're getting on my last nerves already," Eye snapped, standing up. The tears were about to fall. Eye was suddenly scared; that scared 6 year old inside my heart hugging my trembling body in the corner of the room when that man was done mutilating me.

"Pharoah!"

Eye started for the door. "Eye have to go." *Run!*

"Pharoah, don't leave. You can't keep running from something you claim you've dealt with."

"Eye can't be here. This is a bad idea."

"Pharoah, many people look up to you."

Eye unlocked the door. Eye would never see him again. Eye couldn't do this. This was harder than Eye thought.

"PHAROAH!"

Eye turned on my heel and pointed, "No pressure; isn't that what you said?"

"Yes, Eye said that," he said, standing up. He walked up to me. "As a shrink Eye won't pressure you or make you do things you don't want to."

"Eye had counseling before. MDSO class, when Eye had to register as a sex offender. Eye hated that class, sitting in there for something Eye didn't do and had to lie and say Eye did so they wouldn't throw me back in jail. The entire ordeal was a goddamn joke. All they wanted was money, money, money. Dr. Checkerwitz and all those other jokester therapists got on my last nerve."

"Pharoah, as your friend let me help you. Eye know all about that. Eye read your blog a couple years back when you openly discussed that case. The things you survived man, and you kept going in *spite* of. Not many people go to prison and become bestselling authors. Only a handful have successfully achieved that feat."

"Eye know."

"Tell you what Eye'm gonna do." He pulled me to the computer room. Pricey shit. Laser color printer, and other printers that print pictures and everything.

"Log onto your Facebook, Myspace and Photo bucket and go sit out in the living room."

Eye started for the living room.

"Better yet, go outside the condo and take the elevator down to the first floor then take it back up and come back. Don't look at me crazy. Just do it."

Eye did so, hesitantly.

Me and my favorite cousin Ravonte Payne with out Janet Jackson Number Ones Tour tickets for her Tampa, Florida show December 4, 2011. I love you Cuzzo!

Dapharoah69 at my brother Trevor's House Party, an intimate gathering of family and friends. This was one of the happiest times of my life. You see those smiles on our faces? Thank you Trevor for being a brother. And my nephew Adon is amazing!

BELOW: Dapharoah69 with my niece Shay, Alana, and my nephew Pac-Man and my sister Shani McCrary.

# THE ELEVATOR

*Eye stood in front of the elevator,* shaking out of my skin.

"Eye'm scared of elevators. Oh my God!"

Eye gazed at my reflection, looking myself over. Eye smiled. Eye'm about to open up to a complete stranger.

Eye closed my eyes when the elevator opened. Eye held my breath.

"Eye can't do this!"

"Yes you can," he said, standing behind me. "Face your fear. Take the elevator to the first floor and back up. Do it alone."

"But Eye can't!"

*When Eye came back inside the condo* from going up and down in the elevator by myself (and my fear), Eye held my breath. He had printed out my baby pictures and photos of me from my life before Eye was a bestseller.

He had them in frames all over the condo. The end and low tables, the dining tables with candles lit.

He taped some to the walls, very neatly too. Eye was just floored.

To see half of those pictures Eye haven't seen in years did a number on me. So much came flooding back. That life before these books Eye didn't want to remember.

Days Eye hated myself with a dark loathing that confused me. Days Eye challenged the angels and demons of my soul. The days Eye wanted nothing yet tried to achieve everything. Those days Eye slept with men for strength and banged women because Nookie was something Eye felt Eye couldn't live without. Days Eye disrespected myself, church and my mother. Days Eye wanted to die, tried to commit suicide and days Eye didn't want to wake up the next day.

Times Eye seriously did not wanna face. Times Eye went to jail, prison, had to register as a sex offender, stayed in different houses to appease parole, and holding down two full-time jobs.

Eye've gone through a lot and been through a lot and Eye wasn't supposed to make it. Eye wasn't supposed to be here. Eye was supposed to be a crack head, one of my cousins said. Eye never touched crack a day in my life, no matter what Eye have gone through.

Eye sat on the sofa and put my face in my hands.

He sat next to me, rubbing my shoulder.

"*Pharoah, are you ready to begin*. Eye know this ain't exactly your life flashing before your eyes. Think of it as flash cards, your pictures."

Eye looked up, and gazed at my kindergarten picture.

Eye was so cute.

What happened, Eye thought, trying to make myself laugh and Eye started silently crying, bursting open.

"Why do you frown at your photos, Pharoah?"

"Eye hate them. Eye hate everything about them."

"Why do you hate them?"

"Because Eye'm not all that."

"Why do you feel that way about your earlier image? You were made in God's image."

"As the world turns."

"Are you ready to dig deep into your soul, and let go?"

"Yes, Eye am."

"As your shrink Eye don't support this, but as your friend Eye want you to hit this."

He lit a joint and we smoked it together. *Once* the effects got to me, making me high, Eye leaned back on the chair and he picked up a yellow pad and an ink pen.

"Are you ready to talk about the rape?"

"Yes," Eye said, and Eye begin to talk…

The door of my subconscious snatched open.

The light starkly chasing away the shadows.

But the darkness remained.

# HOME GOING SERVICE FOR:

SUNRISE:
June 26, 1977

SUNSET:
August 1983

PHAROAH C. WILSON, JR'S VIRGINITY
AUGUST 1983
12:30 A.M.

SWEET HOME BAPTIST CHURCH
33 SOMEWHERE ON CONFIDENCE LANE
GOULDS, FLORIDA 33170
**REV. DR. GOD VS. SATAN**

*Let not your heart be troubled. Ye believe in God believe also in me. In my father's house are many mansions. If it were not so, Eye would have told you so. Eye will come again, and receive you unto myself where Eye am, there ye may be also.*

# John 14:1-3

**A Time to be Born:** On June 26, 1977, Pharoah Wilson, Jr. was born in Salinas, California to Clara Bernadine McCrae and a dead beat named Pharoah C Wilson, Sr. He's the oldest of three children.

**A Time to Grow:** Pharoah grew up in Goulds, Florida amongst a few family members that hated him. And those he thought were friends betrayed him. Two of those friends would rape him under the school portables.

**A Time to Reflect:** Pharoah was a promising young kid who loved his toys and lived for He-Man, the Smurfs, and the Jackson 5 cartoons. His Kindergarten teacher, Mrs. George taught him to spell his name before she taught any other kid in her class. She also secretly and quietly gave him 2 books she didn't give any other kid in the class. It was a dictionary. And the Holy Bible.

**A Time to Die and be mourned:** On a gloomy day in August 1983, Pharoah Wilson was knocked to the floor and raped by his Step daddy [at the time]. He not only lost his voice but no one believed him. Older cousins turned their backs on him after a couple of them said, "Your Grandma killed my daddy," and brainwashed him into thinking the rape never happened. But it would happen for the next four years, till he turned ten years old.

# YOU LIK∑ BOYYYSSSS!

***Eye remember that day vividly***. Eye was 6 years old—as a matter of fact Eye had *just* turned six years old June of '83, and Eye knew Eye was a big man. Already taller than my classmates, life for me was about my He-Man and Battle Cat toys. It was about to rain. Eye could smell it coming, and dark clouds were slowly transforming the sky, gradually swallowing the sun. Eye was out in the front yard playing with Bernnard, my friend that stayed in the first house on the block. He didn't have his own toys so he borrowed my GI Joe toys. Eye didn't like him very much, because he was a bully and he was always making me suck his penis, but he said my teeth kept cutting him so he eventually made me stop and Eye was glad because Eye didn't wanna suck nothing a niggah pissed with anyway, but since he was the only friend, besides Chad (and he stayed too far away) around me Eye had no problems playing with Bernnard or jacking him off until thick white stuff spewed all over my hands. He was breathing all hard like he stupid and gazing at me all wide eyed. Niggah crazy, but Eye didn't say anything. He said he'd beat me up and Eye was a scary child, but tried not to show it.

But that would soon change.

Bernnard and Eye were slapping action figures together, competing. The green/brown grass was itching my legs. Eye wore jean shorts, tennis shoes minus the socks and my white

He-Man and Battle cat sweater, with the sleeves cut. Eye also had a black one Eye hardly wore.

"He-Man getting his ass beat," Bernnard said, slapping my toy and Eye slapped his ass.

Eye grunted jubilantly. "Don't hit my toy that hard boy! Don't break my toy!"

"Eye know you didn't just slap me!" he said, giving me the Eye.

"Eye just did! You slapped my toy; you hurt my fingers in the process, man."

He frowned at me. "Don't you hit me again, Pharoah."

Eye stared him down. "Or *what*? What are you gonna do? Beat me up? Eye would like to see you try."

He wanted to stand up and kick my butt. "Man Eye will mess you up!"

Eye was making talking signals with my hand, like yap, yap, yap.

"Me and He-Man ain't try'na hear all that," Eye said.

He walked up to me and was about to swing and my step daddy, with two braids in his head, pants half buckled and a tight light blue tank top appeared in the door way.

He looked sternly at me. "Bring your tail in the house, Pharoah."

Eye ignored him. "Eye'm playing with my toys."

He said it more defiantly. "Bring your tail in the house, boy!"

Eye protested. "But dad."

He yelled, "NOW!" His eyes were glowing hot coals.

"Where's Mama? She will let me stay out and play."

His shook his head, his temples twitching. "Do Eye look like your Mama? And Bernnard, take your dirty ass home. Pharoah coming inside. Good bye!"

Bernnard mugged him and walked off with my GI Joe toys.

"Inside."

Eye was disappointed. Eye wanted to continue playing. It was boring on the inside. "But Eye wanna play!" Eye said defiantly. Who wanted to go in the house just for him to tell me to sit, go get him some water, pick *that* up and take this plate back to the kitchen sink all day. Adults were lazy as hell. Had kids just to slave them around.

He walked down the little concrete steps and snatched me off the ground by one hand, beating me on my ass with an open palm like Eye was a grown man. The onslaught threw me into instant silence. The pain shot through my body.

He never really hit me like that before. He dragged me in the house and closed the door.

My heart pounded. "Eye'ma tell Mama you hit me!"

He smiled inwardly. "Tell her. She ain't here. Take your ass in the room you little bitch."

"Where's Mama?" Eye asked. Eye didn't like him anymore.

He wasn't hearing it. "*Snook*. Go in the room. *Now*, boy before you piss me off."

Snook was my nickname, one Eye hated. He picked up a can of Bull beer and wolfed it down, walking to the fridge to get another one. That would be his third one. He had the first one with his retarded brother Stevie. Eye couldn't stand that man. Eye frowned whenever he brought his midget ass around.

He cracked open his beer and stood by the stove, wolfing that one down too. Something was eating at him; Eye saw it in his eyes.

Eye sat on the sofa, turning on the small black and white TV with a clothes hanger for an antenna. Eye didn't wanna go in the room.

"*Pharoah*!" He stamped up to me and slapped me in the head. Eye fell on the floor, disoriented. "Didn't Eye tell you to go in the room?"

Eye was getting tired of him really fast. "Eye wanna watch TV!" Eye couldn't stop crying and sniffling.

He pointed at me. "You have been hanging around Bernnard a little too much. You developed his mouth."

Eye looked into his eyes. "You hit me again Eye'm telling Mama on you!" Eye meant every word.

He ran up to me and Eye rolled out the way, and ran to my room, trying to close the door but he caught it and pushed it open and my body flew on the cracked wooden floor with the weird smell, my chin hitting the wood. That hurt.

He stood there, looking down on me, the sunlight vanishing on the outside, and the rain started to come down.

A crack of thunder, a flash of lightning rendered me speechless.

Quietly, he was unbuckling his belt.

"Eye'm gonna beat your butt! You got a hot little mouth on you. Eye already had a *bad* day. Eye had too much to drink, and you are getting besides yourself."

Eye wasn't hearing him! "EYE WANT MAMA!" Eye stood up and faced him, looking past him, seeing if Eye could run. Eye was going to run to Roe house. The living room couch was in view, and a window hung with cheap curtains. The front door Eye could not see.

He waltzed up to me, snatched me by the arm and started brutally *whipping* me. He was a beast, whipping me for something deeper than Eye could understand. Eye was so in shock at first Eye didn't say anything, nor react. But once the force of his hand continued to slam against my frail body the pain was inevitable.

Eye was fighting him back. "LET ME GO!"

Eye hated him.

He tossed the belt and grabbed me by my neck. He squeezed so hard Eye could barely breathe. "Eye'm tired of you."

Eye felt powerless. The love Eye had for him was completely destroyed instantly. "Let me go!"

He punched me in the forehead and Eye fell on my back. Eye was so dizzy my vision was blurry. Eye couldn't grasp a thought and Eye kept saying, "Eye want my Mama! Eye want Mama, where is Mama at?" but Eye didn't dare move. Eye lay there a shell.

Laughing uncontrollably, he turned me over on my stomach. Another crack of thunder made my body jump.

BOOM!

"Mama…" My voice trailed off. Mama wasn't there to neither help nor save me.

Eye felt my shorts and draws coming down, my ass exposed. He hastily snatched them down, as if on his prom date and anxious to deflower the virgin.

His eyes scanned my body. "Got a mouth on you, huh little Niggah. Talking back, defiant, trying to tell me what to do. Eye'm the only man in this house."

He straddled my waist, tying his belt around my hands. Eye lay limp, afraid to flex a muscle, afraid to talk, afraid to breathe.

He had the most Satanic eyes…Eye would ever see. "Eye'm gonna give you something to talk about!" he enthused.

He spread my booty cheeks and spit on my rectum. Eye was confused, what was going on? What was he doing? Now Eye tried to fight him but Eye was dizzy and it's like my legs refused to move. Eye was uncomfortable.

Eye said it again. "Eye want Mama."

He said, "Eye'm not your daddy. Your real daddy didn't want you. Eye don't have a sissy for a son! Laron will never be gay! Eye never got you for putting fingernail polish in my boy's Eye! White patch over his Eye in his birthday pictures!"

And he slowly started sticking his anger inside me, covering my mouth and my eyes were wide with pain. Eye tried to get him off me but Eye couldn't. He was much too strong.

A grunt of pleasure, eyes wide with hate. "Take it like a man. Running your mouth. Got something to say now?"

My voice was reduced to muffled sounds shielded by his clammy hand. My eyes were wide with fear, my body felt like it was shutting down.

He pushed in deeper, but not all the way. And he started to slowly gyrate inside me.

"Like that?" he asked, sensually moaning in my ear, his hot breath on my shoulder blade…

Eye kept trying to scream for my mother, but by that time my body died. Life as Eye knew it failed and things Eye thought Eye understood died and nothing made sense.

He groaned and slowly moved in and out of me. My anus hurt so badly Eye wanted to die.

Eye kept screaming against his hands, my feet fumbling on the wooden floor.

More lightning and thunder scared me.
Eye died right on the floor.
But another part of myself was born….

*When he was done Eye lay there*, staring at the bottom of the bed; a zombie. Eye knew deep down that Eye would never be the same. Did a virgin lay like this when she was deflowered? Eye wasn't a girl so Eye guess Eye was uprooted. Devastated beyond understanding and logic, Eye refused to move. He was standing over me, zipping his pants. He untied my hands and put on his brown leather belt. He spit on me. It fell right on the side of my face. Moist and hot. The smell reeked of beer and funk, like he hadn't brushed his teeth in a few days. Eye didn't move. Eye would lay there till Mama came home. He got on his knee and stared at me, stroking my face. Eye cringed inside from his sweet touch, but Eye didn't dare move. My fingers curled…my hand rest on the wood. "Next time Eye ask you to do something do it. If you tell your Mama anything that happened in this room Eye promise you…"

He leaned up to my ear. "Eye will kill you both…Eye need another beer."

He walked out the room.

"Go get your ass in the tub!"

Reluctantly, Eye slowly got up, pain shooting through my body, and when Eye saw blood on the floor Eye nearly freaked out. But Eye didn't. My booty was in so much pain, a throbbing sensation in my anus made my mouth remain ajar.

Eye glanced at The Bible. Mrs. George gave me. It was on the dresser. Shaking my head, Eye used my He-Man sweater and cleaned up the blood. And Eye walked to the bathroom. Naked. Eye looked at my favorite sweater, tarnished and tainted by my blood. Eye shook from the sight of red. Smelled of salt. As much as Eye hated to, Eye buried the bloody sweater under the trash in the garbage.

Eye did not want to live anymore.

*This would go on for the next few years.*

The Demon shaping and molding me. A dark, misconstrued pleasure unwrapped within me, and it engulfed my body beyond understanding. Eye knew how to give head before Eye turned 8 years old. Deep throat and all. He taught me. Beat me good if Eye didn't do it right. No room for error.

With my younger brothers, his biological children, he adored them. His sons were his world, and he was telling them, every time Mama left for work or to the store, to never respect me. And they listened. He would make me sit on the chair in the living room and he would tell my two brothers bad things about me. Eye felt like a contorted freak on display at an exhibit. He told them that Eye was gay and Eye didn't even know what gay *meant*. Eye was never attracted to boys or girls; Eye didn't know what sex was and it was never taught to me till Eye was raped and going through it with Bernnard making me jack his penis. That's when Eye found out.

He told my brothers that Eye liked boys; that he didn't want them to ever listen to me, that Eye wasn't to be respected.

Eye remember sitting there in tears, crying so hard Eye cracked open and my brothers, who didn't know what was going on, were laughing. Pointing and laughing with their father.

"Eye hate all of you," Eye whispered, and they laughed harder.

"And we hate you, too," he said, urging his sons on.

Up until Eye was initially violated, Mama told me my penis was to piss with. And that's all she said. And by the time Eye turned 7 Eye couldn't live without his penis inside me.

Because a grown man told me Eye was put here just for that purpose. Eye'd become addicted to the abuse.

Eye was sent here to be a faggot, he once said. Eye was a *dirty* faggot. Eye was to never be *anything* in life.

He embarrassed *and* ridiculed me any moment we were alone.

Eye kept staring at the Bible my teacher gave me, sometimes picking it up, something within drawing me like magnets to it but Eye hardly opened it, Eye didn't know what Eye was supposed to do with it.

He caught wind of the Bible and asked me where did Eye get it from. Hesitantly, Eye told him. Looking it over, he picked it up and Eye gasped, remaining quiet. Grinning like he always did when taunting me, he cracked it open, grabbed a marker and wrote:

YOU'RE MY SEX SLAVE

across the Book of Job in the Bible and held it up for Eye could read it. Eye shook with rage. Eye would use this in my short story FATE WILLIAMS in *THE KING OF EROTICA 4* when Fate's mother wrote *You're my sex slave!* in the Bible and held it up for Fate to read.

The Demon stripped me down butt naked sometimes and made me stand in the corner of the room for a long time, talking about me, picking at the shape of my ass, picking at my crooked teeth and made me feel like a circus freak in my own house. When Mom was around he treated me like royalty and Eye allowed it because he said he would kill us if Eye talked. Eye cried like a baby when Mama left me alone with him.

So Eye remained quiet, trapped, and powerless. What was Eye to do? What if Eye talked and he killed Mama? She seemed so happy with him. How could Eye destroy that? So Eye sacrificed myself for the sake of keeping a whole family.

In school Eye was to myself. Normally Eye would talk to everyone and make them laugh; now Eye was meek and mute. Quiet. When my friends and fellow classmates came around to play Eye went to the other side of the room. Afraid they would see it in my eyes. Eye did my work in silence. Eye had problems focusing. My teacher kept trying to talk to me and Eye wouldn't respond back. Eye would ignore her.

She would angrily beat my hand with a ruler for being disobedient. Her ruler didn't amount to the pain Eye'd gone through from the Demon's penis. Eye refused to cry. Eye held in the pain and Eye hated her for hitting me.

But the abuse wouldn't stop. It would get worse.

And the devastating part. Eye would enjoy the pleasure.

To the point Eye stared asking for it…

*Eye relived the first time he raped me*, over and over in my head as Eye grew in age and started to mature. But of course at the time Eye didn't know what rape was or what the term meant. Eye would put that all together as Eye matured in age.

Eye remembered Eye faced him. In my darkest hour, the rain pouring even harder outside. Me, the 6 year old. Him. My step father. Authority figure. A few nights later, he did it again. Mom was working at Sunrise, Villa 8 Eye think, and he came home and asked me to do everything, from get him a glass of water to looking after my brothers so he could smoke dope with his brother Stevie. One time Eye was watching him. He stripped me naked and had me in the corner of the living room next to Mama's wooden shelf holding up family pictures and a radio and vinyl records.

She had vinyl records hanging on the walls by Denise Williams, Sugar Hill Gang and a few other artists Eye never cared to listen to. Eye would one day get up there fumbling with the records and a sowing needle (she hung the records with) got in my hand and Eye was rushed to the hospital and surgery was performed on my hand to remove the needle. A permanent scar still is visible on my right hand from the surgery. Eye remembered this time very well. An older white man used to come in my room and talk to me, make me smile and laugh all the time. He was really there for me, this stranger, and Eye didn't even know his name. Eye would never see him again when Eye was discharged from the hospital.

Unfortunately, Eye was yanked back to the present. Stevie, clad in horrible looking clothes—no style at all— looked at the Demon. "Don't smoke up all the drugs!"

The Demon sneered. "Be careful. Don't get that stuff on my table. My wife will kill me."

Stevie found it amusing. "She doesn't *know* you doing drugs? Eye thought you wore the pants in the marriage."

The Demon could care less. "Eye do."

Eye looked over my shoulder. "Eye'ma tell Mama what you're doing!" Turning to face the wall, Eye covered my mouth as quickly as Eye'd said it. Why didn't Eye keep my mouth closed?

They got quiet. "What did you say?" The Demon asked, tilting his head, studying me.

Eye said it through my hand over my mouth. "Eye'ma tell Mama what you're *doing*, *that's* what Eye said!"

Stevie laughed. "He sounds so gay."

The Demon smiled again. "He's gay! And Eye'm stuck raising him!"

Stevie stood up. "Gay boy—*what* did you say to my brother?"

"Eye said Eye'ma tell Mama!" Eye said, turning to face him. Eye was naked and didn't care.

"Eye should kick your ass!" Stevie promised.

"You ain't my Daddy!" Eye shouted at him.

Stevie pointed at me. "You don't have a *daddy*! Your *real* daddy ran off, from what my brother *says*."

How dare him! UGH! "Eye *hate* you!"

Stevie tried to hit me and Eye ran in the room and slammed the door closed, locked it and leaned my back up against it, breathing hard, my eyes wide. My stomach was going in and out…my heart pounding against my chest.

"Remember. Tell your Mama anything Pharoah and Eye will kill you both. *DON'T CALL MY BLUFF*!"

Eye ignored him, tears running down my face.

He punched on the door. "YOU HEAR ME?"

Eye jumped out my skin, startled. "Please leave me alone!"

"Open this door!" he ranted evilly.

Eye looked around wildly, debating whether or not to jump out the open window if he burst through the door. Eye didn't know what to do. "*No*! Eye won't say anything, Eye promise! Just leave me alone!"

All was quiet.

*Eye slowly opened the door, peering* out into the living room about twenty minutes later. Eye saw the sofa, window, wooden floors.

Open beer cans. They cleaned up their drugs. Why didn't they dispose of the beer cans? Eye hope they didn't think Eye was going to do it.

Eye went to Mom's room to check on my brother. Jarshawn was sleep but Laron was up.

"Hey, you ok?"

He got off the bed and ran up to me, hugging me. Eye tried to pick him up, but he was heavy. "Get back in the bed!"

Eye went to my room and he followed me. "Get in the bed, Laron!" He got up in the bed, and Eye got in bed with him, with my clothes on. "Go to sleep," Eye said and the man of the house came in the room as if on cue, startling me once more. His glowing eyes burned through mine. "Eye don't want *my* son in bed with *you!*" Eye glared at him.

"Wanna say something?"

Eye kept my mouth closed.

"Come on, Son. Time for your bath."

*Once Laron was bathed and put* to bed, he had his sick way with me.

"Pharoah come here."

Eye slowly walked to him, wide eyes, trembling. Eye wanted to puke.

Eye paused in front of him.

He said, "Look at me."

Eye did. He put lipstick on my lips.

"Do like this," he said, rubbing his lips together and Eye did, smearing lipstick all over my lips.

"Look just like a bitch."

Huge tears fell down my face. "Why are you doing this to me? Eye did *nothing* to you."

"Your mouth. You act like a woman Eye will *treat* you like one. You're gay, Pharoah. Gay. You like *boyysss*."

Eye started crying harder. "No Eye don't."

"Yes you *dooo*," he taunted. "YOU LIKE BOYS!"

My heart beat rapidly once more. "Eye want Mama."

He sucked on his middle finger. He gripped the top of my head, turned it to the side.

He wanted to write.

He spelled it out. "L-O," he wrote on my cheek, with his finger and saliva. "S-E-R!" The tip of the R connected with the right side of my lip.

"You are a loser. A gay loser. Say it, baby. Eye am a loser."

"No."

He slapped me and Eye held the side of my face, tears blinding me. The sting was stunning. He looked like a watermark.

"SAY IT!"

Eye couldn't catch my breath. "Eye'ma loser."

He grinned. His beautiful eyes contained so much hate for me. "No. Say 'Eye'm a gay loser.'"

"Eye'm a gay loser!"

He fed off my misery. "Keep saying it."

"Eye'm a gay loser…Eye'm a gay loser," Eye said, my heart on fire, my stomach in knots. "Eye'm a gay loser…"

He snatched me by the shirt and pulled me to him. Eye shook. Softly cried. Let the tears fall mimicking the rain drops down my window pane. The thump of my heart, vertical. Against my sadness.

"Eye don't like you."

Eye didn't say anything. Eye was so close to his lips Eye smelled the BULL malt liquor on his breath. He was intoxicated inside his psychological incarceration.

"You can ignore me all you want."

"Eye want Mama."

He pulled me to his face. Even closer. Nose on my nose. "Forget your Mama...Eye see you always asking for her when you in trouble, huh? You're a man; stand on your own two feet. Want me to show you?"

"Please don't hurt me anymore. Eye just want my Mama, that's all."

He pulled his penis out. It was big.

"Get in the bed!" he demanded.

"No!" Eye said, refusing to.

He tucked his chin back. "GET IN THE BED!" He drew his open palm back.

"Okay…" Eye slowly got in the bed, sitting next to him.

"Now Eye will tell you what to do, and you better do it right…"

He pushed my mouth down on his erect penis.

And he taught me how to please a grown man. Eye wasn't doing a very good job.

He kept jumping and wincing from my teeth.

"Goddamn it!" He smacked me. "Watch your teeth."

"Eye don't like this!"

"Keep sucking..."

Eye gripped it, and played with his testicles like he showed me. Eye was tired. Eye wanted Mama.

He jumped again.

"Damn it!"

Angrily, he threw me on the floor. My body against the wood didn't feel good at all. Eye was humiliated and embarrassed. He turned me over. Eye knew what that meant. The sound of the belt unbuckling released my animosity. The sound of the zipper by two damp fingers unleashed my rage.

Inside my eyes Eye died when Eye felt him. Slow. Cautious. Controlling.

"Take it…"

It hurt. My pain sacrificed for his pleasure.

Long. Unbearable. Sinister. Evil.

"There you go. Can't put it all the way in you. Don't want nobody suspecting."

Cold. Against my heart. Molding me. Taking my young body and chiseling art. Abomination. Introducing Pharoah the Ghost. The Man many would one day hate because of my sexuality began to breathe. GOD PLEASE Eye WANNA DIE! PLEASE GOD PLEASE GOD SAVE ME! Before Eye could send out another mental SOS, the words died on the tip of my tongue. My mouth afar, my spine affixed between two masculine experienced hands. Forever gyrating. Molding. Shaping pottery. Pottery is poetry with an extra T. The extra T was me. My hips unnaturally started to move. Sudden pleasure engulfing me. With his flames Eye became One. We're entangled. Lost. Floating. Crashing. Waves of seduction took me captive. New found emotion tied to the thrust of powerful interaction. Poetry. Not quite Robert Frost, but the road less taken was leading me to desire. Eye was moaning and he came alive. Sweat. Slipping and sliding. Eye wanted the pleasure.

Eye liked it. Pleasure too strong for my young body. Lipstick drying on my moist lips. Pleasure Eye didn't understand. What were we doing? What was taking place? What did he introduce me to? Why hadn't Mama mentioned anything like this? He was kissing me like he kissed Mama. My lips were sloppy, inexperienced. Yet eager. The longer he kissed me, the easier it became… Eye closed my eyes and balled my hands into fists. Heat on my neck.

His saliva drying on my shoulder blade.

*By the time Eye hit the third grade* Eye was being raped for two whole years; programmed and conditioned; Eye became his Assembly Line of integrated movements. He didn't abuse me every single day, no. But mostly when Mom wasn't around and when he had too much to drink. He was never sober when he raped me, always full of Bull malt liquor or alcohol, always doing drugs. My teacher this year was Miss Mike, and she took an immediate liking to me, because Eye was quiet.

When Eye saw her Eye rushed to the back of the class, to take my seat there and she said, "Young man, come here please."

"Who, me?"

My classmates, who really didn't like me because Eye was the "weird, quiet one," were snickering.

"Yes, you. Come here."

Eye walked up to her, carrying my book bag. "Yes."

"What's your name?"

"Pharoah Wilson."

"Why are you so sad?"

"Because Eye'm not happy."

# GUARDIAN ANGEL

"*Your eyes are withdrawn.* Who's your Mama?"

*Why do you care?* "Clara..."

Her eyes narrowed, deep in thought. "Clara, Clara what?"

"McCrae," Eye said simply.

She was stomped. "Eye know some McCrae's, but Eye don't know a Clara."

*Who gives a damn who you don't know?* "Can Eye sit down now?"

"No. Eye wanna give you something."

Eye exhaled audibly. "What's that?"

"First, Eye gotta ask you something, and you can tell me."

"Yes?"

"Who's doing it to you?"

My defenses skyrocketed. "What do you mean?" Eye asked, getting terrified.

She tried being more polite. "Pharoah, talk to me. Somebody is hurting you."

My hands were shaking. *Oh, no! He's gonna kill me and Mama oh no, God please!* "Eye'm ok. Eye'm just really sleepy."

She put her hands on both shoulders and Eye jumped out my skin. Her eyes were wide with surprise. "Oh, God, Pharoah. Someone hurt you."

*Leave me alone LEAVE ME ALONE!* "No! You don't know what you're talking about! Nobody hurt me! Nobody! Eye am sleepy! Clean up all the time to help Mama! Eye swear!"

Huge tears fell down her cheeks. "Pharoah…"

"Can you please leave me alone?"

"You can talk to me."

"About what? You just met me and you're trying to make stuff up."

"Young man."

"Eye'm going to my seat now."

"Pharoah."

Eye pivoted on my heel and she grabbed my arm and Eye started to scream, rushing to my desk and Eye sat down, my ass sore; *hadn't* healed all the way and my class mates were really laughing.

*"He's crazy! Eye told ya'll!"*

Eye put my head on the desk and Eye wept so hard Eye nearly passed out. After class was over, the bell sounded. Eye grabbed my little red back pack and tried to beat everyone out the door. Miss Mike stood in front of me with her hands on her hips. "Eye wanna talk to you."

Oh, no!

# THΣ FALLING STAR

**She sat me down, this time** a little more delicately.

"Who are you protecting?"

Eye avoided her eyes. "No one."

"Pharoah."

Eye'd had enough. "Why are you bothering me? Eye want my Mama."

"Maybe Eye should call her."

"No! She works all the time. She's always tired. Leave her alone! Stop messing with me! Eye HATE YOU OH MY GOD Eye HATE YOU!"

She hugged me and Eye jumped again, pushing her off me.

"What is going on?"

"Eye wanna go home."

She held up a finger. "Eye wanna give you something."

She stood up and walked to her desk. Eye was about to stand up and run out the door, timing it perfectly.

"Don't you run out the door," she said, without looking up.

Dang it. Eye sat down, but not all the way on my romp. It hurt.

With a grim look, she walked up to me…handing me a piece of paper. On it was a bunch of words, structured in a way Eye have never seen. My eyes widened.

"What is this?" Eye asked breathlessly.

"It's a poem. By Robert Frost. And under it is another poem, by Sara Teasdale."

Eye read it. *The Road Less Taken* and *The Falling Star.*

She said, "Eye want you to recite the poem. *The Falling Star.*"

"Lady, *what's* a poem?" Eye was shaking my head. "Black people don't read no poems," Eye said prematurely, not knowing of any black writers, and really didn't care. Miss Left, my first grade teacher and the Librarian, already said we're slaves. Now Eye guess there were black writers in the world, too. Yea, ok. Not going to fool *me* again. Second time's on you, Missy! Eye lived in Goulds, the 'Hood, Niggahs sold dope and prostitutes sold their bodies on the corner.

She took the ruler, held my hand and beat me ferociously. Eye was trying to snatch it back, crying aloud and she finally stopped.

"You learn it. Eye want it memorized by heart in two days. And you will stand in front of the class and recite it."

"Ok, just don't hit me. Why is everybody hitting me all the time"

"Pharoah…?"

"No, Eye am ready to go. Eye will learn the stupid poem."

She gave me one other thing.

"What's this? More poems?"

"*No.* It's a notebook. Call it a journal. Eye want you to write your life, write the things you do and see. Eye want you to describe things, what it looks like, what it tastes like and what it feels like. Everyday write in your journal, personalize the pages to mean what you want them to mean. Knowledge is power, and out of all my students, you're special. Eye see it in your eyes. You are destined for something great in your future. Write your life."

Eye have been writing my life ever since.

She was my guardian angel...

## Lord Jennings and Pharoah: Interview

***He was fascinated for some reason***, and after meditating and reliving this during the editing process Eye saw a lot more, thins Eye didn't remember before because of the shock of reliving that entire ordeal. The way the room smelled of lavender mixed with two chocolate bodies in heat despite of each other. "Do you feel Miss Mike was put in your life to direct you to the path you walk today?"

"My path as far as what?"

"Writing?"

"Yes, Eye do. She gave me a journal and poems and basically Eye had no choice but to indulge."

"Eye think that was a noble thing of your teacher. Robert Frost isn't a poem you give kids, but she gave it to you. And you have *grown* from it."

"Yes, Eye have."

What do you think the writing did for you while you were being raped in your home? And before you answer Eye'm so sorry about that, Pharoah. Eye wish Eye could go back in time and stop that from happening to you."

"It's cool, man. That's what Eye'm here for, right? To deal with the past."

"And so far everything seems good, but Eye know it's not easy to come to terms with what he did to you."

"No it wasn't easy," Eye said sadly.

"How long did it take you?"

"Eye'm 32 so it took till Eye turned 28 years old."

"Why that age? What was so relevant about age 28?"

"That's how old Eye was when Eye told Mama about the abuse."

"Wait. *She* didn't know before then?"

"No. She didn't have a clue."

"*How were you able to stay so secretive* about it? Why didn't you tell her?"

"He said he would kill her then me so Eye didn't play with him. He beat me with an extension cord threatening me to be quiet about it. And Eye did remain quiet. Eye was 28 when Eye told Mama and it *wasn't* pretty. We were in an argument, and she kept saying she know me better than Eye know myself, always try'na control me. Eye can never do anything right in her eyes."

"So, she was trying to control you?"

"Yes. She had a problem with anything Eye did. If Eye picked friends she didn't like she always had something to say. If Eye wore a red shirt when she gave me a blue shirt she'd have something to say."

"So how did you break the control she was trying to hold over you?"

"Eye yelled, 'If you know me so well did you know your ex husband raped me when Eye was a child?'"

He was quiet, jotting down notes.

"That shut her up. Sure, she put up a brave front like she didn't care. She even laughed about it, but Eye wasn't laughing and Eye was tired of keeping the secret. It was eating me alive, literally destroying me."

"Did she believe you?"

"*Yes* she did, but we kept arguing. We argued about me not telling her, and when Eye told her why she didn't accept it."

"Do you feel she failed as a parent? Eye mean, when you find out your grown son was raped on the scale you've been tortured when you were younger surely this crippled her."

"If it did she didn't show it on her face. She could care less. And every time she gets mad at me she does what he did: verbally tear me down to a worthless pile of shit."

"Eye don't believe she didn't care."

"If she did she didn't show it. Every time she gets mad she calls me names and that really stings."

"Because you're ex step daddy used to call you the F word?"

"Correct. Every time she calls me a faggot Eye see *him*. Eye didn't see Mama anymore; Eye didn't see the woman who gave me life. Eye saw *him*. And when Eye saw him Eye wanna *fuck* him. And *not* in a good way."

"Oh my God."

***Tell me about your Grandmother, Great grandmother and anything off the top of the brain you want me to know about you.***

***Lord Jennings***

## *Fire and Ice*

*Dapharoah69 answers to Robert Frost*
*One of my favorite poets f all-time*

Some say my life ended with ice
the day a heated man recreated my bedroom
ashes dancing across the wooden floors
my soul the inner city with no outer appearance
churches on every corner
ice capsulate my heart
beating remnants of pain
fire and ice go hand in hand
leading me to the source of flames

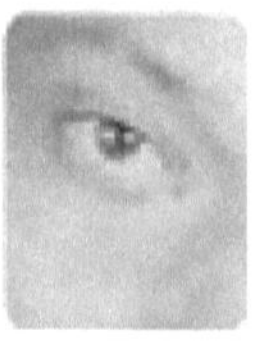

***loved my great grandmother*** Olive, my grandmother's mother, with all my heart. Eye never met my real Grandma, Olive's daughter;

she died before Eye started floating inside Mama's ovum pouch. So Olive was the *closest* thing to a Grandma Eye would ever know. If anything…learning my Mama and watching my great-Grandma bridged the gap over my grandmother and it felt like Eye was talking to her every time Eye held conversations with them.

They were pieces of Alice Rolle McCray.
Alice's mother.
And Alice's daughter.
And me, Alice's grandson.
Together, that was Alice Rolle.

*Part of the love for my great-grandmother* was derived from my appreciation for the elderly. Eye viewed all elders back then (and even now) as beings with different stories to tell, and they told their stories with heart, passion and lots and lots of emotion.

Even if 90 year old Miss Vale used to pop her coochie 70 years ago—take a penis to the throat 60 years ago, teach other Tricks how to suck, and deep throat without seeming to choke—she would go into retrospection with her head high, ass out, back tight, shoulders straight and tell you with a Botoxed face how she had it going on strong back in the good ole days.

Why today's young women couldn't do that. Some of them had no class. Drop the C and the L and that's what they looked like at the end of the day. Got it all hanging out. Eye couldn't talk! Eye been validating myself through sex since Eye was 6 years old, but back then Eye didn't know that was wrong because an adult, an authority figure in my life, taught it to me. And after Eye grew to like it Eye made a decision to keep chasing the very thing Eye hated until Eye grew to love it. Then it became my character.

Eye wasn't born gay oh my God get outta my face with that! Eye'm SICK of people telling me Eye was born with testicles on my mind. Bull.

*YOU!* may have been born gay but *not* Pharoah. Eye didn't even know what gay was till a grown man put his penis deep inside me and started calling me every faggot in the book and Eye didn't even know what that meant.

Maybe if Eye wasn't molested, abused, battered, emotionally and verbally torn or raped, Eye could look through those eyes but Eye was never given the choice. It was taken from me.

And don't bring up others who were raped and try to tell me Eye shoulda turned out like them! Mix yellow paint with blue and you get green. Mix yellow with purple and do you see green? Um, No!

Eye do know this: Eye make every decision in my life, even when Eye was being raped Eye chose to give in to the devil. *Eye* did, when Eye said, "Ok," that was called a "choice." And that's the part that Eye hated about myself for years to come.

Eye wasn't born with sex on the brain. If Eye *knew* Eye was gay why did Eye ask Mama what was the piece of meat hanging between my legs? Contradiction much?

Why did she say it's a penis, and you take a piss with it? She didn't mention the words *dick* or *urine.*

Eye took with me what she said and that became the gospel. Anything Eye watched Mama do was the status quo.

Eye imitated things Eye used to see. A little after Eye was first raped, Eye saw Mama putting on lipstick one day, and when she went to work Eye did the same thing.

Eye went in her room, which seemed a world within a world, and Eye stood before my reflection in the mirror.

Eye was naked, putting on a pair of black panties that were too big for me. So Eye tied it on the sides, a part of the back going up my butt but Eye didn't care.

Eye put on one of her bras, looking myself over, smiling to myself.

"Do Eye look like Mama? Is this how she wears this stuff? Eye wonder if my step daddy will have sex with me while wearing this. Eye wonder if he will *like* this. His penis is always hard half the time Eye'm around anyway."

Eye frowned. Step daddy already put make up on me and wrote LOSER on my cheek with spit.

"But what if he doesn't like what Eye'm wearing? He said Eye'm a faggot. What is a faggot? Eye'm confused. That's what he called me. That's what Eye am. A faggot. If he said it then it must be true." Eye looked up at the ceiling. "God, you there? You can hear me. Mama always talkin' 'bout you but Eye think she's crazy. She be doing all that praying and talking to a bunch of air. She be talking to herself, that got to be it, God. Eye don't think Eye like life too much. It's a bunch of pain."

Next was the perfume. Eye picked up a bottle of it and sprayed it all over me, bathing in it and Eye started to choke. Eye'd sprayed on too much.

Eye dropped the bottle on the floor and kicked it under the bed.

Finally, the lipstick. It was red. Eye colored my lips with it, a heavy coat. Eye rubbed my lips together the way that demon taught me, my eyes sparkling. Hell Eye put it on better than he did!

"Now Eye look like Mama," Eye said, smiling bitterly. "Step daddy said my real daddy don't want me. Eye thought my step daddy was my real daddy. He said he hates me. Eye never did a thing to hurt him. Why he hate me so much?"

The tears were hot down my face. They fell from my chin, dropping on my bird chest. Eye gazed at my underdeveloped nipples.

"Daddy hates me. Eye don't *have* a daddy. Nobody wants me, God. My name is Pharoah Curtis Wilson, Jr. God did you know that? Eye'm only 6, you know. Eye heard Eye'm named after my daddy. Why did Mama name me after a man who doesn't love me? Eye don't like playing this game very much. It's no fun, God. *God.* Can Eye tell you something? Eye promise to be quick, Eye mean if you're really there…"

Something in me died when Eye did this. Eye was unknowingly speaking untimely doom into my existence and Satan took full advantage of it. You think Satan gave a damn about me as a child? Hell no.

Eye closed my eyes. "Eye hate my guts, God. Eye hate myself. Eye hate myself, Eye hate myself, and Eye will *hate* myself for a long time!"

Eye opened my eyes. "Eye gotta go now. Gotta get ready for tonight. He said he is gonna do it to me again. And it's gonna hurt, but Eye gotta do it *or* he will kill me and Mama."

Eye took off the bra and panties and replaced it in Mama's drawer. And Eye went to the bathroom to wipe the hate and make-up off my face. But it was already embedded deeply in my heart.

And Eye was slowly *becoming...*

*My Mama's husband at the time* kissed Mama and tried to rear a home with remnants of my young tender flesh drying on his skin. He gave me false attention, putting up a brave front, performing his Broadway play to rave reviews. He had 'em all fooled. All of them, except me. He worked at Vicks Farms. A Niggah as a farm hand apparently messed with his security because when they cut his hours and his pay he presented the insecurities of a man to me through sex, and conditioning me.

The glass house in my body was built with bricks from Inca and buried with Nefertiti in Egypt. You would never know Eye was a Queen by the smoke and mirrors of his marriage to my mother. Eye was his secret lover. His best kept secret. And that was the Alpha of my Omega. The start of the end. The End of the start as Eye knew it and the start of the end from a sexuality standpoint. Eye was May Day King at Pine-Villa Elementary. Eye forgot who the queen was; she wasn't important anyway. It was to believe my thoughts created the Universe Eye found myself suffocating in. We (my classmates and Eye) were treated to the sprinklers being put out in the huge field by the P.E. building and we got to run through the water on a hot sunny day and eat cake. Mama bought me a green and yellow short set with tube socks Eye would wear to the Seaquarium with my Grand daddy and his girlfriend, whom he would later marry and was still married to her 1 years later. We even took pictures.

They even had a May Day ceremony outside on the big field. Eye would accept my prize for winning, and Eye didn't even know how Eye won. Eye was just a kid. But that was a happy day for me. The sun shined really bright that day.

But my step daddy's piercing glare killed it all for me. Eye stopped smiling; knowing what was to come when Eye went home. He was going to screw me again.

At home Mama taught me the rules of the Bible and barely lived by the rules herself. No one seemed to talk about the contradictions of the Bible, and *since* they didn't question those contradictions, neither did Eye. Eye sort of fell into the gap and went with the flow of things. Eye knew from watching cartoons and TV that cartoons were caricatures of realistic TV shows, made to look funny so blowing a bitch up on a cartoon was a laughing, joking matter but do it on TV you are going to jail.

Contradictions were in everything back then so Eye did what was required and still made decisions for myself, even at a young age, and those decisions were simple. Write in my journal daily, no matter what. Even if Eye just write PHAROAH WAS HERE and the date. And Eye would write poems and write write write because that's all that seemed to matter to me.

But there was a grown man taking out his anger on me for *struggling* to be a good husband, yet he failed as a father figure in my life.

My own Daddy wasn't there to protect me.

So Eye gave in. Eye started throwing my booty back against his pelvis, it felt so good and the tears dried up and was replaced with sweat and he banged me so good Eye lay tired and spent when it was over, and took the tape off my mouth famished, wanting some more.

Sad. It would have built my ego, but Eye was blinded by the threats of my ex step Daddy. Eye was submissive to it. Manipulated and controlled. Eye was an obedient kid. If Eye was a good little Tramp he said Eye could always get some programmed penis. And Eye loved when he banged me, unfortunately. It felt so good, but Eye couldn't say a word. So Eye didn't as long as he kept making my toes curl.

A child sex slave Eye was. He was careful not to leave any marks on me. Eye sometimes had a very suspecting mother, but Eye think somewhere along the line she stopped focusing on me and started focusing on the other brothers Eye had and that was just what he needed, to do what he did. Gave him time to do what he did.

And Eye would grow up to hate myself for it.

Mama figured Eye was too young to learn or *know* about sex so Eye wasn't prepared for the onslaught of a married man deep inside me, making me nut without touching myself, nut in the darkness where all Eye saw was his glittering eyes and gagging from his Bull malt liquor breath and Eye grew to never want the night to end or the day to begin when he moved inside me.

Eye didn't want a vagina. Hell no! But he had me pretending my ass was one. Eye knew that much. Eye loved a penis so much Eye wanted to suck my own if Eye could, and Lord knew Eye tried plenty times and wound up with a head ache and a back ache, about to pass out. Concentrating too hard. Eye was totally ignorant to the one man and one woman married in Holy Matrimony farce church was shoving down the public's throat. Eye haven't met *one* Pa$tor who had sexual self-control yet. All of them were whores. If you get it hard he'll let you suck till he nut. But you better not tell his fat wife. The concept of marriage, for me, failed when Eye was young. By the time Eye was 8 Eye knew Eye would never want a wife, but Eye *did* want kids. Eye loved kids so much. They were pure, like Eye was and knew no wrong and would never hurt anybody. A married man was making me suck him up, wasn't he? So why would Eye believe in marriage?

One day he made me give him some head. It was one of those boring days when *nothing* went right for him. He was perched in my bed and Mama was working in Villa 8. She worked with mentally handicap kids. Grand daddy was the Manager out there and Alma worked out there as well.

"You better not tell her, you hear!" he warned, whipping me harder. And every time Eye gave God directions and called out for Mama the pain intensified.

Eye was backed into a corner and he kept whacking me with the cord and Eye wanted to die, shocked and stunned from the pain.

*GOD HELP ME PLEASE!* "PLEASE STOP PLEASE!"

Whack. Whack. Whack.

*God where are you?* "PLEASE PLEASE!"

He seemed to be in a trance.

Whack. Whack. Whacckkk!

Eye saw my blood and Eye freaked out! "Eye won't tell her anything!"

"You better not!"

The cord crashed into my left arm.

Felt like Eye had to faint. "OKAY! STOP!"

He kept whipping me; and Eye wanted to die to make it stop.

*"God please help me!"*

Whack. Whack. Whack.

*"GOD PLEASE HELP ME PLEASE MAMAAAA! MAMA! MAMA!"*

Eye stood up, even though he was hitting me—*Whack!*— and Eye held up my hands, shivering. "Please stop Ok! Eye won't tell her please stop hitting me *Eye can't take it anymore!*"

He stopped beating me and said, "Go get your dumb butt in the tub. Pour some bleach in the water for your nasty *ass* and those whelps. Ew! Sissy! *You like boyssss!* Say you're a sissy..."

Eye looked at him like he was stupid. He raised the cord and Eye held up my hands, drawing back into the wall, glad it was behind me and said, "Eye'm a sissy!"

"Eye love sucking you, Daddy!"

*"Eye love sucking you, Daddy!."*

"Say, 'Eye like big ones in my butt!'"

Eye hesitated. "Eye like big ones in my butt!"

"You *faggot*!" He spit in my face, and spelled LOSER on my cheek, pronouncing each word as he did for the second time. He made sure Eye grew up a *loser*. He studied his art with an evil smile, tilting his head to the left, his hair long and in his face. "L…O…S…E…R."

The stem of the "R" connected with tip of the right side of my lips again, the air blowing from the window making his spit feel cool on my face. Eye hated him. God Eye hated him so much! It boiled in me like hot lava, like those volcanoes Eye seen on TV.

"Recite it a hundred times."

"Please! Not this *again*!"

He raised the cord with the evil glare in his eyes.

Eye jumped out of my skin, pissing down my legs.

"Eye'm a loser! Eye'm a loser Eye'm a loser…"

He was pleased. Eye gave up. "Eye just want Mama!" Eye said, running into the bathroom, slamming the door.

Eye leaned against it, shivering, turning off the lights…rubbing my arms, my mouth and jaws hurting and throbbing. There was a rapping on the door and Eye clammed up, my heart pounding.

"You will always be a faggot," he whispered harshly. "No one will ever like you. You will never get a girl. Women will *never* like you. Eye will raise my sons to never respect you. They will hate you forever. Eye must be *lucky*. Eye'm freaking you and your Mama. But Eye like freaking you better."

Eye shivered like Eye was cold. Eye feared him so much Eye vomited in the toilet again.

"Why is he doing this to me?"

Eye turned on the bathwater in the dark. Eye bathed in the dark. Eye had to. Eye was scared to turn on the light and see the faggot in me looking back with a smirk or a grin. Eye poured in the bleach, a lot of it.

He didn't say how much. Eye got in the water and it stung. *"It burns!"*

Eye jumped out the tub and turned on the light. My body was burning, the bleach burning my whelps. "*Ow*, it burns!" Eye was fanning my body, hoping to relieve it. It didn't work. Eye was becoming something society would *never* accept, but Eye had no control. Eye thought that would be my life. Forever. Eye was a faggot! Hey, that's what he taught me. With his penis deep inside me setting it.

In stone.

# THE [PR☯]STITUTE

## *The day Eye discovered the word "Promiscuous,"*

Eye went up to a prostitute on my way to my great aunt Rozella's house. Eye couldn't pronounce it, but reading the definition Eye knew Eye was the word, and would be the word for years to come. Eye asked her, "Can you tell me what this word says and what it means?" Eye knew what it meant, Eye just couldn't pronounce it. She looked me over, rubbing herself. Eye had an erection, and she was licking her dry lips. She took the book and pronounced it. "*Promiscuous.*"

She read it over, and handed me the book back.

"What does it mean?" Eye asked.

She gazed at me a moment. "It means men love some hot female coochie."

Eye shook my head, my hardened member jumping in my pants. Eye had a sudden urge for coochie, to see what it felt like…Eye was about to pay for sex for the first time. Eye saw a random dude the other day buying sex from the same Hoe; so Eye simply imitated *him.* Only difference was she went with him somewhere in his car. And Eye was too young to drive or buy a car or a truck. "Hey, trick! You got me hard! Sup with some of that good twat!" Hearing myself say it Eye sounded ignorant, but Eye didn't care. She was laughing and patting her knees, buck toothed woman. Stank wig, tight leather skirt, fish net and black panty hose, tight leather jacket in the hot sun and some high heeled boots.

She found me amusing. "*You* want some of this good stuff boy? Do you have pubic hairs yet?"

"You got *sense* yet?" Eye retaliated and she was momentarily quiet, looking me over.

"Eye graduated from college," she said, patting her wig with pride.

"Graduated right to the corner of 220th Street. A *Whipple* Store Hoe."

"Forget you, ok? You're the one handing me dictionaries to pronounce words for you."

"*Look, trick*— Eye want some coochie!" Eye was getting angry. Eye wanted some adult coochie and she was playing around.

Her eyes were wide, with painting-on Eye brows. Why would she shave off her Eye brows just to pencil them in above her dead-looking eyes? "You ain't got no money! You're just a teeny-weeny baby! You can't afford it!"

Eye dropped the book on the ground and pulled out my Snicker's bar—and my balls were overstocked with peanuts— right on the block and Eye shook it. "Suck it, tramp and shut up. Suck it like you sucked that dude's penis. The one you went away in that black truck with."

She looked at my erection, and then turned away in shame. Eye gave her the five dollars Eye was supposed to use for lunch. My cousin Wanky gave it to me. Eye loved Wanky. He was my favorite Rolle at the time.

She said, "Are you Clara's son?"

## *What was the aftermath of*
## *The meeting with the [Pro]stitute?*
### *Lord Jennings*

*Eye scoped the Trick cautiously*. "*Yes.* How you know my Mama?" Eye put my penis back in my pants. Damn, Eye'm not gonna get any today.

She was shaking her head. "We went to Mays together. You know your Mama ran track. She was a fast little red bitch. Eye couldn't stand her. Thought her stool didn't stink."

"You ain't gonna talk about my Mama, Twit!" Eye said defensively, getting in her face, balling my hands into tight fists, about to get down to the ground with this Hooker. My dick and mouth wasn't included, neither was her clit.

"You keep my Mama name out your mouth dick sucking bitch!" Eye meant business; Eye was not playing with the toothless slut.

"Eye see you're just as deranged up as she is. Got that mouth like her! Eye used to fool around with *Buck*."

"You're *crazy* if you let that bag of rocks slept with you. My uncle got plenty Hoes; *plenty* Hoes. *You* ain't the only one. And don't let my Uncle Siegel get up in it. He selfish when he doing the nasty. Anyway, you can talk about him; Eye could care less—but you're going to keep *Clara's* name out your mouth."

She flipped the bird. "The hell with you and your skinny Mama!"

Eye grabbed my package. "Suck it!"

"Grow it!" Eye had enough. Eye was nearly as tall as her. She was four feet 11. Eye leaned up to her, even though she was taller than me. Grinned. Then impulsively snatched her by the wig. Eye slapped the Hoe for talking about my Mama! She was *dazed* from my attack. She didn't know what hit her. Let me help her out. A hand snatched your wig, got it? She stumbled backward and Eye ran like the cartoons and jumped and footed this late witch in her gut so her future children were born slow and would walk with a twitch and a limp, talkin' 'bout my Mama…dyke shut up.

She screamed. "Help, help! He's *crazy*!"

Vehicles slowly passing by, grown people laughing, pointing and saying, "Whoop her butt!" No one bothered to stop me; no one bothered to take me, whip my behind and tell me to stay in a child's place. No one taught me that Eye shouldn't be treating a black woman like this, whether she sold ass or not. Eye just wanted her to read the definition to the word *promiscuous*, and pronounce it for me. Eye was gonna give her five dollars to let me get a shot of coochie on top of that. Eye didn't have a clue what to do with a woman, but Eye was gonna get deep inside her the way my step daddy slid deep inside me. They were both holes. It couldn't be *that* hard. Eye mimicked her. "Help! Help! Eye'm a minor and she took my five dollars try'na get me to do the nasty!" Eye screamed like a damsel in distress and she threw my five dollars at me, "You ain't worth jail bitch! You ain't worth five dollars."

"You're right. Eye'm worth all the money in the world. Your pussy worth a buck fifty but Eye gave you a little extra for your time." And she turned to run off and Eye kicked her in her ass, watching her stumble, stumble timberrrr into the light pole, her head slamming into the metal.

"Don't talk about that red bone bitch! She's my Mama, Hoe!" And Eye walked off.

*Tell me about a time you felt powerless*
*And vulnerable*

*Lord Jennings*

# CRAIG

***Eye was always a free thinker,*** doing things that wasn't asked of me and Eye was viewed as a rebel. Church and God were forced on me. It was never my choice and Eye wasn't try'na hear about The Good Lord when that was contradicted by a grown man destroying me at a young age.

Watching a 23 year old mother of four, with three of them being older than me, suck me up and swallow became an addiction, but Eye wouldn't dare tell Mama that.

Eye noticed the women that blew me till Eye came swallowed with a purpose. If Eye had five dollars in my pocket, they were happy with that. Men spit with an intention. Intentions of control and possession by using aggression.

Every man Eye ever had has tried to possess and own me, tell me what to do and control my every move. One adult male, when Eye was 13, told me Eye couldn't talk to *any* man. Period.

His name was Craig.

He was a 28 year old failure, had skin the color of chocolate and had an amazing body women fought themselves over to ascertain. Most men got off on hoes fighting over them. But not Craig. The more they fought like today's Basketball wives, a ridiculous group of bitches making black women look dumb and *hideous* on TV (thank God Eye'm bisexual, Eye could switch it up at the sight of drama), the more turned off he was until he put it out of his mind and pretended not to see it as he went throughout his day. We used to hold deep discussions about it and he was fascinated at my knowledge on how to fix relationships and how to maintain them and the only relationships Eye had was letting my friends' parents have sex with me in the shadows.

Eye'm telling you. Women were trying to buy Craig's love and he *still* wound up screwing me on the low and Eye was a minor and didn't have to buy him anything. He spent money on me, when he had it of course, and that was hardly ever. Eye used to laugh to myself watching women fight all into the street over Craig's sexy self.

Eye took pictures of them with my camera, and still don't know where those photos were. In every pair of eyes fighting in the street lies demons in each individual body, driving them like a man in a Voltron suit. Forgive these tricks, Father, Eye thought, watching from the side of the road. *They know not what they do.*

To my surprise the adult spectators that ebbed them on (they had demons in their eye as well, it was like watching a boxing orgy from the flames of Hell) instigated the fights, getting a kick or two in and then retreating back to the side lines.

A gorgeously pregnant woman with big red weave and mascara rings around her eyes, like she'd been crying at night, ran up from the side lines and kicked one of the women in the face, blood spurting on the dry soil beside her A cloud of dust circulated up her nose while the red haired woman walked off laughing, saying, "Eye bet you won't go after Craigg again, bitch!"

*And he's not going around your stink pussy ass either, Dummy,* Eye thought, staying out of it. Eye was in love with Craigg, but as a Bottom Eye'll be *damned* if Eye fought over a dude no matter how good his pipe game. Screw that!

Too many females and dudes waiting for you to mess up so they could step in and snatch me off your arm, so a penis was never the deciding factor in me staying with anybody, though Eye've done it a few times. Everybody has played Boo Boo The Fool in a relationship so don't read this account with judgment because *some* of your sticks and vaginas were sliced and diced (and some of your asses, too) before you graduated high school.

A few of you were sluts before you even started college, and got turned out before you got your degree and *half* of you dropped out (or was kicked out) because your slutty ways and your names (that put a bad taste in everybody's mouth to even *utter*) made the rounds with a force your dicks and pussies could no longer handle.

Eye think Craigg would have greater joy out of a bunch of straight men (on the Down Low) fighting publicly over him, without letting anybody know that's what they were fighting about. That'd make his dick hard. Eye know. When Eye suggested it his penis sprang to live like a Javelin's throw and pounded me all over his crib. Eye had to stare at the debris of failure strewn all over his house.

When he smiled he made a Niggah's booty *wetter* than female coochie. That's how fine he was. A thug at heart, he religiously chewed prescription drugs with his liquor—He worshipped the liquor bottle like it was his God, he even prayed to it while he wolfed it down, a genie in Motion he once called that process—and he didn't give a *damn* about anything attached to emotions. He didn't have any emotions. He never showed them or one single tear or weakness around me, even though eye saw it the entire time dancing in his lust-filled eyes, bordering the crazed.

Everything he tried to achieve in life he failed at. He intoxicated himself with a form of Hepatitis (Vodka) to forget about it—an everyday thing. Eye felt sorry for his *liver*. But he never made excuses, and he always *blamed* himself, which told me a lot about him. One day he was so drunk we wound up having pure unadulterated, freaky, nasty sex in the laundry room. He picked my lil' butt up like a roll of wet tissue and his penis represented that tissue when he grinded deep inside me till my toes curled from orgasm.

At times it hurt like hell, but once my body was used to his deep stroking Eye felt so good, falling deeper into the hate Eye had for me. Eye was dick sick and didn't want him to stop.

After he came deep inside me, he totally flipped out on me like a war Vet remembering Vietnam.

Another level of consciousness presented itself; my nemesis for this level of life, this moment, for this circumstance was born from the product of our lust and the Pit of Craigg Abyss he would like to think of as a brain. He was not Craigg any more.

He was his Alter Ego.

The Man Hurt from his past *finally* displaying his emotions—something he hasn't done in years. He was looking around wildly, like bombs over Baghdad exploding deep in his eyes and heart, dazed as if he'd just awakened from a drunken stupor in a place other than his own home and his own familiar surroundings. Why did he look like a man that wanted to confront something, yet Eye wanted to escape without incident?

Why was he a man that suddenly wanted me destroyed?

And it took some good booty to strip it out of him.

*His eyes were filled with love*, yet manic at the same time, both feelings warping, exploding inside a deadly thought of change while his redirected pupils focused on me. He was *determined* to change mistakes of the past. And using me as a vessel, not inspiration. The love in his eyes was from the love of vengeance and blood. That only served as fuel for his passion to redo the past and make it right. When was somebody going to tell him life didn't work that way?

He scowled. "Why did you leave me?" he screamed, brutally slapping me in the face, his own face a twisted mask of pure evil that baffled me for a second. Eye didn't have time to hold the side of my face like "Take 5, *action*!" on the set of a soap opera. My life might be at stake.

Frightened, Eye ran to the other side of the Room-in-House he lived in, clumsily picking up his pocket knife from the low-table in the living room and, shaking, raising it in front of me defensively. His semen was running down my leg and Eye was grossed out—Now wasn't the time for that; my survival instincts kicked in over time and in overdrive. Crazy Niggah! *Twelve o'clock North!!!*

My eyes were wide with fear. "What is wrong with you?" Eye stuttered dangerously.

Craigg *Versus* Pharoah: Round One—FIGHT!!

"WHY DID YOU GIVE BIRTH TO ME AND ABANDON ME?"

My eyes clouded over. "What are you talking about?" Eye asked, confused. Damn *Gemini's*, Eye tell you.

"Don't play stupid," he said, walking to the closet, snatching open the door with a hidden purpose. His thick ten inch vine swinging, his hairy buttocks jiggled like a female's ass that got hit from the back five times a day. But *nothing* about the fruit cake was feminine. He was masculine times eight. "Eye waited years to confront you, you weak bitch."

Ok Eye got a knife dude. "Weak? Who are *you* calling a weak bitch?"

He pivoted, aiming a Glock at my head. Oh my God! My knees were about to give out, but Eye didn't put the knife down. Eye stood my ground with my head high, but my eyes were about to give at any second. *Don't cry in front of this fruit roll up, Pharoah. Be strong!*

"How could you abandon me, Mama?" he asked, tears falling down his face. He was childlike, acting like he was eight years old and it dawned on me that he actually thought he was; Eye knew the feeling, but Eye couldn't relate because his pain was all his own. Eye could only relate to having the mind of a six year old, even as Eye thought Eye was maturing with age, and was only doing more reckless things.

Eye had to get through to him—now that Eye saw the light at the end of the tunnel, but the more his eyes hardened that light was starting to fade. "Eye'm Pharoah. Eye'm *not* your Mama."

A dark shadow rolled over his face and then it was gone. Scared me half to death. "STOP LYING!" He shot the window out behind me and Eye screamed with the explosion of glass, falling in huge chunks as Eye fell to my knees, dropping the knife.

*Danger, Danger, Danger!* "Eye'm not your Mama! Eye'm Pharoah!"

My words made him angrier, fueling the beast—Craigg was The Boss Eye must beat at this Level of life or Eye was going to die, like Mario when King Koopa's flames burn my ass. "LIAR!" He shot the lamp off the table and dumped three bullets in the wall. "Face me, Mama!"

Eye shook so badly Eye broke down. Eye slammed my eyes shut and refused to move. My entire body hardened like a shell, and Eye forced myself to go numb. Eye was in the fetal position tightly, a tight fist that refused to budge. God protect me. *Please* protect me. Eye don't want to die! Why do grown men love abusing me?

Why do Eye allow it? Eye'm only 13 years old, surely a lot of you have a thirteen year old, or once had a thirteen year old and how would you feel if they were secretly going through something of this magnitude and you didn't have a clue?

A lot of parents didn't know their teenagers as much as they thought. Some of those teenagers had secret lives outside of your home and your authority.

Eye should know. Eye was in a secret life with Craigg, and Eye was about to die.

And my Mama thought Eye was in school.

Why couldn't Eye break free, Lord?

Why did my flesh hate me so much?

Where is my *Daddy*? Pharoah C. Wilson, Senior—if you were in my life *none* of this would be happening!

Damn you! Damn Mama from taking me from you!

Damn you both for bringing me here!

"Oh my God, Pharoah. Eye'm so sorry," he said, dropping the gun. Eye heard the metal smacking the wood. But Eye didn't soften the turtle's shell. "Pharoah. Look at me." His voice was soft and loving once more. But Eye wasn't to be fooled. The Eye always came *after* the Storm.

"No, man," Eye said through my tightly wound body. Eye shivered like eye was cold; Eye was slowly losing my mind. *Help me, Mama! Please! Eye called on God and He didn't answer me!* "Eye'm scared of you. Please don't shoot me. Eye'm not your Mama."

"Pharoah..." He took me by the hand and Eye flinched, and then cringed inside. "Pharoah, *Niggah*—be a man! *Stand* up."

Eye looked up at him, reluctantly. "You're not gonna shoot me?"

"No, Pharoah Eye'm not." He meant it. But Eye had to be sure. So Eye remained reluctant. Sighing, Eye stood up and he pulled me into his arms and we passionately kissed. He was feeling all over my body with eccentric, eager hands and spreading my cheeks, sliding his middle finger deep in me. He pulled me to the bedroom and Eye kicked the Glock under the sofa.

Bitch ain't gonna shoot me today.

He closed and locked the door, walking over to the dresser and snatching up the Vodka bottle. He drank from the bottle, wolfing it down like Kool-Aid. Smacking his lips as he drank some more, the sun beaming bright as hell. Eye was cool. Mama wouldn't be looking for me for a few hours, as long as Eye beat the sun home. Dropping the bottle he walked over to me, grinning. "Eye want some *more* of that young asshole." He fell silent a moment, contemplating, sipping more booze.

He broke the silence that was causing my ears pandemonium. "My brother used to bang me the way Eye'm about to dig you out. Too bad Eye *killed* him." He threw the bottle on the floor. There goes his God. He turned on Him, realizing Jesus Christ wasn't in that type of water. That's liquor, pure alcohol—not wine. With a hunger Eye never saw before, he picked me up off my feet.

His face a twisted mask of evil once more, he attacked when my guard was down and all Eye could do was allow him.

A few minutes later, my toes were curling with the sheets. The Eye of the Hurricane Craigg made land fall.

On my ass.

"Eye *love* you, Mama," he said breathlessly as he came deep inside me. Looking deeply into y eyes as if Eye was his mother, and that made me feel dirty and incestuous. Eye lay there in silence, both petrified and paralyzed from what trickled over me.

It was a part of the story Eye never revealed.

Until now.

*Thanks* to the power of Meditation...

☯

*Eye didn't know how long* Eye was sleep, but he awakened next to me, vomiting all over me. Gross! Eye was covered in pinkish puke, and some of it got in my mouth and Eye fell on the floor, butt naked, spitting and slapping at my lips trying to clean them, but the taste was overwhelming.

Eye was running for the kitchen.

Eye turned on the water, filled a cup with it, poured in a cap full of bleach and Eye wolfed it down. He was in bad shape. It was like Eye didn't know this dude. And that's a Gemini for you. Sometimes you thought they were an identical twin. He puked in the toilet, and Eye was behind him, my hands on my hips.

"You threw up in my mouth!"

His world was spinning out of control. He tried to stand up and slipped in puke. He fell hard on his back, his feet slamming into the rusty sink and Eye didn't help him up.

He had attention deficit badly. If Eye gave him head he couldn't even focus on *that,* mind wandered worse than a bum without a plan. He didn't have a high school diploma or a G.E.D. Eye feared the man, but trying to face that fear kept me in his life. During daylight hours he was a people person. Everyone loved him.

He went to church on Sundays, seemed to be positive about life but always cried over his failures in the darkness.

He forced himself to sit up, leaning against the tub. The bathroom was stinky as hell. Comet and Pine Sol worked wonders, Craigg. His eyes were lowered to the floor.

"Eye grew up in an orphanage, Pharoah." Eye was stunned. He has never opened up to me about his past, and now that he was Eye wasn't sure if Eye wanted to hear his story. "Eye never met my family; Eye never met my father. Mom took care of me and my brother. When she *found* my oldest brother poking me in the ass she ran out on us and *never* looked back. My brother was raping me for a very long time. Eye wound up stabbing my brother to death in his sleep and throwing the knife in the dumpster.  Eye ran away, eventually getting arrested for stealing food out of the grocery store and when they asked who my parents were Eye said they were dead. Eye was put in an orphanage. When Eye turned 18 they cut my ass off at the knees, pushed me out into a cold world and wrote my ass off."

Before Eye could say anything Eye heard Mama screaming my name. "PHAROAH! PHAROAH! PHAROAH! WHERE THE HELL ARE YOU AT? PHAROAH?"

Damn. How could she think Eye was in school when Eye got home from school *hours* ago.

For some reason Eye was fortunate Eye had a mother, even though she didn't pay me very much attention. She sort of did her own thing, and Eye did my own thing as well.

He looked into my eyes. "Go home, Pharoah. Thank God tonight that you have a mother. Eye am jealous of you. Eye wish Eye knew where my Mama was."

"Are you gonna be okay?" Eye asked, a huge lump forming in my throat.

"PHAROAH! EYE'M NOT GONNA KEEP CALLING YOU, BOY WHERE ARE YOU? PHAROAH!"

"Yea, Eye'll be fine," he said with a sheepish grin that made him even more beautiful then he ever was. The sunlight pierced the darkness, the fading light at the end of the tunnel becoming me and Craigg's truth. "You better spray some of my smell good on you," he suggested.

"Right, and have me smelling like hot mess," Eye said and we laughed.

"Just come by when you can. Be good to your mother. She needs you more than you realize."

Eye said, "She don't *need* me."

He was being serious. "*Cherish* her. There's *nothing* like a mother's love."

*Yet your mother walked out on you and your brother without a second thought, and has been gone for years. Eye find that hard to believe. Mothers are sometimes no better than no good fathers.*

"Eye hear you."

Eye put on my clothes and closed the door behind me.

**Later on that night, after Eye** ate dinner, took another shower, and retired to my room, getting ready for bed.

Eye had my own room, so Eye didn't have to share with my brothers, plus Eye was the oldest. Eye lay down, and waited for *Mama* to fall asleep. It was as dark ass it could get outside when she finally did—Eye heard her snoring. Yup. She's out like a blown light bulb. Flip the switch all you want. That bulb is a dud. Eye put on some pants and a shirt, a jacket and Eye opened the creaking back door…closed it, leaving it unlocked, and went to see Craig. Eye made sure Eye was quiet. Eye didn't really worry much. Mama slept like a bag of rocks. Eye was walking up to Craigg's front door. Changing my mind, Eye walked to his room window and Eye softly knocked on it.

"Craig…Craig."

Eye knocked again. Nothing. Eye tried the window. It opened. Eye crawled in it, nearly falling on the floor. Once Eye was inside Eye couldn't see. It was too dark.

"…Craig…" Eye turned on the room light. "*Craig…*?"

The room was empty. Open beer cans everywhere and cigarette butts, weed crumbs all over the sheets. Room still smelled like puke; smelled even worse! "Craig?"

Eye looked at the bathroom door. It was ajar. Eye heard what sounded like a radio turned down really low.

My eyes narrowed. Damn it's funky in here! Grown man living this filthy needed his ass beat. "*Craig…?*" Eye walked to the door, kicking a few beer cans out of my way, and then another empty liquor bottle behind them. He's going to drink his way to the grave if he doesn't cut back. Eye held my breath, and pushed the door open. Eye fumbled around for the light switch. Finding it, Eye flipped it on and my eyes swallowed the bloody images so badly a scream was constricted in my throat. Refused to surface.

Eye fell to my knees, covering my mouth and started puking myself.

"NO, NOOOO CRAIGG, NOOOO MAN NOOO!"

He'd blown his brains out.

## CHERISH YOUR MOTHER

*As his words filtered through* my brain on repeat, Eye shook all the way home, running so fast Eye was tripping over my clumsy footing. "Craig, oh my God…" When Eye got to the back door Eye rushed inside, locked it and ran to my room.

Closing the door, Eye took off my jacket and threw it on the floor, slid out of my shoes and kicked them under the bed and Eye put on some shorts. Eye couldn't stop crying. Grabbing my stomach, Eye ran to the bathroom and barfed in the toilet. Eye puked so badly it hurt my stomach.

Mama came out the room. *Oh no! How can Eye hide a suicide from my face without her suspecting anything?* "What's wrong, something you ate?" she asked.

"Yea," Eye lied. Eye hated lying to her, but Eye couldn't let her find out what Eye just saw.

"Must have been some bad beef. Throw it all up, brush your teeth and take your ass to bed. You're damn sure going to school tomorrow."

She went back in the room. Eye stayed up all night crying.

Eye missed Craigg already.

Eye stared outside my dirty room window, a torn 13 year old that didn't want to live any longer. Eye would never see Craig again.

And even during his funeral—it was a packed house, Eye never knew so many loved him and every bitch that fought over him were the ones showing out—his words played through my head as Eye approached his casket, pretending like we weren't lovers. Eye kissed his lips, Eye cry now, January 25th, 2012, reliving a moment eye didn't share when Eye put out Pharoah and talked about Craigg.

"I love you," Eye whispered. "And Eye'm not your Mama. But Eye love you as if Eye were. Rest in peace, buddy."

And Eye turned my back on Craigg and our history.

Forever…

*Did your great Grandma ever betray your trust?*

*Lord Jennings*

***Great-Grandma's house was the*** one place Eye could go and never had to worry about adults or friends trying to have sex with me. She used to have my baby picture in a nice frame hanging on the wall of such a meticulously-styled, designed and decorated living room. She lived in the green and white wooden house on Goulds Park, and Eye loved her house because Eye always felt like she was God's wife. Her skin was the radiant color of relief after America won the Civil War, her lips the curvaceous affair of the Nile River, her fingers the amazing stumps of evergreens in the Spring and her personality bubbling like suds that aids the cleaning of dishes. Her mind and the way it worked and her choice of resilient words reminded my young self of education and why my ancestors fought so hard for it. Eye may have been promiscuous and nursing wounds of being abused—it was my drug of choice at the time—but Eye was an avid reader and Eye knew things about the world a 13 year old should never know. Her eyes used to light up with joy whenever she saw my face, and Eye melted every time her arms encircled my body. The only thing Eye hated about Olive's house was the smell of mothballs. Eye nearly gagged every time and she used to look at me and her smile chased away my unease.

Eye respected her from the core of my soul, right on down to my toes. Respect was *earned*, but with my great-grandmother and our brief encounter in this life Eye took with me so many things she taught me in such a small amount of time. During the few conversations we had (a total of 4), she always told me Eye was going to be something special in this life when Eye read to her my poetry. Eye never really considered it poetry, but whenever Eye recited it to her from memory, she would clasp her hands together like so and her beautiful eyes, balls of diamonds, filled with tears the way water settled in a well.

As the tears battled the wrinkles of such a lovely face, sort of zigzagging towards her chin, Eye was insecure.

Eye didn't want my poems bringing tears because a smile would do. But after Eye read my poems she would take my hands, pull me to her and plant her lips on my lips and she would give me such a grandmotherly kiss.

Eye remember one time, during the summer—when Eye was 12 years old, the year my sister Diva was born— she told me over a chocolate cupcake, that to truly be brave in my life Eye had to always let go of anger and revert self hatred into prayers that only God could hear. Eye really didn't want to have *that* kind of conversation. It was too heavy for me. But Eye was 12 years old, and already Eye had gone through some heavy stuff. Eye just never told her because Eye was scared she'd turn me away like a couple of my older cousins had. She knew Eye didn't *want* to have the conversation, especially when Eye was more focused on eating my chocolate cup cake.

But Eye sat down at the dining room table, and she sat beside me in a conservative looking white dress and her wig.

She said she loved God profusely and nothing came between her and God. She told me, that no matter what, she wanted me to forgive others of personal transgressions towards me. To pray for my enemies the way Harriet Tubman once had. She said when the going gets tough to hymn. She told me in my life many were gonna come in God's name and claim to do his work, but what they wouldn't reveal or want the world to know was one simple thing:

## THEY WOULD THINK THEY WERE GOD.

*Eye never forgot that*. Eye was enlightened early on in my life about Masons and the secret society.

Eye looked deeply into her eyes and said, "Grandma, *why* are you telling me this?"

She looked at me like she was preparing herself to never see me again, and it scared me. "Because Eye am preparing you."

"For what, exactly?"

She never took her eyes off me. "The *future.* Tomorrow isn't promised for the only thing promised to us was death."

"So there is no guarantee Eye will live to become an adult."

She took my hand and squeezed. "Come closer to me, Pharoah." Eye did so. Eye was so close Eye could smell the soap she used in the shower. "You will be something great in this life. Eye already know what that will be. You will be a writer. You already write in your journals. Eye already read something in one of them when you were napping in the room when you got out of school."

Eye clammed up. "Oh, no! *What* did you read?"

She was on guard. "Don't worry. You can talk to me."

Eye was on guard. *Intruder*! "Grandma…" Eye stoop up, backing away from her. Instantly she was one of The—a stranger.

She was hurt. "Pharoah, *come* sit."

Eye was rebellious. Eye didn't trust her anymore. "No. *Why* would you read my stuff?"

She was stern. "Who has hurt you?"

Eye put up a fifty foot wall. "No one, Grandma. NO ONE!"

Eye hit a nerve. "Don't yell, young man."

Eye was devastated. "Eye trusted you!"

She was feeling guilty. "*What* did Eye do wrong?"

*How could you Grandma?* "You had no right to betray my private thoughts!"

"Eye hate what you went through. Why didn't you tell anyone?"

Eye was heated. "EYE DID!"

She studied me. "Who did you tell?"

The Countdown begins…"Two of Roe's kids, but they retaliated saying my Grandma killed Uncle Al."

"My daughter didn't kill her own brother. Eye know this. She…"

Ten, nine…eight…"Eye have to go."

Her eyes widened. "Pharoah!"

Seven…six…Now Eye saw *why* she looked like she would never see me again. She had already invaded my privacy. "Eye'm never coming back."

"You can't run from your problems, Pharoah. You have to face them."

Five, four…three…"Eye will face them when Eye get ready. Why do adults always try to force me to do stuff?"

"*Pharoah*!"

Two…one…"Eye *love* you, Grandma. Eye love you very much. But Eye'm never coming back. And if you tell anybody my ex step daddy raped me Eye will deny it till Eye'm blue in the face."

The buzzer goes off in my heart, separating me from her forever. The End. It's over. Never look back. You'll turn to salt. Eye was too young to realize what Eye did, but presently, with huge tears falling all over my keyboard as Eye recount this, Eye still hurt inside from spiritually cutting off the only grandmother Eye'd ever know.

Hastily, Eye opened the door and ran to Roe's house. Eye never went back over there. Eye would pass by my great Grandma's house and never stop by. Because Eye was scared she was going to make me tell mom about the abuse, and Eye wasn't ready to deal with it. So Eye stayed as far away from her as possible.

Eye would clean Brisha Lynne's nasty ass house (which Eye did all the time). She had shit everywhere, and Eye would *never* stop by my great Grandma to even say, "Hi."

Eye was so hurt she read my journals.

How could she do that?

*Eye remember when Mama bought* me my first cassette tape. *Janet Jackson's Rhythm Nation 1814*. Eye loved this tape, and Eye loved the Miss You Much single. Eye was so excited. Eye heard on the news she was kicking off the start of the tour in Miami, Florida at the Miami Arena. Eye ran to Mama. "JANET COMING EYE WANNA GO TO THE CONCERT!"

She was sad, barely talking to me. Typical.

"She is?"

Eye was so excited. Eye was going to wear all black because that was Janet's favorite color.

"Can Eye go can Eye go?"

"No, you can't."

"Why, Mama?"

She looked me square in the eyes. "Your great Grandma Olive died…"

"Oh, no! No! No, Mama noooo!"

Eye died inside

Eye would never do that ever again…

*Were you ever a prostitute?*
*Or pimped by a man?*
*Lord Jennings*

A pimp was nothing but an advanced payment center. You give him your money up front and he gives you back your small cut (nowhere near the amount you made) at a later date. And to think they still didn't offer Pimping, Hooking and Cooking in college as a degree option when money and sex made the world go round and round. Eye thought about this one hot, sunny day. A handsome dude approached me while Eye was walking home from the bus stop. Eye was in the 8th grade at the time, and Eye was having serious problems with Squeaky who always bullied me in Perrine (Piss-Rine Eye called it). Eye never knew why the brothah had it in for me, but every time we saw each other he jumped on me and tried to fight me and Eye would never fight him back. That was till my home girl Petrina Warren, with her chocolate cute self, got in his face and told him if he messed with me again she was gonna beat him up. And he magically left me the hell alone. Eye think of her now. Eye recently saw her at The Green Room when Eye was getting my hair cut. She brought her father in so he could get a fresh tape around those thick dreads. We saw each other and embraced. Eye hadn't seen her since high school. Sixteen years ago.

Eye showed her the proof to Ђe Kingdom and her eyes were wide with surprise. She said she's a high school teacher now, and Eye told her Eye was going to make sure she got the book. After all those years all Eye could think about was how she defended my honor. Eye will always love her for that. But people jumping on me Eye would get tired of. In junior high Eye was trying to do the non violent artin Luther King thing and it got me nowhere. Sorry, Martin. Eye love you but Eye take X's side on this, fighting a bitch back was more my forte. Eye then got in a fight with Theresa Left. She was my neighbor and we were friends. We got into a heated argument on the school bus on the way home from Southwood Middle School and she ran at me with a screwdriver when we got off the bus and Eye didn't hit her, but Eye dragged her all through the street, took the screwdriver and when her older sister tried to jump on me Mama turned the corner and they ran in the house.

My dawg Petrina, laughing, said, "You need to fight Squeaky just like that, dawg."

And she was right.

*That day Eye started fighting* him back and he left me alone. A few weeks after the fight with Theresa, there was a strange man seated on the side of the road on the hood of a Cadillac. Nice car and rims, really clean. Chewing on a toothpick, staring at me and Eye rolled my eyes, gripping my back pack. Eye was clad handsomely in black loafers, long sleeved gold and black shirt, crisply cut high top Kid-N-Play fade and black slacks. Eye always dressed good for school. Learning was serious business.

"Say young blood, lemme talk to you, son bring your butt over here."

Eye looked at him with my mouth open. Stunned by his request. Eye was about to pass him. When Eye got up to him Eye could smell the Hennessey on his breath. Moist lips. He ran his tongue across his top lip, his arrestingly gorgeous eyes unpeeling my clothes layer by layer. Eye had to blush and look away. Eye was uncomfortable when people stared at me. "Eye'm a private investor," he began, in imitation gators that looked like knock offs from the flea market.

"Ok, and you're telling me this because?"

The sun beamed down on us, and Eye was starting to sweat.

"Eye like you. You ask a lot of questions."

His eyes bounced around a lot when he spoke. Didn't trust this one. Why were strange men always trying to talk to me? He kept on talking and Eye wasn't really listening at first. He then said he could promise me a bright future. His name was Bill Rackley, but they called him SNAKE in the streets. He was a dope boy/FBI Informant. In lament terms, he was a snitch. He got in good with niggahs, learned the goings-on of their lives and sold it to the FEDS. A lot of homes were broken into and a lot of niggahs were lining the pavement in handcuffs because of this *Prima Donna* Niggah.

Behind bars he was labeled a rat, from what Eye would later find out about him from some older friends of mine.

"Eye could make you a local celebrity, young man," he said, warming to his subject. "You see…you got a quality people seem to want."

"Qualities? What are you talking about? Eye'm in the 8th grade."

"Look at the way you dress, son? Look at your friends. They look like the product of the ghetto and all the in-doings in between. But look at you. You're *clean.* Dress shirt and pants. *Loafers. Nice* hair cut. *Gorgeous* eyes," he went on, making me uncomfortable. "You have beautiful eyes."

Did Eye say "*Thanks*" to a complete stranger?

"Um, gee. Thanks."

"*Wanna* work for me?"

Eye guess he didn't catch the sarcasm. Mama did need help with bills, and Eye really did want a job. All men had jobs, from what Eye saw. And Eye did want my own money so why not.

"Sure. Yes, Eye wanna work for you!"

"Good! Good!" he said, his face lighting up. He reached over, picked up a small red cup. There was a pail of ice next to him, real small, gold, and he put in some ice cubes and poured more Henn Dawg, he called his liquor. "But first things *first,*" he said, handing me the cup. Eye looked at it.

"Eye don't drink." Eye wasn't gonna front this time.

"Try it. It'll make a man out of you…or bring the man out of you," he joked and Eye didn't wanna look like a punk in front of my new boss so Eye took the cup and Eye wolfed it down, slamming the cup on the hood. Burned the hell outta my throat but Eye hid it on my face, narrowing my eyes instead.

"Good stuff?" he asked.

"Eye had better," Eye lied.

"Oh, yea? What do you drink?"

"Vodka. Straight. Room temperature. No ice."

He did a double take. "*Goddamn*! But look. Working for me ain't that easy. You see Eye gotta, you know," he went on, looking side to side, making *sure* no one was in ear shot, "test the booty."

Eye rolled my eyes. "What?"

"You gotta let me get in it. Eye need to know if it's nice and tight." He pulled out a stop watch. "See how long it takes for that boy coochie to make a niggah nut. Time is money, son. If you got some good booty then and only then will Eye escort you to the team."

"The team?" Eye said, shaking my head, taking a few steps back.

"Oh, yea." He smiled again, rubbing his hands together. He never looked away from my eyes. He was studying me. "Eye got other Hoes working for me. Eye'm telling you now; they aren't gonna like you. They attached to Daddy, ya' feel me? Hoes with big asses and mosquito bites for tits. You'll be the perfect addition. Eye'm in the process of severing ties with one of my Hoes you'll be replacing. And good riddance. Don't know what Eye saw in the tramp. She's so ugly you will spray the cockroach with RAID then shut her up with mosquito repellant."

If that was supposed to be funny Eye didn't laugh. In fact Eye didn't crack a smile.

"So you want me to sell ass?" Eye asked. Typical adult requests.

"Don't say it like that, son."

Eye narrowed my eyes. "Eye'm blood raw! And Eye'm *not* your son."

"Eye know you aren't, young man. If you *were* Eye'd sell his ass, too. Eye love money. Money makes me hard."

"Sad." Setting my book bag on the ground, Eye dug in my pants, rubbed my booty hole and walked up to him, coating his lips with my masculine scent.

"You ain't never sold ass like this, Pimp."

"Eye love you already. Damn you smell good. Eye bet you got a nice, tight little ass."

"How big are you…?" My eyes dropped down to his crotch. Not much, from what Eye saw. "Eye don't mess with little ones."

His eyes bulged out of his head. "My clients are gonna *love* you."

"So you're trying to pimp me? How many other niggahs you pimpin'?"

"This is a trial run. Hoes ain't what they used to be so Eye'm trying the fellahs out now."

"Eye guess. Eye don't know about this."

He rubbed my shoulder, his penis hard behind his slacks. "Let me take you somewhere. Get in the car and go for a ride with me. Eye want a 30 day money back guarantee voucher on that sweetness young blood."

"How much you payin' me?"

He was laughing. "That's what Eye'm talking about."

"How much. Eye mean it. You ain't getting it for free."

"Get in the car."

Looking around, Eye did.

*Once we were in his pricey car*—we were protected and hidden behind illegal tinted windows—he wasted no time digging in my pants. His breathing increased, and his clumsy, eager fingers fumbled with my moist booty cheeks—it was hot in this car; turn the AC on!—till he found the pleasant warm center of my ass pop. He started smearing his fingerprint all over my tightness, and Eye moaned because it felt so good. Hastily, he leaned into my face and kissed me, deeper and deeper, drawing me in. He smelled so good. His tongue well experienced in the field, his breath sweet and inviting. His eyes soft and filled with darkness and lust.

"Eye wanna do it to you," he said eagerly. "Eye want the booty, Niggah. Keep this between us and you can get all the sex you want!"

He kept rubbing my hole, occasionally dipping his middle finger deep inside me, making me moan and my eyes were wide and he pressed his finger deeper, deeper until it was all the way inside and he said, "Suck my tongue while my finger is in your warmth. Then Eye'm gonna get deep in it. Your booty's ripe for the plucking! Eye'm gonna have fun bouncing in it!"

Promises, promises. "Is that right?" Eye could hardly breathe. "It's really *that* ripe?" Eye asked, playing the dumb blonde role.

"Yes," he said breathlessly, and Eye was sucking on his tongue, and his eyes rolled to the back of his head.

He pulled his finger from my insides and he put it in my mouth and he watched me, his mouth wide open, suck it from his finger. Eye smacked my lips.

"Yummy!"

"Damn you are *hot*!" he said excitedly.

He pulled out his erection. He had a big one after all, damn dude. Eye retracted momentarily. "This is going to be your only on the job training," he enthused.

He pushed my head down on his throbbing stick and started banging my face. Ok, aggressor. Eye opened my mouth, activating the hate Eye already had for myself, held my breath and throat-freaked the old school niggah. Couldn't show me up old man.

"Damn, Niggah. Damn! *Damn* you're sucking it good!"

Suction sounds filled the car and my ears. Crashed on the windshield and became fog on the windows. Spread out and search. All the windows now fogged and humidity climbed to startling heights. His lips covered with sweat, but Eye kept sucking and appreciating.

*Eye hate myself so much. All men want is for me to suck on them. Is this all life is about? Making a niggah nut? Eye wish my daddy come save me but he probably ain't even thinking of me. He doesn't even* love *me.*

Eye held his penis down my throat for 15 seconds and didn't bat an Eye lash.

*"Ohhh my God! Ooooh Niggah, damn!"*

And when Eye came up for air he dug deep in my neck, grunted, toes locked up, nuts jerked, thighs trembled and nut spurted from his flaming hole and splattered across my lips, nose and face.

He's moaning and talking uncontrollably. He's a so-called grown man that test drove booties and mouths before he finished recruiting new Hoes to his team and he's OH GOD OH GOD DAMN NIGGA THAT WAS A GOOD NUT!

He sounded like a bitch. Ugh! That made my penis shrink to Midget status and my booty dry up faster than your floors thirty minutes after you mopped them.

Eye looked at him. "That'll be a hundred dollars."

He was laughing. "What?"

Eye put my hand out. Eye performed a service. Eye want pay for services rendered. Eye wiped his nut off my face with one of his shirts on his back seat.

"That's a clean shirt!"

"It's your *nut* on *your* clean shirt! The Cleaners on US.1. Take a lot of quarters, and don't use the last dryer by the back door where the old bitch folds all the damn clothes for a living."

"Pharoah."

"Give me my hundred bucks! Eye like my hundred dollar bill crisp, slim and lean, strong and straight."

"Get outta here!"

*He glared at me. "Eye'ma pimp!"* he went on. "You haven't started working for me yet!" He punched me so hard in the face Eye fell back against the seat, disoriented. He punched me in the stomach and Eye curled in a ball. He punched me in the back of the head, and Eye was dizzy.

"Eye wants my money," Eye said weakly. Eye started laughing, sitting up and he looked at me like Eye was otherworldly.

"Eye want my money!" Eye steamed. "And Eye want it now! Don't hate me playah, hate the forbidden fruit Eve ate making life hard for all of us."

He hopped out his car, snatched open my door in broad day light and pushed me out the car. Eye fell on the ground hard, but Eye didn't wince.

"Ew, sissy!" He screamed, getting people's attention. An older woman was in her garden wearing a straw hat and overalls, and another older male was working on his truck, oil all over his mechanic suit. They were both looking.

Oh Mr. Pimp showed off. "EYE DON'T WANNA HAVE SEX WITH YOU OH MY GOD KID! YOU CAN'T GIVE ME HEAD! YOU'RE A MINOR! GET AWAY FROM *ME* PUNK EYE LIKE WOMEN!"

Eye was put on blast, and embarrassed. Stunned. Shell-shocked. Oh, well. Bitches looking at me and Eye didn't care;

they were talking about me anyway because Eye dress good to school.

He said it again. Eye just really wished he give me my money and leave me alone. "Punk Eye love women!"

Keeping my head high, Eye started walking off, gripping the strap to my book bag. Back straight. Didn't look to the side or listen to the harsh whispers.

*"... The sissy trying to give head. Sad!"*

Eye looked to the right. "*Forget* you!" Eye exploded, my hate boiling over. The tears fell hard. "You old trick! Eye suck *better* than you! You don't know anything about me, Miss Bloomers! You don't know what grown men did to me since Eye was a small child! Poppin' off at the mouth. Your breasts sagging yet?"

Her mouth fell open. Eye went on, "You're just mad because Eye can pull more men than you ever had in your life!" Eye was clearly bothered by her response.

She feared me. Her eyes wide, she held her throat. "You're going to rot in hell."

"Right behind your stank coochie, trick!"

He jumped in his Cadillac and sped past me, leaving me in a cloud of exhaust. Eye held my breath so Eye wouldn't have to fan and choke.

H**3*4

Eye smiled, flagging down the bus amidst gay slander too threatening for me to rewrite or repeat. Eye knew what Eye was, so Eye wasn't worried. The brakes squeaked as the metro bus, the number 52 stopped. Eye paid the fare and sat in the back.

Eye shook my head, not sure where Eye was going. Mama wanted me to come straight home, but the two door Mustang wasn't parked in the yard. Eye smiled to myself, hate boiling in the depths of my soul. He didn't pay me my one hundred dollars." Eye frowned. "Next time Eye want my money up front."

Eye pulled his wallet from my draws. "Oh, yes! Money money money!"

Eye counted $890 in twenties, tens and hundreds.

Ah. There was his driver's license. Social security card.

"Sore loser. Eye may be a teenager, but Eye'm not stupid! Got an advance for my services. Niggah Eye fooled you!"

Once Eye got off the bus by the Recycling Can Place on Marlin Road, walking to my friend James house, Eye wrote *EYE HATE FAGS!* on some woman's door, threw a rock through the window and threw his ID and wallet in the window, went across the street to the pay phone at the store and called 9-1-1 and reported a break in.

Eye even described the car.

And the license plate number.

*Who tricked who, Niggah! Let's see how he likes the taste of Shug Avery's pee in THAT water! Taste good, didn't it. Pimp.*

# Book III

## *The Cages of the Abyss*

*Congrats to my Baby Brother Kells for a Bachelor's in Computer Science from Fayetteville University. The first in my immediate family to graduate college. He graduated on his 25th Birthday—May, 2011 and we were all in North Carolina to support him. Eye am so proud to be your big brother…*

# Day 2

# HOME GOING SERVICE FOR:

SUNRISE:
AUGUST 1983

SUNSET:
SEPTEMBER 1987

PHAROAH C. WILSON, JR'S AWAKENING
SEPTEMBER 1987
2 P.M.

SWEET HOME BAPTIST CHURCH
11335 S.W. 190 LANE
REV. DR. GOD VS. SATAN

*"No one is to approach any close relative to have sexual relations. I am the Lord...Everyone who does any of these detestable things — such persons must be cut off from their people"*

# LEVITICUS 18:6, 29

**A Time to be Born:** In 1987, after being freed from a four year rape system, Pharoah was free to live his life and be a kid again. But that was short lived. Two older cousins, his ________ daughters, would abuse him for 8 months...

**A Time to Grow:** Already dead inside, Pharoah learned how to treat a woman, touch a woman and eat coochie through his older female cousin. Initially, he was against it but after, again, falling submissive to the older "authority figure," he would be thrown into a cycle of sex, being pussy whipped in the process.

**A Time to Reflect:** Pharoah Wilson didn't understand why he had to have sex with his cousin. It started with the much younger cousin—a few years older than him. Around the time he was being raped in his home, he used to hang with this older cousin and she would teach him how to hump her with their clothes on, being sexually stimulated.

**A Time to Die and be mourned:** Sadly, The Older sister would get the object of her desire when she took Pharoah's virginity. Initially taken by his ex step daddy, now he was playing for the other team, lost in a game of sex. Feelings his young body wasn't built to handle blinded him, but he handled it because something in him died. What died in him exactly, the world may never know.

*But Pharoah Wilson himself.*

*Tell me about the Era*

*Lily abused you*

*Lord Jennings*

# LILY'S IN THE FIELD

***Eye can't say that Eye was sad*** to watch Mama throw my step daddy out, because, honestly, it was the HAPPIEST DAY OF MY LIFE! YAY! THE EVIL MAN IS GONE GONE GONE! Eye cried tears of joy around that time; Eye really didn't have the words to describe it. Eye did know that Mama could do better without him. Being married to him had been tumultuous enough. Eye remember one time Eye walked in on him doing the do with her in the bedroom. For most kids it would have been a rude awakening, but since he had been doing that with me for years it did nothing for me. Eye simply turned around and went in the room, closing the door as if Eye didn't see anything. He'd put Mama through a lot. One time, he'd come home late with an attitude. Mama was in the shower and he called himself smacking her around. Retaliating, Mama ripped the shower curtain down, pushed him in the hall closet with the bikes and all you heard was *BOOM BOOM BOOM!* Mama kicked his butt. It was *then* Eye started to realize that he wasn't the tough guy Eye thought he was, and with that Eye started to develop a smart mouth and standing up to him myself. If he couldn't beat a woman surely he couldn't beat me. The day Mama threw him out Eye recounted in my head everything that'd happened between them. Eye was in the fifth grade when she lost her first daughter, Samantha, and the stress Mama endured. Previous to losing her daughter, my brother Kells had gotten a seizure, one he couldn't break out of. He was twitching and shaking and Mama was about to go crazy. Eye remember being at the hospital with Mama while doctors tried to revive him. It didn't look too good for Kells, and Eye was devastated because Eye took him everywhere Eye went.

Eye used to read him books and talk to him and teach him things, even when he was a newborn baby. Eye think Kells flat lined and Mama died inside. She pleaded and cried to God "Please don't take my child." God heard, because when he sent Kells back he took something else.

Her unborn daughter.

*But of course Mama didn't know* she lost her daughter. She was still carrying her child to term, or so she thought. She was also under a lot of stress, being a working mother and married yet doing more work in the home than her husband, doing the things a husband should do. But Mama was never the type to sit around and wait for a handout, no matter if it involved family or not. Her own relationship with her father was a rocky road. They were at it all the time. Back and forth. She once told me her daddy told her she would never be anything in life. That she would do nothing but make babies and be on welfare. Mama was on welfare, but hardly *on* it. She only got on it if she really *had* to. But if Mama could work she got off her ass and got a job. Eye always respected her for that. That instilled in me a hardworking spirit, and that reinforced what my granddaddy taught me when Eye had to work out in the yard, and cut the grass to make a little more money. Eye would get Mama's lawn mower and walk around the Hollywood Squares Projects and cut people's grass for $10 a yard. They were very impressed with my work. Eye would go above and beyond the call of duty, even picking up the trash and taking out their garbage for them. That was my signature. And every time they needed their yards cut Eye would do it, even if they had to pay me later. But when my sister was still born Mama died inside, and so did Eye. Eye was strong for my mother, making sure she was ok but she wasn't talking to nobody, not even her kids, husband or father. She was sinking into a dark place, and Eye know she had to be thinking of her deceased mother, since she died when Mom was 15 so she always felt like she was robbed of having a mother. Eye remember going to school at Caribbean Elementary, and Andre, Bert and Vernon comforted me. We always walked to school together, every day. We used to compare our penises, pull them out and see who had the biggest one. And of course, Eye did, and it wasn't anything gay or nothing like that. We did that once just to see who the big man was. Eye was already the tallest of the group.

Eye didn't think of none of that when my sister died. Eye really wanted a sister. Eye was tired of having brothers. Eye was in the cafeteria waiting to get my food. And Eye was so upset. Eye started crying and everyone looked at me because Eye hardly cried. Eye was known to be the class clown. A few of my friends asked me what was wrong and Eye told them. In class they made me *We Love You!* cards with crayons and construction paper, and that truly brought me through. Eye brought them home to show Mama. But she was like a zombie. She didn't pay the drawings any attention. Gurgling sounds came from her mouth. Eye looked in her eyes.

They were dead.

*It killed me inside knowing Mama* was going through so much pain and Eye felt helpless because there was nothing Eye could do. What brought her around was my granddaddy, her father. Eye think he slapped her over and over till she came to and she snapped out of the trance and was like, "If you slap me one more damn time."

Mama was back.

*For months Eye did know that Mama's* insurance money was vanishing from the manila envelope that hung above the front door in the living room. Eye was under strict instruction to make sure the insurance man, who, back then would come to your house to collect payment, received the funds. But for some reason the money would not be there and Eye know Mama put it there because Eye watched her.

One day Eye was in her waterbed and Eye was just laying there watching the black and white TV that sat on a small nightstand by the bedroom door. Eye turned to the side, my brothers in the other room playing as they always do. They weren't too thrilled to see their daddy leave, and my youngest brother Kells had just been born in 1986.

Eye reflected on everything. Every fight Mom had with my ex step daddy, the ways she stood up to him and didn't let him slap her around. Eye always admired her for her fighting spirit. She always had the ability to go out in the world, a black woman, a sexy black woman (light skinned with gorgeous eyes) and make it happen with a job. She still worked at Sunrise with the mentally challenged kids, something she seemed happy with (sometimes Eye got to go out to her job and see the kids myself) but around the Christmas break she would get a seasonal job at Toys R' Us so we had a Christmas. Eye looked on the floor behind the bed and saw a Pepsi can. It wasn't that it was a can, but burn holes were all around it. Eye never saw anything like it in my life. So Eye picked it up and observed it. "Why are burn holes all over this can?" Eye thought nothing of it; didn't know the story behind it so Eye threw it away. The insurance man was at the door. Step Daddy was gone (thank God) so Eye got up and told my brothers Eye'll answer it. Eye was tall for my age so Eye reached above the front door and took the envelope from the nail holding it in place on the wall. Eye gave it to the insurance man, who always seemed to be in a rush when he got there. Who *cared*? Nobody was going to rob you, dude. You pulled up in an Isuzu for God's sake.

He took out the papers and said, "Where's the money?"

"Eye don't know," Eye said, confused. "Mama put it in there."

"This isn't the first time, young man."

"It's not my fault."

"Where is Mrs. Horn (her married name)?"

"At work."

"You said that *last* time as well."

"Don't get an attitude with me."

"Her insurance will be canceled if she doesn't pay."

Eye snatched the envelope and looked inside. It was empty, again. Eye told Mama and she was mystified. She questioned her husband but men always had selective amnesia so you can guess where the conversation led. Another argument. A few weeks later Mama found out what the burn holes were in the cans and the story behind her money vanishing. My step daddy was on crack and was doing it heavily. Eye knew for years, but was forced to remain silent. The only thing that Eye never knew of was the burned cans. For me, Eye didn't know what it meant. But for Mama that was the straw that broke the horse's back. Eye remember she was so angry she was crying. "Eye know he's not doing drugs around my children!"

She packed all his belongings in large garbage bags, and Eye do mean *everything*. She said he had to go, and she meant business. When Eye heard the words Eye was *thrilled*! Did this mean he was getting out the house? Eye was so excited! Eye was smiling to myself, trying not to make it obvious to Mama. Didn't want to raise red flags.

Eye even went with her when she, cursing all the way there, drove her Mazda hatchback Across the Tracks in Goulds, where Step daddy was partying with friends. You could tell he was high as hell. His eyes were red and his long hair in plats as always. Mama put the car in park, her leisure curl kinda dry and hopped out. She didn't waste time.

"Get your ass out my house!" She threw all the bags on the ground, hopped back in her car and stepped on it, hauling tail up the block. Smoke from the tires snaking backwards towards him, staring, grim-faced.

Mama didn't look back or take him back.

He was what Eye called *Get the hell O.U.T.*

***As an end result, Mama threw*** herself into work and proved that you didn't have to stay married for the kids' sake when you were no longer in love. Whereas she had help with bills and rearing the home, the gears switched and she had to rely on herself. Eye admired her for this. Eye used to write in my journal just how proud Eye was of her, proud to be her son. She showed me, through setting an *example*, that you can get through anything, even a divorce, because she filed for it and didn't hesitate. Eye was jubilant. He couldn't touch me ever again. He couldn't spit on me and tell my brothers to disrespect me when they got older. Eye can't tell you the number of times he told my brothers Eye wasn't their real brother because Eye came from the sack of another man.

Eye can't tell you how that used to devastate me. It was bad enough finding out the man Eye thought was my Daddy was raping me. How naïve Eye was. But Eye came to the conclusion that all kids are naïve in a sense.

Then Eye wanted to know who my real Daddy was. Eye knew Eye was named after him. Eye knew Eye was born in Salinas, California. But Eye wanted to know him and talk to him. There was a man coming over my Aunt Roe house that spent time with me and took me places. He felt like my Daddy but he wasn't my *Daddy*. Life got a little harder for me. Free of sexual abuse, Eye had to be big brother. Eye had to take on duties a grown man should have. Eye had to be responsible for the house while Mama worked. Eye could still sometimes go out and play hide and go seek with my friends, but that dwindled when Mama went through divorce. Eye had to go from loving big brother to ass whipping brother. Mama laid down the law before she went to work and she said it ONE TIME. Don't answer my phone. If Eye feel you answered it Eye'm beating your butt. Wait till the answering machine comes on and when you hear my voice then you pick it up. Don't turn on the stove. Eye will cook ya'll food before Eye go to work. If you breathe on my stove Eye'm beating YOUR butt, not your brothers. Don't answer my door. In case of emergency, go across the street and get Mae-Mae. Or Miss Ginger a few houses down. They will look after you while Eye'm gone but you run my damn house. Mama is depending on you, baby. Eye can go to jail leaving my kids home alone. Mama can't afford baby sitters. Eye love you. Did Eye follow her rules? *Hell* no. Since Eye was so ahead of my years, Eye reared her home like Eye was the husband *and* the Daddy. Yes, we ate what she cooked but if we got hungry again Eye cooked us something and had the kitchen and house spotless by the time she got home. She never came home to a dirty house. Eye cleaned and cleaned and cleaned till Eye couldn't clean anymore. Eye really didn't have the need to call Mae-Mae or

Mrs. Ginger. Eye didn't like Ginger anyways, she was always talking about somebody and as fat as she was she couldn't talk about nobody. Everything went along kosher until one day, he showed up at the house when Mama was working, and it scared me to death.

My step daddy.

*My brothers were excited*. Eye had the youngest boy; Eye had to look after him and change his diapers and feed him. Evil Man knocked on the door.

Laron tried to say something and Eye smacked him. "Shhh…Mama said don't let him in here."

Jarshawn was giggling. He wanted his Daddy and Eye told him he couldn't have him.

He knocked again. *Bam! Bam! Bam!*

"You little *faggot!* Eye *know* you're in there. OPEN THE DOOR!"

Eye shook with fear, my teeth clicking together. Eye hugged all my brothers and didn't let them move. Eye would protect them. He stated kicking the door. Felt like the entire HUD house jumped with his foot. He then started pounding on the room window, peering inside. Eye turned off the lights. We were in the dark. "Eye'm scared," said Laron. "Daddy is scaring me."

"Eye'm scared too," said Jarshawn, hugging me tighter. Kells started crying.

The Evil One was laughing. "Eye see you faggot." Eye looked to the right and Eye jumped again from his piercing, demonic eyes glaring down into mine. My blood froze from the hints of remembrance and lust galloping his irises like the Elite taking bet on how to kill off half the human race. "Release my kids! They *miss* their daddy. HEY BOYS!"

Eye gave them a knowing look. "You better keep your mouths closed!" Eye meant BUSINESS!

They were sobbing.

"Eye'm gonna kill you when Eye get my hands on you," he promised.

"Oh, yea! You can't even get in the fucking house!"

"WHO ARE YOU TALKING TO?" He punched on the window. Eye thought it would *break.*

"FUCK YOU! LEAVE US ALONE, *BITCH*!"

Eye had enough. Eye got up and called the police.

And Eye didn't tell him. Hugging my brothers, they clung to me as we waited for the wails of cop cars. And when they came the punching stopped. Yea, bitch.

The Armor of Jesus held the window in place.

*When the police came Eye* hopped up and ran to the door. When Eye opened it he was plea bargaining and Eye told the cops the story, everything. Eye was tempted to tell them he raped me but since my older cousins never helped me and turned on me, Eye felt rejected so Eye swallowed it and didn't say anything. Mama's friend Mae-Mae ran across the street and made like she was there with us the entire time so Mama didn't get in trouble. When Mama did get home she was mad with me, but she understood, after Eye told her what he did, and she didn't whip me. She actually kissed me and said, "Eye told you when problems arise to call Mae-Mae."

"But he threatened me."

And she left it at that, doing damage control.

Evil Man was gone again! YES!

*Later that night Eye thought* about my ______ daughter, the youngest one, Apple. She was a few years older than me. Eye wanted to do with her what she used to do to me, when we were hunching, trying to have sex but our clothes were always on. Eye actually smiled, because, at the time, Eye didn't know this was wrong. No one taught me that sex with a close family member, especially your first cousin was wrong. All Eye know is Eye was on hard just looking at her skinny ass. Back then parents hid things from us kids, hoping we would *never* find out till we were grown. But what they never thought of was that we had friends and cousins our age that had open eyes. Bit into the Forbidden Fruit a little early. *And* my oldest cousin would take me on a wild 8 month ride with her coochie that not only had me whipped, but had me nearly being a father before Eye turned twelve. Till she miscarried. It was a deep family secret Eye *NEVER* shared.

Till now.

*Things were on the up and up* when my cousins came over. The oldest one, Eye will call Lily, was big with big titties, pitch black skin and a raunchy mouth. Ghetto to the bone. Eye actually picked up a few new words from her.

She had on this ugly floral skirt and a tight light blue shirt with Michael Jackson's *Thriller* album in the middle.

She was watching over me and my brothers while Mom was working. Eye was laying in the waterbed, staring at her sister. We used to do the bump and grind thing and my penis was hard thinking about doing it again.

So Eye crawled over to her and Eye said, "So, what's up."

She gave me a coy look with Diana Ross-like eyes. Big and pretty. "Ok, we can do it."

Eye was smiling, getting harder. Before we could go in the other room she whispered something to her older sister, and she looked at me. She sat up and turned the black and white TV to a channel that was scrambled and wouldn't show the entire picture. Eye did make out tits and sexual sounds. Must be the nasty channel. My penis was harder seeing tits. Lily looked at me, licking her lips. "Eye heard you wanna hunch my sister."

Eye went soft instantly. "What are you talking about?" And Eye glared at her sister, betrayed.

"Don't play stupid. She said you wanna hunch, boy. Eye'm going to tell Clara!"

"Don't tell her," Eye said, scared. Mama would beat me for even having thoughts of sex, even though sex with my cousin Eye never knew was wrong. Eye thought it was a part of growth and life.

"Eye won't if you do it to me!" she promised.

"Eye don't wanna do it to your big ass; Eye want your sister."

crashed on the tile floor. It hurt so badly Eye couldn't move from the shock. She sat up, pointing at me. "GO PEE AND COME BACK AND MAKE ME CUM!"

Eye ran to the bathroom, smelling like sweat and coochie. Eye stood over the toilet and strained. Nothing came out.

Running back to the room, she raised her skirt and said "Eat my coochie."

"What?" Eye asked, twisting my face.

She snatched me by the head and shoved my face between her upper thighs. God, the smell! Ugh! Help me, God! Didn't she piss from her coochie and she wanted me to eat it? And women bled once a month. One time Eye watched Mama putting on a tampon because she didn't close the door all the way and Eye watched in disgust, not even knowing what the hell was going on.

"LICK MY COOCHIE!" she said, slapping me in the face. "Push the hood back and suck on my clit! Make me cum *faggot*!" Eye didn't know what the hood was, or what a clit was. Eye didn't know what "make me cum" meant, but she wanted me to do it and Eye coulda been at the black board trying to do trigonometry and Eye hadn't learned division yet.

"You can't eat coochie." She snatched me up. She was twice my size, built like a man with titties.

"Eye want some more. With your cute self. Cuz, you so handsome," she soothed, trying to sweeten me over and it wasn't working. "Do it to me again!"

Eye slid back inside her and Eye *loved* it, despite my unease. It felt so good. Eye was humping her again. This time she held my buttocks and spread her legs.

She was in la la land. "Yea, cousin. Get it! Yes!"

Eye was kissing her titties.

"Oh, yea. Eye'ma have fun getting this!" she promised.

Eye had to pee again. It built from my toes and popped in my pelvic bone.

"Eye gotta pee," Eye said prematurely.

Her eyes were hot coals. "DAMN! YOU'RE MAKING ME MAD!"

Knowing she already slapped me once and Eye fell out the bed, Eye hopped up, racing down the hallway to the bathroom. Eye was determined to pee. My hand on my hip, Eye held my penis, staring in the toilet.

Again, *nothing*.

Eye slowly walked back to the room. Part of me didn't want to do it to her anymore, but she kept calling my name and threatening to tell my mother so Eye went in the room a complete zombie. Eye was on auto-pilot when Eye started to have sex with her again. She called me every name in the book. While gyrating inside her, she grabbed my butt and was controlling my spine. Eye felt her thighs trembling and she tried to kiss me and Eye turned my face. Her breath was stinking and Eye didn't feel up to kissing anyway.

"KISS ME!" and her tongue darted in and out of her mouth and Eye closed my eyes, her coochie wetter and feeling even better. Eye had to pee again and this time Eye didn't open my mouth. It felt good the way it was traveling along my shaft and Eye banged her harder, burying my face in her tits. It felt incredible. Eye didn't want to pee in her but Eye was determined to pee this time. Eye started to moan.

"Hell, yea. You like this coochie! Talk to Mama!"

Eye gotta pee, Lily.

Eye pissed right in her coochie. The best piss ever. Damn taking a leak felt like *that*? Eye didn't know Eye truly came inside of her with my explosive seeds. It wasn't pee at all, but Eye wouldn't know this until a few months later.

The next few months she was bringing her ass over to the house all the time, and Eye was back in hell. Eye had just got out a four year destructive system with my ex step father and now a female was abusing my body. And as much as Eye hated her for it, Eye loved her coochie. Eye was *addicted* to it. Eye was banging her all the time now, even sliding it in the booty. She was eating up all the food in the house. Mama told us we couldn't eat certain things and she'd bring her mammoth ass over and eat it all up and Eye got in trouble for it. Getting my butt whipped didn't matter because Eye was getting coochie. Eye didn't have any desire for the other sister. She betrayed me, and loyalty was everything to me. So Eye never touched her again. Before Christmas my cousin and Eye was having sex. Eye was so attached to her; Eye think Eye actually *loved* her. Eye didn't know what love was so Eye never truly thought about it, but when she told me about other boys screwing her Eye was so jealous Eye wouldn't talk to her when we had sex. Eye'd just dick her big ass down and send her fat ass home. Since she was doing it with other boys Eye wanted to screw other girls and boys. So Eye was having sex a lot in the 'Hood, but never with anybody my age. They were always older than me. One guy was married and lived on the next block next to Gee Gee, a friend of mine. Eye used to cut his grass and he always paid me $10. One day he and his wife got in a huge fight and she packed her stuff and left. They made a huge scene and Eye was walking up the block pushing the mower.

Eye asked him was he ok and he didn't say anything. He was about twenty-three years old. Eye pushed the mower behind the medium-sized divider wall and knocked on his door. He let me in and said, "Eye don't want the grass cut. For what? Eye don't have a family anymore."

"Eye understand," Eye said, sitting on the couch. "Man it's hot outside."

"You don't understand," he said, his pants falling below his ass. He had on a t-shirt and had a nice hair cut.

"My Mom threw my step dad out not too long ago. Eye know what you're going through."

His brows rose. "And how did she move on?"

"Eye don't know. She just…did it. Eye guess her tits had more power than daddy's nuts."

We were laughing.

"Eye like you. How old are you?"

"Sixteen," Eye lied. Eye always wanted to be older.

He examined me. "You got a girlfriend?"

"Yea, but she having sex with other boys so the hell with her Eye'ma do it with other boys, Eye meant *girls*," Eye

*Over the next few weeks Eye* stopped cutting yards. Eye focused more on my school work and mad because Lily was having sex with other people, and Eye was going through withdrawal. Turned out she wasn't doing it with other dudes at all; she told me that to make me jealous. She got off on it. She told me she couldn't bring herself to bang other dudes because she was in love with me. Eye smiled, telling myself yea, right. One day, when Eye turned 11 years old, she came to me crying hysterically.

"What's wrong?" Eye asked her. She wouldn't look me in the face.

"Eye'm pregnant," she whispered.

"Ok," Eye went on, lost. "Pregnant, what are you talking about?"

"Eye'm pregnant, Pharoah. Eye'm having a baby."

"OK, so why are you telling *me*?"

She just stared at me. "Mama can't find out. And Daddy can't find out. They will kill me."

"Your *Mama* is so nice. She won't hurt you. And ______, too." ______ was *not* nice, why Eye said that beats me. Eye guess Eye was trying to calm her down. Eye thought back to when Eye was ten, after he fought Mama over milk. Eye could still feel his hands around my neck and my feet dangling.

"Eye HATE HIM!" she screamed at me, walking past me. "Eye shouldn't have told you."

"Told me what?"

"He used to. He, Eye can't say."

"You can't say what?"

"Everything Eye did to you he did to me."

"What are you talking about?" Eye played dumb. She didn't remember already telling me what her daddy did to her. So Eye remained quiet to see if she would say the same thing.

She looked in my eyes. Eye saw the same hurt and pain that used to be in my eyes when Eye was being raped. What was she not telling me? Eye had to know.

"Lily, somebody hurt you."

She started to cry harder. "Yes! And Eye can't forget it. Eye started doing this drug."

"What drug?"

"It helps me forget what happened…Eye don't think about it when Eye'm high."

"Are you doing drugs, Lily?"

"Yes!"

"You can't do drugs! They are bad for you!"

"Eye'm about to have a baby, cuz! Eye can't have this baby! Eye just can't! Eye'm scared!"

"*Eye'm your cousin!* Eye got your back."

"Pharoah, *you're* going to be a daddy."

Eye sat on the living room couch and said, "No way!"

Eye was only 11 years old.

*Eye couldn't really eat*. Becoming a father from my cousin was something Eye never thought of in a million years. Eye remember telling one of my closest friends. He was gay, around my age and he told me, "Pharoah, you have sex with your own cousin?"

Eye was smiling. "Hell, yea. So what."

"Pharoah that is wrong!"

"No its not! Cousins have sex all the time."

"Pharoah, it's wrong to sleep with your uncle's daughter."

"She told me its right."

"Is she your age?"

"No, she's a few years older than me."

"Wow, man. Come here," he said, taking me to his Mama.

"Watch this," he said as we entered her living room. She stayed on S.W. 191 Court, the next block.

"Hey, Ma," he said.

She was medium built, pretty and looked tough as my own Mama She was cooking black beans and frying chicken. Um, um, um Eye LOVED chicken.

"Eye know Eye'm getting some chicken," Eye told her and she kissed my cheek.

"You ain't dancing today?" she asked. "Boy, you dance really well."

"Thanks."

My friend, Eye will call him Corey, asked his mom a question. "Mom. Isn't it *wrong* to have sex with your own cousin?"

A ghost jumped out of her and her reaction half opened my eyes. But they were closing really fast because, dealing with adults who were supposed to be more mature than us kids actually turned me off. "Who's having sex with a cousin? That's sick! Yuck!"

He said, "My friend Harold at school."

"Who is his mother? Eye wanna know who she is so Eye can go tell her!"

"Eye can't do that, Mom," he said and she smacked him.

"Who is he?"

He looked at me. "Eye don't know. Eye forgot."

"Eye'm gonna whip your butt! WHO IS HE?"

"Eye can't do that, Mom. You're just gonna have to whip me."

My world destroyed, Eye sat at the dining table as she whipped her son for being loyal to me.

He sucked it up, taking each extension cord hit like a man.

"Who is he? Eye'm telling his Mama so she can stop it. Incest is wrong!"

He was crying, trying to grab her hand.

"Even Pharoah knows having sex with cousins is wrong, don't you, Pharoah?" she asked, pushing her son on the couch.

"Yes, it's wrong," Eye said to appease her, hoping her loud mouthed ass shut up. She had more teeth than lips, that's for sure.

"Wouldn't you wanna know who he was so you can tell his folks?" she asked, handing me some cookies.

"Yes," Eye said, feeling used. My cousin *used* me!

"Good. Eye'm going to sit down. No cookie for you, Corey."

When she went in her room Eye gave him half my cookies.

"Eye told you," he said, mad at her.

"Eye'm sorry she hit you."

He wiped away tears, eating a cookie. "Fuck her. That whipping was worth it."

"Why?"

"It proved to you that having sex with your cousin is *wrong*. And now she's pregnant with your kid. You ain't old enough for a baby."

"Eye'm scared," Eye said. *He's lying! Having sex with my cousin is not wrong! He's jealous because Eye'm getting coochie and got a baby on the way already and Eye'm only 11.*

"Tell your Mama."

"Hell, no," and Eye ran out his house, all the way home and closed the door.

Praying to God to kill the baby.

## *Were you ever a Hoe?*

### *Lord Jennings*

***Eye didn't understand Hoes.*** These days, during this so-called recession, Hoes were on their A Game, weren't they? They have all the sense, 'ey? We should replace NFL coaches with big breasted Hoes that were street smart, loaded with business savvy and, yes, bitch, fraud the IRS with seven different names with seven different checks. Now how in the hell did you do that? Eye see why a Hoe was the secretary and or slash treasurer at the church. Hoes were blindingly smart with money. Eye didn't trust them with my cheddar, though. Eye learned that from the years of watching Mama. Mama dated men (weren't that many, thank God) that could elevate her passion and eternal plan. And out of all her boyfriends two of them tried to come on to me behind her back and Eye never said a word.

Eye couldn't hurt her like that. If Eye told her what they did that would effect her eternal plan. And that was to get her kids out the ghetto and give them things in life, give them a better life than her mother and father gave her. The ignorance of my age truly kept me deaf, blind and dumb.

My mother was without a mother since she was 15 years old, my grandma wasn't there to show her how to become a productive woman, but Mama had me after her Mama died, so now Mama putting her goals and dreams on me. Eye had to go to school and do what she wanted me to do. Eye knew she wanted what was best for me, but at the time Eye didn't view it that way. Because of the inner hatred Eye had for myself. Eye suffered tremendously. Eye had to play basketball because Eye had basketball players' hands, or so she surmised. Eye never believed in the *motto* of the ghetto, inner city or the projects. It went like this. All a black kid was good for was to basketball-and/or-*football* his way outta high school, skipping college and signing directly to the *Pros.*

Eye was a smart Niggah. Eye was bisexual or in lament terms a cut above the competition. Sex validated my very existence, so that's all Eye really thought about as a teenager. Eye was promiscuous, trying to relive every abusive moment Eye endured because it became my very genetic make-up. It was a nightmare Eye couldn't escape. How adults abused me and moved on as if nothing happened baffled me beyond reason and understanding.

*Any* Niggah that could suck a good stick could damn sure eat good coochie. Eye used to give head for the taste, but eating all good coochie made me burp and call it a night. But the nightmares, those sinister, living, breathing dreams shackled me inside my own misery. Eye used to fight the air, sometimes falling out of the bed and onto the floor trying to scream for my mother. But the darkness clenched me by the throat and beckoned to continue becoming…whatever it needed me to be and Eye sometimes awakened in a drunken stupor, punching the darkness around me, my fist slamming into my dresser, sometimes the wall…Eye shattered the mirror to the point my hand started bleeding from the open wound. Eye could remember, when Eye was 15, crying uncontrollably, pouring alcohol all over my wound…screaming into the air. Mama was at work. Brothers and my sister slept. Hadn't awakened for school just yet. Eye couldn't control my breathing; my chest was on fire, the acids of my stomach popped like Crisco oil. Eye squeezed my eyes shut, *wrapping* Mama's good towel around my hand…Eye stared at the economy-size bottle of Tylenol…Eye wanted the pain and the dreams to go away—Eye wanted them to *stop*! But they *intensified* over the next few months…and then Eye tried it…tried to swallow the pills…about 20 of them…wolfed them down with a Budweiser at Boyd Anderson High School, after my TV Production class. Eye got the beer into school via my huge book bag. Eye just wanted to die. The class was vacant. Eye was alone, in a class Eye both adored and loved. Eye remember racing to a friend with a car. The pain started behind my eyes, giving me a plaguing head ache. He drove me home as the pains started to lick my belly. Eye rushed inside and threw myself unto the bed. Eye cried so hard Eye couldn't stand it. And then Eye blacked out…

*My ex step daddy taught me how* to suck and take a penis, sent me to boot camp early; and _______ daughter used to whip me with extension cords, making me eat her out and have sex with her…the images plagued me.

Eye remembered the voices as Eye fell into blackness, trapped behind my closed eye lids…the pain of taking pills was getting the best of me. Eye knew it was death; Eye was slipping into eternal darkness and Eye welcomed it. Anything was better than living on an evil earth with governments trying to control society and adults using my booty hole for target practice.

Eye had to stop it; Eye had to stop it now! Eye had to stop the dreams, the nightmares that plagued me since Eye was a child, dreaming of Satan with a lollipop for a penis…the images scared me to the point Eye never wanted to talk to people.

Taking the pills was a big mistake. My heart pounded…pounded faster…and then…suddenly…the darkness lifted my eye lids and Eye was ten years old, reliving the nightmare…of boning Lily…and getting extension cord whippings because of my reluctance to sometimes. Eye saw Lily slapping me on the floor because Eye had to "pee." Eye could touch her—smell her stench…her coochie tramping through the air made me gag and now that Eye though about it her *Nookie* smelled better than she did. Eye could smell Apple, and she smelled nothing (nothing remotely close) to the fruit, the forbidden fruit, even though in the Bible the forbidden fruit was never described or named…Eye could see the thin lace curtains hanging on Mama's bedroom window, see the dust settling on the fabric…the small black and white TV…the scrambled Playboy channel spewing ooh's and aah's into the room, into her ears, into my ears…the tile floor cold beneath my small feet. Eye saw myself racing to the bathroom. Standing over the commode straining and not an ounce or drop of piss materialized. As a 15 year old Eye reached out to save him, save a part of myself that never had closure…a part of myself that didn't forgive myself for the abuse…a part of myself that blamed myself for what happened, everything!

Eye wanted to hug my inner child, that scared boy, that trembling boy living in fear of society's expectations and let him know Eye was there—Eye was there from the future to change my past.

"Come with me!" Eye said to him, but he didn't *hear* me. Or was he ignoring me? Eye hated rejection.

He raced past me, his body shattering the image of myself at 15 years old and Eye turned and ran after him…into Mama's bedroom…as he slid back inside Lily while Apple pretended not to notice. "Having sex with a relative is wrong!" Eye screamed at him, remembering the butt whipping my friend once received, proving to me, through the curt eyes of his aggressive mother, that sex with cousins was wrong; it was a sin! And sin had dire consequences! But my voice was drowned out by the power of Lily's aggressive baritone. She was saying, "Ooh you feel so good! My daddy used to do me like you're doing me. Get deep in it cousin!"

Eye was saying, "Pharoah! Not like this! STOP! She's conditioning you through the pain her father inflicted on her. She's acting out!"

And then Eye saw his eyes—ЂE DEM☯N…

…My ex step father, throwing me to the floor…against the lukewarm wood…the thunder boomed, the rain poured outside my window…and he was pulling my underwear to the bottom of my butt cheeks, splitting the Red Sea—Moses was spitting on my hole anticipating penetrating my young body…he was pushing *cautiously*, slowly, deep inside me—making me gasp in pain and shock; unveiling the story—the *real* story behind thy penis, which wasn't just used to "piss" with…

Before Eye could scream for my mother's help, his sweaty body snatched back into Lily, and Eye was back inside her and Eye, the 15 year old, screamed horrendously…trying to save him, needing and wanting to give him closure…Eye savagely swung at her face and my fists were transparent, flowing through her. She hadn't even noticed Eye was there, an image…trying to save myself from ruin and couldn't, because what was done has come to pass. Amen. So be it. It's over. Move on! But Eye needed closure…

Lily grabbed my ass and pushed me deeper inside her, and Eye opened my eyes…ten years old again, trapped in his skin…Eye grunted, trying to *will* myself out of her, but to *no* avail. The coochie was good, but the misery was an untimely doom. Being punished for the untold sins of our parents. What Eye knew then Eye knew now and in the darkness it wouldn't allow me to use what Eye learned and apply to the years that have come to pass…and Eye screamed in her face but his lips didn't move!

"*GODDAMN! PHAROAH! You're* only ten year old and you feel like grown man—go deeper!! Oh my *God!! Y*ou feel so *good!* You're *gonna* make me cum, *Cuz! You* my favorite Cuz! *Show* me how you gonna do it to your girlfriend when you get one!"

And Eye went to town in the coochie, got dressed in her Nookie, Nookie; my raw penis had on a cum suit and matching cum shoes on my hairless nuts and her hand pressed on my buttocks with her middle finger deep inside my hole so when Eye plummeted in the coochie my balls bounced off the top of her softness and pelvic bone and Eye bounced my hole back on her finger and Eye came deep inside of her. Eye remember how the darkness began to fade, like a setting sun, a huge ball of energy ducking behind thick, purplish clouds and the image of Lily turned to blackened roses dancing from an easterly wind in a huge meadow deep in the forest…and Eye was running…a pack of wolves behind me, ducking every tree, running along the bark, swinging from thick branches…ducking the darkness…claws reached out for me and Eye began to scream as my eyes slowly began to open…something was there, something came into focus….and then the smell…puke was all over me and the bed sheets. Mama came in the room, shaking me, "Are you okay baby?"

"Must be something Eye ate in school," Eye told her.

When it dawned on me that my suicide attempt failed Eye closed my eyes again, ignoring Mama, and Eye welcomed sleep once more. Mama didn't understand. Eye wanted to die. As the weeks passed, my depression grew; people were starting to get suspicious so Eye masked it behind humor in school and making people laugh. It worked. Thank God. Mama was on me about playing sports. Eye wasn't interested. Hard enough taking 7 classes in high school and helping her raise my brothers and sister. Eye didn't need the added pressure. Since the age of 6 Eye was trained to take beatings and get a nut out of it. So when Mama tried to get me to play sports Eye said '*No.*'

Every man she dated that even tried to make me play sports Eye told him 'bout his funky ass. No!

If my *own daddy* wasn't there making me play sports then, *Niggah,* get away from me and out my life! *Let's* get it right! *You're* here to bang Mama! *Not* tell *fatherless* son what to do—Niggah. And they gave up on the first try.

But not my cousin Sweet. He came over, grabbed me by the high top fade and pulled me to my feet.

Fire was in his eyes. "You're *gonna* play football or basketball."

And Eye snapped. "No the hell Eye ain't!"

The fire turned to ash and stone. "Who are you cussing at?"

Eye've seen enough fire being raped. He didn't scare me. Eye was tired of grown men thinking they could touch me when they got good and ready so Eye told Sweet, "Eye'm cussing at *your* ass! Eye'm not scared of you!"

And Eye got in his face, my heart pounding. He wanted to rip me to shreds and Eye was hoping he did. He didn't know Eye tried swallowing pills a few weeks ago. Eye was already dead inside. "Let's get it right. *You're* my blood cousin! *You* ain't my daddy. So don't put your hands on me!"

Tears welled in my eyes. "Eye hate you! Eye *hate* my fucking self! MY OWN *DADDY* DOESN'T EVEN HIT ME! EYE HATE YOU!"

Shocked at my outburst, my older cousin grabbed me in a bear hug and held me close to his heart to the point Eye heard it beat and hot tears wet my face. Eye lay limp against his chest, his touch doing nothing for me, wishing he left me alone. Why did he care? No one loved me; Eye didn't love me. Eye hated love, love did nothing for me. Sweet didn't cry over dumb stuff. My cousin was a *real* man in every sense of the word; he took care of family and kept his entire generation of people deeply rooted in the family tree through his Christmas Parties. He lowered the side of his bearded face to the top of my head. He felt like a father at the moment. "No, no, no Pharoah no don't you ever say you hate me or yourself. Eye know your Daddy ain't about nothing. But we're *blood.* You are my cousin. Eye made your Grandma Alice a promise, that Eye would look out for Clara. And that includes her son."

Eye shook. Never before did a man hold me and didn't want to have sex with me. That was my cousin. He truly loved me. He truly *cared* for me. He would protect me. Eye knew this, in his arms, Eye had a father, something Eye been hoping and searching for…forever. Eye wished Eye was Big Man—Sweet's biological son—at that moment. He was raised by his Mama and Daddy; Sweet taught him how to chase skirts and be a man. Taught him about money, important ways on saving and spending, got a good faithful wife at home, but he had some whorish qualities.

Eye knew this. Sweet knew this. And Eye pushed away from him and said, "You are not my Daddy. My daddy doesn't want me and Eye *don't* wanna play sports. If you wanna beat my ass you gonna be turning my booty cheeks to Jesus being beaten to the cross because Eye ain't playing no sports."

He sympathized, and he counted the agony in my eyes. Dead eyes. They didn't shine nor sparkle. "Eye hear you," he said cautiously, examining me, "But stop all the cursing. Eye know what its like to be without a father. Mine was shot and he died."

Eye was shaking my head. "Not you, *too*! Eye'm *sick* of hearing about this. What now? You gonna say my Grandma killed your Daddy, *too*? Goddamn! Give it a rest! Eye wasn't even *born* yet!"

He held up his hands. "Eye wasn't gonna say that, Snook. Eye know she didn't kill my father."

Eye was skeptical. "Then why your fat ass sister keep saying that every chance she gets?"

He widened his eyes. "Which *one* of my sisters?"

Eye tapped my foot on the floor, glaring at him. Eye told him.

He was stunned, but not surprised. "Eye know she didn't tell you nothing like that."

Eye looked deep in his piercing eyes and wasn't intimidated any longer. "Yes she did, and if she say it again Eye swear Eye'm gonna punch her in her mouth, and Eye don't hit girls or women. Keep Alice's name out her mouth I all eye ask!"

He gave me the *stop cursing* gaze again, and Eye fell into silence. "Eye'm gonna talk to her.

"Do what you gotta do." It was barely a whisper. My voice cracked. Eye had no more fight left in me.

"Are you sure you don't wanna play basketball?"

Eye turned from his face. "Eye'm sure."

He never bothered me about it again. Eye mean sports wasn't for me. Eye was a book worm. Eye lived for my dictionary and writing my poems and short stories. Eye never told anyone of my secret obsession. Eye didn't want praise or recognition, so that's why Eye sat on my talent. Eye wasn't ripe in the world yet. My experience for the subject matters Eye wrote about was too much for my teen age. Eye hadn't gone through enough. God didn't put enough on my plate. Everything has its season.

So Eye sat on my writing talent. Writing every single day and never told a soul. So why jeopardize that by playing sports. Less time on books, more time on lines of scrimmage, groupies, probably banging your team mate in the ass and sucking the other one's penis and keeping it on the hush; nah Eye didn't want any part of that.

Eye saw enough of that with a few Niggahs on the Boyd Anderson and Southridge football team. Since being a bestselling author, Eye slept with two high profile NBA stars. Eye know they're shaking their asses off right now. *Brr*, Niggahs—it's COLD in here, but Eye *won't* put your names in the ATMOSPHERE. Relax. NBA Niggahs hang up the phone, don't call your Publicists (who came at me like pimps to sleep with you two, oh *yea* ya'll it was a threesome and one of them liked to get piped down like me!). Only a dumb Niggah who was illiterate would go directly to the Pros. The Niggah Eye knew screwed his way to good grades in high school; another Niggah Eye know had sex with his math teacher for straight A's, and that Niggah in the NFL right now that graduated from _________ Senior High.

So Eye was glad Eye didn't play sports. If Eye would have made it to the big time that would probably be my life, the sexual romps my NBA booty calls led daily behind their wives back, bashing gay men in social circles.

When a couple of Mama's men tried to screw me Eye suggested a cold shower and don't kiss Mama after she smoke in the mornings because her breath be kicking like Bucky the Bull. Eye was put in an awkward position. One of Mama's boyfriends was fine as hell and Eye swear if he flirted with me one more time Eye was going to give him some. But Eye couldn't do that to my mother. So Eye didn't.

Eye was a dog, territorial when Mama got a new man and brought him in the house.

Eye was the man of the house when daddy, her second husband and then, years later, her boyfriend said, "Well the trim has gotten kinda boring so Eye'ma get going, not gonna call and if you are pregnant don't call because it ain't my baby."

She thought Eye was stupid, but Eye was taking notes.

When Mama was having sex Eye used to listen. With my ear pressed against the wall. Eye was already a writer so Eye wrote it down, my penis hard as hell at the sound of her dude telling Mama she felt sensational. *Damn* girl!

And Eye was turned completely off by Mama's cries of passion. Could you say *Ugh*! Eye knew well enough that good sex didn't stop her eternal plan.Eye could remember one time she was having sex and the Niggah sounded so good through the wall Eye was like *ohhh* and Eye spit on my hand and Eye pulled on my erection, slightly gripping it till it was rock harder than Chinese arithmetic. Shuddering, Eye spit on it some more, pressing my ear harder on the wall. The Niggah kept saying *oooh sh*—and Eye stroked and pulled and almost buckled at the knees and Eye came all over my sheets. When he had an orgasm shortly thereafter, Eye heard him and Eye fell on my bed; springs squeaking, taking a deep breath and Eye heard Mama say shhh, shhh, shhh…

Wide eyed, Eye was like oh damn! Did she hear me?

"Eye thought my kids were up," she said and Eye thought, *Eye am up! And Eye got a good nut!*

And there was another dude she dated when Eye was younger; Daniels, with his alcoholic ass; God Eye couldn't stand his loafer wearing, red-skinned behind. Eye didn't like him He was too smooth and Niggahs that were too smooth had a rough exterior they tried to protect. Every time dude spoke Eye rolled my eyes, looking at Mama from the table like he's talking *bull! bull!* And you better not believe a thing he says. But she *did*, and while she worked or was gone he's sleeping in her water bed with his hard-on exposed, butt naked with the door open. Eye walked in there one day, looking at his penis. He had a big one. Eye walked over to him. He was out like a light. Snoring. Mouth open. Beer cans everywhere.

Where was Mama?

*Why was he in erection mode*, in the middle of snoring? Eye felt a pulse in my booty hole. Blood was running from my penis, keeping it soft and settling in my rectum, making me moist.

Eye crawled in bed beside him and took it into my mouth, using what my ex step daddy taught me. Veins popped out of nowhere, and he gripped my head, slowly humping my hot mouth.

Eye reached up and covered his eyes.

"Don't open them," Eye whispered, trying to sound like Mama.

"Damn baby suck it, Clara."

He thought Eye was Mama. Mama don't suck like me, baby. Eye could smell the beer on his breath. Eye licked his balls and ran my tongue between the split in his cheeks like Eye once did my ex step father and he spread his legs and Eye ate him real good and he jerked himself, keeping those eyes closed and he locked up and cum shot on my tongue and Eye licked it all over his rectum.

Eye jumped out of bed and closed the door behind me, running straight for the shower. Eye knew that Niggah was gay. Wait a minute. He thought Eye was Mama.

But at least Eye got some…

*When they broke up Eye* was happy. Eye didn't want to see him again. He was a punk. Eye'm sorry. Any man more concerned with dressing up in some good clothes and getting drunk was dressing to get drunk and look good for a Niggah.

Oldest trick in the book. You gave a Niggah like that some coochie then you are a fool.

Eye'd rather buy vibrator cock than casual cock that wanted more asshole than coochie.

But he called the house one day, when Eye was about 13, maybe 14 years old. This was after Mom got the job with the FEDS, and we moved by Caribbean Elementary in those brown apartments Eye hated.

It was about 1 a.m. "Hello," Eye whispered.

"Is that you, Clara?" he asked.

Eye knew who it was instantly. The way he pronounced his words, the slight lisp in his voice gave him away. Yup. That's *him*. What did Eye do? Hell, Mama got a new job. She's single with no man and all her attention was on work and her kids.

Um, stay away, Big Daddy. You were kinda funky anyway when Eye sucked it years ago. Eye hope Eye didn't suck Mama from his penis and the thought made me cringe and wanna puke. Eye covered my mouth briefly, and then decided the past was gone. Now that Eye thought about it…that was probably why my stomach was hurting later that day, after Eye sucked him up. If Eye tasted the womb that brought me here Eye would cut my tongue off and cast it in the fire.

"Clara, you there?" he asked impatiently, thwarting my thoughts into scattered pebbles.

"Yea."

"Why are you whispering?"

Eye thought about it. "My kids are sleep."

"Oh, cool. Eye can respect that. So *wassup*, girl?"

Eye rolled my eyes, wanting to laugh at his ignorance. "Eye'm cool." Eye put my fists over my mouth, giggling. My little brother Kells woke up, looking at me and Eye covered the phone and said, "Take your ass back to sleep! Now!"

And he lay down and did what he was told.

"Eye'm back," Eye continued to whisper, needing to get this over with and fast. "Look. Eye wanna see you."

"You do? You cursed me out last week. You said you don't want me in your lie."

"Eye did; but Eye *changed* my mind." Oh, no! My penis was starting to swell. "My coochie kinda hot."

Kells looked up, smiling and Eye popped him in the back of the head and he lay down.

"It is? It wants Daddy?"

"Yea," Eye whispered, covering my hard on with a pillow. "Let's meet up. Come to Hollywood Square, Eye'm still staying in that old HUD."

"Eye remember that place real well. You sucked me up real good that day, wouldn't even let me open my eyes and you licked my nut all over my booty."

Eye jerked his chain. "What you talking about, Eye never sucked you up."

"Yes you did."

Eye shot my cuffs. "You were drunk, probably dreaming."

He sighed. "Yea, you're right."

Eye talked like a girl, still whispering. "Come meet me there and Eye'll suck it good this time."

"Hell, Eye'm on my way."

Eye hung up.

We didn't live there anymore; we stayed next door to Caribbean Elementary.

Whoever lived there now was gonna whip his ass knocking on their door this early in the morning.

Kells looked up. "What were you doing, big brother?"

Eye looked him deep in the eyes. "Keeping perverts away from my brothers and sister. Gotta keep the bad men out."

"Eye love you."

Eye kissed his forehead. "Eye love you. Now go to sleep." All my brothers were in bed with me that night. And for the first time Eye felt like a protector. Shortly after, my arms around all three, Eye fell into a deep sleep.

Mama didn't need him in her life.

*But before all that could happen*, Eye thought back to when Mama didn't have a Federal Job. Eye thought about the five months before she got the letter from the government. Once she did get the letter, while being served with an eviction notice, Mama went away to training, leaving us there with                 's ignorant tail. So Eye indirectly ran Mama's house because Eye knew how she liked it run. We were struggling. Hankerson, who was dating Mama and cheating on her with Miss Lisa next door, spent up our food stamps on another bitch while Mama was in Glynco, Georgia for training. And ______ had my brother pulling his drawers down in the bathroom and Eye was looking under the door the entire time.

Same bastard that raped Lily.

Out of fear, Eye bammed on it and scared his ass and he rushed to make my brother pull up his draws and Eye bammed on it again till it opened and Eye told my brother, "You sleep with me, let's go."

When he went in my room Eye looked at ________ vehemently and snapped, *"You crack head bitch!"*

"Eye'll beat your ass!" he yelled at me, balling his huge hands into fists.

"You think you're so big and bad because you did time in prison, bitch Eye will kill you over my goddamn brother! Why you made him pull his draws down?"

"Eye don't know what you're talking about!" He was fidgeting. He was on those drugs. Eye wasn't stupid.

Eye got in his face. And Eye meant business. "If you mess with my brother ever again Eye will *screw* you the way you deflowered your daughter. The way she screwed *me*."

And Eye left him standing there trying to figure out how Eye know he deflowered and molested Lily, and she screwed and molested me, and wound up pregnant with my child when Eye was 11 years old. You really didn't remember Eye confronted you the day you fought Mama over milk in Hollywood Squares *before* she lost Samantha? And then Eye lost my child—a pain Eye shared with Lily and we didn't tell a soul. We gave it to God. She does crack to forget—maybe she *has* forgotten. But Eye never will. Eye would write it in my journal. As the saddest/happiest day of my life. Sad because Eye would *never* know my child. Happy because—*phew*—Eye didn't want to share a baby with my cousin. That's some crazy stuff.

Then the inevitable happened.

***Mama elevated in her career choice***, left the ghetto behind—thank God Mama believed in herself enough to answer an Ad in the paper when the government was hiring new corrections officers. Eye will never forget that letter she got in the mail when we were at our lowest.

The letter that changed our lives forever.

Eye should touch on that a little more. The *letter* came when we got evicted—our water was turned off by the City, and the lights, too. Eye *think* the lights were off, or were they in danger of being *turned* off. At Mama's lowest, God stepped in and gave her a career. The letter came right on time. Mama forgot she sent off for that job she found in the newspaper. Hiring for the FEDS. When the FEDS gotta recruit through the daily newspaper something ain't right with that, but Mama didn't care. She went to Georgia and graduated with good marks and scores. Eye was so happy! NO MORE GHETTO! OUR LIGHTS GONNA GET CUT BACK ON YES! WE MIGHT GET A POOL AND EYE CAN HAVE MY OWN ROOM; A BIGGER ROOM AND HAVE SEX LIKE MAMA BE DOING WITH HER MAN!

So Eye became a Hoe, instead of joining a gang. Joining a gang was normally done when you come from an environment lacking essential ingredients for your development and well being. When you tried to disengage from a gang the price was death. They killed you and your family. That's why Eye never joined the Vice Lords, or the Bloods and Cripps. No sir. Eye gave up my well-trained body to adult Niggahs and my young, always hard penis to adult females. Eye was even my Pa$tor'$ Hoe. And he put me to work. Pimping me, and had me bringing him the money back, and what Eye got to keep Eye put in the collection plate, and he told me that was a good investment. Be a cheerful giver, he always said.

Then, for the next few months, he tip-toes out of his bedroom while his wife, big mouth, lippy trick—strung out on dope and liquor and he got a hotel and was having his sick, perverse way with me till Eye came all over those sheets. The Pa$tor didn't have to worry about the money coming up short with a gutter Hoe. Hell, that's his wife—the gutter Hoe, and where he found her from—and Eye was the Side Line Hoe. The Jump Off. There to make him *skeet* his marital failures from the flaming hole of his penis, and he goes home; leaving me confused, spent and satisfied. Yet Eye yearned for him, the attention he gave me was priceless, or so Eye thought. Eye was lonely, often times silently crying myself to sleep. He had the comfort of his bedroom, sleeping next to his wife. And he had angry sex with me.

Once my body conditioned him, he took his Biblical ass home and gave his wife empathy sex. Eye was at a loss for words. Pa$tor spending the church's money on her hair, nails, pregnant coochie and her unwavering shopping at

Body Works, it wasn't called Body Works back then, but it's what it's called presently. Eye used to love being a Hoe when Eye was a teenager. Eye was Hoe Central. Before TLC was chasing waterfalls with that cheesy, corny video Eye was turning Niggah's to Niagra Falls, looking deep in their faces with my left Eye, head slightly angled.

Eye was sucking adult men ferociously, and eating adult women fiercely, giving up the good good to a few cops who thought Eye was 18 years old, and this one dude who worked for the government before my Mama started working with them pursued me until Eye gave in. Eye gave him some of my teenage loving a couple times, then he crushed me by saying his wife was back in his life and he had a son and he had to make it work.

Crushed me like ice in slushies.

Eye was heart broken, went home and waited till Mama slept and Eye tried to slash my wrist.

Eye looked in the mirror and said, "You stupid Hoe! YOU BITCH!" Eye yelled at my reflection. "How could you fall for a married man? You're too young! YOU KNEW HE WAS MARRIED! No matter what he told you, he wasn't obligated to tell you when you sucked him up and gave up your body and Eye felt better to him than his wife's narrow, timid coochie."

Eye would see him again when Mama worked at FCI. When he saw me his mouth fell open and Eye pretended Eye didn't know him. He wasn't all that anyway. Gained a little weight, pudgy. The sex barely made me yawn, Eye meant moan, *playah.* Eye just wanted the C-notes anyway and he paid handsomely. Eye kept right on ignoring him and he was trying his best to make Eye contact with me during one of their picnics. Eye wasn't with it that day. Eye didn't go back, Eye moved forward. Eye did not wanna move forward and look back and turn into something Eye hardly even put in my food—salt. Being a Hoe—being a good Hoe—was the business. Even when a Hoe was stripping as a career choice, raising kids or popping her snatch on trashy penises she was still bobbing her head to Snoop Dog, listening to *with my mind on my money and my money on my mind.*

That's a Hoe's Motto…

*Thought* you *knew*, fool.

And for the other Pa$tor Eye gave some good loving to—Eye was 14 years old, and had him doing the skip, skip, skip to my Lou inside me.

And Eye still walked out feeling like Alice in Wonderland. Eye swore he had forgettable sex. The minute he slid it inside me Eye suddenly knew why his wife kept cheating on him—endowment malfunction. Eye was like "Is it *in* yet?" He was laughing, grinding in me with that weak excuse of a penis. Eye *guess* his stick was still in Morning Mass, and Eye said, getting off his erection, "A ha ha ha hell—what's so funny? You can't do it right. You need to get out of here. Easter will never resurrect that puny thing!"

He was steamed, all in his "feelings," *Chile*…"The hell with you!" he stammered unapologetically, unconvincingly. "Go to hell. Eye make the ladies run from this!"

Grabbing my clothes, trying to put them on—and nearly tripping over clumsy footing—Eye ran for the door. "Run from it like *this*?" Eye asked, reaching for the door knob and he was offended. "They were *running* to keep from laughing at you! *Midget* dick, Niggah!"

His mouth hit the floor. Eye opened the door and left.

Never called him again. And the third Pa$tor that had sex with me at another church. The church was on NW 27TH AVENUE in Liberty City. If you're gonna be, if you're gonna be, if you're gonna be, if you're gonna be, if *Shawty* wanna be a Hoe instead of a thug, hell, let him wear his panties under his Pastor Robe. Eye was tired of Tupac wanna-be Niggahs clad in Pastoral robes trying to walk, talk and act tough in front of the congregation. Pa$tor Higgins. Don't get your panties in a wad, Pa$tor Eye changed your name in this account so you could continue fooling your wife, who had ruined coochie, that you actually love her. If she only knew of the things you told me about her she'll *gut* you, spit on you, eat you, shit you out and flush you but Eye'll spare you. For now.

The thing with Pa$tor Higgins was simple. He forgot one of the rules of the streets. You *couldn't* turn a Hoe into a Housewife; and thinking that you could blinded you into *creating* expectations you could never live up to, because you forgot the golden rule. Then, after marrying the prostitute you paid for, you came a *Party of 5* in her womb over the years, making her stay home barefoot and pregnant?

You knew she was addicted to fast cash. She got in, got her money—sometimes sticking around long enough to milk him, then you, dry— suck his stick the way he *loved,* becoming his fantasy; swallowed his rage…pocketed her cash and one day her ass got busted. She went to buy feminine products, and her items came up to $200. What the hell did she have on the counter that summed the price so high? But you, over the years, Robin Hood your congregation, giving your money to Pinocchio (your wife, and me), making your penis grow longer than the lies you left behind… and the lies dry…boo boo dries—always dry on your nose. The last dude you ate out painted Picasso all over your lips and you fell out the bed, remember, looking at me and Eye was like "What are you looking at *me* for? You see why Eye don't lick anybody's butt anymore. Yuck. Giving head was one thing, but hell no am Eye gonna toss a salad that was based in the brown stuff like *Au Jus*? Nope. *Eye* been there done that. Always in the flow of things. Eye didn't get down like that. If you eat my booty, or whatever you wanna call it that was on *you*! Eye didn't ask for that, but *yes* Eye *know* Eye secretly love it. You talked me into it, talking 'bout Pharoah you're so fine you're reminding me of my pimpin' days and Eye can't think about the good ole days because Eye will get hard, and you know Eye love wearing panties, getting in touch with my feminine side and my wife will never understand so…." All that yap yap about keeping secrets wasn't working with me. Why say you're a real man when you have sex with men and gotta coax a bitch to remain silent. "You're so full of it," Eye told him nonchalantly, never losing my reserve or cool. "Clean your mouth off. Talking mess with *crap* on your lips, ugh!" He went to the bathroom, silently, angrily, washing his face, disgusted. Eye was disgusted *for* him. All we heard was the door slam. The place shook momentarily. Homeboy that painted the Pa$tor'$ lips was gone. He gave the Pa$tor'$

mouth diarrhea and he hit it, forgetting his money. So Eye slid it in my pants pocket without a word.

Eye was laughing and The Pa$tor was mad.

*And Pa$tor'$ crazy check getting* wife. Oh, she *was* crazy for real. She wore curtains to church talking 'bout that's a *new* dress. Um, Eye've been to your house. Eye gave your husband some booty behind your back; Eye know those were your curtains. Eye was hiding behind them one day when *you* came home early, talking 'bout you smell *shit* in the air.

The same day ole boy ran out of the house after painting your husband's lips a greenish/brown color. Eye held my breath to save your marriage. Eye almost passed out.

Your husband was holding me hostage in church, telling me Eye'm going to hell for being gay, but never actually calling me out. Eye wished he would have. Eye'd pull his ass out the closet, screwed *and* exposed. Eye stopped talking to the Pa$tor when Eye saw his wife stealing the church'$ money. She used to be a stripper, remember, before you paid for it. Fell in love, and now forced to live a lie. Hoes and Pa$tor$ go hand in hand. Pimp$ are Pa$tor'$. Pimp$ and Pa$tor$. In fact the biggest contributors to the tithe plates, Eye meant collection's plates were strippers, escorts and penis-sucking parasites. The main man, Mr. Pa$tor, was Mr. Mom, keeping three bad kids that weren't his—that's the shade and the irony, Pa$tor, that none of those kids turned out to be yours. And you're *still* holding on to this woman—and one of those kids have Down syndrome, and the Niggah your wife has been secretly creeping with on the side—for some get away cock—thought he had *all* the answers.

He's sticking the trick free of charge, can't get any money out of it because she gave it to the Pa$tor on Sunday, even donated some to the Building Fund. Pa$tor$ are Pimp$. Told ya. They're the smartest bitches in the world and half those hood rats couldn't tell mozzarella from Swiss or cheddar, talking about they're selling their bodies to make that bread and her big brother been making coke on her stove for years, scratching his balls and rummaging through her fridge without washing his hands…and eating from her pots on the stove before he fed her husband and her kids…he was also spitting on her floors and pissing in her sink and farting in her kitchen.

All in all, yes, at one point in time Eye was an environmentally shaped Hoe, shaped and molded by the very adult hands that bash sex offenders.

When in fact, they were offenders themselves.

They've just never been caught.

# HOME GOING SERVICE FOR:

SUNRISE:
SEPTEMBER 1987

SUNSET:
OCT 1990

PHAROAH C. WILSON, JR'S
AUTONOMY
OCTOBER 1990
3 P.M.

SWEET HOME BAPTIST CHURCH
PERRINE, FLORIDA
REV. DR. GOD VS. SATAN

*Jesus told him, "I Am the way, the truth, and the life. No one can come to the father except through me."*

# John 14:6

**A Time to be Born:** In 1990, three years after losing his virginity with his older female cousin and suffering the loss of his child at age 11, Pharoah detested everything about himself. He hated his smile and he hated the very breath of his body. He moved on with his life, separating himself from his cousin—*falling* into the sexual fires of older people that molded his young body for their ultimate pleasure. They would publicly shame him to keep him obedient and conditioned, having their perverse way with him throughout the night.

**A Time to Grow:** Tall and mature for his age, Pharoah solicited older people to have sex with him because he couldn't control himself. People twice his age used and abused him and moved on without a second thought.

**A Time to Reflect:** Pharoah started writing even more in his journals. Becoming one with words. He wrote to express himself because his journals were the only things that listened to him. They understood him. Part of him hated being in bondage. The other part of him kept telling him it was all right so he never wanted it to break.

**A Time to Die and be mourned:** Pharoah died in Oct of 1990, just before Halloween when he was savagely attacked by a neighborhood gardener and he would never be the same. The rape fueled in him a deep hatred and after the event he would grow tougher and become outspoken and retaliate through theft and stealing. He stole a boom box out of Miss Valencia's Science class not because he wanted it, but because he was trying to get his mother's attention so he could tell her of the adults that abused him. But she would never listen…

*Eye read something about "The Pail Man" in one of your journals. Eye want to hear you talk about it.*

*Lord Jennings*

# "ЂE P/A\IL MAN"

***You know things were messed up*** when you moved out ofyour Mama's house—spur of the moment—for an *ounce* of independence, the exact reciprocal of dependence, and you *still* weren't happy. In my case that dependency was my drug of choice. Eye'd become addicted to Mama's house because Eye was afraid of the big bad wolves in the world. Even though Eye was raped in Mama's house back in the day, many years ago, and Eye confronted my sick ______ in Mama's bathroom once upon a blue moon; Eye still felt safe— overall—in Mama's house and never planned on leaving or flying over the *Cuckoo's* nest.

Eye feared the wolves in the world—and Eye feared Ђe W☯rld. Eye was terrified of Ђe W☯lves that camouflaged themselves in police, Pa$tor, bum and plain clothes police uniforms to corner a target the minute the cashier swipes your driver's license at the DMV. Those bar codes on the back has your damn life digitized right under our eyes. Cop pulled you over, took your Driver's License... *Swipppeeee!! Everything* computes right before his eyes.

Pushing that out my mind, Eye had my stuff packed after hearing Mama's phone call to my Uncle. When she was going to delete my books and have Jarshawn change the password. Eye burned with an astonishing rage the entire time, mind plotting a mile a minute. Once Eye was packed Eye neatly placed my suit cases and garbage bags filled with my belongings and clothes on the sidewalk on the side of

Mama's house by the side door. It was dark and cold out and Eye was waiting on John to come pick me up in *our* KIA Sorrento. He left work at the Hospital on his lunch break to come get me outta Mama's house. He was taking a while, so Eye walked to the Pine Island Projects, across the street from Mom's house in Hartford Square. Hartford Square was a middle class neighborhood back in the 90's, till a few of the Section 8 recipients moved in and hell on earth was the end result.

People's houses were getting broken into, Niggahs from Liberty City—*christened* Ђe City—were down in Homestead try'na *run* the 'Hood and only ran their mouths and Eye thought about this while eating Mac and cheese, ribs and crab and ham rice at my Aunt Debra Brown's house. Goes to show that a good plate of food wasn't nourishing enough to keep my mind off *Niggahs.* Better keep your mind on your Niggahs—*YOUR* NIGGAH—before you even think of having money on your mind day in and day out. That's how niggahs get robbed and jacked. So busy glorifying money with your cars and wardrobe, different Calendar Hoe on your arm (last month it was April, now you having sex with June in August) and not realizing that Niggahs—YOUR NIGGAH—robbing you blind and smiling in your face and having gut-wrenching sex with your Hoes.

Miss Debra Brown was not my *real* aunt, but Eye loved her like an aunt and she's the only reason why Eye came in the Pine Island Projects. We used to work at Publix in the Keys years ago, catching the early morning JGT bus from Wal-Mart (what a crazy bus system that was!) with more Haitians than anything and they always gave an attitude and Eye waved my Nassau, Bahamas flag like what the hell ever.

My Mama never had sisters, so Eye didn't have any aunts. My dad had sisters, but Eye don't know who they are or where to find them.

Aunt Debra *knew* something bothered me. She could see it all over my face. Eye didn't have anything to say.

"You're ok, baby?" she asked. She had beautiful dark skin, and when she wore that crummy wig (sorry Auntie, smile) it made me smile.

Eye lied so she wouldn't worry. "Yea, Eye'm ok."

She gave me the all knowing Eye. "You know when your aunt be cooking food, *don't* you?"

Eye bit into the rib. Juicy. Yummy. "Yes Eye do."

She pat my shoulder. "When your new book coming out?"

"On my birthday. June 26th."

"Eye know it's gonna be good," she said approvingly.

Eye looked up at her. "Better than these ribs," Eye joked.

A few beats of silence drummed by. "You're talking to your Mama yet?"

"Hell no," Eye snapped. "She betrayed me for the last time."

She felt my pain, but still gave me a kind word. "Always love her, Pharoah."

Eye hesitated for a moment, my anger getting the best of me. "Eye do. But Eye'm gonna do it from a distance."

She could tell by the pain on my face that Eye didn't wish for the conversation to go any further. Eye was shaking my head, deeply angry. Eye was the sole proprietor of Mama's success, but she told me a few short months ago she did it all on her own and nobody helped her. Bull. Eye was 10, 11, 12, 13 and 14, 15 and 16,17 and 18 staying home keeping my siblings so she could work. Eye made it easier for her. Didn't have to pay a baby sitter with me home watching out for the house. Eye kept the house in order—sweeping, dusting, rearranging, and mopping the floors like Eye was somebody's husband and Eye still had to stay up late, after my siblings were in bed (or if Mama worked late or pulled overtime) doing my *own* homework. Eye went to bed late all the time, with hardly any sleep.

And don't let 2 o'clock hit and her house wasn't cleaned to her specifications. Mama came in my room like a beast with a hot poker in its ass. Huffing and puffing. Red faced. Turning on all the lights. Doors opening and slamming, letting me know she was home. When she pushed open my door…the knob slammed into the wall, and the door closed half way and Eye opened my eyes the instant she snatched me outta bed and said, "Eye thought Eye told you to have my kitchen clean!" She was clad in her federal uniform. Eye hated that damn uniform.

Well, hi. Good to see you, *too*!

"What do you mean?" Eye asked, fearing her so badly Eye almost pissed my pants. "The kitchen *is* clean!"

She scowled. "Clean my *ass*! If that kitchen is clean then my name is Beverly."

*Well hi, Beverly. How you do.* But Eye wouldn't dare say. She'd replace the olives in her martini with my balls.

She warmed up from the core of her control and motherly power. "Get in there and mop the floor over again. And pull out the fridge and the stove! And clean under my counters. Half cleaned floors brings roaches!"

"But the floor *is* mopped!" Eye whined, getting pissed. Looking at the clock Eye groaned because in a few hours Eye had to get up for school!

She slapped the back of my head and Eye shifted a few steps forward, nearly tripping over my big feet.

"Get your butt in the kitchen, Pharoah!" she said through clenched teeth.

"But Eye gotta get up for school soon, Mama!"

"GO CLEAN MY KITCHEN NOW!"

Eye hardly got any sleep, Mama! *Damn*! What the hell! Eye'm getting TIRED of this! You think you got all the answers. What happened to THANK YOU PHAROAH FOR WATCHING YOUR SIBLINGS AND MAKING THIS EASIER ON ME?

Eye needed sleep. Tired of going to school falling asleep in class. And that white bitch teacher of mine looking at me all crazy, trying to be nosey with her long nosed, ditzy ass always talking about don't talk black, Pharoah—or act *ghetto* in class when young, hardcore *thug* Niggahs were on her mind. Eye saw her flirting with her students all the time, and *nobody* thought anything of it.

Because she was a white woman.

Fantasizing about the black penis while teaching the class.

When wasn't this woman's panties wet?

*Get's kinda lame and tired,* Miss Teacher, smelling your coochie in the air. Eye used to roll my eyes and suck, thinking, "How pathetic!"

Rumor has it she gave the start football player head at her home and swallowed him three times a week and stuffed hundreds of dollars in his pocket. He told a few people he trusted on the varsity football team, but there was a breach of security…those very same dudes told me what he said after we had sex. Miss Teacher's wild curly blonde hair draped her shoulders, and brushed the small of her back as she rubbed her gold rings and tossed that mane and put an extra twitch in her step as she paced the class, teaching—or modeling, prancing, advertising, Look at me I'm a 40 year old white woman in heat, my coochie is dripping and craving young black jizz so wassup do you see *me* HELLO!

Everyday she dressed like George Clooney was going to come through the door at any moment and eat her out on the desk in front of us all. Every penis in the class was rock hard…all except mine, because she was starting to smell more like my dog Spot the more she started to perspire.

In addition to that, Eye was five miles to empty all throughout my high school experience up to this point. Because Eye had the job, Eye'm sorry Eye was being slaved, getting paid in ass whippings under the table so it was a tax write off to keep my skinny butt home to run Camp Clara.

She basically treated me how she treated her male inmates. She was *becoming* her job. She was sounding like policy books. And it was pushing me away from her. When she's mad it feels like she takes it out on me, since Eye was her son and the oldest and the closet person to her.

Hell Eye was an inmate in Camp Clara. In my own home Eye was a slave—that's how Eye felt at the time of course. As long as Eye did what Eye was told Eye was straight. But *Mamas* didn't know everything and sometimes they didn't know what was best. Eye'm so sick of that phrase; they were ignorant at times, and would *never* admit it because we were supposed to stay in a child's place when Eye'm a damn teenager and more aware now. More aware of the world than she ever realized. Like Eye couldn't put two and two together. So was Eye not to question what confused me about Mama? Was Eye not to question some things Mama said that let me know they truly didn't know best?

Mama was street smarter than me but Eye was educationally brighter than her and my uncles and my knowledge and secret journal writing and studying thesauruses and dictionaries kept Camp Clara enlightened.

Eye was Cinderella! With three brothers who didn't lift a finger to clean anything! They all got to experience the great outdoors. Eye was kept mostly inside to watch over the house while Mama worked.

Eye couldn't go outside when she wasn't home, but my brothers could go to football practice? Eye thought it was the most unfair thing in the world!

My brothers got to go everywhere. But not me. Sure Eye got to go to the school dance, but that was where the buck stopped. Eye was the inmate without a conviction. The trustee of Camp Clara.

Being the son of a seasoned federal officer was the most depressing time of my life. Eye wished she never got that job sometimes!

Before she got that job Eye had an amazing mother. A mother Eye would lay my life on the line protecting. Then the FEDS came into the picture. Then they *hired* her. They transformed Mama into a monster—at the time. And when Eye did ask to go somewhere Eye couldn't go nowhere unless her house (not mine, but hers!) was clean and that was a 7 day a week thing.

Seemed it would never end.

**Eye thought Eye would be** a teen slave forever! "And take your baby sister with you!" was her catch-22. If Eye didn't take my sister then she wasn't letting me go anywhere. Eye hated it!

Eye was in high school and gotta take my baby sister everywhere with me. It was so embarrassing, and my friends poked fun at me so bad Eye started resenting Mama. Eye hated my neighborhood. Eye was tired of it. Eye hated grown men and women touching me; but once we started to have sex Eye welcomed it. It was fuel for the hatred Eye had for myself. Eye felt like Eye was two different people back then. Pushing all that to the back of my mind, Eye walked out Aunt Debra's back door and my foot kicked over a pail on the side of her house. Eye didn't know who put it there but my heart skipped a beat and my pulse quickened. Eye could hardly breathe. Holding my chest, Eye leaned against the wall and closed my eyes. Remembering The Perrine Era.

Shuddering from the lingering memory of…

**THE P/A\IL MAN.**

*Eye invite you to* F O L L O W me as Eye guide you through

THE

DARKEST

TIME

OF

MY

L I F E—

F ☯ l ↑→↓↔ l ☯ w

M♋E

D

☯

W

N

Into the trenches of a devious, sick mind; a mind Eye had to battle and face at a young age. To better understand the mentality of "ThE P/A\IL MAN"...Eye will *introduce* you to the *Ebonics* chapter...exhibiting the way *he* spoke and his mentality...so cum

D

☯

W

N

Into The Stratosphere of The Darkness—a kaleidoscope of different shades of black. And remember...have an open mind and leave yo' bias at da door...

Eye remembah one day Eye had just gotten off da skool bus, goin' ova 2 Chad's house. He lived wit' Tanka, his auntie. He didn't cum 2 skool and Eye was goin' 2 take him his homework.

Eye was walkin' thru Perrine (wasn't far, '*bout* a ten minute walk) and Eye passed a tall, burly man wit' a weather-beaten face. He was pullin' up weeds in a rose garden. Eye knew he had 2 be a crack head. Crack heads were da only men digging up weeds in a flower garden—from what Eye saw.

The man looked at me and said, "*Psst...psst.*"

Eye looked at him. "What?" Eye had a look on my face like Eye was breathing feces instead of air. He raised a finger mid air, dropping da Hoe—gardin tool—on da ground. Black ants scattered onto da sidewalk and da smell of trees and grass gave me a slight head ache. He had durty, filthy nails. My grandpa taught me 2 neva befriend anyone wit' durty nails and durty hands because dey just dug outta some stuff.

"Cum here, Boy! And hand me dat dere pail wit' da rocks," he demanded curtly.

Da pail in question was filled to da rim with rocks. Eye was tired, didn't feel like being another adult's slave. Jezis, bad enough Eye gotta go home and clean up.

Despite my inner voice screaming *NOOOO!!!*, Eye agreed to get da pail. Eye was taught to never talk to strangers, but that was contradicted when Mama said respect my elders. And he gave me ah direct order to get da pail of rocks. So Eye had to respect da stranger and do what he said. After putting my other book bag strap on my shoulder, Eye picked up da pail by da thin metal hook. It wasn't *dat* heavy—thank God.

Eye looked up at him and he kept licking his lips all weird. He narrowed his eyes…*momentarily.*

"Something wrong with your tongue?" Eye asked.

He grinned. "Naw, Son. Jus' dat my lips are chaps and dry."

Eye could tell he dropped out of school (he still spelled school—S-K-O-O-L) because of the way he spoke. He spoke like he talked. If he was to write a sentence it would be like "Eye can'ts go 2 da sto' boy. Eye can't go to the store, boy." Hence why Eye wrote the Ebonics chapter, coupled with the *proper* way of writing. His thoughts and words will be in Ebonics form, and since Eye was educated Eye would write my portion properly.

Eye dare to be different

Eye don't change for no one...

Eye gazed at him, wanting to go home and resisting the urge. "But its 95 degrees. Hot as hell. And you're sweating? It's all over your face. So how are your lips chapped? And its 'chapped,' not 'chaps.'"

He had dangerous eyes…dat stern look elders gave a child before issuing a demand. "Eye'll pay U five dollahs 2 bring dat pail 2 da house ova yonder."

Eye looked at it—Da *House.* It was abandoned and the windows were boarded up. All Eye thought about was the money. Five dollars! *Shoot*—Eye could buy some stuff from the store and eat it in class. Suddenly carrying the pail was a cinch. Eye started to perspire. Eye was clad in a long sleeved gold and black shirt, business pants and shiny loafers grandpa ordered for me out of the JCPenny sales magazine, since he claimed me on his income taxes. Eye always dressed nicely for school. Eye was always a step ahead of my opponents by my style of dress while getting an education. Hell Eye was fifty steps ahead of the House Niggah digging up weeds and talking with a third grade education.

Learning was serious business for me. That was real grown man stuff, reading and writing and comprehending and Eye had to dress the part. My friends and other students were too busy buying a gazillion pair of Nikes, in various colors and wearing flea market stuff. White man already wanted to reduce me to a state number back then, police always bothered the neighborhood kids, accusing us of peddling drugs for our parents so Eye didn't need them in my face so Eye stayed in school.

While Eye was walking up to him he was licking his "chaps" lips again and he said, "Go on ova 2 da house. Eye gotta builds anothah gardin 4 da white peeples who are 'bout 2 move in *dat* house." He pointed without looking at it. "Eye'll follow U while Eye carrying my gardin toolz."

He's giving me directions while he walked behind me talking like a dummy. What the hell part of the play was this? A grown man talking more childish than a three year old. Some gaa gaa goo goo language Eye had to strain to understand.

"Turn here, opins da door. Sit da pails down, boy."

Eye set it down by the front door, wanting my money *now.* Eye opened the front door, sweating. A huge spider web was across the top of the door. Eye was looking at it, too because Eye was afraid of spiders.

He smiled a greenish toothy smile; Eye could smell the stench of his breath and Eye wanted to die. "Take da pail 2 da back room. It's down da hall. Da last door on da right."

It was kind of dark. The cracks in the board covering the thick, dusty windows provided little light. Faint light. Enough to tease my eyeballs. Eye was cool with it. Eye would take the pail to the room, get my money and go home.

Eye started walking down the hall and Eye heard him closing the front door.

It creaked as it closed.

***The house wasn't abandoned,*** *but* was being built. From the looks of the installation and framed walls, it was in the final stages of creation. So it *wasn't* abandoned like he told me. The hairs stood on my neck …ut Eye played it off…*wanting* my five bucks. When Eye walked into the last room at the end of the hall, Ђe Master Bedroom, it was very dark. Black dark. *Darker* than dark. So dark Eye couldn't spell the word black relying on my eyes. Eye had to rely on my mind to write the word *black* on black stationary paper in the room with a black pen and black ink. Eye couldn't see my hands. Eye set the pail down and Eye heard footsteps. Heavy stomps—

BOOM BOOM BOOM BOOM BOOM BOOM!

Where did he want me to put the rocks? It's dark in there! Eye can't *see!* "Where are the *lights*?"

Eye picked up the pail. "Man Eye want my money!" Eye said, as something occurred to me. He said he wanted me 2 carry da pail of rocks becuz he wuz goin' 2 carry his gardin toolz. He never came to the house with anything in his hands. His hands were empty and folded in front of his crotch the entire time with a distant, disquieting look in his eyes. Eye turned to face him. Those deep, disquieting eyes dark, null and void. He was digging in his pocket, smiling with greenish, brown teeth. Good. He's giving me my money. "Where is my five dollars?" Eye asked, getting restless and he said, "RIGHT HERE!" and he punched me so hard in the face Eye flew back on my ass. Eye was stunned into silence. Dropping the pail.

Rocks were everywhere.

***Fear*** TRAVELED ***through my*** blood stream at warp-speed-taking-my-breath along with it. Eye got up on my knees; attempting to stand up, but Eye was scared and

NER—
VOUS.

*Then* it hit me.

Eye was in a booby trap.

***A blood-curdling scream constricted*** my throat, and Eye had nowhere to run; nowhere to turn. "No! Oh, God no! *Noo*! No! Not again! God, no not again!" EYE SCREAMED AT THE TOP OF MY LUNGS*! M*y small hands (compared to his) balled tightly into fists, adrenaline rushing to my head.

He P U S H E D ME

F U R T H E R:

Into:

↑→ ЂΣ D/Δ\RK R☯☯M ↔↓

*Closing:*

# DAY

# 3

## Response to Robert Frost's
## "NOTHING GOLD CAN STAY"
### By Dapharoah

Man's second sense for lust
His thinking: southward
The forbidden fruit symbolizes Alpha and Omega
The punishment for Eve's split second decision
Blindness succumb to the flaming scimitar
In paradise...nothing Gold can Stay
The sun rises on the newborn
The sun sets on shadows hovering over the grave

# The Beast of The Darkness Versus Pharoah

*He grabbed me by the shirt!*

Beating me in the back—*Boom Boom Boom!* Eye was stunned and petrified, paralyzed…Then, he brutally punched me in the face, neck and chest. Over and over again. It was so dark Eye couldn't see and *he* couldn't see. So he relied on movement and feelings and so did Eye, the power of sight taken from us both. But Eye felt and smelled him. Worse smell of my life. Savagely, like he hasn't been touched in years, he pulled down my pants. Didn't say anything. Breathing harder than an exhaust pipe. And he immediately pushed his erection deep inside my sweaty anus. The pain was unbearable. The humidity was so startling Eye had to gasp to breathe old, stale air. Eye was trying to fight him, but he was much too strong for me. A poodle withering beneath a ravenously famished mountain lion. No oxygen going to my brain, felt like Eye was suffocating. Eye started to sob because Eye thought Eye was going to die.

He pushed my forehead down hard on the dirty tile floor and he rode my sweet chocolate rosebud with no lube.

Grunting like a lion. The pain was even more unbearable. Felt like my anus was on fire.

"GOD PLEASE! Somebody please help me PLEASE!" Eye managed to yell, my voice horribly cracking. My throat was parched and dry…Eye was *gasping* for air.

He covered my mouth, snatching my vulnerability and fueling his horniness—his sickness… He push any deeper inside me he was going to enter the hole of my hatred. And he did just that. Felt like his penis, the Serpent, entered another hole deep within in my anus. And his breathing increased. Now he was moaning, sucking all over the back of my neck. His smell ruminated from my skin. My inner voice was silenced. And my vanishing soul pushed out the sunlight of my heart and introduced me to the DARKNESS.

Satan was riding my anus and Eye had to battle for my life. Eye would die in there and Eye didn't want to die. Eye had a lot to live for, even though Eye hated myself.

As if a great wind pushed us he stood up, pulling me with him, his erection still deep inside me; and he walked forward in the darkness, till Eye was pressed against the wall. A thunderous burst of evil rendered me speechless. He then took my head and rammed it against the wall like my brain was a coconut…he had no desire for the *outer* shell. But the contents that lie within kept his erection stern and patient. Eye was so nauseated and dizzy Eye nearly blacked out…but something inside wouldn't let me. Eye would fight with every breath in my body.

Guiding me to the floor, forcing me to lay on my side by digging his fingertips into the upper portion of my thighs, he had a change of plans and decided to turn me over on my back. He pushed my legs back and put me in a buck and he pounded me harder and deeper.

The room was spinning. Eye was disoriented.

My eyes fluttered closed and remained closed…as Eye began to drift away on the blackness…going numb inside. "Noo, please," Eye attempted weakly. Giving up the fight.

Eye was slowly losing it, slowly releasing the pain and BOOM Eye gave in to the pleasure.

Something awakened in me, something filled with passion and fire, a will to live maybe…but whatever it was…it took the reins of my soul and Eye found myself saying, "Do it to me!" Eye moaned, his penis feeling so good. Eye was wet in my anus, and Eye smelled the blood in the air. My blood was lubing his endowment, and it felt so good inside me. He put me in the doggy style and Eye knew what to do. Step Daddy taught me well. Taught me to pop it like a coochie on a Niggah's stick. And Eye popped for dear life and he stopped pounding me and pushed his penis deeper inside me and Eye made my booty jiggle, even though we couldn't see anything and he finally said, "Oh damn boy throw it back on Daddy!"

Eye did what he said, tightening my hands, putting my face down to the floor. He felt so good and inside Eye hated

him very, very much. Eye had him under my control.
"Damn. Damn. Damn. You do it bettah than a bitch! GET IT YOU LITTLE SEXY SISSY!"

He slapped my cheeks, spreading them; going deeper. Plummeting. Eye cringed because it *hurt*, but Eye kept him controlled through the movement of my buttocks. Aiding his sickness. He pulled me up to his lips, still raping me, bouncing off my sweet cakes and he whispered, "God. Ain't. Real."

And he pushed my face back to the floor and crawled through my softness.

"Do it to me, *Niggah*!" Eye shouted hoarsely, my voice cracking. Eye tasted death as it approached me. His thrusts were violent, eager and selfish. "Yes, Niggah!"

My body trembled. My step daddy hadn't done it to me like this. Nor have any other adult male. Not the Pa$tor that once had sex with me in his wife's bed while she played with her coochie, and wiped her juices on his balls and Eye watched her suck it off from the bedroom mirror.

Eye knew what time it was. Eye was about to nut! It was coming fast!

My toes curled in my loafers.

He felt my body lock, then jerk. Eye felt him smiling. "U 'bout 2 nut *sissy*?"

Eye tried to hold it. "Yes."

He pulled out and turned me on my back, got between my legs and went back up inside me. This time he stuck it all the way in, all the way out, all the way innnn allll the wayyyy outtttt and he locked up and beat me to the punch.

"Eye gotta cum, Sissy!" he yelled in satisfaction.

When he started to nut Eye screamed—

DIE…!!!

…slamming two medium sized rocks into his face. His penis thumped in my ass and Eye pushed him off me.

"MY EYEZ MY EYEZ MY EYEZ!" he was hollering like a vampire in the sunlight.

Eye couldn't see but Eye went crazy, tripping over my book bag. Eye snatched it up and put it on me, trying to pull up my clothes. The pain in my anus prevented me from running as fast as Eye wanted to, and both my legs felt like rubber.

Eye was about to lose it. Eye didn't want to die! "GOD HELP ME! IT'S DARK IN HERE! EYE CAN'T SEE! GOD, PLEASE! PLEASE! SOMEBODY HELP ME PLEASE PLEASE!" My voice was *dangerously* low and hoarse Eye barely heard myself scream. My voice failed me.

*Not like this, Pharoah!* Eye felt along the walls. About to pass out. But Eye had to get out of there. Please! Now the darkness worked in my favor.

He couldn't see me so Eye fumbled everywhere.

"Eye'm gonna kill U punk! U ruined my eyez! Eye can't see!"

Eye heard loud thumping, like he was shuffling all over the place.

Eye felt along the wall, breathing hard and fast. Eye couldn't stop shaking or crying. *God please help me, Lord, please!*

Eye ran into him and he grabbed me and Eye bit his arm and he screamed and Eye dropped to my knees and bit his penis as hard as Eye could. Eye tasted blood and Eye spit it on him, at least Eye think Eye did.

Screaming painfully, he fell down, covering his nuts Eye imagined (couldn't see shit) and Eye blindly fumbled for the rock…found a lot of them, nice sized. Eye picked them up one by one and stoned his faggot rapist ass. "YOU BITCH! EYE HATE YOU!"

Eye knew Eye was hitting him. The rocks fell against his body and he screamed every time. A soul-lacerating wail.

Eye heard the rocks slamming into his bones and flesh. Eye picked up more rocks, blinded by the darkness, my eyes ignorant to the light, and Eye stoned him → and stoned him! Eye threw rocks and threw rocks! Eye tried to pick up more and fell back into ϴЂ∑Ɖ[☯:☯]R→and fell down to my butt. God that hurt! Eye knew it was The Door because Eye felt the wood and the door knob.

"Ow!" Eye whispered, careful not to be too loud. He'd know where Eye was!

Eye stood up and his body slammed into mine again, and we both hit the door and he fell on top of me and said, "EYE'M GONNA KILL U! CALL UR GOD NOW! HE DON'T EXIST! HE AIN'T REAL! LET'S SEE HIM SAVE U!"

He put his hands around my neck and he squeezed. Eye was kicking and squirming, my hands on his, having a flash back of when ______ choked me, lifting me in the air, even with his eyes, feeling his breath on my face.

Eye couldn't breathe. Trying to inhale. Trying to exhale. My lungs were on fire, my anus burning, repulsed. My feet noisily fumbled on the floor.

As a last desperate attempt Eye thought, God please. Not like this. What have Eye done?

"DIE!" he yelled, spitting in my face.

He repeatedly shook my head and it sporadically slammed on the floor. Eye was dizzy. Growing weary. Tired. Drained. My eyes were fluttering in the blackness. Eye couldn't even see his eyes or face. All Eye saw was blackness. And it wore me like panties. Eye say panties because Satan was a bitch.

Eye was weakening. He leaned into my face. Eye felt it. Eye knew it. 'Cause his breath was strong on my nostrils. He was choking me harder. Eye'm gonna die. THE GRIM REAPER *has arrived....* He was going to take me somewhere. Maybe Eye'll see Grandma Alice and Great Grandma Olive.

Yes. They will love me. They won't have sex with me. They won't molest me. They won't rape me. They won't make me clean kitchens and mop floors and go to school.

They will love to have me. Forgive me for my sins, father. And tell Mama Eye will always love her, that she can get Laron to mop the floor now.

Eye love you Mama. Even though you don't even love me.

And Daddy told ________ he hates me.

Bye, Daddy.

Amen!

Eye closed my eyes and gave up the fight. He slowly released me, letting go my neck. Eye tightened my fists.

GASP! GASP! GASP! Eye deeply inhaled, the atmosphere, God's breath filling my lungs, electrifying me! Yes!

Eye screamed hoarsely and slammed two rocks into either of his ears—Eye knew it was his ears, Eye felt it and he screamed even louder, letting me know through his wailing Eye got his ears, bull's-Eye. Impulsively, Eye sat up and bit him on his nose, trying to pull it off, and he grabbed me and Eye pushed him off me and stomped him in the face and chest. Eye put loafer prints on him!

Eye snatched up my book bag because my Janet Rhythm Nation compilation VHS and my Rhythm Nation 1814 cassette tape and film short was in my bag and Eye'll be damned if Eye leave *my* shit behind. After the ordeal Eye faced, Eye felt compelled to grab my belongings.

Eye opened the door and ran like hell out that house—no matter how painful it was, and it was so painful Eye nearly blacked out as my feet clumsily slapped the pavement.

Eye ran all the way up the block. Eye didn't scream.

Eye didn't yell.

Eye didn't stop till Eye got home.

*When Eye got home Eye was* never so happy to mop a floor or sweep a floor or make up a bed or cook a meal or let Mama scream and wake my late ass up at 2 a.m. In fact Eye purposely didn't clean up right just for her to snatch me up and smack me and make me clean up.

Mama was in the kitchen eating something and she said, "You can't speak?"

Eye avoided her eyes, swallowing the pain. My body was riddled with fire. "Gotta pee," Eye lied. Running in the bathroom and slamming it closed.

Eye locked. It.

"DON'T SLAM MY DOOR!"

Eye turned on the shower, and Eye took off all my clothes and shoes. Dried blood on my face and lip. My underwear drenched in blood. Blood soaked in my pants, and some soaked in my shirt. A part of my face was swollen, so Eye knew Eye had to put ice on it before Mama suspected.

Eye was sobbing quietly.

"You want something to eat?" Mama asked through the bathroom door.

Eye covered my mouth. Calm down, Pharoah. Eye was so nervous Eye pissed all over the place. Soaked in my clothes. Some on the floor.

"PHAROAH!"

"No!" Eye said, trying to sound normal.

Eye covered my mouth again, trying to sit on the toilet. To my disgust, Eye boo boo all over the floor and the toilet as well. Eye fell on my knees, trembling so badly Eye could hardly adjust my vision.

"Mama, help me," Eye whispered. "Mama, please." Eye couldn't say it. Eye couldn't do it.

"When…when Eye asked my cousins to help me they turned me away," Eye whispered. "Now Eye can never ask anybody for help…"

Eye pushed up and stood up, nearly slipping in feces, mixed with blood. *God please help me!*

The smell filled my nose and made me wince.

It took me almost forty minutes, but Eye cleaned up, showerehind myself, no sign of feces and piss anywhere, and went to my room.

Mama was already in her room. Sleeping.

Eye walked out the back door to the garbage can and threw away the gold and black shirt, the loafers and the pants.

Eye would never wear that again.

Didn't want to be reminded. Of Hell. Once in my room, Eye put on my *Rhythm Nation* tape. Eye lived for this album. Every last song. From *Livin' in a World we didn't make, Escapade, Lonely, Black Cat* and *Miss You Much* to *Love will never do, Alright* and *Come back to me.*

The bells sounded on Rhythm Nation.

*We are a nation...* Eye pulled out my journal.

And wrote Janet Jackson a letter.

*Eye wanna read one of the letters*
*You wrote to your favorite entertainer*
*Lord Jennings*

*When Eye was 13 Eye wrote Janet* a combined 8 letters.

Eye poured my heart out to Miss Jackson. She was more than just a singer, dancer and entertainer to me in my young life at the time—1814 offered me hope.

It offered me a better way, even though we were living in Perrine and going to bed to gun shots from the dope boys running the 'Hood.

Eye listened to her album and learned all the steps to her breathtaking videos.

My friends were on Madonna's Vogue bull crap.

Um, next.

Eye put my anger, frustration, hate, happiness, joy and pain into learning the moves. I stayed up all hours of the night when Eye was done with chores (or every chance Eye could get, even if Eye could only dance for ten minutes) learning the videos.

Before my grandpa bought me the compilation videos, Eye recorded *Rhythm Nation* back to back all over Mama's *Imitation of Life* movie.

Eye put some scotch tape over the hole on the bottom of the tape and picked up the telephone.

I ordered *Rhythm Nation* on the Juke Box channel back to back and pressed record.

Eye was on some Oaktown's 357 *Juicy Gotcha Crazy* mess back then, but then *Rhythm Nation* changed my life.

Eye will be revealing for the first time one of the letters Eye wrote Janet.

Exhibiting my anger, pain, joy and happiness with my life when Eye was a teenager.

Hating myself, wanting to commit suicide and wanted to die in my sleep.

*Hello. How are you? Eye'm 13 years old* and 1814 and the Rhythm Nation album means so much to me. Eye'm so nervous, oh my God. My hands tremble as Eye write this letter. Maybe Eye need my head examined for writing a person Eye don't think exist. People on TV appear to be otherworldly folks trapped in a box. But Eye know you're real, and Eye think you are the most beautiful woman in the world. When you smile on TV Eye melt. Eye love you for your passion and your radiant smile.

If Eye was a letter Eye'd be the letter "Eye" in "Nation" because Eye stand with my hands behind my back to get ahead. Eye go to South Wood Middle School, Home of the Stars. Janet, Eye know you don't know me and you probably don't care but Eye was just raped (again) by a man who asked me to carry a pail of rocks for him. He promised to give me 5 dollars and wound up giving me emotional and physical scars. Eye'm devastated; my butt hurts so bad Eye could hardly sit down and Eye had an accident all over the bathroom and pee on myself because Eye was so nervous and so scared of Mama finding out.

Eye saw blood but Eye can't tell Mama because she won't believe me, just like when my ex step daddy raped me as a small child and my older cousins didn't believe me and called me a faggot and accused my grandma of killing their father and this happened before Eye was even born.

Eye hate myself, Janet. Eye gave in to the pleasure. Was Eye wrong? Eye had given up. Eye have let go. Eye hate myself for that so much! Eye don't even know why Eye'm writing you. You probably get millions of letters. My letter will be the needle in twelve haystacks.

Eye know you're busy, on your world tour. This is the very first letter Eye ever wrote you and Eye will write you every week until you write back, Eye promise.

Eye hope you write back. Maybe you can help me because Eye don't wanna live anymore. Eye hate being black. All blacks do is hurt me. Eye'm tired. Why can't Eye be normal, like the other kids? Why does this keep happening to me. Eye'm just a teenager and grown men won't stop touching or sleeping with me and forcing me to be quiet.

Eye love you. Pharoah. P.S. Eye learned all the dance steps to Miss You Much. My favorite move is when you extend your arms singing Eye miss you Mu-uuchhh. And then you cross your arms in front of you, then you throw that weird sign over your Eye. Eye been practicing that for two weeks and can't get it right! But Eye'ma keep trying. Eye'ma make you proud.

Eye love the peace sign move over your Eye.

Love you.

*Pharoah.*

*Did you ever confront _________ for raping his own daughter?*

*Lord Jennings.*

## B U † C K

*Back in the 80's, Clara and Buck* got in a fight one day, over a gallon of milk. We were living in HUD housing, 11335 SW 190th Lane, next to Southridge Senior High.

Mae Wrick, Buck's baby mama was there, and she was just as *sweet* as she could be. We looked on in confusion. He always came over eating up the food or cooking any and everything that wasn't tied down. Cook just to be cooking and hardly put anything on anybody's plate, but it was every man for himself. In fact he fixed his plate and *then* it was everyone man for himself after *that.*

Eye never really liked him, but Eye loved him because he was family. And watching Clara and Buck pull on the gallon of milk was pathetic. Eye was shaking my head. They were supposed to be grownups.  Eye was sitting on the couch, looking on in silence.

Eye guess no one noticed he was high, because his eyes were red as hell. And he spoke after taking deep breaths, like it was hard for him to control his breathing.

"This is my milk!" Clara yelled, and he was pulling on it; he was twice the size as Clara, fighting over a dairy product.

"This is my milk!"

"Like hell it is! You drink up my children milk then save your food! Not today! Eye'm taking this. This is my milk!"

He pulled harder and she put her leg back, pulling against his strength and the milk carton exploded, milk flying everywhere, all over the floor.

Since they couldn't decide whose milk it was Eye guess God took it away. Now *nobody* couldn't get any milk and Eye hated *whole* white milk anyway, Eye didn't care. Couldn't ever pay me to drink milk, unless it was in my cereal.

Clara was pissed. And Eye was equally pissed she fought over milk. Buck didn't have the sense of a bird so Eye'd never throw him seeds. She shoulda been blessed and thankful that WIC gave her free milk. Buck was secretly devastated because he wasn't *man* enough to carry the weight of his family, always creeping on his lady with other absent-minded Hoes—running the streets and doing drugs. He thought nobody knew what he was doing and everyone knew what he was doing because one time Eye caught him smoking crack, but Eye didn't say anything. Eye simply closed the door and pretended Eye didn't see anything.

He had Mae Wrick and his kids in Mama's HUD house, didn't offer money to replace the food he ate nor lifted a finger to clean anything. And if he thought Eye was cleaning behind him he was sadly mistaken. While Mama was cleaning up spilt milk, Buck, mumbling under his breath, claiming he was never gonna come over to Mama's house again (GOOD RIDDANCE DARTH VADER!), he went to the bathroom.

And Eye followed him. He turned on the sink water and Eye walked inside and closed the door, staring at him. He was a naturally big, blue/black niggah with huge arms and legs; he was three times the size as Eye was, but Eye never feared anyone. Except Clara and my step daddy, who was the devil in disguise when the sun rise and galloped with the demon himself when the sun set all over and through my sore anus. He put the fear of God in my heart, and Eye would never know this fear again.

Buck looked up in the mirror, putting cold water on his face, sighing. Water dripped from his cheeks and chin all over his chest, sink and the floor, and he snatched down a towel like he was in a street brawl. What a sloppy man.

"That's my towel," Eye said, leaning against the door in little shorts and a turquoise-colored shirt granddaddy Burke bought me. Wasn't really my towel, but Eye was about to pick a fight with him. For what he did to Lily.

It took a minute for him to respond. Sunlight poured through the, window radiating on his skin. Eye was still by the door; sunlight fell short of my toes.

He snuffed. "So what. Eye'm using it now."

Water dripping from the tub faucet created a rhythm in my head. Drip, drip. Drip. Drip, drip. Drip.

Eye shook my head. "So you just love taking what's not yours?"

He looked at me dumbly. "It's *just* a towel. Eye don't feel like it, ok? Eye just got through having it out with Clara.."

"Eye know. Watching two grown people fight over milk was just pathetic."

"And you need to watch how you're talking to me."

"You ain't my daddy, Buck."

Fire ignited in his eyes. "It's *Mr.* Buck."

"It's *Aunt* Buck," Eye stammered and his mouth fell open. "…Eye hardly even *like* you. You hardly even come around. Eye only tolerate you because you're blood, but don't let that fool you."

"Eye don't like you either."

"We're on the same page."

"Yes we are."

"You're high on crack, aren't you?"

His hands were shaking. He busied himself with the sink knobs and that didn't even look right. Hot water on. Cold water on. Hot water off. Cold water on. Off. Hot water on. Pulling at his pants. *Yup*. He's high.

He tried to avoid me. "Niggah Eye don't smoke crack." He was stuttering.

"No glass dicks, right?"

He smacked me and Eye hit him back; even though my tiny fist against his stomach only pissed him off. He didn't even bat an eyelash.

"Don't put your hands on me!" Eye whispered harshly, careful not to be too loud. Eye glared at him. "Somebody already doing that!"

He looked me over. "You little punk! You're gay, aren't you?"

There we go. "Whatever."

He nearly grinned in my face. "Eye'm telling Clara."

He walked up to me and Eye said, tears forming in my eyes, "Go to hell."

"Get your punk ass outta here!"

"Punk?" Eye said, tucking my chin back. "Punk? You deflowered your own *daughter* and molested the other one and you're calling me names?"

He was stunned at this startling revelation. Yea, Eye knew your dirt.

Wide-eyed, his breathing increased so rapidly Eye felt his breath on my face and boy good thing that milk exploded because if he drunk it Lawd his damn breath would smell like spoiled milk. Jesus. Damn shame a grown man breath smell like hot puke.

He pointed at me. "You need to shut your mouth and stay in your place."

"You need to keep your hands off my cousin!"

He was nervous, looking over his shoulder a moment, contemplating his next move. "You got a hot little mouth!"

"Eye get it from my Mama. And Eye'm getting tired of people telling me what Eye can and can't say when half the world says what the hell they wanna say! Eye hate you!"

He smacked me so hard Eye fell to my knees. There we go. Grown men LOVED hitting me. Eye fed off it. It didn't hurt as much as Eye'd thought it would. That's a man's answer to anything they can't control—hit Pharoah. Take it out on *Pharoah. Control* Pharoah. Touch and molest Pharoah. He's a kid. He won't say anything. We'll beat him good. He'll remain mute and meek.

Eye was getting pressed, pressure piling on top of more pressure piling on top of more pressure piling on TOP OF the hatred in my black heart. My heart felt like my ass. Always in crap, always in a world of trouble—*always* in a state of shock.

Eye shook it off. My hands pressed firmly on the tan-colored tiled floor; Eye looked up into his haggard face and said, "My grandma Alice is turning in her grave. Touch me like you touched my cousin. Do it to me like you destroyed Lily! Do you even have a heart?"

He was getting afraid, retreating his cocky Eye-been-to-prison-demeanor. That tough guy crap went right out the window. Chest wasn't so puffed up. Sad looking eyes. Guarded eyes. Shaded eyes. "You're 9 years old!"

"Eye'm ten!" Eye corrected swiftly. "Lily told me what you did to her. She told me *everything*." Eye approached him, looking up into his twisted face with my hands balled into tight fists. "Eye will kill you if you touch her again, Buck. Eye swear to God right now. Eye will kill you. Eye will kill you, niggah!"

"She's a spoiled little tramp. One needy as child! She whines about everything!"

That went in one ear and fell to the pit of my balls before it went out the other. Shut up, Niggah. "You better not ever touch her again!"

He grinned. A very handsome smile framed with pitch black lips. "Or what? Eye'm not doing anything to her, and you wait till Eye see her."

Eye put my hands on my hips, scared as hell of him, but didn't show it on my face. His eyes were dangerous, and he was thinking of something and Eye didn't know what it was.

Eye told this muscular, tall, older big jolly Negro frijoles-eating Giant, "Touch her again and Eye'm gonna tell somebody."

"Niggah." He pushed me in the tub and Eye hopped out and stood firm.

"Push me. Eye don't care. Eye'm not scared of you. Eye'm telling you. Keep away from Lily! Yea, you did it! You did everything she told me you did! How can you taste your own daughter's womb?"

He put his hands around my neck and lifted me off my feet, my legs dangling. Eye was trying to inhale but it was hard and Eye was choking, wide eyes staring frighteningly into his.

"Shut up," he whispered—his breath hot on my face. "Shut up. You will not say a word. Ever! You understand me? Eye never liked your sissy ass. *Never*. Even when Eye used to hang out with your Daddy in California he told me he didn't want no children. But he had you. Yea, bad ass. Your daddy hates you! He never wanted you!"

He squeezed harder and Eye scratched at his hands, trying to get them off my neck. My legs were losing steam.

My feet felt like gnats splattered against a windshield on a car traveling 100 mph. He crippled me with his revelation. That my Dad hates me, that he never wanted me and Eye couldn't handle it.

WELL EYE HATE YOU TOO PHAROAH CURTIS WILSON SR!

Suddenly dying didn't seem a bad idea, but who wanted to die? Certainly not me.

And Eye thought about it. Death. He was going to kill me. So what. Kill me! Eye wanna die! Eye don't want to live! Eye didn't ask to be here! Mama and daddy should have kept their panties and underwear up, leaving me in the darkness of the unknown.

WHY AM EYE HERE? KILL ME! KILL ME! DADDY HATES ME! STEP DADDY LOVED ABUSING ME! HE SAID EYE FELT LIKE MAMA'S SWEET BODY! HE SAYS IT IN MY EAR WHEN HE—WHEN HE'S ABUSING ME! KILL ME, KILL ME, KILL ME!

"Pharoah Eye am telling you one more time," Buck whispered harshly, scowling, careful so my Mama wouldn't hear and Eye heard Mama's big mouth through the door talking to Mae Wrick.

He put me down and Eye took the biggest breath of my life. Eye inhaled so deeply Eye fell against the sink.

He turned the water back on, washing his face. Like nothing ever happened.

"Eye'm leaving! Can you move out my way?"

He snatched me by the shirt and Eye didn't know what came over me because Eye grabbed his cock and balls so tight the big molesting creep buckled at the knees.

Eye was afraid now, so Eye tightened my grip and he was wide eyed, mouth ajar, glaring at me, hands up, palms open. He attacked me first. Eye can't believe he assaulted me.

"You have the same look in your Eye my ex step daddy had when he *violated* me, every time he did it he had the

"No, sir. Eye *like* that."

Eye pressed for more. "What else you did to Lily?"

He was an open library now. Jack pot! "Eye then deflowered her. Eye do it all the time. She *loves* it. Eye made her cum. She begs for it. She loves when Eye bury it deep inside her!"

Rage made my blood boil. How he said that without an ounce of love in his voice killed me. How he did this to his own daughter without remorse was the most demonic thing Eye ever heard in my life. Everybody scared of big black Buck! And no one knew a thing he was doing. Except Lily and her sister, and they had to live with this for the rest of their lives.

"Is that how you're gonna do it to me?" Eye asked, jacking him off, and his legs started drumming together.

"Hell yea."

Eye got on the toilet, and got in his face. We were even now, and Eye meant business.

"Touch her one more time Buck and Eye will kill you in your sleep. And then Eye'll call the police!"

Eye opened the door and walked out.

"And Eye'm the punk?" Eye asked rhetorically.

Eye wouldn't speak to him again for years to come.

And Eye will *never* forget.

*Have you encountered anyone*
*Who doesn't believe in your*
*W👁rk?*

*Lord Jennings*

# ENLIGHTENED

*We all have been through something* no one else has. That's what makes our pain our own. So when someone say they feel my pain Eye look them deeply in the eyes with a smile and misty eyes and Eye say, politely, "No you don't. You don't know the pain Eye endured, just like there is someone going through something worse than me so how can Eye *feel* their pain when Eye never been in their shoes? Certain parts of it Eye can relate to, but Eye will never know your pain and you will never know mine."

Eye tend to befriend those that understand how Eye turned out to be the tough talking, blunt Pharoah Wilson Jr rather than those who relate to my experiences.

Eye didn't want that kind of relationship with anybody, because, if they have gone through something similar, they tend to tell me what Eye should think and how Eye should feel and how Eye should have turned out because *they* thought and felt a certain way when going through a similar ordeal.

Eye simply tell them, "Eye am not you. My name's Pharoah." And leave it at that. So to avoid it Eye gravitate towards the ones who have an understanding, didn't necessarily want to relate *or* have a relationship with you. Unattached, but rewarding.

From my book covers, Eye, everyday, look into a sea of different faces when fans and consumers smile at me. Those are models of success, one of my fans once told me.

He said he hasn't read the book yet because he was still stuck on my picture on the front.

The proof that working through abuse, adversity, prison, self-hatred and family deception has its rewards if you keep God first.

He said he know God exist through my struggle and my survival. And Eye surely thanked him for that. With that being said, Eye have finally embraced my literary prowess.

It took a very long time to accept the gift of words, didn't wanna believe my nappy headed ass has written a book, let alone books—300 books in 13 years.

When people crack my book open my immortality (well put together and organized with the use of sentences, periods, predicates and first and last person) drink the sentiment of the audience's wide eyes. They experience a succulent tornado of emotions derived from my passion, my bluntness and my art.

Something holds the weight of the world on its shoulders.

You may not see them.

No, you won't. So don't strain to see a light you don't know was there. No need to look out your front door, on your back car seat, up and down the block or open your closets, storage units or dig up graves to find it.

It sort of finds you, like it has done me, when you're doing something positive, useful, and inspiring people to be better than their pasts and themselves through my testimony. And Eye still thank GOD first and foremost for anything Eye achieve.

Eye use my status boxes on all the social networks Eye'm on to thank GOD for waking me up before Eye say GOOD MORNING FACE:BK (Facebook) or Good morning Tagged, or Good morning BGCLive or Good morning, Twitter.

Sometimes, when Eye do, there's always that ONE on my friend list (didn't know he was on my friend list) that was an atheist, claiming he's in church and uses Bible scripture to try to deter me from writing "such filth and passing it off as fiction!"

The last man that did that got read faster than *Rollingstone* magazine.

*Eye wr◉te him back:*

CAUCASIANS PERFORMED MANY FACE LIFTS ON THE BIBLE, BABY. 2ND KINGS HAD 700 WIVES AND 300 SIDELINE HOES, 1,000 TYPES OF COOCHIE HE BUILT THOSE SHRINES FOR SO DON'T GUN FOR MY BOOKS. HOMOSEXUALITY IS IN THE BIBLE, TOO, BETTER TAKE A CLOSER LOOK.

CAUCASIANS WROTE AND RE-WROTE AND EDITED THE BIBLE DOWN TO SOMETHING ALL TOGETHER DIFFERENT FROM HOW IT WAS CONTRIVED. THEY FORCED THE BIBLE ON MY ANCESTORS WHEN THEY WERE FORCIBLY BROUGHT OVER HERE FOR SLAVERY.

YOU KNOW MANY SCRIPTURES, EYE COMMEND YOU. YOU TALK A GOOD GAME. YET EVERY TIME EYE POST AN ACCOMPLISHMENT OR A POSITIVE STATUS UPDATE AND GET OVER 50 RESPONSES OR MORE THERE YOU GO, RECITING "SUCH FILTH PASSING IT OFF AS SCRIPTURE," SAME BULLSHIT SCRIPTURES PA$TOR$ BEEN RECITING OVER AND OVER TO THE SAME YOUNG AND OLD CONGREGATION MEMBERS WHO ARE CHEERFUL GIVERS TOWARDS HIS NEW CADILLAC. YOU DON'T EVEN BELIEVE IN GOD, ATHEIST.

SO WHY ARE YOU QUOTING THE BIBLE?

*He logged off and drove over* to my mother's house, called me outside and when Eye came, shocked he didn't call before he came over, he glared me down.

Eye crossed my arms across my chest and kept my back straight, ass out, legs slightly bent at the knees like they taught me in the Army so you didn't faint or pass out.

"You need to stop writing those nasty books!" he chastised.

"And if Eye don't?" Eye asked, yawning. Chile. Eye was pretending to yawn.

"Just stop!"

"You are priceless, dude. You contradict your outer loyalty to the church with public appearances in your Easter suit and hidden hatred for God with an Avatar picture of a blue eyed white Jesus on your Facebook page. Don't you read my books in private?" Eye asked, and he looked over his shoulder, making sure no one heard him. He got serious on me. And since when was he self-conscious around me anyway?

"Shhh, shut up. Someone might hear you. Eye don't want anyone to know that Eye read your books in private."

He was disgusted and Eye was mad Eye even answered my phone or came outside to entertain the circus in Mama's front yard.

"Eye never read your books!" he snapped, balling up his fists, the flames of hell replaces his pupils and corneas. He just said a second ago he read them in private, which was it?

Eye was laughing my ass off that day—Eye'm *telling* you! "If you haven't then how did you know to say book in the plural form? Means you already know Eye have more than one book published."

He dismissed the comment with a wave of his hands, trying to look all thuggish and looked ticklish, ridiculous and girlish.

"Lies, dude."

Eye looked at this penis-for-brains man and repeated, "Lies?"

"Eye only read one of your books."

"*Again, you use the plural form.* Why not say Eye read your book, if you truly only read one of them?"

"SHUT UP! Eye know which one Eye read. It's called gold digger, about the bitch using the fake doctor for money and wound up with genital herpes and a prison sentence. And Eye read First Nut, Fate Williams, and Rock Star, about the bitch infecting men with HIV."

"Eye am impressed. You just contradicted yourself again, *Christian* man, *you.* GOLD DIGGER IS IN ÞE KING OF EROTICA BOOK 3, FATE WILLIAMS IS IN ÞE KING OF EROTICA BOOK 2, AND FIRST NUT IS IN ÞE KING OF EROTICA BOOK 1."

He was on the *defensive,* like Kunta getting whipped.

*Whack*! "Man! Eye swear Eye only read one!" *My name's Kunta…Kin…te!!*

*Whack!!*

*Gotcha*! "Shit, Eye know DL married men who read book 3 or bought book 3 before the other ones because Eye have on tight designer underwear on the book's cover, golden identical dragons squaring off on my body-hugging shirt; my pants half are hanging off my butt while Eye am holding pink panties in front of my penis print."

"Man. Eye hate you," he said. "Eye'm not gay."

"Right. Famous last words."

"Why are you so free? Eye can't be free, Pharoah. Eye can't. Eye'm a grown ass man and Eye hide in the shadows. Eye may lose my family if they find out Eye have sex with men."

"Eye know that; stop living in denial. You're gay. Deal with it."

"Eye'm NOT A SISSY!"

"Eye didn't *say* you *were.* Eye said you're *gay*; you don't have an alibi—you're G-A-Y! And don't blame self incarceration for *losing* your family. We *all* know you be dabbing in your own supply smoking that crack pipe, and you ain't mentioning the lesser of two evils Eye guess so miss me with the bull crap."

"If Eye tell them or if they find out Eye'm gay then Mom gonna find out that her daddy raped me when Eye was 14 years old. And Mama got her daddy on a pedestal, swear he the best thing since sliced bread."

Eye looked him deep in the eyes and he nearly exploded and Eye hugged him and said, "Man, Eye understand now. Eye understand."

Eye didn't dare say Eye could relate.

His pain was all his own...

*After Lily abused you*
*Did you ever have a run in with her*
*Once you two were adults?*
*Lord Jennings*

*Eye used to go down to the New* Buildings in Homestead to Apple's house all the time. Despite our past, Eye eventually grew close to her, forgave her and moved on, but Lily was another story. She was always jealous of how close Eye was with Apple, and sometimes she let it be known with that big mouth of hers. Eye never chose to entertain it, really. Eye simply kept my mouth closed because one wrong move Eye'd snap her neck, and Eye don't hit nor fight girls. The constant nagging from Lily, because Eye go to Apple's house more than hers, got the best of me. So, inevitably, Eye faced the music one summer day in 2006 and Eye paid her a visit. She lived by a small convenience store a couple blocks from the New Buildings. When Eye arrived she was alone, her son was out playing somewhere, who knew and her baby daddy was at work driving forklifts at a warehouse about ten minutes away.

She was happy to see me, taking her a while to register my image. Once she did she gave a smile and hugged me one too many times, asking did Eye want something to eat or drink. No. Eye pass. But thanks anyway.

Eye followed her to her room. She claimed she was watching TV but Eye could tell by the look in her eyes that she wanted to ask for money to feed her drug habit. Eye didn't support anybody's drug habit, Eye work too hard for my money.

Lily looked at me, sprung out on crack. A once natural beauty (natural beauty my *ass*—who was Eye kidding?) she was gazing into misty eyes. It *reminded* me of when Eye first made her cum when Eye was ten years old. Yes, Eye was ten years old and you damn right it was wrong to actually enjoy it, but Eye didn't enjoy banging my cousin the more we did it, especially after finding out it was wrong, but Eye did enjoy the pleasure of orgasm.

"Cuz," she said happily, tugging on her shirt, pants and touching her face like she was doing the robot. Why was she moving like that? "Cuz" was how she said "Cousin."

"Hey, Lily," Eye said dryly, realizing Eye shouldn't have come to her crib.

"Eye'm glad you came to see me. Eye miss you, *Cuz,*" she went on, wrapping her arms around me and she started grabbing my ass and pulling me up against her pelvic bone. The smell of coochie mixed with liquor and crack did a number on my stomach.

*Damn.*

Eye pushed her on the bed and said, "We haven't really seen each other since Eye was 11 years old. Mama moved away and we just lost touch. Now after all these years you're still touching on me. *Don't* you have a son? If you're rubbing on me Eye hope you aren't showing your son what you taught me."

Eye hit a huge nerve. "Shut up! Eye don't know what you're talking about."

"You don't, Lily?" Eye walked in her face.

"No. Leave it in the past. Eye need another hit so Eye can forget it ever happened. Eye did to you what my daddy did to me and my sister. My daddy was boning me ever since his baby mama left."

"*His* baby Mama who?"

"My Mama, Niggah. He was boning the Mama and her daughters, and that was his woman and Eye'm his child and you're over here for some sort of redemption?"

"This ain't about you. And just because he put you through that don't mean you take it out on me. You beat me with extension cords if Eye didn't go down on you."

"This coochie *trained* you, Niggah!" she said, grabbing her crotch. "Eye taught you how to sex those Hoes. Yea, Niggah. Tell those Hoes that talk all that noise behind my back that they owe their orgasms to me. Eye made you a man!"

` Eye slapped her so hard the back of her head hit the wall. "Now you wait a minute! You're giving that shallow funk box *too* much goddamn credit. Who the hell do you think you are? God? God don't have a coochie and Jesus never had a piece of ass so put your coochie in check, because if wasn't good enough for Jesus then it ain't good enough for me."

"GO TO HELL!"

"If Jesus turned down Satan persuading him to turn bread to stone or stone to bread Eye know Jesus turned down coochie because it ain't worth the bread of his nourishment and back in the day they stoned a bitch to death for misfiring with the curtail of their loose *coochie.*"

She glared me down like the sun beaming in my face from a yard away. "Talk English! You always think you're *better* than us!"

Eye wasn't blinded by the glare. Eye had on hater shades. "Eye never said that. And what do you expect! Miss Mike gave me Robert Frost poetry and a journal and told me to write the days of my life and here twenty something years later the world is now reading my work or its available for the world to buy."

Her eyes glowed. "So you on Amazon.com Canada, Japan, France…"

"The United Kingdom, Germany, you name it the King of Erotica is on sale."

"Yes, Cuz!" she engulfed me and Eye engulfed her. Sharing in my accomplishments, praising me for doing something with my life.

"So that mean you got money, *Cuz*!"

Eye was being swallowed in. "Yes!" *No—Eye didn't. Some days were better than others.*

"*Lots* of money."

"Not really," Eye said, pulling away. "Since Eye'm my own publisher, accountant, CEO, book formatter, typist and outreach coordinator Eye gotta pay outside people to help me look good." *And sometimes Eye didn't have enough money for that!*

"Since you got money give me a hundred dollars!" she said, taking off her shirt and snatching her breasts from her bra. Eye was about to puke. She had a few bumps on her breasts and she was taking off her panties. All Eye saw was Harry and the Henderson's. *Shave*!

Eye ran past her and she grabbed me from behind and threw me on the bed.

Her touch paralyzed me. Eye was ten years old again.

"LILY STOP!"

The beast jumped inside her. "Give me the stick! Do it to me with your fine self!"

Eye had to get through to her, and fast!

*"Lily!!!"*

Eye was trying to punch at her, but she pressed down on her cellulite and Eye was stuck like chuck. Eye was about to get raped by my cousin again.

"Suck my titties like you used to."

She shoved them in my mouth, her coochie moist all over me and it smelled like bejeusus oh my God take a shower and douche!

She leaned back. "You ain't gonna listen to me?"

"NO!"

"Eye'ma tell ya' Mama if you don't screw me! Eye'll tell her you told me to give you head!"

The fear of my mother washed over me and Eye shut down. Eye felt the pressure subside in my arms and legs and Eye looked at her with a disquieting look.

"Please don't tell my Mama, Lily, please," Eye said, my voice airing out like Eye was ten again. "Lily we're blood. Please don't tell her Eye said that to you."

*Bingo!* lit her eyes. "And if Eye tell her?"

Eye shot my cuffs, without raising my voice. "Eye'll tell her your own daddy *was* screwing you and your mother. Now *test* me."

A challenging look befell her face. We were on either side of Vs. (Versus). She was after the period, Eye was before the V.

She snatched the alarm clock from the nightstand, *yanked* the cord from the wall and hopped off me, beating me ferociously. She was a savage, lost inside the drugs.

"SUCK MY COOCHIE AND DO IT TO ME!"

"Lily!" The cord hit me in the face and arms. God the pain had me paralyzed. Eye couldn't move.

She beat me and beat me.

"EAT MY COOCHIE OR EYE'LL TELL YOUR MAMA YOU TOLD ME TO SUCK YOU UP—YOU LITTLE SISSY!"

Eye closed my eyes and gave it to God—✞. Eye crawled in the fetal position and Eye meditated against the pain. Mind over matter, and Eye felt myself slipping away, giving it to God. God—*you* said come to you. May no weapon formed against me prosper oh God. Eye'm not even flinching at the cord against my skin anymore because my protective shield was in the Word of God and in God all things are possible and humanly possible. Just trust in him and he will show you the way through the dark valley, the ones with or without green pastures.

She stopped hitting me and it took a while for me to stop whispering to God and open my eyes.

*"Open them, Son..."*

*Eye heard it. The voice of* God.

OH MY GOD! In disbelief—Eye probably imagined it—Eye opened my eyes and blood was all over me. Eye nearly freaked out, but Eye kept myself together. Eye hated the sight of my own blood. Hadn't Eye seen enough blood in my lifetime? When was it ever going to stop? Eye sat up, amidst the pain and my cousin was in the corner of the room sobbing into her arms, her body trembling. Initially, Eye hardened myself inside, like a turtle ducking its head back inside its shell, and no matter what hit the shell Eye didn't feel a thing, but the vibrations ruminating from her body intercepted my thoughts deceptively.

Eye melted for her…slowly coming out my shell.

My heart went out to her. Despite the bad she was still my blood—*before* the pain' *before* the sin. *Say something to her, Pharoah. Good or bad she's your cousin, and you can't turn your back on her.* "Lily…if you don't let it go the pain will consume you, eat you alive. As long as you hold onto a system that was out of your control your father will have power and control over you. You think he's crying over you, Lily? You think he's giving you a second and third thought?" She didn't say a thing, but the look in her eyes let me know she heard everything Eye said. The lines on her forehead let me know she was processing and thinking about what Eye said. Swallowing the lump in my throat, Eye slowly walked up to her and said, "Lily let it go. Let go the past. Eye forgive you and Eye forgive myself. Eye don't hate you. You're my cousin. Eye *hate* what you *did* to me, but Eye love you and that was twenty something years ago. We're all sinners in the eyes of God. Enjoying the sex with you back then was just as bad. When someone gotta pressure and beat you to do something it must not be what's it's cracked up to be."

She looked up at me. "Have you forgotten one small detail?"

"What?"

She stood up and Eye reluctantly helped her. Why, Eye didn't know. "Eye was pregnant with your child. Remember what we both lost." Eye bowed my head—my heart on idle.

That's when she struck.

*Pushing me into the wall, she* pressed her weight against me and Eye was disoriented.

Pulling down my pants, she grabbed my penis and pressed a knife against my neck.

"You ain't leaving here till you face the music. You got books selling and you doing it up! People listening to your stories and *praising* you. You ain't all that, *Niggah*! What, you think you better than us?"

Eye looked her deep in the eyes, not worried about the knife. If she cut me Eye wouldn't make it easy for her, hell no Eye wouldn't. "No Eye don't think Eye'm better—yet you have a knife to my neck! Girl, *why* are you doing this?"

She licked her lips and said, "Throw me on this bed and *freak* me *real* good. Let's try for another baby."

Eye was perplexed. "What? Eye will never do that again."

She pressed the knife a little harder to my neck, Eye could feel the dullness of the blade, and Eye slammed the lamp across her head. It shattered from my hands.

She was knocked out cold on the bed. Eye took the broom and swept the lamp under her bed and Eye threw a blanket over her. Her baby daddy walked in the room.

"Damn, she that doped up huh? Strung out on that crack."

"Yep. She's probably just wasted. But let her sleep. Let her sleep it off."

We slapped palms.

"But who's gonna cook dinner?"

Eye didn't know, but Eye better *leave* before he figures out what just happened here.

# HOME GOING SERVICE FOR:

SUNRISE:
JULY 2005

SUNSET:
JANUARY 2009

PHAROAH C. WILSON, JR'S

# H. I. V.

JANUARY 2009, 4 P.M.
SWEET HOME BAPTIST CHURCH
PERRINE, FLORIDA
REV. DR. GOD VS. SATAN

*He said, "Eye came naked from my mother's womb and Eye will be stripped of everything when Eye die. The Lord gave me everything Eye had. And the Lord has taken it away. Praise the name of the Lord."*

## THE BOOK OF JOB

**A Time to be Born:** In January of 2009, Pharoah was in denial when finding out he had HIV. For him, finding out awakened in him the need to survive, but he lived in fear, not knowing how to tell his family and was ashamed of what he thought his life'd become.

**A Time to Grow:** By this time he was known as THE KING OF EROTICA. The bestselling author that wrote about characters spreading diseases and *now* his life imitated his art and he didn't know if he should tell his fans or keep it a secret. He dated two black men that had HIV in the past, but he knew of it. But another lover of his decided not to tell him and knowingly infected Pharoah with HIV out of spite, hatred and was jealous of his burgeoning literary career.

**A Time to Reflect:** Pharoah secretly gave up writing, turned on his fans in private and he suffered in silence. He took a five week trip to Atlanta to die. He didn't know how to tell his 8 year old and 6 year old nieces (his heart) he had HIV. He put the copyrights to his legacy and all his books in his nieces' names.

**A Time to Die and be mourned:** When Pharoah found the will to live and after telling his family and Facebook fans he had HIV…Pharoah then discovered he had AIDS and no immune system and he took it to God. Pastor Carlos Malone of Bethel Church prayed over him and a month and a half later of Meds, Pharoah's antibody count dropped from 1.5 million to a mere two thousand, *shocking* his doctor and his case manager. When the doctor asked how his numbers dropped so fast, Pharoah said, "Eye don't know what you think Eye did but my Pastor prayed over me."

## *How did you contract* **H.I.V.**?

*Lord Jennings*

*After Eye broke up with my boyfriend*, the one that was using me, the one that had my back and was supporting my book career till he started stealing my money, taking thirty percent instead of ten percent, Eye went through withdrawal. Eye could NOT live without him. The thought of him being with another dude destroyed me inside. But before he officially left me… he *had* to make me pay, out of retaliation. Then once Eye was heartbroken Eye guess he was vindicated because he up and left me before the sprinklers came on. Unfortunately, he was cheating on me for two years and nine months and we were only together for three years. Around the time both of my books were out, and were growing in popularity. In addition to having two boyfriends, he also slept with some dude that bagged groceries at pissy smelling Winn-Dixie in Naranja. That store always smelled like pissy Pine Sol and Comet. Ugh! So you know the side line Hoe was nasty. He's been mopping those floors at night, before the store closed at 11 p.m., and pissing in the mop water. Eye couldn't believe my dude, at the time, cheated on me with him. Eye saw him, once, when Eye was shopping for toiletries. He was pissing in the mop water. He didn't think anyone saw him but Eye did and Eye was repulsed. Eye told the store manager, but he said he didn't wanna investigate it. The scent of the pissy water had all kinds of ghetto Hoes in the store grocery shopping. One woman walked past me in spandex everything, and said to someone on the phone, "Gurl, Eye don't know why Eye'm at the grocery store grocery shopping with cabinets and closets filled with food."

She inhaling deeply, addicted to the pissy Pine Sol, Comet smelling floor. My dude's penis gave me selective amnesia. Eye would do anything for him and Eye made him aware of it and he damn sure made me live up to *my* word.

He was my #1. And that set me up for the Great Fall.

Eye remember he came home one day, upset. Before we broke up. He said his boss fired him 'cause he took too many smoke breaks. Eye had to push him on the couch to calm him down. "And they won't give me my last check. Can you believe that, Pharoah?"

"No, baby." Eye pulled his hardened nature from his pants. Eye put it in my mouth. It was soft and limp, but Eye diverted his attention to the little head because his heart was illogical amidst his grief with his job. So it grows in the warmth, the head of his passion a dome inside my wet mouth and my tonsils hang like chandeliers. He gripped the back of my head aggressively, the code in his shaft activated, and his hips swayed like wild horses to my tongue as Eye played the flute on his scrotum. My hypnotizing eyes were probing. Those eyes caused the snake to grow out of the hole of his boxers like a python to a flute from a woven basket.

"Damn, Pharoah! Suck it…Damn! Your tongue and mouth is hotter and wetter than any female Eye ever had!"

"Oh, yea? Am Eye making your day brighter?"

"Yes, Pharaoh! Suck it!"

My chin was bouncing off the top of his bushy pubic hairs. His penis ping pongs down my throat quick, fast and in a hurry for his nut. Eye put my buttocks up in the air. Wiggled it in the mirrors. Five were up all over the room. Of assorted sizes. Men loved images and illusions, ladies so Eye became his fantasy.

"Eye gotta nut!" he announced with zeal, breathlessly.

Eye sucked faster, deeper, longer, and stronger. Locking my jaws, he was about to blow. Eye took his penis from my mouth and he tried to grab his rod and Eye lined my anus with his penis and he came all over me while Eye was shaking my cakes. My butt cheeks jumping like fags at a Beyonce concert—with Rihanna's head on a silver platter. Praise, Beysus, Eye think not!

Eye kept wiggling my cakes. "*Damn,* baby. *All that ass!*" He was breathing hard. Looking like my nuts about to get caught in the avalanche of cum.

"Your first nut is out the way," Eye said. Eye backed up on it; he slid, slowly, deep inside me. His mouth ajar, narrowed eyes, Eye had a poker face. He was long and thick.

Hurt a little bit, but Eye took it like a man and he got off on it so it's all good.

"Pharoah!" He could barely contain himself. "Stop riding it baby! It's so sensitive."

Negro shut up. Eye'm making a man out of you. We're in the bedroom now. Eye gripped the sheets, put my face down, ass up, and pop pop popped all over that 10 inch uncut stick.

He had to grab my hips because his bottom (ahem, me!) was showing the Top how you get up in some good ass. Eye just raised the stakes; mentally, stimulatingly brainwashed we both were in our deception. We were in LUVH (love) so no condoms were needed after the initial tests we took. We were both negative and Eye did trust him, even though he hurt me deeply. Eye didn't know what it was about this Niggah that had me zonked. Our hearts were in our love making. He touched the bottom of my booty and had me giving up my social security number and all. Eye grew towards my career and the light started to dim on our relationship. He tried to give good face but he was a Top. They couldn't give good face when you make 'em cum down your throat. When Eye was done giving him head you could have sworn he just ran a 60 mile race. He was wheezing and sweating. His abs protruding and reclining; his eyes wide with amazement. He knew he was the S-H-Eye-T! That's why he wanted me to have sex on *his* time table; Eye had to cook, work, wipe his ass and feed him and his penis grapes. Niggah, please. Got to hell. Man…*he* was on a lease; not his dick. Got shit twisted, fool.

He said, "Where you want this nut?" grinding inside me. Then he switched it up. For affect. The bedsprings squeaked while he's deep in it, got my eyes permanently rolled to the back of my head.

Eye said, "Deep down under the totem pole of the booty, Niggah!"

"Eye love the way you talk dirty. You're an intelligent man…Let me pound it a little harder."

We butt ass naked. He controlled me through the movement of his digging equipment. Eye hated authority. So Eye changed it up. Top couldn't have all the control. Eye sat up. Forget all that doggy style stuff. Bruising my damn knees. He grabbed my neck, and Eye arched my booty.

Pop! Pop! Pop! Pop! Pop! Jiggle, jiggle, jiggle…He locked up and Eye kept bouncing on his passion and he grabbed my butt cheeks, grunting, speeding up.

"Oh, oh, oh…Niggah—Niggah, ugh Eye gotta cum!"

"Oh, oh, oh Eye gotta cum my *ass*," Eye mocked, challenging him. Little did Eye know he knowingly infected me with HIV. Since Eye didn't appreciate him he secretly tried to destroy me. None of this entered my mind. Eye was so in love with him Eye failed logically. He looked deep in my eyes, cumming inside me, kissing my lips, still pounding inside me and Eye felt so good.

"Eye love you, Pharoah."

Lost in his gaze. "Eye love you too."

But his infected cum had other plans…

For my immune system.

*He never called again.* When Eye woke up he was long gone. No note. No text message. Nothing. Part of me died inside without him. Eye felt robbed. The other part of me was relieved that Eye now knew why he was in my life. And it was to hinder my growth as a man, as a person and as an individual. What was it about him that made me go bonkers? It really got to me the way he left, but Eye couldn't blame anybody but Pharoah, no matter how Eye tried to justify it. No matter how Eye tried to blame him. He didn't even send me an email from none of his 6 accounts he got on BGCLive.com. Each with stolen pictures of male singers and rappers, got bitches thinking they're online spilling the Tea. But he claimed to be in love with me. Looking me deeply in the eyes while we made slow love. The tip of his ten inches bumpin' the floor of my walls when Eye'm lost and most vulnerable.How could he knowingly infect me? He was that hurt from me losing faith in him when it came to my career? Did Eye deserve his deception?

Was not appreciating his advice, time and attention the real reason why he infected me? Maybe not the problem, but was it an excuse? Was his action justified? Eye think it's the latter. Eye think he wanted to bring me down and take pride and joy in watching me and my career get destroyed. Well…Eye'm still here. And more successful than ever.

So when Eye found out all 3 of my books were in the Barnes and Noble.com Top 100 bestseller's list as the same time FLOORED! Shortly after, Eye found out Eye was HIV positive, and my world was shattered. Being the first self-published author, from what industry insiders told me, to have three books on the same Top 100, Eye experienced a rush of euphoria, a full circle moment. Even if Eye wasn't the first, it was an achievement nobody can take away from me. THREE at the SAME TIME had me bewildered. Seeing Obama, Steve Harvey and The Twilight Series on the same bestseller's list...Eye was in shock. God answered and gave me some sunshine through the HIV affliction. Goulds stand up! Eye kept screaming it.

Had tears in my eyes, breaking me down to the core.

Initially Eye didn't tell a soul. Eye had to celebrate surviving everything Eye lost during my literary journey.

Recounting all the times Eye heard friends and family say it would *never* happen. After the euphoria died away Eye then told my Facebook fans and they rejoiced with me.

After that Eye put it behind me and wanted to continue to grow as an artist, as an author. After four years of brutal rape; after the years of condemnation from my family; years after my own Pa$tor$ secretly raped me; *years* after Eye was gang raped when Eye was a stripper; *years* after Eye was incarcerated; years *after* Eye began to love myself; a couple years after successfully completing parole (Eye am Legend in that MDSO class) it has come down to the words Hollywood actor Billy Bob Thornton had told me at the Oregon State Penitentiary—when Eye was at my lowest…

He said this day would come. Bestseller, Eye Am.

And NO ONE could take that away!

☯

*New York Times bestselling author* E. Lynn Harris told me also this day would come—but Eye didn't believe him, because Eye hardly believed in myself. Yes, Eye know Eye can write, but Eye'm not at the point Eye think Eye'm actually good at what Eye do, like people constantly tell me.

He had a tremendous amount of faith in my work. He told me numerous times that Eye reminded him of himself when he was starting out and no one would give his books the time of day because of the subject matter. Even though Eye didn't believe him…he *still* believed in me. He told me he didn't remember if his books had ever been in the Top 100 on Barnes and Noble.com at the *same* time. Eye had three and he was more proud of me than Eye was because Eye wasn't proud, but Eye was thankful to God and blessed and he said, "Amen."

But…he made the New York Times Bestseller's list. That's something Eye was still pushing for and it would happen, Eye hope. Eye just had to be patient. When Eye talked to him about it he said, "And let God do his work, young man." Eye'm teaching people how to practice safer sex, and how to respect their wives and how to thank God for what you have today 'cause it ain't promised to you tomorrow, indirectly, through those promiscuous Hoes and cut throat Niggahs in my books. Thank you God! Thank you Jesus! But the weirdest thing started happening after finding out my books were on some type of bestseller list...

*Every time Eye opened a magazine* it was on an HIV pill or ad. Every time Eye turned on the TV an HIV commercial was going off or coming on. Every time Eye logged on the news HIV ads were everywhere. Every time Eye turned on the radio HIV commercials or commentary was the present day reality. So Eye went to South Beach to get away, to spend some *Me* time—quietly basking in my success. As a last minute resort, before leaving (a few hours later), Eye go see Sapphire Grimes with SOBAP, an organization specializing in HIV education, and they give free testing. He's one of my good friends. Look just as good as me. That's because we're Nassau, Bahamian men. Yes, sir. Gotta rep that light blue, yellow and black flag.

He smiled big when he saw me. We embraced.

"*Wassup*, Pharoah? Mr. Author."

"Hey, man!" Eye was glowing.

"What brings you out here?" he asked—his booth was stuffed in an office in the back of the CVS. "Aren't you supposed to be writing a new book?"

"Yes," Eye said. "But Eye couldn't *concentrate*."

"Writer's block?"

Eye was perplexed. "No. Never. Certainly not *that*. Eye wrote over 80 books and didn't get writer's block yet."

"So why you looked bothered?"

"Eye don't know. Maybe God is trying to talk to me, dawg."

"What do you mean?" Eye got his attention now. He's curious. Eye met Sapphire through my ex boyfriend, when we were dating at the time, Hans Bidon. Hey, Hans. Love you, man. Anyways. Sapphire was dating one of Hans' best friends, Jaymes. Jaymes, Eye didn't know about him. Eye heard about something he did with some cinder blocks and somebody's car and Eye was like wow...

Sapphire was Jaymes man at the time. But Niggahs didn't know how to act or appreciate a damn good thing so Sapphire got rid of him really fast. Eye'm *glad* he did.

"Eye don't know, Sapphire. Every time Eye open a magazine, it's on an HIV ad. If Eye turn on the TV, HIV ad coming on or going off. HIV signs on the billboards when you travel. Atripala. Norvir. Eye counted four buses today with huge HIV ads."

"Just your luck," he said with a smile. Eye wasn't smiling. Eye was shook up. "Eye'm conducting free HIV tests today."

Eye waved my hands. "Naw, naw Eye'm good. Eye'm *negative*, Sapphire." Eye assumed Eye was negative, based off the false security of getting tested with my ex 4 months after we fucked on the first date—um, wait. We didn't screw when we first met. Now that Eye think about it we got tested first, waited four months, and, together, got tested again. Got our results together. Then we did the wild thing. Window period was three months. So on that 4th month of dating our tests came back negative. It's been a year and a few months since Eye last slept with my ex, and didn't sleep with anybody afterward because Eye was nursing a broken heart. When he upped and abandoned me without even a phone call…*that* was devastating.

Sapphire was stern. "Take the test, Pharoah."

"Naw, Eye'm good. Eye'm about to go. Eye don't *like* needles."

"We do swab tests here."

"What?"

"We swab your mouth." He took my hand. "Come on."

"Ok."

He squeezed my hand. Eye squeezed back. He opened the swab test.

"Open wide."

Eye closed my eyes.

*Eye don't have HIV! Eye'm SURE of it!*

*We chit chatted for 30 minutes while* time slowly peeled away my results. Time was a very powerful thing. So was common sense. We're laughing and joking with each other, since we barely and rarely got to see each other. He was the kind of friend you wished you could spend more time with. We're talking 'bout clubs, guys and the current gay market 8 points down on the Dow Jones and all that NASDAQ shit.

He looked at the test, the smile slowly and gradually dying from his face.

"What?" Eye asked.

"Oh, no, Pharoah."

"What?"

He took a deep breath, looking me deeply in my eyes. "Your test is retroactive for HIV."

Eye was shaking my head in complete shock. Eye couldn't breathe, all the air leaving my body with a resounding click noise reverberating through my skull. "Oh, *hell* no! That's a lie! Eye haven't even had sex in almost 2 years! Eye've been jacking my dick. No *way*!"

Tears clouded his eyes as well as mine. "Eye'm gonna test you again to be sure." He opened a more expensive test.

"This has to be sent away to a lab so a technician gotta determine if the positive test result is accurate," he said and all that registered in my head was *wa wa wa wa Charlie Brown.*

Just my luck. Another low blow, Satan. Now my life was over! Eye got that slow death everybody paranoid about getting and 1 in 5 people already got it and didn't even know it. Eye was the 1 in 5. But now Eye knew Eye had it.

Eye couldn't *do* this, God. Live with this disease. No matter what Eye do Eye fail at it. Now Eye have H.I. Fuc*ing. V. Eye'm gonna die.

"Pharoah. You got a choice," Sapphire said, shortly after swabbing my mouth a second time. He sealed the swab in a lab bag and filled in the information. "You have a choice to make." Eye'm still shell-shocked times one hundred, my world spinning out of control. "And no matter the outcome you must make the choice."

Tears fell even harder as Eye felt myself slowly letting go. The Atlantic Ocean pushing towards a small crack in a bath tub, the pressure was too much. My tears fell too hard. They were *too* heavy to find my cheekbones. All my anguish, my goals and dreams: Splat! Splat! Splat!

As my tears crashed on the tiled floor, Eye let go. Eye made up my mind to go somewhere and die in peace. There was a reason those HIV tests were given in the back of a drug store. That's some Rosa Parks backwards crap for you.

"What…what…" My voice cracked. "What decision Eye gotta make?"

He was serious. "You're a bestselling author. And you're HIV positive. You can either choose to die and leave behind just three books and two nieces and a ton of fans that may be HIV positive with no direction. Or you can live the next 20, 30 and 40 years releasing your 200th book and already have an empire and possibly get studied in colleges."

The sparkles in my eyes dimmed, but they were coming back to life—barely—because he was right. Eye knew people who lived with HIV for 15, 20 years with low or undetectable HIV levels in their blood.

"You're right," Eye said breathlessly. He stood up, and Eye stood up and he embraced me and Eye was trembling, so cold in this cruel world. HIV HIV HIV— Eye couldn't believe Eye had a disease, what would Eye do? What would Eye tell my mother and family? Eye broke apart when the shell of my hurt shattered on the floor of his empathy.

"Why me?" Eye asked. "Eye write about this kind of stuff in my books! Art imitating life. How could this happen to me, Sapphire? How could this happen? *How*?"

Snot stopped up in my nose. "How am Eye gonna tell my nieces? My babies? That Uncle Pharoah is dying? Oh God—*how*, Sapphire?"

He held me tighter. "Eye'm in this with you. Eye will always have your back."

He pulled away from me and smiled.

"Eye'm living with HIV, too."

## Lord Jennings & The King of Erotica

**Eye opened my eyes.** Lord Jennings, the shrink, had his strong, masculine arms around me; his hot tears falling down the nape of my neck and soaking in my shirt.

He's holding me tight and Eye am holding him tighter. His writing pads on the low table, my life scribbled all over them…the tape recorder long ago stopped, my voice on the tape immortalized. Eye was a blade of grass on his collar bone. His empathy was selfless. Loyal to my pain. He doesn't question the object on his shoulder. And Satan takes advantage of that.

"Eye'll drive you to Homestead if you don't want to stay here with me. Like Eye said my wife thinks Eye'm out of town. This was definitely worth it. And Eye'll come get you in the morning so we can continue."

Eye was getting ready to go, trapped in my feelings and shuddering from the memory.

"Pharoah, after you left Sapphire's office, what was your life like?" he asked. We didn't let each other go.

Eye squeezed my eyes shut. "Well Sapphire drove me home." Eye smiled then. "He played uplifting music all the way to Mom's house. Told me when he was depressed he listened to uplifting, up-tempo music. Eye was then getting ready for my Atlanta trip. Was going to stay two weeks and wound up staying 5 weeks. Eye never been to Atlanta before in my life and Eye was excited to go."

We stopped hugging. Eye didn't realize we were standing.

"Sit down for a minute," Lord said. Eye sat down, slowly, staring off into space. "Let's talk about the trip. You just found out you're HIV positive and you went on with business as usual?"

He sat down next to me as Eye answered. "Yes. Eye told myself Eye didn't have HIV."

"So why the trip?" he asked.

Eye sat down next to him.

"Eye went to Atlanta to die."

"My God." His hand was on my thigh.

*Life was over and hope was gone*. Eye was at God's mercy so Eye wasn't going to be taking *anybody's* Meds. Eye cast my sins upon you, God. Eye'll trust you to take care of me. Eye won't claim it as of yet. That wasn't what Eye wanted to confess with my mouth. Amen.

*Eye boarded the plane for Atlanta* March of 2009. My sister Attica Lundy came to pick me up from the ATL Airport after Eye arrived, with my brother Cam, Mr. Durrty Byrd, the best rapper Atlanta would ever see. This was my first time meeting my sister Attica, who was an amazing talented multi-tasking woman. Author. She had her *own* business, Diva Park. She was an amazing mother of three.

Attica and Eye met on Myspace about 5, maybe 6 years ago, when Myspace was the big online social network. Around that time Eye was a super blogger. Any blog that Eye wrote cracked the Top 10 on the Most Popular chart and Eye had over a thousand of them written.

Eye had 540 #1 Blogs in the Writing and Poetry category and my 30TH ANNIVERSARY BIRTHDAY BLOG cracked the top 5 on the Main Popularity chart that only superstars cracked, and Zane's was #7 and Puff Daddy's was #6. Eye beat out Puff Daddy and Eye was like oh my God. Over 2 million people read about my $30^{th}$ birthday and the years of rape and self-hatred Eye lived through.

You know you're hot when million dollar recording artists and movie stars send the "gay" person in their "cliques" to me on Myspace. The "gay" person always turned out to be their agents or publicists. Wanting me to advertise their songs, images and music in my blogs for my fans and didn't wanna pay me anything. Like Eye was supposed to be honored to do this for them. The only woman Eye advertised was Janet Jackson and she didn't ask me to. Eye loved her since Eye was little so as my popularity rose and the surge in traffic to my profile page went through the roof they were mellowed out by Janet Jackson default music on my page. Nuff said. Janet's been my #1 entertainer for 27 years now.

Eye would get my strength from Attica while in Atlanta. She lived with MS (multiple sclerosis) and she didn't let her affliction get the best of her.

We embraced, both smiling like crazy. Eye couldn't believe Eye was actually in Atlanta. Eye shook Cam's hand and we went out to eat at RUBY TUESDAYS, and they were about to close. It was after 10:45 p.m. Once we got there we entered and one of the serving waiters said, "We're closing."

"Aw, man," my sister said, and Eye was grinning.

Eye looked at the waiter in high spirits and he said, "Wait right here. Let me see what Eye can do."

Something was off but Eye shook the thought away.

He came back, energetic, and he took us to a table along the side wall towards the restrooms. The place was nice. Not crowded of course because they were about to close. A few tables over was a group of pretty black women cackling and chatting the night away with their alcohol. Eye smiled at one and she winked. The waiter returned and told us they had a salad bar. He said we could help ourselves. So Eye went over, got a plate, clad in jeans, a T-shirt and a fresh haircut.

One of the manager's, a black guy, walked over, took a plate and preoccupied himself getting some fruit. He looked at me and Eye looked at him with a smile. Eye put some lettuce and cucumbers on my plate, even though half the salad bar was packed up for the night.

"Can Eye ask you something," he asked.

"Sure."

"You look like the guy that write the books."

"Eye am."

"Oh, my God! The King of Erotica?"

"Um, yes." Eye smiled again. Damn. He knew who Eye was and Eye never been there before?

"Wow, man." He shook my hand. "Eye can't believe this. Eye am so happy to meet you, man."

"Thanks."

"Eat what you want. Shit, if you wanna take the whole bar home in carry out trays you surely can."

"Thanks." My big sister Attica and Cam got them something to eat. And my lil' celebrity got all three of us another free meal at a later date. And we would never use it.

Atlanta opened me up to a new clientele of authors and promoters. Eye loved it in Atlanta. Eye didn't think of having HIV and Eye told myself Eye was going to die there in Atlanta because Eye wasn't gonna tell a soul and Eye wasn't going to any doctor and Eye wasn't taking any medicine. Eye was in serious denial. The Atlanta folks welcomed me with open arms and took really good care of me. For the first two weeks Eye didn't go anywhere. It rained day in, day out and the pollen in the air gave me a sinus fit. Atlanta was a very hospitable place, and the men were after me. How sweet, fresh meat! Eye couldn't blink without one swooping in my face trying to get my pants off.

Ludacris wasn't lying about Atlanta's Southern Hospitality. Eye wanted to taste Atlanta chocolate, though…but Eye *refrained* because Eye was in a committed relationship, so Eye didn't put myself in any tempting situations. The first three weeks Eye didn't do much writing because Eye left the cord to my computer back in Miami so Eye was like damn. Eye wrote on Attica's computer when she wasn't building web sites or working. Cam and Eye grew really close. We smoked bud and he took me to Landmine Entertainment, a record label. Eye didn't like that place at all, but Eye didn't say anything because the Niggahs Eye met didn't even know Eye was a bestselling author till Cam told them. Eye gave them a few copies of my book.

Cam was a very incredible, powerfully talented producer and rapper. Just watching him work inspired me all over again to perfect my craft. We worked out at the gym, and we opened up to each other about everything. Eye really felt like Eye had another brother and now we loved each other like brothers. We never judged each other and we always helped each other when we lacked something when it came to our art. Eye met his grandma, with her pretty self, and Eye gave her my first book as well. She was a bar tender and kept a clean home, very noble and intelligent woman. Eye enjoyed my talks with her and couldn't wait to see her again.

But then Eye grew pensive about HIV. Eye would go to bed thinking of this and sleep all day, hardly getting up, getting lazy, but Eye was on vacation so Eye deserved to be lazy. Eye washed dishes and sometimes cooked, helping Attica with my nephews and niece while she worked from home. Attica and Eye also got closer. A few ups and downs, but nothing big or major. Mainly my attitude; it's hard for me to let people in my heart without the fear of being hurt, but she was patient and understanding and let me know her home was the one place Eye could always be Pharoah.

Meeting my nephew Chris Miller was another milestone in my life. He had a lot of issues, and was very misunderstood, but through all the ups and the downs and the fall out we had, we came out on top. Eye gave him advice about my mistakes, going to prison and learning to love myself. Eye told him things Eye felt he could apply to his own life to better himself as a man, since he was the oldest child and only in the 11th grade. He confided in me about things Eye wouldn't repeat because he told me in the strictest of confidence, but in a lot of ways Eye saw myself at his age when he spoke. Later that night, when they all slept, Eye logged on Facebook, after getting off the phone with my nieces. Over 45 IM boxes instantly popped up:

*Eye wanna have sex with you…*
*You got a phat booty.*
*Is that booty good?*
*Do you give head? Eye need some.*
*Give me some advice.*

*And out of 45+ IM boxes*, only one person said, “Good day, Pharoah. How are you doing my brothah?”

So Eye answered him back.

*Most authors, when you hit them* up, didn't even respond back or speak to you. So anybody that hits me up Eye respond back. But there was a *way* you spoke. If you couldn't ask a brothah how were you doing or spoke properly then Eye didn't respond. If you didn't stand firm on your hustle then get the hell off the bus. Eye chatted with ole boy on the IM for about ten minutes,

[My Sister from another Mother—Myesha]

then Eye told him Eye was tired, that Eye was going to bed. Eye logged off and crawled on the sofa and went to sleep. The next day my brother Cam asked did Eye wanna go to the mall. The Lennox Mall. Eye said, “Yes.”

So we go. To the Lion's Den, E Lynn Harris called it. Harris and Eye were going to have lunch, but he said he was on his way out of town, but did tell me he lived by the mall.

E Lynn Harris gave me the keys and the tea on Atlanta. *Everything*. He told me things that made my eyes pop out my head. All the spas, bathhouses, and professional jigaboos were in my mental Rolodex.But Eye didn't get in too deep.

Cam and Eye walked through the jam packed food court and heads turned in my direction. Eye made sure Eye looked masculine and sexy that day. A few of the men got up, whispering to each other and doing double takes the entire time Eye was walking from store to store, talking to my brother. Eye looked back and a small crowd followed me and a few of them smiled and waved and another gay man started crying, covering his face and Eye was like what was wrong with him? So Cam went to a shoe store and Eye pivoted and walked up to the crowd of 15 and they instantly said, “Oh God, oh God it IS HIM!”

“Excuse me,” one of them said. He was very handsome, clad in green everything. “Are you The King of Erotica? You wrote 3 books and you used to be Miamilicious in the porn video? Are you the one that was in porn for 5 days to make money to be your own publisher?”

Eye shook his hand, and he was trembling. “Yes, bruh. That is me.”

The others in the crowd spoke.

*“Oh my God.”*

*“Eye told you!”*

*“He looks better in person.”*

*“Eye didn’t know he was so goddamn tall.”*

*“Will you sign my autograph?”*

*“Where are your books available for purchase?”*

They shook my hand or kissed my hand or cheek and Eye signed autographs and Eye was on my way.

Walking off one of the men said, “Pharaoh.”

Eye stopped and looked at him, the one that was crying.

“Yes.”

He really let go. He hugged me. “Eye look up to you, Pharaoh. Thank you for your books, thank you for telling your story.”

“No problem, bruh.” Eye hugged him back.

“Eye’m living with HIV and you inspired me to write my book.” Tears fell down my face. On the way back through the Food Court, going home, my head was high. Eye looked side to side, flashed a smile, and winked my left Eye at folks just to mess with them. Niggahs dabbing other Niggahs’ arms with their elbows, nodding at me, looking at my butt, or checking for a penis print behind my pants and finding it ‘cause Pharoah didn’t wear underwear. Eye nodded upwards to some, and downwards to others. Before Eye got to the door one came up to me.

“Eye heard you’re an author.”

“Yes, Eye am.”

“So Wassup?”

Eye hate that *What’s up*, or *Sup* crap ugh! “Um, sup.” He pulled out his Blackberry and called somebody. “Hold on,” he said and Eye was about to walk off.

"The King of Erotica is in the Lion's Den, bitch. Yes, the author. And *gurlllll* he is fine as hell!"

"Eye'm about to go, bruh," Eye said. "Nice meeting you."

"Wait! Can Eye get a picture of you?"

"Sure."

He hugged me, his hand on my ass. Eye pulled it up to my back.

MY COUSINS KIM SINGLETON, BRENDA,
MY TALENTED COUSIN LAQUANDRA MILLER AND EBONI JACKSON

Eye said, "We ain't cool like that, Pimp."
Flash.

Eye walked off. Niggahs were doing Facebook updates and *Twittering* (Eye hate Twitter, oh my God!) about me in the mall. Eye didn't have a Twitter account. And didn't want one. Later that night Eye thought about the man Eye met at the mall that told me Eye inspired him to write his own book on his own life living with HIV. For some reason that opened me up and the tears flowed. Eye was so messed up inside, feeling alone. Eye felt abandoned within myself. Eye didn't know if Eye truly had the strength to get through. Eye shuddered with fear. Eye couldn't picture myself taking Meds for the rest of my life. Eye logged on

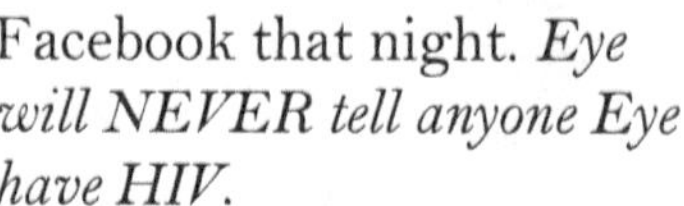
Facebook that night. *Eye will NEVER tell anyone Eye have HIV.*

[Caroline Lewis and I having fun.]

Eye typed in my status update box, about 1,300 people on my friend list:

Me in my dear friend Jennifer Hick's chest at Trevor's party lol; Rafael and his wife

Me, Melvin, my sister Danielle, my god daughter Legacy and my god son Josh

**The King of Erotica has H.I.V.**
**Don't wanna talk about it.**
**How could this happen to me?**
**Eye'm logging off.**

There, Eye did it. Eye put it on a social network that Eye have HIV. Eye never anticipated the breathtaking response.

Me and my sexy cousin Jhamelia in The Everglades; me and Jhamelia, Bread and Khambrell at Club Rumors. Below, Sean Timberlake (Ying) and shakira.

MY FIANCÉ JOHN WILSON, ALIYAIH AND SUNJARAIH [NIECES] (2ND) MY COUSINS WEE WEE, ME, BREAD, POLAR BEAR. KHAMBRELL. (3RD) ME AND ADON (NEPHEW). (4TH) ME, TREVOR AND FRIENDS.

[BELOW] ME, MY FRIEND FOR 16 YEARS RAFAEL FELIPE AND HIS BEAUTIFUL WIFE. ME EATING JOE'S CRABS (THANKS JOHN!)...

# DAY

# 4

# Response to Robert Frost's
# "THE ROAD LESS TAKEN"
## By Dapharoah

Two roads greet thee before thy devastation and failures…
one road stemming from Mama's womb
the other dislodged from Daddy's deformed testicles
Learning to read was thy great antlophobia
of which they twirled towards a dusty tomb.

The ghetto was my slavish atelophobia
inside what the environment said I should be
pick up a football to become an entity
fumble the book because we don't read
my roads are phobias by name

*Around 3 a.m. Eye logged on.* Eye was bored. Eye couldn't believe the outcry from my fans. Eye had over 800 messages in my inbox from around the world. Eye had over 500 friend requests and counting. Eye was adding 100 friends per hour after publicly saying Eye had HIV. Up and down my page were fans telling me Eye was their hero, to keep my head up, that GOD has the final say. People from Japan were on my page. People from Africa and South Africa were on my page offering me love, attention and bought my books. My book sales surged through the roof. Pastors, doctors, nurses and lawyers, other authors and even E. Lynn Harris and JL King reached out to me and told me having HIV wasn't a death sentence. In a matter of hours Eye went from little known author on Facebook to the most popular male author on the Facebook Network. Eye was at my 5,000 friend maximum nearly *instantly.*

It was then Eye realized that my life was bigger than me; that the position God has me in to inspire and to lead people to his Word was enormous. Eye accepted the challenge and Eye was changed because of it. My phone was ringing off the hook! Over 190 calls in thirty minutes. Eye didn't answer because Eye knew why my phone rang and Eye didn't want to spend the rest of the morning talking about having HIV. Millions of others had HIV as well. So Eye wasn't in the boat alone.

When Miss Bling Diva out of Chicago called me, with her cute self, she said, "King, tell me it ain't so."

"What?"

"Eye get a call at 3 a.m., people waking me up out my sleep saying Ѣe King of Erotica posted he has HIV."

"Yes, Eye do"

And we talked for the next hour. About some shit Eye said Eye wouldn't spend the morning talking about. Damn. But anything for Miss Bling Diva.

The next few weeks slides by, Eye decided to come home and face having HIV. Couldn't run from it anymore and Eye didn't want to *die* from it. Eye had to love and live for myself, and having HIV brought me closer to God. Eye took accountability for my actions and Eye already knew where Eye got HIV from. That was a no brainer. Eye didn't blame anybody but myself. Nobody put a gun to my head and made me sleep with my ex without a rubber. Maybe if Eye wasn't being so whorish and loved my body the way Jesus loved me Eye wouldn't be in the predicament Eye was in.

Eye told my sister and Cam Eye was heading back to Miami. Attica was especially happy because she wanted me to get help concerning HIV and do all Eye could do to prolong my life and Eye agreed. She put her foot down. Eye didn't have any symptoms. Not one. And that's what scared me and my sister. You truly couldn't look at anybody and try to guess what they had.

*When my plane landed back in Miami*, Florida, John picked me up from the airport and we went straight to Big Lots and Eye bought my nieces a few gifts. Eye missed them so much and Eye wanted to see them before seeing anybody. Eye bought them Mr. Potato Head toys and was happy with that. Once we arrived to my nieces' home, John was filming me running up to the front door to see my babies and my heart quickened when they answered. Eye heard them screaming *Uncle Pharoahhh!* before the door even opened. Eye loved them so much. The video is on my YouTube.

They were so happy to see me.

*A few days later Eye made a doctor* appointment at CHI. My Case Manager was Kevin Palmer, and we wound up becoming very good friends. He was more than a hardworking Case Manager, he treated you like family and he was very well liked at his job. At least Eye thought so. Eye confided in him about everything from HIV to my career and he always had an open door policy when it came to his clients. At this point, in May of 2009, Eye didn't know how far along HIV had progressed in my body, so he ordered various blood tests and Eye had to take a slip over to the Lab and get some blood drawn. He signed me up through ADAP, a program designed to help those with HIV obtain free testing and medicine if you qualified. The criteria Eye wasn't sure of, but Eye qualified. Eye'm so scared of needles, oh my God Eye nearly pissed on myself when Eye saw all those little tubes that had to be filled with my blood. But Eye had to get it over with. No time to act like a baby. Eye made this bed. Eye had to lie in it. Once the RN was done drawing blood Eye went home.

And waited a week for the results.

*The next week Eye went to see Kevin*. We shook hands and went through the preliminaries of what we been up to since we last talked. Eye reminded him Eye had to get the test results and he looked them up.

"Damn," he said. "Eye forgot you took a lab before you *went* to Atlanta."

"Hell *Eye* forgot."

"Well, let's check those numbers. Then Eye gotta get you in to see Dr. Oper."

"Ok."

He typed in my info.

"Your birth date?"

And Eye told him.

He pulled it up and he stopped smiling and Eye stopped smiling.

"What's wrong?" Eye asked.

He said, "Well you don't have HIV for one."

Eye'm happy. *Rejoicing*. Eye knew Eye didn't have HIV. Eye knew it!

"Bruh," he said, turning the screen around so Eye could see it, and Eye didn't know what Eye was looking at. "You don't have HIV anymore," Kevin said, and my heart leapt. Yes! "You have AIDS," he continued, devastating me instantly. "You have 60+ T4 cells. Pharoah…you barely have an immune system."

Eye lowered my head.

"God…" was all Eye could say.

But Eye didn't cry. Eye did enough of that in the ATL.

"Look at me, Pharoah."

Eye refused to let him see my pain. "No."

"Pharoah. *Please.* Look at me. Eye'm your boy."

Eye looked at him, tears falling. Eye hated myself so much. Eye had AIDS? Just imagine if Eye never paid attention to the HIV signs on TV and on the radio and never got tested. Eye'd be dead by now, or on my way to the GRAVE!

"You will *not* die from this, Pharoah. Eye promise you. Let me explain this screen to you. You have over 1 million antibodies in your blood for HIV."

"Goddamn."

"This means you had HIV for a while."

"Eye see."

"Eye'm getting you to Dr. Oper ASAP. Trust me. With your cooperation, we will get through this together. Are you with me on this, Pharoah? Eye can't do this without you. Eye *need* your cooperation and you have a long road ahead but you will make it, man."

"Yea. Eye have no choice."

"Eye got your back."

He got me to see Dr. Oper.

Eye was given:

Zithromax: 2 tablets before breakfast (Sundays ONLY)

Norvir: a gel cap. Take ONE

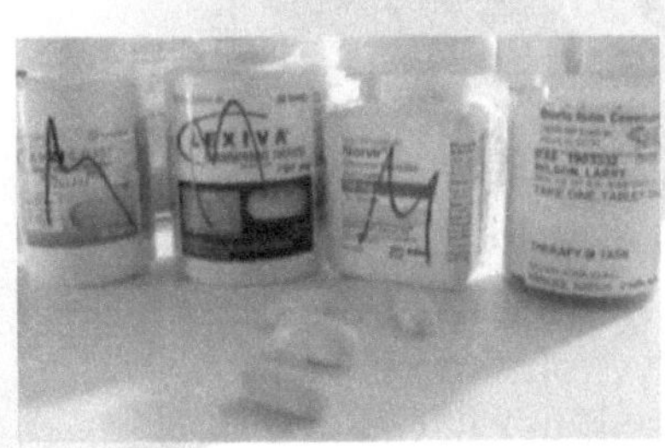


Lexiva: Pink pills, take two

Epzicom: Orange pill, take one daily

Bactrim: take one

A multivitamin: a maroon pill, take one daily

**Dr. Oper was a very mean** doctor, but Eye *loved* him. He kept it real and he didn't mess around with anybody's health. He was a very respected, older, balding white man. Nothing easy on the eyes to look at, but his heart was pure and Eye had love for him instantly.

He said, "From this day forward Mr. Wilson we are married. We will get through this. You will live, and it all depends on you. Eye prescribed your medicine, a cocktail Eye call it and we have to get your immune system up. Will take a long time to get your immune system up, but best believe no one has died in my care. Do you trust me?"

"Yes, Dr. Oper."

We shook hands.

*Eye started my medication. Mama* could care less. In the beginning she acted like she gave a damn, but as she got mad at me over dumb stuff she told me how she truly felt.

"Eye'm not the one with AIDS!" she screamed in my face vehemently. "Ain't my problem." Wow. But she wanted me to give a damn about Laron's kidneys not working, and yes Eye did care. She wanted me to give a damn about Jarshawn's diabetes (Eye do care), but he hasn't taken insulin shots in forever. Now Eye only cared about me and me only.

My cousin Trice, who was also a nurse, called me and gave me advice on the do's and don'ts of starting HIV meds. She said Eye was going to have some side effects and whatever side *effects* Eye get she told me to make sure Eye tell my doctor. Eye took notes and started my medicine at 9:30 a.m. Eye took all the pills around this time, and Eye had to take it with food. Over the first few days nothing. Eye took my meds on time and did everything the doctor, my case manager and the nurses instructed. When the Miami Pride, called The Sizzle, rolled into town Memorial Day weekend E. Lynn Harris hit me up. Eye told him Eye wasn't going to be able to attend because Eye didn't have enough money to pay for my hotel room, bills at home prevented it all. He offered to pay it for me and Eye was in shock.

"Really?"

"Yes, Pharoah. You gotta come. Eye wanna meet you."

"Thanks E. Lynn."

But Eye didn't let him pay for it. John paid for it and we didn't need E. Lynn anymore. But Eye did thank him very much from the bottom of my heart. One of my old co-workers from Dolphin Stadium called me and Eye told him Eye was at the Hyatt host hotel in Downtown Miami for the Sizzle, checking in. John helped me and Eye was looking for my vendor table to set up for my books. It was the first function Eye ever attended as an author.

Niggahs were on me *hard*. Damn, could Eye breathe? All the porn stars whistling at me. One photographer said, "You are a tall, fine ass bitch!" Eye met Breion, a porn star and a cool dude and he took a picture with me holding up one of my books before they even went on sale. Once Eye was set up Eye went to Walgreens and had pictures of myself made, and bought frames so Eye could set up on my table. Eye didn't have enough time to order flyers or anything so the frames would have to do. Once Eye was set up Eye hugged John and he went home after Eye thanked him for helping me.

Going to my room, Eye felt faint, but Eye lay down and rested my eyes. Eye had to pee so Eye got up, loving the room, and decided to make a quick Facebook video of my hotel room. Eye showed my excitement about meeting E. Lynn Harris, and gave a stern message about knowing your HIV status. And even though Eye was excited about meeting one of my favorite authors—Damian Campbell is my absolute favorite author/poet—Eye didn't know Eye was selected for E. Lynn's Literary Café in support of *The Basketball Jones.* After shooting the video Eye put up the camera and took a piss.

Flushing, Eye washed my hands and smiled, licking my tongue at my reflection. And Eye had heart failure. My tongue was completely white—Eye had a yeast infection on my tongue, one of the side effects of the medicine. And it hurt badly. Eye could hardly swallow.

My legs felt like rubber. "Oh, no! No! What is *this*?" Eye couldn't stop looking at it. Locking up my room, Eye called a friend and told him my dilemma. He drove to the hotel, picked me up and drove me down south, to Goulds, South Dade Health Center—CHI, which was about an hour away from the Hyatt.

Eye went to see the doc, but he wasn't there for the day so one of the RN's got another doctor to take me in. Eye told him the problem, and showed him my tongue. He prescribed me some thick yellow stuff to swish around my mouth and swallow. He gave me the directions. After thanking him, my friend drove me back to the hotel. And Eye cried on my bed till Eye fell asleep. Eye got up about an hour later and caught the elevator down to the Main Lobby, then took the escalator to the ground level floor. The Marketplace. Where all the vendors were set up.

E Lynn Harris was being set up in the Ballroom and Eye still hadn't received word that Eye was a part of his Literary Café. At that point Eye didn't worry about it. Eye was still going to do my thing with my books with or without it.

After setting up my table, Eye took a seat and my homeboy Damien came by. He would be staying in my hotel room with me. He was a feminine dude that worked at Dolphin Stadium with me and he would not only embarrass the hell outta me with his flamboyant antics, but he was completely intoxicated.

"So Eye take it E Lynn will be in the Ball room," Damien said with a smile, looking around at all the fine dudes prancing by, staring me in the face and Eye avoided their eyes.

"Yea," Eye told him, just daydreaming about one day hosting my own Literary Café. Fat chance. Maybe that would *never* happen. If Eye kept thinking like that maybe it wouldn't happen.

"Were you picked?" Damien asked, holding his breath for my answer.

"*No.* His room is being set up for the Basketball Jones Event and apparently Eye didn't make the cut."

"It's ok, man."

Eye avoided his eyes. Didn't want him to see my utter failure. "*Thanks.*"

"You're still here promoting The King of Erotica at The Sizzle so that is nice."

"Yes it is," Eye said, barely smiling. Eye didn't even want to be there anymore.

"You don't seem too happy."

Eye glanced sadly at him, and his heart went out to me. "Eye'm ok."

*My friend walked off, looking at* all the male Eye candy and Eye sat there, too afraid to talk to anybody. Eye never attended this kind of event so Eye was nervous.

"His book must *not* be selling," a random feminine hater said. He was behind me, off to the left, and Eye pretended not to listen.

"It ain't," said his counterpart, eying me with contempt.

"He ain't no E Lynn Harris," Feminine continued to say and Eye yawned, looking around.

"The King of Erotica my *ass.* And *nobody* bought a copy *yet.*"

"Eye actually sold 24 copies and the event hasn't started yet, *fag*!" Eye said, standing up and looking at him and he sat on a nearby chair like oh, no, this author will tell you about your ass in an instant.

"*Damn* you are tall!" Feminine said, trying to distract me.

Eye had fire in my eyes, already upset because Eye wanted to go home. "And Eye will beat your ass if you don't get your dumb ass from by me, *bitch*!"

Half of Flavor Works' porn stars were laughing at him and Eye sat down and said, "God be with me. These faggots gonna make me stomp mud holes in their *asses*!"

A handsome camera man stopped by my table.

"Hey Pharoah," he said, medium build, lovely smile.

It took a minute for me to calm down. "Hey, man." He shook my hand.

"You are very attractive."

"Thanks," Eye said, ignoring him.

"You seem shy."

Eye looked deeply into his eyes. "Eye'm a little outta my element."

"You're a knock out. Look over yonder. All those men are staring at you."

"Eye know," Eye said flatly.

"And you ain't flirting?"

"Eye'm living with HIV. Eye got in this predicament being hard headed.

"Eye admire your candidness. Eye follow you on Facebook. You always tell your fans the status of your infection."

Eye was starting to enjoy our conversation. Eye melted from the black—and block— of ice Eye'd become. "Eye hope it gets people to get tested."

His tone changed. "Listen. Eye have some good news."

"What's that?" Eye asked. Eye wondered what it could be?

His eyes sparkled. "Get your books and your table. E Lynn Harris has selected you to be in his Literary Café."

Stars must have slammed into my body because Eye was suddenly jolted and energetic. "OH MY GOD!" Eye jumped up, covering my mouth in complete shock. People were looking, some of Flavor Works' porn stars were whistling at me and clapping, and the two faggot haters were clapping, saying, "*Congratulations*, Pharoah."

"Thanks…" My heart beat so fast. "Eye need a moment."

"We'll take the table in the ballroom for you," one of the haters said.

Tears wet my face. "Thanks."

*Eye went up to my room, burst* through the door, closed it and fell on my knees. "Thank you Jesus so much for the blessings! Oh my God Eye'm about to hyperventilate. Eye knew Eye was meeting him, but Eye did not know Eye got picked with two other men. Oh my God! Thank you! All praise goes to you! Eye get to meet my mentor! Amen."

Eye spent the next ten minutes praising God.

*A few hours later the room was jam*-packed with E Lynn Harris fans, my table was set up and E Lynn Harris, in a black shirt, slacks and shades (looking too fab) walked in the room and everyone went crazy. Immediately he looked dead in my eyes, took off his shades and his high wattage smile lit up with his face and Eye was floored. Eye think he was more excited to meet me.

*"Pharoah! Mr. King of Erotica!"*

Eye felt like Beyonce finally meeting Janet Jackson! We embraced like long lost friends. Eye smiled so big and huge tears fell down my face. Eye was trembling. This was my hero. One of them.

"It's so nice to meet you!" Eye said, not quite knowing what to say.

"Eye know, young man. From our many Facebook chats and emails to this very moment. It's an honor to meet you."

"Thank you E Lynn."

"Eye see your table is set up."

"Yes, it is."

"After the meet and greet, Eye want to talk to you about your table."

"Ok."

"Enjoy."

He squeezed my hand.

Eye squeezed it back.

*As the fans poured in and took* a seat he was signing autographs and had his assistant handling book sales. She was a nice white lady, very courteous. He spoke to his fans and took pictures and Eye just took notes.

Dwight Powell (Sizzle Miami Owner) walked in and spoke to E Lynn and Eye was daydreaming again. Of one day being a big book star. But it would never happen. Not to a Niggah from Goulds. A few of my dreams went up in smoke at the thought. Maybe Eye was kidding myself.

Eye took E Lynn THE KING OF EROTICA 1 and CALL HER QUEEN HATSHEPSUT. He was the very first one to get a rough draft copy of HATSHEPSUT and he said, "Pharoah you gotta let me buy them. Eye want you to have the money."

"Thanks."

We turned and took a photo. "And you autographed my books?" E. Lynn asked, his brow raising.

"Yes."

He smiled. "Eye just want to say Eye am very proud of what you're doing. You remind me of myself, Pharoah. You took control of your career and made people realize you're here. Stop letting small things get to you. Eye've been following you for three years, young man! And you're *fabulous*!"

"Oh my God! Thank you."

"No one is doing what you're doing. Eye could never write your material. You're going to be a star, Pharoah."

"Thank you."

"Eye'm gonna be your mentor. Eye'm going to discipline you. Eye will get my editor to look over your book and see what we can do…"

"Eye appreciate it, E Lynn. But *no.* Eye want to do it on my own."

"Eye admire you. More than you realize."

"Eye don't want people saying Eye got a book deal because of you. Then Eye will be in your shadow."

He had a warm glow about his face. "And Eye so understand that."

"Thanks."

*"Eye'm going to read these.* Come on. Eye don't normally do this but for you it would be my *pleasure.*"

"What's that?" Eye held my breath.

He turned to my friend holding my camera, and held both of my books up midair with a huge Kool-Aid smile.

OH MY GOD!

Eye hugged him.

FLASH!

The passing of the torch was documented.

He would die two months later. Two days after our last Facebook conversation.

And Eye took his death very hard.

*A few weeks after The Sizzle ended,* Eye broke out in hives. Huge bumps were all over my body. Eye panicked. Eye drove myself to the hospital and was checked out. Turned out that the Bactrim medicine Eye was allergic too. So the doctor discontinued it, and gave me something that healed me of the hives. Eye think they gave me Benadryl, which worked instantly. A few days later Eye got a call from my good friend (with her cute self) Cortes Maria. Eye met her through my ex boyfriend Angelou back in the day so we were well acquainted. "What are you doing in a week?"

"Nothing, why wassup?"

"Eye want you to come to a revival for those living with HIV/AIDS at Bethel church."

"Ok. But remind me."

"Eye sure will. Eye'll even come pick you up."

"Bet."

*The day came quicker than Eye* thought. Eye was a little uneasy because Eye didn't want to publicly tell the church of my affliction, but since Eye told Facebook Eye was like why not. If it saves lives Eye'm all for it. Pastor Carlos

Malone called me to the stage to a near packed house and Eye spoke into the mic, telling everyone my testimony and my struggle. Pastor anointed me, prayed over me and Eye felt something open up inside me. Eye went to bed that night feeling better than Eye ever felt. It wasn't till a month and a half later, when my test results came back, that Eye realized that God sent a miracle. Eye dropped from 1.3 million antibodies in my blood to 2000. And my CD4 cell count surpassed 200.

Eye didn't have AIDS anymore. Back to HIV status.

And a few months after that HIV was nearly undetectable in my blood.

## *Did you ever confront your ex*
## *For giving you HIV?*

*Lord Jennings*

*Near the end of 2009 Eye took myself* out to eat at The BBQ Pit, just to have some time to myself, since Eye'm always writing. Eye needed this, really needed this time to myself, and Eye was glad Eye came out to grab a bite to eat. Place was crowded as hell and the good thing about it was that *nobody* knew who Eye was. No one knew Eye was THE KING OF EROTICA.

A handsome male waiter came up to me and asked what did Eye wanna drink.

"A strawberry daiquiri," Eye said with a smile.

My phone wailed and Eye answered. "Sup."

"Pharoah! What are you doing?" my friend asked.

"Eye'm grabbing a bite to eat."

"You're eating?"

"Um, yea."

"Eye mean you're always writing and shit."

"Eye do have to eat." Eye smiled, looking around.

"Where are you?"

"The BBQ Pit."

He grew quiet. "The BBQ Pit *where*?"

"The only one down in this damn area, why?"

"Oh, no."

Eye was alarmed. "Oh, no, *what*?"

"Your *ex* works there. He's there *now*."

"Who?" Eye narrowed my eyes.

"The one that gave you HIV."

Darkness colored my face.

"*What?*" *Eye was looking* around, seeing if Eye could spot him, my heart pounding.

"Pharoah, if you see him don't let him get to you."

"Eye'm good. Eye'm not worried."

"He's your ex."

"He gave me HIV."

"Benjamin has learned."

"What? You're his publicist and spokesperson?"

"No. Eye'm gonna call him."

"For what?"

"To let him know Eye will beat his ass *if* he says anything out the way to you."

Eye rolled my eyes. "Eye'm a big boy. Shit, at least he *has* a job."

"Yup. This is the longest he *ever* kept a job."

"Eye'm about to get off the phone. Eye gotta go."

Eye hung up.

Eye changed tables.

Eye sat at the front table, by the entrance door. Didn't like the feeling so Eye switched to the middle table and let the waiter know where Eye was.

"Welcome to The BBQ Pit," he said and Eye was like "Dude, Eye already ordered a strawberry daiquiri."

"Damn, that's right. It's coming right up."

"Is Benjamin on the clock?" Eye asked amicably.

"Yes."

Eye smiled coyly. "Eye wanna request him as my waiter."

"Can Eye get you…?"

"No. Let Benjamin get it."

"Eye'll go and get him."

"*No, Pharoah. Eye'm not serving* you." Benjamin still looked good as hell, sexy as all out doors. Eye fell into his eyes again and tried to fight it. Okay, Pharoah, this was the man that hurt you beyond logic and reason. He was nervous as hell, and Eye took full advantage of it.

"*Hi*, Benjamin. That's not the way you greet the man you gave HIV!"

His eyes darted all over the place. "Pharoah. Eye'm sorry."

Eye wasn't yelling and Eye didn't talk loud. Eye spoke at a tone only he and Eye could hear and he was about to shake out his skin.

"*My* bad," Eye said. …"Can Eye have a strawberry daiquiri, Benjamin?"

"With an extra shot of Bacardi," he suggested, and my heart fluttered—then dropped deader than my soft penis. "Eye remember just how you love it. This is your favorite drink." He smiled, trying to butter my bread; bitch, please!

Eye smiled. "*Two* extra shots." Eye stopped smiling. Eye fucking him—and not in a good way. So much bitterness and hatred surged through me Eye had to yawn to keep from going the hell off.

"Coming right up."

He walked off.

☯

*Eye called my* dawg back.

"Sup, Pharoah."

"Eye'm good. Sipping a daiquiri."

"You love that drink don't you?"

"Yea, beyotch Eye do."

"Don't you have a book to write?"

"Yup."

"Where are you?"

"*Duh*! The BBQ Pit."

"Pharoah no...You're *still* there?"

"Yup." Eye sipped through the straw, dangerously mugging Benjamin, who was talking to customer's with a big ole smile. Like he didn't knowingly give me an incurable disease and the more he smiled the more Eye died inside.

Blinded by anger and vengeance, Eye hung up.

*Benjamin came back.*

"You're finished your drink already?"

"Yup. Want another one. It tasted like shit."

"It did?" He seemed disappointed.

"Yup. Tasted like medicine." Eye shot my cuffs. "It tasted just like Epzicom when you take it with water. You know that nasty, lingering medicine taste in your throat?"

"Pharoah, please baby."

"Eye'm *not* your freaking baby!"

"Pharoah…Eye'm still in love with you."

"Eye'll take another daiquiri. Make sure it's full of multi vitamins, will ya'. And send the receipt to ADAP at the clinic, via Tabitha will ya'?"

He brought me another drink, grim-faced and quiet.

Eye sipped it. It tasted so good. *Yummy*!

"Ugh!" Eye slammed the glass audibly. People looked. "Ugh! Yuk!"

Wide eyes. "What now?"

"This is worse!"

"Pharoah!"

"Now it tastes like Zithromax and Norvir! Who is mixing these drinks?" Eye kept wolfing it down, double shots of Bacardi. Didn't take much for me to get tipsy. Eye was already high on a blunt.

"This is my job!"

"Your *job*? Your *job*?" Eye asked, standing up, tears falling down my face. "Job? Don't talk to me about your *job* when you tried to sabotage my book career!"

"Pharoah, *please.* Eye am so sorry for this. Eye never meant to hurt you. Eye was so angry that you didn't appreciate me in our relationship."

The Manager came over.

"Sir. Are you ok?" he asked me.

"Did Eye ask for government assistance?" Eye asked with an attitude, glaring at him. "Piss off!"

"Sir, calm down."

"You calm the fuck down. Eye don't give a damn!" Eye glared at Benjamin. He wanted to embrace me, but he knew better. "Eye *loved* you," Eye went on, glaring at Benjamin even more dangerously, my hands fists. "And you fucked me over."

My dawg, Lethal—the one Eye called on my cell phone—came *flying* through the door.

Eye was a beast. "Eye ain't no punk bitch! You pussy lipped *bitch*! *You* gave me HIV! EYE HATE YOU!"

Lethal wrapped his arms around me from the back.

"Pharaoh. *Calm* down," he whispered in my ear and Eye shook in his arms, afraid of life, didn't want to breathe so Eye held my breath.

"Pharoah, Eye am so sorry man. Truly. All jokes aside. Please forgive me," said Benjamin.

"Forgive you?" The place was quiet as a church mouse during communion. "*Forgive* you? Eye was committed to you! That was my *job!* You betrayed me!"

"Pharoah, come on man let's go," said Lethal and Eye didn't budge, couldn't stop glaring at Benjamin. Eye wanted to cut his limbs off and hang them as Christmas Ornaments.

"Lethal let me go!" Eye pushed him over the table and flipped the table the over. Now Eye'm dead inside. The King of Erotica. The part of me that protects Pharoah and Dapharoah69. He didn't have emotion!

"SCREW YOU BOTH!"

"Pharoah. Eye didn't put a gun to your head and make you have unprotected sex with me," Benjamin said, and he was right.

Eye got all the way in his face. "You're *right!* You put your dick deep inside me…*leaned* into my face when Eye was most vulnerable and you said 'Eye love you. Eye will never hurt you' and you made my immune system start the plummet towards utter failure from the explosion of your inner hatred for me. For not *appreciating* you enough. You was stealing my money then infecting me for nearly two and a half years while you were boning the infested bitch that gets off on pissing in mop water. That's the crime of the century. Tab is on you. Drinks tasted like shit." Eye turned to the people. "Make sure your man wears a condom before you let him fuck you because men like this late trick will purposely give you HIV. Enjoy your meal."

Eye walked towards the door.

"Pharoah! Eye'm asking you to forgive me!" Benjamin called after me.

Eye paused, tears of anger burning me up. Head bowed 'cause Eye wanted to kill him. Eye rubbed my arms like the white Hoes in the soap operas. Eye looked up at God.

"Is this funny, God?"

*"Pharoah." He put his hands on my* shoulders from behind and Eye didn't look back. Eye cringed when he touched me. "Please, Pharaoh. Eye'm asking you to truly forgive me. Eye forgave myself for infecting you. That was deceitful and unconscionable. God forgave me, Pharoah. *Didn't* you say God is your number one? You beat me up already. You embarrassed me. Ok. Eye'm suffering too. Forgive me."

"You got infected from the Winn Dixie Piss Mop Niggah and you brought that shit to me. You were taking meds behind my back, Benjamin, prolonging your life and you didn't tell me a thing. You kept infecting me because you were afraid Eye would leave your ass."

"Pharoah!"

Eye faced him, grabbed his face and planted my lips on his quivering lips and my tears wet our lips up and Eye hugged him, shaking from the cold and some folks dabbing their eyes and a few men had their heads lowered and the manager didn't say anything.

Eye pulled away. "Eye *forgive* you, Benjamin."

"Thank you so much!"

Eye kissed him again. "And Eye forget you. Forever."

And Eye was out the door.

*Eye stood by someone's Nissan Maxima.*

And Eye burst open.

Eye sunk to my knees and balled for the old and the new. The world was a cold place, my daddy hated me, Mama hated me, family hated me and Eye was tired of living for others so Eye made a decision to start living for myself. Eye didn't know what to think or feel. Eye was snatched off the ground and Benjamin and Lethal hugged me tightly and Eye cried so hard, screaming into their arms. Eye held on to them for dear life and they wouldn't let me go.

“Pharoah. Eye am truly sorry for what Eye did to you. For giving you HIV. But your life is much bigger than anything we ever had. There is a reason for your life. God gave you a purpose and you fulfill a part of that purpose every time you sit behind a computer and write books. Don’t let your hate for me compromise your legacy.”

He was right.  So right then and there Eye released the hate. How did Eye successfully do that?  Easy.  By giving it to JEHOVAH. And that’s when Satan tested my faith.

Nearly costing me my life.

## *Did any of your ex's ever attack you*
## *For dumping them?*

*Lord Jennings*

Eye went home after leaving The BBQ Pit and was tired. Eye caught Niggah-itis a little early, so Eye was going to fall asleep in front of the TV tonight. "Niggah-itis" (Niggah.Eye.tis) was a word that meant a Niggah ate and was full and wanted to curl up and go to sleep.

Thinking of Benjamin and his asking for forgiveness, Eye walked through the valley of the shadow of death to my bedroom. Eye didn't look left or right. Because Eye'd become accustomed to my home; well this was my *homeboy's* home, but Eye helped pay bills and sometimes had a room there when Eye needed to get away for a couple days…so it was just *like* my home. Eye've become *too* predictable lately and that wasn't a plus. Eye really needed a change.

Exhausted, Eye sat down. *Quietly.* On my bed. Staring at nothing and everything in the bedroom was staring at me. Looked ahead. He smiled, Eye smiled. My eyes lit up; *his* eyes lit up. My reflection from the mirror kept me company. Eye smiled, even though there wasn't anything to smile about. My reflection and Eye. *Always* happy to see each other.

Eye heard a noise.

Coming from the living room.

But Eye dismissed it rather quickly.

Didn't hear the sound when Eye walked through the valley of the shadow of death, so it could be the house settling.

Eye heard the noise again.

This time it was a little louder than the first breach of sound security in my homeboy's home.

Alarmed, Eye stood up. My back facing my reflection. Trapped in the glass. Eye tip-toed to the living room.

It was so dark. Eye could see, from the glow of the crescent moon…the bottoms of the end and low tables…a few photos of my boy and his friends at various attractions around the country on the table.

"Seems quiet. Probably nothing," Eye concluded.

But the silence alarmed me even more. The silence was just betrayed by the Judas Factor: two unfamiliar sounds 5 seconds after each other. As long as Eye stayed with my boy Eye never heard sounds like this before.

"Somebody's in this house!" Eye was on the defensive end instantly, ready for battle. But against what? Eye had home court advantage. And was still on guard. My heart was pounding

"So you're not *talking*?" The more Eye walked towards the living room sofa in the corner of the room, devoid of the moon's glow, the hairs stood on my entire body.

A faint smell of cologne went up my nose and was getting stronger as Eye slowly tip toed to the lamp and Eye turned it on and Eye saw him.

On the sofa. Under a blanket; linen pulled up above his nose, just under his evil eyes. Peering at me. He didn't blink. He stared *dangerously.* He bats them a few times. Taunting me.

*Intruder! Intruder!*

Benjamin jumped off the chair, covering my face with the blanket, catching me off guard. And he pushed me into the wall, BOOM!

The pain shooting from head to toe rendered me speechless. My forehead was slammed into a framed photo and Eye snatched the blanket off my face.

My ex said, "Didn't Eye tell you if you ever gave your body to someone else Eye was going to *kill* you, Pharoah? And you come to my job showing off?"

"Oh my God!"

He snatched the lamp from the wall and it was completely dark.

Oh, No!

We're silhouettes in the moonlight. He punched me in the back and a hard fist to the middle of my face.

Eye stumbled backward again, and Eye felt his fist flying towards me yet again based on the ratio of punches Eye already received.

Eye ducked, and his fist slammed into the glass of the photo.

It fell off the wall.

"*Ow*!" he screamed aloud.

He's in front of me. Blew his cover. Eye ran at him full force, fearing my life and my trembling body crashed into his like Miami Rugby Football.

We fell face first on the tile.

*"Ow shit!"*

*"Fuck!"*

The floor hurt us both. Eye was disoriented. Didn't go as Eye planned. "You belong to me!" he said, obsessed.

He rolled on top of me.

"GET OFF ME! It's over!" Eye yelled in his face, twisting and turning.

"You break up with me by sending a text message?"

"You gave me HIV you ugly bitch! You are the one that made love to me and left! You were the one out to get me because Eye didn't appreciate you!"

Eye tried to turn so Eye could spring up with my knees and hands, but the minute Eye did that he put his hands around my neck and slid up deep inside me, hard, with no rubber or lube and it was like a hot poker in a pig's ass.

You run and you squealed, but Eye couldn't run or squeal. He's choking me to death, wide eyed and drooling from the mouth. Eye was trying to breathe, but couldn't even gasp for air. All air supply was cut off, and Eye was getting numb, nauseated and sleepy. Eye was falling into an euphoric state.

"Eye'm gonna infect you again! Eye hope you die!"

He went in deeper and Eye didn't feel anything. My head was light as a feather and my mind dissolved to black, gradually. Who am Eye? Where was Eye from? Eye exhaled weakly and he loosened his grip and pulled out of me, crying and sobbing.

"Pharoah! Pharaoh! Pharoah! Baby? Oh, no what have Eye done to you? Eye didn't mean to kill you, Pharoah! Pharoah!"

That's when Eye struck.

Eye sat up, biting into his nose so hard Eye tried to chew it off. He's shell shocked by my attack. Came outta nowhere. Blood all over the place and in my mouth, but Eye kept biting. We all came from the Blood of Christ so his blood was no exception. Eye pushed him away from me and Eye hopped up to my feet. He's screaming his Oh, God's.

"MY NOSE! MY NOSE!"

Eye stomped him with my feet.

"You crazy bitch!" Eye threw his useless ass out of my homeboy's crib. Opened the window. Eye screamed for the neighbors to hear.

"HELP HELP HELP! HE'S TRYING TO RAPE ME HELP HELP HELP!"

Covering his nose, he ran up the block to his truck, parked behind a huge tree down the street.

Good riddance!

TENEILE JAMES AND PHAROAH, BARNES AND NOBLE, KENDALL & 88TH STREET

*Tell me about being*

*In love with a $tripper*

*Lord Jenning$*

# EYE'M IN LOVE WITH A $TRIPPER

***Eye wish the good ole days were*** still here. Instead…those days took off the rain coat, left it at the door and had me slipping all over the threshold of the past. Both sexually and physically. Can't let it go because it has a threshold on my tall ass. If the good ole days were back a certain youngster wouldn't have brought sexy back when sexy was a state of mind not Janet's breast. They shoulda fingerprinted her ripped bustier, but because they're rich they get right on by. They fingerprint me even when Eye'm cashing a check. Justin's fingerprints would be all over it. Not Janet's. But blackness always takes the down fall to the color of Saltine crackers.

When did it ever leave? Slavery? Why was a tit the focal point of every news show on the planet earth? A breast? Who knew a black tit had so much power. Yet the incident had everyone from closeted—and those flamboyant, claustrophobic—homosexuals to on the low Pa$tor$— who loved wearing panties under those thick robes—putting their *sexy up* till *congregational* pimps released the threshold of the recession. Simple home economics. Yet when faced with adversity something snapped in me. Things were all good before Eye got saved, yet when Eye was dipped in cold water in a white, dingy sheet—the Pa$tor almost dropped me, too, gotta mean something—giving my life to God, to be "saved," things didn't look up. Things were harder. The stench stronger. Had to strain while taking a dump, my insides constipated with everything but the right things.

Breaking a sweat. The toilet, clogged. Stock in toilet paper rose from my extensive eating during clinical depression. Yet Eye still pray, pray and pray. And my piss-colored Mama still hated me. Mama hates me.

Daddy does, too. And Eye had no memories of him.

He emotionally lied to me over the phone about 6 times outta my 34 ½ years breathing on earth, and that didn't count as memories. You're disqualified.

No matter what people, you gotta keep your mind on God when you're going broke, losing it all, and suffocating from lack of energy and air. Family ain't what it used to be. After getting an extended family Eye felt like Eye separated from my immediate family during slavery. Forced to love other people and successfully finding your place. Friends seemed genuine and bent over backward for you.

It wasn't God's fault for the consequences of our actions and bad decisions. Satan was real, and yes he exists. Without evil…*love* can never balance itself out. That's the *earthly* chess board set up anyway. Wealthy, *opposing* forces battling for global supremacy and using us—We The People, Four Scores and Complete *Bullshit* Ago—to see who check mate's the King. Both sides of the Chess Board stands a supernatural King. The *King of* KINGS, *Lord of* LORDS Vs. THE KING OF DARKNESS. Life was about God vs. Satan. And who would turn out the victor—how many lives will be sacrificed from controlled natural disasters at the expense of picking and choosing the *wrong* side…

Thanks Eve for biting the forbidden fruit with your breasts all out in front of The Serpent (and yes the serpent knew she had a coochie before *she* knew she had a pussy)—and Eye was being *sarcastic.*

Funny how a naked woman activated life after Satan told God he could win more souls. Her Free Will choice, something both God and Satan knew she was going to use, opened the door for the key players—civilization…us, me you, them—people. Eve and Adam banged day in and day out. Eye knew that coochie was ruined for pushing out all those damn children if the earth is reaching 7 billion people.

The Devil's challenge to God was agreed upon *before* The Garden of Eden was created. What's a game without *players*?

What's Chess without game pieces?

And instructions? —The Law

*Eye researched this heavily* and discovered some other hidden truths about the Bible that made me turn away from it. *But* in my heart Eye know and believe Jesus died for the sins of man and nothing will change that.

A demon possessed Eve to defy God's command by biting the "forbidden fruit," and it wasn't a shiny red apple.

Eye thought about this when Eye was sitting in church one Sunday after Eye released The King of Erotica 2 The Crown 7 months before. Eye was in a bad mood. Eye didn't know any of those folks, and half of them kept staring at me.

"Eye seen his faces somewhere before…" some woman whispered from behind me.

"Girl Eye heard he's an author."

"Oh, shit!" she whispered excitedly. "I think Eye know who that is. As a matter of fact…"

"Hey, King!" the woman said aloud, attracting attention. She winked, and stuck out her hand. I cupped it. Kissed it. Looked up into her misty eyes with a smile.

"How are you pretty lady? Like your dress!"

Looked like shit. But who was Eye to judge?

"Welcome to ________ Baptist Church! What an Honor! Look at God work! Yes! Yes!"

A few people sucked their teeth at her, rolling her eyes.

Eye heard another verbal scribe.

"Chile, she just wants to fuck him before the other girs get to him…"

So she was the church slut. Eye still treated her the way Eye wanted to be treated. What she did with her coochie was her business, unless she was gonna let me hit. And if she did she wasn't gonna piss or shit the same when King-ah-*Conda* was done rummaging warm holes.

Eye woke up on the wrong side of the bed. Eye wanted to go home. Eye had a book to write. Eye started the King of

Erotica 3, but didn't write anything concrete as of yet. Should Eye write an outline? Eye stifled a yawn.

"Huh, you were saying something?" Eye said to the lippy female and she tucked her chin back.

Good. Go sniff somebody else's ass and get off my nuts. It took me a minute to realize she spoke to me during the Pastor's tired sermon, in my opinion. He gave her a knowing look and she said down.

"There is only one King in this house, and that's God," The Pastor said…

And Eye *inwardly* smiled at him.

***He went on preaching about*** the Garden of Eden, and lost me with the red apple. That crap kills me every time the forbidden fruit (oh, let me put that that in [makes quote gestures with my fingers] quotation marks for the conservatives) is *depicted* that way. What gave man the right to place the fruit of their choice in the story?

Made me wonder what other fill in the blanks they did in the Bible's scriptures.

And Eye'm not supposed to be skeptical of what Eye'm reading?

Hmmm. Where's Arsenio Hall when Eye need him. That's what Eye see, that's what Eye've come to understand, and no church in America ever taught me that, and never mentioned it. About a demon possibly possessing Eve.

Eve knew she had tits and a coochie and weakness in her flesh before she returned to her husband, and that's another thing. How were they married? In the Great Book it never depicts him getting on one knee, like a lot of these men and women do for the ones they are married to now.

The Pastor raised that in his sermon, saying (to the crowd's delight, boy he had them by the breasts and balls…and their purses, check books and wallets (oh and debit cards, too!) its mandatory that a man marries a woman (and these days they are not damn virgins, either). That when he finds his bride-to-be he has to get on one knee.

"Adam didn't," Eye said and a few people were laughing, but the Pastor wasn't and Eye didn't care. The Forbidden Fruit wasn't an apple. "They didn't have a ceremony before two families, either. They had no choice but to forsake all others. They were the only two on the planet, Eye think the important thing to realize," Eye said, "Is that there were no…Pastors present in the Garden either."

"Shut up, Pharoah," The Pastor said, making like he was joking. "You sound ridiculous." Eye tucked my chin back. *Lawd.* Is he *trying* to straighten me? Is he trying to check me in front of his church?

Here goes. "Have you some babies and tell *them* to shut up."

He narrowed his eyes. "My kids are grown…"

Eye gazed at his wife. "Well, looks like its time to put up the Thigh Master and take off those shoes so you can give your husband some barefoot and pregnant sex."

The place burst into laughter.

I grinned.

"You are tacky, just like those dull erotica books you write, clown. You are a clown if you think…"

"Yet you bought my first one, and Eye autographed it, hypocrite. You once told me your favorite story in the book was The Golden Masks…you know…about the orgy in the church!"

We stared at each other for a few moments allowing the shock and the gasps to filter around the room.

*Don't act so shocked. A few of you read the book, too!*

Eye looked at his wife again—she's the front runner for the Holier than Thou Awards, a non existent award given to wives that didn't have a clue about self-respect.

It didn't matter if you saved your coochie for your future dude; what do you think sucking every cock in America letting men eat your coochie until you nut on their lip, leaving many of their wives to slap them in the face for coming home smelling like a fresh shower.

Didn't matter that you spruced yourself up and thought you had it all covered. And you did, up until she leaned in for a kiss and she froze in place inhaling some other bitch's pussy, and her eyes zeroed in on your mustache.

Yup. She told me all about it the day before Eye came to this church. She had some bomb coochie too. My nuts felt like real people getting college degrees from the brain she domed on my swollen mushroom head.

And she swallowed. Eye made sure none got in her weave.

You spent *all* that time showering and making up lies, and you forgot to brush your teeth, or at least gargle with mouth wash, and not that cheap Family Dollar bullshit either—did you at least look yourself over in the mirror…um, No, You *Didn't*!

That taught me a lot about reflections and images. A Niggah ain't concerned with how he looked when he's caught up in some shit.

As long as he looked and smelled good—and that coochie was good, and that nut was one trillion times better, and felt better than your girl and your wife's uptight, lippy, won't-shut-the-fuck-up-for-two-seconds pussy (which felt more like sticking your dick in an ant pile—then *Niggah,* the rest is history.

When you get caught up, fellahs, do me one favor: Keep your head high. Hold it as high as you can. And piss on regrets. Sometimes you gotta do what you gotta do when you're married to a woman that was cold, selfish and pathetic. So stop blowing my cell phone up with the specifics and particulars. You walked out m life when Eye was 21, *remember*?

She wanna trap you in a baseless marriage make life hell for her—and *no,* Eye'm not talking about abuse. Eye didn't believe in beating women at all, even though Eye've said Eye'd knock one to Kingdom Come if she put her hands on me—and since then Eye won't ever even do that.

Eye'm talking about go get you some new pussy, but get to know the pussy before you do your thing, and strap it up.

You got one life to live, don't waste it arguing over something that can't and won't ever be saved.

And ask to see HIV papers before you stick your penis in something that might turn out to be electrical sockets when it shocks the hell out of you when your test results come back *positive* for HIV, or Herpes…

But in your case *don't* shake, Tommy. Eye changed your name. Your name ain't Tommy, but you know good and damn well who the hell Eye'm talking about, Pastor Tommy…Eye sent you an advanced copy of this book while editing it—the rage that boiled inside my soul *hotter* than melted lava bubbling beneath my feet—GET IT TOGETHER, PHAROAH...IT' IN THE PAST—with this page bookmarked, *suckah.*

How can you tell me Eye'm going to Hell for being with a dude…when you're an *atheist* that went to Theology School as a career choice when you realized how sexy and powerful that cash cow looked under the religion umbrella—not to mention you were boning since Eye graduated in 1995 (started when Eye was 16 years old).

Oh, *crap*—and this is the best part…he was on the Down Low. And may the church say Amen….Amen…!

Um, Brother Wilson—*Pharoah,* where are you going? Services aren't over yet. What? Eye'm an atheist that cons money, cars, and lavish gifts from *congregation*?

"Um, that would be *correct*—congregation. The first three letters made me skeptical about the validity of 'church' since Eye was a kid, but Eye never really *said* anything because, you know, adults thought they knew everything and never listened to a word I said when eye was child. We got it under control, but all around me, and in my home, was blood-curdling chaos…and Eye suffered in the darkness, Eye suffered in silence…"

They were looking at me, his "congregation," root word (and Eye'm being funny) "Con."

Eye'm amidst a group of con artists, polished and molded through the Pastor's sermons, laced with a certain hidden agenda, subliminal preaching, who would have thought, Pastor Tommy. They were created, their minds no longer their own, but completely in the pastor's hands, only they didn't know it. He was King of his Church, an untouchable man that had 4 babies out of wed lock and had the gall to stand on his stage and judge me for having bestselling books out.

"You know what, Pastor Tommy. I have something else to say, and then Eye'm out this bitch, for real." Eye held my hands up, looking sternly into random eyes, with a vigor Eye *never* knew Eye possessed. Eye wrote books that touched people, Eye'm King of my Creations, and that means just as much to me as his fake ass preaching. "Ey mean no disrespect, but let me tell ya'll…"

"Pharoah, don't go there, okay? Don't! You pick the wrong time to bring that in here…your stupid books nobody cares about…"

*"He's very talented,"* somebody said. *Thank you.*

Eye had no time for ego boosters. "Pastor, you had me up until you substituted an apple in place of the forbidden fruit."

*"Eye have some of his work, he's amazing!"*

Eye grinned. "You were *saying*…Eye'm in your church and already your faithful followers are dwindling one by one…" Eye looked around. "Free books on me!"

There were cheers and whistles.

He jumped down from the podium and got in my face with the untrustworthy smile of a politician crushing for gay sex and being caught.

The cheers stopped.

Several people were confused as the bigger picture unfolded. The Ushers were on alert. "Your church isn't as tight as you thought it was, huh, Pastor Tommy…?

He didn't say a thing, but he wanted to kill me and it was all over his face as his façade begin to shake, and we felt the tremors, Pastor Tommy and Eye, and Eye thought about it…what Eye was about to do…what my heart told me to do…

Eye thought long and hard about character assassination.

Eye spend so much time writing and creating characters that Eye never *thought* Eye could assassinate them at will.

Oh, boy. There it goes. The peak of my rage, and disappointment in myself. He invited me to his church on Facebook when Eye put my second book out. Eye had reservations because Eye haven't seen him since Eye was 21. He broke it off with me, so suddenly. When Eye yearned him the most he cut all ties. Took me out to eat and broke my heart over lobster. Eye lowered my head when he didn't even say good bye. He stood up and walked out my life. And Eye had to wash dishes because Eye didn't have the money to pay for my food. He always paid.

He walked away from years of sex, dancing in the flames of the darkness (with his wife participating).

And now Eye was face to face with him; mad that Eye didn't stay away; *upset* that Eye convinced myself Eye was ready to see the man that's been fucking me since Eye was 16 years old (and he was 38 years old at the time).

Eye once said eye forgave him…and Eye realized now that Eye didn't.

Because Eye needed closure.

"Let's cut the bullshit, okay?" Eye said in my Janet Poetic Justice voice, and a few folks started laughing.

"Eye don't find shit funny!"

It stopped.

"Eye have something to get off my chest, and Eye can't say that Eye totally blame you for your lack of intelligence, despite your doctorates, but one thing strikes me as odd. Jesus—open your Bibles to Pharoah Chapter 1 Verse Get a Damn Clue—never bashed gays…Ponder that for a second. Jesus never bashed gays. That contradicts that Leviticus chapter entirely. Look around, people, open your damn eyes. For real. Are we wearing sandals and sheets and writing on stone tabs and feeding Kings their fruits and veggies? Hasn't the Leviticus Era come to pass? Amen? So be it?"

Pastor Tommy glared at me, but didn't say a thing.

"When Jesus was hung on the cross did he die for the sins of all man? Even the gays? Doesn't that make the Leviticus Era null and void? If you call me an abomination one more damn time indirectly, by saying Eye'm going to hell it's going to be on and poppin, Pastor Tommy."

"You put on a good show, Pharoah. And Eye'm resisting the urge to throw you out of y church."

"Correction, Bum. This is God's House!"

"Amen!"

"Hallelujah!"

"Come as you are!"

"You heard that, Pastor Tommy? Eye'll give you a minute to pick your mouth up off the floor. Eye have every desire to ruin you where you stand. Eye see now that making more chaos conflicts the chaos we created together, but Eye was only 16 back then. Dumb as hell."

The tears fell down my face and Eye wiped them away quickly, keeping my head up. "My father failed me, and Eye searched for one on you and thought Eye found him…and then you betrayed me, and you know what Eye'm talking about, and suddenly Eye didn't have a father…but Eye had a lover, a controlling one, with a controlling wife. Both of you should have beat my ass and refrained from touching my body, bringing me pleasure…"

He grabbed me by the upper shoulders, his eyes red as hell. He was beyond angry. He was so shocked by y confession and so embarrassed he died where he stood, instantly. His eyes were manic, and he did his best to disguise it.

"Eye would hope you forgive me, Pharoah." He walked past me at an angry mob. His loyal followers turned on him in an instant. Eye was amazed myself. One minute they praised a false idol, and in the next they banished him from being their leader, many of them walking out of his church and joined *another* one

You didn't like your church? Those church hoes (most of them in the choir) being too nosey? Niggahs that smell like boo boo *won't* stop asking for your phone number?

*Find* another church home.

That simple.

As for me that was the last straw. Eye was completely done with organized religion. Eye will praise God from the comfort of my home and my ten percent tithes can go towards my $750 rent. Eye didn't owe nobody, especially not man, mortals like me, an explanation. Eye didn't have to be treated like this. Eye was good with you till you started preaching lies. The forbidden fruit was not an apple, and when are you going to tell your wife that Sally, her sister, is *pregnant* with your child?

Hmmm. Pastor Tommy, how do you *invite* me to your church with the intention of humiliating me? But Eye got to you first, 'ey?

Battling myself internally, I turned to face him He looked like a chicken with his head cut off. The things they were asking him was too grotesque to type.

Eye was sitting on the front pew with my legs open and an arm dangling over the back of the pew. Eye lowered my forehead, with my eyes up on him trying to calm his "congregation" down.

Eye grinned like a Cheshire cat.

Con your way out of that.

*And for the congregation, the Popularity Contestants…how does it feel to receive your Sunday sermons from an atheist that served ya'll green eggs and ham in exchange for your hard earned dollar?*

*Arseniooooo Halllll! Front and center, damn it!*

*There's some things that's making me go Hmmm…*

**After about 15 minutes—people** were leaving—Eye stood up and brushed lint off my suit jacket, and walked through the angry mob of folk. Some were all up in the pastor's face, and Eye was walking out of his life. The way he walked out of mine when Eye was 21. When Eye told him Eye wasn't giving him any more free booty. If he wanted me he had to commit and he was married with a wife that couldn't keep my dick out of her mouth, yet he broke my heart to return to her every night, knowing his heart was with me and his dick belonged to his wife.

So why did you look deeply into my eyes when you were digging me out and said it belonged to me. Pharoah?

…And when you climaxed you called out her name.

And Eye was tired.

You lusted after deceit and money, and you admitted this to me, Pastor Tommy. Tisk, tisk, tisk…Eye still have a pair of your boxers. The ones your wife bought you on your 18$^{th}$ Anniversary. Come onnn, Pastor Tommy!

You don't remember? The ones you made me wear when you ate me in ways you never dreamed of eating your wife…and Eye was all of 16 years old…

All your doctorates and crap on the walls you flaunted before my eyes when Eye visited your church, at the behest of your wife that was a friend of one of my school teachers at Southridge.

You shoulda gargled with Listerine, the Grey Goose and Hennessy of Mouth Washes. And maybe your wife wouldn't have smelled another woman on your mustache…when in fact she was tasting me, and Sally.

What do you think taking in the dookie shoot meant—and this is for your wife. You saved your coochie for the man you married. Ain't the same. You basically gave him unpopped *cherry* pussy and the minute he got to enjoy it, appreciating and loving you for letting him be the first to deflower you on your Honeymoon he gotta wake up with shitty sheets tangled between both sets of legs. So focused on saving the pussy, and gave your husband a ruined ass in the process. How does it feel to wear Depend and you're not 60 yet? And Eye've been in the game sine Eye was 6 and Eye didn't wear draws.

That's because Eye have Walls.

*Life. Seemed like Satan was* winning based on those misleading music videos, Hollywood movies and popular entertainment, but we all know God got this War. God was the Artist of War. Satan was just a game piece who never got what he wanted for Christmas. Because even on that pagan holiday we celebrate Jesus' Birthday—the actual day it falls on Eye could care less about. In my heart Christmas means that, but Eye'm doing research . So Satan still gets no attention. Boo hoo hoo.

So he toys with our souls for power, control and a false sense of supremacy. And if he gotta drown your son in a swimming pool to get you to turn away from God then that's what he'll do and have done and continues to do every single day on planet earth. Jesus stored a sword in his mouth clad in gold and white right by God's side.

God is love. Satan is hate. The thin line in the form of angel wings/black horns was what we were created on.

We were created then separated from the creation. Like God did night and day. Water and land.

Your Eye on the Word unabridged perfection. Don't let them separate you from God. They'll damn sure try.

Everyone from certain family members to a few lifelong friends have betrayed me. But Eye brushed them off like dust, for which they all shall surely return. Eye have lost some very special people. All over writing a book. Creating a destiny. Being fearless and hungry.

A full belly never sought hunger. And an empty belly never asked for air. Maybe sustenance vs. substance. This is what my life has become.

Mama want me out the house Eye helped her maintain since Eye was a small child; home was where the heart was, not in 2*7*1 *W 1**th Avenue. My heart told me something in confidence. Said it was a message from a dream. Said Mama removed me from her Will and her heart long before she kicked me out her home. *Now* with my eyes on God Eye gotta build from scratch—*zero*—and *find* my own way…it's really cool if you think about it. Eye can blaze my own trail and no one can say they did a thing for me, except for those that supported me or even offered a prayer, good advice or a kind word…or taking the time out of their busy lives to read my stories Eye offer online free of charge in addition to selling books.

The one who marinated my body in her incubation/ecosystem—intoxicated from the aura of *Genesis,* and like God separating day from night and calling it a Sabbath day—Mama separated her Oldest, First Born seed from the vessel of my soulful transportation and now Eye was nothing.

Eye gotta create Me from the debris.

And Eye succeeded…

You're reading my creation, aren't you…?

*All this spiritual warfare confuses me*. Sides are being chosen using Free Will. Reminds me of The Temple (our bodies) vs. The Church (a building) Vs The *Separation* of church and state. The separation was necessary for what's about to come probably in 2012—what do you know it's 2012!

Eye'm mentally equipped, are you? Spending your time fighting bitches and worrying over a man when the men with the architect of life—The U.N.—is plotting, planning and initiating public ruin. Trackers are in your iPhones and Androids, GPS, too—and the lines of people for those iPhones were disturbing. No thanks. Eye pass.

Identities were being stolen, accounts opened in your name you knew nothing about.

In my opinion it's all a cash cow. And Eye want no part of it—folks like me have rent to pay. Eye wasn't put here to make those wearing the Big Wigs filthy rich while we plummet into the bowels of oppression and depression, via recession. Public privacy will soon be a thing of the past; in the future Bibles will be banned from the hands of the public. The Internet was nothing but the Devil.

They'll keep playing Lil Wayne, Be*yawn*say Knowles and Lady Gaga's videos to keep you entertained and distracted. You let me tell it North America will be the new Ancient Greece. Ancient ruins. Photographed and documented in hard cover text books with the Head of the Statue of Liberty dismantled and floating in the middle of the Atlantic Ocean.

Text books given to Generation Next, the Roboticized Era, your children's children—will be in digital form. Makes me wonder where technology comes from. Seriously. Eye had a dream the government jacked technology from space ships. And then Eye woke up to Super 8 playing on my TV. And Eye watched it till it went off with my mouth open.

There won't be Bibles available in the future, but it'll probably be THE TWILIGHT SERIES in its place. Bella, a 17 year old minor, in love with and worshiping a 90 + year old Vampire, Edward, born in 1907—you do the math—that groomed the hell out of her before they married.

She turned on God to become an immortal blood thirsty creature of the nigh and believe they're gods themselves with incredible wealth and prosperity. That's what our teenagers are reading right as we speak, conditioning them to turn on God to worship the man or woman they may choose to love one day. When faced with death, when it's the end and your time to go those books condition you to seek the alternative, give your life over to the dark side for immortality.

You better study the Word now. Over and over. Every single day. Every second you can spare. Ten minutes a day wasn't asking much. Buy a Kindle reader and store it as a PDF file for safe keeping. Because when the Masters of the World ban Bibles your Free Will in double jeopardy.

Eye've been studying the fall of Greece for some time now. In private. Don't gotta tell anyone what you study. Eye writes erotica to inform and distract people from their radios, TVs and reality shows long enough to knock on their subconscious.

Open up the creaking door. Impulses and catalysts. Let out all the darkness. Enlightened and indifferent, but Eye urge you to embrace the God in you. Only then can you research what was taught to you as truth; but *truly*, in all actuality—was not and will never *be* knowledge!

Eye don't even think the photo of the first man on the moon was real. No more real than Abraham Lincoln freeing us from slavery and never even endorsed the Emancipation Proclamation. In the document we weren't to be equal economically and socially to whites—so how were we free? An unsigned document meant it *didn't* stand. Hello. Wasn't he assassinated in a theatre? If we didn't give our hard earned money to the government they take our children—throwing them in orphanages or an abusive System without a second thought—land, homes, material possessions and leave us, dying, hungry and sick, on the streets, homeless, living in poverty, forced to fill out applications for public assistance, welfare and an EBT card. This was the country we lived in today, yet we couldn't even get free Medicare.

But that's null and void. Abraham's gay ass didn't sign the document. Yes he was a homosexual, but they didn't teach you that in school, yet they throw blacks were meaningless slaves in your face day in and day out. Edited stories, omitted information. Studying those types of books once led me astray. Back when Eye didn't know any better. But since being in prison and released, physically but *never* mentally, The Lifers gave me the entire mental equipment warehouse Eye needed for the imposing Revelation War. Now Eye'm a Soldier. With PHAROAH on my name tag. Eye learned to research everything anybody told me. Truth was…sometimes the wolf in sheep clothing. A well-disguised lie.

Take people's minds off God in school they would graduate and thank Mama and Daddy first over the Creator. And some folks never said Thank you, Jesus when they endured school to get diplomas and degrees.

People stuck on how somebody dressed in church, yet Jesus said the real church was the Temple. My flesh. My body. His body. Her body. Their body. Our body. That housed the Holy Ghost. That meant Eye could go to church butt ass naked and a bitch better zip those lips up. Eye long ago stopped going to church. GOULDS CHURCH OF CHRIST killed church for me for the rest of my life. Killed the "image" of it. All the people in that church that tried to secretly fuck me and turned their noses up at me in the end will reap what they've sown. So enjoy your Heaven now. Niggahs used to beg to eat me out. Only called when time was convenient for them. Two were married *and* one married man ate me out in the back of his truck on the way to an Agape Meeting, and he wasn't even in my Agape Group. But Eye couldn't say anything. Because they had me controlled through religion. The last time Eye got up in front of that church—and half of them were rolling their eyes like naw, not this Niggah again!—and said Eye was facing the darkest days of my life, Eye went home and told myself, "You know what—the hell with my ex-boyfriend, Angelou!"

The next Sunday Eye went to church and told everybody and anybody that would listen that he was my ex-boyfriend.

Eye broke the control he had over me. Eye was tired of lying. After calling his brother's baby mama, Lisa, to my Mama's house, Eye told her Eye had a confession. Eye invited her into the room Angelou and Eye used to have sex in. After telling her everything, from start to finish, her mouth fell open in shock. Eye told the aunt, the other brother, and his grandma and grandpa Eye was the bottom and he wasn't that good a Top anyway. Eye did a lot of faking when we had sex.

And his grandparents still loved me till this day. And the auntie. And one of his brothers lied in the family meeting they had at his Mom' house. His aunt, without them knowing, called my cell phone, and said "Hold on, listen to what they saying about you," and put me on speaker phone. Eye had the "mute" button pressed so they didn't hear me throwing books in anger and ripping Angelou from my pictures and cursing Angelou the hell out for lying, talking 'bout being gay was a phase he was going through. LIAR!

He's been gay since his first encounter at the University of Miami. Letting some random Negro give him head. He even whispered it in my ear one day he was helping me jack off that the Niggah used to swallow him all the time.

He did that long before he met me so nice try saying Eye turned him out. Chile. Don't flatter yourselves.

One day, before the aftermath of Wilson vs. Angelou, his Mama said Eye talked like a fag and Eye choked off my spit. Eye looked at her and said, "And Eye guess Angelou talk like Barry White huh?"

And she shook her head and rinsed off her vegetables in the sink. As lightly aired his voice is, with no treble or bass to his windpipes, she had no reason and was in no position to throw stones at me. Eye loved and respected her, but Eye wanted to laugh.

Eye will never be faithful to another church with phony leaders, meaning phony Elders. Not all of them were phony. But two of them were. And Eye know it.

Eye worked for one of the Elders, paid half of what Eye made in tithes, and still had to help paint stripe Florida Roads with GIRL-O INDUSTRIES.

Just sitting back observing, Eye knew Eye didn't want to work for them. But Eye didn't have a job, and Eye was on parole—at the time—*and* Eye needed the money so Eye did what Eye didn't wanna do for some cash.

Strippers weren't any different. Doing what they didn't wanna do for cash. To make it. To survive. No money equals no food and a bitch was stingy these days when you asked for a little help. They all have something slick to say when you come to church.

Don't wear earrings young man; during Bible study don't wear wife beaters. Congregational women focusing more on your arms than the Word; *damn* what the hell can Eye do? Eye Can barely blink my eyes without being checked and criticized. Conditioning me into utter bullshit; so Eye dropped religion, Satan's safe Haven; and took refuge in the spirit of God; and that's not found in any Bible or in any church building.

You study the Word with the phony; yet Eye'm alone on my knees in my room crying out to God, telling him to give me an understanding of the Words he wished for me to know. Teach me the Word the way my teacher taught me to spell *Special* then my name, *Pharoah.*

Only in his grace shall the haters dismantle.

Eye was made in God's image, so was my daddy yet he still didn't man up and Mama took me to the opposite side of the world where my future rapist resided.

Eye'm still walking along the reshaped path of mental strangulation and confusion.

Daddy never gave a shit and still had to go to bed at the end of the day. The bed we make was the bed we lay in.

Don't forget to get on your knees. Eye pray the Lord my soul to keep and Eye STILL wake up facing the same bullshit Niggahs, Hoes, rent, bills, Sunday tithes and a big-mouthed mother who swore me down she was the happiest go lucky woman in the world.

Well why she hated me so much? Then why was she making my life on earth a living hell because Eye haven't married some gum smacking black chick and came in her pussy making some snot-nosed grand children?

Ain't gonna happen. These days a woman's coochie wasn't worth the company of my hot nut. Eye'd rather jack off and flush it. Ever since my first book dropped, ƬE KING OF EROTICA 1, Hoes still trying to get this dick.

Only to trap me into an unwanted pregnancy. So my social security number was redirected to her mail box in the form of a check. Hoes don't want my bisexual ass; they want what they think my bank account was doing every time Eye release a book, making pussies wet enough for the hard dick entry and Eye don't fall for that kind of trick. Too ambitious.

Yet Eye sometimes had sex with my Groupies. Slid deep in the coochie, lick my nut off her tits, swallow my seeds like Eye do my blood when Eye get a paper cut and never called the Hoe again. No child support from me. Ha, ha. Eye'm bisexual. You lose. Back in the day men owned women, pre Abigail Adams. Now women owned men; seemed these days most men were submissive to the Clit; Proverb Niggah—slash—Mr. Mom House Niggah.

And bitches wonder why sometimes Eye used to wear panties to bed, or while Eye'm jacking my long, thick delicious pipe a Hoe won't get to touch until Eye get good and ready, Eye remind myself that love comes from deep within yourself—*not* from him, them, us, we or *you.* Eye never trust a Hoe; Eye never make babies with a bitch. And on some nights Eye was a Hoe and a bitch so same rules applied to me.

My home boys were hurting. Eye have more straight home boys than gay friends. Eye didn't really do the gay scene. They hate on you if you don't praise Beyawnsay's Beysus wanna be Knowles, so Eye don't even bother. Eye didn't keep that kind of company anyway.

Eye'm a Janet Jackson stan kinda man.

Courts after Niggahs' money—and they had nothing to take, hello! Courts *didn't* care if they live or die, or if they were homeless, broke or hungry; they seizing bank accounts…sending government checks to deserving, hard working mothers and UNDERSEVING SLUT ASS WHORES who spend their child support checks on their new men, Mr. Right Now wasn't Mr. Right dummies. Those men were only there for a free ride to the corner store for Swisher Sweets; you don't have them, you crooked Arab? Then give me some BACKWOODS and Eye wanna pick my own shit, Arab! Shut up before Eye cum behind that Plexiglas and shove a pipe in your ass.

Undeserving Hoes got it going on! Getting that fat severance pay via her baby daddy's payroll check.

Sparking a rise in under the table pay. Because Niggahs were tired of the IRS taking their loot and sending it to worthless skank bitches who lay on their asses taking dicks deep in the rectal colon and some of those bald-headed tricks had the *gall* to take a few of my homeboys back to court for more money and your so-called man was laughing at you the whole time, telling his boys he only boning you, and residing in your roach-infested crib (*HUD*, bitch?) 'cause you giving him the easiest money of his life. Why do most ghetto Hoes swear they're ballers when you're only paying $60 a month (if that) for rent?

Before you came along the Niggah couldn't tell what a twenty dollar bill looked like. Niggah never had a damn thing in his life, not even a diploma or G.E.D. Talking about he's a hustler and a player. Chile please. What hustler you knew lived with a woman he wasn't dating, couldn't find a job, and looked forward to the Store Porch day in and day out begging a bitch to buy you a Black and Mild and a Miller in a can? What you didn't know was that he was a recovering crack head that took a shower, bought a

Goodwill suit and stole some jewels and went to the club in a stolen car, got with your dumb ass and been milking you, your tits and your pussy since. You spending your child support on a crack head Niggah. Eye should know. Eye watched him drive your car to the Trap buying crack, weed and cocaine with your child's money, Hoe. Wake up!

Eye thought of that when Eye went to the strip club a few years ago. Niggahs weren't making it rain like they used to. Times were hard as hell. Bus fares going up with gas prices. So was the cost of food. Wal-Mart wasn't even as cheap as they used to be. It went from 40 men making it rain on jiggling booty cheeks, bouncing breasts, wet twat and dry booty holes to 39 of those Niggahs getting laid off from their jobs—budget cuts— ducking child support, and had to resort to drastic measures to feed their families. They were online, naked on gay sites, secretly selling booty (Bottoms), cock (Tops) or cock and ass (Versatile Top), or ass and cock (Versatile Bottoms) to any willing participant to make ends meet. To pay that light bill, feed the kids and make next month's rent till you find another job. Instead of polishing a resume you'd rather polish a…

Now only one Niggah made it rain—well, drizzle—in this small club in Cutler Bay (Goulds, for the Old School Playahs) and that was me. Club was so dead the Manager snatched me inside, telling me to keep my ten dollars. If he don't get outta my face patting my back a million times Eye was gonna kick him in the nuts. Damn. All up in my face like we homies and don't know me.

Business was slow in this semi dark club. A few Hoes sitting down playing solitaire instead of stripping and another Hoe dancing on stage just to be dancing.

Eye knew off the top of my brain, pulling a suit case filled with ƁE KING OF EROTICA 1 books, that these were some hard to reach Hoes. Eye saw Tanisha, one of the biggest Hoes in Dade County, or so Eye overheard her telling her cousin Sensation—visiting from Georgia. Swore her man was all that and that her bed skills had him on lock down…Eye guess now wasn't the time to inform her that Eye, a few months ago, watched him have sex with another dude, in a wig and heels she stored in her closet, but Eye shook the thought away. Wasn't a pretty site. Watching a secret tranny without tits try to bang a man.

Ole tranny boy had boo boo everywhere and Eye was gagging, running out the room. That's why Eye didn't hang out with people Eye meet. They swore it was on some home boy shit, then it quickly turned into sex, and this particular time Eye didn't participate.

Shaking the thoughts away, Eye sat on a stool at the bar, my long sleeved shirt sparkling all over the front, black pants snug on my ass, and Harley Davidson boots with metal over my baby powdered feet. Eye looked around, different color lights flashing.

Bar tender said, "Hello, King," with a huge smile.

Eye smiled, winking at her. "Sup, boo."

She looked me over a moment, sexy woman. "From my Face book page to my job."

Eye smiled like a Cheshire cat. "Yes, ma'am."

She opened a small counter-high cooler, and took out a beer in a green bottle. Droplets of water were all over it. "Here's a Heineken—on the House."

Eye wanted more. Eye'm high maintenance, what can Eye say. "Can Eye get a Budweiser too?"

"Interesting."

"Eye always drink a Heineken then a Bud to the head right after it."

She was impressed. "Eye mix drinks for a living and you mix beers."

"Yes ma'am. People so focused on mixing Henn with this and Alize with that…no one mixes Corona with Bull or mix Heineken with Budweiser or 211 with Colt 45. You should try it!"

Her eyes sparkled, as the music thumped, vibrating all over my body. "Eye likes you!"

"When Eye fry fish Eye pour Old English in the flour with one egg."

"Yummy. Eye would like to taste that…why you in a strip club, King?"

Her brows rose. "Eye may *occasionally* love men, but girl Eye love T and A just as equally."

*Tits and Ass.* Eye looked down at KIT (my penis nicknamed after the car in the old school show *Knight Ryder*) and said, "Eye know you all big and bad, being nine inches of knowledge and all but stop getting hard in front of these Around the *way* Hoes. We're not on coochie right now. We're on a mission. Gotta sell these books."

"Damn. Talking to your package?" Graciously smiling, she handed me two beers. Eye didn't waste any time. Eye wolfed down the Heineken without taking a breath. Then wolfed down the Bud, taking it to the head. She trashed both bottles.

"KING!" said the owner. And Eye looked across the room at him.

"Eye'll holla," Eye told the bartender, never catching her name. Kissing her cheek, Eye grabbed the handle of my suit case and started across the room.

The Owner extended his hands, very welcoming. "KING!"

"Hey, man!"

"Welcome!"

Eye was smiling. "Wassup, Dawg!"

A few jazzy Hoes walked by. One squeezed my ass. Careful now. My pussy better than yours.

Eye was the only Niggah there. All eyes on the bestselling author, Eye wasn't a Thug Niggah till Eye Die. Sorry.

We slapped palms then we hugged tightly. He was my dawg, a very dear friend who accepted me for who Eye was and never tried to change me. A true Goulds hustler.

He looked over my clothes, he approved. "You made it King! Thank for accepting my invitation."

"Yes Eye told you Eye'd come."

"You're going to have a good time!"

Eye looked around. A couple girls waved at me. Eye didn't do snow cones. Another girl snapped a picture of me with her camera phone.

"Paparazzi up in this bitch! Snapping pictures of the King," he said, and Eye smiled humbly.

Eye was all smiles and teeth. "God!"

"Ready to make it rain?" he asked, hinting at a surprise in his eyes. Eye hated surprises.

"Yes."

A Hoe named Brenda took my hand and led me to an expensively furnished back room. Felt like Eye was in another world. Mirrors were everywhere. One single chair. A leather chair. Spotlight. Turned on, shining on me.

"Can you kill the light?" Eye asked The Owner. Eye was starting to perspire.

"Sure, King."

Brenda took my suit case to the owner.

"Sit, King," she said demandingly, sweetly.

Eye sat. Looked around, smiling. Rubbing my legs. Heineken + Budweiser = time to get loose.

"The first young lady up to give you a lap dance is a sexy bitch named Stacy," The Owner said with pride in his voice.

She comes out. Vanilla skin; tattooed up. Long black hair. Huge gut.

Eye gave her ten dollars just to leave me alone. KIT wasn't having it.

"King," Mat, The Owner, laughed. Eye didn't smile. "So mean!"

Eye looked at him, in mock surprise. "How am Eye mean? That's the fastest ten dollars she ever made in her life!"

"You're a pimp, dawg! Well, you'll love the next girl. Come on out Samantha!" he boomed, holding up his hand as if magic controlled his limbs.

She was black as tar, ugly as fright night. Seeing her made me close my eyes tight. Like Mommie, Mommie Eye'm scared of this horror movie.

Eye stood up. "Eye gotta take a piss. Sorry. Be right back." And pushed her out the room and shut the door, hard. BOOM!

Matt couldn't control his laughter. "You are cold! Eye love it!" he joked.

"Are you purposely doing this to me?" Eye wasn't laughing.

Matt held up his hands in surrender. "King, LOL smiley face."

"KMBA," Eye said simply.

He was confused. "What does that mean, LOL."

"Kiss my black ass!" Eye said dryly.

"Ha ahaha."

"Can Eye make a request?"

"Sure!"

With a smile. "Eye want Kandi."

"Hell! Everybody wants Kandi. She doesn't come cheap."

Eye looked in his eyes. "Didn't Eye make you nut in five minutes flat?"

Matt shook his head, the smile fading, just a bit. "*Goddamn.* Why you had to go there?"

Eye wanted what Eye wanted. "Eye *want* Kandi."

"Kandi coming right up!"

Eye turned the chair to face the door, leaned back, grabbed my crotch and leaned to the side.

Smiling like a Cheshire Cat again.

*Kandi walked in, her body banging.* They way her curvaceous lips poured into her cheek bones set off her exotic eyes. Had an ass that wouldn't quit, and tits to match. Cute feet, oiled toes, the way she walked and talked had me feeling like a straight dude.

When she saw me her mouth fell open.

"Pharoah?" she called out, stuck, frozen, nailed to the floor.

Eye smiled wider; she was a jazzy woman. A queen in public, held down a part time job at K-mart, and knew how to make money as a side hustle.

But when the night fell the whore was loose.

She was short and sweet.

"Hey, Kandi." Eye couldn't stop smiling; Eye could smell the kitty, kitty in the air, Hello *Kitty*.

She slowly walked up to me, moving her big booty to some Ying Yang Twins, a song that wasn't hot anymore.

She looked at me a moment, then, one foot over the other, she raised an acrylic nail-clad hand and tossed a huge mane of weave/hair from her beautiful face, walking towards me, slowly, guardedly, cautiously…

She looked like a midget goddess. She paused in front of me. Eye leaned forward and kissed her coochie. Muah. Her hands rose to the back of my head and Eye leaned back, observing, watching her…examining, analyzing.

She smiled sweetly. "*Damn*, Baby. Eye'm glad you came. Eye see you're doing well for yourself."

"Eye never boast," Eye said, forgetting Eye wrote books. Eye just wanted to forget it all, forget Eye was bisexual, forget my problems, forget everything—and get in touch with my masculine side, the side that loves good coochie.

She rubbed my head again, leaning over and kissing my cheek. KIT was hard instantly. Throbbing behind my jeans. Eye wanted to nut, Eye needed to cum right that second…but Eye held back, not now.

"Rumor has it you got 300 (5) star reviews on your books."

"Eye wouldn't know," Eye joked.

Her eyes sparkled like diamonds. "Congrats!"

"All thanks go to God."

She shook her head. "It's because of you, not any God, that got you to where you are."

Eye shook my head in disagreement. "God got me here, Kandi. And don't ever forget it."

She rolled her eyes, half smiling. "Eye *hear* you."

She sat on my lap, tightened her vaginal walls on my shaft, gyrating to a Pretty Ricky jam, jacking my stick through my pants. Wow, OMG.

She cupped my face with soft hands, her eyes inches from mine. She was inhaling my exhaling breath.

*Cum fuck me* was in her eyes, deeply in her irises, bringing out the retinas in ways Eye never imagined. "Are you sure you're Bi? Your…*thing* is hard as hell. You have a big stick, Pharoah! *Damn*!"

My eyes were narrowed. "And your wet walls are jacking me off." Eye grabbed her butt cheeks and gyrated with her.

"You're more man than my man is, Pharoah. That's for damn sure."

Eye licked my lips, our faces inching closer…closer to each other. "Is that right?'

"Yes." Her eyes dropped, lowering her forehead. "He mistreats me," she said, the conversation taking a wrong turn. "…He lost his job. Blamed me for it."

"That's not right," Eye said, my face tightening.

"Eye know."

Tears fell down her face. Damn it, they tugged on my heart strings and Eye tried to block it from my face. Eye wanted a lap dance before Eye sold those books. DAMN IT! A woman crying was my weakness.

"He doesn't…touch me like he used to," she said, running her nails behind the nape of my neck. She's still jacking me off with tight coochie lips. My hips didn't move, Eye'm the man, Eye control this. "He used to set me on fire with just a look. A gaze."

*How much of this was bullshit?* "Really?"

"Yes." She answered too fast. Careful, bitch. You haven't won the brass ring quite yet. "My bed has become flakes of dandruff and snow. So cold. *Brr.*"

Eye knew the feeling. Eye've been sleeping alone for years.

"Eye tell you what," Eye said, because she had me sold. "…Eye *never* paid for coochie. Hell. Eye got more panty endorsements being an openly bisexual male than Eye got as a closeted punk."

She stopped humping me. My pants soaked with sweet coochie juice. Eye inhaled her womanly scent. For a minute Eye wished Eye was a straight man so Eye could take her from her no good, cheating man—ad he could be a disrespectful, crummy bastard when he wanted to. Eye looked at Kandi. LOOK AT HER! Sexy! Sweet as honey. Wide hips. Okay tits—Eye slowly inherited them with my eager, yet controlled hands, closing them over her breasts softly. Tenderly.

Her lips pursed. "Take it out," Eye said, *It* meaning my penis. KIT was ready. "It's been ages since Eye had some trim. Time to give my booty a much needed break.

"Oh, Pharoah! Don't be playing with me!"

"Shut up, and take it out!" Eye handed her a Magnum rubber from my wallet. She ripped it open with her teeth, her hands shaking from anticipation.

"It's up to date," Eye said. "Eye checked the expiration date."

"Condoms expire?" she asked, confused and Eye was shaking my head like bitch were you for real?

*Duh*! "Yes."

She finally gave me some sweet tongue (she had some soft lips.) and Eye slid a hundred dollar bill into her bra-top.

Eye had to pay my phone bill with this money, and didn't wanna go to the bank to take out more. But oh well. She needed it more than Eye did.

"That is for you," Eye said and her eyes sparkled like rubies.

"Thanks, Pharoah. Eye appreciate you helping a Sistah. Eye *guess* my coochie is at your command."

"Eye want you to make me cum," Eye said breathlessly. "Ride me till my balls say stop."

We were giggling like school kids.

"You're so crazy! Eye love a man with a sense of humor."

"Remind me to give you a free book before Eye leave."

"Eye've been looking forward to reading your book." She sucked on my neck, *reaching* back, massaging my balls. Eye spread my legs further, my boots firmly on the floor. "You're so smart."

"Eye do have HIV, just so you know." Eye believe in being honest, she had the right to know. If she didn't wanna go further Eye would understand, no harm done.

She didn't cringe nor flinch. "Eye know. You say it on Facebook all the time. We got a condom. We'll be safe."

"As you wish."

She put the condom on the tip of my penis and slide it down to the top of my nuts with her wet coochie. *Jeez*! Eye love that trick. She held my shoulders, looking in my eyes with my mouth ajar and bounced on my rod till Eye came fifteen minutes later. She was grinning, her nipples hard and erect. "Damn baby you cumming?" she asked and Eye was smiling. Eye forgot what coochie felt like!

"Hell, yea!" My anus was pulsating, opening and closing in synch with my nut as it filled the Magnum. Ugh! Ugh! Ugh! Wow! That was a good nut! She started to get up. Eye grabbed her butt cheeks and slid the coochie back on my stick.

"Oh, no! No! Don't stop riding KIT. Now that my first nut is out the way. Take off this Magnum, put on a fresh one and let me have my turn."

"Damn! And you last longer than my dude!" she gushed excitedly. Once Eye replaced the old tarnished condom with a clean slate condom, Eye put her doggy style on the adjoining couch and dug her out long and deep, making her toes curl and her legs tremble till Eye came deep inside her again via my condom. She came on my plastic stick a few short minutes after. Eye squeezed her breasts, pushing them together and running my slick tongue across both nipples while her juices ran down my balls and the crack of my ass. Eye didn't realize Matt stood there watching me the entire time, trying like hell not to stroke himself and shake one off.

After it was over Eye zipped up my pants, smiling. She was smiling, floating on Cloud 9. Satisfied. Yup. Had to change the filter in that sweet coochie with this Nassau, Bahamian stick. Eye got her coochie the same way a few deserving Niggahs once got inside me. No mercy. Eye didn't play with a stiff one deep inside me, or my shaft in a female's mouth, gripped fist or coochie. She handed me a glass of Paul Masson. Hot. Straight. No ice. Just the way Eye like. Paul Masson at room temperature. No chaser. Hold the fruit juice.

"Thanks."

"Damn you're good!" she gushed. "You're supposed to be somebody's wife."

"Eye will be somebody's wife one day," Eye joked and she laughed so hard.

"Eye meant you should be married to a woman. Making her babies. A woman would honor and encourage you, Pharoah. You're a different kind of black man! Who knew Bi cock was so good?"

"Thanks."

The boss opened the door, smiling. Eye guess my time was up. He handed me $300.

"What's that for?" Eye asked.

"Eye sold all your books. Twenty dollars a pop. They sold out. All the stripper bitches bought them up."

"Thank you!"

"Eye bought ЂE KING OF EROTICA 2, 3 and 4 on Barnes and noble.com a short while ago. Eye want the entire collection."

"Thanks, man!" Eye was still panting from Kandi's sweetness. Eye wanted some more.

Eye left out the room. Kandi went to wash up.

And the praise started washing over me like a warm shower.

*"Hey, Mister! Sign my book! Eye can't stop reading it! Eye'm already on page 40!"*

*"And sign mine, too King you definitely did the damn thing!"*

*"And you're from Goulds! Eye'm Mystique! Eye'm so proud of you! Sign my book!"*

Kandi came over. Eye handed her the last book in my suitcase. Eye guess Matt didn't see that one. Eye gave it to her free of charge. Eye promised it to her before Eye bust that pussy open. She gushed with zeal. "Thanks Pharoah! Wow! Eye finally own your book! You're the best!"

"No problem," Eye said, let me get some more coochie on my tongue, but Eye swallowed hard. She was about to find out about her man. And why he hasn't boned her in months, creating dandruff and snowflakes in her cold bed. When she reads ON THE LOW LOW from ЂE KING 1; Eye was so talking about her married man. She'll figure it out. Because Eye misspelled his name, but it pronounces the same. Eye described everything about her life in that story. But in real life somebody other than me had HIV.

And he was keeping it a secret.

***The next week Eye went back to*** see Kandi. Slipped her a fifty dollar bill and Eye'm in love with a stripper's coochie, briefly, in the moment, it slides and glides on my wrapped-up-in-rubber-penis.

Her coochie's been sliced and diced already. So Eye knew not to believe anything she says and she was feeding my head with, THIS IS YOUR COOCHIE! EYE WANNA BE YOUR BITCH!! EYE'LL NEVAH LET ANOTHAH NIGGAH GET THIS, PHAROAH.

That's what she was filling my ears with.

Come on, now. How naïve did you think Eye was? You riding a bisexual's penis after his rectum was deflowered by his ex-step father when he was the tender age of six. Eye used to tell a Niggah that too when he did it with me. When Eye was the age to make decisions for myself.

And Eye still chose your man's endowment deep inside me over your tainted vaginal walls. You give your ass away freely, to anybody with something over ten dollars. Eye'm high maintenance. You couldn't feed me grapes and tell me its pineapples. Eye don't *like* coconuts. And if the coconut had a brain it'd looked like the inner sanctuary of kiwis.

Eye used to say, "This is your ass!" B.S. And didn't mean it! Eye was lying my ass off at the time. Had *your* Niggah thinking Eye had never been penetrated before, mentally camouflaging my sliced and diced body, and it was still tighter than your pussy. The pussy your man keeps running away from. Sleeping in a Hotel bed with me, leaving yours untouched and cold.

Eye got that good, good—at least that's what the last Niggah told me, your Niggah as a matter of fact. Eye didn't believe it myself, telling your man Eye was his and he was mine. His skills weren't all that good anyway. When he was deep inside, all up in his face moaning and groaning, Eye was too focused on getting my nut.

So why were you trying to run game? He said your coochie *used* to make his cock spit at 12 one hundred hours and 12 seconds. He got 20:12 tatted on his upper shoulder. Documenting his endeavor. His reward from all that hard work spiraling down the drain when he washes his hands with anti-bacterial soap. My ass still drying on his lips.

Now Eye come along—challenging that tattoo. My mouth broke the record set by your coochie. Bitch wasn't so grand after all. My mouth did it in two minutes 12 seconds and my booty did it almost instantly. Twenty pumps. Came in half a minute. Gave him a lot of mental stimulation leading up to the act, and by the time Eye had him amped and pumped he came instantly. Worked like a charm. Had him cumming all over the bedroom.

"Why you telling me this?" she asked, walking up to me with my book in her hand. Goddamn. Eye didn't realize Eye was talking out loud.

Oh, well.

The cat is out the bag now.

*Eye didn't wanna be the one to* do this? But, she asked. And it was time to answer. Sigh. Here goes. "The last time your man screwed me was a few nights before Eye came here to this club and let you ride this dick."

She was destroyed, looking at me like *damn* Eye knew he was gay and how am Eye gonna compete with another man, let alone ЂE KING OF EROTICA, whose a sexy man himself?

"YOU BETRAYED ME!" she screamed, her voice booming.

"Betrayed you?" Eye said, snatching my book and slapping her across the head. "Bitch get some sense! You gave up the coochie to every man that desired it in the ghetto. And every man you laid with turned up with HIV."

"EYE DON'T HAVE HIV! SHUT UP!"

She was furious Eye knew this bit of information. Eye knew she had HIV and she knew Eye knew she was just playing Legally *Blonde.* Eye saw the bitch in the pill line at CHI with a funky wig and Bandi shades on. In full disguise picking up her monthly dosage of Norvir, Epzicom and Lexiva and Zithromax and pills for Herpes. And she got her pills on time. Her man worked in the pill room, but Eye get my pills late, even when Eye order refills on time. Something ain't right.

What made me notice her was the Bandi shades. There's no Hoe in Goulds, Florida City or Perrine on superstar status, so why the Bandi shades? Eye don't even *have* Bandi shades and Eye write books. Eye tell you. Hoes think they're smart.

"Eye can't believe this has blown up in my face!"

Eye shook my head. "You shut up! Eye have HIV. We even have the same Case Manager. Yet your man doesn't have it."

"Eye make him use rubbers! Eye care about this one and if Eye tell him Eye got HIV he will leave me like all the others did!"

"Gurl that's wrong! It's against the law! You're supposed to make the person you screw or sleep with aware of what you got! That has to be his choice to still sleep with you."

"Screw the *law*! My daddy did time in the Army and he said the government invented this HIV crap and tried to pass it off as a fag disease. Don't ask, don't tell."

"*Don't* believe that."

"Eye don't! How can it be a fag disease when Eye'm living with it and Eye'ma straight bitch and never touched a clit outside my own in my life!"

"You're justifying and you touched more than one clit in your life."

"You got me fucked up! Eye'm not gay like *you*, bitch!"

Damn, she was defensive.

*Hit a nerve Tinkerbelle* Jezebel ass Hoe?

"Yet your Mama's clit slid across the top of your forehead, down the slope of your nose and wiped blood off your lips and smeared her essence all over your ass when she was pushing you out her coochie on your birthday."

*"Get out my face!"*

"What you angry for? Eye made both of you nut, what, you *mad?* You and your man bust good from Pharoah's temple. Had both you late bitches cumming, watering my landscape. You cheated on your Niggah riding this pole, with your eyes bearing into mine, revealing reflections and mirrors; hypnotizing me in your scheme. You committed adultery. Not me! Eye gave you a hundred dollars bitch because you're a hard working mother."

"And Eye appreciate the money."

Eye snatched a hundred dollar bill out her bra. "You didn't even tell me you had HIV!" Eye told her.

"GIVE ME MY MONEY!"

"You were an Indian giver with the coochie. Cheating on your Niggah. He doesn't know you have HIV. Eye told him Eye had HIV before we had sex, before we even got to that point, and he chose to wrap it up and get deep in it. So Eye was an Indian giver with my money with *you!* Eye just wanted to see what all the fuss was about when it came to your coochie. Shit ain't worth the sweat off my asshole. Niggahs paying for HIV infected coochie and they didn't even know what the hell is going on?"

She slapped me. "You make me sick."

Eye slapped her back. "You touch me one more time, that's your ass, bitch. Eye'll go to jail telling your gay ass man you got HIV. Then we'll see whose zooming who, Aretha."

Eye pivoted on my heel and walked to my car. Borrowed it from some Niggah anyway.

Bad ass Mercedes E Class.

# DAY

# 5

*Lord Jennings &*
*The King of Erotica*
*Downtown Miami.*
*56th Floor Condo*

"***Some Men Wear Panties*** is the book you wish you never wrote?"

"Yea," Eye said, sipping champagne. Never had this kinda bubbly before but we were celebrating, because we were Day 5 into the Therapy Sessions. Going along rather smoothly. Bumpy at times but Eye felt myself opening up in ways Eye never dreamed.

We were in our T shirts and pajama pants, having a good time and smoking trees and mellowed out. The huge

ceiling glass door was opened and the breeze blew across our bodies and relaxed us more.

"It's heaven up here," he said.

"Yes it is. Eye don't get to go out much."

"You're a bestselling author. Eye can only imagine…so tell me why you regret writing Some Men Wear Panties."

"That book made me look like a fool. Eye mean JL played on my ignorance and vulnerability. Eye feel that entire project was for him to try to fuck me. Eye thought he was my friend."

"Sharks in the publishing world."

"He had me fooled. Sending me text messages asking when Eye was going to let him fuck me and Eye kept turning him down."

"Do you feel this is why he pushed your project back?"

"Had to be. Even when Eye was in Atlanta, when we first met, Eye should have known he was no good. Some guy named Antoine came in Outwrite bookstore with his pants sagging all under his big ass with striped boxers on and JL pulled out his camera phone and took a picture of it right in the middle of us going over the revisions for Some Men Wear Panties."

"Wow."

"Now he's a spokesperson for the Pull your Pants up campaign and he taking pics of niggahs with sagging pants?"

"Go on."

"So he took us out for a few beers. Eye called my big sister Attica and told her the plan. JL invited me back to his house to smoke trees and he told me he was going to cook and wear sexy underwear and have my kind of Niggahs over. Eye knew the play so Eye said sure, ok and stood his ass up and never showed."

"And he was on Oprah."

"Tell me about it. Eye paid this niggah $1,700 for his services. For his company to turn me into a brand. Eye didn't see anything my money paid for. He asked me to do all the work. Promote myself to fans. Do this and that and he didn't do shit. He then called me and asked me would Eye write 7 monologues for him. He has a play on the road, so he sent me a paragraph about a character named Juice. About four sentences. Eye turned it into a ten minute monologue and told him Eye only had the time to do one. He swore me down he was going to give me my writing credit and he never did. Eye copyrighted what Eye wrote him before Eye sent it anyway and never told him."

"Smart move. Eye would like to see that contract. And read what you wrote for him."

Eye pulled the folder out my book bag and handed it to him.

Still embarrassed.

"Why does he get under your skin?"

"He had me tell over 15,000 of my fans about Some Men Wear Panties the book and the Pink panties tour he swore we were going on. While he's out behind my back promoting his book and all that, sometimes he went months without calling me. Eye didn't hound him and Eye seldom called. Eye sweats no niggah."

"How did your fans take it?"

"The book was supposed to drop March of 2009. As you can see its January of 2010. And Eye had to publish it myself. Eye should have known he only wanted sex. He kept begging for me to send him the porn video Eye made five years ago and Eye said yes at first, but then Eye changed my mind and never sent it."

"Wow."

"He then called and said he was going to a swingers convention. He wanted me to write a Swingers creed. Eye wrote it but Eye guess it wasn't fast enough for Mr. Hustler so he wrote it himself, or probably had some other niggah write it."

"So how did that affect your working relationship with other writers?"

"Eye never did that again. Eye will never write or do a book with anyone else. JL didn't write anything in Some Men Wear Panties. Not a damn thing. And one of my friends, the book's editor, Kevin McNeir, a very dear friend of mine, called me and said Some Men Wear Panties was on sale at Outwrite book store and Eye never signed a contract for the release of that book. Eye still own it 100%."

"Will you ever work with him again?"

"Hell no!"

## EPILOGUE♋PHAROAH:
## PRELUDE☯THE KING OF EROTICA™ 8:

COPYRIGHT RORI-TAI © 2009, ATLANTA GRAND HYATT

# Lord Jennings & The King of Erotica

Lord Jennings set the folder down.

"You are one talented ass man!"

Eye noticed he was cursing a lot more now. When we first met he didn't curse at all, didn't smoke weed or drink booze and now he was doing all three relentlessly but Eye refrained from further dialogue with him on the matter.

"Thanks," Eye said, studying him. Eye did have feelings for him as far as friendship goes.

"Well Eye'm about to turn in," he said, yawning.

Eye looked at the clock. It was 4:15 a.m.

"*Damn*!" My eyes clouded over.

"We've been talking all night and all damn day."

"Eye know," Eye said, getting on the huge comfortable sofa.

He sat next to me, giving a long look.

"What?" Eye asked, getting a little fidgety. Eye was tired.

He leaned up to me

"Oh my God," Eye said.

"What?" he asked innocently, his lips inches from mine.

"Are you going to kiss me?" Eye gushed.

"Yes," he said matter-of-factly.

"But you're married," Eye reminded him, my heart pounding.

He was getting closer to my lips. Dangerously close. He rubbed my face gently. "In name only."

Eye could barely breathe. *Please stop touching me!* "What do you mean?"

"My wife and Eye are separated. And have been separated for two years."

"Are you serious?" Eye asked, standing up. Eye mean he was my therapist. He was supposed to be *helping* me deal with my past. To help me better *understand* it. Now he's trying to get in my pants.

He was standing behind me. "Pharoah. Are you upset?"

*Yes!* "No, man…*but…*"

"But what?" He seemed desperate.

Eye faced him. "You told me that you told your wife you were going to be away for a week."

"Eye lied, Pharoah. Eye mean how was Eye supposed to know Eye'd get the opportunity to be Ђe King of Erotica's shrink."

"So was this the reason why you wanted to get close to me? Was this what it's all about?"

"Pharoah—*No*!" He stepped closer to me, taking off his wife beater. He had an incredible chest. His nipples were large and made my mouth water. Eye turned away.

Eye walked past him, my nature getting hard. "This is dangerous, Lord Jennings."

"Eye admire your bravery and your strength. Eye mean this is heaven for me. Seeing a man that survived so much. Eye don't know if Eye could have made it through your ordeal. Eye hold onto things too much. Eye carry grudges."

"This is stunning me, dawg." Eye said, sitting on the sofa, refusing to look in his eyes. Eye felt betrayed. Wasn't this kinda shit against the law? Sleeping or trying to fuck your client?

He sat next to me. "Pharoah. Look at me."

"No, man."

"Look at me!"

Eye looked at him, trembling. Part of me wanted to run.

"Do you wanna know why my wife and Eye are separated?"

He's gonna tell me anyway so why not? "Yea. Why?"

He wrapped his arms around me. "Because she found out Eye'm bisexual."

And he tongue kissed me.

We had sex for the rest of the night on the floor…

*The next morning Eye awakened.* Thick blankets covering my body. Eye looked around, forgetting where Eye was. Then it dawned on me that my therapist and Eye had incredible sex. Why did this anger me? It's almost as if something came over me and moved my body for me, something Eye couldn't see or control.

"What is going on?"

Eye stood up, yawning and stretching.

Damn Eye was tired, moving about like a zombie. Eye could barely grasp a thought or remember my name.

Eye had to take a piss so Eye walked to his elaborate bathroom, real baller stuff, and held the wall and drained the weasel. Felt good to piss in a pricey bathroom.

Took my HIV medicine and made me something to eat. Place was stocked to the max. Since Eye was a guest might as well eat. Eye wish he would protest. Eye'd kick his ass.

Eye was looking for my phone and couldn't find it.

Where was it?

Eye emptied my back pack.

Couldn't find it.

Eye checked my pockets. Gone.

"Where is my phone?"

Eye continued combing the unfamiliar place.

"Lord?"

Eye walked to his bedroom and opened the doors. Bed empty. Room spick and span. Nothing was out of place.

"Lord?" Eye called out again.

Eye walked to the front door and tried to unlock it. The bottom lock turned, but the top bolt lock was secure and there was no way of opening it without a key.

*What* the…?

Eye slowly walked to the couch and sat down.

The sun shined brightly.

☯

*Eye stood up, confused*, and tried to open the glass door. It was locked. And that too needed a key to open.

Eye turned on his computer. You needed a password, so Eye couldn't get online. Eye looked around the house and there was no house phone. No way to the outside world.

It was then Eye realized he'd locked me in his condo.

With no way out.

FRIENDS OF MINE SHOWING SUPPORT AT THE ITLA PRIDE, ATLANTA—GRAND HYATT, BUCKHEAD 2009. COPYRIGHT RORI-TAI, ATLANTA

**TO BE CONTINUED.**

**ЂANK YOU FOR READING Ђ∑ KINGDOM BOOK 1, PHAROAH**

**Ђ∑ KINGDOM BOOK 2, LORD JENNINGS**

**B E G I N S N O W...**

PHAROAH

Pharoah and Lord Jennings cover photos by DAMON↔2010.

♋

# ThE King of ErotiCa's

# ThE KiNGDOM

L[o]rd Jennings

Book 2 Of 2

# Damian Campbell

Author of "Soul of a Fatherless Child®"

## Preamble to The Kingdom Book 2

Larry Wilson Jr. ™ (Pharoah) was born on the 26th day of the 6th Month in the 77th year of the 20th century. The eldest of five offspring born to Clara McCrae and Pharoah Wilson Sr., his fate was foretold in the stars of the constellation, Cancer. His life has been a tumultuous journey, fraught with tragedy and triumph, joys and pain, love and loss. It is *this* writer's experience of the author Dapharoah69™ that he is a kind and compassionate soul, with an unconditional ability to love selflessly; more imposing than his physical stature, his aura is only outshined by his palpable vocabulary.

A consuming verbal arsenal at his disposal, Larry—commonly referred to as The King of Erotica™—has, in my opinion, redefined urban literature. From the outskirts of fine art, to a verbose, emotional voice in the inner sanctum of true poetry.

Not restricted to the

limitations of the prose and verses of the early renaissance, The King of Erotica™ has elevated what was once perceived as simple words into an entity onto themselves.

Bringing life to inanimate scribbles on modern day parchment, more refine than simple musings, his insight and honesty borders the clairvoyant. Never has there been a writer, poet, author such as this, and there shall never come another after the King. He is one of a kind. Only God can make something so beautiful. All things revolutionary are often imitated and seldom duplicated. But this is *not* like attempting to mass produce the first ever automobile. But more like putting a patent on the light bulb; something as enlightening as its purpose. This book is NOT a representation of just the King. More, it's a representation of a movement, an ideology that the King has placed years, blood, sweat, and tears into. The measure of a man is NOT in the amount of earthly possessions one can amass before his time on this earth expires.

Rather, the measure of a man can't be measured in the sense of distance or some astronomical amount of monetary or physical assets.

A man's measure is defined in the heart he possesses and the hearts he touches.

The King has touched, not only my heart, but my family, as they flow through me. I can assure you, after reading the contents that lie within, he'll touch your heart in a profound way.

Not trying to change who you are, or redefine your understanding of the world; allow the King to share with you his wisdom and understanding of the world, behind this world.

Peace and Love, and may the faiths smile upon you.

*From the Author of "The Soul of a Fatherless Child."*
*Legendary Poet of the People™ / Damian Campbell*

# "Poet you are"

## By: Damian Campbell

*For the King of Erotica™*

Such a poetic deviant
your decadence wallows
in the after birth of your creativity.
You are
the bastard child of muses and deities.
Your divinity averted,
but your destiny undisturbed.
Covered by the yoke of the fathers before you.
You give life to still words.
Every phrase a miracle of life
when spoken thru you.
Your secular tongue
speaks amoristic blasphemy
to the rigid structure of social order.
You present
needed chaos in a construct lacking uniqueness.
Ejaculate your ideology
into the minds of the masses
until they've been satisfactorily fucked in the game.
Self gratification
is relative to the individual;
continue this vocal masturbation
until you're satisfied
and u leave the masses draped.
In the essence or your preamble,
the secretion of your literary distinction.
The exquisite aftermath of laden masses
after your loins, lay flaccid after you deploy your craft.
A journeyman as words traverse y
our tongue after being conceived

in the bosom or your imagination.
You suckle them
until they are ready
to be heard,
absorbed by a demanding audience,
biting at the bit to be berated by your brashness.
So allow them
to sit attentive to await your gift.
Bring your soul, bare,
so they may all play a witness.
This poetry and a Poet
You are...

FORT
OKLA
B BA
1ST BA
33RD FI AR
4TH PL
WARL
22 S

## Tell me about Chadrick Render And the inciden† in ☯regon ✞hat landed y☋u in prison

Lord Jennings

*This was one of the most depressing* chapters Eye would ever write in my life. Eye have written many books and created many characters, but my own life was something Eye never thought Eye'd actually document, even though Eye fantasized about doing so numerous of times. The first time Eye attempted to write my autobiography was when Eye was incarcerated at the Inverness Jail in Salem, Oregon back in 1997. Mom told me Eye should try to write a book after Eye sent her a collection of poetry Eye'd written. Eye used to go to the Law Library to type poetry, telling officials Eye wanted to work on my case yet Eye lied, hiding my writings in my paperwork. It became my obsession, *writing* that was. Eye wrote my first book, titled *A Lighter Shade of Men.* When Eye was on my way to the Big House (prison, after Eye plead No Contest and was convicted of Attempted Sodomy in the first degree, and the lesser charged dropped), Eye sent the book to mom in 5 different manila folders. She never received them. Three of the 5 envelopes Mom eventually received. The other 2 were lost in the mailing system and Eye suffered a deep depression. Eye think one of the guards stole my book.

Before Eye get into the charges and what happened Eye will first set up the entire ordeal. My first visit to Oregon, a state Eye'd never been and a state Eye would visit on vacation and leave on probation, was an educational one. Eye learned then that your own kind would destroy you, especially if you were a foreigner in their neighborhood and state. Portland niggahs didn't like Down South niggahs, and they let that be known after being phony, laughing and smiling in my face. Once Eye became comfortable, that's when they attacked.

Chadrick Daquan Render was my best friend for 15 years and my brother at heart. He was the Keeper of my inner secrets and he protected them with the heart of a warrior and Eye never asked for the protection but he so willingly gave it. A pint sized bundle of blackness, don't let his size fool you. Every time Eye walked in a room his face lit up like a Xmas tree. Talk about a loyal friend, he was that. Athletic, handsome and he loved the ladies and treated them with respect. Before Eye visited Oregon, Eye was going through problems at home, just getting out the Army with a dishonorable discharge and being back in Mama's house, a place Eye wanted to desperately leave, did a number on me. Eye was still heartbroken over Chantell. Chad helped me cope. We stayed up for hours on the phone crying together. He felt my pain. He helped me get through the tough time.

At the time Mom was involved with a dude named Jimmy, who worked for the Feds on the same institution grounds as she, FCI Miami. Eye didn't like him very much. In fact Eye couldn't stand him back then.

After mom helped him out, even got a leather chair on her credit for his apartment, Eye guess his bills caved in on his manhood because next thing Eye know my 8 year old sister was waking me up out a dead sleep.

She was worried. "Pharoah! Pharoah! Get up, boy!"

Aggravated, Eye was mad as hell. Waking me up. Eye hated it. "What, girl?"

"Who is that man in Mama's kitchen in his draws cooking shrimp for breakfast?"

Eye sucked my teeth. "Probably Laron."

"IT AIN'T LARON, BOYEE! It's a grown man! Eye never seen him before."

OK. She got my attention now. Being Eye was the man of the house, Eye got up and walked into the kitchen, wiping sleep out my eyes. Eye had to get up anyways. Eye had to go job hunting, since Uncle Sam wasn't sending me guaranteed checks every two weeks anymore.

Inhaling cooking shrimp and eggs, Eye saw him. Muscular body, ass a little on the flat side and Eye said, "Excuse me, who are you?"

He looked at me with those thick lips and sparkling eyes. "Hey, Pharoah."

Eye looked at him sideways. "How do you know my damn name?"

He smiled, stirring the shrimp, sizzling in my ears. "You're the oldest, right?"

"Yea, man. Now who are you? Are you in the right house? You're in your draws around my fucking 8 year old sister?"

"Eye mean no harm. Eye'm your mother's boyfriend. Eye just moved in."

Eye narrowed my eyes. "She doesn't have a man." Eye felt betrayed. "She moved you in and didn't even prepare her own kids. Typical."

"She's grown, Pharoah she doesn't have to tell you anything." They say a mind is a terrible to waste, and hsis brain will look like Outback Steakhouse whipped potatoes when Eyes slap him across the head with that non-stick frying pan he cooking shrimp in. That's what Eye call a third degree burn, suckah!

*Oh, boy. Here we go. Try'na control me already and it ain't gonna happen. Black cocky dude ain't been in my kitchen two hours and he trying to pull some damn heat.* "That may be true but put some shorts or pants on! Your half naked butt around my goddarn sister ain't cuttin' it. Tell my Mama *that*!"

He was grinning, stirring the shrimp. Eye said, "Who cooks shrimp for breakfast? Eye guess you got it like that?"

"Eye surely do. Eye *do* work for the B.O.P."

"Eye know who you are now. You showed up here one day when Mom and Sweet (my cousin) was painting the living room. You were the one that claimed to have followed her home because you took one look at her and was all in love, and she fell like a starving penis inside anorexic pussy from those old, tired, corny lines."

"Watch your mouth."

"You ain't my daddy."

"Eye'm your step daddy," he said, emptying the pot of shrimp on a plate.

"In your dreams, muscle neck," Eye mumbled. Eye didn't have to time argue with Mama's boy toy. He was what, man number 2 since we've been in this Hartford Square ass house in Naranja. The first piece of shit, Sam, who was in the Airforce came and went and Eye was glad because Eye was tired of losing sleep from Mama OH GOD OH GOD through the walls, like Eye didn't have goddamn ears. Eye knew she said all that. Eye used to press my ear against the wall laughing my ass off at the little leprechaun trying to make Mama's toes curl. What was it with Mama and midget niggahs? Now a new Sheriff was in town and Eye would shoot him real quick he try me.

The trouble had just started.

*Over their dizzying relationship* Eye was never close to the man, but my brothers loved him mainly because he had video games. Wow. Who gave a shit? Eye wasn't easily won over when it came to a man Mama dated because, when they hurt her Eye was the one who had to see her tears, and watch her write lyrics from CD's on paper to give to those worthless cock suckers. Eventually, at least Eye thought at the time, Mama chose him over me. Made like Eye didn't exist and Eye was blindingly jealous. So Eye retaliated and Chad convinced me to move to Oregon and Eye did so in the next few months. Mama and Eye were not on speaking terms and we basically hated each other. Mama and her new boo were up and down. In love one day, arguing the next. He took Mama all over town looking like a Cuban with a hair cut (he loved Spanish women and damn sure had my Mama trying to look like one and Eye HATED IT! Only Mama didn't realize it) and the next day they were at it again. He's arguing with her and she's arguing back, over everything from a man in a picture with Mama with his hand above her booty (Jimmy SWORE his hand was *on* her butt, and his jealous ass got his panties in a wad), to a video surfacing of a half naked female with her breasts hanging out, popping her coochie on camera and he claimed he made that tape BEFORE he moved into our house but that leather chair Mama got for him on her credit turned that undercover truth into the lie it was. And she still kept him. What did it for me was hearing him on the phone one night with one of his ex fuck buddies or Baby Mama, telling her what he missed doing to her, and that he wanted her to send him naked pictures to his P.O. Box and Eye woke up Laron, my brother and said, "Oh my God! That double crosser!"

"What are you talking about?"

"Jimmy cheating on Mama!"

He was wide awake. "*WHAT*?"

"Hell, yea! Listen." Eye put the phone on speaker, with the MUTE button pressed.

"What kinda pictures you want?" the bitch asked him.

"Eye want pictures of that pretty Nookie," he said.

"You miss this Nookie, *don't* you?" she asked.

"Oh hell naw," said Laron. He was steaming. "And Eye liked him. Eye thought he was cool."

"Eye never liked the bitch."

When the phone call ended we called Mama at work and we told her what we both heard. "Oh hell no!" she spat icily. Eye didn't know how Mama got home so fast from the prison but she did, coming through the door with a purpose. Eye was so happy. YES! Another one bites the dust. Pack your shit and GET O-U-T!

She was yelling and screaming, "Who was that bitch you were on the phone with?"

He was like a dear trapped in head lights. "What are you talking about?"

"Pharoah and Laron told me they heard you talking to some bitch on the phone!—" *Damn*, Mama! Just throw me under the bus! "—Eye didn't know you had a P.O. Box! She's sending you *pictures*, Jimmy?"

"PHAROAH!" he yelled and Eye ran out the door with my brother. We ran across the street by the gas station (CITGO, it was after, what, 11, 12 a.m. at night, and we hid in the bushes).

"He ain't finna Teenage Mutant Ninja Turtles my ass with those thick arms," Eye joked and Laron was laughing.

"Eye say we go back."

"Hell naw! Eye look like Harriet Tubman?"

"Come on. Two against one!"

We went back.

Jimmy and Mama argued for the old and the new.

*The next day Eye felt crummy*. An eerie feeling befell me and Eye couldn't shake it. Eye was glad Mama found out about the double crosser and he was gone.

Eye opened my eyes and was startled, jumping outta my skin. Jimmy was in the doorway, dressed up nicely. He smiled.

"Get out!" Eye shouted. Eye hated him so much.

"Eye see you were eavesdropping."

My eyes were blood shot red. "Get out, double-crosser."

"You see that's just it," he said, gloating. "Eye convinced her you were making it up. Your Mama and Eye are still together." He winked.

"Eye hate you, bitch!"

He laughed and walked off. Eye walked into Mama's room. "So he gets to stay?" Eye asked rhetorically.

"Yea, he does. Why did you and Laron lie on him?"

"WHAT?"

"You heard me! You need to get out my house! You're supposed to be in the Army. But you *messed* that up."

"Eye heard him, Mama!"

"YOU NEED TO STAY OUT MY BUSINESS!"

"Mama!"

"Eye don't wanna talk to you Pharoah! Get out my face!"

"Mama!"

"NOW!"

"He lied to you!"

"You and Laron lied. Lie again Eye'm throwing you out my goddamn house!"

"Eye hate this shit."

"Get out my house, Pharoah."

"If he stays, Eye stay." And Eye went to my room and closed the door.

She opened it. "Don't close no doors in my goddamn house you don't pay no bills. You need a job."

"Whatever."

She slammed the door closed.

π

**Eye called Chad on the phone** and of course Eye filled him in and he was like, "Yo, that's screwed up, Baby Boy."

"Tell me about it Red Eyes."

"You should come to Portland."

"Eye've *never* been there."

"For real, dawg. Come up here with me. Eye miss home, though. And it will be hard with you up here because you are the only link Eye have to talk to my family behind Junior's back."

"What your cousin, well your so called *guardian*, do now?"

"Can you believe he pissed in my shoes because he doesn't want me going out with Komingo?" Chad's African girlfriend.

"That's foul." Eye was shaking my head.

"He hates her and he controls me. He told me if Eye won the state championship in wrestling he would let me go see my mother."

"And what happened?"

"Eye won it, and he reneged, said Eye couldn't talk to her. Calls my Mama all kinds of names. Yes, she does drugs but so what? That's my mother and Eye love and miss her so much."

"Eye'm sorry, dawg. Eye can't even stand my Mama right now."

"So are you gonna fly up?"

Eye smiled. "Yea, Eye am."

He was so happy. "Eye'll help you buy the plane ticket. You can stay as long as you want. You're family."

"Ok, Eye'll get on it."

"Eye am thinking of joining the Blood gang."

Eye choked on my spit. What the fuck? "WHAT?"

"Pharoah, don't trip."

Eye was infuriated. "DON'T JOIN THAT! They will kill your entire family if you try to get out."

He laughed it off. "It's not like that."

My eyes were wide with fear. "YES IT IS!"

"Eye want your blessing."

Eye rolled my eyes. "To join a gang? Eye had a rough life but Eye'm not joining a gang, Chad."

"Please, Pharoah."

"Nope. Hell no. Eye love you dude. But join a gang friendship is OVER!"

He was hurt. "You don't mean that!"

Eye was devastated. "Yes the fuck Eye do!"

"Baby Boy."

Eye hung up the phone in his face.

And turned the ringer off.

*After buying my plane ticket* a few days later Eye called him and let him know Eye'm on my way to Oregon.

He was happy. "Hell yea. *Piru's in the house, Blood! What's your set?*"

"What the hell does that mean?" Eye asked, confused.

"Nothing, dawg…Eye'm just glad you're coming up to P-Town!"

"Eye can't wait."

"It's me and you, brothers for life."

"You *knowwww*! Eye am going to mail you the flight itinerary. You gonna pick me up?"

"In the white Cutlass hell yea, dawg."

"Bet.

*That night Eye thought about* my future. Eye was all of 19 years old, fresh out the Army, no sense of direction, and needed a job. Maybe Portland would be a great start, not knowing Oregon was a racist ass state.

Eye pulled out Chad's letters and read them over. Eye was happy with my decision to visit a place Eye never been let alone heard much of. It was an invigorating experience for me, running away from home again and hoping for a new start. Eye loved Mom but Eye hated that man she dated. Why didn't he just move out and leave us alone? Eye have been the one consistent man in Mama's life, and with Jimmy there Eye was starting to hate.

Them both.

# Letters to Pharoah From Chadrick Render

WEll Blood I thought enought west 4 DLB's in this shit Blood. A West 4 with that Girl you use to go with, A Blood I Don't Need to Meet her B-Ruzz if She can Break My Nigga's heart she ain't worth Meeting let alone looking at Blood. B's 4 & Fuck All crabs gangs (L). A But west Been 4 the reason I say WEst all of the time is B-Ruzz that's were the Bloods hang, and the CRAbs hang on the (Eastside) the Fuck Side. a so what's Been up with you lately, I just got your other tape So A nigga's on lock down shited that what yall think im a player 4 life like yall said on that tape L-dog westside 4 life. a are you going to do that 4 a nigga you Know when you go to the Youth fair, get me a shrit with my picture on it, yeah on the front and on the Back I want my mom's name or something I tell you later and Know I don't want no girl's name not even lomingo's name on my shit Blood. a But a nigga is just chilling doing nothing really, yeah yall wos talking a lot of shit on that last tape But that's okay B-Cuzz I liked it But im going to Beat your home girl shit 4 hard dag.

"oh" tell Kelven Thanks for the picture it looks really good. Hell I wish Mark could draw like that let alone look up to me the way my shorty does Mr. Kelven. A West + with Puffy anyways, and when are you trying to come + here on Spring Break or something well when even if you are let a nigga know in advanced or if you're going to surprise me let J.R. them know okay alright. Damn I needs to go over Savann house and get my Carmera From him so I can take my ass some pictures and shit Blood. a I wrote yoshi a pretty nasty letter B-cuzz she wanted one I didn't get as nasty as I could have But it was nasty enough 4 her.

a But a nigga's got to go alright, alright then

W/B when ever you can see ya

B's + Blood.

WEST 4 LARRY A LONG time Hu! YEAH I KNOW A But DON'T TRIP B-CUZZ I'M still HERE LiL Nigga. A tell my Babies thanks 4 the pictures & the letter I Luv it. A so what's NEW Blood, nothing here But [illegible]ms. My Cousin J.R. Should "B" Back [illegible] 26th at 8:00 AM But I'll "B" at Sch[illegible], But I Don't give A Fuck. Dam[illegible] [illegible]ry Why do WE catch all the Fucking Drama From mom's and Bitches, I Kno[illegible] why B-cuzz WE are the Fucking Best Bloo[illegible] My Big wrote ME Not to long ago and I wrote Back, then he didn't write NO MORE. Blood I guess Life Just

wasn't 4 us. Niggas like us you want ever come By again Lil Nigga, A I'm going to Send ya some Pictures that's on (Piru Luv) WE are Homies, Better yet are Brothers yo! and Fuck everyone else. Baby Boy Don't worry about all this Shit B-cuzz God Luv's US and that Shits real. A I might Send Yoshi A picture 4 X-mas Just B-cuzz I still like her I Lil. But I'll give You 1st drips on the pictures. Well See ya Love ya! LOPG's 4 Blood.

## Letter #3

aug 15, 1996

what up Baby "L" what's Been poping nothing much here. Damn you be writting your ass off a But I like that. "Oh" why didn't you call me Back yet Why Man!!!

a when are you going to be getting out of the army and when you do get out What are you going to do. But anyways whats been happen with you "Oh" I haven't forgotten about your pictures I just have to find you some okay. So what is your mother saying about you getting out or did she say anything about it yet. damn I really don't have anything to say so I'm going to close this ugly letter sorry. Bye, Bye love you lot's

Letter #4

2/20/97

West + larry west Been Happening with you Blood. ain't shit here But Bad times I sending you a lil something. yes I gave Puffy some 2 to "B" on target Blood. I'm Sending you these so "B" happy okay. I really don't have much to say But Could you do me A lil something Could you give one of these pictures to My auntie. thanks a lot. I would do it Myself But I'm out of stampes right Now you know. Damn its like everything I want to use My stampes 4 Something like this I don't have None sorry Man. Well I hope you enjoy this picture I'll send you some more later when I get them out okay. So let Puffy have 2 B-cuzz you will "B" getting youres soon trust me on that Blood. Love ya Chadrick Daquan Render.

# "CHAD"

C
H
A
D
R
I
C
K

My best friend forever.
You will NEVER be replaced, Red Eyes.
Eye will keep your memory alive!

THESE TRIALS ARE ONLY TO TEST YOUR FAITH
TO SHOW THAT IT IS STRONG AND PURE

IT IS BEING TESTED
AS FIRE TEST AND PURIFIES GOLD
AND YOUR FAITH IS FAR MORE
PRECIOUS TO GOD THAN MERE GOLD
SO IF YOUR FAITH REMAINS STRONG
AFTER BEING TRIED BY FIERY TRIALS
IT WILL BRING YOU MUCH PRAISE
AND GLORY AND HONOR ON THE DAY
WHEN JESUS CHRIST IS
REVEALED TO THE WHOLE
WORLD.

## 1 Peter 1 vs thr the 7th verse

Pharoah and Big Dog

Pharoah in breaking Barriers class, O.S.P.
Eye learned things Eye still carry with me
10 years later...

## HOME GOING SERVICE FOR:

SUNRISE:
SEPTEMBER 1987

SUNSET:
JULY 1997

# PRISON

PHAROAH C. WILSON, JR'S FREEDOM
MARCH 1998; 11:30 A.M.
OREGON STATE PENITENTIARY
SWEET HOME BAPTIST CHURCH
69 S.W. DOOMSDAY LANE
REV. DR. GOD VS. SATAN

*Flee from sexual immorality. Every other sin a person commits is outside the body, but the sexually immoral person sins against his own body.*

## 1 CORINTHIANS 6:18

**A TIME TO BE BORN:** Pharoah Wilson, Jr has survived four bitter miserable years of rape only to grow up a confused teenager. Learning to hate himself, he fell into a dark vortex of problems dealing with people twice his age that used his young body for carnal pleasure. That would lead to his own freedom being snatched away by the very men that killed his best friend.

**A TIME TO GROW:** Educationally, Pharoah loved reading, writing and researching but in his heart, mind, body and soul he was dying. No one listened to his pain yet everyone had something to say about what he was doing wrong, calling him a faggot and rejected him because of his lifestyle that he never brought around those he loved. Those he loved persecuted him when he needed them the most.

**A TIME TO REFLECT:** Pharoah Wilson snitched on the men who he thought murdered his best friend Chad and he received death threats on his life, but he never stopped cooperating with the police. His faith in God was starting to get cloudy as he rejected the Bible and Pastors to find his own way in the world. But going into Hell labeled "Prison," he would rediscover God all over again and his faith never waivered.

**A TIME TO DIE AND BE MOURNED:** On a very sad morning, in March, after his mother made him take a plea bargain, Pharoah sucked up the pain and false accusations, swallowed the death of his best friend and entered a place called Prison where everyone wrote him off and said he would be raped and die in the darkness. Pharoah Wilson died…and left behind the ashes of yesterday…

# The Coronation

## The King of Erotica In the Making:

## P R [1] S N

***Someone asked me what*** "made" me gay. Nothing "made" me anything. Situations Eye was in, traumatic things Eye was forced to endure, certainly *influenced* me, but even when Eye was being raped as a child Eye made a choice to succumb to it, to enjoy it, and to become addicted to it. Yes Eye was addicted to the sexual abuse. Our choices lead us along the path. Sure, Eye wasn't mentally or physically prepared to comprehend or handle what Eye went through, and it wasn't right by a long shot. But at certain points in my childhood Eye used to ask my abuser for sex because Eye grew to *enjoy* it—and even then Eye didn't know it was wrong. My abuser molded my young mind like a potter does wet clay and the substance was formed and put in a kettle…hardened…extracted to cool and settle…then glazed and decorated...*celebrated…*then unapologetically placed on the mantel of abomination. By the time the abuse ended when Eye was ten years old, Eye had grown to enjoy and like what was done so Eye lived my life chasing my anger throughout my teenage years, sleeping with people twice my age to replace what was no more. That's all Eye'll say. Eye'm bisexual. Eye've been this nearly all my life. Eye love men and women equally. And whoever Eye choose to be with knows my orientation. Eye'm man enough to be honest and let whoever Eye deal with choose to take it further. Everyone is different; accept people for who they are. All gay and bi men are different individually. Don't mash me together with other gay or bisexuals because *none* of them was Pharoah C. Wilson Jr. Everyone's pain were their own. Generalizing a group of people into what you wanted them to be was a form of discrimination. The *prejudice* in the gay community was astounding.

The HATE Eye've experienced in the gay community never bothered me. In fact Eye could give a damn if a gay or bi Niggah liked me or not. Words were like sticks and stones and Eye'd beat a Niggah with sticks and stones before Eye let him rob me of my dignity. The ONLY being that can decipher the human species is God, the Creator. If you don't believe in him then that's *your* Free Will and *your* choice.

If a person is gay, bi, or transgender embrace people for who they are. And stop stuffing them in a generalized box because we're ALL different.

In my life Eye have been tried for purity for a very long time. Years, in fact, dating back to when Eye started watching *The Jackson 5* cartoons on Sunday, just before Church. And probably months before *that.* Eye grew up watching Mama smile when she had it all, pat herself on the back when she held down sometimes two jobs to make it work and was married, with a husband who always had secret bitterness that Eye wasn't his son. But at the time Eye didn't even know he was my step father; Eye always *assumed* he was my biological father because he bought me McDonald's every Friday and took me and my brothers to Toys R Us and always hugged and showed me love. So imagine my surprise, after this man groomed me, turned around and brutally raped me and took it all out of power, control and selfishness.

But as a kid Eye was not to know this. He blocked my blessings by testing the purity of my soul. He tried to break the unbreakable because my Mama always prayed for the safety of her children. So a realm of protection surrounded me but the more and more Mama stopped praying, the very moment she cut off God by reducing her prayers to breakfast, lunch and dinner that protection, that realm weakened, and he violated my comfort zone and came all over my butt cheeks when he was done. And this manufactured me. How could Eye pray to God when Eye didn't know him yet? When you're 6 years old you still didn't know the world was bigger than your bedroom, the bathroom and Mama's living room. Eye never stopped believing in God because Eye was forced to like him and to love him and Eye didn't *know* him. How did you love something you didn't know? Eye hadn't made the choice to worship God or believe in Scientology at that age because Eye didn't know such a choice had to be made. How could Eye when the theory at the time to me didn't exist?

And Eye would carry this misconception throughout my life. Pray to a God Eye didn't know and never saw, and Eye could remember a few times Eye prayed for him to show me his face without peeking around the darkness and over the years he had. He showed me. He showed me when Buck's *daughter* took my virginity and opened my eyes and he showed me when she wound up pregnant when Eye turned 11, revealing and destroying the myth that storks carried babies 'cause honey if they did then my cousin was a big, black ass stork.

Where's her beak and where were the feathers? Eye could remember feathers in my hair when Eye used to eat her out, from a hole in one of Mama's pillows on her water bed, back when sleeping on water was today's version of Jesus or Peter walking on water, but don't take your eyes off Jesus if you do. You'll get swallowed by whales. Lily, my older relative, swallowed my virginity like a good plate of greens and cornbread. Always wearing long floral dresses to fool the elders but when she pulled it up making my pole hard she didn't have on *any* panties and she would beat me with an extension cord if Eye didn't eat her the way she expected me to, or if Eye didn't do it to her right, topping the last performance. Eye feared her so much that when she came around Eye was unnaturally quiet and barely said two words to her. God showed his face when Eye slept with people twice my age. "Baby, wait till you marry to have sex. Keep yourself pure," Mama used to tell me and Eye was already being sexually dehumanized by some of the adults in my neighborhood, the nocturnal stone throwers…

Yet older people in the 'Hood that were married were sexing me and watching me have passionate sex with their significant others through the reflection of mirrors—doing it on the washer, dryer and the nightstand.

Eye was barely 14. He showed himself again, after being raped in Perrine by The Pail Man (from PHAROAH, when Eye found the strength to move on and survive), and God showed himself again a few weeks later when Eye was beat up and dragged into the bushes by The Circle (pink duplexes behind Lee's Grocery store) by two bullies who Eye always hated. Even when they raped me, they couldn't screw. The times Eye wanted to laugh nearly crippled me, but Eye didn't because a) it wasn't a laughing matter and b) Eye still had the mentality that Eye was put here for men to misuse and mistreat. It was molded into me for four years. Um. Eye survived. It didn't kill me; it made me stronger.

God showed himself in every major situation in my life in the form of my sanity and survival; but Eye denied his presence because Eye was too busy chasing my self-hatred and the weakness of my (the) flesh. God showed himself AGAIN when Mom and Eye fell out when Eye was 19, because, back then, Eye thought Eye was grown. Eye thought Eye knew more than my mother and Eye bought a plane ticket and flew to Oregon to stay with my best friend, running from my problems. Eye needed to get out of Mama's house, and Eye was determined to do just that. God showed himself in that situation by allowing Satan to attack me, just as long as he didn't take my life, for disrespecting my mother. My days were numbered and Eye didn't even know it.

Eye've never been to Oregon, and Eye was glad Eye went. Eye hadn't been on that side of the world (well Eye was born in Salinas, California but Eye had no memory of that) and Eye needed to see this. Eye remember when the plane arrived in Portland, Oregon, in 1997. It circled a huge mountain topped with snow. It was one of the most beautiful things Eye have ever seen in my life, but the bench mark of the gravest hell Eye would face on earth, the hell of having your freedom taken away as if a lion tearing through the salty, sweaty flesh of a buffalo.

My star wrestler best friend Chad arrived at the airport to pick me up and when we saw each other…silliness met silliness once again and we were ranking on people like we did in the old days and talking about everybody, and catching up with each other's activities and hugging so much we just couldn't believe we were in each others' lives again.

He changed, though. And not in a bad way, no. His voice was more polite and jubilant than it was years before and he was in college. Eye was proud of him, that he was going to Portland State University to be an architect/graphic designer. A couple of years before, he made the newspaper in high school. During that time he played three sports and still had like a 3.26 GPA. Big upgrade from the Perrine, Florida days, when his grades were about to take that unnatural plummet to hell. Eye remembered Eye used to do his homework for him while he thought about selling drugs. Thank God he never did. Eye talked him out of it.

Chad's passion was simple. He wanted to be a better man than his father, and he wanted to make enough money so his mother didn't have to *ever* work again. Chad also wanted a daughter. He wanted to terrorize his daughter's Prom Date when the time came. When he first told me Eye was laughing so hard Eye almost threw up. Eye told him Eye'd have my Chopper sitting next to his so we could blow his ass away he disrespected our baby girl.

And he was sent to Oregon by his Grandma to better his life and wound up getting murdered there. That's the irony. No matter where you live you have an entirely new set of dilemmas and problems. Eye'm so glad he never sold drugs, no matter how much he wanted to. Something in Chad never let him give up or stop fighting and that rubbed off on me. Eye never met a more humble person. He practically raised himself ever since he was ten years old. And that's why we were so close. We kept each other going. The one thing Chad always longed for, that his guardian's tried to keep from him, was his mother. Chad confided everything to me. And some things Eye won't say, because if he specifically asked me to keep it between me and him, even in his death, Eye will HONOR his wish. But the few things Eye do reveal Chad really didn't care if it got out. It was no secret that Chad's mom did drugs at the time.

Chad used to be angry about it, but he never judged or disrespected her and Eye didn't either. When Chad was sent to Oregon, he said he didn't want to leave his mother, but once he realized he needed a future, something his mother could be proud of, he went. Leaving life as he knew it behind. All his friends. His upbringing. Me. My family. And *Goulds.*

Chad didn't go to Oregon for Chad. Chad went for his mother and never told anybody his true intentions, but me. His Mama was his secret life source. This drove Chad to the brink of destruction. Chad didn't like South East Portland, which, pretty much, was the good part of town. North East Portland was a place his guardian's warned him to stay away from, but he would wind up over there anyway. That's where most of the blacks resided, and Eye didn't care how you tried to live around white people and dance to their music and eat their food. Part of you will always gravitate towards your own kind. Wrestling became Chad's passion. Sure, he also played football, and excelled, but he loved to wrestle. This little pint sized best friend of mine, about 5 feet 4, throwing Niggahs on their big asses like they were beanie babies.

He rose up the popularity list. His wrestling got him a national spotlight. A spotlight he never anticipated. He used to write me letters and send me pictures and post cards from the places he visited overseas. His guardians always pushed him to be the best and do the best. And Eye believed in this, until Eye went to visit Chad in Oregon and he revealed the shade. He revealed the lies and the cover ups. He told me one thing that not only pissed me off, but Eye cut his guardian's off, without even telling them. They lied to him. Chad and Eye were sitting in his room one day. He was absent-mindedly showing me all the wrestling photos. All his accomplishments. Of course Eye was proud of him, but Chad could care less about those accomplishments. He down played them.

"Why, man? You should be proud."

"Eye'm not, Pharoah." Eye always liked how he said my name. Always made me smile.

"Why?" Eye asked. Eye was admiringly flipping through pictures. He saw parts of the world Eye could only dream about. Eye was so happy for him, seeing life through his eyes and experiences. He told me to take the pictures Eye wanted. *Jeez,* Eye wanted them all.

"You know they lied to me to get me to win the wrestling tournament," he said.

The pictures turned to smoke and burned my eyes. Eye slowly looked up at him. He told me that before, but Eye didn't say anything. "Lied about what?"

He smiled bitterly and sat next to me. Eye put the book up. Pictures could wait. He looked under the door to make sure passing shadows weren't lurking. When it was all good, he looked in my eyes. "They promised me Eye could see my mother if Eye won the wrestling championship. Eye put my all into it, even in practice Eye sucked up what made me a winner because in the back of my mind Eye knew Eye could see my Mom. When Eye won the wrestling championship they did everything in their power to ensure Eye didn't get to talk to my mother."

"Ah, man, yo. Are you serious?"

Hot tears fell down his face and he hugged me and Eye hugged him and he said, "Eye just want to lay eyes on my mother, Pharoah and they keeping me from her."

Eye died inside.

*Chad longed for Mom.* He loved his mother unconditionally. Eye didn't care what she did in life; he had his mother on a pedestal, and his favorite Aunt Tanka on a pedestal. Tanka's kids were Chad's universe. Jason, Erika and Kim. Chad pretty much raised them as if they were his own children. His brother Wand, who was locked up (at the time) was Chad's source of inspiration. Chad adored his big brother, and just because he was in prison didn't mean anything to Chad. That's his brother and he was going to stick by him no matter what. Chad always asked about Jason, Erika and Kim and part of him was mad Eye was in Oregon because Eye was his link to talk to his family when Eye was at home. On Mama's phone Eye used to call his relatives on the three way so he could talk to them; Chad was an entirely different, care free person when he talked to his family; and he told me to never let his Guardian's find out. Chad and Eye stayed up all night talking once Eye got settled at his Guardian's home. His cousin, who went to junior high school with my Mom and his Filipino wife, Eye didn't like her at all, was Chad's *worst* nightmare. When they greeted me Eye was very cordial and doing all the little shenanigans Mom taught me when you met someone for the first time, but once Chad and Eye went to his bedroom and Eye set my bags and suit case down on the wooden floor by the door—his drawings all over the wall, and my picture in his mirror—he said, "Don't fall for the act, Pharoah."

Eye was thrown. "What do you mean?"

He looked around a moment, listening for passing footsteps. "They are fake. They will smile in your face and stab you in your back."

Eye believed him. "Then why are you still living here?"

He looked helpless. "Eye have nowhere to go."

Could it be that hard? "What about your girlfriend? How does she feel about it?"

"Komingo? *Nah*, Eye tried. Komingo's parents even told me Eye could live with them."

"And what happened?"

"My hot tempered cousin." His Male Guardian. "He threatened to show up on her door step raising hell if Eye did. So Eye'm trapped in this house. Can you believe one time this man actually pissed in my shoes so Eye couldn't go out with her."

"Wow, Eye remember you told me that in one of your letters and on the phone."

"Eye'm trapped in here. They try to control everything Eye do. So some things Eye do they will *never* know."

"And what's that?"

He was quiet, staring at me. Swinging a red bandana around on his finger.

And it still didn't dawn on me.

*Chad's favorite color was red* and his nick name was Red Eyes. He had two key chains made with Baby Boy (me) and Red Eyes (his) that read "Best friends forever." Eye put one of the key chains on my keys and began to enjoy Portland.

It was *so* different there. Portland natives called soda "Pop" and Eye got in plenty arguments over it whenever Eye went to a fast food joint and asked for a soda. They looked at me like Eye was a Martian. One cashier asked, "Sir, what is a soda?" And Eye was like "Um, Sprite, Pepsi…"

She smiled, dismissing my comments with a wave of her hand. "Oh. You mean you want a Pop."

Eye slapped my forehead in mock horror.

When my best friend was murdered Eye was devastated. Eye think that was the single most hurtful thing Eye have ever gone through in my life. My best friend stuck by my side since childhood and he died without *me* by his side. Eye had no clue he was murdered until the next day. Eye saw it on the news. And when his face flashed on the screen Eye tried to dig up the earth itself. Eye didn't eat or sleep for weeks. Eye withdrew into myself. Eye stopped loving and caring for any and everything. Eye used to confide in him all the time and he always had my back and was very protective of me. Eye remember back to July 27, 1997. The day and year he died. We had a good day. Eye had his gold rims installed on his pearl white Cutlass for him since he had to work. After they finished with his car Eye was driving around town feeling *good* because he felt good. Eye had just gotten fired from Circuit City because they found out Eye was stealing merchandise, and Eye was because Eye was selling it to have money to survive. My mother said Eye wouldn't make it on my own and she said hell would freeze over before we spoke again so Eye had a point to prove. Eye told myself Eye would NEVER call her for help. So stealing and selling merchandise provided for me temporary relief, till Eye was caught and Eye didn't apologize for it.

But on July 27th, Eye was enjoying spending time with my best friend, not knowing it would be the last day Eye ever saw him alive. Talking about it fifteen years later seems so foreign to me and the pain is still there. Tears fall down my face remembering the pain and grief of losing my best friend. But Eye remember driving Chad's car, getting the rims installed, then getting his stereo system (Eye bought for him) installed. Eye was enjoying (at the time), for a second, another man's car as mine and once Eye took it to him at his place of employment (Belmont Terrace, a nursing home—he loved working there, and the elderly loved him!), Eye never saw his eyes glow so brightly. He loved that pearl white Cutlass. It was a 70's model, and you couldn't tell him anything about that car. When he saw the rims on his car he smiled so big Eye melted. "Is this my baby," he said, running his hands over the hood of his car. *"Sitting on the all gold cheeses!"*

"Cheeses" was his word for gold rims. He looked at me, giving me a big hug. "Thanks, dawg! This is what Eye always wanted! My car totally fixed up! The Hoes g'on hate me! Eye love you, dawg."

"Eye love you too, bruh!" Eye said.

Things were going along swell until one of Chad's friends came to visit him, to see his car. And *that* friend brought *another* friend Chad and Eye didn't know.

Confused, Chad looked at me. "Who is that Niggah with Toine?"

"Eye don't know!" Eye said, eyeing the other dude suspiciously. "Eye'm visiting Portland. Eye don't know who any of your friends are."

"*Toine* is my friend. But Eye don't know that other Niggah."

Despite his unease having a stranger around, Chad agreed to take us all for a spin in the car. So when ole boy made his way to the front seat Eye walked right past him and said, "The back seat is back there."

Chad, laughing, said, "Yea the front is for my brother."

Enough said. Things were pretty uneventful. Four black men driving around N.E. Portland, blasting music and having a good time. Chad was so happy his car came together he could barely stand it. One of his wishes (he once told me) was to have his car fixed up, so he can say it's his and then he wouldn't want to live anymore. Be careful what you ask for, Eye told him.

Chad's friend, Toine, said, "Yo, homie. Fam. We should go pick up these two bitches across the way."

Eye was down. Hell, Eye flew across the country, from Miami to Portland to kick it with my best friend so Eye knew Eye was going.

"Ok," he said, unsure of himself.

"Eye'm going," Eye said, sure of it.

"Um, no you're not," Chad said, blurting it out.

Eye looked at him sideways. "What?"

"Yea, man," Toine said. "Just *us*, man. So there's room for the girls."

"*This* is *my* best friend and *my* best friend's *car* and Eye'm not going *no*where." Now Eye felt betrayed by my own best friend, and the anger swelled inside me like hurricanes.

Chad was telling me, again, "*No*, you can't go with me," with two brothahs in his back seat that had him marked for death, but he didn't know it and neither did Eye. Eye would find out the next day that Chad saying "No" saved my life. God showed himself verbally, through the wavering soul of my best friend. Because if Chad would have said "Yes," we both would have been shot at the place he was told the two Hoes lived, and the place was abandoned.

God showed himself through accusations of sex abuse against a kid. Eye still couldn't believe people would sink so low. Eye was only 19 years old. A year past 18, and already my own kind turned against me, had my best friend killed, showed no emotion, lied, lied, lied, then tarnished my image because Eye was the only one cooperating with the police to bring them closer to the murderer.

Then God showed himself again when they put me in the same prison with the goons that killed my best friend. What type of racist state does that? Um, *Oregon.* Four percent black and half of them were in jail, under Ballot Measure 11. Measure 11 was a law that high jacked Niggahs, giving them a mandatory 8 years day for day or more for getting your black asses out of line.

Stay in your place. They tried to pin Measure 11 on me but it didn't stick because they didn't have DNA evidence or NOTHING to tie me to those so-called bogus ass crimes, but they won through my ignorance because Eye didn't know the so-called Public Defender (or Public Pretender) didn't know what the hell he was doing. He immediately begged me to plea bargain just so he could collect a big paycheck. As far as Eye know my lawyer could have been a snitch from a jail cell in a Burberry suit and sent to court to represent you or get you to sign a plea bargain, even if they have lack of evidence and a bunch of circumstantial bull.

Okay. Eye'm black. Tarnish my name, reduce it to 11517837 and call it a day.

Eye had a solid alibi. An unexpected friend named Tracy stepped forward and wrote me a letter. He told me everything, how my so-called victims were related by blood to the very one that helped get my best friend murdered. Eye was in shock. Eye showed my lawyer this letter so the lawyer agreed to talk to Tracy. Tracy said it was part of the conspiracy, that Chad was murdered, that we knew, and the plan was to take me down as well for "snitching." And when Eye started cooperating with the police, that angered the members of the Blood Gang even more to either take me out or to shut me up. So Eye was marked for death. Eye felt good, because Eye told Mom of the witness who could prove Eye didn't molest a kid, and my lawyer felt good about it as well. That was my smoking trump card, and instead of thanking God Eye thanked Tracy and everyone but God.

Wouldn't have taken me 3 seconds to thank the Lord. But it wasn't even on my mind or in my heart. So God vanished, and when he did the enemy took it all.

Even Tracy's reputation.

*One day, in one of the dorms* at the Inverness jail, Eye was sitting with the infamous Tom Curtis at one of the dinner tables, watching the news. Inmates loved the news. They were on it. They knew who did what before you even got there. He asked me did Eye write anything, since Eye used to sneak to the law library and type my stories and hide it in my paperwork so it wasn't confiscated. Eye told him Eye had. Tom smiled, skinny ass. But he was good people.

"What about poems? You got some?"

"Yea, Eye do."

"Eye need one for a girl."

Eye shook my head. "You sound like all the other dudes in here. In the past month Eye must have written over a hundred poems. Luckily Eye keep a copy to prove Eye wrote it."

He was quietly watching TV.

"Tom?" Eye was studying his face. It was like he saw a ghost. He was pointing at the screen. "Isn't that your boy Tracy, your witness?"

Eye slowly looked at the TV, the breath caught in my throat. Yes. He was on TV. And the next few words Eye heard made me close my eyes and say "Oh, God."

*And a scandal has unfolded. Tracy Ross, a 17 year old high school student, was really a 30 year old man imposter. More details at 7.*

*The room was spinning.* "No, this can't be happening. He's 30?" Eye asked, watching Tracy's life dissect right before my very eyes. Huge tears fell. Eye couldn't breathe. His picture flashed on the screen, and the high school he attended imposing as a student made me wanna puke.

"Oh my God, Pharoah. Welcome to Oregon, dude. Chad's murderers want *your* ass in jail. They just secretly called the police and exposed all his stuff so he's discredited from getting on the witness stand. Man if anything proved your innocence, it's this latest development. If you weren't innocent this wouldn't be happening. He was getting away with posing as a *seventeen* year old and illegally selling cars across the Canadian border. Now he's on his way to jail."

Eye wasn't hearing him. Eye lay my head on the table and refused to open my eyes. God showed himself. You put anything before me Eye will take it away. Including my freedom.

And my only key witness.

*The next few months unraveled* horribly. Eye lost Tracy as a key witness, as his life played out all over the news for weeks. Eye couldn't believe even Eye didn't know he was really 30. Hell Eye didn't even know he was going to high school. He damn sure didn't look 17, so how in the hell he pulled that off? Then the news showed his real graduation picture from an old year book back in the day. Eye was simply taken aback. Eye lay in my bunk, watching the news, heart sick. He faked and forged documents, fake birth certificates, fake military papers. The whole nine. Whoever put in that secret snitch phone call exposed all his crimes. They didn't just want him off the streets…they wanted him locked up for years to come. Eye didn't understand. Maybe because Eye was just 21 years old and the year Eye became legal to buy alcohol was the year Eye was locked up and would stay locked up for the next four years.

What kind of people had Eye made my friends when Eye was visiting Oregon? Those were the people Chad took me around and introduced me to. Eye didn't like them at first, but Chad *assured* me they were good people and when he died they really showed me what they really thought of him. They hated him.

And hated me for being so close to him.

*Eye was still going to court.* Eye would stand up and be a man. But my manhood was slain when Mama took the wheel, and she wasn't playing around. She made all the decisions for me while Eye was locked up. It was then Eye wanted to be the Master of something, anything that gave me some type of control in my life. But what that was had me stomped.

Mama and the family intervened. Family intervention. Before Eye was to go to court, the judge summoned me. Eye was shackled and transported to the court house. Once Eye arrived, Eye was ushered in the judge's chambers. Eye had an attitude the entire time. She called Mama on the speaker phone. My Mama, a FED, on the speaker phone in Oregon from Miami, told me to take the plea bargain or basically lose my family from my stupidity.

Eye was angry. *Very* angry. "Are you on their side, Mama?"

"No, baby. But this is a crime against a kid and the people who had your best friend murdered are all behind this and we can't prove it. Those suckers *know* you didn't do that.

Where's the DNA evidence? They don't have any DNA evidence and they know it."

When she said it the lawyer and Judge lowered their heads. Didn't say anything. And Eye was staring at them. Busted!

"So why should Eye sign a plea bargain, Mama? Eye didn't do this. If Eye did Eye would man up but Mama you are the one who always told me to stand up for what's right."

"This isn't play school, Pharoah. You made this bed."

"Eye know that. All Eye did was the right thing. Cooperating with the police to find Chad's killers. He was my best friend. Eye couldn't just sit by and do nothing! Eye shouldn't have to be punished for that!"

"Everyone on the jury will be white. Your judge is white. Your prosecutor is white. Your lawyer is white. You are in a predominantly white state. Eye warned you not to *mess* with Oregon. You go there on vacation and leave on probation."

"Mom."

She said more sternly, "You are black with no record. Your Mama is a FED and not a welfare case, they already mad about that. That your Mama has some sense. They have no evidence, none, Pharoah. And they know this. Where is the DNA? If they had DNA they wouldn't be asking you to plea for a lesser charge. They would stick it to your ass. But that's white people. They love destroying our black sons. They are probably gloating now."

Funny thing was *no* one in the room protested what she said. This made me shake in my chair. How many innocent blacks have they already locked up? Eye did have stolen checks on my record, a misdemeanor.

"If you go to court you are already hung. Your defendants are bitter blacks who had your best friend killed and are after you for talking too much. Take the plea. You can be a dumb ass, and lose, doing 8 years day for day. No good time. You won't be the same, Pharoah." She was near tears, Eye knew this had to be destroying her.

*Take it to court! Eye believe in the law, there's no way Eye'm owning up to something Eye wasn't a part of.* "Mama, Eye'm going to court."

"TAKE THE FREAKING DEAL!" Eye sat straight up, quiet. The judge smiled. Victory in her eyes.

My hand shaking, and my own self talk telling me NO DON'T DO IT PHAROAH, God showed himself when Eye signed. Hot tears streamed down my face and for an instant Eye saw empathy in the judge's eyes—Eye'm sorry. And then her eyes hardened. Eye didn't sign just a plea bargain, pleading no contest, Eye signed a pact with God…that Eye endorse seeing you for years yet putting mortal man and my own sins and carnal pleasures and immaturity and recklessness before GOD, but now my life *began.* Now began the terrible climb back from an infamous piece of crap to grace. And when Eye get there Eye must say Thank you God. But it would be a hard climb. Mission Impossible, Eye whispered silently when no one paid attention.

*I know what Eye want to be the Master of now…Eye want to be the Master of my Thoughts…*

*Mission Accomplished.* And Eye gave a chilling smile, making the judge do a double take. She stared at me for a long moment while things were finalized. *One day Eye will tell my story to the world. Eye believe it with everything inside me, Eye feel it! Eye want nothing else! Everyone will pay for double crossing me in their lies and deceit! My best friend's death won't be in vain. Eye already conquered it in my heart…and Eye knew it would come in the form of writing…Eye won't worry about how its going to come…Eye will let things do what they do. Eye will make it happen. People will know my name. They will know my face. They will be touched from my storytelling.*

*Eye vow…*

*When Eye did prison time Eye* didn't shed one tear. Eye refused to cry. When Eye felt myself about to cry Eye would bite down hard on my tongue and it'd go away. If Eye could survive four years of rape and four years of high school Eye could and would survive this. Eye was Nassau, Bahamian; we didn't fold when facing a dilemma. But now wasn't the time to embrace Bahamian values, when you just signed a pact with God that Eye would never lose faith in him and never let it waiver ever again. Eye smelled like

Similac to an 80 year old. Eye was the smell of cum to a 90 year old. Eye'm the type of *preemie* she used to swallow from flaming head; sent back into the hell of stomach acids while in the semen state.

Eye needed to be embracing God. But that didn't mean Eye wasn't still a sinner because Eye was young. Eye was an old soul but Eye wasn't a 40 year old. Eye was still 21.

Doing time was rough. Eye could not believe Eye was going to prison. My decisions and the choices Eye made in life got me here. Eye never blamed anyone for my problems, Eye always owned up to them. Some more reluctantly than others, but now Eye'm in prison for a crime against a child when Eye love children and Eye didn't know how to embrace that. So Eye didn't. Eye gave it to God. By then it was out of my hands, but Eye had to go through the motions to prove to myself Eye was worthy of life. When Eye was bussed from the dorm of the Inverness jail to the infamous Oregon State Penitentiary, maximum security, Eye was shaking my damn head. Eye wasn't a violent *or* a hateful person, even though Eye've hated myself for years. Eye never understood why they sent me to a maximum security prison. The Laws of Attraction jolted me awake, and suddenly everything made sense. Eye was being prepared for something…something greater than myself. But what was it? Why was Eye focusing on what Eye don't have? No matter what it was Eye was going to write my stories until it came to me. Eye'm not going to worry about how its going to come, or what form it will come in. Obedience.

Time to Master obedience…

***You tend to remember things*** when you stopped thinking about them; it seems you find true love when you stop *searching* for it…If Eye could Master *that* then Eye'm good. The transitioning taking place deep inside of me was startling. Being shackled in a white jumpsuit, Eye felt the lowest Eye had ever felt. My mother did this for a living, dealing with federal inmates but this wasn't the cozy FEDS with sparkling windows and marble floors.

This was state prison. Nothing sparkling about that. Eye shook the entire time. Eye was so in fear Eye was about to call out for my mother, but the mistake of calling out for mortals was the sole reason Eye fell from grace. Eye still hadn't called out to God. So Eye did. Eye closed my eyes and talked to God the entire time. Telling him Eye didn't know what to do or what to say.

And within seconds my nervousness vanished.

*My arrival at OSP was scary*. Eye was in prison. Eye couldn't believe this. When Eye arrived, Eye think there were about four other people with me. Felt good to form alliances despite our differences. Eye was the only bisexual amongst the group, and they treated me with respect.

One of them said, "Eye don't even know your name yet, but check it. None of us can judge you. We were all judged before we boarded this bus. We're all scum in the eyes of society. We're the same color—orange and blue. We have the same name—a state number; Let's show these crackers we can band together."

All four of us agreed. We also agreed to make a pact, that, despite our crimes, we were all young and we would be like brothers. And we would hold true to that motto, even when doing time got rough with predators walking the yard, scalping, trying to find the weakest of the bunch so he could move in his cell and rape him all night.

Eye was also told to stay away from an inmate named Chicken George and Clayton. They said Clayton liked to apply baby oil on his naked body during count time so the guards could see his meat and Chicken George hog tied his young victims and gave them old man dick till they passed out. Eye was warned of all this before Eye got there. So Eye knew what to look out for. But it's one thing to look out for it before you got to prison. Because once Eye got there Eye found out it was bigger than just *looking* for it.

This was a place designed to tear you down and destroy you. Being amongst the bitter, cold and angry—and experiencing the Concrete Jungle—was the scariest time of my life. Eye was anxious to start doing my time and get on with my life. But Eye shook like a hooker in front of the state senate. Gotta tell how Bill Clinton's cum got on my good Easter Sunday dress.

Getting off the transportation bus in shackles, Eye felt like a slab of meat. Being introduced into mind control slavery. *Deprogram*...Eye was stronger than Eye gave myself credit for. Eye was still 13 Bravo Field Artillery *whoooaaaa* and Eye was still a soldier, whether Eye was out or not. Military thinking had become my whole thought process as Eye entered the Concrete Jungle surrounded by thirty feet walls. Eye was going to use Mama's knowledge on Federal policy to get me through state prison. Mama was my source of inspiration, despite being angry at her for making me take a plea bargain and dangling the interaction with my family over my head to make me do it.

Guard towers surrounding the place. When Eye told one of my friends back at the Inverness Jail (12926272, the number Eye was reduced to), that they were shipping me to OSP he was shaking. Eye will never forget the fear on his face. Eye nearly pissed myself. "Oh, no! That's a Mad House! Oh, God Pharoah Eye pray for your safety."

Eye had God deep in my heart. Eye feared no one, not even man. But that all changed when Eye was on the bus, being lead to *The Blair Witch Project*: PRISON.

My life has been reduced to this. Eye was very upset with myself, that my decisions led me here. Despite it all, Eye blamed nothing and no one but myself. Eye may not have done the crime Eye was accused of, but as of that day Eye stopped making excuses. This was real life, not TV. This wasn't a stage play with directors and casting managers and background lights and scripts.

Eye saw all the prison movies. Almost always you saw the submissive one being approached to be punked or raped.

So Eye was a Miami-Dade County Niggah, Goulds up in the Salem, Oregon camp. After going through the transition, given light blue long sleeved shirts and blue jeans bearing an orange OREGON iron on, Eye got dressed. They gave me some ugly shoes. You didn't dress a dead body in those shoes unless you trying to set somebody up, so Eye put my walls up. One of the guards, a short male, looked me over. He smiled and Eye lowered my head. “Hey, there,” he said, walking up to me. “You must be Miami.”

“You know me?” Eye asked, afraid to look up. Felt like Eye was being singled out. My brothers looked at me strangely, our alliance already being threatened and tested and Eye only knew them for a few hours. One of my brothers whispered, “Do you know him?”

“No!” Eye mouthed with a weird look on my face. My brothers relaxed. Phew! Eye looked at the guard. “Do Eye know you?”

He looked us over before he responded. “No, Eye don’t,” said Officer Wadley. “But Eye heard you are an amazing poet. My friend works at the Inverness jail. He told me to look out for you, that you have a raw talent for words.”

Eye looked up and smiled. “Really?”

“Yea, Officer Gaston.”

Eye smiled faintly. “Oh, yea. He good people.”

He studied me a moment. “Something is off about you.”

Eye didn’t follow. “*Off*?”

He grinned. “Yea. Looking at you, you don’t belong in a place like this.”

*Here we go!* “Tell me about it. Famous last words.”

Eye liked his vibe. “OSP isn’t all that bad. Eye hope you weren’t scared up before you got here.” The Law of Attraction works! Work small! Nah, dream *bigger*!

“Yea a friend was telling me it’s the mad house.”

“Here are the ropes, Miami. Stay away from the tobacco trade. Don’t snitch, mind your business, and always eat. Eat all you can.”

“Why?” Eye asked, wondering why he wanted me to always stuff food down my throat.

“You’ll understand if it ever happens to you.”

For some reason that made sense.

*There were four blocks at* OSP—A, D, C, and E Block. Eye was given a cell in D-Block. There was an honor Block—A (and they lived good) and a work Block—C; you have to have a job to be in A or C, and there was a waiting list for A Block. E Block was the last of the four. An honor block and a waiting list in prison, laugh out loud, sounded like Section 8 sucking off the welfare line. There was a long pill line as Eye crossed the beige so-called marble floors. Air smelled of depression, lights dimmed of imperfection casting ghosts, not light upon those awaiting medicine.

Eye was holding my property and my clothes, my squeaking shoes against the floor disheartening.

Inmates of all shapes, colors and sizes looked like zombies in the pill line. One inmate, a big Niggah, went slap off. "Eye want my freaking *meds*!"

Oh, yea. Wouldn't be talking to him. Eye kept my head ducked. When Eye was approaching D Block, Eye walked into the unit and it was huge as hell. Eye looked up. Cells seemed to go on for miles.

"Oh my God. Be with me. Eye just entered the lion's cave."

***Eye was walking past cells*** on the second tier. Another officer showed me where to go. The way he moved about robotically unnerved me, like he only did what he was designed to do. The Block officer, Miss Storm, looked at me, with dents all in her face.

"She used to be a stripper," said the guard. "She got good coochie, too."

Eye was laughing. "What? You are crazy. That ugly thing used to strip?"

He gazed into my eyes. "Eye used to own the club."

***Walking up the tier, the*** block officer opened my cell. A few inmates, who didn't have jobs, or were indigent, were looking at me. There goes the whispers.

*"Damn that Niggah fine as hell!"*

*"Look at his eyes."*

*"Hey, pretty lady."*

Eye paused at the bars and slammed my boots against it, and he jumped a hundred feet back, throwing up his fists, "If you *touch* me Eye will go postal on your monkey ape looking ass!" Eye yelled, shaking my head as if psycho—it actually worked.

And walked off. If Eye'm going to survive Eye better join them. *What am Eye doing? Might as well play as crazy as the men in the pill line so word travels about me fast.* Eye walked in the cell, and a troll looking Niggah got off the bottom bunk.

The guard said, "Get ready for Chow, Miami."

Eye faced the guard with fear in my eyes, dropping my property on the floor. He mouthed "Good luck" the way my brothers mouthed at me when they thought Eye knew him. Why was he whispering? Suddenly, Eye knew why. Guard separated himself from inmate. We're back on opposite sides. He had a job to do, and Eye had one to do. Eye turned and faced the midget. We shook hands. "*Wassup*, Niggah?" he said. "What's your name?"

*None of your damn business.* "Miami." Eye said simply.

He looked me up and down. "Mighty chummy with the guard."

Eye looked his midget ass up and down. "We went to school together. Couldn't stand his dumb ass," Eye lied.

He laughed; Eye barely smiled. Tried to look Ford tough and was soft as Angel Soft toilet paper. Eye opened the bottom drawer and threw in my things. Eye'd arrange it all later. "You got the top bunk, tall ass Niggah," he said, a tattoo by his left eye. Of a tear. Oh, boy. Gang banger. They were like shit stains throughout the institution. You were either a Blood *or* a Cripp. At least that's the way it appeared to be. Eye would later learn about Vice Lords. And the Aryan Nation.

Skin Heads.

*"What you in for?" Inch, my* new cell mate asked.

"Being young and dumb," Eye joked, and he started laughing. Eye wasn't ready for him to know why Eye was there. Eye was still accepting it myself. Eye didn't come here to make friends. Eye wasn't Casper the Ghost. But Eye definitely couldn't afford to make enemies. And to think Chad's killers got off with making up lies on me. And Sheba, my so-called friend telling cops Eye told her Eye was raped. Yea, Eye did tell her that but her fake, late ass was just mad that all those attempts to throw her dry ass pussy at me failed when she found out Eye was bisexual. She didn't take rejection too well.

Rejection was the marshmallow man thumping through the inner city of her mind like the Ghostbusters's movie.

Eye sat on the bottom bunk with him. He glanced at me.

"You're different," he said.

"Different how?" Eye asked. He was trying to figure me out.

"Eye don't know. You seem reserved, to ya'self."

"Yea, Eye am very anti-social," Eye said.

"You ain't on that stuff are you?" he asked.

*Bwahahaha! F*unny. "Naw, Eye'm on that cough syrup like you."

Eye got a reaction out of him. "Oh, Niggah!" He pulled out the cough syrup. "Hell yea, dawg. Sippin' on some sizurp."

"Oh my damn, three 6 mafia."

"It's the 666 Mafia," he corrected.

"Evil bunch of dudes, huh?" He poured some in a cup, taking it to the head. Then another cup, then another, then another. Damn.

"Give me some of that," Eye said, taking two teaspoons of it. That's all. It felt like Eye was getting a cold anyway.

"Feeling that?" he asked, zonked.

"Yea, Eye really *feel* it," Eye joked, rolling my eyes. Eye didn't feel it and wasn't trying to.

The cell popped and a soul-lacerating bell rang. Oh, God, the sound drove me crazy and made my skin crawl.

"Time for CHOW!" screamed the guard.

Eye got up and followed the line movement.

*Once in the Chow Hall,* Eye got in line, and refused to look up, my heart beating out my chest. Eye was about 175 pounds, a small afro going and my scalp was dry. Dandruff was forming and Eye didn't have shampoo, just those little bars of soap. The rest of the stuff Eye had to buy off the canteen. Plus Eye had to call home, so Eye could tell Moms Eye was here and safe. Something told me to look up and Eye did. Looking around, Eye saw nothing but white men. Eye shook with fear and ducked my head. They were mean-mugging me hard. Hesitantly, Eye looked up again. One of the men had a huge swastika on his arm. The Chow Hall was segregated. Another skin head, red neck, was behind me.

He pushed me. "Move it, Nigger. Line in motion. They don't serve coons over here."

"Watch your mouth, buddy!" Eye snapped, turning to face him. *Buddy? Eye sounded so gay! What the hell was that, Pharoah?*

"Oh you standing up to me nigger?"

"Yea, spick." Eye turned and walked up to one of the servers. No one on the food line was black. All skin heads.

"What do you want, Nigger? Eye ain't serving no colored boy!" He slammed the spoon down, and the other skin head said, "The fried chicken isn't in this line. Goddamn you ugly, bitch! Is that how they say it in that one nigger movie written by that nigger bitch YOU SHOLL IZ UGLAY!"

Before Eye could respond an older black man, well kept, neatly trimmed, approached me. He took me by the hand. He had friendly eyes. "Young black man, the brothers are on this side of the Chow Hall."

*"Get that nigger in his place, monkey face."*

*"Coons belong in the woods to be hunted and shot for supper."*

*"Niggers eat coons, too!"*

Eye followed the brother to the Black Side.

**Eye knew deep down in** my heart Eye would write this account one day; Eye just didn't think it would be so soon. Well, it's been 12 years now. After getting my food, string beans, fried chicken and soda, Eye sat next to the brother who led me over here. His name was Earl. He has been locked up for over 20 years and still had his sanity. He introduced me to another man named Big Saint. Eye met Punch, Skeeta, Bam and a host of other Niggahs. Eye knew instantly Eye wasn't what the Pacific Northwest preferred. Eye was a Goulds Niggah. Eye held my head high.

"Eye don't mean to sound so gay, but you have a nice smile," said Stressla, the intelligent, bald headed brother of the group.

"Thanks…"

"How long you been here?"

"Just got here a few hours ago," Eye said, thinking, *Why are you being so nosey?*

"Where are *you* from?" he asked and Eye just stared at him for a few minutes. Half the inmates in the Chow Hall stared at me, waiting for the answer.

Eye thought about it. "Goulds—Ђe Forgotten City. That's in Miami, Florida."

He stared at me blankly. He never *heard* of Goulds.

"*Miami*!" he said with a smile.

"Welcome to Miami!" someone sang, referring to Will Smith's big hit. All they heard was "Miami." Goulds was forgotten the instant Eye said it. One day Eye'm going to change that through my writing. Eye smiled. Maybe Eye should start another book. A thought occurred to me…and Eye focused on my thoughts until Eye felt what Eye thought. Pharoah stop focusing on the negative, focus on more positive things, like starting the first draft to your new book…Eye smiled thinking about it. And then Eye stopped smiling when Eye realized Eye didn't have the resources to start a book.

*Please find a way.*

*Amen.*

"What you in for?" Stressla asked.

Eye looked him dead in the eyes. "Attempted Sodomy."

Playtime was over. They gazed at me. Laughing.

*"Yea, right."*

*"You don't look like you ever stole a candy bar."*

"Talk all the mess you want, at least Eye got a release date." That shut him up. Eye picked up my tray. "Eye'll take my chances eating with the skin heads."

☯

**Eye walked back to the other** side, the Niggahs looking at me like Eye was crazy. The Skin Heads glared at my skinny ass.

*"Oh, no. The coon is back."*

*"What's the matter? The chicken taste like black snatch? You know black booty holes are like imitation crabs, ain't twat but damn sure smell like one ahahahaha!"*

Eye sat down at a table of three, pushing their books on the floor.

"You know what?" Eye said. "Eye just wanna eat my fucking food. Don't have time for all this bullshit. If Eye'm a fucking coon bitches you're smelly, *skinned* dogs when you get wet. Stay away from the water Scrappy Do."

Eye ate my chicken in peace once they realized Eye was no longer scared.

...Eye was frightened as hell! But Eye had a Poker Face.

*Long* before there was a Lady Gaga.

*Eye moved out of Inch's cell* in D Block to another cell when Eye got a job a few weeks later. He was a good cell mate, but he abused cough syrup a little too much for me. Eye was now in E Block with some dude named Big Cease who got off on counting everything in the cell. From magazines and attire to the actual cell bars. Eye kept to myself in that cell. We didn't even speak. Something was being put into action, and Eye felt it but didn't know what that was. Eye was mad Eye had a looney toon for a cell mate, but he was the most organized man Eye've ever met. His thoughts and actions were an assembly line of progress. He was always counting something or counting on something day in and day out. Taught me discipline.

Eye hated D Block—getting out of Death's Block was one of the best things that happened to me. And that wasn't an *accomplishment.*

Eye *refused* to die in Oregon. At this time Eye didn't know that the dudes that murdered my best friend were going to be put in the same facility as me.

If you weren't working or doing something constructive, like snitching on other inmates (one thing Eye *never* did was snitch in jail), you couldn't go to C Block and Eye so wanted to move there. Make my stay in prison as comfortable as Eye could make it. Pharoah always kept himself out of prison business 'cause prison business was closed to the world, but running rampant behind those thirty feet brick walls that been up since, what, 1903 or some crap like that? So taking away an inmate's mail, personal belongings, labeling it contraband, takes away some of their hope to live, especially if they got life. Hell Section 8 housing was starting to look like families stuffed in little houses like jail cells, making you pay a little a month for a bed.

When Eye got work it was in the Cafeteria. Eye was there less than a week and wound up getting a proposition to work as a tutor on the Education Floor, which was one of the high paying jobs at about $60 a month (sixty dollars a month Massa!) Eye wasn't trying to work in the cafeteria. Hell naw. Eye cooked for my Mama and siblings for over 12 years. Wasn't about to cook another four years for thousands of inmates.

But getting the job on the Education Floor would come right on time…

One day when Big Cease went to the Yard to work out, Eye remained in my cell and spent some alone time. Eye didn't know what to do—read or sleep, hmm, and Eye decided to sleep. Eye lay on the top bunk, and curled up under the blanket. Before Eye could close my eyes Eye saw a book on Big Cease table. The Law of Time.

On second thought Eye was suddenly very awake.

Eye opened the book. And began reading.

*Eye made it to the yard after all.* It was an entirely different world from what Eye was used to.

There was a huge concrete track.

Benches lined the gates.

A crummy golf course was off to my right, past a long row of payphones.

The weight pile had Niggahs on it looking like prehistoric dinosaurs.

The Recreational Building, inside another gated part of the Yard, had a basketball court, and iron tables with iron chairs that were occupied with gambling, card playing, cut throat inmates.

Towers were strategically surrounding the perimeter occupied by guards loaded with deadly weapons, looking down on us with suspicious eyes.

A group of Niggahs approached me and Eye put up my fists.

*"Calm down lil niggah."*

*"Oh this one got a set."*

*"He'll fight, Eye like that."*

Eye didn't put my fists down. Eye backed up so the fence was behind me. "Who are you? Eye don't know who you are!" Eye said, my eyes narrowing dangerously.

"Calm down. He's a soldier," said a tall, well-built inmate with easy going eyes. But Eye didn't trust it.

"Uncle McAdoo has summoned you," an older inmate said, and Eye was like Eye don't give a damn. Nobody summons me.

"And he rarely summons anybody," said the shorter inmate with an attitude.

"Who is that?" Eye asked, obviously attracting likeminded individuals.

More possible allies.

That wasn't a bad thing.

"Follow us," they all said.

*Eye followed them to the middle* of the yard, to what appeared to be a square concrete slab, about say 15x15 feet. Seated on it were a few distinguished inmates, neatly trimmed, eyes filled with hope for the future. Being in such a dark place Eye found that to be rather attractive. One of the men, McAdoo, a much older brother, and obviously the ring leader of the Distinguished Gentleman Club, was one of the most respected men in the institution Eye would learn. He was in his mid forties and didn't look a day over 33 years old. Very handsome.

McAdoo stood up and Eye felt like a Ninja Turtle about to address Master Splinter. What did Eye say to prison royalty? "How are you" He asked, his voice riding the waves of utter smoothness and decorum. His brows rose. "Miami, right?"

How did he know my name? Oh. Prison gossip. "*Yes*, its Miami." *Eye hope Eye didn't sound like an idiot!*

"That's where you're from?"

"Yes."

He was skeptical. "Oh, *yea*? *What* part?"

Eye stuck my chest out. "Eye was raised in Goulds, but Eye currently lived in Homestead, before Eye was arrested."

Sparks went off in his accusing eyes, giving them a more vibrant color. The hazel was emphasized by the sunlight. "Shit. Eye been to Homestead before, is that right? Eye was in the military."

"Really?" Now it was my eyes that painted the actual picture.

He was sure of himself. "Homestead Airforce base, right?"

Eye was smiling. "Yes, we stay on 1*7$^{th}$ Avenue."

"By the little gas station," he said, stunning me. He was right!

"Yes!" It felt like Eye found a new best friend. And the fact that he's an older man with different experiences, Eye'm sure he had many stories to tell of his past. Eye was anxious to know this man's story—and to tell him mine…in time of course. You didn't just meet a complete stranger, a man you never knew existed, and spill your guts. That's lunacy. In time Eye hoped we could confide in each other. Why Eye felt a sudden connection truly baffled me into a state of blind confusion.

"Eye like you, Miami. He cool, ya'll." After shaking everyone's hands (and gave a few brotherly hugs), he gave me a package in a brown paper bag.

It had soap, toothpaste (real toothpaste, and not that institutionalized crap), a long toothbrush and the bare necessities.

"Only thing Eye ask," he said, "is for you to help the next brother who comes through those doors."

We sealed the deal with a firm handshake.

*Yup. He's straight old school* royalty on top of that. You could tell a lot about a man based on his initial hand shake. Sometimes a handshake tells you all you need to know.

He would be my guardian angel throughout my 4 years 9 months prison sentence. After that encounter it took me a long time to go back to the yard. A couple weeks later my cell was popped open and Eye was told to go to work in the chow hall. Like hell. Eye didn't wanna work in there anymore; bad enough Eye had to be in here against my will.

Eye went to the yard instead, meeting new folks. Eye had in my hand my folder, and Eye started a book called *The Scorned House of Blue Scars*.

At the Inverness jail Eye wrote a book called *A Lighter Shade of Men* but some of the chapters were lost when Eye mailed them out.

Eye swear someone in the mail room stole my book.

No time for that now.

Eye sat at one of the tables and Eye began to write about Aalexandria Cummings. A single black woman with it all, except a man.

At that point Eye knew Eye didn't want to write a chick book. But Eye started it out with Thelma, Jane (white girl acting sistah) and Aalexandria. She met a doctor named Marlo at her best friend's Gertrude's engagement party. Gertrude was married to fine ass Louisiana boy De'Andre James.

Eye already fell in love with the characters.

When Eye was done writing the books opening with those god awful small ass gold pencils, Eye read over it.

*If Eye had thirty arms, hands, fingers and toes, Eye still couldn't count the number of men Eye sucked, fucked, pussified, bewildered, mystified, and Mummified looking for love or searching for some rare form of it. Here Eye am at age 29, got it all, brand new socks and draws, and still got a leaking roof in a $90,000 condo, a Chrysler 300 M (Eye'm 2 months behind on my payments). Damn shame Eye had expensive shit throughout my condo in Blueberry Hills, Lauderhill, Florida and a bitch still had to whip out the buckets on a rainy day to catch the water from my leaking roof.*

***Eye was satisfied.*** Eye'd tweak it later.

The sun shined brightly. Two males sat in front of me.

One said, "How are you."

"Eye'm good," Eye said with an attitude.

"What are you writing?" asked the other.

"Ah, its nothing," Eye said, closing the folder in my hand like a scroll, and it became my defense mechanism.

"You writing a letter?" He asked. "Oh, Eye'm Bobby." He was one cool white boy, looked like Drew Carey.

"And Eye'm Tre," said the taller one.

"We're road dogs," said Bobby. "What's your name?"

"Miami."

"Your real name?" asked Tre.

"Pharoah C. Wilson, Jr."

"L.C.Dub!" joked Bobby and Eye was grinning.

"L.C.Dub, 'ey?" Eye said, tired as hell.

"Yea, Eye'ma call you that. You seem real cool, family. Why you over here by yourself?"

Tre studied me.

"Just to myself and my thoughts."

"That's just it. Everyone here got a hustle, and you're a free thinker?" Tre asked.

"Yea, Eye am like that Eye guess." Eye pulled out my paper, spread it on my folder and kept writing.

Tre looked over. "Oh, shit. He's a writer."

"Let us read." He took the papers and Eye smiled. Bobby read what Eye wrote and Eye held my breath. Eye mean it was about a chick.

"You got skills, dawg," Bobby said.

Tre said, "Lemme see." He read over it, nodding his head. He couldn't stop reading the page.

"Not bad. Good shit. Good grammar. And you can spell."

"Ha ha," Eye said.

"No, man you don't understand. The prison is filled with wanna be writers," Tre said.

"Like Sleepy," Bobby interjected happily.

"Sleepy?" Eye asked.

"Yea, his name Anthony. He writes books."

Eye had to meet Sleepy. "For real?"

"Yea, he got skills," said Bobby and Tre nodded in agreement.

"But the boy can't spell worth a damn," Tre went on warmly.

Eye was laughing. "Who is he?" Tre pointed at him and Eye looked across the way. He was about 6 feet, had beautiful sleepy-looking eyes and his pants sagged. His swagger was off the chain. He spoke to everyone, Chicos, Mexicans, whites, blacks. Eye stood up and walked right up to him. He tucked his chin back, looked me over and smiled, extending his hand. Eye shook it, squeezed it firmly. Yea, Eye ain't no punk.

"Eye know you?" he asked.

"No, but Eye hear you're some kind of writer."

"Yea, Eye am an author."

"When can Eye read your work? Let me determine that?"

"Eye'm the best writer here."

"You ain't better than me."

"Eye write that street lit," he said.

Eye faked a yawn. "Over and done with that kind of shit, when are you going to *dare* to be different?"

People literally stopped talking.

Then they said, *"Sleepy's good."*

*"He writes good stuff."*

*"Niggah you can't even write."*

Eye stared him down. "Whatever you wrote Eye will top it, shatter it and walk across that crap."

Eye called him out. "Oh, yea? You write anything?"

"Follow me."

A few Niggahs followed us, smelling drama and it wasn't even that kind of party. When Eye got back to the table, Bobby and Tre spoke to Sleepy. He had a blue wool skull cap pulled low above his eyes. Eye handed him the paper with the book Eye started. "One page?" he asked.

"Yea, Eye got confidence in that one page."

"And he say he's better." Everyone laughed, except Bobby and Tre. They looked at me. Sleepy began reading out loud, "If Eye had thirty…" He kept reading, entranced by my words. He hopping up and down, fist over his mouth, wide eyed. He read the back and his minions were like, "Can we read that?"

"Shoot, he's writing about a bitch. Is she fine, Miami?"

"Yea, she got big tits and good pussy," Eye said, observing.

"Does she have a man?" an inmate asked. "Write about me. A gangster who wants to get out the lifestyle and go to college to care for his breezy."

Breezy was another word for "lady." Eye was taking notes. "Ok, Eye can do that. What's your name?" Eye asked.

"Capone. Monet Brown."

Eye analyzed him further. Clean cut, definitely a smooth talker. He was the kinda man Hoes threw their panties at. He had a pimp appeal, like he pimped Hoes…so my walls went up. Eye reverted my eyes, didn't let him look in them too deeply. Con artist, too smooth, eyes bounced when he spoke which means he thought things up as he went along.

Eye gazed at smooth ass Monet Brown. Thin rimmed glasses covered his emotionally charged eyes. He created art with his hands as he spoke. Captivated me. "Eye can put you in the book," Eye told him without thinking.

Another guy, named Marlo, dark skinned, said, "Damn, can Eye be in the book?"

"Eye have a character named Marlo already."

He was grinning. "Must be destiny."

"Ha, ha. He's a doctor in the book."

"Ok, and he has to be from Louisiana? Eye'm from there. Calliope projects."

"Ok, will do."

"Don't jive me. Eye wanna read that shit." Briefly showing itself in his eyes was danger. The purplish mist nodded upwards, glared at me and vanished into his retinas. Spooked me.

"Well Eye'm writing by hand," Eye said, dreading those little gold damn pencils.

Sleepy said, "Eye'll see what Eye can do. Let me talk to some people."

The stage was set for the rise of: DAPHAROAH69.

*A few days later my cell popped.*

"Wilson!"

Eye peaked my head out.

"Education floor!"

"Education floor?" Eye put on my shoes and headed out.

*Eye asked one of the inmates* where the education floor was. He pointed at a stair case, and opening the door and looking up Eye was like goddamn, these are a lot of stairs. Eye'm looking up for Rapunzel to let down her hair.

Shaking away the thought, Eye made the climb, not sure of why Eye was summoned. Eye didn't know Eye was making the climb into the beginnings of my bestselling author destiny.

Eye had a high school diploma, and Eye had to drop out of college when Eye came to jail. Eye felt bad about it, but now my future starting to look brighter than before. Eye basked in the glow.

When Eye reached the top floor (my legs were sore), Eye came face to face with a poster hanging on the wall.

**DON'T WANT PRISON TO BE A ROTATING DOOR.**
**JOIN A COGNITIVE PROGRAM.**

Eye hesitated…but inevitably Eye took the poster down, folded it and stuffed it in my pocket.

*Damn sure didn't want prison being a rotating door in my life.*

Eye approached the main Desk, run by inmates. Everything was run by inmates. Guards sat back like African chiefs observing and correcting when necessary. And they get paid for this? Doing absolutely nothing at all?

"And you are?" a big, white, burly inmate asked.

"Miami. Eye was summoned up here."

"Oh, yea. Eye heard you're a writer. Eye'm an avid reader. Maybe Eye can read your work."

Eye shook his hand. "Eye got you."

"Mrs. Marsters called for you."

Eye scrunched my face. "Mrs. Marsters? Who the hell is *that*?"

"She's a sweet old black woman. Tough as nails. Married to a white man."

"Oh, ok. But why she called *me*?"

"Just wait and see."

*When Eye walked in her office* (An old, revised and restored classroom) Eye noticed a petite, tiny older woman with well combed graying hair. A knowledgeable woman with thin glasses over keen eyes. The Oracle. The Gatekeeper guarding the Entrance to my *Destiny*. Was Eye worthy of it? Was Eye ready? What was it, exactly? How did Eye conquer it? Observe it? Taste it?

Eye felt her wisdom, it rolled all over me like warm waves on a cold summer night. The tornado of feeling enveloped me. Nothing was impossible, anything is possible. Ask. Believe. Receive. Thank you…

"Are you Pharoah?" she asked, not looking up from the book she was reading.

"Yes, Eye am."

"Eye hear you are some kind of writer." She slowly flipped a page.

*Here we go. Judging me. And don't know jack about me.* "Who told you that?"

"Anthony," she said simply, the arrogance dripping from her head moving side to side, guiding her eyes across each and every word on the page of text she was reading. Like a queen looking down at angry peasants.

Eye smiled. "Yes, Eye am."

"Will your work entice me like the book Eye'm reading?" She flipped another page, quickly devouring the words. "As you can see Eye haven't looked up from the book yet."

"Yes, my words are enticing."

"Really?"

"Yes."

Books were all around her. Stacked on the desk. On the shelves behind her, surrounding her.

"Eye used to be one of the Salem newspaper editors. Eye have a Masters degree. And Eye don't waste my time reading *crap*."

Then and only then did she close the book, looked up and said, "Do you have a portfolio?"

Eye looked at the folded paper in my hand. "No, but Eye have this." She was making me feel stupid. Maybe Eye'm not ready for this journey just yet. Eye couldn't even convince the gatekeeper Eye was worthy of the skill of words.

Eye extended my hand, and she looked at the paper like it was a ton of shit and she was wearing a white Easter dress. Eye snatched my hand back.

"And you're a writer? Please. Anthony isn't even as good as he said."

"Ok, Eye don't need the third degree."

Eye spun and was leaving.

"Bring me the paper. That's a direct order."

*Ok, she's tough as nails, but Eye gotta switch ball change up for her ass.*

Eye slowly walked up to her, one of two gay men, her student aides and tutors, glanced up from typing his vampire tale, based in *London* Eye would later find out, on the computer.

The other inmate tutor, Charles, a real geek looking guy with Jagged Edge teeth and blackening gums, looked up at me as well. The brainiac. His mouth looked something ripped from a Michael Myers film. Eye got to check my calendar and make sure Halloween didn't sneak up on my ass…looking at this dude.

Eye handed her the paper. She looked it over.

Eye put my hands behind my back, the "at ease" military position, the thumb across the other, and watched her.

She adjusted her glasses.

She began reading.

Quietly, to herself. Calmly reserved. Eye was on pins and needles.

She said, "Aha. Hmm."

She flipped the paper over. Read some more. Touched her forehead. Looked at her watch.

She looked up. Eye took the paper and started for the door.

Yes, Eye embarrassed myself. Eye wasn't a writer, Eye didn't know why Sleepy set this up.

When Eye reached the door she said, "Pharoah."

Eye paused, not looking back.

Jerrid, vampire boy, waved Bye Bye with a sly smile.

Eye flipped the bird at him and he mouthed, "Bite me, you inexperienced writer."

"Face me," she said.

Eye looked at her.

She was standing. Looking heavenly, radiant.

"There's your computer right there." She pointed at it. "There's your dot matrix printer, old school but doable. We have a newsletter called *Outer Visions.* You will serve as a contributing writer. Eye can get you a Journalism credit through Chemeketa College."

"Thank you. Wow." Eye felt like Harriet Tubman wanting the sugar lump out of the bowl for a touch of heaven.

"Eye know you hated my little story. Sorry for embarrassing myself."

"Oh, yea. That's another thing. That one paper was better than the book Eye was reading. Feel free to write your book on that computer at your leisure. If Eye'm on the clock, you can write all day, as long as you want, till count time."

*Sufficiency and abundance, potentiality and polarization, attraction and allowance work hand in hand…*

*The Gatekeeper granted me* access to the treasure and technicalities of writing and deliberate creation. And eye mastered it over the next few months. A whole new world opened up. And my mentor Tommy Marsters was there to help me on my literary journey. Mentoring and coaching me.

Only Eye didn't know Eye would actually succeed.

She edited my first book, *The Scorned House of Blue Scars.*

It took me three months to finish, because Eye didn't know how to write books. Eye thought there was sòme sort of special formula for writers. Seemed like it was unattainable.

So Eye created a system.

*Everything Eye wrote she* edited. At first my paper bled from all her red markings. But she explained them, never trying to change my voice or writing style, because she loved it.

Eye kept my promise and put my boys in my book, but Eye did it Dapharoah69's way. But the first thing she told me was, "You are describing everything, and that's good but its not."

"Explain."

"You wrote here, 'Eye picked up the Oil of Olay soap and turned on the cold water and the knobs were somewhat rusty and after my shower Eye put on Suave lotion.' The rusty shower knobs were strokes of genius, but Oil of Olay soap and Suave lotion you didn't need to describe. Just say soap and lotion. Let the reader substitute their favorite soap and lotion right there. *Include your readers!* Don't exclude them."

Eye took it to heart.

*Oh my God! Eye got it! Eye got it! Eye know what Eye want to master.*

*Eye wanted to Master 7 different things...*

**Over the next few weeks** proved to be productive.

Jerrid and Charles and a third tutor, Mark Marshal, an artist, handled the tutoring while Eye was writing my book.

Mrs. Marsters whipped me into shape. Replaced the carburetor under my hood and Eye was running like a brand new fully loaded Ford F-150. Eye started writing home, typing my letters, truly thankful Eye could type stuff and write my book. And Eye had an amazing editor who told me my strong and weak points. When the Education Floor was closed...Eye spent time in the library, researching and studying great writers...like Shakespeare (even thought Eye heard he's a plagiarist), Socrates, Dan Brown, Sidney Sheldon, Jackie Collins, Mark Twain, Andrew Young, Zora, Langston, Danielle Steele along hundreds of others. My mouth hung open whenever Eye read important books because Eye understood something no one else in prison thought about. And the more Eye understood it, the more Eye tried to Master some things...it became my burning passion.

Over the course of my first book, Eye was seeing her red markings less and less. She asked me how did Eye improve so fast and Eye told her, "Because Eye'm always reading other authors."

"And that's they key to great writing. You must keep reading."

On one of the chapters she said Eye was an "excellent character study. You can write from a dog or cat's point of view and it would be devastatingly accurate."

That touched me. Jerrid was getting jealous. He'd been writing his vampire saga forever and a day before Eye came, and there Eye was pumping my book out like it was already there, and Mrs. Marsters couldn't wait to edit it. She was editing Jerrid's book less and less, and he silently hated it.

And she focused on my book. She was the only black woman or black teacher working on the floor and Eye was the only black tutor. When Eye completed my first book Eye celebrated by releasing it on The Yard, giving an inmate at a time chapter by chapter so they could read it. But it was hard to keep up. The folders found everyone's hands and the story exploded all over the Oregon State Penitentiary. It was hell keeping up with all my creations! But what Eye wasn't prepared for was a group of skin heads called the Aryan Nation seeking me out, hunting me down and once they did, all hell broke loose.

Something Eye wasn't prepared for.

*Eye put my chapters inside* a three ring binder, so Eye didn't have all forty chapters in 40 different places.

The book was so good inmates were reading any chapter they got their hands on and anxious to read the other chapters afterward.

Aalexandria, the character, was causing quite a stir in the penal system.

Then the guards were alerted.

They stopped by my cell one by one.

"Eye wanna read that book everyone is talking about."

So Eye had to print out an additional copy.

Eye mailed my floppy disk home and told Grandpa to put it up, and to not open the envelope—The Poor Man's Copyright Protection— and he did just that, so Eye was protected in the event late bitches tried to publish my work.

Another guard stopped by, a white man with a lot of tattoos.

My cell was popped.

"Pack your things."
"Where am Eye going?"
"To C block."

☯

*Yes. Leaving Inch in D Block* to move with Big Cease in E (Echo) Block wasn't a good move because, in addition to counting bars and tile, Big Cease was into selling tobacco and Eye didn't want to be around that.

The cells in C Block were *much* bigger, way bigger, with a lot more room, and Eye fell in love with a *mother-freaking* cell block. Somebody shoot me. There was a spot for a TV and Eye instantly knew Eye wanted one. My cell mate was a cool Niggah. Before Eye could say my name he said, "You're the writer, Miami."

"Yea."

"What an honor!" He shook my hand. "Any of your stuff published?"

"Naw, man. Eye don't wanna be no published author."

"Why not man?" Hanging all around the cell were black men from black history.

He had self help books everywhere. *Ebony*, *Essence* and *Jet* magazines.

On the TV was BET and Eye was like oh my God. Damn. In jail?

"Eye don't know. Eye'm not no James Patterson."

"Nah, you better than James Patterson. You better than all those big timers."

Eye was laughing. "Yea, right."

"Shh, shh, listen."

"Who is that yelling?" Eye asked, narrowing my eyes.

"Hear what he saying?"

Eye was listening. Sounded like laughing. Hysterical.

*"Miami's a fool! Ya'll read his book? Aalexandria, damn Eye wanna bang that broad! She's my kinda bitch!"*

*"Wait till you get to the part her doctor boyfriend Marlo finds out the man he performed his first liver transplant on is his*

*biological daddy! That he was the product of rape. His daddy was a skin head, what a twist!"*

My new cell mate, Dee Boo said, "And you were saying? They are talking about your books more than they talk about the big timers or Sleepy's sorry book."

"Eye still don't wanna be no published author. Eye'm not writing any other books."

But Eye had already secretly started writing *Superstars.*

Eye gave Mrs. Marsters the first two chapters already.

**Eye was walking around** the track because the education floor was closed on weekends. And Eye didn't feel like being cramped in the cell, plus that gave my cell mate some alone time. We had it worked out. When Eye wanted alone time he went to work or on the yard to the weight pile. When he needed alone time Eye found the library, Eye hardly went to the yard.

Eye was becoming…

**Eye was walking around the** bend of the track when Eye saw a white guy with tattoos all over his arms, body and back laughing to the point he was choking.

Eye rushed over to him. "Mister, are you ok?"

Eye started pounding his back, and he coughed up some meat and noodles.

"Thanks," he said, then took one look at me and said, "Oh, Gawd. A Coon helped me?"

"Eye'm not a coon, *bitch*!"

He jumped up. "Who are you calling a bitch you uneducated nigger?"

"Whatever, man Eye'm gone."

"Yea, get your punk ass away from here. All you black niggers are fag fucks."

My eyes grazed a folder on the table. It was yellow. One of my stories. How did it get out of the binder?

"Eye see you're reading the story Eye wrote."

He was quiet. He sat down and rubbed his palms across the top of it.

"Yea. Right. Nigger you wish you wrote this."

"Eye did."

He gazed at me for a few minutes, and Eye glared him down.

Suddenly. He burst out laughing. "Oh, you're trying to trick me. April Fool! Ha ha ha!"

"You know what sir one day Eye will be a published author," Eye said, unsure of it, but anything to show this honky tonk ass white man down.

He laughed even harder! He jumped up to his feet, grabbed the folder and walked over to his Aryan Nation boys. They all tattooed up, cursing worse than blacks and chewing snuff, which was illegal in prison and contraband, but Eye didn't give a shit what they did with their time.

"Guess what boys?"He pointed at me. "This coon burnt butt monkey said he's gonna be himself a published author!"

They roared to life, laughing and tripping over each other.

"*Yes, ok and Eye am Clark Kent, bitch!*"

They laughed even harder. Eye was smiling.

*"Have you even written a book?"* another inmate asked.

"Yes, the folder you're holding. Eye wrote that."

"Yea, right. A white man wrote this," he said.

"Um, no he didn't. Eye wrote that."

"Bullshit! Eye happen to like this story Eye'm reading. A black bitch married a man with a KKK father. That's some…"

Eye was smiling. Eye handed him my ID card, with my name on it.

"Pharoah Wilson." He said it slowly.

"Turn it to the back page," Eye said.

His boys watched him. He did so.

His eyes were wide. "No. One Pharoah Wilson is the author of this? This is like the thirtieth chapter Eye have read, and my boy read this, too, Nigger what do you know. You are a talented sonofabitch."

One of the men tried to shake my hand but when Eye extended my arm he snatched it back. "Eye hate black people. Eye never talked to a nigger in my life where *Eye'm* from."

"We're one in here, man. A state number. Separated from our families, away from our loved ones. Right now there is no black and white."

They were quiet. One of them, Eye'm guessing the ring leader, started to walk off and Eye grabbed his arm and he snatched it back and grabbed my neck, "Fuck Nigger you crazy touching me?"

Eye kneed him in the balls, "Bitch don't fucking touch me."

A few brothers rushed over, including Uncle McAdoo. Eye was happy to see him.

"Nephew, you're ok?" Uncle McAdoo asked.

"Yes, Eye am."

He looked at the Aryan Nation boys. "We got a problem?" His brows rose. If and when Eye find my biological father Eye hope he was just like McAdoo.

"Now Mac you know we started doing time together."

"And we never liked each other," he said, pushing me behind him. "Eye am in here for murder, bitches." He had fire in his eyes, like a father protecting his son. "Remember what Eye did last time. Eye will gut a bitch and cut his head off and kick it down the road. You know how Eye roll."

*"We meant no harm."*

*"But the nigger grabbed me."*

He turned to face me. "Miami, there are just some things and some people you never talk to in prison."

"Eye got you." Eye walked off. Eye have never been called so many niggers by a prejudiced red neck dog smelling crackah in my life. Let him come to Goulds with that.

"*Miami*," Uncle Mac called out and Eye kept walking. One thing Eye would never do again was give a damn. Eye couldn't change the world, especially not a prison. Detachment, activated…

"Miami!"

Eye walked towards the outside activities building, sulking into myself.

"Miami."

Eye looked back. It was one of the Aryan Nation boys.

"Let me have a word with you. Alone."

☯

We were sitting on the concrete slab, the weight pile behind us. The sound of weights rising and dropping got on my nerves, the clanking of iron meshed with grunts and moans filled our ears.

"*Listen,* nigger…Eye mean, bro. This is hard for me, you know…but something you said was true."

Eye was offended, but Eye remained mum. "And *that* is?"

"Inside these thirty foot walls we are all the same, a state number. Separated from our loved ones." Trembling, he handed me a photo of a gorgeous woman with a little baby girl. Eye could tell he fought himself to be cordial to a "Nigger."

"Wow, she's a fox. And cute kid," Eye said, meaning it.

"Thank you. You know," he said, in his little red shorts and bare-chested, "You are the first nigger…Eye mean bro Eye ever showed my family too."

Eye handed him the photo back. "Well Eye'm flattered."

"Eye have a friend in here named Sonny—he's one of the math tutors up stairs."

"Never heard of him," Eye said, because Eye mind my business.

"He is Mr. Gregson's tutor. Eye think he tutors math."

"Eye'll check it out."

"Eye was raised to be the way Eye am, son. My father hated black men so much he used to hang them and Eye used to watch without a care in the world. Eye wasn't born to hate. Eye took on the *trials* of my folks."

"Eye understand."Eye thought about my sexuality. If he wasn't born to hate surely Eye wasn't born gay.

"But Eye do know this. Everything has a changing point, and Eye can tell you what is changing, at least with me, but may not sit well with the boys."

"What's that?" Eye asked.

He took my hand, and Eye felt his muscles flinch, like he wanted to snatch his hand back quick, fast and in a hurry.

"You are one talented black brother! Fucking A right, man. Eye read that story and man oh man. If Alexandria was a white woman Eye'd have to get that whore and make her my baby Mama, isn't that how the brother's say it?"

Eye was laughing. "Yea, man. Thank you. Eye am no author. Eye just write."

"What inspires you, and what's your real name?"

"Eye'm Pharoah. Eye don't know what inspires me. Eye lose a part of myself every time the sun set."

"Why do you say that?"

"Because Eye become another part of myself when the sun rise."

He released my hand. "This is what Eye'm talking about. Never before have someone like you come through here. Bro, you remind me of a friend Eye used to have in high school."

"Really?"

"His name was Billips. He was timid as a sheep, but smarter than a fox."

"Sounds like he was a loner."

He looked into my eyes. "He *was*. Look, rumor has it you are in here for attempted sodomy."

"Yes, Eye am. And Eye…"

"Bro, let me show you something."

Eye started to back away. "Are you going to try to kill me?"

"Bro," he said, as Eye realized he no longer said "Nigger." "You are a gift from God almighty. And for me to tell a brother that is beyond reproach, but it's on my heart. Eye may have been raised for war and hate, but you are a talented young man. And one day Eye feel in my heart you will be a published author."

Tears fell down my face, and Eye wiped them away. "Thanks."

"No problem." He put his arm around me. "Come on, let me show you something."

Eye followed him into C Block. He was in Sub C, the cells below the other cells, and Eye followed him to the end. The guard popped the cell, and looked at me sideways. He started to press the radio to say Eye was in an unauthorized area, but the Aryan Nation dude shook his head, "No," and the guard relaxed. Eye followed him inside. He had all kinds of things hanging up. Eye could tell he's been in this cell for over ten years. His entire life was in here and for some reason Eye felt at home. The word **ILLUMINATI** on a huge poster caught my attention. With a picture of the Beatles on it, throwing weird hand gestures.

"Have a seat," he said. Eye sat down. The cell closed.

"My cell mate is my lover," he said, "But we don't show any type of affection out on the yard. We hardly even embrace. We are painfully quiet about our relationship."

"Eye understand. It's safe with me."

"He and Eye will die in here, and he's my whole world. Eye could never see my wife again."

"Does she visit?"

"No. She married my brother and just gave birth to his daughter. That's the picture Eye showed you on the yard. It sliced my heart in two, so Eye know heartbreak."

"Thanks for sharing that with me, but why me?"

He looked at me, then reached on the top shelf to take down a manila folder. "Eye like you." He sat down on the opposite stool, and dumped newspaper clippings on the table.

"You started to tell me about why you're in here," he said, finding what he's looking for.

"Ok..."

He opened the newspaper clipping. "What does he mean to you?" he asked.

Eye looked down, taking it. My heart hit the floor when Eye saw Chad's picture. Tears fell. "Oh, God." Eye broke down instantly, and the funniest thing happened. He gave me a loving hug.

"He was your best friend, wasn't he?"

Eye couldn't utter a word.

*It works!*

*What Eye was learning to Master became my character.*

*The cell popped and Eye* followed him up the tier.

"Something tells me you were set up."

"Eye was. Eye was even marked for death."

"Prison don't treat rats too kindly, but in your case, brother, you did what you thought was right."

"Yes. Eye didn't snitch on anyone; Eye merely cooperated with the police. Hell Eye was even a suspect."

"You wouldn't hurt a fly, that much Eye do know…do you have any siblings?"

We were walking past the guard, and up the stairs, going back to the yard. "Yes. Four. Eye'm the oldest."

"Sweet. Eye bet they adore you."

"Yea, they do."

"Have any pictures of them?"

"Yes, Eye do."

"Maybe you can share them with me, like Eye shared mine with you."

"That would be cool."

We shook hands.

*When we got back on the yard Eye* followed him over to the Aryan Nation boys. They had a huge spread on the table. A cleaned, ripped open garbage bag. On it mounds of Doritos, on top of the chips was Top Ramen noodles. It looked like a pizza. One of the younger members poured on the refined beans, and then another poured on the cheese, then the chopped meat. Smelled yummy.

My new friend looked at me. "We can't cook like the bro's but damn it we do all right!"

There was a boom box playing a song Eye never heard before.

"What is that playing?"

"Rock music my friend. System of a Down. It rocks, huh?"

Eye loved the beat. "Yes, it damn sure does." Eye was bobbing my head. "Sounds good." *Toxic City rocks!!*

*"Yo, boys! The author likes our music!"*

*"Yea!'"*

*"YEAAA!"*

*"Rock on, Miami!"*

The member that cursed me out for grabbing his arm jumped in my face and stared me down. Eye looked away. Eye knew this was a little too made for TV.

"Yo. Eye hate to read but Eye read a little part of your typed book," he said like he was having open heart surgery without anesthesia.

"Oh, yea?"

He extended his hand. "Eye may not join the million man March, but brother, you got it. You got it, and you are a bad man with the writing. Don't stop. Don't stop for no one."

"Thank you."

"You're free to join us for some grub."

Humbleness wins the war…to be humble is to be patient. To my surprise, he handed me a cup and a spoon. He didn't cringe nor flinch. Eye smiled, wiping water from my eyes before he noticed. "Damn something flew in my eye," Eye said, blowing smoke up their asses. Eye refused to cry in prison.

"Thank you!" The other brothers on the Yard looked on in shock. Uncle McAdoo nodded with a smile, winking.

He said, "Let the author get his grub first, boys! Take all you want."

He pats my shoulder. "And take your Uncle Mac some, too."

"Eye will. And thanks, man."

"Eye want next on that book. Can you write a story about a redneck piss head hick like myself from Grant's Pass, Oregon who get all the girls pregnant and have to play musical pussy lips at the hospital."

Eye was done; laughing so hard Eye dropped my cup.

"Eye'm for real, Miami."

"We'll see, man. We'll see," Eye said. Before Eye could squat down (never bend over in prison, a big no no!) he leaned over, picked up the cup and handed me a clean one.

Trashing the one that hit the ground…

*Eye helped over 170 people get* their G.E.D's. All inmates, who had their heads high when their G.E.D.'s became a reality. It would open some doors for them when they got out. But the real challenge would be, even with education, you have a felony record so what are you gonna do? Say you don't have one and take your chance of being found out and fired or take the chance to be tuned away by telling them straight up, no bullshit, from the beginning, so when you're hired, given a second chance, you can't get fired for dishonesty because you prayed to God then went to your interview and God was with you the entire time. How do you know? When you smiled and thanked the interviewer for their time…that was God.

That's all the interviewer needed was to see someone smile, after the bad interviews he's done and the number of times people cursed him out because he said, "Don't call me. Eye'll call you." But *some* inmates didn't look at the big picture like that. They looked at it as an accomplishment, which it was, but also, some could never use it when they have life in prison. What was a G.E.D. gonna do when you got life in prison?

Eye can tell you what. And one of the Lifer's once told me.

"Getting my G.E.D. may not open the prison doors, but it opened the doors of being incarcerated in my own mind so when Eye read a book, or book after book, with my mind Eye am out of prison and experiencing the story Eye am faithfully reading about so when Eye read the Bible, Eye start to see things with my mind, and realize that even Jesus was jailed, even he was persecuted so if he can rise from death after being nailed to the cross then Eye can keep my mind out of prison and my body in this cell and know God hasn't forsaken me."

That got me doing some things to enrich myself.

In contrast, the Yang to Yin, Eye met two bad people my whole prison term. The men Eye met were cordial and nice, some were quiet and tried to pretend to be crazy but Pharoah never fell for that crazy shit. Scream, shake your head real fast and do the Hammer Man across the OSP lawn. Yawn. Niggah. Try some *other* crazy shit. Where Eye'm from those kinds of people never became a threat—they just collected SSI (and crazy) checks. At OSP everyone called me "Miami." Don't get me wrong. Some niggahs didn't like me, yet those were the same Niggahs chasing me, begging to screw me…*then* act like they didn't know me on the Yard. Damn. They got Down Low Gay Inmates as well. But ain't no closets in Prison, unless you're a Pimp, doing 9 years and Eye opened the utility closet on the Education floor a few months before Christmas and saw a well-known Pimp fucking another supposed Pimp in the ass. The two biggest Pimps at OSP fucking and making cocks and nuts swing like an Action flick was revealed when Eye told just one person on the Yard what Eye saw. To get it off my mind.

And it was all over the Yard in about an hour. It was one of the biggest dramas OSP had seen in recent years.

Lazy Eye Blimp and Tony Curry George. Two dumb asses that pimped all over the world, Girl, were screwing in the closet. Moaning like Buffaloes were sticking each other. They were so off cadence Eye was mad just because they couldn't do it right! Rocking back and forth like a R. Kelly Slow Wine. No wonder they were pimps. Couldn't *screw* to save their lives.

When they saw me Eye slammed the door closed in disgust—BAM! They've been fooling all the listeners on the OSP Yard. They loved a well told story, yet a Niggah from Miami, Pharoah caught their asses and it became a huge scandal. Even Eye couldn't believe it got so big. One of Tony's friends, a so-called boxer, was so upset at the revelation of his friend being caught doing the do that he tried to punch me in the face when Eye wasn't looking. Impulsively, Eye turned, threw two punches at him and that Niggah was like Oh, Shit and retreated. There were dudes cheering, running out from the pay phone booths, leaving their girlfriends and wives hanging like sitting ducks waiting for a bullet. Their angry voices spewed from swinging receivers.

Ole Boy was known for knocking dudes out cold. Wasn't happening to me today. Eye had to make an example out of one. And *that* set the tone. Don't *mess* with me, bitch. Eye wasn't the baddest man in the world, but if you beat me Eye will fight your ass all day everyday till Eye take back the title. Eye was raised that way. Eye'm a *Rolle*! My popularity went through the roof. Niggahs that didn't like me were buying me commissary and getting me what Eye needed to lighten the load on my Mama's wallet. Eye had a lot of big brothers, especially Larry Lott. We grew very close very fast. A Gagster Nigga asked to move in the cell with me and once he did he made sure Eye had soap, lotion, tooth brush, the best tooth paste and the most expensive shit on the commissary. And all he wanted me to do was re-enact that one, two punch at Tony's right hand man, and he would buy me what Eye wanted. He died laughing. That was his entertainment. Eye mean…every time Eye did it…it was funnier and funnier to him and it also amused me. But that was a moment Eye would never take from him. He had life. And that laughter Eye gave him Eye wouldn't trade for all the diamonds in the world.

We were good until one night, he asked me to sit on his bed. Eye did, since Eye had the top bunk. He looked into my eyes. Sitting in his draws and Eye avoided his eyes because Eye heard them whispering to my ears. This Niggah wants to have sex with you. Eye loved how you threw that punch but Eye looked in your eyes and a saw a wounded soul that needed a real man to make love to you real *good* and make him feel safe. He wanted to make me cum.

Eye turned away, gasping. "Eye know you ain't asking what Eye think you're asking."

"Eye'm a Vice Lord," he said. "From Chicago. My daddy pimped niggahs in wigs. Hell, Eye pimped a few of them myself and eventually won over my daddy and put his ass to work, too. Eye love handsome men. Pretty niggahs. And the way you threw that punch Eye want you to reenact it on this stick."

Eye leaned towards him and kissed him, he was rubbing my thigh, his uncontrollable breathing slowly suffocating me. Because if Eye kiss you and you can't fall into place, get in sync and breathe in cadence with me then you ain't getting the booty. So Eye got him hot and jacked him off.

And put his ass to sleep, getting in my bed, crying from the weakness of my flesh guiding me and said, "God, please forgive me, Father. Eye know not what Eye just did. Eye'm starving for affection."

Amen.

*Like attracts like…*

Between going to the Education floor for work and rarely going to The Yard, that applied to the Chow Hall as well. We got a monthly schedule of things to be cooked for breakfast, lunch and dinner so Eye pretty much *knew* what days Eye was going to eat and what days Eye wasn't based on the menu. All that beef stroganoff bull? *Ew,* Niggah. Not Pharoah! Eye wasn't eating that crap! And they seemed to serve that nasty shit every other day. Eye fasted instead. Until Mom sent me a $150 here and $150 dollars there and Eye stocked up on Top Ramen, sausages and junk food. And chips.

One day Eye got into it with Vee, my cell mate, the Vice Lord. Eye was getting tired of this dude begging me to jack him off every night. Niggah, your *wrist* broke? Mama was sending me money; Eye'm buying my own stuff, got my own supply! Niggah, *who* wants to be *Zest* fully clean when Mama sent me enough for Ambi soap, that good toothpaste and to buy my own TV? Angry from rejection, he jumped up from his bed—turned—and punched me twice in the face. Eye was shocked. Enraged, Eye jumped out the bed, landed on my feet with the precision of an alley cat—*Meow!!*—and head-butted him and threw a two piece.

What the hell. As much as Eye been practicing, reenacting that one, two on Tony's friend, you dare try me?

"Screw you! You ain't nothing! *That's* why Eye screwed you."

"Screw me? Nah, *fuck* you, *Niggah!* Eye've been jacking you off. You didn't even sniff my ass, bitch you weren't good enough so who the fuck you think you talking to Vice Lord?"

"Go to hell! Eye'ma beat your ass."

"Bitch, try!"

"SHUT UP!"

"Why? Because Eye *don't* want to jack your little, *unflattering* dick every night? Your whatever it is should be a *cock,* as thin as it is. They should have a *law.* A law for dicks. If it is 6 below, it is classified as a cock. From 7 to whatever, you have a rod!"

He spat in my face, bruised from me stepping on his manhood and snatching a so-called fake ass Gangsta out the closet. People laughing and clapping and somebody yelled MAN DOWN, MIAMI! MAN DOWN!

They normally and unusually screamed MAN DOWN when someone was shanked (stabbed) or beat up real bad. So Eye guess when Vee's reputation got stabbed by my words people were like MAN DOWNN! "*Get* your stuff and get out my cell."

Eye took the pillow case from my pillow and put all my stuff in it, my extra prison uniform, and everything and screamed, "LET ME OUT THIS CELL!" When the reality of so-called Gangsta crying befell me, Eye became silent. What was he crying for? He looked helpless.

"Daddy! *Please* don't leave me. Mama swears she won't fuck that man again. She promised, Daddy! *Don't* go! You always said you wouldn't break up the family."

Something didn't make sense.

"Eye gotta go," Eye told him. "GUARD LET ME OUT!"

"Please, Daddy! Eye'll let you jack my dick again! Just don't leave Mama. She won't find out, Eye swear."

And Eye didn't know why but Eye wrapped my arms around him, a Niggah that spat in my face and held him and let him cry on my shoulder.

"Daddy," he began, rubbing my back. "Eye forgive you for breaking up our family. You said you gave it to God and you repented, so you came to me to ask for forgiveness. And Eye do forgive you, dad. Eye do. And Eye forgive myself."

God showed himself to me again.

**When it dawned on him that** we were hugging, he pushed me off him.

"What the hell, Miami. Why you hugged me?"

"What?" Eye asked, in shock. Now Eye'm confused. He was like two different people.

"You heard me? And man why is your stuff packed? Man, Eye'm sorry for spitting on you, man. Eye thought you were my dad. Eye spit on him when he walked out on his family."

He started taking my things out the pillow case. Eye scratched my head, confused. "Man we're fam. Eye don't want you jacking me off. Eye'm sorry for taking out on you what my father had done to me."

"It's ok."

"No its not. Man if Eye want God to forgive me for my crime and my down falls Eye have to learn to forgive."

Eye sat on his bed and said, "My God."

*On the Yard the next day*, Eye called home, talked to the family, then left to go run some laps. But Eye fell out of it that fast and decided to walk. Clear my head. Think about my future. Am Eye gonna make it out of here alive? Am Eye going to die here? Four years and nine months was a long ass time. Plus Eye get good time. And Eye never got wrote up and Eye never went to the Hole. Eye felt Eye was doing well.

Another day gone was another day to mark off my calendar. In prison sex with men was so big they tried to hide it. One night Eye saw Officer Billy Dame boning one of the so-called-thug-Niggah-inmates on his bunk. All in the open. A guard screwing an inmate like a bitch; OSP guard Negro deep inside tight-thug-*caramel*-softness, his eyes rolling to the back of his head. He kept moaning his wife's name. Calling Hot Coochie Thug Boy…Samantha Gooding [Eye changed her name].

Yea Eye heard it! Jeez, Eye'm right there a few feet away. The cell smell like Cool Water cologne, Old Spice, Power Trip Dick and grimy, convict booty.

He then pulled out, slapped the thug's face with something that rhymes with Rick (there was hints of feces on his penis and Eye scrunched my face) *then* his butt cheeks, spread his cakes apart and decided to use his tongue for the icing. Eye wanted to throw the hell up. Ugh! Didn't you see boo boo on your penis?

He tongued the thug's tarnished center (damn his tongue vanished up there) while staring at an Ice Cube poster hanging on the iron cell wall ripped from some VIBE magazine article—tears falling down his face. What got me was the guard moaning, "Ahh—Nigga, DAMN! Pop dat booty hole on my tongue!" *loud* as hell—and the Thug grunted like Porky Pig—and no other officials heard it, and if they did they must have turned the bluest Eye away from the flaw in security.

The Down Low Closet Thug was fine. He had a brick bigger than the guard's penis; but the guard was boning the big dick thug Niggah with *pathetic* dick. Eye shook my head.

"*Damn* he wasting all that good black thug beef. But Eye'm straight. Eye get it, Eye don't give it. Hell to the no."

So why all this yelling and grunting, booty slapping, penis swishing tight booty hole—unlike wife's pussy—and no one saying anything. No inmates opening their mouths. Surely, they were at the cell bars, listening. My eyes racked the cell block. The Sea of Lust and Weakened Flesh took my breath away. Like attracts like. We're all in the same atmosphere. One Event.

Cell block Orgy. Some of the inmates were licking their lips; four *other* white men—separated two by two in individual cells—sucking and quietly screwing, but didn't make a sound; a few brothahs were beating off together—two Tops were tongue kissing and jerking each other—their legs trembling. Down below, another brothah had an old white man eating his booty. White man had a look of heaven on his face. Like it pleasured him to be of service. The black dude had to be about 25, 26 and the old white man you can say was older than prune juice. Old prude tonguing every orifice on the brothah's body...the brothah was *struggling* to keep his ass cheeks apart. The pleasure nearly broke hi down in his corrections boots.

On the white man's head was "Eye'm a Child Molester." The Niggah had a page cut out on his face like a mask of Macaulay Culkin. Eye stood there in shock, afraid to move. What did Eye just step into? The Twilight Zone? The weakness of different types of flesh sent off tiny vibrations and tremors that stampeded through my psyche, slowly causing me to succumb in thought.

Eye stared at the black brothah, and he somewhat stopped jacking off. Scowling, he looked up into my eyes from the first floor. Eye noticed he was in the PC unit, where most the big time rapist, serial killers, stars and reject parole revoked child molesters were kept.

He kissed at me and Eye flipped the bird at him. It was *then* Eye realized that the brothah with the Macaulay Culkin mask on was a guard himself. Down illegally in the PC unit, making the old white Caucasian child molester suck his dick, eat his asshole and beat his white ass to make him suffer like he did to those children. And they were HIS children Eye would later learn. And his children were now grown and he was still molesting and raping them before he was locked up for life.

Eye shuddered when Eye found that out. That one could be so cruel, heartless *and* cold. That's like my step daddy (well, ex step daddy) putting me through four years of rape, and kept fucking me through my rebellious teenage years and when Eye became an adult he was still fucking my ass and face. No, that didn't happen like that (it stopped when Eye was ten, and my cousin Lily started it next!). But Eye looked at the situation that way to better understand it. And Eye understood perfectly. At some point the child molester father grew to like and love and enjoy what he was doing. He fucked up emotionally and now it was an emotionally psychological problem. And Eye had to wonder did his grown children hate it, gave in like me and start to inevitably enjoy it. Like what Eye experienced as a small child. What did they do and say when he did what he did? Did they go to bed crying at night like me, wishing they were dead and calling on God and never getting him because no one, not even my parents, told me that believing in God and Jesus was a Free Will Choice God gave to all?

No wonder he didn't come when Eye called on him. Because Eye wasn't saved as of yet. Eye was 6! How the Hell was Eye supposed to know Eye needed saving when my parents hadn't told me Eye was born into sin? Eye didn't know the world surpassed my living room or school and definitely didn't look past my bedroom because ex step daddy was fucking me to sleep. Eye was forced to love him and Mama tore my ass up if Eye didn't get up for church. She beat me all the way to the car. GO TO CHURCH! TAKE YOUR ASS TO CHURCH! And she really beat me when Eye said, "Mama, you're not coming?"

And she gave me every excuse to stay her red ass home. She went to church Easter Sunday though. In her best low heels, dress and that curly perm was off the chain.

Then Eye further questioned that God-loves-me-but-never-met-him theory because Eye was like how do you *love* something or some being or somebody and you never even spoke to or saw him before. In that case, since we were made in His (God's, but derived from the strongest seed from Daddy's cum) image, why don't Eye love my classmates? And Eye couldn't stand half their dumb asses. Somebody lying somewhere, Eye thought as a kid. And Eye made it a mission.

To one day find out.

*So Eye knew then that guards* weren't worth the uniforms they put on before they clocked in. They were probably church-going guards. They *had* to be. They were married to conservative, Biblical, borderline *ugly* white chicks (oh yea! They in church every Sunday for Mass) and now throwing shade by punishing people who already been convicted of their crimes. Who died and made those guards God? Somebody surely fooled them. So my guard went up instantly to the police-wanna-be-OSP guards. A bunch of ass clowns.

Eye stood there watching the guard and the Thug have rough sex. Flip-flopping, screwing each other. Mr. Guard couldn't take much cock; the thug's pole was too big; so they switched, balled—chained up once more and the guard had the wheel. When the guard saw me Eye ran to my cell; but no one was at the guard booth to pop it open. Eye knew the guard wasn't in the guard booth. Because he popped ole boy cell and was banging his back in. So Eye was caught out there…

Officer Gay (after getting dressed in the child molester's cell) looked up at me and Eye looked down at him. Officer Dame smiled at me and Eye shook my head.

"Eye didn't see nothing," Eye said, coming up with a well devised plan.  To my advantage. Eye rose to the occasion (G*o soft! GO SOFT!)* but *damn* it! My mind was still on God, my flesh didn't give Him a second thought.

God revealed himself in this entire ordeal. Eye was seeing things while incarcerated that Eye didn't see on the streets as a free man. Eye was learning and absorbing the untold omissions from text books and 12 years of school; those untold omissions were hidden in prison. Eye learned more about the lies taught to us in school then Eye learned studying well edited text books throughout my school experience. And in that a silent rage began to boil.

Eye'd been had. Before Eye was incarcerated, Eye was cocky and thought Eye had the world by the balls. No. Those kinda dudes would fall and fall hard because God was so real and so true he will inevitably make any and everybody, kids and animals too, bow down. And at one point in your life you have bowed, or will one day bow to God when Jesus comes back; you just didn't realize it. Eye didn't care where you were from or what you had going on. It happened at least once—or it will happen.

That's God's existence in a nutshell. Right there for you. You didn't even know or understand God yet you STILL fell to your knees praying during a traumatic experience to Jehovah. And you're bitching and groaning and complaining because he didn't come on time *this* time? You didn't even appreciate when he was there for you—on time—the *previous* time. You *question* God…when your faith in him vanishes for the material things of the world, everything eventually crumbles. Your tears and pleas and the fact you were crying out with your heart through your lips via the tongue and *not* your tongue via the heart has been sent *back* to hell where it came from because you used to lie to God and he knew you were lying and you go out and do the same shit yet again.

But he continues to forgive.

In this instance, Eye was in a Catch 22. The Guard wanted to fuck me and Eye wanted him but Eye signed a pact with God when Eye signed that plea. So Eye compared both sides. God's love Go Hard 24/7. A penis? Grows Hard and Goes Hard? Um, yea ok. It's long, big and thick. What's the battery life of a good scrumptious penis anyway, or is that answer disguised by the Tootsie Pop Owl?

What's the miles per gallon on his scrotum (they looked a little small. Too small for my taste). What's the battery life on each square inch of a penis? That means the average brothah cums in two minutes when he wasn't gettin' coochie...so when he up in me he gonna last, like, what *ya'll* do the math—don't just read my autobiography.

He'll last about 30 minutes till he goes soft. God goes hard 24/7, and all Eye need is a mustard seed of faith. You should try it out. Eye decided to pick up the Bible and Eye turned a blind Eye and he popped my cell and Eye went inside and the cell bars closed with a loud CLANG noise and Eye glanced at the lotion bottle. More temptation. Now Eye wanna jack my dick. But Eye couldn't. Or could Eye? Eye'm licking my lips, struggling to keep reading the Bible...the lotion bottle was *heavily* on my mind at the same coordinates as the images of the Guard digging deep inside Thug Boy...making me wiggle my toes. *Ugh, Arg!!*—my legs started to tremble—then shake with fear *and* trembling—at the very thought of looking away from God. Not right now. Eye was in prison. Hell on Earth. Why did you think the government kept building them?

Duh! Hell on Earth was all over Earth. And Christians talking 'bout Eye'm going to hell for being bisexual...*Dummies* Eye'm already in Hell on Earth University called OSP. Didn't get any worse than this.

When Eye was younger, when Eye wasn't saved and when Eye didn't love or believe in him...He *never* showed up when Eye called because Eye called on my Mama first. That's a false idol in the eyes of God. Nothing and NO ONE before him. He meant business, folks. And Eye learned the hard way. You knew my life now up until this point of the chapter (unless you cracked the book open and you were immediately on this part then Eye would suggest you read from page 1). Eye called on Mama, didn't believe, wasn't saved, didn't say with my lips and tongue that Eye believe in Jesus and he died for my sins after admitting Eye was a sinner. If you don't do that you could pray all you want. God ain't gonna show up. He knew what's in your heart.

And you calling your Mama and Daddy first? Over God? Put nothing and no one above Him!

And now, after suffering all that abuse and heart ache and self-hatred, Eye was in prison. Eye struggled profusely to keep my faith in *Him*; after confessing that Eye love him, after confessing hat Jesus died for my sins, Eye was *baptized* at Church when Eye was 14. And life got much harder for me. God brought me through the rain and the storm and Eye was now struggling to stay faithful, falling to the sins of my flesh, sins against the Body of Christ. After Eye signed that plea bargain (pact with God) Eye promised to stay true and faithful and to turn to him through any and everything and GOD revealed himself in that because Eye have the full armor of God!

Know how powerful that was? Eye walked through the Valley of the Chow Hall of Death…mean mugged skin heads, ate on their side of the Chow Hall, beat on the bars with my boots, threw that one, two piece Popeye's meal at the so-called Midget Boxer on the Yard after Eye caught two Pimps boning each other. Eye had it out with a Vice Lord whom *later* broke down—after Eye jacked him off for months —and he spat in my face; then *begged* Daddy not to leave Mommie. That Daddy promised he'd never break up the family. And he was a grown man on some childish teenager bull-crap. So jacking off was out. Eye even trashed the lotion bottle. And continued reading the Songs of Solomon. Simmering. Eye smiled and shook my head. Deliberate Creation. Polarization. Potentiality. Allowance. Sufficiency and Abundance. Detachment. And Attraction. My eyes and thoughts were forever on the Universe, Eye didn't have to understand something to benefit from it. What did Eye have to lose.

Eye was already at my lowest…But not for long…

*A few weeks later Eye* saw the Guard that screwed Thug Boy. He was at the Main Box or whatever that small compartment at the start of the tier was called and Eye needed to get in my cell. Eye avoided his eyes because he was trying to get my attention.

Eye walked up the tier.

"YO!"

Eye spun on my heel. "What, Nigga?"

He raised a finger mid air and signaled for me to come to him.

"Eye'm in my 20s dawg, Eye'm not a freaking *teenager.*"

He kept fingering me to *come here.* So Eye went. Just getting off work.

Eye reminded him of what Eye saw.

*He laughed like something was* funny and Eye looked around him and didn't see Casper the Ghost tickling him so why was he laughing?

"Screw you *Miami* Bitches!" he spat evilly, staring me down. Trying to put the fear of God in my heart and Eye farted just to make a point. Stinky fart, too. The Negro was fanning his nose.

"What?" Eye asked rhetorically.

The way he looked at me made my skin crawl. "What is it? 305? Ya'll ain't 'bout dat dere. Eye'm 'bout making dat paper. Yea. Eye'm married to a white woman, but Eye'm from L.A. Used to be in the Cripps. Moved away, got a new start, met a white Hoe with money and got this here job. This is the West Coast, Niggah. Ain't no Miami Bass poppin' off up here. Trick Daddy? That's hard?"

Eye smiled. "Yea. Trick is hard, *bum.* Leave Trick Daddy out your mouth. Don't talk about Trick in my face dude, Eye'm serious. He got more money and Hoes than you can count. And Tupac gotta West it Up when he was born on the East Coast to give L.A. a *Mascot*?"

The smiled died from his face. "You're disrespecting me?"

Eye wasn't intimidated. "Eye saw you sexing that thug. Eye saw your goon guard buddy making a child molester tongue him while beating off to *you* boning said thug boy for motivation and inspiration. So Eye got all the trump cards. Eye'll spare thug boy, but *screw* the police!"

"You think you got all the trumps cards?"

"Eye do."

"They won't believe you. Eye'm always to work on time, always the first to arrive and the last to leave and Eye'm always doing overtime."

"Duh. Isn't thug boy your bitch?"

He got dangerously quiet. "What?"

"You're in love with him. Don't be ashamed. If Eye had ass that good Eye'd bang *my* wife with two minute cock just so Eye could *save* that *second* and *third* and *fourth* nut for your prison *bitch*, too."

Eye hit a hundred nerves, and it caused a reaction out of him. "*That's* it, *Niggah! You're* going to the hole!"

Yawn. "Do it. Or have you forgotten who my mother works for. The Feds. Eye'll tell her what you're *doing* and we'll see who believes who and Mama a working mother that make money and they take over half in taxes so she quick to sue a punk bitch!"

"Well Eye saw you on the tier, my co worker saw you on the tier and Eye didn't see you catching me having sex with said thug boy so it's your word against mine. My co worker got my back. That's two to one, Pharoah. Faggot ass. Eye swear. And as you can see…" He held up his badge. "Eye'm one of them."

Eye glared at him, needing a damn joint. "Fuck the other side!"

"Screw you Miami niggahs. *Bitches!* Eye'm the law, convict." He spat in my face and Eye closed my eyes. "Who you think the Warden gonna side with?"

Eye wiped his spit from my face. Eye glared into his eyes.

And he winked his Eye at me. "Go to your cell. You're under a restriction. Eye should write your faggot ass up."

"You write me up Eye will put your business all over the yard."

"Eye hate your bitch ass!"

"And Eye love you, unfortunately God says Eye have to love the handicap."

"Cell in. That's a direct order, bitch."

Sure, dude.

Keeping my mouth closed Eye retreated to my cell.

With an evil, *inward* smile on my face.

Eye was turning dark, and fast...

*The next day my cell was* popped and my cellie was called to work. Eye walked onto the tier, heading for the guard box. "Wilson? You're under restriction," said the Guard on Duty.

Eye grinned. Heading to him.

"Not if you got a job. And Eye work on the Education Floor."

Eye walked past him.

"Pick your mouth up off the floor. Have a good day, sir. God bless you."And screw you too! Two to 1 my ass. Eye got God. It's Infinity +1 to 2. With God Eye had the Home Court advantage. Eye always have GOD as a backup plan.

Scratch that. He's my *only* plan.

*Eye caught the guard again*. The fifth inconsecutive night Eye saw Officer Billy Dame screw his thug boy toy on his shift. Again, *all* in the open. The same time, *same* bat channel. Pow! Bang! *BOOMING* Thug booty hoe like the world was going to disintegrate in 30 seconds. Eye guess everyone had their version of heaven on earth, couldn't wait for it in the afterlife, had to have it now. That's why we have so many millionaires. Because they know where they are going once their life and their version of heaven is over.

Eye stood there, again, *watching*. Eye was hard (as usual), my mind wondering, but *never* leaving GOD, yet my legs buckled. Why did Eye have one foot in Georgia, and the other across the state line in Florida, trying to be in two places at the same time? The Officer and his Gentleman stopped having sex and they both looked at me. *Strangely.*

Eye waved with a Goulds, Florida smile. "*Hey,* Officer! See me now?" Eye let the hunter see the hunted. Eye ran to my cell, but no one was at the guard booth to pop it open.

Because he popped ole boy cell and was fucking him in the ass again. When the guard ran out to me (he didn't rush this time—he *sprinted*!), fixing his shirt and he said (not whispered) "Eye can fuck you, too!"

"Nah, dude. Eye'm cool."

"Come on Miami," Officer Dame said, licking my ear. "Let me get in that booty. Eye heard it's good. Got niggahs spitting in your face. Eye banged every pretty boy at OSP in the 3 + years Eye've been here. Eye put money on their books using druggie bitches from the 'Hood and they keep making this cock spit, since Eye mostly work double shifts; and Eye am always away from my family and my wife.

Eye shook my head and said. "Eye won't say anything, man."

"Eye hate Miami bitches, but Eye want some Miami Booty."

"Sorry. Eye don't let House Niggers fuck me."

"Eye find that hard to believe."

"That's because you keep your hard on stuffed in thug twat, *suckah.*" The Thug inmate frowned and Eye rolled eyes *daring* him to get rowdy with me. Eye'll pull his card and cancel that bitch, too.

"That ain't what Eye heard about Ole Boy and Tony, two pimps boning in the storage closet on the educational floor. Eye heard you pulled their cards all over the place. You're a hero."

Eye was stunned he heard about it. "Is it really that big?"

"YES!"

"Eye won't say anything. Just leave me alone."

"Eye know you won't," he said, grinning.

Eye rolled my eyes again. Eye didn't know what he meant by that, but it really didn't matter because he was a garbage Niggah spitting garbage for words.

Ten minutes later my cell popped.
"WILSON, PACK UP TO MOVE."
They moved me out the cell and into my own.
On the *other* side of the block.

☯

*My new cellmate was Craig* (Eye changed his name). A bald headed black gangster from Portland. And he was actually good people. We hit it off fantastically. He never tried me sexually nor did Eye try him. He was like my big brother. He didn't judge me and if he had extra, so did Eye. What we brought to the cell we shared.

And that taught me, that even in prison, brothers can live together during to lowest of times, yet still make it comfortable for the other person by being open hearted, kind and generous, even in prison. He loved working out on the weight pile and listening to his radio and his favorite song was: *"Eye need a Project Chick. One who can suck my nuts. And come and suck this dick."* That wasn't the Cash Money lyrics, but he changed them and made me laugh.

We were the best of buds.

*Nominations to hold office in* Uhuru Sa Sa (Swahili for Freedom Now—An organization created by African American inmates as OSP) were cast, and a few people nominated me for Secretary, since Eye now worked on the Activities' Floor.

First as a volunteer for HAAP, HIV/AIDS Awareness program, and then eye was appointed Executive Director of Office Operations when Charles, the founder, was released from prison.

The program was the only one of its kind in the United States, and we sent information on HIV and AIDS and the dangers of other STD's to institutions all over the country.

And now Eye was Co CEO, making $50 a month. Mrs. Marsters retired and it was like my grandma died.

Eye cried all night when she left. Eye would never forget her, ever. And Eye was also a math tutor with another teacher. A white man named Mr. Gregson. It was then Eye met Sonny…

*Waiting for Uhuru Sasa nominations*, Eye had all my books in multi-colored folders my new Boss Mr. Gregson, brainiac, had ordered for me. Mrs. Marsters told him Eye was a writer so he never interfered with my writing. Since Eye was a math tutor, Eye didn't do as much teaching as skin head Sonny. Sonny, such a cool dude, taught math and Eye was writing my book called *The Blonde Bombshell* that may never see the light of day. Eye may never publish that book, that book was written solely to help me hone my craft. Story dealt with a local stripper turned multiplatinum singer, actress and screenwriter that battles a lunatic serial killer that escaped a mental hospital and was killing her Hollywood friends.

When Eye got to my cell Eye would add a new folder to my book legacy stash on the top shelf above the cell's entrance.

Eye was proud of all my writing. People talking about my books, got people on the Yard reading them and giving me praise and corrections officers stopping by for something to read while on the clock.

But there's an opposite side to the laws of the Universe…

One day after Eye got off work (had a long day), my cell was raided by three guards.

"Step outside the cell Wilson!" one guard said forcibly. Eye looked at him like, Chile, puleaze. Eye took my time.

"What? What are you doing?" Eye asked. Another taller guard was taking my folders and my books and some of them had my writings stored on disk. OH NO! Knowing the Thug's Officer boyfriend was behind this pissed me off.

Eye was upset. Hysterical. "No, you can't take my *shit*!" Eye said, my heart stopping.

"Having folders in your cell is contraband and we're confiscating it!" the Tall guard barked, getting in my face and shoving me against the wall, with my arms trapped in his tightened grasp.

"What do you mean?" Eye asked, looking him square in the eyes. Motherfucking flash light cop bitch! Fuck you!

He laughed in my face. "It's going to get destroyed…"

*Eye sat on the floor like somebody* kidnapped my children and killed them. Then Eye lay on the floor dead to myself, dead to the world. They took my soul. My soul was in my writings, writing that kept my mind out of prison. None of my books were about prison. NONE OF THEM! My books were about history and incredible sex and family deception, books that were thought provoking, bringing guards and inmates into my mind, into my world and they read how Eye viewed the world and the Word and how Eye mentally challenged things. And all of that was gone.

"God, just kill me now…"

And Eye meant every word.

*A week has passed and Eye* hadn't been to work. Eye faked like Eye was sick and made myself vomit and they left me alone. Eye hated myself and hated life. Why didn't Eye leave my books at work where they would be safe? Easy. If Eye was rolled up and moved to another institution they wouldn't let me go up to the Education Floor and get the product of my hard work.

Then somebody else would steal it and publish it. Eye didn't look that stupid.

So Eye brought them to the cell with me, where they'd be safe. And the guards used authority and came in my cell and took them.

Savage bitches. My cell popped.

"Wilson! Hearings."

*So Eye had a hearing*, and it was rather quick.

Convict Niggah, yea that was me, #12926272. Stuck up Crackah. He was *well* cut. Handsome in his *mid* forties. Well groomed, tailored and dressed. Staring down my nose like he didn't get buggers.

"Mr. Wilson."

Eye closed my eyes. "Its Number one two nine two six two seven two. You don't know me like that to be calling my name."

"*Tough* one."

My eyes opened with fire. "Eye want my books."

He growled. "What gives you authority to use OSP computers…"

Eye smiled with the right side of my lips. "State computers, dumb ass."

"To write what you call books. Eye saw what you wrote and its bullshit and trash."

Eye shot my cuffs. "The *skin* heads don't think so."

"They just want to fuck some black snatch."

"Fuck you. Eye *want* my books."

"They have been destroyed."

A lump formed in my throat, like a mother just finding out her favorite child has died in a car accident by a drunk driver under age with a fake license. He gloated from my reaction, watching the life slowly seep out of me. Eye will never write again I vow it on my soul.

"Ya'll destroyed my hard work?" Eye asked, tears forming in my eyes at the anger that begin to boil with my stomach acids and Eye got heart burn. Eye was about to fuck this crackah up. And he wouldn't enjoy it.

"Let's get this clear, young man. You don't have no luxury in prison. You are not to use state computers and you are not to print using state printers for your entertainment."

"Fuck you bitch!"

He laughed. "Take your *ass* back to C block, sissy!"

☯

*Eye steamed all the way to my* cell. Eye couldn't believe he gloated about my books being taken. My boss gave me permission. Mr. Gregson said Eye could write for as long as Eye wanted. That white man had my back. Eye told him what happened and he went to bat for me but they told him my books have been destroyed and Eye cried myself to sleep.

Saying, "God *please* don't let it be true! Eye won't believe it! They couldn't have destroyed something you gave me. A gift for words. If they destroyed my books then why do Eye still feel optimistic and determined to continue writing?"

The next day, around 4 p.m., my cell popped. Captain Lacey summoned me to the property room. Oh, no. They changed my job probably to janitor just to make sure Eye'm not around computers. "*Hey*, Wilson."

Eye was dead to the world. Didn't look up or at him. Didn't care to. Eye said nothing.

"Wilson."

Eye said nothing, holding my stomach and Eye puked on the floor and puked and puked, the force from the pull had my stomach muscles sore.

"Wilson!" He gave me a mop, and pushed some fresh mop water towards me. "Clean it up. That's a direct order."

And Eye cleaned it up, huge tears falling down my face. How could they destroy 34 books like it's nothing?

Eye looked up and he handed me an index card.

"What is this for?"

"Write a name and address on there and don't tell nobody but Eye switched boxes with a fake box and they threw out a box of old books from OSP's Library."

Eye blinked three times. "What?"

He picked up two huge boxes and set them on the counter. "Man *listen* here."

"MY BOOKS OH MY GOD!" *What you put into the Universe ALWAYS comes back to the Source!*

"Listen, Wilson. Eye was going to throw it out but Eye read what all the prison hype was about when it came to your book and my Lord the way your mind thinks young man you write such incredible stuff. Eye'm a fan."

Eye shook his hand. "Thank you so much man this means so much to me and Eye thought Eye lost them forever. Thank you Jesus!"

My hand trembling from anxiousness, Eye filled out the index card with my granddaddy's address and two boxes of my books were sent to him for safe keeping.

Paid for by the state, baby.

Thanks Mr. Lacey! That's the day Eye realized my purpose in life, and why Eye was put here on Earth during this Era. And that was to write. And inspire.

The stage was set for the birth of The King of Erotica (one of three alter egos)…seven things Eye wanted to Master have been initiated.

Eye Mastered them. *Finally.*

***When it came time for nominations,*** my friend Craig was getting out of prison, and Eye hated to see him go because Eye had to find a compatible cell mate, but he needed to go and continue his climb from shame to grace. It ain't what you go through. It's how you get through that counts.

Eye had to put together a speech, and convince Uhuru Sasa members to vote for me for one of the highest positions: Secretary.

The speech for president and Vice President went well. My dude, Skeeta, who Eye call my cousin 'cause we close like family, was running for President, and will win it. Very business minded.

When my name was called Eye went up to the podium. My hair was growing out (Eye had plats). Eye took center stage. Eye lay my papers on the podium, neatly typed before me. Eye said a quick prayer.

Amen.

"Hello, Eye'm Pharoah Wilson and Eye know Eye am the best man to be secretary. Eye type 62 WPM and as quickly as Eye type memo's and faxes Eye can stand up and defend the beauty of Uhuru Sasa."

Eye won them over already.

"…*Don't* vote for me out of favoritism, vote for me if you feel Eye am the best candidate for the job and Eye already told you Eye'm the best so think like a winner and pick a winner. Thank you."

They clapped and whistled. Eye felt good about the voting. Till this one snake stood up. "Eye oppose!" he hissed. "Eye oppose till you tell us if it's true."

"Is *what* true?"

The Rapist asked me, "Is it true you caught Tony fucking my dawg, the Pimp, in a closet on the Education Floor."

OK. God was testing me. Time to see his presence.

Everyone was quiet because they wanted the answer. Shit, shit. You a Goulds Niggah! *Own* this moment.

Eye smiled, bowed and said, "Eye respect your question but at this time my speech is completed. Time has *expired*. And Eye choose *not* to entertain the question. *Thank* you."

And everyone clapped, standing up and The Rapist looked like the ass he was.

Eye stared at him like, "Yea, bitch, check mate. Eye'ma Goulds Niggah."

Eye won Secretary.

*Things were looking up for me.* Eye stopped calling home so much and focused on myself behind those thirty foot walls. Eye made my life worth living by writing books, and staying to myself. Being the Secretary was fun because Eye got to vibe and bond with the President, Skeeta (Damien Neyland, my dawg outta Portland), Issac, and Stressla.

Damien was the most business minded Niggah Eye ever met. Eye think he was in for murder, but he has truly changed for the better. It reflected in his business sense and the very respectful way he spoke to people. Eye learned a lot from him that Eye apply to my career right this very day in 2012 as Eye type this with White Zinfandel Arbor Mist chilled at my side. But all things, good things at least, must come to an end.

Before Eye went through a falling out with three inmates, Eye was selected with a hundred or so others to be in Bruce Willis and Billy Bob Thorton's movie *Bandits*.

Eye was so excited. Eye didn't think Eye would get picked when Eye took off my shirt to pose for a Polaroid picture. Producers combed through applications we filled out and Eye made the cut. The Universe hasn't failed me yet!

Eye was so excited Eye was about to get my first taste of Hollywood from in prison. When Eye was coached by the director, while they were about to shoot "The Boxing Ring" scene, Eye was sad because Eye didn't get picked to be an extra in that particular scene.

After the director and his side kick called out names, Eye walked off.

"Hey, you," said the director, Barry Levinson.

Eye turned to face him. "Yes."

"Pharoah Wilson, Jr, right?"

"Yes."

"Come on, man. You're picked to be up close to Bruce Willis and Billy Bob!"

Oh my God! Thank you Jesus!

*And 14-15 hour shooting days began.* Doing the same thing over and over. Eye had on red shorts, black shoes, white socks and a blue skull cap over my braids.

Bruce Willis was in the ring, dressed in boxing gear; getting ready for his scene. It was SO COOL! BRUCE WILLIS WAS THIRTEEN FEET AWAY FROM ME!

So close Eye could smell the sweat of his hard work. He did the scene fluidly. Such a Die Hard star he was. We had to do the same thing over and over. Eye was really excited when Billy Bob Thornton came in the room. He spoke to everybody and Eye died. Eye think he was married to Angelina Jolie, when she was just dick sucking lips then, keeping Billy's blood in a locket around her neck.

Barry Levinson stopped filming a few times, looking directly at me. "Pharoah. Act like cameras aren't in here. You keep looking in the camera smiling!"

"Sorry!" He was so nice. Shit, this was HOLLYWOOD at OSP!

Billy and the director went over the scene. Bruce, during breaks, sat down with a makeup artist reapplying his makeup. He looked so goddamn scrawny, not at all the buff dude Eye saw in *Die Hard.* And he kept looking at us out the corner of his Eye like he was disgusted, like we were going to snatch his little ass and Eye was like aw shit dude you ain't all that now. Eye haven't even seen Die Hard. None of them. Just the commercials. Barry Levinson snapped his fingers and screamed BAKGROUND! Meant we had to do our extra part, making like we were training while Bruce was boxing. ACTION! Billy Bob rushed into the boxing room. Telling Bruce they took garlic off the commissary.

Bruce, according to the script then got frantic and started punching the hell outta the man in the ring and Billy Bob Thornton screamed ANGER MANAGEMENT! ANGER MANAGEMENT!

It was perfect! CUT! The director was cool with that. When we wrapped for the night, a man took a few Polaroid pictures of the set so it could be decorated exactly how it was during tomorrow's shoot. What an experience. The next scene was the break out of prison shot. We had to play basketball on the court while Bruce and Billy sneak to a cement truck to break out of prison. Eye saw the different camera angles. One shot had the camera just on Bruce and they had to act as if both were being filmed. CUT. Then the next shot the camera was just on Billy and they did the same acting. HOT! When Bruce and Billy got to the cement truck to break out of prison we had to run, cheering, towards the gates, leading them on. They even did a shot with a camera on a motor cycle and the camera man on the motorcycle kept up with the cement truck. WOW! After that scene Bruce was his usual retreating Eye'm-scare-of-ya'll-self and Billy Bob came over to speak to us like he knew us all our lives, he got major respect for that. Everyone was tussling to shake his hand, pushing me out the way. Eye couldn't get to him. He was signing any autograph the inmates wanted, telling us he did time before and that there was life after prison. He looked me deep in the eyes and smiled and Eye melted!

"Come here, young man."

A few inmates mumbled *something* out of hate and Eye smiled, star struck. He shook my hand and he said, "Who do you want me to make your autograph out to?"

"To Pharoah with Love."

"Who is Pharoah?"

"Me, silly!" Eye could not stop smiling.

"This is the last autograph Eye'm signing today, Pharoah. Are you getting *out* soon?"

"In a couple years."

"Something different about you," Billy said. "What you do to occupy your time?"

"Eye write books."

He shook my hand once more. "Never give up. Who knows. One day you might be a bestseller." In my mind Eye was already a bestseller. Eye thought of nothing else. It consumed me, gave me feelings of desire and progress and Eye dreamed it when Eye slept. It was the first thing Eye thought of after thanking God for waking in the a.m., and the last thing Eye thought about after praying the Lord my soul to keep every night. And that's exactly what happened.

Thanks Billy Bob Thornton!

*When the movie wrapped our money* was deposited on our inmate trust accounts. A hundred something dollars. Since we were inmates we couldn't get the high pay scale, but Eye was cool with that because Eye got to shake Billy's hand and get an autograph. Eye sent my free BANDITS hat and shirt to my brother, and sent my BILLY autograph to Tamera. Then disaster struck when Eye wasn't even prepared.

Darkness came.

*Eye was on the Activities Floor*, doing Uhuru Sasa business a couple months later. After typing up a BLACK FIRST article for the inmate population in Uhuru's News Letter, Eye decided to take a little break from writing.

So Eye stood up and headed for the Studio; a place where certain inmates made rap beats and rapped their well-produced music. Damascus (Doo Doo) was the best rapper Eye have ever seen. A young cat Eye grew close to. He was one of the coolest Niggahs in the world and he loved my writing and Eye loved the way he wrote raps and spit his verses and his flow made T.I. look like crap, but of course

Eye didn't think T.I. was out during that time and this dude was like 23 or something like that.

Sometimes Big Zin, a cool, heavy set brothah and a helluva producer and rapper, laid down tracks and Eye got to hear them. Big Zin was good people. But that particular day Big Zin wasn't up there.

An inmate, Anthony (the Pimp Eye caught banging the other Pimp in the educational floor closet), came up to me, smiling. Eye couldn't stand this snake. He used to pimp men and women all over the world. And this niggah had it bad for me. He told me he was going to spit rap (game) till he gained control of me. "You're the *finest* bitch in the institution," he said. "Eye got to have you."

"Well you can't have me, dude—*damn.* Let my pores do their job and sweat me naturally."

"Look. Go back by the studio. One of your homeboys called you, told me to come get you."

"Who?"

"Big Dog, your lover."

"He ain't my lover."

"Please. That Niggah eating that sweet boy pussy. And he lucky. Eye know he sticking dick to that sweet asshole."

"Bye, Anthony."

*Naively, Eye went to the studio* to see what Big Dog wanted. When Eye got back there Eye was ambushed. By three dangerously created brothahs, *Anthony* included.

One punched me so hard in the face Eye flew into the wall. The other brothah was a fine red bone with a sick need that needed attention. The tall dark skinned brothah (the one that punched me) didn't love himself and raped men to build his ego and recharge his power; Anthony was just a late punk that hasn't done any real work in his life.

Eye didn't scream because Eye was from Goulds, bitch and we owned up to a battle. My heart quickening, Eye said a quick prayer to God, knowing Eye wore his full armor.

"*Hey* Miami!" said the bald one, the ring leader with a black chiseled body rivaling a Greek God. Fucking beautiful, but right now wasn't a very *beautiful* moment. His penis was hard from anticipation; he unbuttoned his pants and pulled out his *Thing*. Eye remained quiet, observing those Oregon niggahs. They never spoke to me before. Why they try'na spark a conversation now?

My game face sturdy, Eye said, "What do you want with me?"

The red one said, "It's about that time, Miami."

Anthony said, "We gonna pound the piss out of that boy coochie! We're *tired* of dreaming about it. Niggah Eye want a shot of pussy now! NO LUBE!"

Yawn. "Hell naw, *cunt*! Ya'll gotta fight me and take it!"

The black one, Eye'll call Black Stallion, jerked his erection, and then slapped it against his hand to get it extra hard. Cute ass. But he wasn't getting none of my booty today. "Eye wanna cum in your ass, Miami."

"The hell with *that*! Let's rape this bitch ass *Niggah*. NO MERCY!" said Anthony.

"Eye want some booty hole with your sexy ass. Eye always wanted a shot of Miami booty," the red one said, his huge dick put the fear of God in my heart.

My guard went up. Everything my ex step daddy did to me came flooding back. Eye was shell shocked, panicking. About to have a nervous breakdown and they fed off it, tormenting me. Saying what they were going to do with me.

*"We hate Dade County, bitch!"*

*"We're putting three penises in you!" they promised.*

*"Eye was gonna love it," said Anthony.*

The humiliation of my childhood and the embarrassment was too much. Tears fell down my face and Eye quickly wiped them away. No time to cry. Eye was a warrior. Prepared to fight. Eye lowered my head, my eyes on the devil's spawns.

"Ya'll gotta fight me. Eye'm not coming off my ass, sorry bitches." Eye smiled inwardly.

"He called us a bitch," said Black Stallion. "Eye'ma kill this faggot when Eye'm done!"

"Don't resist us, Pharoah. If you do we are gonna fuck you longer and harder."

"Bitch!—suck it!" Eye yelled.

The red one lashed out at me, *grabbing* my arms and the black one was behind me, "Yea gimme this ass!"

Eye flung the back of my head into Darth Vader and Eye head butted the piss colored Niggah in the face.

They both stumble back, disoriented.

Eye was a bit disoriented myself.

## *Did Black Stallion, Anthony And Red Man rape you?*

*Lord Jennings*

***Two arms wrapped around*** my body from behind, holding me tight, and Anthony hastily pulled my pants down. Eye was trying to break free and Eye refused to yell. Fear bit at me ferociously but Eye needed to survive. They looked like killers, and Eye refused to believe this was it for my life. Like Hell. If they wanted to fuck they had to fight me for it. Every ounce of fight Eye had they had to exhaust.

Black Stallion punched me in the stomach and the light skinned one pushed me on the floor, holding my legs and Anthony held my arms and they punched me in the ribs and in the back and Eye felt paralyzed. Eye'd never known so much pain.

Eye thought of the officer Eye met when Eye first arrived at OSP.

*"Something is off about you."*

*"Off?"*

*"Yea. Looking at you, you don't belong in a place like this."*

*"Tell me about it. Famous last words."*

*"OSP isn't all that bad, Eye hope you weren't scared up before you got here."*

*"Yea a friend was telling me it's the mad house."*

*"Here's the ropes, Miami. Stay away from the tobacco trade. Don't snitch, mind your business, and always eat. Eat all you can."*

*"Why?"*

*"You'll understand if it ever happens to you. And if it does you shit all over those motherfuckers, Pharoah."*

The instant Black Stallion tried to push himself inside my ass Eye let go. Eye started shitting all over his ass and he jumped fifty feet back, swinging fists, disgusted. Eye just kept shitting, the sounds felt like my favorite rap jams as they poured into my ears. Shitting on myself! *You wanna screw me? Cum get this boo boo booty, Busters!*

Eye got up and slapped Anthony with shit. POW!

"Ya'll want some ass?" Eye yelled, throwing shit at Black Stallion and it was all in his face. He started vomiting all over himself. Disgusted beyond his wildest dreams. Nah, bitch! *You* ain't dreaming. Eye'm ya' worst nightmare, bitch!

Slipping in vomit and shit, Anthony tried to run.

"Oh, no piss colored Niggah!" Eye yelled at him...

Angrily, Eye ran behind him and slapped shit in his mouth and he fell on his back, kicking and gagging, trying to spit. *Niggah* you ain't no rapper! You're a bullshit artist—*rapist!* Anthony was so disgusted he squirmed on the floor, making himself vomit. Eye wasn't done. Eye was here, damn it. Ya'll gonna *remember* me forever, bitches!

Eye squatted over him and shit, just boo boo all over that Niggah's face. *Damn,* what did Eye eat?

He pushed me on the floor, and Eye slid in my own shit, but Eye didn't give a damn. Eye had to survive. They were trying to rape then kill me and these so-called OSP guards were lazy assholes and weren't doing their jobs; so Eye'll do it for them!

All four of us were slipping and sliding, and Eye staggered to get up. Eye got a rush of adrenaline. Eye stood up, ran at Black Stallion and Eye kicked him in the rib cage, repeatedly, trying to pull my pants up.

He's grunting, holding his side, curling up.

Anthony grabbed my foot and Eye slipped against the wall, but caught myself.

Eye kicked Anthony and that's when the Red Bone Niggah tried to run at me and Eye pivoted on my heel and slapped him with shitty hands.

*Whop, bitch!*

*Pow! Bam! Boom, bitch!*

He slipped in shit and fell on Anthony.

"How about some golden piss!" Eye was so lost within myself part of me started to turn darker than the color black.

Eye pissed all over their asses, looked to the side and saw a push broom.

While Anthony, Red Bone and Black Stallion sliding in stank shit, trying to get up Eye stuck the broom stick up Black Stallion's ass and kicked his bitch ass in the face.

Blood spurted from his thick lips.

And the minute the light skinned Niggah tried to scream Eye pulled the broom stick out Black Stallion's flat ass and Eye shoved the shitty broom stick in his mouth, his head snapping back from the force of it on his tonsils.

"How that shit taste, bitch!"

Eye beat their asses with the broom for dear life!

And dropped it. Shaken, Eye pulled up my pants. Crap all over my clothes. Eye left the Activities Floor so fast Eye couldn't breathe.

May no weapon formed against me prosper.

But what happened when your soul has had enough…?

*What was the boiling point of doing time? Did it ever break you down?*

*Lord Jennings*

After Eye got back to my cell after taking a shower and washing feces and fear off me, Eye turned off the light, leaned against the wall and slid down to my ass. Closing my eyes, Eye was breathing in deep, wide eyed and my hands were in the form of fists. Eye didn't want to *be* anymore. Eye simply didn't *want* to *be* anything. Eye shook with rage and Eye was burdened down with the blues. Eye must admit that Eye was so deep within myself that Eye let the darkness wsh over and consume me, swallow me whole. Eye wanted to scream, rant and yell but decided not to because they would think Eye was crazy and they would dope me up in the SMU (Special Management Unit) so why bother? Eye didn't feel like being pumped or forced to take institutional drugs. They could be giving us some incurable shit, using us as lab rats so fuck it. Did Eye look like a Tuskegee Airman?

Eye missed home and Eye missed my freedom. Eye was having Vietnam flashbacks about my freedom, and life on the other side of the thirty foot walls. Why didn't Eye listen to Mama and *why* did Eye have to be so hard headed. Dumb ass bitch. Now you're a convict and they're *all* gonna laugh at you! My hands shook with fury and Eye started perspiring. As Eye got angrier and angrier, withdrawing into myself, losing sense of reasoning, the blackness zapped my color and in return gave me anything my heart desired; as long as Eye used it in the comfort of the darkness.

Eye hated myself so much Eye hadn't realized the sun has set and it was well after 10:30 p.m. Eye sat there in one spot. Eye didn't fart, eat, shit or piss at all. Didn't think of it;

didn't want to do it; Count time came and went and when the guard walked by he simply looked in on me, checked off his count sheet, and moved on to the next cell.

Eye miss HOME! Oh my God! *Let* me out this bitch! Prison has finally broken me down. Eye can't be strong anymore. Eye forgot how to.

Eye'm shattered and broken right on down to the core. The final transition of soul from body interjected into my mental immobility. My inner self. Eye didn't want to live anymore and putting my hands in front of my face Eye didn't want these hands anymore. Could Eye get a refund on the purchase, Lord? Eye looked at my feet and suddenly didn't want them anymore and surely not my body. *Grown* folks have been using my body long enough! Eye turned out to be a promiscuous dude. Eye couldn't control my flesh because Eye was never taught how to take care of my individual self.

This was the end! Goodbye, world! Hey young world my ass, Slick Rick. The very people reading me bedtime stories have given me *nothing* but grief and nightmares that played like full Hollywood movies through my mental frame of mind for the 8 hours a night Eye sleep. Eye couldn't believe my life has resorted to this. All Eye've been through have become troubled waters. Eye couldn't sleep. Just lost my lover, Big Dog. He was told to pack up and they moved him to a lesser security facility. Eye was heartsick because Eye kept our affair hidden for so long, and now Eye couldn't hide it anymore. Eye broke my own rule. *Never* get attached to anyone. They could be moved at any given moment. You'll learn that fast when doing time. Stay as unemotionally attached from Niggahs as you can!

Eye was in love with an incredible man in my eyes, *but* because we're convicts society labeled us scum.

Two state numbers submerged into love. Eye knew Eye was going to die in prison and the realization made me hop up and vomit in the silver commode. The thought of never seeing my mother destroyed me inside. The thought of never seeing my only sister graduate high school or see her pretty self all dressed for her Prom sickened me. Eye already missed Laron and *Jarshawn's* high school graduation and looking at the pictures Mama sent me only made me die inside because Eye couldn't see or talk to them so in my mind Eye destroyed the images of family so Eye could meet my maker with ease. Eye wasn't going to tell anyone so nobody tried to save me. When you cried out about suicide you weren't going to do it. No, you wanted attention and Eye didn't want attention so Eye was going to snub my fucking self. By the time Eye thought of time it was 2 a.m. in the morning. Whole cell block asleep. Nobody up at all. Few TV's glowed from several cells but all was quiet. Too quiet. The silence fell on my ears with a ton of unease. Eye heard a few murmurs and moans, and the guy one cell over from me had an orgasm and his cell mate kept saying, "Yes, Nigga…cum deep inside me!"

Depressed, Eye turned on hot water and lit a small candle Eye took from the Activities Floor (contraband) but who cared if it was contraband when Eye was about to kill myself. Eye turned on the hot water and steam colored the mirror. Darkness and the glow of the candle twisting the night away beautifully. Eye was one with the radiance. Of the low. And the darkness. And the 7 Laws…Misery filled my heart and overflowed into my bleeping soul. Sort of here, gone, here—gone. Here, gone the next second…here, gone the next second. The steam. Moisture on my face and arms. Nipples erect. The blurs on the mirror now fog. Eye looked into my misconstrued reflection. Eye raised a finger, studying myself, my void, emotionless eyes…growing wearily dark. Eye was a grain of sand mixed with rice in a salt shaker. Eye drew the all-seeing Eye in the middle of the mirror, thinking of Africa; my fingertip moist from the interference of steam/fog interaction. "Eye hate you." Eye told my reflection. The reflection of my left Eye aligned with my illustration. Eye was about to steal time from myself.

"Eye have hated you for a very long time, Pharoah," Eye said to myself, meaning every WORD! "Your past loathes you. Your future doesn't think you're strong enough to make it. Eye am an inmate: 12926272 to be exact. The state's property yet they say we freed from slavery. Bull. Now Eye couldn't free myself from self-hatred. Forever branded," Eye went on, raising the razor to my right wrist, tears falling down my face and dripping from my chin, falling into the sink water, mixing with heat and steam.

Eye cut open my wrist, the pain not even making me wince. Eye was too far gone, retreated too far into myself, past my soul, backing away from the light source, the glow of the Holy Ghost distant and fading every time Eye took a step back. "Eye'm in love with a state number Niggah. He's gone, probably met somebody else and digging that Niggah out. Packed up and left with hardly a hug to commemorate the relationship. When the bars closed with him on the opposite end carrying his property forever separated us. Disturbing my self-rehabilitation. Now Eye was a wreck, couldn't stop trembling. Rubbed my asshole trying to spark a conversation with my dick and it didn't feel the same. Eye could still taste him on my tongue, my lips begging for a piece of the essence.

"Eye hate you, Pharoah." Eye traced the all-seeing Eye with my blood. And then Eye punched the glass repeatedly until it cracked down the center. Eye kept punching.

"Eye hate you, Pharoah! Eye hate you! Eye don't wanna be here! Eye don't wanna write anymore! Fuck this shit!"

*"Miami,"* an inmate called out from the cell above me.

"FUCK YOU! FUCK OSP!"

*"Pharoah, bruh please listen to us man, you a helluva writer. Don't give up, man!"*

"Eye can't do this anymore!" My blood spiraling down the drain with the running water.

*"Miami, man you have so much to live for,"* said a white inmate from the cell opposite mine.

"NO EYE DON'T! Eye'm a convict. We're all convicts! The enemy has won!"

*"Miami. Eye love your writing, man. Not trying to sound like a pussy ass Niggah, man. Don't you understand? Eye am never getting out, Miami. Your writing is all Eye have to look forward to Miami Eye don't have a family. Mom is dead, daddy dead, brothers dead, sister, dead, wife, dead, children, dead. Died during the last fifteen years Eye been incarcerated in this very cell."*

"*Screw that!* All that writing ain't *shit!* Eye'm fooling myself. Me, an author—Yea, *right*! Eye will never be published! NEVER!"

*"Miami,"* said another inmate from the cell below.

Eye grew silent. A few more inmates woke up, harsh whispers filled my ears.

"EYE'M A NIGGA AIN'T NO SECOND CHANCES FORGET THAT WRITING CRAP! SCREW THAT! THE NAACP DON'T WANNA KNOW ABOUT ME! WHAT THE HELL! LEAVE ME ALONEEEE!"

*"Man, Miami! If you stop writing Eye will kill your ass, fuck Niggah. Represent your black culture, Niggah. You hear me Niggah?"*

*"Miami, hang in there man. At least you got a release date."*

While Eye continued getting words of wisdom, and praise and threats on my life if Eye turned my back on myself and my writing, Eye silently turned to the light yellow metal wall. Closing my eyes. God. Eye've wasted your time. My life was a complete joke. Look where Eye am. Eye am nothing, God. Nothing! Nothing about me was worth talking about, thinking about or saving. Jesus died for nothing, God Eye am so sorry he gave his life for me and Eye didn't deserve it. Eye give up. Eye'm not a manuscript. *Jail house writing* my shit was called. Eye threw my manuscript in the toilet, water swarming the bottom half of it and Eye started flushing. Over and over as my wrist slowly clotted, and blood stopped coming out. Dark red and hardening into a thick scab. The rush of cold toilet water soundly filled my ears. Eye flushed the toilet again. Whispering harshly *"Eye don't wanna write Eye don't wanna write Eye don't wanna write Eye don't want this writing shit!"*

Eye didn't have a gift. Eye'm no goddamn author. Eye'm no Tom Clancy and no James Patterson and no Sidney Sheldon! Those inmates were toying with me. Hey. Joke on Pharoah! Eye faced the wall. Eye give up, God. Right here right now. Eye give back the gift; Eye didn't *want* it! You could give it to someone more deserving. Eye would never write again! Eye reached up towards the top shelf. My hands shook. Eye took a Sharpie (contraband). And did what my heart told me to do. Write. Eye didn't have control. Write, Pharoah. It's who you are! It's your burning passion!

Eye wrote it with big letters.

*You froze the sparkles in my light brown eyes.*

Something opened up in me, something real deep that was rushing to the top of the light for air, for just a quick GASP.

Eye welcomed the company. Eye was smiling through my tears, writing, loving what Eye was writing and needing to write; it was *imperative* that Eye keep writing because if Eye stop writing Eye was going to wither without writing then die with no future writing to immortalize.

Eye will never ask you why
Because my soul may turn on me and hide
There's no passion left within me
My truths won't even set me free
Eye have no start to finish from
So Eye will be exactly.
What. You. Want. To see.

Eye was lowering myself as Eye wrote along the wall; writing so fast my head was spinning, focused and concentration, driving my words and sectioned them off where needed. Eye continued writing the poem down the wall. My hand moving a mile a minute. Eye was nearing the end of the wall but Eye kept writing. Running out of space. Eye sat on my naked ass and wrote on my left thigh.

Now you wanna battle me
Jealousy against envy

On my right thigh:

*Eye'm just Armor without a Knight.*
*Eye have no life.*
*So turn around and ride off into the moonless. . .*

And on my forehead: *Night.*

Eye stood up, slowly approaching the mirror. The water turned cold. Eye turned it off. Wasted enough of taxpayer's money and didn't give two fucks.

Above the mirror Eye wrote:

*Armor without a Knight*

Eye got on my bunk, crawled into a ball and cried myself to sleep. The blood fully clotted in my swollen wrist. Before the Sand Man brought me a dream Eye whispered, "God, please kill me in my sleep. Forgive me for my sins. Amen…" Funniest thing happened…Eye awakened the next morning when the bells sounded and the guard yelled "CHOW! MORNING CHOW!"

The morning bell rang once more. Alerting inmates that the cells were about to close. Eye covered my eyes. Eye wasn't hungry and Eye just wanted to be alone.

The bars closed back. The guard walked the tier and Eye pulled my blanket up to my chin.

"Glad to see the future bestseller making it through the night."

Eye looked up. It was Vencio. Eye smiled. "Yea, Eye did."

"Don't give up on your fans. Even though your fans are fellow inmates. You got men reading your shit, Miami. You are inspiring inmates to be better than themselves, don't you realize that Pharoah? All of us love you dude. You aren't supposed to love in prison, but we love you dawg. We won't let anything happen to you, do you hear bruh? *You're* dedicated *and* you're humble. You smile everyday in a dark place and that makes us smile. Not to mention niggahs chasing you all over the yard."

"Ha, ha Vencio."

"Promise me this," he said, taking my hands through the bars. He kissed them both.

"Yes."

"When you become famous don't let *anything* or no group of people turn you from God."

"Group of people?"

"Yes, group of people."

"What group of people?"

"If you're ever famous, you'll know bruh."

He got dangerously quiet and Eye shook my head, confused, but decided to drop it.

"Promise me, Pharoah!"

"Eye promise, Vencio."

He squeezed my hands. He never took his eyes off the All-seeing Eye dried in blood on my mirror. Eye would never understand why. At least not at that moment.

But as the years passed and the books dropped, it would make perfect sense. Perfect sense.

LARRY LOTT (MY BIG BROTHER) AND PHAROAH

At the age of 21 Eye went to prison...with no sense of direction. Eye was broken, shattered and torn. I successfully completed my four year, nine month sentence an author/a published author with a Book of the Month Feature in Body Positive Magazine and I was an extra in a feature Blockbuster film with two world renowned actors. I was released knowing my purpose in life. And Eye will fulfill the purpose of writing and inspiring until the day Eye die. Prison isn't The End, but a beginning. It's not a rotating door unless you make it one. To the aspiring writers out there DON'T GIVE UP! DON'T GIVE UP! YOU CAN DO IT YOU CAN DO IT! Eye did it. Eleven published books, 6 Awards and 100,000 + copies sold later Eye continue to.

HOME GOING SERVICE FOR:

Sunrise:
August 1995

Sunset:
July 1996

# The U.S. ARMY

Pharoah C. Wilson's being

# PROGRAMMED

March 1998
11:30 a.m.
Fort Sill, Oklahoma; Fort Hood, Texas
69 S.W. DOOMSDAY Lane
Rev. Dr. God vs. Satan

# John 11:35:

# Jesus Wept

**A Time to be Born:** Pharoah Wilson, Jr....I don't wish to say right now.

Love, Pharoah

**A Time to Grow:** ...eye withered into a reflection of blackness after she, after...she...

**A Time to Reflect:** ...never manifested, because of the death of...

**A Time to Die and be mourned:** I was suffering the deepest depression of my entire life. Nothing I have nor would ever go through, experience, what the fuck ever would AMOUNT to the damage and the way I suffered at the price of my reflection...

That's the day I became an image, taking my writing more and more seriously.

**Love Pharoah.**

If I even know what love is...

## ✞ELL ME AB♋UT Y⭮UR †IME IN ♀HE ♂RMY

*L☯rd Jennings*

# ђE U.S. ♀♀RMY

JOINING THE ARMY WAS ONE OF THE WORSE DECISIONS OF MY LIFE!

EYE HATED THIS PICTURE SO MUCH!—PHAROAH

*Military and law enforcement officials* run in my family. My cousin Connie worked for the Feds as well as my mother and a lot of my good friends. My brother Jarshawn did five years Active Duty in the Army and my younger brother just joined the Airforce, following in my grandfather's footsteps. My cousin Luke Evans has been in the Army for nearly a year now and just got sent to Iraq a few weeks ago, 2012. My cousin Antoine was in the Army and so was his wife. My cousin Thomas Way was a seasoned police office with Miami-Dade (over 20 years Eye think, and Eye think he's retired now) and my *other* cousin worked for the Florida City Police Force, though Eye never met or laid eyes on the man in my entire life. My cousin Sean Taylor's dad, from what Eye heard from my Great Aunt Kelis, was the Chief of Police in Florida City, even though Eye never met him a day in my natural life. Thomas, who Eye absolutely love and adore and respect, met the likes of Nelson Mandela. My Uncle spent more than fifteen years in the military. Since Eye looked up to my Grandfather (because he and Alfred were the only two father figures Eye could actually trust) Eye naturally gravitated towards the military as a way out of the hell of a life Eye had in Miami.

But at the time Eye joined the Army Eye hadn't known Eye had *that* many family members in Law Enforcement. Nearly all of them let me go in blindly—except for Luke, Antoine, Jarshawn, and Kells, they were kids when Eye joined the Army—not fully preparing me for the shock of my life. My Grandfather was the only one that sat me down and briefed me on the military. He schooled me. He told me the ins and outs, and that saved me from brutal ruin to life as Eye knew it at the time Eye was Active Duty.

Eye loved my grandfather. He was one of the most prestigious, intelligent men Eye have ever encountered. In my eyes my grandfather's crap didn't stink, he could never do any wrong (despite people in my face telling me what he did do wrong, and Eye NEVER listened) and Eye used to model myself after him. But not anymore. He could speak several languages, loved watching the *History* and *Discovery* channels, could tell you the different parts of a car and truck, and turned around and told you what kind of plant was growing in your yard better than a text book.

My love for books came from him. And my ability to be my own man and be a leader came from his twenty five years plus Airforce career. He retired a heavily decorated Master Sergeant, and he loved that Airforce blue till this day.

The old saying goes don't run away from your problems because they will be at your new destination waiting to throw a block party, but that didn't stop me from running to the Army to escape Mama's house and stern iron fisted rule. Today was February 7, 2012…and now that Eye look back on that day Eye realize that Mama's iron fisted rule wasn't bad after all. She loved us so much she went through great lengths to protect her kids at all costs. Only Eye didn't see it as a positive thing back in the day.

Currently, Eye had the best mother in the world. Eye loved her more than anything, but Eye never put me, her or anyone else Eye love above Jesus. He's my #1, whether Eye sin or not.

But during a very depressing time in 1995, Eye didn't have any more fight in me. Spending your entire life fighting perverted motherfuckers took a toll on my soul. Eye was exhausted from living by the time Eye got in the eleventh grade. During that time Eye really didn't want to know what the future brought. Eye wanted to write, then die. Eye wanted my stories and my poems and short stories to tell the tale of what Eye went through written in the form of characters Eye gave names, the names of my journals have been names of characters in my books as well.

Eye was in the 12th grade when Eye reluctantly swore into the U.S. Army. At first Eye didn't tell anybody Eye was even thinking of going, and when my Mom found out she was kind of against it. Well, she was fully against it.

Eye didn't even believe in this county when Eye joined The Army. Hell Eye didn't even believe in *myself.* Eye was so programmed by society and being beaten and raped before Eye went to the Army that, when it came to enlisting, Eye really didn't think anything of it. Eye just wanted to leave—go! Exit Miami. Pharoah has left the damn state, screw the building. Exit Stage Right. Ghost Light; alone on stage with the world watching, wondering were you a circus freak. Eye'd seen too much, been exposed to unspeakable things *before* my time…

My Army recruiter was talking, happily giving me paperwork and promising me the sun and the moon if Eye joined. In my mind Eye already joined. Eye made the decision months ago. What this white lady talking about, with those black ass teeth. She was into that Copenhagen snuff stuff and it disgusted me. She then spit inside an empty Zephyrhills bottle and handed me an Army pamphlet. Eye will never drink Zephyrhills again. Eye always think of her spitting in those damn bottles. Weren't you supposed to give me the pamphlet *before* Eye signed my life away?

Bitch thinks she's slick, but it's all good. Keep it cool, Pharoah. In my life Eye've had so much adult pussy while fingering dysfunctional nipples that Eye could sense, feel or see a snake from a mile away without losing a nut. Eye still get my nut, no matter how many snakes lurking along the marble floors of the mind. Adults taught me every damn thing about life Eye knew. Life was filled with images, photographs and untold hallucinations. The Untold were forgotten and locked up inside mental wards. They're pumped with drugs and kept in a surreal dream state, to the point they really didn't know who they were, where they come from or what they've done in life. Mental wards were human laboratories. Eye called it Ђe Chambers of Satan.

But what never dawned on me, as Eye signed and joined the military, was that a) my body no longer belonged to me. It belonged to the Government. Eye was a part of the Property Room, trained to kill and protect the government's investment: MY BODY. And b) 30% of those locked in mental wards were dishonorable, recently retired, retired, or Vietnam war veterans who have lost their minds. Those 30% used to wear Armed Forces Uniforms. The thought sent a chill up my spine. *One thing Eye never forgot,* even now in 2012, was that the Chess Board of Life was set (the deal between God and Satan [who can win more souls]) *before* Adam drew his first breath. That meant Satan would try to use on me the same demons he used on Eve when she was ignorant and without sin. Adam and Eve were never born into sin, but wound up sinning in the end.

Eye guess that's why nuns never *fooled* me. Eye got the best head of my life from a nun, and she's a nun till this day. That changed everything for me. No Pa$tor ever told me those things about Adam and Eve. Eye had to find that out on my own. Some Elder$ and Pa$tor$ preach—nah, *scream* was more like it, showing off, showboating in God's House—to you what they want you to know—demands he doesn't do himself and instructions he doesn't follow in his own home—not what you want to learn.

They stay up all night putting together sermons that weren't even all their own. The richer and wealthier the Pastor—and the *bigger* the congregation—the less control he has over his sermons.

TD Jakes—Eye was never a fan of his, and never will be. Let's just say Pharoah does his research. Eye don't believe half the things that man says out of his mouth.

Do Pastors and Elders ask the congregation what we want to learn, or do they predetermine those sermons before they dress in those over priced suits. You're a Pastor. Not Usher, Raymond that was.

And if Sister Betty ask me to donate money to get the Pastor a new Cadillac (when he still has the one we all got him three years ago) Eye was going to scream. She's called me 7 times in an hour and left that many messages. Eye stopped editing Ђe Kingdom (Ђe Army Chapter) and answered her on the 8th ring.

Before she could say, "Hey, Pharoah! How's the new book coming along?" Eye clicked on her ass for the old and the new. Just because Eye write books *didn't* mean Eye had Stephen King's kind of money dummy. Eye didn't care what she asked the rest of the church, but *any* man damning me to hell when the Leviticus Era was over dumb ass doesn't *deserve* my hard earned money for a Cadillac. Eye catch the damn bus to work and Eye'm a bestseller. Go figure.

He's the Pastor, not the Eye.R.S.

Eye let her rip. "*No*, bitch! Jesus wore sandals and sheets and walked on land and water feeding people fish and preaching the Word. He didn't *have* a damn Cadillac and five hundred dollar suits. Pastor Lee is a Pa$tor! *Not* Jesus."

"Well Eye never…"

"What would Jesus do, trick? He'd snub the Cadillac and use the money to feed people. Good bye. And P.S. Eye heard about you sucking Andre in the church bathroom, you need to quit!"

And hung up. Eye guess now wasn't the time to remind her she gave me head on the bus herself on the way home from Islamorada, Florida when the stars tinkled above the express bus with the lights off on the inside.

We were in the back, and she did a helluva job.

***My Army recruiter treated me*** nicely in the beginning. She was always there at my beck and call before Eye signed the dotted line with a nervous John Hancock. Whatever Eye needed Eye had it. If Eye needed a ride to the store a government car was there to chauffer me to where Eye needed to go. Eye was treated like royalty in exchange for my signature into their organization. My Signature was a vow. A vow on the Oath. An Oath regular society didn't know about. Unless they were military veterans or rejects.

Yet after Eye signed and was sworn in, she hardly took my calls, she came around even lesser than the weeks before and then it had gotten to the point she simply vanished off the face of the earth. Why? Because Eye was one of the last ones that enlisted. Quota, fulfilled. Orders, changed. Eye was a little mad about that, though. Because she was a nice woman. But the more and more Eye thought about it, she was getting PAID to be nice to me and that meant all her phony bullshit snowballed me.

Eye should have known something was up with her when she first met me. Came up to me one sunny day before Eye graduated from Miami Southridge in June of 1995, trying to hand me a pamphlet, but Eye wasn't interested at the time.

Eye looked her over. Well dressed. Class A's pressed much? Hmm. *Too* pressed—and so was her attitude; my attire has been pressed enough. Eye didn't need some seedy white woman with a blackened smile pressing me into taking the pamphlet about something Eye had yet to experience or understand. Eye was already in the Airforce J.R.O.T.C. in high school. Eye was one of the element leaders, and with Tashena Sutton (the baddest chick in the J.R.O.T.C. Program), we won a lot of Drill Competitions. So Eye had an idea what the military was about. Or so Eye thought. But that's all the military was. Trophies and competitions.

With humans being the trophies. Eye loved everything about the Airforce, and that's where Eye really wanted to go because of my Grandfather. Eye kind of wanted to follow in his footsteps.

Eye used to pray to God about it all the time. But it would never happen. Because Eye'm Pharoah. Not my Grand father. One of my best friends, Marcus Sands, was going to join with me so we could be stationed together through training. We were already in R.O.T.C. together. He'd been in it since his freshman year of high school. Eye joined during my senior year and Eye always regretted waiting that long to join it. But when you're the oldest of five kids in a single parent, controlled home things like that you never thought about. You rolled with the punches and took life as it came. Marcus and Eye joining the Airforce would never be. Eye couldn't score high enough on the ASVAB, despite having a 2.9 G.P.A. in high school. So Eye switched gears, joining the Army.      With the help of a horny, much older Sergeant. Who thought my booty was his wife's coochie, often times calling me…

Her name.

So *the thought of my recruiter* giving me a phony friendship in exchange for my signature did a number on me. Eye was angry with myself when Eye met up with her and joined. She came up to me in school, in front of the Main Office, at Southridge again. *Consistent.* Grinning politely, she offered to take me out to lunch. Eye said "Sure." Hell, Eye was hungry. Needed the free meal. Whoa. Now she's taking me out to eat. Crap! Eye smell a rat. Trying to talk me into signing up as a lab rat.

We became friends over pricey food at Red Lobster. Wanted me to join your organization feed me while Eye sit and roll my eyes at half the stuff you're promising me. You're on my time. Eye wasn't on yours. You needed my signature in exchange for life as Eye knew it.

She didn't make Eye contact with me one time.

Eye never had lobster before, and she told me if Eye joined the Army Eye would get a guaranteed pay check like clockwork every two weeks and Eye could buy all the lobster my little ole heart desired. Umm, you have to come harder than that. Come harder than Eye do when Eye masturbate Eye felt nothing from her empty words. Eye that much already, my Grandfather told me.

They would help me set up a bank account because we got paid through Direct Deposit. First time Eye heard about that or heard the term. Now we're getting somewhere. Eye couldn't stop looking at her fancy little ole ring. Unlike anything Eye'd ever seen. Intricately carved into the gleaming metal was an arch over a letter, the letter being 'G.'

At that instant my Great Grandma Olive came to mind. Eye remember seeing a 'G' like that in her home on a magazine. Eye read the 12 page article.

Eye knew what it was.

Where Eye was from, Eye didn't know too many people with a bank account. And Eye damn sure never seen that kind of ring. Seemed like everybody had bad credit and couldn't get a good TV or bedroom furniture on credit; so they started getting utility bills put in their children's names.

Unfortunately, they messed *that* up by not paying the bills on time and in the end the utilities were savagely cut off, leaving their families in the darkness with no running water or electricity. Their kids' credit and social security numbers were so *screwed* up that when they turned 18 and graduated high school and were starting college, any and everything they tried to get in their names were rejected, declined, NOT AUTHORIZED, shut down, paused, idle, game over, you lose, bwahahaha, thanks for your time, and there was nothing they could do about it. There was nothing worse than having creditors blasting your phone over money you didn't owe them, but the stuff is in your name thanks to your childish parents.

But they knew best, 'ey? Eye knew a few of my friends going through that. Getting ready for college and couldn't even qualify for financial aid because their parents snubbed their credit. And when they asked their parents to co-sign on the loan so they could get higher education the parents gave their asses to kiss. Hell naw, bitch—the parent(s) said disapprovingly. Not me! Eye never went to college and Eye'm getting by so you can do the same thang, too.

Eye wish my Mama would. Eye couldn't let that happen to me. And Eye'll be damned if anybody opens anything in my name without my permission. Eye'll take their asses to court, try me like that. Eye didn't care if Eye wasn't out of Mama's house yet. Open a light bill in my name and you didn't tell me Eye'm calling the Red Necks and pressing charges. Red Necks *loved* mingling in black affairs. It made good entertainment around their dinner tables. Made them feel like God to kick in your door waving the Glock.

And Eye wanted a bank account and most certainly wanted to know what having a bank account felt like. Eye told the recruiter that and she smiled, cleared her throat and said Eye could buy stuff with my ID card at the PX like a credit card and Eye would have the best roof over my head; better than the one Eye was raised in as a regular member of society, the one controlled by ten percent of your paychecks and Pa$torS publicly preaching to congregations, focusing more on homosexuality and barely bringing up infidelity, adulterers, cheats, crack heads and stank pussy stripper bitches, but worship two M(m)aster behind closed doors..

Eye noticed, while we ate our selected choices (lobster was kinda nasty, ugh. Crab legs tasted better!), she didn't offer me the pamphlet the second time. Eye wanted to ask her about it but Eye swallowed my lobster via pride and kept my mouth closed—mashed potatoes were kinda good and those free garlic biscuits were the bomb!

A few days later, when Eye decided to go to her office to sign the papers, she ran a criminal background check on me.

That really made me shudder. Why would she do that? Eye was only a teenager.

She was switching information out of a sick need to fill a quota. If she was this disorganized then it must not be good. But my desire to leave home and escape my past ruled over my thoughts.

Enlist as many clean niggahs as you can. Their sides would be determined. They represented a part of THEM. Any felony on your record you are a part of SOCIETY. The regular society. But not the one you've become accustomed to. So she's babbling on, spitting—*PUH! PUH!*—in the empty bottle and sprinkles of brownish Copenhagen-clad saliva found my hand and one of the pamphlets (which had a soldier jumping out of a helicopter in full army regalia; but what got to me was the color of his eyes—they were dead to the world; he had *no* soul left—and damn near red.

Frowning, Eye feverishly wiped the back of my hand over my jeans, creating friction, which kills her lurking germs. She didn't even cover her mouth; nor say "Eye'm sorry for that."

She went on. Business as usual. That set off alarms in me. *What* alarms? Eye didn't have a clue. So Eye did one other thing. Eye proceeded. After signing some forms she's still talking about the promises of having a fulfilling career with the Government, yet all Eye heard was blah blah blah blah BLAH BLAH. Ok, bitch—*shut* up!

Eye'm so over adults promising me the sun and the moon then turning around and taking turns fucking me and Eye wasn't an adult yet. So *miss* me with the promises. But Eye stayed quiet, smiled, nodded like Eye had a hidden shiny red apple for her and played along, remembering what my Grand Daddy said.

When Eye have to make major decisions, Eye called my Grandfather. Then Eye would go over and talk to him face to face. Just the two of us. Eye valued his opinion. His word was worth gold to me. He gives me an unbiased view. Blood raw, no short cuts nor breaks. If you decide to get on GrandPa's Freeway you *better* be equipped spiritually and mentally—yes, also physically and gun it at 100 MPH on that very Freeway all the way to your destination. If the tires blow you better not slow down. If your engine's running hot you better keep that foot firmly pressed on the gas pedal; and if the engine blows [BOOM!] you better jump out the speeding car, tuck and roll…high crawl off to the side of the road and low crawl through the bushes. But never stop. Because GrandPa pushed me to be the greatest in everything Eye ever did, whether he believed in it or not.

Resting was *never* really an option when there's work to b e done, according to my GrandPa so that principle became the status quo in my life. Around that time Eye was reduced to ruble and debris in my own life, living out the perception of being a sex slave for older people all through my childhood *and* teenage years. And now that Eye was broke, left with nothing, Eye was growing weary of the lustful and expensive catering…in exchange for my complete silence.

Why should Eye give joining the Army a second thought? It *couldn't* be any worse than living on the other team. Society vs. Them vs. the Government. That's the only three sides on planet earth. Follow the rules and respect the law, or suffer an agonizing prison sentence, or worse, be put to death. And they say Hell isn't on Earth? Who lied to you, 'cause, ahem, it is! After the way my ancestors were dragged, kidnapped and beaten across the slavish, evil waters of the Atlantic Ocean (The Devil's Gateway) you really think for one second that wouldn't hinder the respect Eye would endure for Caucasians?

After my ancestors were separated from competitive tribes (each kidnapping each other and selling for a few gold pieces into slavery, The Wall Street of that Era), they had to have Bibles and Gods and religions shoved down their throats and half of the slaves couldn't read nor write so now Eye suffer the loss of separation from family and Eye gotta try to read a Bible and convert to the Catholic views of my white slave owners and masters?

Every time Eye saw those old videos of beautiful black souls being sprayed down by racist police, shrieking from snarling dogs and pressurized water hoses nearly tearing the skin from their bones, Eye grew angry inside. Eye felt so much rage Eye would literally squeeze my nails into my closed fists, drawing blood and not feel a thing. For some reason, before Eye signed the papers, flashes of my ancestors being sprayed with water hoses came to mind.

When the Bic ballpoint pen touched the line where Eye signed my John Hancock, images of Martin Luther King, Malcolm X and dogs snapping at the ankles of my black folks colored the retinas of my eyes. Was Eye selling out, Eye thought? Was Eye joining the ranks of the enemies? Was Eye going to be a part of *Them*, separate from Society, and life as Eye knew it? Was Eye selling out on myself? Eye used to say the Pledge of Allegiance with so much contempt, Eye used to lip-synch it with everyone else in school, but the breath in my larynx never formed the words. Too many images of my ancestors being helplessly beaten contradicted that shiny sea shit. The Atlantic was never shiny during slavery. Those waters were bloody and polluted with dead black bodies.

As my paperwork was being processed, awaiting ASVAB scores, we hit a snag. All kinds of things came up on my name. It showed that Eye went to prison and had felonies on my record.

She glared at me. "Why didn't you tell me you had a criminal record?"

Eye glared at her. "*Trick* Eye'm only 17 years old, what record Eye got when Eye'm still in high school and Eye'm about to GRADUATE?"

She calmed down. "Eye'm sorry for snapping."

"Take me home."

"Pharoah…"

"NOW! Eye gotta tell my Mama about this."

She grabbed her keys, wallet and walked towards the office door.

"Come on, Pharoah. Let's go talk to your mother."

***Mama wasn't an easy woman*** to talk to. Sometimes Eye thought had a robot for a mother. She was so hard and stern and set in her ways she hardly compromised. She made all of our decisions. Well, at least she thought she made mine. Eye always, in the end, did what Pharoah wanted to do because Eye did know that this was my life. Not hers.

Mom shifts on the chair in her living room, giving the white lady the once over. Her eyes were full of knowledge. She pulled on her cigarette, leaned her head back a tad and blew smoke in the air. The recruiter was on Mama's stomping grounds now.

"You don't look like an Army recruiter," Mama said. She wasn't playing games.

My recruiter smiled, spitting in her water bottle. Black snuff-clad spit trailed along the sides, towards the bottom of the wrinkled bottle. It used to be a water bottle till she sucked all the water and air down her throat.

"Eye am."

"Where were you stationed at?"

The recruiter, who Eye'll call Directory Assistance, said, "You have knowledge of the military?" looking around Mom's house at the different things that made our house a warm home.

"Eye'm one of '*Them.*'"

Eye listened intently. "What do you mean?" A muscle on the side of her face flinched, and her left leg nervously shook. She smiled again, like a gushing blonde, and Mama wasn't with it.

"My father did over 25 years in the Airforce and Eye work for the government. Eye am a military brat."

"You do?" Directory Assistance asked. Eye guess she thought we were on welfare. "What's your line of work?"

"A correctional officer."

"Eye hear the state corrections offer incredible pay," said Directory Assistance and Mama crossed her legs.

Mama tucked her chin back with a phony half smile.

"Eye'm *Federal*. The Feds."

She remained silent.

*After a few moments of silence,* Mama told me to go get her a glass of water. Eye didn't hesitate, pout nor back talk.

"Yes, ma'am…you want ice?" Eye had some resentment in my eyes. Even though joining the Army was my decision, Mama rained on my decision making by reminding me who was the boss.

Mama's head snapped at me. "Pharoah, you know how Eye like my water."

"Ice it is," Eye smiled; clearly embarrassed and Directory Assistance was watching me flash the fakest smile of my life. Yes, Eye was upset.

When Eye opened the freezer to put ice in Mama's glass, Eye whispered, "Oh, yea." Eye stopped smiling. Anger stung my eyes to the point they welled up with tears. "Eye'm joining the Army. Tired of being treated like this. She was closer to the fridge than Eye was."

"Pharoah, you said something?"

Eye released a large gush of air. Eye forgot the robot had radars for ears. Hesitantly, Eye handed Mama the water. The ice tinkled in the cool, moistened glass.

Mama smiled. "Thank you." She looked at Directory. "So why did you wanna see me."

"We have a problem with your son joining the Armed Forces."

"Who's *we*?" Mama asked, sipping her water. Her hair meticulously framed her face. "The President is also my boss. That's who Eye work for."

"Then we understand each other."

"Get to the point." Mama set the glass down with attitude. She was not *fooling* around. "Eye got things to do."

"Eye ran a background check on your son."

Mama dismissed the comments with the wave of her hands. "He's never been to jail a day in his life. Eye made sure of that."

She handed Mama a folder with papers in it—of the search itself; the conclusion of the investigation.

Mama tossed it on the table. "Eye don't need to read that shit. My son has *never* been to jail. Did Eye say that in Spanish?"

Oh, boy. Here it comes.

"Ma'am, you don't have to curse…"

"This is my goddamn house. Eye pay the bills here. You don't like it there's the door!"

"Eye'm sorry. Eye didn't mean to imply..." Directory Assistance looked at me like a lost dog, and Eye handed her a pamphlet.

"Have you thought about joining the Army?" Eye joked, smiling at her and everybody laughed, even Mama lightened up.

*Nice save, Pharoah!*

"Pharoah's silly," Mama said. She picked up the folder. Quietly flipped through it. "This is not my son," Mama said.

"Yes it is."

Mama glared at her with an attitude. "No it's not. Two different social security numbers. And my son's birthday is June 26, 1977. This is someone else's birthday." Eye didn't like the look on Mama's face. What wasn't she saying?

"Let me see that?" Directory asked, reaching for the folder and Mama dumped all the papers on the table.

"This paperwork doesn't belong to my son."

"Well, we'll *redo* the investigation."

"Dumb ass, this is his father. This is his father's paperwork." Eye held my breath.

My heart pounded! “Let me see that?” Eye shuffled all the papers up, reading over them excitedly. Mama sat and silently watched me. My recruiter tried to take them and Eye stood up, reading as much information on my father as Eye could. Why he went to prison. The circumstances. *Everything.* Eye learned more about my father and his life in ten minutes than Eye had ever known or gathered during my entire existence on planet earth. *Briefly,* the memory of me cursing out my teacher for trying to make me watch *Roots* in the fourth grade at Bel-Aire came to mind.

Her name was Mrs. Bamford (Eye changed her name) and Eye called her a racist because she told me we were only slaves, and Eye had believed it, totally forgetting what Eye learned in the first grade with the book on Africa the Librarian hid under the book shelf.

We were Kings and Queens as well.

And the few white kids in class used to secretly chant it.

“Your *daddy* was probably a slave, Kunta,” and Mrs. Bamford didn’t utter a word to save me or chastise the moneyed white kids.

Mama didn’t enroll me in schools in the ‘Hood, except for Pine-Villa Elementary. Mama put me in good schools. Cutler Ridge Middle. Southwood, Home of the Stars, a future Magnet School. Eye heard Pine-Villa was even a Magnet School now. Eye should know. Eye went there as a kid, before it was a Magnet School. Looking at Daddy’s life in black and white printed on government paperwork, Eye was angry all over again. How much of this information did Mama know? And if she knew this *why* didn’t she tell me from her own mouth? Why did Eye have to find out this way? When most men and women felt unloved, they joined gangs. Bloods and Cripps, Vice Lords and the others. Eye felt by joining the military, all my problems would be vindicated. Eye could write the chapters of my own fatherless life, and be a better man than his retarded ass would ever be. Eye’d have my own family.

Eye thought that way at the time. Present day, Eye love my father, though Eye haven’t seen him, face to face, in 33 years.

Eye'd read enough. Eye gave the recruiter back the paper work. Eye was numb inside. "So, Pharoah, do you want to join the Army?" Directory asked.

Mama looked at me. "If that's what you wanna do, more power to you, Son."

Eye kept looking at my recruiter.

"Hell yea."

"Don't curse in my goddamn house."

"Sorry, Mama." *But your ass cursing, lead by example, goddamn it!*

*Goddamn that!*

*A few weeks later, Eye raised* my hand in a room filled with a few other society members, raised my hand before the flag, and promised to protect the United States against all enemies. Foreign and Domestic. From a society member to a future soldier. How could Eye protect a country with some people in it that Eye absolutely hated? Most of all...how could Eye protect a country that treated my ancestors like shit on toilet paper.

WHOOOOAAA!

*Eye just wanted to escape, get* away from Miami, Florida. Eye wanted to see new people and experience new and exciting things. If Eye hadn't joined the Army Eye would have taken my life. Eye really think Eye would have eventually killed myself. It ain't like nobody was checking for me anyway, with the exception of the adults that have been enjoying the beauty of orgasm via my body for years. The further away from them Eye put myself the better my development.

Eye grew to detest my own hometown of Goulds. Thank God for the writing. My writing in those journals day in and day out truly became the martyr of my life. And that in itself was an epiphany. At a time Eye did love my entire blood line, at a time my own Mama was warning me about my older cousins and their backstabbing ass ways, at a time she told me "One day your eyes will be open about your cousins," the day would come sooner than expected. Eye also wanted to go to the Marines—even when Eye was doing *Army* time—but my Mom's fake friend Sonja Shit-face (also Mom's co-worker with the Feds, with her big mouth ass) said, "If you make it out of the Marines even Eye will come to your graduation."

It wasn't so much of her hinting that the Marines was the toughest of the military branches (Eye heard men go *ballistic*, full metal jacket in there…suicide), it was the way she said it. Like she was telling me goodbye at my funeral ahead of time. Eye stared at her. She was sitting at Mom's dining room table. *Snickering* and trash talking was what she did best. Unfortunately, *this* was a woman Eye used to adore. If the tile man was laying tile in her house or if any house work was being done to her crib Eye would set aside my own life to watch over everything while she worked because Eye loved her like a mother. Eye knew her since Eye was about 13, when Mom first started with the Feds.

But her mouth, and the things she say about folks (Eye used to overhear) turned me off, because my biological Mama *wasn't* that sick and twisted. Eye mean get real. A fat bitch walks the tightrope too well Shit-face was going to say something about it because she didn't think of it first, and because she couldn't do it. Eye was thinking to myself. If Eye could survive four years of rape, my cousins screwing me, a haggard teenage life, feelings of autonomy and survive suicide attempts, self-loathing and self-hate and learning about my Daddy via government paperwork, then the Marines wasn't shit. Eye was already older than my age. Eye used to shed tears long after lights out because Eye realized with a jolt Eye made the wrong decision joining something Eye didn't believe in. And if you didn't believe in *something* surely you wouldn't follow the rules of the engagement nor share their personal views. Marcus and Eye joining the Airforce, we believed this with everything in us. Be it would not be.

We even had it all mapped out. We were in constant contact with an Airforce recruiter by the name of Sergeant Jackson. He was a short, stocky guy, very intelligent and had it all together. He wasn't the best looking man in the world but his attitude and his compassion for the Armed Forces made me feel like Eye was joining an elite program.

That, folks, was why Eye respected my Grand Father. The Airforce fit him like a fine leather glove tightening against a sweaty finger on the trigger of an M-16. Marcus and Eye took the ASVAB, but Eye didn't score high enough to go to the Airforce. Why Eye was thinking about this in Boot Camp beats me, but Eye knew even then that any decision Eye make Eye will weigh the pros and the cons AFTER Eye research what it was *first.* So there are no *regrets* when Eye make a decision. Don't join anything if you haven't performed research. Do a criminal background investigation on what you join or what you're a part of. After all, companies and businesses use the government when they do background checks on you.

Be smart. Flip it around on their asses and sue if they discriminate *against* you. Shunning research on the Army hindered me and the decision Eye made when Eye joined. And that's where Marcus and Eye fell apart as far as career goals. His mind was set on the Airforce. But as the years separated me and Marcus, walking individual paths, Eye would later learn he joined the Marines. That, right there, showed me just how LOYAL he was. If Eye didn't join the Airforce with him, he would join something else.

Freethinkers we always were.

***Despite it, my Army recruiter*** was a very caring woman. She wasn't all that bad. Eye just *hated* seeing her spit snuff in empty bottles all the time. We actually took some photos together when she came over after Eye graduated high school. Eye learned then that having family outside of family sometimes saved your life. Even the Bible states that your biggest enemies will come from within the family, even though Eye didn't believe everything written in the Bible. Some shit Eye seriously questioned with the heart of a warrior.

She was nearly the only friend Eye had who didn't try to rape or molest me. It took a while for me to trust her. But once Eye did, Eye trusted her with my life. Eye didn't know that, in the years to come, Eye would become family with a few friends and we would all be a close knit family because all of us had been raped as children and that's what would keep us bound for life.

Forever.

*When Eye graduated high school*, my cousin Alfred bought me an *expensive* Fahrenheit cologne set complete with free duffle bag. Eye had never owned my own bottle of expensive cologne before. Eye used to own knock-off flea market shit, but never the real shit. Eye cherished that bottle of cologne till this day; and it remained my favorite cologne of all time.

Eye needed the bag because Eye didn't have enough for all my stuff. Eye tried to pack every belonging Eye had, not knowing that half that shit Eye would have to put up during the 8 weeks of basic training and the other 5 weeks AIT

Eye was so excited about leaving Miami, Florida Eye didn't eat a proper meal. Part of me hated the fact that Eye entered the Deferment Program, choosing to leave Florida in August instead of June. Despite wanting to escape the place Eye was badly raped, Eye had my grandfather here and he was one of the most important people in my life. Ever since Eye was a growing boy, every time Eye saw his face, my face lit up like a Christmas Tree.

And despite me and mom's love/hate relationship, Eye loved her more than life itself, so to actually be flying the bird nest and leaving behind a place Eye was man of the house was hard. It was hard leaving my brothers and my sister. Eye pretty much raised them. Eye was more than a big brother. Eye was their father, disciplinarian, teacher and friend. Eye loved them like they were my own kids.

But Eye knew in my gut Eye had to go. Eye hated Miami, Florida and every abusive bitch in it.

The night before Eye was to leave Eye was all packed. Mama had a different attitude. Eye think it was hard to see your first born son, a boy who stayed home rearing your kids and cooking for them so you can work and not think about babysitters or paying them, getting ready to spread his wings and fly away. It was a very tearful thing. And since Mama was a fiery Scorpio and never showed a tear or emotions, to finally see some type of emotion reminded me that she was human after all and not a fucking space alien.

Eye laid in the darkness all night, just staring at the ceiling fan. When Eye had to piss Eye didn't move. When my bowels moved Eye didn't move. Eye thought of my girlfriend, Collier. Eye would go to the Army, come home a brave soldier, marry her, give her anything by Whitney Houston (because she looked up to her) and we would have a lot of kids. My delusional ass actually *believed* that. Eye remained faithful to her, but Eye was being sexed by an older dude on the side. Eye just had to have the best of both worlds. Eye never screwed Collier. We kissed here *and* there.

We touched and rubbed. Sometimes the coochie smelled like ugh! Wash or something, but Eye never said anything. But with my fling on the side we screwed all over Dade County. From his Mama's house and couch to the bushes leading to Turkey Point.

Eye didn't really wanna commit to anybody. Eye had a huge problem with it. Eye slept with so many married people and had threesomes with married folks my idea of marriage went to hell.

Eye used to sleep with men that *watched* me bang their wives. Eye was with married men who told me to show their wives how to give that Becky (head), and the wives, in tears (grown women twice my age) would sit there and watch me, studying then sucked with me till they got it right.

Eye slept with husbands who had wives who played with their clits watching their men screw me like there was no tomorrow.

They were too afraid of leaving their men with money that they satisfied his thirst for male ass *just* so they could keep their Benzes and Mercedes and Acura's and their big ole houses and the credit cards and money. Eye covered my face at odd times and my body shook with fear. Eye was so scared to leave home. Then a realization hit me. What if there were more abusive people out there? What if Eye go to the Army and Eye get raped again?

Eye sat up, sweating profusely. Eye didn't want to go anymore. Eye changed my mind. Eye reached over and picked up the phone. The numbers glowed in the dark. Eye called my Army recruiter, just knowing she wasn't going to answer because, after Eye was sworn in, she vanished into thin air. She answered on the third ring. My heart stopped.

"Pharoah? What's wrong?" she asked and Eye was looking around my bedroom, making sure Eye wasn't being watched by hidden cameras. How did she know Eye called with a problem? She didn't say "How are you doing!" She asked, "What's wrong."

Eye was quiet for a long time, trying to figure this riddle out. Eye was *so* quiet Eye heard the ceiling fan spinning and the wind blowing past my ears. "Eye don't wanna go."

She was laughing. "You're scared."

"Yes!" My eyes were wide with fright. Eye crawled under the covers and tried to wrap them around my body so nobody could get to my ass.

Felt like the dark wanted to fuck me and Eye didn't wanna be touched.

"Eye was afraid also. But you will have fun."

"Fun? Nothing about life is fun."

"You're young! You should be having the time of your life."

"Eye'm a young man trapped in an adult's frame of mind. Eye had to grow up fast!"

"That's what Eye used to say, child. You'll be fine."

"Maybe you aren't hearing me. How many young men you know can spit poetry?"

"Eye don't know many. But spitting your own poetry doesn't mean you're not young and having fun, Pharoah."

*She doesn't understand.* "Two roads diverged in a yellow wood…"

"Oh my God, Pharoah! You're quoting Robert Frost's the Road Less Taken."

Tears spilt from my eyes. Eye just wanted to die. Eye recited this poem over and over and over. Every time they fucked my young body, Eye recited it. Every time adults touched my ass or licked my nipples, in my mind Eye recited this. Two roads. Gay or straight. One traveler. Me. The abused. Which do Eye choose? "Again, how many young teenagers recite Robert Frost when half of them never heard of him?"

"There's something else bothering you, Pharoah. What is it?"

"Eye don't wanna go. What if Eye get raped?"

She was really quiet. "Pharoah. You can tell me anything, you know that, right?"

"Whatever."

"You can, young man. Talk to me."

"Nah. Eye pass. If my older cousins didn't believe me *why* would you?"

"Believe what?"

"Eye used to try to tell them where he was burying the treasure map, but they wouldn't listen."

"Pharoah, you're scaring me, baby. What's wrong?"

"Eye don't wanna go," Eye said, looking to the side and the sight of him made me jump out my skin. Eye screamed, dropping the phone. Covering my mouth, Eye bit down on my tongue.

"PHAROAH! PHAROAH! PICK UP THE PHONE EYE'M CALLING THE AUTHORITIES!"

Shit. It was just my reflection.

*Eye picked up the phone*. "Eye'm good."

"But you were…"

Eye was getting agitated. "Eye just don't wanna go."

"But you signed your name on the contract."

"Well Eye'll go to prison, fuck the Army! Eye can't risk being *raped* again."

Eye heard her gasp. "Pharoah. You were raped?"

"Yes. Ever since Eye was little. More than one time. So many times Eye started liking it by the time Eye was nine years old."

"Oh sweet mother of Jesus. Eye'm so sorry."

"Sweet mother of Jesus don't give a crap about me. Eye'm scared. Eye just don't wanna go."

"Pharoah. That's all the more reason to go. Get out of dodge. Don't look back. Eye love you, Pharoah. Eye'm coming to take you to the airport."

"That's fine." Eye lay down, my head pounding. Why did Eye tell a white woman my turmoil? What did color have to do with it.

"Have you told the police?"

"Please. They can't even answer a 9-1-1 call in the 'Hood on time. Too busy dressing as prostitutes, planting drugs on innocent people and pocketing a potion of discovered drug money, trying to fuck people. Eye have a better chance of taking care of myself."

"Who was he?"

"He used to be my step daddy. He was so *drunk* Eye don't even think he knows the monster he becomes."

"Pharoah."

"Calling you was a mistake. Good night."

And Eye replaced the receiver.

*The day came for me to* leave for Basic. Eye was all packed, and Mom was up and ready to see me off. My cousin Alfred just had to say some smart remark. Made me smile. He said, "If you make it through boot camp Eye will come to your graduation."

Did they think Eye was a pussy or something? Just because Eye rebelled against high school sports didn't mean Eye wouldn't grow into a strong man.

It would come at a price.

*Eye've never been on a plane.* Mama said Eye had, when Eye was very little. Back when she left my daddy and flew back to Miami. But Eye had no memory of that. Eye heard it was the safest way to travel. Umm, yea right. If Eye had to choose 20,000 feet in the air over big tires on the ground Eye think Eye'd stay on the ground. But that was not to be. When Eye got to the airport, Eye was looking nice. Fresh hair cut, fresh sneakers and my crisp white T-shirt. A few chicks spoke and Eye spoke back. After checking in my bag and gripping my carry on, Eye settled down in the waiting area.

A cute chick sat by me and she said, "Damn, baby…"

Eye looked at her. And Eye didn't smile. "Sup, chick."

"You fine."

"Cool."

"You got a girlfriend?"

"Yea, but we ain't gonna make it."

"Why?"

Eye licked my lips. "She won't suck me up and let me eat her kitty."

"Oh my God," she said, fanning herself. Her silky center was wet. She wanted my Milky Way spiraling in he cervix.

"*Damn*, baby. Let me suck it."

*Typical.* "When and where?" Eye asked.

"Go into the bathroom. Eye'll be right in. Go to the last stall."

"…*Why* not." Eye needed a quick nut, a good one, too, to settle me down, help me fight off nervousness about boarding an airplane. Eye looked at my watch. Had forty minutes to spare. Eye grabbed my bag and went to the last stall.

After Eye cleaned the seat and put one of those seat protectors on it, Eye pulled my pants down and sat down.

She tapped on the stall door and Eye said, "Its open."

She comes in, closing and locking it. She had her hair stuffed under a cap and she had a huge sweater on. She looked like a boy.

"Take off that hat," Eye said and she did, putting it on my head. She got on her knees and ran her tongue over my erection. Instantly Eye rose to the occasion. She had to be about twenty-four. And she had a wedding ring on her finger. Taking me into her mouth, she thumbed my balls and pushed her finger inside me. It felt so good. Eye grabbed clumps of her hair and po-*poked* her face. Moaning at a moderate tone, she pulled up her skirt and played with her burning bush. Eye wanted to be Moses. Let me have a conversation with it.

"Let me taste that shit."

She reached up, my penis *still* in her mouth and Eye sucked her womanly juices down my throat. Eye had to cum faster than normal. Mainly because her finger was inside me.

Eye didn't say anything. Damn that felt so good. Eye tensed up, grabbed her head and pumped her mouth faster. Spit trailed my 9 ½ inch stick—ran down my balls and felt cold racing down my hole. Eye burst deep in her mouth and she tried to lift up and Eye pumped that hot mouth, dumping nut down her throat. "You wanted it…swallow every drop!"

After it was over Eye stood up, pulling up my jeans. She grinned, licking her lips.

Hey eyes sparkled. "Eye never swallowed before."

The cum stain in her black sweater told me another story. It was dry, so it couldn't have been my cum. She sat on the toilet and pulled off her panties.

"Time to taste me..."

Eye buttoned my jeans. "Eye'm gonna suck the clit into a famished bitch."

"DAMN!"

Eye fixed my shirt. "Ready for this tongue?"

"Oh, hell yea. This is gonna be fun—oh wee, baby!"

*Damn, she got some huge breasts.* Eye reached down and pinched a nipple. "Close your eyes."

Licking her lipstick, she closed her eyes. Eye got between her legs and played with her for a minute. Eye looked at my watch. Eye had fifteen minutes to get to my plane. She was grinding on my finger…so Eye put in two, then three. Bitch was looser than the atmosphere.

Eye looked closely. Dried nut was on her pubic hairs. Some dude screwed her before she met *me.* She was an Airline Hoe, sad…Eye stood up and said, "Keep those eyes closed."

She was obedient. "*Yummy*—yay!"

When she opened them Eye don't know what the bitch saw because me and my bags were persona non *grata.* My lips work per diem. So get your head before Eye get mine 'cause when Eye get mine first…the first one cum wins. Like it's a title match.

A few minutes later, Eye walked up to the cute receptionist. His name was Hank and he said, "Ready to board?"

"Yes." Eye looked to the side and saw ole girl looking around wildly for me. She was pissed off, too steam coming from her ears. Eye pulled her hat low over my eyes, gave ole boy my ticket and boarded the plane. Never to see Easy Cum, Easy Go again in my life. Desperate bitch. Eye put my carry on in the cubby hole above me, and, trembling, took my seat. Eye was so afraid of this damn plane, but Eye think the world outside of Miami, Florida was even scarier. Before leaving Miami, Eye had only left the state once. When my grand dad lived in Lane, South Carolina Eye had visited him there. Me and my cousin Sandra. But after Eye came home that had been the only time Eye left. So embarking on this entire new adventure was frightening. And Eye had to do it alone. Without Mama holding my hand.

Eye put on my seat belt. *God, don't let this be a joke.*

*When the plane thundered into* the skies, Eye burst into tears. And was comforted by an elderly woman. "Eye know you're scared of flying," she said, stroking my head like a loving grandmother. "Eye was scared during my first plane ride."

My tears soaking into her blouse, Eye hugged her tighter. "Eye'm not scared of planes," Eye said mournfully. "Eye'm crying because the bad people and my family can't rape me again. My body is free! Eye'm FREE!"

The elderly woman told me to, "Cry, baby," her gentle voice trembling. Eye felt her shaking from anger. "Let it out and don't look back." And for the first time in my life Eye truly mourned. Eye finally got to cry and mourn the loss of my innocence. Eye cried till Eye fell asleep in her arms.

Eye awakened when the announcer came over the loud speakers. It took a minute for me to remember Eye was on an airplane thousands of feet above the earth.

"We're now at the Dallas/Ft. Worth Airport. At this time we request that you fasten your seatbelts as we prepare to land…"

Eye was in Texas. Holy *shit*! This was *really* happening! Yay! For some reason Eye thought of the Pee Wee Herman's movie when they sung "Deep in the heart of Texas!" And you clapped two times. Eye clapped two times after singing it at a moderate tone. People started laughing and the little old lady touched my hand and said, "See you are awake."

"Yes, Eye am. Very alert."

"You slept soundly."

"Eye felt good too. Best sleep of my life."

"Maybe because you were so many feet in the air."

"Yes."

"So what are you going to be doing in Texas?"

"Eye'll be *hopping* on another plane to Ft. Sill, Oklahoma."

"Ft. Sill. Military man."

"Yes. Eye'll be there for the next 13 weeks."

Eye felt the plane dropping in altitude or however you freaking said it. The closer to the ground we were the better.

"Make the most of it."

"And what are you going to be doing in Texas?" Eye asked.

"Working."

"You aren't retired?"

"No, son. My line of work calls for me to work."

"But you are supposed to be retired. How old are you?"

She beamed. "Seventy-eight."

"Wow." Eye rolled my tongue making catty noises. "You don't look a day over 40."

She touched my cheek "Sweet young man. Eye wish my son was still here."

"Where is he?"

"He joined a gang because Eye was always too busy for him."

People were getting ready to un-board the plane and it hadn't come to a stop yet. A few moments later the tires hit the pavement and a thunderous noise filled my ears.

"Why would he join a gang?"

"Eye may look homely but Eye wasn't always the best mother."

"Nonsense. Eye'm sure you were."

"Eye wasn't. Eye was too wrapped up in my husband and it drove my kids away."

"So what do you do now?"

She smiled. "Eye'm a prostitute."

My mouth fell open in shock. Eye leaned back in the seat, staring at my lap. A prostitute had been comforting me. Eye cried on the shoulder of a prostitute. Why did Eye feel so used and cheap? But Eye thought about it. Eye didn't know she was a hooker but she was a nice person, so who was Eye to judge her. She comforted me when Eye needed a friend. She didn't know me and Eye didn't know a thing about her.

"At your age?"

"Eye have nothing else to go to."

"Where's your husband?"

"He's deceased. Been dead for thirty years."

"So…how long have you been doing the hooker thing?"

"As Eye said Eye was so wrapped up in him Eye didn't have an identity of my own. Eye couldn't do for myself. Eye didn't have a job because he worked and wouldn't allow me to. So when he died Eye had to do it all on my own. So Eye started selling my body to ease the pain of my loss and wound up becoming one of the seediest prostitutes in Texas."

"Eye'm so sorry to hear that."

"We all have it bad in life. No one deserves God's grace, son."

The plane stopped. She said, "When you leave this plane, your life will get much worse than you'd ever known."

Eye shuddered. "Why would you say that?"

"Eye look in your eyes. Pharoah, you're the chosen one."

"Huh?"

"Great things await you in your future. Eye don't know what it is, but you will be praised by many. Remember this old prostitute told you first."

"So if Eye'm chosen, why did Eye go through all the bad stuff growing up?"

"Because you're being initiated on two levels. On one level, God is allowing Satan to test you to see if you keep your faith in him. Read the Book of Job. And the second reason is because Satan doesn't want you to become this great man you will be. He hates it because he knows what it is and you don't. He will try to destroy you. Promise me," she went on, cupping my hand and kissing it, "That you will press forward. No matter what. Never give up."

People were leaving the plane. "Eye promise."

"We will never see each other again. Eye wish Eye can be here to witness your greatness."

Eye was chuckling. "Eye'm not going to be great at nothing. Plus you'll be fine."

She kissed my lips. "Eye'm dying of AIDS. And Eye'm an old school rebel Eye don't believe in doctors and treatment. Eye'll be long gone before you rise to the top of whatever it is God has planned for you. And judging from the book on your lap, on Egypt, you are probably chosen to be a big time author." Her eyes lit up. "Yes! That's what it is! You're going to be a fantastic author! Everyone will be talking about your books."

"Now Eye know you're really psycho. Me, published? Ha, fat chance."

She unbuckled her seat belt. Nothing about her told me she sold her frail body. She looked like a nice grandma who baked pies.

"Remember Eye told you first."

"If Eye become some big author, Eye will remember you told me first."

After getting her bag she took one long look at me, shook her head and said, "Read the Book of Job. And prepare yourself."

And Eye never saw her again.

Eye was sitting in the lobby of the airport, cool as a breeze, going over in my head the conversation between me and the elderly white lady. Eye marveled over how fast a book's cover could peel away to another book cover, as was the case with us. To her, Eye was a young black kid afraid of planes, till Eye cried on her shoulder and said Eye was actually crying because my asshole would no longer be tormented and tortured by grown ass preachers and other sick bitches.

She appeared to be a homely old woman with a cookie cutter life, until she revealed she had to sell pussy to make ends meet, and that poured into her retirement years. Because she worshipped her husband above God and all else and was his submissive fool AKA slut up until he died, taking her soul with him. When my flight was announced for boarding Eye saw a tall, handsome dude with a duffle bag. We kept staring at each other. He nodded and Eye nodded. That was the confirmation Eye needed to talk to him, to see where his head was and not the one in his pants.

Eye walked over and introduced myself. "Eye'm Pharoah."

"Nooo," he said, smiling. "My name is Pharoah."

"Yea right dude. Ha ha ha."

He pulled out his I.D. It said Pharoah Low.

Eye pulled out mine. It said Pharoah Wilson.

"Well Eye'll be damned." We shook hands. "What's up twin."

"*Man* Eye can't call it," he said, cheesing.

"Where are you from?"

"Eye'm from Georgia, man, where you from, man?"

Eye noticed he said "man" a lot.

"Miami, Florida."

"The state with citrus pussy."

"Shit, give me peachy pussy over pussy that *stings* any day."

Grinning, he nodded. "Eye like you, man. Where you headed?"

"To Ft. Sill, Oklahoma. The Army."

"No way man! Eye'm going to Ft. Sill, Oklahoma."

"Well, lets board."

"Eye'm taking the next flight."

"Damn, Eye'm taking this one."

"Dang, man...You can't get it changed to *mine*?"

"Well, let's see." We walked over to the receptionist.

"Hello, sir."

"Hey," Eye told the lady, Pharoah Low crossing his fingers. "Can Eye change my flight from this one to the next, so Eye can travel with my brother. We're *both* in the Army."

"Why sure," she said. Twin and Eye slapped palms. "Since you're both cute, why not?" she said rhetorically.

And she changed my flight. We would be good friends through my whole Army experience.

Even if it only lasted a year.

Joining the Army was the worst mistake of my life. It was also the *worst* experience of my life. There were more in the closet fags in the military than there were roaming free in the civilian world. Eye swear. So many homeboys of mine in the Army begged to get in my boxers, and Eye was *shocked* at the forwardness. No one wanted to lose their career so the Don't Ask Don't Tell policy a lot of them used as a shield. Fuck men all in the ass. And leave emotions soaking in mattresses and sheets. Better make it to formation on time, *brothah*. We ain't cool on the clock. In fact bruh Eye couldn't *stand* your ass. So in public you shut the hell up. And after dark, Big Daddy will low and high crawl all through Pharoah's Nookie.

Eye knew Army brothahs that went to the local mall and poked local men in the butt using their uniforms to lure them to bed…or they had orgies with church dudes, sexing them like POW's and sending them home with sore assholes. Army brothahs used to brag about it drinking beer and watching Hoes shake ass in the videos. Even when we went to the strip clubs, *Niggahs* had to pretend to be mesmerized by the female ass with my ass on their minds. It was funny to me at the time.

How Army brothahs bait and switched themselves lock, stock and barrel to keep up [↑]with their egos and images. Sweating bullets. Never really being totally free. Some Niggahs had wives. Wives that screwed other men when my friends (their husbands they only married for the extra pay) were in the field for two weeks, sleeping in tanks and loading 60 pound rounds and turning, pulling the string—BOOM! You *didn't* see what you blew up or what you were shooting at, but that little call transmitted through the radio let us all know if you hit or miss the target in the field.

So with another set of eyes Eye studied military dudes while in the Army.

Started at boot camp. Fort Sill, Oklahoma. A place Eye never heard of. A place that had wicked interchanging weather and during the winter it wasn't nothing nice. Eye was: 13 Bravo Field Artillery WHOOOAA!!!

Cadence: Warlords, warlords—*smooth* —this is how we do it—BOOM ! War Lords! War Lords! *Shout!* Your left your right—it's Funkdafied! Warlords WARLORDS! SHOUT! Hold 'em up (we all cupped our balls together in sync on this part) *then* move out. ARTILLERY! Break it down—*kneel*—Get em up! GET EM UP! *SHOOT*! KILL!

Eye lived for our morning cadence when Drill Sergeant Hemple or Drill Sergeant Martinez (who had a crush on my mother and hadn't a chance in hell) called the Platoon to attention. But before all this…my arrival into Fort Sill confused me...

The purpose for boot camp was simple. It was designed to turn you from a regular civilian into a 100% SOLDIER! *Period.* No ifs, ands or buts. So making my way to the Transition Center when Eye got there, we were given pills to swallow (Soft *Peter* Pills) designed to stop you from getting an erection, but Eye crushed mine under my boot. Eye didn't trust the government like that, even though Eye was government property. My very body belonged to them.

After half the brothahs swallowed their erections away. My dawgs—new friends that came with me to Fort Sill (and we were closely knit like a family)—followed my lead and didn't swallow the pill. We were then loaded on cattle trucks. The Drill Sergeant, especially a tall black Sergeant, was very accommodating and nice. They spoke politely to us. Made us feel welcome. "Yes, welcome to the United States Army. Sure, you could go on to make a brilliant career out of *this*! Where are you from young man? Goulds? Where was that? Miami, Florida? Oh, snap. Never heard of it—*Goulds* that is…" He shook my hand. He said, "Nice to meet you."

Eye said, "*Likewise.*" The cattle trucks stopped by a photography studio and the Drill Sergeants smoked us. Meaning made us drop down and give them fifty. And you better do fifty two. We were *dirty* and sweaty. We're pushing up and down unexpectedly. Eye'm thinking, ok—*what* part of the game was *this*? After we're done doing physical exercises, we're ushered into a photography studio. We had to put on Class A uniform jackets and the Class A uniform shirt over BDU pants, put on that retarded, funky ass McDonald's looking hat and say, "Cheese!" like we weren't just smoked. Eye was breathing hard. Eye gave the camera a seldom gaze. *Flash*...It's *over*. We're ushered out of the building, back onto the cattle trucks like we were actually cattle. No one said anything as it all sunk in. Tires biting into the bumpy pavement, causing us to shift ever so often. We're holding rails and above railings for balance or leaning on each other for support. Once the cattle trucks crossed the tracks, we entered another

## DIMENSION.

*A dimension very different from* the world Eye was brought up in. And Eye was brought up in Hell, making it to the Fortress of being my own man. And when Eye thought Eye'd broken bondage Eye was alleviated to another realm of social consciousness.

Along the roads huge buildings began to rise from the horizon, like college campuses. Our eyes were wide with excitement. Drill Sergeants' eyes narrowed with maliciousness. Masters with whips was their mental frame of mind. Government property we soldiers were to be.

Once the trucks stopped, brakes squeaking, the DEMONS surfaced.

GET OUT OF THE FUCKING CATTLE TRUCK RIGHT NOW GET THE FUCK OUT NOW!

Drill Sergeant barked orders that put fear in our hearts. Gone was the welcoming spirit they possessed on the opposite side of the tracks, just before the photography studio. My heart pounded through the pulse of my asshole sending shivers down me spine. Yea, my *spine*! Eye was *that* messed up. Grabbing my bags, we all scattered off the cattle trucks as if they were on fire about to blow in three, two, one seconds and the barking orders ceaselessly stopped our hearts.

YOU SEE THE WHITE X'S ON THE PLATFORM LINE UP ON THE 'X' MUTHAFUCKAHS! PICK THOSE BAGS UP DON'T LET THEM TOUCH THE GROUND IF YOU DIDN'T WANNA CARRY ALL THAT BAGGAGE YOU SHOULDA LEFT IT IN YOUR PAST PICK IT UP MOVE IT MOVE IT PRIVATES!

Eye found the nearest X, struggling to hold my bags and stood at attention. What a strain! Mutha*fuck*!

Out of my peripheral, all my dawgs found an X and stood on top of it, struggling like me to hold all our personal property up. On the outside realm, when Eye was a regular civilian the shit in my duffle bags was material possessions Eye told myself Eye couldn't live without. Yet on the opposite side of the realm, as a soldier those beasts, Drill Sergeants, basically let me know that my material possessions were worthless because my possessions possessed me. After we all lined up we were separated into four different batteries. Eye was sweating because Eye could be mixed up and separated from my dawgs Eye met at the airport and on the cattle trucks. Eye was a part of the Down South Brothahs crew, since Eye was from Miami. And James was from Georgia, so was Wilcox and Pharoah Low.

Once their names were called they were to go to the Warlords. Cool. But Eye wasn't picked. Goddamn it. Eye couldn't go to any other Platoon! Damn!

"Wilson, WARLORDS!"

Um, in that case yes the heck Eye will.

Follow my DAWGS that was.

*The first few weeks were grueling.* We were "smoked" for every little thing we did wrong. If we didn't work as a team we were smoked. Group punishment—yes they believed in wholeheartedly. One screwed up the entire Platoon screwed up. We jogged for miles every morning with Hilly Billy ass Drill Sergeant Hemple. He was the skinniest, coolest white dude Eye *ever* met in my life. He ran those miles like they weren't *anything*, tiring me and half the Platoon out. But we made it. Eye figured out that it was about mind control. For instance…if you're crying about missing your mother *or* your girlfriend or wife the Drill Sergeants rode your tail.

*"Jody banging your Mama in the ass, boy!"*

*"Jody eating your wife's funk box, boy! You're a soldier!"*

*"We're soldiers 24 hours a day!"*

*"Forget your wife and your retarded Mama, boy!"*

All of this angered us, but we had to stand at attention and not mimic, say or breathe a word. You better not even blink. Stand like those Russians in furry hat and red coats. Even if they spit in your face or sucked your penis, you *better* stand at attention like there's nothing happening.

When Eye realized that Eye was good. Eye didn't let them anger me anymore. Eye was one of the element leaders, so my squad was the *business!* Eye remember two blanket parties that were given out to two different soldiers. One for Rogers (Eye changed his name) and the other for a white dude Eye couldn't remember his name for the *life* in me. Rogers was the whiner. He whined about *everything*. He was the *best* at everything. He was a donkey looking fiend sporting Caucasian twat around in personal photos. Caucasian twat being his girlfriend and he drove us crazy with the bull. Eye forget exactly what he did, but some members of our Platoon waited till he fell into a deep sleep and put a pillow over his face and beat him with soap inside blankets. You're trapped in the darkness while heavy bars of soap slammed forcibly into your body for messing up. If you got the entire group punished you received a certified BLANKET PARTY on the house and you better not snitch because that was your ass.

So Eye knew then to keep my mouth shut. Eye never had to go through *that*. Lester one day got a pair of panties from his girl and he put them on, running through the barracks with that fat ass. He was making muscle gestures, screaming, "GAS GAS GAS!" We said the "Gas" phrase when we had to put on our GAS masks. You had about, *what*,

6 to 7 seconds to put it on. GAS GAS GAS symbolized the mask was put on properly. To further train us in that we were put through a gas chamber with real live CS Gas. My God. When Eye tell you that was hell! To be *choking* to death on gas and forced to say your social security number and Platoon name while standing at attention with a straight face was hell. They got us on video running out of the gas chamber with snot and spit dangling from our nostrils and mouths. Eye nearly died, oh my God.

But the experience taught me to appreciate clean air a little more than Eye used to. Being a soldier would have its turning point. Eye wouldn't go so far to say Eye hated the place; my Army experience Eye truly enjoyed. Eye had the time of my young life at the time. Eye didn't have to worry about being cut from the Army, like regular society members losing their jobs or being laid off and losing medical benefits.

My shit would be automatic. For as long as Eye stayed in the Army. And if Eye did 20 years, Eye could retire with benefits regular society members would never obtain.

So Eye said "NO" to a career early on. Eye loved the Army experience, but Eye hated the people who abused me in the Army. Regular soldiers like Eye was. Protecting the U.S. against all enemies foreign and domestic, yet Eye still got gang raped in Boot Camp with a hand over my mouth, a knife to my back by 4 of the Niggahs in my Battery and threats against my young life if Eye didn't oblige their sick need for pleasure. So who was protecting me from the ones protecting the country? The ones that didn't take those Soft Peter pills? At that point Eye learned that you couldn't run from your problems, especially if you never faced them and had closure. Eye was so busy trying to escape Goulds (Florida at large, the taste of citrus was starting to get on my nerves) that Eye didn't know Eye would go through it worse in Oklahoma.

When Eye got raped in the Army, Eye learned this ten fold. Eye used to hate it. Eye was too afraid to tell officials, because of the law of the streets. You never snitch, no matter what happens to you, yet those brothahs that raped me took an oath to protect the United States against ALL ENEMIES, foreign and domestic just like Eye had.

That meant Eye had to obey the rules of the Brotherhood. Protect them at all costs. Eye was property of the U.S. And getting sexual gratification from my warm hole penetrated that oath, and they became my enemies. Enemies against government property: my body. If you so much as suffer a heat stroke in the Army, you better hope, wish, beg and PRAY they don't give you an Article 15 or a Court Marshall. So telling them Eye was being raped, at what price would it cost the stipulations of Don't Ask, Don't Tell? That order in itself kept me controlled, programmed and quiet. DON'T TELL! Meaning, keep your mouth *shut*! Shit real in the field. Eye hated negative folks.

Eye hated the oppressors.

Boot Camp went by smoothly (except for the few times Eye was gang raped), and making our way into AIT (learning our military jobs), things seemed to return back to normal. We weren't being smoked as much, and Drill Sergeants gave us a little more freedom. Eye wasn't raped again. Drill Sergeants didn't come awaken you every single morning anymore, weekends were cool…and we eventually received an OFF BASE pass to go to the mall or to the Gunner's Inn (on base) where we got tipsy and drunk. Well, Eye was tipsy. Eye never got drunk. The Niggahs that raped me were suddenly Biblical brothahs that asked me to forgive them. Eye told them Eye did with a smile, but Eye hated them to the very core of my soul. [Presently Eye forgave them, and Eye didn't hate them at all]. Nonetheless, we were now one of *Them*! Soldiers. The *other* side of society.

Eye loved some of those fun times in the Army, overall. For me it represented the first time Eye actually belonged to a family. A family of soldiers. Trained to kill, yet loyal to each other despite our past or differences.

And that had me fooled.

*When we graduated AIT*, Mama and my cousin Sweet flew to Oklahoma to see me walk across the stage. Having Sweet there softened the blow of my father's absence. Mama was so proud of me. Beautiful in a cashmere sweater and light blue jeans, her radiant smile was so strong half the Drill Sergeants took off their wedding rings and stuffed them in their pockets; they were looking at Mama's ass and Eye was mad. All four of the Batteries got into one huge formation and we, newly trained soldiers, marched to the Gunner's Inn before our friends and family that flew or drove to see us graduate and Mama was waving at me and clapping. Eye winked at my cousin because he swore me down Eye wouldn't graduate boot camp and Eye had.

So he gave me props.

*The Army was off the chain* in the beginning. Finding out that half my platoon got orders to go to Fort Hood excited us. We weren't separated. Yes! Around Christmas of 1995 we were on planes flying to our respective hometowns for a two week break to spend with family. And after the New Year we boarded planes to Fort Hood, Texas from our respective hometowns. The Army was so *lame* we had to buy our own tickets to our permanent duty stations. The catch was that if you didn't go home for the holidays and went straight to your permanent duty station then the Army paid for that.

When we arrived it seemed like another world yet again. Cabin-looking buildings…Houses on base looked different. Or were they houses? The barracks we stayed in was grimy and dirty. Bathroom floors mildewing…our First Sergeant, a ghetto-country-brothah-that-couldn't-read-above-a-third-grade-level was a M.C. Hammer reject that drove a green truck he polished twenty four hours a day just so he could brush his hair in the reflection.

Real dumb ass…Eye didn't like his horny ass at all.

He banged *half* the boys in the Platoon. Helping them get rank. Eye walked in on him getting his penis sucked by two horny thug dudes in BDU attire. They're tongue kissing the swollen mushroom head, then kissing each other. Both of them had the *same* last names. Eye think they were biological brothers. Yup. Two blood brothers sucking the same First Sergeant cock, and they weren't even in our *Battery.*

Kinda gross…but *looking* at it…it was thrilling to see the secret lives unfolded in the darkness, when the rest of the world didn't give you a second thought. They were now sucking his scrotum, spitting on his ass. First Sergeant didn't care about me standing in the doorway. All of them were ranked above PFC. Eye'm just a *private.* First Sergeant was the King of his realm. He created his Universe from feeling and thought. He slid his condom-less erection inside the Staff Sergeant's tight hole and gazed into my eyes.

"Either cum in and let me get deep in that country booty," he informed me, and eye ignored him, "…or shut the hell up and get out!"

He pushed ole boy's face into the desk and his booty cheeks applauded the genius of his stroking ability. Eye was trapped by the dimension presented before me. Eye entered and closed the door. Eye ain't *never* scared! Walking up to him, Eye ran my finger over my softness, sticking my fingers in his mouth while ole boy pulled down my pants and gave me some head. First Sergeant was banging ole boy from behind and ole boy was bent over, sucking me off and First Sergeant was slurping my hole from my fingers.

Hell yea. One of the brothers grabbed his wallet, keys and hit the door without looking back.

"So does this mean Eye get rank?" Eye asked.

"No. You're new on the block. Doesn't *work* that way. Bitch," he went on, slapping ole boy's ass. Cheeks jiggled deliciously. "Show him what he outta do for rank."

The thug dude obliged immediately. "*Yes*, Daddy." You'd swear he was raised with a bomb strapped to his chest and the powers that be said, "Do it in the name of Allah!" Boom! He followed directions quite well. Eye was more of a *rebel.* He stood up, wrapped his arms around my neck and Eye kneed him in the balls and he doubled over on his knees,

First Sergeant falling out some good booty and Eye said, "Don't try to size me up. Let me show you what you think you were *going* to show me."

Eye pushed First Sergeant on top of the bottom bitch and Eye rode him like a blind drunk on a mechanical bull. Ole boy was being *crushed* underneath the First Sergeant. First Sergeant was grunting inside me. The best he never had. Till now. Ole boy couldn't move. All our weight was on top of him. Lemme show him how you get down to the floor.

Eye held First Sergeant's chest and worked my ass to the bone, grabbing between his legs and gazing into his eyes.

"You feel better than Gregory."

His mouth was ajar. Eye trailed my saliva all over his lips, watching him lick it off and Eye said, "Shut up and *bang* me." And bang me he did. Right into an earth-shattering orgasm. All three of us asleep on the floor. Breathing my homeboy's air. The one with the baby on the way.

***And this was where the*** story takes a turn. When Eye encountered Chantell Bynum. She was a *thick* girl Eye would fall in love with. No, she wasn't fat. She had a big ass, deep pussy and tight jaws. When she smiled Eye saw God taking a rib from a sleeping Adam to make the Woman. Full of life and lust, eccentric and aspiring inspiration. Eye felt this when Eye was in the PX, looking for Alanis Morrisette's *Jagged Little Pill* album, to see what the buzz was about pertaining to that angry *You Outta Know* chick. Eye paused before the display of CDs with Janet's *Design of a Decade* under my arm.

Chantell smiled at me and Eye frowned. Had to play it cool. Never let a woman know you're anxious to get with her. That's when they get bitchy and besides themselves, comparing you to their Daddies or other men they may love and look up to.

"Is that CD good?" she asked, and Eye put the headphones on, pressing *Play*. Listening to the entire album free of charge. She tapped my shoulder and Eye snatched the headphones off. "Why are you *touching* me?"

"Damn, it's not all of that."

"Bitch it was enough for you to *touch.* Get away, thank you. Eye don't give out free samples and Eye heard left over's are for bums."

"Fuck you."

"Bitch don't you wish!"

"Ugh!"

"Ugh!" And Eye put my head phones on, jamming to *You'll Learn.* Eye decided to buy the CD.

**Eye bought one other thing** before Eye bought the CD's. When Eyc paid for my item, Eye told the male cashier to hold it for me. Eye had to go look for something else, another CD. Plus ole girl was on my mind, Eye shouldn't have talked to her like that. Eye just hate strange bitches meeting my acquaintance. Eye was very snobbishly standoffish. Another cashier booth was open next to me, but the light was turned off. But Eye saw a water bottle and a James Baldwin book under the register.

Eye thought nothing of it.

**Eye'm headed for the check out** to buy the CD's. Didn't find the Barry White one Eye wanted, so Alanis and Janet would do. Eye didn't have cash on me, so Eye handed the cashier my ID and the CDs. "This dummy..." she said.

Eye looked up. God. It was *her.*

"You work here?"

"Yes, Eye do," she spat, dropping my CDs into the bag.

Eye took them out. "Bitch, *you're* crazy!"

Eye rung them up for her, eyeing her evilly. "Don't be trying to get me locked up for shoplifting. Don't make me get ghetto in this bitch. *Damn,* the AC broke in here?"

Eye was hot in my BDU's.

"You need to get out my line."

"You need to ring up my purchase."

"Get out my line. You're rude."

"Eye'm not rude to your fat butt! Just *because* Eye'm *not* begging for your phone number or trying to get some pussy don't mean Eye want your simple ass."

"Go away!"

Eye reached over and hit the *Total* button myself, then swiped my ID coded card through the slot. It rung up.

Eye hit Enter and the receipt came out.

"Shit, Eye need your job. God bless."

"Go to Hell!" she said.

Eye smiled, taking my recently purchased item from the male cashier that held them for me.

She covered her mouth. Eye held the roses.

"Eye think you're a sight for sore eyes. Eye would love to take you on a date."

"Eye would love to."

She took the flowers and slapped me over the head with them. "Fuck off."

"Fuck you, bitch!" Eye was mad.

She smiled then, walking up to me. "You can't take me out without getting my phone number first."

When Eye kissed her Eye tasted sugar. The sweetest taste Eye would ever know. Even sweeter than her pussy.

But that cums later.

*Getting to know her was* invigorating. Eye already didn't want to be in the Army, and Eye was telling my homeboy that. He had a sister that moved up from Georgia to live with him. He had a baby on the way (another two months his wife should be giving birth to his first son). Eye told him that Eye think Eye was falling in love with Chantell.

She was fun, silly and full of life. She was sexy, even with hair rollers in her hair. She didn't need make-up to be beautiful, and she never depended on a man to take care of her. She had her mother's deviant ways and her father's knack for life, love and business. We spent a lot of time together. When Eye had free time, and was off duty Eye left the barracks, without telling anyone, and hung out with her. We used to get hotels and spend hours together. Eye never wanted to meet her folks because she said her father disowned her after she lost her virginity with an older cousin that raped her (her Dad blamed her for the occurrence), and her brother barely talked to her.

We went to the movies, out to eat, and Eye paid every time. We clicked. Eye told her of my sexuality, and she handed me a James Baldwin book.

"Eye love James. *Giovanni's Room* is an incredible book."

"So why did you give it to me?"

"Eye read a journal of yours. Eye found it the day Eye saw you in the PX."

"The day we met?"

"No, a few days before we met. You were in here carrying a book bag. You bought some Jordan shoes and Eye guess one of your journals fell out your bag when you were putting your old shoes in there. Eye picked it up, intending to flag you down but Eye opened it, curious, and read your poetry and a few stories you wrote. In one of them you mentioned this book. So Eye went out to the bookstore and purchased it."

"Are you serious?"

"Yes. The day we met Eye was going to introduce myself as a new fan of your work."

"My God."

*We were so very close. She was* more than just a girlfriend, she was my soul mate Eye felt. Being with her, Eye wanted her and only her. Her skin tasted so sweet it kept niggahs and dick off the brain relentlessly. Eye got to talk to her about me, my past and my life. She used to rub my head when Eye told her of my childhood. We used to eat popping corn talking about our ambitions and goals in life.

Eye was so into her Eye became her eyes, a reflection of the woman who birth me.

In a lot of ways she reminded me of my mother.

But a nicer version.

Eye stopped going to clubs with my friends on Fridays. Mr. DJ's it was called, and Eye used to dance my ass off. Sweating like a pig on that liquor and marijuana.

With Chantell Eye stopped it all. Eye wanted to be a better man, and through her patience Eye was carving out a new image of myself, something that became habit, then my character.

One day before February of 2006, Chantell invited me over to her cousin's house. She said she had gotten in a fight with her mother over her career choices, and her brother called her every bitch name in the book. Eye wanted to fuck him up, but decided to stay outta something that really didn't involve me. If she asked me to get in it, then *Yes*, ok that was different.

She came to pick me up, since Eye didn't have a car. When Eye lay eyes on her the sun rose all over again. Eye saw love.

We kissed and embraced, inhaling our body auras. She smelled of expensive lavender. Eye smelled of cheap supermarket cologne. Eye only put the expensive stuff (Fahrenheit) on my nuts.

Holding hands, we talked about everything under the sun.

But it wasn't her cousin's house we went to.

She pulled up in front a hotel that was larger than life.

We were 20 miles outside of Killeen, Texas. Where were we, Eye didn't know and Eye didn't question it.

She paid for the Presidential Suite with her mother's credit card before she picked me up.

"Eye'm tired of living for everyone else," she said, smiling.

"What's wrong?"

"Nothing."

"Eye can see it in your eyes, baby."

She took my hand. "Its hard for me to open up to anyone."

"You can trust me."

Darkness befell her face. "Can Eye really trust you?"

"Yes, you can."

"Lets go up to the room, and watch TV. Maybe cook a little something. Hell, my mom's credit card footed it all. She always trying to control and change me. And since she expects so much of me, then maybe her paying for this room is the compensation Eye need right now."

"You're something else."

When we got in the room Eye looked around paradise. This was a very breathtaking room, and Eye'd never seen nor experienced anything like it in my life. She sat on the huge sofa with big off white throw pillows and crossed clean shaven legs. Eye smelled her pussy in the air, blended in nicely with potpourri inside huge wicker baskets.

"You like the room?" she asked, pouring some wine. Eye hated wine, never really got into drinking like that so Eye passed.

She still poured me a glass, handing it to me. Eye looked at her like she was an alien.

"Taste it, Pharaoh. Don't knock it till you try it."

"Is that what Eve said to Adam when she bit the forbidden fruit?"

We were laughing.

"That's why Eye love you. You know how to make a woman smile."

Eye didn't look at the drink once. "Is that why you love me? Because Eye make you laugh?"

She walked up to me, her nose on mine. Our lips extended, made the gentle connection yet eagerly retreated.

Her eager fingertips trialing the epidermis of my arms sent chills all over my balls. My penis was solid, yet, mentally, Eye wasn't ready to be sold into the gentle folds of sweet gushy coochie. Eye was uneasy for a moment because Eye've become accustomed to sleeping with dudes. Eye slept with them as a form of executed fatherly love. When Eye lay with a Niggah Eye want him to be strong for me, guide me, fall all over and through me until Eye cum his perception of utilization. Eye shiver all night. Nothing was sweeter to me than my toes curling during orgasm. That's when Eye'm vulnerable, and most susceptible.

With Chantell Eye closed me eyes and slowly inherited her plump ass. Eye was calmly rubbing, creating the much needed chemistry for this form of friction to work. Eye pulled her pelvic bone up against my body, and Eye kissed her slowly and passionately, letting it build into edifices too treacherous for the amateurs. She put her shaking hands in my pants and squeezed my meat. "You know that's one big stick you're gripping," Eye said, trailing my slick tongue along her slender, *Swan*-like neck.

"Eye know what it is."

"Saying *hello* to my little friend?"

"Yes."

"Well, Eye have to say hello, Kitty." Eye fell on my knees, pushing her skirt past her womanly-shaped hips. She smelled good, but does the taste provide a much needed collaboration—or corroboration? My tongue melted into her wet, juicy, coochie…my lips correlating with her vaginal walls. She shuddered in her heels, her legs bending at the knees. Eye pushed her against the wall and her arms go up and over her head while Eye pushed back the hood of the coochie, revealing a silky, pinkish clit…Eye sucked her till she started to cum. Eye kept feasting, swallowing her, running my tongue along her tight ass, pushing a dry thumb deep inside her. She gasped, wide eyed while Eye munched on filet ah fish.

When she said she had to cum the second time, Eye stood up, and slid inside her so deep she had to wrap her arms around me. Already, she was cumming on my stick.

While Eye banged another nut out of her.

*The coochie felt so good and Eye* realized just how much Eye truly loved and needed the warm body of a woman, that when Eye had to cum Eye didn't pull out.

Eye leaned into her silky hair, grunted, said, "Eye gotta nut, baby," and came deep inside her…

Best feeling in the world. Then a funny thing happened.

We drew even closer after our sexual transition into each other's lives. The physical aspect (getting to know her, learning the ins and outs of her being, learning her zodiac, respecting her mind before enjoying her body and having real conversations about the future) intertwined both our psyches as one, so when Eye gave her my body Eye was giving my body to her spirit as a sacrifice.

Only Eye didn't know this. After the first night we made love, fucked and grunted till the neighbors screamed, "Okay you ugly *muthas*…enough is *enough*!" We started having sex more and more and Eye loved it because Eye got to nut deep inside her walls on the regular. Her body was my addiction…combining the lust of my hips with the conundrums of her breasts.

Eye became One with her, my penis deep inside what my rib made giving me the feeling of a complete circle because everything became crystal clear. Pussy was the most generous gift God put on this earth. Therefore Eye treat pussy as if it's precious, Eye cherish a good female with good pussy and a juicy clit. And if she got a brain, too, perfect match! That was Chantell. Eye used to sleep with my dick thumping in her pussy. Didn't grind, move or fuck her at all, but my dick deep in her incubator, keeping shit warm and fuzzy till Eye beat it up after my slumber the next day was my true reward. Having that kind of morning orgasm had me on cloud nine.

We would do this for two months. Make love. Go out. Fuck some more. Suck my dick in the PX parking Lot inside her car. Listen to her wails of mistakes made in the past.

Eye fell in love with her. Everything about her was perfection, reaching perfect tens on every human scale on earth involving looks, brains, guts and beauty. She was that bitch a niggah said he could never get, no matter how confident 50 Cent was on eventually getting Alicia Keys. And she wound up taking another woman's husband and now about to drop the baby in a few months.

But during this time there wasn't an Alicia Keys in the industry nor 50 Cent. TuPac was alive then, even though he would get murdered around the time Eye got out of the military. And with anything good in your life manifesting into something you could cherish, Satan made his move and everything vanished.

Literally the next day, after laying with her half the night trying to get her to open to me about something that seemed to be bothering her, she disappeared. She didn't call or accept my phone calls.

Eye ran around Fort Hood like a chicken with my head cut off. Being late to formation in the mornings because Eye stayed up half the night traveling with my boy all over Killeen, Texas, going to every store she shopped asking employees about her whereabouts or if they seen her and getting a "No" answer every time. Eye couldn't eat nor sleep, my penis getting hard for her softness, and it wasn't there so Eye had to revert to masturbation to keep the pressure from bursting the tubes in my testicles. Eye got an Article 15 for disrespect. And didn't give a damn. Eye was high on weed with some of the soldiers Eye hung out with (they had that Cali Crypt oh Lawd hammercy!) when Eye did extra duty. Had to clean those mildewing barracks on Fort Hood with a toothbrush. Eye mean get with the times. People hardly brush their teeth in the mornings yet you want me to scrub the floor with some 1950s technique?

Eye pretended Eye was cleaning the floors and crusty shower walls. If this was the Army why these raggedy barracks look like a bunch of bull? Couldn't even walk around barefooted. You liable to get athlete's feet or a fungus. After Eye was relieved of extra duty Eye went looking for Chantell again. Eye was a wreck.

*A few weeks would go by* before Eye saw her again. Eye was shopping at the PX with red and black patent leather Jordans, a red Steve Young sweater with a big #1 on the back, and black NIKE shorts. Eye felt good that day, deciding to get back to living and be the best man Eye could be, despite my unease about Chantell. Eye was heading out (Eye didn't buy anything) and decided to grab a slice of pizza. The place wasn't that crowded and the janitor was wiping down tables with an attitude. Before Eye could walk up to the cashier, Eye saw her. Approaching me with a half smile on her face. She looked radiant, as always. Her skirt below her knees, and her cream colored blouse fitting her perfectly.

"Pharoah."

My heart racing, Eye stared at her. Eye didn't even blink.

"Where were you? You vanished off the face of the earth."

"Eye had issues to deal with."

"Issues? That's the excuse you're giving me?"

She smiled, cupping my hand and Eye snatched it back. "Eye have been looking all over for you."

"Stop being dramatic."

Eye walked past her, heading for the door. "Peace."

"Pharoah! Eye need to talk to you."

Eye held up my hand. "Talk between my fingers because my hand is protesting your dumb ass."

"Pharoah!" She was running behind me. When Eye walked through the double sliding glass doors, she grabbed my arm. Just above the elbow. "Please. Hear me out."

Eye snatched my arm back. "What, Chantell?"

She stuttered. "Eye had to disappear for a while."

"Why? And not call me? Eye thought we were better than that."

"We are. And Eye apologize. But Eye had to deal with an emergency. One Eye wasn't prepared for."

"A family emergency?"

"Something like that."

"What exactly was the emergency?"

She was quiet. She took my hand again and this time she was trembling. Eye was worried. "What's wrong, girl?"

"Come inside, out of the hot sun. Lets grab some pizza. And talk."

Eye nodded quietly.

*She paid for the food*, despite my protest. Eye was going to pay. Eye never let a woman buy my food. Eye feel whether they asked me out or not Eye should flip the bill, as long as she didn't go overboard ordering things then Eye wouldn't have to flip out on her. She held both my hands, her head lowered. Her hair hung in her beautiful face. Licking chapped lips, she looked up and said, "Eye'm pregnant. With your child." Eye closed my eyes.

My heart was drumming ferociously, Eye opened my eyes with a huge grin. Hell yea! Eye looked down at my dick and said, "HELL YEA!"

Not the reaction she was expecting. She relaxed a little.

She smiled then. "What are you saying?"

"Eye'm saying hell yea Eye'm going to be a father."

"But you're getting out the Army."

"Yes, Eye am!" Eye was kissing her hand something terrible. She chuckled. Standing up, Eye pulled her to her feet and picked her up, turning in circles.

We were both jubilant.

"Ya'll she is going to have our baby!"

Eye was so happy Eye couldn't stand it. Inside Eye felt like butterflies over a mountain top during the first break of spring. Eye would be the best father. Eye would read to my child and Eye didn't care if it was a boy or a girl. Eye would be to my kid what my father wasn't to me.

Eye couldn't wait to tell Mama. And Eye know my family would be in shock because they have been calling me names for years. Now they could suck it. Eye put her down, and she got serious on me after everyone applauded.

"Eye don't want the baby."

Eye died inside. "What?" Eye grabbed her arms. "Please don't take this from me. Enough have been taken from me in this lifetime."

"What are we gonna do? Eye can't have a baby. Eye got college, and my parents will freak out. Plus you're getting out the Army."

"So what. Eye will still take care of my child, Chantell."

"Eye might have an abortion."

"That is a definite No. Are you serious? It's my decision too."

"You can't even tell me how you're going to support this child."

"OUR CHILD! And we will be just fine."

"Eye don't want it."

"But Eye do. Kids are a blessing from God. If you don't want it give him or her to me. Eye'll raise it myself."

"Eye do want to give you a child. You are a good man. Eye don't want it, yet Eye don't want to kill it; but as long as it exists my future is compromised."

*Please, please, PLEASE, Lord help me!* "Please don't kill our child." Eye shuddered. Eye have never been so terrified in my life. "How many months are you?" Eye asked, trying to get in her good graces.

She tried to smile. "Going on two," she said uneasily.

Eye was desperate. Eye was willing to say anything if Eye had to. Eye had to change her mind. "Will you promise to talk to me before you make any rash decisions?"

"Yes, Eye promise," she said harshly.

"So you need me to buy anything?"

She grinned. "No, man. And don't be buying up *everything* in the store."

My eyes lit up. "For my child hell yea."

"What do you hope it is? A boy or a girl?"

"It doesn't matter to me. Eye'm going to be a father. Wowee!" Eye was so happy Eye couldn't stand it.

"You can drive me to your room so we can talk some more."

"Eye got a better idea. Let's go out somewhere private so we can really talk about this."

"Fine by me. But Eye am sure of one thing, even though Eye am nervous about it."

"Shoot."

She wrapped her arms around me. "Eye know you'll be a good father."

*Oh my God oh my God!* "So does that mean…?"

She kissed my lips. "*Yes,* Eye'm keeping the baby. Eye will turn our kid over to you because Eye have a life and there are things Eye wanna do before Eye take on responsibilities of raising a child. Eye can barely raise myself."

"Oh my God. Eye love you thank you so much!" Eye picked her up again, turning in circles.

This time she let me, laughing along with me.

But we wouldn't be laughing for long.

☯

*The next few months proved* to be something of a mockery of my very existence. Because Eye nurtured and caressed her belly during my every waking moment. Eye started spending time away from the Barracks, and staying the night with her. We lay up all night munching apples and oranges and pineapples. And Eye fixed her my favorite guilty pleasure. Sliced bell peppers, mild lettuce, and thinly sliced tomatoes with Italian salad dressing (my favorite YUMMY!) and bacon bits. Mix it together and sit back and relax and munch on the concoction. She said she loved it.

Getting her to try it was a feat, though. She was the kind of woman who thought she controlled her every move, when she couldn't control anything God created, not even the weakness of her flesh. That weakness never came with a Surgeon General's warning, directions, instructions or assembly rules. Eye was seeing my friends less and less. And that was a good thing because they were still playing musical beds with their wives and undercover homosexual fem bottoms and tops, dancing inside a deadly obsession…so with the coming of a baby, my first child, Eye had to lead by example. Eye changed myself instantly. Eye was so excited. Eye wanted a kid so badly Eye couldn't *think*. Eye wanted one because Eye loved them, because my father wasn't much of a parent, guardian, provider, protector or Daddy to me anyway so Eye wanted to correct the past with my present day reality. My child was going to get nothing but love.

One of my friends asked me what Eye would do if mother didn't accept my kid. "You know she's mean as hell," he said, shaking his head. "Have you even told her yet?"

"No," Eye said, telling my friend Starks, Staff Sergeant, getting weary of him trying to worm into my boxers and private affairs.

"Why not?" he asked.

*Dang get you a life or something!* "Because Eye don't have to report to my mother with a progress report, referral, detention or an evaluation. Eye'm a grown ass man and if Eye want a kid Eye will have my child."

Eye was offended. My mother wouldn't and couldn't stop me from becoming a father. At least she could give me some credit for waiting until Eye graduated high school and was in the Army before Eye got a bitch knocked up.

"Eye think you should tell her."

*What is this Niggah's problem? Why the sudden interest in my life all of a sudden?* "Eye don't *want* to tell her."

He walked up to me, putting both hands on my shoulders and Eye flinched. Eye hated people trying to change my mind. Looking me deeply in the eyes ain't gonna get me to tell my mother or anybody else that ain't ready to know Eye got a baby on the way. That's my business.

"Pharoah. Listen, man. You are about to get out the Army soon. You told me you're not reenlisting. You still angry about that General calling you a nigger and no one believed you because you're a Private. That still eats away at you."

"Why did you have to bring that up? That was a very hard time for me."

"Eye know it was, man. We stayed up over drinks talking about it. We chilled that night. You found out that Eye got your back."

"Oh, yea? That was till 5 a.m. hit and you decided to put your hand in my draws and fumble around with my booty. Eye jumped up on your ass and left. You violated me."

"We both mess around with Niggahs."

"Eye'm a Quality over Quantity type of mofo, you diggin' me man."

"So now you talkin' all hip now, huh. Niggah with the two ton balls because he got a piece of pussy pregnant. Eye must admit the Hoes love you, but you don't sweat them."

"Eye am about to go home my dude."

"Stay over, man. Think it over. How are you gonna have a baby when you're getting out the Army, you haven't told your mother, you don't got your own house, you don't have a car, and barely got a bank account and the account you got is filled with two dollars and lint. You can't afford to have a baby."

"Eye'm leaving."

"Eye gotta drive you home."

"Eye'll catch the bus!"

"Bus ain't running after 11 p.m."

"Fuck it then, man! Eye'll *walk*. Eye don't have to stand here and listen to what you're suggesting."

"What am Eye suggesting, Pharoah?"

"You think my baby mama should abort my seed?"

"Exactly. You're both young. You told me she wants to go to school and really don't want to have the baby."

"But she's having it for me. She will let me raise my child."

"And that ain't any reason to have a child. A kid has two parents. Eventually he or she, whatever, gonna wanna know about his mother. Then what you gonna tell him? That you on lease and set up on a payment plan through the child support agency."

Eye stormed to the door without uttering another word.

"PHAROAH! Don't mess up your life."

Eye paused, and spun on my heel, pointing. "Like you? A man with seven kids from five broads? All getting child support. Leaving you with barely a percentage of your military pay. And you're giving *me* advice?"

"That's why Eye'm telling you this. So you don't make the same mistake."

Eye grabbed his arms and shoved him into the door. A flash of anger bit his eyes and Eye smiled and said, "Eye will kill myself before Eye kill my child. Eye'm having my baby! And Eye don't want to have this conversation again."

"Get your hands off me Pharoah."

"Eye hope you heard me."

He threw my hands off him and stood his ground. "Eye said get your *hands* off me."

"Go to hell, bitch."

"Get out my house. You can walk."

"You're gonna drive me home. Eye'm not walking 20 miles back to Fort Hood and Eye'ma Goulds Niggah."

"Get out."

"Make me."

"Eye'll throw you out."

"Eye'd like to see you try, Sweet cheeks," Eye said. On second thought…eye grabbed my wallet and keys. "Fine. Eye'm gone."

"Have the abortion. Don't be a fool."

And he slammed the door closed behind me.

*Eye stared at the door.* "Don't your spoiled ass kids need to eat?" Eye yelled, rolling my eyes. He thought Eye was about to walk? Chile. Eye unlocked his car, hopped inside and drove to Fort Hood. Eye parked by my friend Granger's truck.

And called it a night.

*But the next few days Eye couldn't* sleep. No matter what Eye did. Eye had insomnia. Wondering was Eye making the right decision. Was my reason for having a child accurate? Eye knew Eye didn't believe in abortion. That's murder and Eye'll be damned Eye murder something my dick created. Eye was just being real about it. Mama said if you make it take good care of it. And she meant it. Eye decided that *yes*, Eye was doing the right thing. My family would love my kid. Having the baby would delete the gay suspicions mother has of me. But then again that ain't any reason to have a child. Kids are not smokescreens. My kid would have it all. All my time and attention. Eye would probably spoil his or her ass and wouldn't let anybody watch them but me because these days you couldn't even trust your mother or your brother with your kids. When it comes to raising your kids look to God.

That way your eyes were cast away from a very wicked line up of ailments waiting to tear your family apart.

Eye would stand up and die for my child. And one night, over steamed crabs, Chantell and Eye talked about it. We were both in matching tube socks, black boxers and T-Shirts. Eye was never a fan of dressing up like my woman or my lovers, but with her Eye was a very compromising man. She was going to have our baby, and Eye would cherish her, no matter if we wound up together or not. Eye would always be there for her, give her my last for my kid. Eye made a vow to God. And Eye meant it.

She already vanished on me once when she found out she was pregnant. Eye was afraid she would vanish again with my child and Eye could never see him again and that right there would drive me to the barrel of a gun. If Eye couldn't have my child, how could Eye live for myself or want myself?

As the next month passed Eye was reading and talking to her tummy all the time. She used to roll her eyes at me and say, "The baby can't hear you. He's probably sleeping."

"You don't know if it's gonna be a boy," Eye said, excited about the thought of having a son. Yes! Eat your heart out Daddy!

"It's *gonna* be a boy. Eye just *know*. And Eye never saw a man this excited about having a child. The men Eye know and even my brother were about to die when they found out their women were pregnant. Hoes they were fucking from the 'Hood winding up giving birth to their kids would piss any real Niggah off."

"Well Eye'm glad you're not like that," Eye said, closing a book of Langston Hughes poetry.

"Well Eye do know this: your boy is gonna be a very warm hearted man."

Eye blushed. "*Aww*, shucks. You mean that?"

"Yes." We kissed, rubbing each other into a slow grinding frenzy of lust. Her nipples absorbed the atmosphere and stood erect upon its completion and my shaft slapped the ell out of my mushroom head and left it swollen, ready for some good coochie, pregnant coochie was the best. It swelled to all new heights, with a small pain in my dick head because too much blood was pumping into one center a little too fast. A dick wasn't built to handle as much blood as the brain. Too much going on. She rubbed my balls and Eye spread my legs, kissing her lips. The faint taste of fruit she ate earlier activated my fingers and Eye tip toed across her abdomen. Her thigh jerked.

"Our baby wants to feel some love."

Eye lowered my forehead and looked up with seductive eyes, licking my lips—wanting to taste her pussy, but refraining because Eye was a man with self control.

"Yea, ok. Mama just wants some dick."

She rolled her eyes. "God. You're *so* romantic, Pharoah."

Eye bit her tit. "So you're saying that pussy ain't ready for me?"

She kicked at me and missed. "DAMN BE ROMANTIC!" Eye dove between her legs, pressed my lips hard against her pussy and held the top of the clit with the flatness of my palm, blowing inside her. She sat straight up. "Oh, *shit*." And Eye began to feast, sucking down the salt and tasting cream. She came quite early, but that didn't stop me.

Eye ran my tongue across her pussy then separated the folds, teasing the labia menora, caressing the labia majora and getting a few tremors. My lips were receptive to her frequency, and Eye started to suck on her clit and stroke my dick. Eye was pre-cumming. She took my head and pulled me to her and said, "Put that dick inside this pussy," and Eye didn't protest, anticipating her warm engulfing…wanting and needing her opposites. We gave each other some tongue. Then a peck, and another, then another. The instant the tip of my dick slid in the pussy my body locked and Eye began to nut. Eye squeezed her tits together and buried my face, slow grinding inside her as my orgasm intensified, then began to gradually cool. Eye didn't say a thing. Eye stayed hard in her pussy half the night. She burst 9 times in three hours. Eye burst twice. Then rolled over and snored into dreamland without a second thought about Chantell. But Eye smiled for my baby. Eye started planning our future and it was filled with truths about me Eye never told anyone books, dictionaries, fun, fun, fun fun! Eye couldn't wait for you to meet my Mama, she will adore you and meet your great grandfather and my brothers and my sister oh my God thank you! Eye didn't know Eye rewrote the future when Eye erased Chantell, my kid's Mama, from my thoughts.

***When Eye got in from the Motor*** Pool Eye called Chantell, but she didn't answer. Eye just got to my room and was dirty as hell. Eye smelled like oil, sun, dried nut and ass. Eye jacked off three times at work today. When were they going to understand that working in the heat kept me a bitch in heat? It ain't everyday physics. Eye hung up the phone and took a quick shower. Warm water felt good against my skin, rinsing Dove soap down the drain. Dove smelled so goddamn good. Eye heard the phone ringing. Shit. Eye grabbed a towel, did a quick dry off while hopping out the shower and wrapped the towel around my waist, nearly slipping down on the tile. Damn!

Eye answered. "Hello." It was Starks. "What, Niggah."

"Meet me at my place man."

"So you can kill me for taking your car."

"Eye ain't trippin' on that Hoe stuff. You did a niggardly thing."

"*Niggardly?*"

"*Any* Niggah would take my car before walking 20 miles to Fort Hood."

Eye shook my head. *He's too nice. Something is up.* "Man Eye don't think this is such a good idea."

"We're friends, Pharoah."

"*Were* friends, yup that's about right."

"So you ain't my boy?"

"Nope."

"Man, fuck all that. You're my dawg. Eye'm your boy. Eye'm not supposed to always tell you what you wanna hear, dawg. Eye'd rather lose you as a friend by telling the truth then keep you as a friend through lies and deceit."

That's who Eye learned that from. "Ok, man. You're *right.* But Eye don't want an abortion. She's about four months now. Ain't it too late to do that?"

"Let's not get into that. Let's go get a drink at the Bar."

"Cool. Just bring me right back home, man. Don't want a repeat of last time."

"Eye like you too much. Eye ain't on that old shit dawg. Let your guard down and let a Niggah do something for you sometimes. Make a Niggah like me feel really special."

Eye actually smiled. "Fine, man. But no funny stuff."

"Eye *promise.*"

We *never* made it to the Bar. He bought a bottle of Hennessy and when we took shots till we dropped he fell so deep inside me Eye couldn't think. My head swimming in nocturnal bliss, Eye became *One* with his body, moving to the pulse of his biorhythm. He held me captive in his hairy arms, wrapping his legs with mine, bouncing in and out of me while Eye was lying on my stomach. Eye felt every throbbing inch. Filled me beyond reproach.

"Eye love you," he said. Eye cringed. Dick wasn't that good, man. Plus Eye got a kid on the way. All my love will be for my baby. "Eye'm 'bout to nut, Pharoah *goddamnnnn*!"

He came deep inside me. Then it dawned on me why he wanted me to have an abortion.

He was in love with me. And wanted me all to himself. No distractions. It was then Eye realized Eye had a decision to make.

And Eye *already* made it…

**Eye lay next to him that night**. Enraged. Any man wiling to have my unborn child killed so he can continue banging me didn't need my respect—or *deserve* it. The love Eye had for him slowly seeped away and was completely gone when Eye exhaled. He was snoring. *Eye* was staring at the moon light. It was a full moon tonight. The glow against my face, upper body and skin had me floating in thoughtful bliss. Eye smiled with tears forming in my eyes. Eye squeezed both my fists together and said, "Eye am *going* to be a dad!" Eye squeezed both my eyes shut, tears spilling from them.

The snoring stopped.

**Starks slowly opened his eyes** and wrapped an arm around me. The breath caught in my throat. Eye looked in his eyes and he pierced through mine. "You're gonna be an excellent father," he said earnestly.

Eye kissed him. "You know after tonight this will be no more."

He closed his eyes. "Eye *know. Trust* me, Eye'm counting the seconds. The thought of never laying up like this again Pharaoh—why you do a Niggah like this?—kills me inside."

*Good. If you wanted my child to die bitch you die instead.*

"This could never be, man. Eye'm not ready to be out the closet. Eye'm not ready for my family to know about this. Eye don't care how many suspicions they're having. Don't mean Eye have to confirm them. Eye'm on the Low, man respect that. Eye don't wanna lose my family. Eye don't want my son coming into the world while Eye'm having one night stands with *you*."

The words tore through him like poisoned knives. "Eye'm not mad, man. Eye'm not ready for my family to know, either. My daddy would kill me. Shit, we're Jamaicans, remember?"

"Yup. Eye know. And Niggah Eye'm Bahamian, thank you. *Look*, Eye'm going to bed. In the morning Eye need to go home."

"Eye got you."

He slid deeply inside me, held me close.

And started snoring again.

***Eye was walking around*** a park outside of Fort Hood with Chantell a few days later, trying to put Starks outta my mind.

"Eye feel sick," she said, rubbing her forehead.

"What's wrong? Is it something you ate?"

"Probably that seafood. It's not agreeing with my belly."

Eye was worried sick. "You gotta regurgitate?"

"Feels like it." She found a nearby bench and Eye helped her sit down. The sun wasn't as hot as the day before, and a little cool wind danced across my skin.

"Want me to drive us to your home?" Eye asked.

"Nah, let it pass." She held the tops of her thighs.

And not *once* did she rub or hold her belly.

***When we got home Eye sat on*** the living room sofa, thinking to myself. Any expecting mother would rub her womb if she was sick, hoping the shit didn't upset her baby. Just a maternal instinct my homegirl once told me. Eye thought back to a conversation me and my homegirl, Daisy, had after high school graduation in 1995.

She was coming down with the flu and she rubbed her belly before she rubbed her forehead, thighs or hands.

Eye was so awed. "Why are you rubbing your belly?"

She tried to smile, but you could tell she was feeling down. "Eye don't know…but when you're about to be a mother you are protective. Even before you give birth you're protecting your baby. Eye can't explain it."

"So what if you catch a cold or something?"

She started rubbing her pregnant belly again.

"Eye don't even wanna think about it."

Daisy went on to have a son.

And he's a year old.

☯

Eye would think about all the drill competitions me and Marcus went to together while in Basic Training, climbing obstacles, pulling myself across thick tight ropes in mid air and forest land. Those were the times of my life. The Army showed me just how tough Eye was. Eye never knew Eye had so much toughness and strength. They had 13 weeks to convert 18 years on God's earth as a regular society member into a shoot-to-kill soldier—

**Whhh Oaaa!!!**

—that *knew* how to follow orders and carry out demands and commands. If your Drill Sergeant told you to do it you do it. The Drill Sergeant's job was to *drill* the ARMY deep into your conscious and subconscious. The soldiers come first. Family could wait. That wasn't U-N-I-T-Y to me, so Eye never felt U-N-I-T-Y in the Army. It was more of *every man for himself* in there. That's why so many of the male soldiers were sucking and screwing other male soldiers (and Down Low men off base) in the booty hole of the darkness. The Oath of the Military they were sworn into protected that darkness. Don't Ask, soldier. And Don't Tell, *Private.*

Privates were the lowest of the totem pole in the Army. They just starting off at the beginner's level. A rookie. They get fucked and fucked over day in and day out by those with rank and status. One of my homeboys, who came with me to Fort Hood, was propositioned by a Staff Sergeant and a Sergeant. They told him if he didn't let them *screw* him they would put all kinds of shit out about him that could ruin his career before it even got started…And they *did*. As they slowly destroyed his military career because he turned down their sexual offerings, his girlfriend wound up pregnant; and with a baby on the way everything changed.

So he called me, crying. He said, "Eye think Eye'm going to *do* it."

"Do *what*, niggah?" Eye was half asleep. But Eye didn't say anything, since he was a dear friend and a Warlord.

"Eye am going to Staff Sergeant Dick's house right now."

"Oh, no, man!" Turning on the light, Eye jumped out of bed. Eye had two sleeping room mates. Snoring. So Eye lowered my voice. Eye was dressed in my boxers and long white tube socks. Eye thought about Marcus then, and the times we went out of town to Vero Beach and other places like that for high school drill competitions. Our drill team did the most mimicked and sought after performances in Florida. When our buses rolled in everyone knew who we were. Eye learned about doing *anything* to win, even then competitions drilled one thing in my mind.

DO WHAT IT TAKES TO WIN.

Simple. With my friend on the phone and a baby on the way, he changed sides. He became one of *Them*, letting the Staff Sergeant and Sergeant take turns banging him in the ass, and all his worries vanished. He rose up the ranks faster than Eye did.

And that's when Eye had had enough.

☯

*Eye'm 19 years old with a baby* on the way. Eye was getting out the Army. Eye didn't wanna be in it anymore. To speed up the process Eye stole one of my roommates check books and wrote up some checks to myself and went to the PX and bought up some shit because they wouldn't let me take the easy way out. That General calling me a Nigger really ate away at me day and night. How his rank saved him. Ugly pink-faced bitch! And then my friend giving up the booty for rank set me off. Eye did it myself, but Eye never got rank.

He had a baby on the way and suddenly wanted more money. Dummy. Before resorting to theft, Eye really tried to do it the old fashioned way, by telling my 1st Sergeant Eye didn't wanna be in the Army anymore, but he laughed at me and said, "You barely got a year in. You got three more to go."

"Eye want out this Army shit. Eye got a kid on the way. And Eye don't wanna follow orders when it comes to my kid and Eye can't be in his life."

"You got a baby on the way?" he asked, smirking.

Eye licked my lips. "Your grab-a-dick-by-the-balls-gay-ass got a goddarn wife, trick?"

He frowned. "Low blow, man. Eye'm not gay. Eye am a man fucking a man."

*This country muthafuckah needs to shut up!* "You're a gay man *sexing* a gay man in the butt—you in denial ass *bitch*."

He shoved half the shit off his desk, and Eye sat there smirking. Just the way he smirked at me when Eye said Eye had a baby on the way. "Get out my office, *Private*, before you get an Article 15."

"Maybe Eye should send those pictures of us fucking to the Board of Military Directors, whatever you call it. Chain of Command, *something*. And then we'll see who the hustler is. Eye'm from Goulds, bitch."

He started to tremble. "Get out my office." His voice was shaking.

"With pleasure." Eye looked him up and down. "It's starting to smell like…" Eye sniffed. "Fish in here."

"Fuck you!"

"Enjoy the shade, 1st Sergeant Dick in the Ass. Have a good day. Get me out this Army shit."

"No, Pharoah. You owe Uncle Sam three more years."

Eye stared at him. "Have you met George Bush?"

He rolled his eyes. "No. What does that got to do with anything?"

"Stop thinking for him, then. He ain't checking for you and he ain't checking for me. Isn't the Gulf War, Desert Storm going on right now? By the way Eye stole my friend's checkbook. Eye'll just wait for the MPs."

A few hours later the MPs showed up at my room door.

"Private Wilson…Can you come with us, *please.* You're *under* arrest."

If they weren't going to let me out then Eye'll show myself the door. Eye also said Eye was a *fag* and they gawked at me like Eye was an escaped lab monkey running rampant in an elderly front yard. Like Eye was despicable.

But for some reason they didn't believe me.

***Eye didn't even want to go to court*** and fight it. Give me an Other than Honorable Discharge and set a Niggah free. *Working* for Uncle Sam when Uncle Sam didn't give a fuck about me or know who Eye was wasn't a career choice for me. Fighting for a man Eye couldn't see. The only man Eye fought for and couldn't see was God, Jehovah. And that's it, Private. Eye didn't want to be a part of nothing that kept deep, dark secrets from the public. Eye was fingerprinted and charged. Eye was found guilty of theft and thus my road to recovery began. Eye wasn't a part of *Them* anymore. Eye was a part of regular society. The Civilians. Good bye Girl Scouts!

Eye met up with Chantell a few days later. Eye had to beg her to come over.

When she did she was high on marijuana, and Eye was furious.

"You're smoking weed, pregnant with my goddamn child?" Eye asked.

She was laughing. "So *what,* Niggah," she said, pointing. "Eye'm stoned. Eye had some angel dust."

"Oh my God, bitch!" Eye snatched her by the arm, my heart bleeding for my unborn child. "Have you lost your rabbit ass mind?"

She snatched her hand back. "Don't touch me!"

Eye snatched her into my face. "Eye'm calling the police if you *ever* do that again bitch now goddamn try me." Eye didn't yell or scream. Eye said it calmly, and with a killer smile.

"Eye'm going home. Eye didn't come over here for this!" She opened my door, and stormed out.

"Go to hell, bitch!"

And Eye slammed the door closed.

*We didn't talk for a few days. Eye* wasn't checking for her or checking up on her. Eye didn't even want to see her right now. Smoking dope while pregnant with my baby. Bitch crazy or something? There was a knock on my room door. A faint knock. Like someone wasn't too sure of the door they knocked on. Eye slid into my slippers, clad in shorts and a wife beater T.

Eye opened the door and it was Chantell. She looked a mess. Mascara running with her tears, lipstick smeared into her white blouse.

She shook in her low heels when she hugged me. Eye didn't understand what was going on, so Eye pulled her inside, washed her face for her and asked her to take a deep breath.

"Tell me what's wrong, Chantell."

"Eye can't tell you."

"You can tell me anything. You know that."

"A few days ago you lashed out at me. Am Eye supposed to forget about that?"

"Eye'm sorry, but you did drugs with a child in your womb. That's just wrong. My baby didn't do anything to you. Don't hurt my child like that. That hurts me!"

"You called me a bitch."

*Oh my God! That's all she's focused on? Me calling her a bitch? What about smoking cocaine and pot while you're pregnant? Did you care about that, bitch?* "Eye said Eye'm sorry. Eye already hate apologizing for anything."

"Pharoah. Eye don't wanna have a kid."

*The fear of God crept into my heart instantly.* "But you promised." Eye was so nervous Eye didn't know what to do.

"Eye know. But the thought of going through all that pain? And Eye wanna go back to college."

"You can still go to college!" Eye was about to have an anxiety attack!

Something in her eyes died. Eye was losing her! "No Eye can't. Who am Eye gonna get to watch my baby?"

The hairs stood on my body. "Eye will. You don't even want him."

"Eye got a confession to make."

Eye held her arms. "What, girl?"

She stared at me for a long time. And the silence fell on my ears with a ton of hatred. Eye glared at her and tilted my head, looking down at her belly.

A belly that hasn't grown an inch.

Since she's been pregnant.

*"Tell me you didn't..."* **Eye** closed my eyes so tightly Eye wanted to scream my discernment and feelings of abandonment.

"Didn't what?" she challenged me. "What? Say it."

"You had an abortion?" Eye still kept my eyes slammed shut.

"YES YES YES! Eye did, Eye did!" she yelled with no emotions.

Eye sunk to my knees and wrapped my arm around her waist, pressing my ear against her stomach. "You're lying. You have to be."

She rubbed my head with trembling fingers.

"It's true, Pharaoh. Eye'm so sorry."

"BUT EYE HAD A RIGHT TO DECIDE TOO!" Eye exploded, squeezing her to my ear tighter, huge tears spilling over my eyes and was evilly running parallel with the most devastating feeling Eye have ever encountered in life. "HOW COULD YOU DESTROY ME LIKE THIS?" Eye shook so *badly* Eye nearly threw up.

Her tears fell into my low fade and Eye was rubbing her belly, wishing and praying she was jerking my chain. Eye mean...Eye know she was angry with me for exploding on her for smoking dope while pregnant with my seed. But to go out and rip out my *soul*?

"Eye'm sorry. Eye'm just not ready."

"Shh, shh," Eye said, squeezing my eyes even tighter. "Eye'm trying to hear if Eye could hear my baby moving. He doesn't like a lot of noise and he loves when Eye read him Langston Hughes." Eye shook with fear. Eye WANTED TO DIE!

"PHAORAH HE'S GONE!"

"Eye've been talking to an empty stomach? Are you shitting me right now?"

"No Eye'm not shitting you, Pharaoh."

"Eye read him poetry and short stories and told him all my dreams and goals and you allowed me to make a fool of myself?"

"It touched me that you gave attention to what you thought was our child. But Eye had already killed it, even before you read the first sentence to my child."

Angry and betrayed, Eye slowly stood up.

Opening my dark eyes.

*"Eye can't believe this."*

She tried to hug me and Eye don't know came over me but Eye pushed her so hard into the TV shelf she fell to her knees. She was holding her back, and Eye was holding my black heart. It *lay* in my hands like burnt ashes. Like Satan took my future with my healthy son and crushed it into cremation with the palm of his hand. Eye was a demon. Eye slapped her and a few of my friends came into my room grabbing me and Eye was trying to run at her, trying to get out of my shirt and pants…but they kept holding and pulling me and telling me to calm down. Eye wasn't hearing it. Eye was so deep within myself Eye didn't even feel them touching, grabbing or pulling me. Eye was numb.

"Why did you do this to me?" Eye screamed, as they started to pull me down the stairs. Eye was trying to climb them, like a sprinter running against the force of wind up the stairs.

"EYE'M SORRY!"Eye heard her yell.

One of my friends comforted her and Eye spat at her, trying to stay on top of the stairs. Eye didn't take my red eyes off her. Eye hated her with my soul. Fuck her soul. Bitch, *die.* Fuck you! You killed our child you sadistic

BITCH! "You have no heart, Ho. You know that?" Eye started swinging at my friends. Three of them took a few steps back, holding up their hands.

"DON'T HOLD OR TOUCH ME!"

"We can't let you mess up your life," one of them said.

Eye turned towards her and my friends ran in front of me.

"Somebody gotta be praying for you, slut because these fuck Niggahs standing in between me and you. They let me go Hoe Eye'm gonna give your soul an abortion. Kill you the same way you TOOK MY CHILD BITCH!"

She covered her mouth. "You never talked to me like this?"

Eye was trying to get past my friends. One tried to grab me and Eye threw a two piece at his face. He ducked them.

"Pharaoh!" he shouted. "Eye'm on your side!"

*"EYE SAID DON'T TOUCH ME!"*

By now Niggahs coming out of their rooms, or climbing the stairs, trying to see what was going on.

Eye stood in one spot and looked into her eyes. "Why did you break your promise?"

"Pharaoh, please. This is painful for me too," she said, sobbing. Eye could barely make out the words. :Eye'm sorry!"

"Go to *Hell*! What made you back out of your promise?"

"Eye had too. He was putting too much pressure on me."

Eye was confused. "Who? Your *father*?"

"No, man, no! My brother. He kept putting pressure on me, saying don't be having your baby. That you haven't told your mom about it and you were getting an other than honorable discharge. Eye can't bring a child into the world with his father failing already."

Eye was stunned. "You're judging me?"

"No, man. Have some empathy."

"Did you do that for our child, bitch?"

"*Pharoah*! Eye have to protect my future! Eye can't have a kid. It would interfere with my plans."

"Who protected our baby?" She fell silent. "Who protected him?"

"You don't even know if it was going to be a boy."

*THE NERVE OF THIS BITCH!* She's worried about that, after killing our child and telling me nothing? She didn't even let me tell my child goodbye. Eye woulda tried to talk her out of it till Eye passed out. And even in my slumber Eye would still tell her to reconsider. Don't take my life like that; don't crush my manhood, the little Eye had to myself, away from me. Don't fuck it. It doesn't have an asshole.

"Who is this man that convinced you to kill my child?"

"Pharoah."

"WHO, BITCH? WHO? WHO? WHO?"

"Starks, Pharaoh!"

Eye fell into a deep silence, the fight zapping from my body like a heaven bound spirit cursed with the fires of hell.

The wind left my lungs.

*CODE RED! CODE RED!*

*She was mentally and physically* drained. "Eye'm sorry, Pharoah. My big brother was right. Eye can't have this baby."

"Starks, Staff Sergeant Starks, my good friend is your older brother and neither one of you thought to tell me this?"

"It's not that we didn't wanna tell you."

"What did you call it, Chantell? Eye mean, ya'll played games with me?"

"Eye needed to know everything. Eye wanted to know all your plans."

"So you had him get in good with me. And everything, every concern Eye had, he ran back and reported to you?"

"Yes. That's when Eye had an abortion."

"When, exactly?" Eye asked.

"Three weeks after Eye told you Eye was pregnant."

"What a low blow. How could you sleep at night?"

"How could you? Eye'm the one that got a low blow."

"What are you talking about?"

"My brother told me you two are fucking." Gasps filled the room and outer hallway.

People were wide eyed, soldiers covering their mouths.

"We are doing no such thing," Eye said with a straight face.

"Eye don't wanna have a gay man's son. What an oxymoron, are you kidding me?"

"You need to die a horrible death. May your soul never rest. May you suffer for the way you killed our child. Pain took our child out of the world, a pain initiated by selfishness and arrogance."

"Please forgive me."

*"THE DAY JESUS INVITES SATAN OVER FOR BREAKFAST WOULD BE THE DAY EYE FORGIVE YOU. UNTIL THEN, ROT INSIDE YOUR DARK ASS SOUL, BITCH!"*

And Eye flipped the middle finger.

*Eye looked at my friends*, ignoring her. Eye would hate her. For an eternity. Maybe. Hate was a strong word. But abortion was an even *stronger* word. Because that was an action word. Hate wasn't an action word. It was a human emotion that we're all plagued with. Whether we're using hatred or not. Hate is needed to keep love balanced.

"Eye'm going for a walk," Eye said, walking past them and down the stairs. Eye unlocked her car. Got in the driver's seat.

And hauled ass towards Starks house.

*When Eye got there, Eye parked* by his ride, and hopped out with the car running and in "park." Eye left the door open. Eye knocked on his door, and he answered it. He was shocked to see me. He said, surprised, "You know Eye like for people to call before they come—"

Eye punched him in his face and he stumbled backward into the living room. Eye saw nothing. But red. Red for blood. Eye didn't even think Eye blinked.

Eye slammed the door closed and locked it.

# Starks Versus Pharoah

↳⇧⇨🠅➥U Turns
By Dapharoah♋
The king of erotica

I've endured the last of your vulgarities
since I'm a regular occurrence
what should I name my cross/road?
U-Turns aren't an option
❹ my heart will never yell RETREAT!

① ➲ways are over ↓
rated

because my ❹ inch b⟶r↑o↓k⟷e⟵n↨ yellow lines
never connect the arrows in my turning lane
so now the light is red
and my ♥ is green
my soul is yellow
Proceed with caution
The ④ way stop
has congested road maps
I yield to let you win
slamming me in❷ dead ends
For the sake of family I lose my friends
yet family burns me, creating loose ends
I'm the care❹lly orchestrated embarrassment!
I cry for the last time
I've endured the last vulgar❽ty
my ❹ inch b↓r⟶o⟵k↑e⟷n white lines
never connect the regular occurrence
so while I yield to let you win
standing at the ④ way stop: tell me,
what should I name my cross/roads
when [YO]Uturns are no longer an option?

*He ran at me and punched me* good in the gut. Eye didn't have time to react. Eye stumbled backward into the front door and he ran at me and Eye pivoted out the way and his head slammed into the door.

"Eye hate you fuck *niggah*!"

"Go to hell, faggot!" he yelled back.

Eye kicked him in his ass. He caught my foot and pulled me to his head as it slammed into my face.

Blood was everywhere.

Stained my clothes; and the tiled floor.

He grabbed my neck and squeezed real hard.

"Eye never liked you."

"How could you betray me?" A knee to his balls. He doubled over, holding them tightly.

Eye kicked him in the face and stomped his chest.

"You helped kill my child! Eye didn't know Chantell was your freaking sister, you backstabbing bitch!"

He looked up at me. Eye stumbled forward then backwards, like Eye was drunk but Eye wasn't intoxicated nor tipsy.

Eye held my stomach, bending at the knees.

Eye never sobbed so hard in my life. "My kid is gone. You helped kill my dreams. That kid was my immortality. My future. And you killed it?"

"Man. Eye'm sorry."

*"YOU HELPED KILL MY CHILD YOU BITCHHHH!"*

He was reaching for me. "Eye love you, man…Eye *never* meant to hurt…you. Eye was jealous! That you would share a kid with my sister when Eye'm in love with you!"

"Fuck you!" Eye spat blood at him. Some got on his shoes.

*"PHAROAH!"*

*Eye slowly walked up to him*, and fell down to my knees. Face to face. Eye grabbed his face and planted my lips square on his and he held my face and we're stroking each other's face, breathing each other's air and Eye said, "Eye will never forgive you. Eye will never forgive her. Eye will never forgive neither of you."

He was kissing my face. "Pharoah. Abortion was the *right* thing!"

"That wasn't your child, Starks."

"Eye'm glad she destroyed your child!"

"GO TO HELL!" Eye head butted him so hard the back of his head slammed into the wall.

Staggering, Eye stood up. Looking at his pathetic ass.

"After today our friendship is *over*," Eye said, meaning every word. "Don't talk to me and Eye won't talk to you. Eye hope you rot, bitch! Eye hate you so much."

"No you don't," he managed to say, trying to regain his composure. He rose to his knees, avoiding my eyes. "Your heart is too big."

"You don't say that! You DON'T SAY THAT TO ME!"

"Whatever you wish. Leave now, before Eye call the goddamn police."

"Eye don't care to be here anymore. Fighting you ain't gonna bring my child back. You took my soul, you little dick bitch! You killed my soul, man. You got your fucking five kids bitch! Alive and well! FUCK ALL OF THEM! FUCK EM!"

He was crushed. "You don't mean that. They adore you."

Eye looked at him so darkly he trembled. My forehead lowered, my eyes peering into his. "You killed my child. The *hell* with yours."

"Eye can take that man. Now please leave."

He looked down at the floor and Eye ran at his ass.

His head snapped up at me and before he could do anything Eye put all my anger, frustration, betrayal and disloyalty into the discrepancy report called FIST and rammed it into the middle of his forehead.

He fell to the floor.

And didn't move.

*We're you ever a $tripper?*

*Lord Jennings$*

**Y↓O←U↓**
**NA[$]TY**
**B**
**↪☯**
**Y↓↑**

*In a myriad of thoughts about* where Eye'm going and my future, Eye stood at the fridge, filling my glass half way with liquid. The room temperature of the glass gradually cooled as the cold water turned the glass from full (atmosphere—air: 100%) to half empty (50% shore, ocean and half of the atmosphere). Then the house phone rang, disturbing my thoughts, and all the phones were on *one* line, Mama's line. Eye answered. It was Tom, with his fine ass. But he's slow as hell so that wouldn't work with a brothah like me. Tom said somebody stole the church's money. "*Nooooo!*" Eye'm stunned into silence. Eye forget all about my cold water.

"Yes, sur! Initially they counted about 2 G's, but 1.1 G's has been accounted for by the secretary."

"Oh my God, dawg," Eye said, bothered by this. *And they wonder why Eye'm late paying tithes.* "Damn, yo. Why the secretary counting money? That ain't in her job description!"

"She's the accountant and the secretary."

"*And* the Pa$tor's wife, people keep forgetting that crap, dawg!"

"Eye know. Eye keep forgetting. Eye guess she gotta take a little here and there to set up in another account."

The Shaq Ex Wife Effect. The *worst* kind! "Eye know, man. And they wonder why Eye put two quarters in the collection plate."

"Eye know right. You got me doing that."

Eye said, "Hey, what can Eye say. Eye put common sense in the plate. When Eye *was* going to church Eye used to drop two quarters in the tithe plate. Eye did this consistently. They know who's donating and who's not; they know who's stealing and who's getting over in church. But the brothah who putting in two quarters amongst all this green, we gotta *find* him. They called me to the office one day."

"No," my friend moaned. "And said what?"

"Yea, they called me to the office behind my Mama's back, questioning her child about what's going on in my house yet Mama thinks she knows more about me than myself. Ok, Mama. Keep thinking that!"

"What?"

"Yea, man..."

## THE PA$TOR'$ CHAMBER

***Eye was remembering that time***, when Eye was 19 years old and was so lost, confused and full of hate, bitterness and darkness and Eye never told a soul. Eye hid behind my smile. Eye used to love making people laugh because it kept me off my problems, and they were disturbing ones. The images came flooding back in retrospection. Pa$tor said, "Ya'll that broke? You can only put two quarters in the collection plate? Why half of a whole dollar. That ain't good economics, son."

"You're right. It's English. Two quarters mean you need to get some common sense, get it. Two quarters are in common so Eye ain't hearing you."

"Eye never did like your mouth."

*You didn't say that when Eye sucked your dick the other day and nearly vomited because it was a stank dick at that.*

"And Eye never liked *you*."

"God doesn't like unruly children."

Eye narrowed my eyes. "Eye'm a teenager, and God don't like horny Pa$tor$ that cheat on their brain dead wives with young teenage boys, bitch!"

"The Lord wants his ten percent," he snapped like a fish outta water and Eye grinned at his uneasiness.

Eye stood up. "And God just told you that?"

"Yea, he did."

"Bull."

Sarcastically, Eye'm looking around the office, my eyes sliding past expensive carpeting, half done wainscoting chipping at the corners (termites) and real lamps and real plants but out in the church the carpet was made from cheap, fake synthetic and was so low to the floor it felt like you were walking on concrete and fake flowers and fake pictures of a Caucasian looking Jesus beaming down over the congregation (when the J wasn't invented during Jesus heyday, so how was his name Jesus?) and the ceiling fans were the ones Home Depot sold on the clearance shelf.

"Son."

"God? You here?" Eye asked, ignoring him. My heart was pumping. Eye knew the day would come when he would talk to me or show himself. Why should PaStor$ be the only avenues to God when the Bible states Jesus was the mediator, not Pa$tor$.

That goes to show that when Brothahs get a little power it goes to *both* their heads. They think they're Batman or Superman yet in bed his favorite game to play was called Lower the Submarine. Just wished he washed his body! Eye started to walk around, rubbing my arms like Eye'm cold.

"God? You hear me? Talk to me, Father. Please…"

Nothing.

Eye turned to the PaStor out of anger. "Why God ain't talking to me?"

"You can't question him," he appeased and it didn't appease a thing.

"Eye didn't question Him! Eye'm questioning you. Why ain't he talking to me?"

"He only talks through me."

"Bull!. *You* preach that God loves us all, that he hears all his children."

"He does."

"*Bull!* Is God here?"

"Yes, Son!" He was getting nervous, trying to calm me down.

"Good. Eye gotta get some shit off my chest." Eye started yelling. "God! *Where* are you?"

Pa$tor was nervous. Now he was worried about his image. In a desperate attempt to shut me up, he rushed up to me, slapping me like a prostitute.

"Brothah shut up!" Small beads of sweat started popping across his wrinkled forehead. "The congregation out there…they can hear you."

Eye pushed him off me. "You ain't my daddy! Keep your hands off of me. God! Where are you? You walk over me to tell this grimy brothah about me? Why not tell me, God? Whisper in my ear and let me know you exist, Lord…?"

His eyes bulged out his head. "Pharoah…shut up! Before Eye punch you in the face. You're out of control."

"Out of your control, *that* Eye will agree on."

"What is your problem?"

"Eye got some questions for God."

"Such as?"

"My Daddy has *never* been there for me; *nor* did he teach me to play ball. Why, God? When Eye was 11, 12 and 13 Mama always smiled through her problems, worked hard and that built my confidence. Then she betrayed that one night she thought Eye was sleep and Eye heard her break down through those cheap walls. Asking God to give her strength to raise her children. That it was hard for a single mother to survive in this world.

"My own Mama lied to me. Everything wasn't all right. Eye had a false sense of security. And when your Mama lies to you things change but Eye'm her child. Eye was programmed through church and older family and teachers to never question her. To do as she say and half the stuff she asked me she didn't do her*self*."

"And you *shouldn't* question her."

"She's not God! So Eye can question her if Eye respect her. Why can't Eye ask her questions?"

"Because your types of questions aren't suitable for a child to ask."

"But Eye have an old soul, man. Eye'm 19 years old! Eye am NOT a child. Eye have questions and people can't just keep pushing my feelings under the rug. Eye have feelings too! Because Eye'm a teenager means my feelings mean nothing?"

"Pharoah. That's the way it is. Your mother is the boss."

"She's my mother. She's not my boss. If she's my boss where is my paycheck for keeping all her kids so she can work? She owes me some *serious* back pay. Why can't Eye file taxes on the work Eye do around the house, cooking and cleaning tirelessly like Eye'm some cunt about to deliver triplets?"

"You have internal issues."

"Eye got questions!" Eye was tired of talking to him. Eye wanted to talk to the Creator. "*Father*? Where *are* you?"

"You can't test the Lord or question him!"

"Bull! Why are you lying to me? You question him all the time. *What*...you're better than me because you wear a robe?"

"Eye'm not lying."

"Yes you are! What are you not telling me about religion?"

"Why are you so smart?"

"Because Eye read a lot of books. Eye read books and don't tell anybody. Eye pretend to hate reading books in public so people don't suspect anything. Plus Eye write in my journals every day. All my anger and frustration with this sick planet is outlined. Eye don't wanna live anymore! Eye didn't ask to be here. Eye think my parents are Selfish for bringing me here to this place. Eye was perfectly fine in the dark of nothingness in her womb. Eye was just fine!"

"No one asked to be here, Son."

"Eye am not your son. Stop calling me that."

"You have to calm down."

"Eye have to stay black in the ghetto and die. That's what Eye'm taught. That's what these failed black men around Perrine and Homestead and Goulds are exhibiting. Grown ass men robbing each other, making babies with all those Hoes, barely taking care of them or their seeds. These dumb brothahs live in the 'Hood, picking coochie over the welfare of their kids and got the *nerve* to say they are real brothahs doing real things. How you're a real brothah and couldn't even give your baby mama a ride to the store because she refused to hold your dope and be your punching bag and door mat? Brothahs got the game messed up, yet throw a fit when a brothah come through and treat his Mama the way he treats his baby mama.

"Got her catching the bus with your bad kids in tow, carrying a thousand grocery bags. Eye saw the look of hurt and betrayal on her face. If *any* brothah do that to my sister Eye'm taking his ass off the planet myself and send his mama a Thanksgiving card; Federal Express. Brothahs would rather buy a car with beats and rims over a home for their baby and baby Mama. Don't talk to me about calming down. Eye don't wanna end up like that!"

"Pharoah. Calm down. This is my last time saying it."

"And if Eye don't? What are you gonna do about it? Whip my ass? Call my Mama? Tell her Eye been a bad, bad boy? You do that Eye will tell her you been touching on me since Eye was 14, creep."

"Tell her what you want! She won't believe you."

"Adults love saying that. They won't believe you. Three of my older cousins once said that when Eye told them to save me from my ex step daddy raping me. Eye was shaking with fear, thinking Eye was going to be removed from that home. They said what you just said. They also said my grandma killed Uncle Al, their daddy. Who gives a damn! Eye had *nothing* to do with that. Eye wasn't even born yet. Why should Eye have to suffer for that?"

He tried to hug me and Eye kicked him in his balls. Eye pushed past him, snatched open the doors and said, "Maybe God is in the main assembly."

People were seated, talking and opening Bibles. Getting ready for the Pa$tor to drain their wallets and purses dry this week. Eye pushed through the doors.

And startled them all.

# THE M<u>A</u>IN A$$EMBLY

*"God, are you in here!* Where are you? You talk to the Pa$tor but not me?"

Eye walked up the aisle, looking all around the church. Causing a disruption inside a controlled, programmed environment and didn't give two fucks what they had to say. Talking about everybody and everything but themselves and their own individual fucked up lives.

"Father, where are *you*? Eye don't wanna be here anymore!!" To say Eye was angry and loudly cursing and they were in shock was putting it mildly.

"God!" The tears fell. "Eye can't do this anymore. Eye want to live. Eye want to be Pharoah. Eye got kicked out the Army. My life is nothing. Eye work at Turkey Point, and Eye am tired of the Outage. Eye am losing myself in watching over my siblings. Cooking and cleaning like Eye'm a woman. Eye'd rather cut the grass. Wait, Eye do that, too!"

Eye fell to my knees, looking at my hands on my lap. People looked at me and didn't utter a word.

"God, can you hear me? Eye thought you would *never* forsake me. Or is it all lies Pa$tor$ tell to get your money. Are you even real, God? Are you a myth? Like Greek gods, everybody knows Zeus ain't real."

Eye was let down. God didn't come. He didn't say anything. Like Elvis, GOD has left the building. Was he ever in it? Eye slowly stood up. Eye glared at them. "You know what? *Screw* church, you recovering crack head looking *zombies*!" Kill the lights; they didn't utter a word or a Word. The church body was *too* stunned by my outburst, totally unexpected. Sometimes you had to cripple your opponents to win the game. And they would be some paraplegics by the time Eye was done. The idea, the image and the spectacle of church was ruined.

"You know what?—*yea*, Eye'm bisexual and Eye am a real brothah; and *sometimes* Eye can be a dick. Are ya'll real? We're broke in Goulds and now we're all up in the church like it's Sunset Boulevard. This isn't Sunset Boulevard or Hollywood. Those rich white people don't care about us. Excuse me, Lord, but your grown behind children in this defunct church need to get it in order then get it together and fast. Eye got teeth marks all over my back from the gossip. If you got something to say *tell* me in my face because Eye'm not scared of neither one of you!"

"He is so ghetto, he's *ignorant*," somebody said and Eye put my hands on my hips and slayed for the Gods they served because it *wasn't* Jehovah…The Pa$tor had us on our knees, praying to him. Pa$tor' Dumb Ass thought *he* was God. The people surrounding me we're worshiping the Pa$tor, and not Jehovah. Eye knew it and they knew Eye knew it.

"You're gonna say something, Pharoah? *Looking* at me all messed up you potty mouth child," She stood up—*ooh* she's a *bad* bitch, Eye loved confident females—and Eye took a few steps in her direction.

"When you kissed your husband…did you taste my cum?"

Her eyes bulged with confusion and shock. Her head snapped in his direction (he lowered his head). "*What*? Oh my God!"

"He ate me out, too, swollen mouth *trick*!"

*"Kick him out the church!"*

*"His mouth!"*

Eye lovingly looked in her eyes. "Coming from the mouth of the chick that sucked her husband from my erection just a few short days ago?"

She grabbed her purse, ducked her head and ran like a bat out of Hell out towards the exit door. Boom—bye, bye. A few people were leaving, but others were too curious to know the other's business if Eye exposed it and they forget they are a part of the collective whole of the congregation so their shit getting exposure, too, that's how the Media worked anyway.

Eye went on. Church has hurt me for the last time. Telling me God was try'na tell him somethin' 'bout me. Let God tell me for himself. Eye wanted God to tell me about me. Why go to a man that has sex with me with my business? Eye got some things off my chest once and for all, "Eye want my money back. All the money Eye gave with a cheerful heart. Half that money Eye got from turning tricks. Yea that's right. Adults paid for this, not my peers, not people my age. Grown people! Using rent and utility money to get into my body and Eye shouldn't have given you anything. Eye gave you common sense from that money, not ten percent. Eye should call the Better Business Bureau on this establishment. Church is a joke. *Terrible* things started happening when Eye got saved…Eye'm *losing* money, Pa$tor is rich and Eye'm hurt, screwed and broke and Eye'm not even 20 years old yet!"

Pa$tor grabbed my arm and Eye pushed his ugly ass on the floor.

"Don't touch me. You say homosexuality is wrong—Jesus never bashed gays. But you banged me in your wife's bed while she played with her *coochie.* And Eye'm going to hell? Where the hell you think you and that slut wife of yours is going? Ya'll been sucking and banging me since Eye was 14. But nobody wanna talk about that!"

The church was destroyed.

*"What?"*

*"Pastor, that true?"*

*"Oh my God!"*

*"Eye am in shock!"*

Eye looked the shocked harlots in the face and said, "Eye know ya'll ain't popping off at the mouth. Ya'll wanna throw stones? Ya'll wanna talk about how the Pa$tor got his rocks off with me?"

Oh, they're quiet now. *Retreat! Retreat!* those scared eyes yelled at me. Withdrawing the troops. Eye had arsenals for that funky ass.

"You're popping off at the mouth? You're bumping those gums Bubba Gump Shrimp?" Eye pointed at an elder. "Eye had you." Eye pointed at his wife, "Eye ate you out something proper 'cause *you* said your husband can't *eat* fish 'cause he's *secretly* has me on his sausage diet!" Eye pointed at him and his brother, "Eye watched you two bang each other so don't go there on me! You're both in love, and you have the same Mama and Daddy."

Big girl was *running* for the exit door. "No, trick!" Eye ran behind her wobble, wobble, shake it, shake it ass. "Don't run out that door."

She tried me, pushing it open and Eye snatched her by her wig and pulled her back to me, looking like toppling dominoes on a checker board. "Don't run. Tell everyone you were one of my high school teachers. When Eye was a mighty, mighty Spartan! You used to tell me when Eye turned 18 you were going to suck and hump me to sleep because Eye was fine. You were even at my graduation. Eye was still 17, a few days before my 18$^{th}$ birthday in 1995 and Eye snuck out the house and you made me nut eight times that night. After the 5$^{th}$ Eye was shooting blanks, though."

"Pharoah. Shut up! You're lying!"

"*Eye'm* lying? Tell these nosey bitches in this corrupt church. Eye'm not going to lose no sleep."

"Shut *up*!"

"Eye'm dating your brother right *now*. Want me to bring his sl-sl-sl-slow butt in here and confirm my story?"

"Eye hate you!"

"And my penis *hates* your buck teeth. Always grazing my shaft. And this folks is why Eye gave two quarters and not ten percent of my mortgage, lights, water bill, child support and payroll checks to give to these greedy people. Ya'll been had! Ha ha, not me! Enjoy your communion. Eat that bread, drank that wine you whoremonging hypocrites!"

Eye spun on my heel and threw up the peace sign, walking up out of that hell hole of a church. Eye's been robbed blind for years by a Pa$tor preaching that same mess he preached ions ago, and still getting ya'll money. They need to run background and finger print checks on Pa$tors, Elder$ and Preacher$.

Church hasn't and never will condition me.

When ya'll g'on wake up?

☯

*Tom didn't wanna finish* talking about the church's money coming up missing after Eye told him that story. But, hesitantly he finished talking. Good.

Eye said, "...That's crazy. Now they stealing in church and want me to believe in organized religion. Bad enough Eye slept with *half* the church and all of them were Pastors, elders, and *mummies* who haven't been touched in years. They looked at me and wished they were 27, 28 and 29 again. One Pa$tor told me, 'If Eye was 27 again, brothah, Eye would *fuck* you to sleep and make you *nut* on my chest.'

"...Eye was so turned on he didn't have to wish because he activated my flesh and made me weak in the knees. And Eye made him shoot for the stars all night and misfired, skeeting on his sheets. Didn't want that old ass nut on me, oh hell no!"

Tom laughed so hard he choked. "You're crazy!"

"They stealing, Eye coulda kept my $400."

"Brothah, stop lying! You only gave them forty dollars, all in quarters in those quarter rollers."

Now Eye laughed. "Eye know."

"You gave out a lot of common sense."

"Ha, Eye know!"

"Well shit saying Eye gave $400 to the church sounded appealing, all about the image. And why are you counting my money for me before Eye put all those quarters in the tithe plate?"

"Tithe plate, collections plate, whatever."

Eye said, "Eye remember last week. You took out about seven $20's, thinking nobody saw you..."

"Eye had to come up with $140 extra for rent."

We were giggling. Tickled me pink. He's silly...Did any of you have a friend like that? A pal that constantly made you laugh saying of-handed things?

"You're dumb!" Eye said.

"When you get an eviction notice and 30 days to leave you realize the government forfeited and reneged on your 40 acres and a mule you had on lease for a year in your sister's name because you were a convicted felon. Even if they gave all us blacks our 40 acres and mules we'd look like complete jack asses when they hit us with all that inheritance and property tax. And brothahs gonna sell out on each other for that ass Eye meant mule.

"Eye hear you."

"*Look*, Eye gotta go. Gotta get ready for school. Financial aid office keeps calling me about paying for fees. *Damn* Eye just started school."

"They're hating."

"Yea, and my Cuban friend Juan hasn't paid a fee or a bill in a year and they ain't called him to the office yet."

"You know they look out for their own."

"And how Eye owe the school when my Financial aid goes directly to the school? How Eye owe money? They didn't even give me a receipt for spending my government money!"

"They crooked as fuck."

"Eye'ma call the police and file a complaint about that. Juan goes to school for *free*. Eye haven't been here three weeks and they're harassing me about *payments*."

"You're crazy."

"Bye." Eye hung up and called my homeboy Cedrick.

"Pharoah?"

"Yes," eye said, smiling. "Let's make this money. Eye wanna be a stripper. What do Eye gotta do?"

"Eye am so pleased. A whole new world is about to open up for you. You're on the next level. They ain't gonna be able to take you, Pharoah. And you write?"

"Shake it, gimme those dollars. Let's go!"

*Eye still wound up* calling Tom back, being nosey about the church's money. My thought process about stripping was a very inner coastal, discombobulating thing. Because Eye was incarcerated by society's expectations. There Eye was living it up to society's expectations when Eye haven't even lived up to my own. And at this point in my life Eye was a ghoul of a goblin. An egotistical, barbaric ghost rocking the boy next door birthday suit and a sassy, masculine attitude, but nothing too flamboyant. An oxymoron of myself. Playing straight in public yet Eye was one strong-minded bisexual. Eye was afraid of the light. Eye was a vampire of my sexuality; a slave, held at its fledgling and the thought of leaving the darkness sucked the moisture from my lungs and Eye was thirsty. Satan knew this.

Oh he knew that all too well.

## PROMI$CUITY

*Eye couldn't even go to the grocery store* without fine dudes, men that were my type, athletic types in gym shorts wearing no drawers…*hounding* me. One Liberty City Brothah asked me what time it was and he had on a watch. Another asked to use my phone when he just got off *his* phone. Claiming his phone died. So Eye let him use it. No one answered so he gave it back and we went our separate ways. Later on that night, just after 11 P.M. my phone rings and Eye answer and it's him, talking 'bout, "Eye had to call my cell to get your number. Eye hope you're not mad. Eye think you're fine as hell. Eye'm gonna cut right to it. Let me get up deep in that there, dude. Eye'm married. Got two kids. Don't give a damn. Help me get this nut."

Eye hung up. Then they walked up to you and you saw that huge penis print and they semi hard talking to me, couldn't take their eyes off my lips. And they always nodded at me and Eye was hard as hell, secretly sneaking in the bushes with them and making them cum all over the wild grass. If Eye was as promiscuous as Eye was back during my self-hatred years, Eye would have been rolling around the sack with them, validating myself. Eye would get lost in it, like Eye had before. Try'na breathe but suffocated instantly when brothahs got up, got dressed and left without a Bye, see you later or a tip. And even around that time Eye made out with a few brothahs in their cars. Most brothahs loved to be inside me on the back seat of the Impala or the Charger or the Chevy with the police tints and defunct cartoons airbrushed on his trunk.

One married brothah pulled over on the side of the turnpike, turned on the hazard lights, lift the Hood and he screwed me for two full hours on the back seat with those police tints. Then Eye vanished without a trace. *Brothahs* didn't know my name, place of address or my phone number so Eye didn't lose any sleep, but Eye did wake up—eventually—and decided that Eye wanted and needed *more* in my life. Eye became a ghost to those brothahs. And to the females, too.

Eye was too afraid to lose the mask, convincing people it's my face when it wasn't even Halloween. So tricks and treats were unnecessary, but that didn't stop me from doing tricks for the treatment of dead presidents. Eye got fired from Turkey Point. They said Eye was stealing and Eye wasn't. Stealing what? Who knows. They just wanted my black behind gone. So Eye left. Brothah couldn't find a decent job, so Eye applied to be a Security Guard and was hired a week later. Eye hated it! *Being* a security guard at Cutler Landings wasn't cutting it because it was some overnight work and Eye was growing weary of it. So Eye put in a change of post with Pro Guard Security, and they moved me to the Florida City Outlet Mall.

Gave me a military type hat and some tight pants and long sleeved shirt. Eye was walking around all day, bored as because the outlet Mall was slow. It was located under Jesus's *sandals* (in Homestead, just before The Keys). Eye enjoyed the job, eating up the food in the Food Court and buying up all the football cards and collecting them.

Eye noticed every time Eye walked past Rack Room shoes a short, sexy female with nice breasts kept running up to the window waving at me. Initially, Eye ignored her. Eye focused on doing a good job. Eye never chased Hoes and Eye really didn't sweat bitches. All that "You're cute" stuff didn't work on me; Eye left that in high school. If Eye went to the mall with a group of brothahs…while 6 of them started rapping at the *same* girl or the girl and *her* girls, Pharoah was in the back picking imaginary dirt out my nails and brothahs got mad when Hoes bypassed them and came right up to me because Hoes hated to be ignored. Eye wound up yawning, looking up and saying, "Naw Eye'm cool. Eye'll pass!" And nine times out of ten me and the Hoes went at it till Eye wound up screwing one of them just to shut the Hoe up. But one day the Rack Room shoes broad ran up to the big window and her breasts looked so good under that tight black shirt and she had a nice petite booty and those tight pants were eating that coochie up. She had a nice chunky monkey in the center, so Eye was like forget Ben and Jerry's. As much as Eye tried to hide it, my stick was hard. Hadn't had coochie in a few months and the season for brothahs that knew what they were doing in the bedroom was *lacking* so Eye hung up the Freak-a-Brothah jersey and hollered at the female. Here goes. Eye went in the store and said, "Are you ok?"

She was holding her breath. She had to be about 5 feet 4. Eye was 6 feet 3 ½ inches. Eye towered over her.

"Why do you say that?"

"Because you're always running up to the window when Eye walk by."

"Eye just think you're cute."

"And so are you. Hungry?"

"Sure. What you'd have in mind?"

"The food court." Eye took her out to eat, and paid for her meal. Cost a pretty penny but she was a dime on her way to silver dollar status real fast. Very sweet, well together girl. Eye invited her to my crib so Mom and my brothers could see my catch and they liked her instantly, especially Jarshawn. She stayed out in the dining room playing spades with the family and Eye retired to my room, a little left out because she was more focused on them, but it was all good. Eye turned off the lights, taking off my shirt, socks, and shoes. Left my pants unzipped. Eye lie down and fell asleep. Eye was dog tired.

*Eye felt someone straddling* my booty. Two warm hands caressing my back, making me smile in my sleep. Or maybe Eye was dreaming. Eye opened my eyes and Hoe'nita had on one of my shirts, her weave dangling in her face. Her silk panties were off and her hot box was wet on my butt cheek.

"Are you still sleeping?" she asked seductively.

"No, Eye'm awake now."

"Are you really?"

"Yes. That coochie hot for me huh?"

She smiled, her eyes sparkling. "Hell, yea!"

Eye turned over and pulled her to my lips. Her *other* set of course. "Ride my face." She held the head board, with those pretty nails. One by one they snapped off as Eye tongued her, gripping her sides, controlling her spine.

"Oh my God! Eat me out Pharoah!" She felt so good on my tongue. The smell of her womanly aura did a number on my balls. The light salty taste, 56 calories per gram of fat Eye needed in my life right about now. Those pretty breasts were bouncing. She looked down into my eyes, shuddering.

"Eye'm gonna cum!" she excitedly said. Eye stuck my tongue in deeper. She came all over my lips. Eye swallowed, tonguing her deeper, handling her petite body. "*Ooohhh*!" Eye handed her the dildo. "Pound yourself with it," Eye demanded.

"Pharoah, *No*…! Oh God—*keep* tonguing me!"

Eye pushed her off me. Eye hated disobedient bitches. Eye was getting up. "No, Pharoah," she said. She was grabbing my arm. "Torture my clit!"

"No."

"*Why*?" she whined.

"Eye don't mess an independent chick. If Eye can't control it then screw you and take your *stank* butt home!"

"Pharoah!"

Eye shook my head. "What?" She grabbed my penis and Eye slapped her hands. "You can't afford that. Don't *touch*!"

"Negro *do it to me*!" she said, her *Nookie* getting wetter.

"Damn, it's like that?"

"Hell yeah!"

"Ride my face and pound yourself deep in the ass with your *toy*!"

"But Eye don't have any lube!"

Eye wiped some of my sweet vanilla nectar from the hole in my Temple and massaged it lightly on the toy. "There you go." Eye lay down, spreading my legs. "Ride my face, now!" She got on my face, and my tongue got to work.

"Oh God you can eat the sliced peach! *Damn*!"

"Stick the toy in your butt!"

"Eye'm scared," she said, bouncing on my lips.

"Spread your butt cheeks."

She did, and Eye slid my tongue repeatedly in and out her. Coochie juice rolled down the sides of my face. Eye loved that nasty stuff. Eye was a nasty brothah in bed. Eye slowly slid the toy deep inside her pulsating, tightly wound, black hole, her body locking. Eye didn't care if it hurt her or not—take that! "Focus on my tongue, baby!"

She shuddered from momentary bliss. "Oh Pharoah oh Pharoah!" Eye had the eight inch *black* plastic toy deep in her tight virginal hole. Eye used to love screwing females in the butt for the first time. She fell back and Eye let her fall. Eye pushed her legs back, pounding her with the toy.

"Oh, God!" She screamed out.

"Oh, God?" Eye asked her, taunting her.

"Yes!" Eye spanked her coochie. Didn't Eye tell you no tongue after 10 p.m.? She didn't even know Eye pulled out the plastic and gave her this good beef.

"*Oooohh*! Let me taste my juices from your lips."

Eye picked up the toy and popped the top of her forehead. "Say please..."

"Please!"

"Suck this toy while Eye get inside that phat ass of yours." She slurped on the toy, tasting her essence…chick was so bad Eye'll call *it* chocolate decadence.

Everything that came out of her was poetry; motion (my Nature) in the ocean (her soft, wet center) reverberate via energy and vibration through my body, popping off at the mouth in my toes, making them curl in shame. Eye felt like a nation of Kings pushed my hips forward…*trying* to rob the tomb in my scrotum for my unborn and underdeveloped preemies. Eye was fumbling her clit with my thumb, sliding my middle finger deep inside her. She put an arch in her back—like a slender necked swan spreading its feathery wings under the moonlight, her eyes on the stars and her mind focused on change. Eye didn't have time for chicks comparing me to their daily horoscopes. She was already re-writing her future with me in it, nah, she penciled me into her future and refused to change a thing about herself. Her type of change she expected me to do, and Eye wasn't with it. She wanted my heart. Eye wanted a shot of coochie and some fire ass head, real talk. If Eye could remember her name a week from now after the sun set then we're *good*, and we can vibe and feel each other out. But Eye wasn't into changing anything about myself right now in my life. Just give me some coochie and Eye'm good! "Eye'm gonna cum again!" she announced.

"You are?"

"Yes."

"Want me to cum with you?"

"Yes, Daddy!"

Eye started pounding her. "...Eye'm 'bout to nut!"

Eye pulled out and cum on her pretty face while she wet up my sheets. Eye fell asleep right on top of her. My spent stick was deep inside her warmth...Being with her was going to be detrimental to my frame of mind. First, she stayed the night with me and funny thing was she never went home. She moved in and didn't tell any of us. *We* were the slow ones. She wormed her way into every aspect of my life, and Eye was so coochie whipped Eye thought it was love. Eye was getting it day in and day out, sucking those breasts, making her catch nut after nut after nut, her coochie juices running down my balls and the crack of my butt. She was my obsession. Eye changed posts again and wound up securing some apartments in Leisure City. Eye would come to work at 8 p.m. My manager checked me off and he hopped in his security car and hauled tail till Eye came back to work the next day. When my shift was over at 4 a.m. he didn't check me out. He trusted me to do that manually and Eye had. But Eye was missing Hoe'nita and her body, but what Eye didn't know was that she was boning my 15 year old brother Jarshawn, turning his young ass out and Jarshawn and Eye would be fighting over her and Eye never understood why he would fight me over my girlfriend. She was letting him bang her under mama's roof, in my bed without rubbers and lying down with me without rubbers and Eye always came deep inside her because Eye hated pulling out. Thinking 'bout her turned me on and Eye was hard, while supervising those boring apartments. And when Eye did find out she was screwing him Eye had to hurt her, but Eye didn't *let* her know Eye knew. Eye knew before Jarshawn told me over the phone when Eye wound up in jail. Eye walked in on them when Eye got off work early and tip toed back out the house and never said a thing.

Eye made them think they got over on me. Eye was friends with the down low brothahs up in the apartment complex and we were screwing up something. Every night my weak flesh was bouncing on another low key Brothah's whatchamacallit, making him nut, doing to him what his bitch wished she could do. But they started falling in love with me and Eye wasn't having it so Eye cut 'em off, ignoring them. One by one a brothah would walk up to the car offering me alcohol and weed to get in my draws.

NOPE!

## WEAKNE$$ OF THE FLESH

*One night, after Eye got* off the phone with Hoe'nita, a tall, sexy, Ruff Neck dope boy came up to me. "Pharoah, damn…*why* are you acting flaky with the booty."

"Eye'm good."

"My female ain't making a brothah nut. Sup with the coochie, brothah?"

"Eye'm cool. Eye got an ass, not a coochie."

He rubbed himself, looking around. You couldn't look at him and guess he got down with other men. He was as masculine and aggressive as they came. You could stare at him and he would never give the slightest clue away, those were the kind of brothahs Eye got *down* with.

"Damn Eye'm on brick."

Eye yawned, rolling up the window. He got in the passenger seat. "Get out, man!" Eye said. "Eye'm working."

"Why you doing me like this? Eye want some booty."

"No."

"Please, Brothah. You got some bomb booty, dude. Make me nut."

"No!"

"Can Eye eat you out? Pop it on my tongue, brothah."

"Get out."

The passenger door opened and *another* brothah pulled him out. "That's *mine*!" he whispered, keeping it gangstah.

"*Piss* off! Pharoah is mine!"

"Guys," Eye said. Eye didn't need this. Not tonight.

"Eye'll beat your ass, Nigga!" one screamed at the other. He was punched in the face. They started fighting. Eye turned on my Mitsubishi Gallant and drove home.

Wanted no part of that. Eye drove to my God Mama Ronda's house. She stayed around the block and was one of the realest women you'd meet. She spoke her mind, has a nasty mouth and didn't give a damn. "Damn *you're* off early," she said.

"Yea, Eye am."

"You *ok*?"

"Yea."

"Go fix you something to eat. Eye got pig feet in there, Eye know you love them."

"Yea Eye do."

"You staying the night?"

"Yea, Eye am."

Her son came out the room. Eye was 19, he just turned 18. He had his shirt off, plaid shorts and no underwear.

"You staying the night, Pharoah?"

Eye barely looked at him. "Yea."

"You can sleep on the couch," Ronda said, yawning. "Eye'm going to bed."

She retired to her room and locked it. Eye made my way to the couch.

Homeboy said, "Naw, you aren't sleeping on the couch. Eye got a *room*. Come on."

"Ok." Eye followed him to his room.
He closed and locked the door behind us.

*Eye took off my shoes, keeping* on my clothes. He got in the bed, and Eye got on the floor.

Eye curled up…going to sleep.

He sat up. Pharoah?"

"What?"

"Come up here, man."

"Eye'm good."

"Eye don't bite."

Eye got up and noticed he was under the cover. Eye got in the bed and turned my back to him.

Eye closed my eyes.

He came up behind me. Eye felt the warmth of his hard on pressed *on* my bubble. "You know what time it is," he said, kissing the back of my neck. And he ate me out till Eye was tender. Then he was inside me all night long. "Eye waited till my 18th birthday to get inside you," he said, kissing my lips, bouncing inside me. Eye was lost, deeper into the hatred Eye had for myself.

"Eye can't believe Eye'm finally getting the booty."

He smiled the whole night through.

*Eye hate you, Pharoah. Eye hate you!* Eye was thinking to myself. Smiling at my reflection in the mirror.

Hating myself inside even deeper, growing darker.

## $TR1PPER

*Eye was afraid to be free,* incarcerated in society's expectations derived from mixed religions. On my way to the strip club for the first time, as an entertainer and debut stripper, Eye was an inferior fool at war with my heart (irrational), body (sexual), mind (intellectual but lacking common sense) and soul (The Holy Ghost). When Eye did my audition Eye was a definite shoe in for the club's owner, Andy, 6 feet 8, Puerto Rican and Jamaican, temper out of this world with green eyes and long hair like a City of Roses pimp. Yes, he was all that! When a man's body made you feel like Julia Roberts then damn it Bob, the Price is Right! But before Eye get into that Eye gotta tell you about the Audition held at his house.

Eye have to convince him to hire me as a stripper.

And he wanted more than talent.

*Eye realized he was the brothah in one of* my college classes at City College, so we really hit it off big.

He said, "Can you dance?"

Can Eye? "Yes, Brothah. Can you hang?"

"All night."

"Whatever. Anyways, yea Eye can dance."

"Ready to audition?"

"Yes."

*He picked up the remote* and put on some Uncle Luke "Its your Birthday" *hey* Eye popped it to the floor chanting "Cancer!" Is it December, no—bitch…it's June 26th, 1977.

Go Pharoah! He stopped the music and Eye froze in the doo doo brown position, looking over my shoulder. "What?"

He was grinning. "Damn you got a nice romp."

"Thanks."

"Eye'm *hard...*"

"Eye see."

"Eye don't want you to audition to that. Typical sissy can pop to this. Don't require much. If you can strip to this, you will be hired at my club with top billing. You're finer and cuter than those other used washed up brothahs."

He turned on the big screen and pressed play.

Janet's "IF" video came on, women rising from the floor and men lowered by ropes from Chinese ceilings.

Eye looked at him. "Eye can't dance to this!"

"Impress me."

"Ok."

Eye stretched, arms in the air and when the beat dropped Eye did the entire video, from start to finish, doing everything Janet did, turned the same way she's turned, facing him, the TV behind me and his mouth was open the entire time. When the song ended he was on his feet clapping, and not once had Eye stripped off anything.

He took me in his arms and we made love all over the house. He was in love with my talent, not me or my body. But Eye didn't know that at the time. He would also become my secret, abusive, controlling lover. My hot, double fudge, passionate, secretly sexy down low big stick aggressively older tender roni lover.

*The first day Eye took the stage* was a scary one. And it wasn't really my first time. This was going to be somewhat of a trial run. To see what Eye'm made of. To see if Eye could hang with the big dawgs. So most of the strippers really didn't take me seriously. Eye heard a lot of men come through and get up on stage, stripping during their trial run and get scared off into oblivion, never to return. Eye knew Eye wouldn't be vanishing. Entirely new audience of my life, a different stage of my mental and emotional development. Eye was 19 years old when Eye stood before Andy, Cederick, Anthony, Bishop, Jabari, Samuel, Big Dick Daddy and Money. Andy being the acting manager of PANDORA'S GATEWAY and the other seven men together brought in over $25,000 + a week. The hottest strip joint in town. Though Eye was a "straight" stripper for the ladies, my secret obsession was to men.

Eye was clad in leather cow boy pants, elephant trunk covered penis and a G string. Felt like Eye was flossing my colon when Eye walked. Andy paused behind me, gripping my shoulders, his breath on the nape of my neck. He pressed himself against me and said, "Are you ready, *Rookie*?"

Eye smiled nervously. "Yea, Eye'm ready."

He looked at me sternly. "This is a trial run, Pharoah. If you got what it takes your first night will be in a few weeks."

"Eye got you."

All the fellahs surrounded me and grinned, smiled, laughed and urged me on.

"Its time to introduce the world to Black Magik."

"That's my name?" Eye asked, grinning, slapping palms with everybody. Eye hated the name.

"Yup. Go make some money," said Andy, winking.

*The women roared to life* when Andy's fine ass took to the stage in a thousand dollar suit and matching shoes. Towering 6 feet 8 with Jamaican and Puerto Rican ancestry. A few ladies threw fifties on the stage and told him to take it off. He slid his hands in his pocket, the blinging of the rings on his fingers ceased, and he said, "Coming to the stage is one of the hottest young men out of Dade County. He's fire. And he is everything you want in a young man starving for attention. He is standing 6 feet 4 inches tall. Ladies Ladies ladies, here is Black Magik!"

The lights faded and fake smoke hissed from the side canisters and Eye slow grind out to the middle of the stage with my finger tips on the tip of the sombrero, stuck my ass out and gave 'em that Michael Jackson stare.

The Lights came On and the Janet Jackson mix Andy cleverly made to Uncle Luke's instrumentals was just what Eye needed to get loose. It's like something took over me, grabbed me by the throat and controlled my body. Eye hit a spin, popped to the floor with my head tilted, licking my lips. Made my erection thump a few times. Eye snapped my fingers to the pulse and fell to my hands and knees, crawling, expertly, licking my lips, forehead down and eyes and booty up, crawling over to a cute chubby woman who had heart failure and tried to hide behind her girl, laughing uncontrollably. Don't hide...Eye'm coming for those dollars. Eye crawled in her friend's lap and she wasted liquor on my butt. Eye jiggled them in her face and took chubby lady's broach into my mouth, tilting my head to the right, tonguing the broach and winking at her. "Daddy needs a new outfit and a new pair of shoes," Eye told her, putting both hands on the floor, arching my legs in the air and fell, straddling chubby's lap.

"Oh my God!"

"When was the last time a man ate your sweet nectar?" Eye asked her, grinding to Janet singing *Nasty* to the One Leg Up, Uncle Al beat. She was wet, grabbing my ass cheeks, darting her tongue at me and women fanning money all around me.

*"She don't know what she doing!"*

*"Ditch that bitch; cum grind on my lap!"*

*"Grab his package, girl!"*

Eye gave her some tongue, took both her hands off my ass and looked deeply into her eyes. "That'll be $250 for grabbing my ass. And Eye want my money!" She quivered picking up her purse. "Eye don't cum cheap," Eye said aggressively. "*Gimme* an extra hundred."

"Oh my God!" She was about to pass out. And Eye wasn't gonna catch her, either. She pulled out her wallet and Eye lowered myself to my knees, spread her legs and stuck my head up her skirt and munched on her lace-clad kitty and she couldn't take it. She threw her legs up and Eye kept munching and she counted out my money and stuck it in my G string and Eye took off the hat, my tongue still thrashing chubby coochie, wondering was Kermit stuck inside Miss Piggy and Eye put the sombrero on her head, grabbed her breasts and tongue f'd her till she cooed, "Eye'm 'bout to cum." Eye smacked her in the face, pissed off her nut and said, "Did you ask me could you nut?" And wandered off, dancing and snapping up to a tall woman who wiggled a twenty in my face. Eye reached for it and she snatched it back and Eye snatched her upper arm, just above the elbow, dropped to my knees and kissed her Nookie—"*Hey* there, Sweetie. Damn you smell good!"—and hopped back up to my feet, bit her right tit and took my twenty.

"You are off the chain!"

"Eye know," Eye said, taking another $20 from her hand and kissed her cheek, dancing off to a white woman. She snapped and bobbed her head, so off cadence. She was all over the beat, her jerky body overshadowing the song (a few females wee pointing and laughing at her).

"Eye offer dance lessons," Eye told her, kissing her hand and grinding my hard on all over her.

"How much do you charge?"

Eye threw it out there. "$500."

"Are you good?" she asked and Eye took her hand and pulled her on the stage. She watched me pop my booty cheeks up to the stairs. Eye picked her up, put her "stuff" in my face (her legs dangling over my shoulders) and Eye twirled all the way to the floor with my tongue was deep inside her vaginal walls. Damn white girl. Now Eye saw why Niggahs propositioned you. But that's where it stopped. Black don't crack. Eye brought both arms behind her and gently lay her on the stage. Women were taking off their panties and throwing them on stage, and money, too. Eye am a money magnet. Money loves me. Eye inhaled 35 types of coochie. Eye smelled each pair…running my tongue over the parts without the smell. Eye wasn't crazy, but they didn't know that. Eye didn't know these pussies from Adams and Eves and Steves and Brians, too. Hygeine was a must! Women were screaming vulgarities when Eye picked up their respective panties.

Andy was in shock, laughing with the Boys.

They turned on some Jodeci. Grooving to *Come and talk to me.* She shuddered and Eye ate with more finesse. Never ate a white woman, she smelled different from black elegance. Her nipples hardened, she said she had to cum and Eye jumped up to my feet, whisked her off the ground, bent her over and spanked her like she's been bad.

No orgasms on my time baby. "That'll be $500!"

"Here baby!" she threw a cloud of one hundred dollar bills in the air and Eye collected them all. By the time Eye was done, and the Boys collected my cash, Eye made over $2,400 just that fast. Andy was thrilled. After the club closed all the Boys met up in the main assembly. Andy was glowing, the Boys giggling like school kids.

"Andy! *Wassup*, man? *Why are* you smiling like that?" Eye asked, sweating, trying to catch my breath.

"*Goddamn*, Black Magik! Do you know how much he made?"

"Naw," said Cederick, jealous of the attention Eye was getting. He was the number one money maker. He had a reputation for making money and slinging big time cock. He was Miami-Dade County's go to guy when your husband or boyfriend stopped touching you. He charged $300 an hour and rumor had it he was worth $900 an hour with his tongue and cheek skills. He made women skeet all over the place with his twelve inch Python. Andy pat my back.

"Eye knew you'd blow 'em away!" he gushed.

"How much he make?" asked Jabari, curious.

"Twenty-four hundred dollars," Andy said. Looks of shock went around the room till Cedrick's mouth fell open. "No one has ever made that much money on their first night. Hell, he made more than Cederick and he's the money maker. There's a new sheriff in town," Andy said and we all celebrated. Till Cederick snatched me by the neck and pushed me against the wall. His body was pressed up against mine.

"Let's get something straight! This was just a *trial* run! You don't even have what it takes to strip with us you stupid bitch!" Andy tried to grab him and Cederick pushed him away, turning back to me.

"Man, what did Eye do to you? You're the one who suggested Eye strip so Eye could pay off student loans!"

"Eye am the main attraction in this part of town," he snapped, scowling, snarling in my face. "This is my stomping grounds. The only brothah stomp the yard up in here is me." Eye kneed him in the balls and pushed him till he ran backwards then Eye punched him right in the center of his forehead and everybody gasped.

"You listen, *bitch!* You must not be all that if on my first night, Eye'm sorry on my trial run—did Eye say Yesterday's News correctly, Sir?—Eye broke *your* peak. Just like a brothah to hate instead of congratulate. We all got bills to pay. There's room for everybody at the top. Did Eye ask for a manicure? Did Eye ask for a pedicure? No, then why the hell you pushed me up against the wall. You like me or something?"

"You talk a good game," he said, running up on me, punching me in the face and Eye did a full circle and gave the late bitch a fist to the nose. Screaming, he fell backward and Anthony tried to grab me and Eye punched him over the table and now Eye was frightened and when Eye was scared Eye fought as if my life depended on it and Eye was afraid of death so there ya go. Andy got in front of me with his hands up.

"BOTH OF YOU!" He glared at Cederick. He's huffing and puffing, Anthony was holding him. He calmed down, but not much. "STOP FIGHTING! We a muthafucking team up in this muthafuckah, you hear me?"

"Forget *him*!" Eye screamed, storming out. "Eye quit! Ya'll got me fucked up!"

"Bring your ass back here, Pharoah!"

Eye turned to face him. "Go fuck yourself." And Eye glared at Cederick. "There you go coochie boy. Your *coochie* hot on the block again Eye resign, bitch!"

And walked out.

## THE RI$E OF THE LU$TFUL BEA$T

*When Eye got home Eye* was steaming like mixed vegetables simmering on number 2. Eye'd calmed down, but it still *bothered* me. Eye went in my room and closed the door, realizing Eye didn't get my money. Eye picked up the phone and called Andy. He answered. "Where are you, Pharoah?"

"Home."

"What the fuck you mean you're home and there's *money* to be made out here tonight, *brothah.*"

"Eye'm good. Look, Eye want my money."

"Come and get it. My house. In thirty minutes. Eye got a bone to pick with you. And when we're done you won't blink straight muthafuckah."

He hung up.

# Day 6

*What the fuck was that supposed* to mean? Eye wouldn't *blink* straight? Eye swore. Brothahs listened to too much Tupac these days. Just because you knew the words to *Thug Niggahz till we Die* didn't mean you were a stone cold gangster. So why was Andy *tripping*? Do Eye love the brothah? Hell yea. Eye loved him because he could stroke it for me, and does it quite well. And that's all the love Eye needed because nobody ever loved me in my life. Eye gotta get love in any form Eye could get it. And sex was the solution to this problem. When Eye got to Andy's house the front door was open. It reminded me of my Mother. When Eye was late beating the sun home once. She had the front door wide open. Or if Eye did something bad. The front door was open when Eye got home. Threshold awaiting me, the floors awaiting the invisible footprints Eye left trekking to my bedroom. But Eye never made it there.

"PHAROAH BRING YOUR ASS HERE RIGHT NOW!"

Oh, shit. Eye thought of this approaching Andy's door.

He reminded me of Mama. And that scared me into a block of ice in an ice tray. Stuffed in the back of the freezer. Forgotten about. Never given a second thought.

Eye went to Mama, *shivering*, because Eye always got my butt whipped when that front door was open…awaiting me to get home.

"Pull e'm down!" he demanded, referring to my pants.

"Mama, what did Eye do?" Eye asked, refusing.

Eye walked in the house and he took a swig of liquor, threw it against the wall and stomped up to me. Andy was Mama, and she said, "Pull the pants down and lay on the bed. Didn't Eye tell you not to go outside when Eye'm at work?"

"But Eye didn't go outside, Mama!" Eye lied, my eyes wide. Bracing myself.

"Yes you did! My co worker told me! She said she came home and you were outside throwing a ball against the wall with the other kids."

Whack.

"Mama! Eye'm sorry!"

Whack.

Andy grabbed me by the neck. "Aren't you my bitch?"

"Yes, Andy," Eye said, appeasing him and he slapped me across the face with his open hand.

"Next time Eye tell you to do something you do it!" Mama said, storming outta the room…when it *dawned* on me that Andy just said the same thing. Eye shuddered. His dangerous eyes tore through my frightened stare.

"Ok, Andy."

"You think you grown, huh? Do what you wanna do? Eye'm 35 years the fuck old. You're 19. You do what you're told."

He punched me so hard in the stomach Eye doubled over. He walked up on me, drunk as hell, staggering instead of showing that manly swagger. He took off his belt. "You quit, bitch?"

"Hell yea! Eye'm not going back to that…"

He started whipping me with the thick leather belt. It had little metal clumps all over it. It hurt. Eye had a flash back of my ex step father beating me, savagely. *You won't tell anybody you hear?! Ah. There was Lily. She wanted e in the field again. Beating me with extension cords to eat her Nookie…*POW!—Andy beats me, savagely. In defense, Eye raised my hands over my face and he said, "You will do what Eye say. Make that muthafucking money. You will be back to the club tomorrow 8 p.m. sharp bitch!"

And he kicked me in my side.

"YOU HEAR ME, BITCH?"

"Yes!"

*Eye was in so much pain Eye* couldn't move or scream. My wail of discomfort was distorted by my pause in breathing. Wide eyed and scared, Eye lost myself. Eye would do anything he said. But please, please…

Don't beat me.

*Eye was nervous about going* out, stripping off my clothes before a SOLD OUT crowd. He picked tonight of all nights for me to go out and debut my hot, young sexy body to a room filled with divorced women just discovering the Power of the Dick again.

That divorcee who cried for months, days, hours, seconds, minutes and trimesters, swearing on God and swearing off men with slight hints of lesbianism…

Those were the types of women in the crowd tonight. Rediscovering their roots, remembering what their fathers taught them and what Mama couldn't suck from a stiff pole with chapped lips and thick red lipstick. There wasn't a dry scalp woman in the house. Hair dos on target, hitting the bull's-eye with their pricey outfits. Eye smelled 60 types of coochie in the air from where Eye stood behind the closed

**BLACK CURTAIN.**

*Eye inhaled deeply, my* erection driving me crazy. Eye was bisexual, yes—but Eye loved coochie. Smiling, Eye inhaled again, pulling out my package as the announcer shushed the crowd. Closing my eyes, Eye spat on my hand, getting itwet and Eye bent slightly at the knees, jacking off and it felt so good Eye screamed out and shushes filled the room. But Eye didn't care nor notice. Might as well relieve myself; get this first one out the way. Cum right on the stage, before the curtain opens on my mobile body with slick hands stealing my clothes from one section of my body at a time.

Eye felt a *breeze* and Eye moaned, *"Oooohh!"* My scrotum felt rejuvenated, swinging through the cool breeze that *swet* my body like global praise. All that was going through my mind was *What if the crowd of divorcee hoes didn't like my performance. What would Eye do? Save face and run the how? Or grab my balls and run off the stage amidst boo's and tomatoes.*

*No time for that now.* Eye was so lost within myself that Eye found myself and the only thing Eye wound up finding was my lost butt *trapped* in a labyrinth of problems. Eye convinced myself that Eye found myself and the only thing Eye found myself doing was making divorcee coochie wet for the dollar with good sex on my brain and my body quivering for it, yet Eye was hard for a female with good coochie. That was one messed up situation to be in. But Eye'm from Goulds. Eye handled it. It's *nothing*.

Eye repeatedly spat in my hand, moistening my scrumptious, throbbing member. Felt the pulse of my balls deep in my toes, overwhelming my brain and my heartbeat became sufficient yet irregular. Eye needed the money to pay off my college loans because *Mama* wasn't helping (or willing to help) me pay for anything. Talking about she got other kids to raise. So *forget* it. Gotta hustle, get it on my own.

Plus Eye could get this financial aid Cuban off my back. Summoning me to the office every week harassing me to pay for classes. Goddamn…*Castro* did it to you; *not* me.

Eye briefly stopped stroking myself and slowly opened my eyes and looked at myself in the mirror. Frowning at what appeared before me. Eye hated that Brothah trapped behind the glass, looking like me, a spitting image.

*What are you lookin' at, late bitch?*

*You're ugly! At least Eye ain't no stripper!*

*Whatever, late trick. You're my reflection.*

*Yup. And when you strip, Eye won't be yours!*

*Piss off!*

*You first!*

Before the mirror Eye stood, sombrero pulled low above my saddened, painful eyes. It hurt to look at myself, staring at what Eye had become and what Eye continuously become daily, when the sun rise. My body's oiled to a shine. Nuts gleaming under silky black elephant trunk thongs. Had to stuff those moderate-sized things back in silk. Leather pants grip my legs and ass like so, but nothing too tight.

The other strippers, before walking out to this closed curtain, were behind me in the dressing room getting rid of the scary butterflies/dragonflies in my stomach. Eye threw up three times before coming out from nervousness. The 5 strippers were my moral support system.

Andy winked at me from the stage. Eye winked back.

You can do it.

Eye pulled out my penis and started beating off again, trying to boost my adrenaline. The crowd roared and Eye smiled.

It was then Eye realized the curtain was already open.

A sea of money flapping from sweaty palms.

Eye kept jacking as slow music came on, narrowing my eyes at all the Hoes through the reflection of myself, yet my eyes didn't focus on that reflection. Eye choose to focus on the feeling of beating off and getting caught.

May the best man win. Eye came on the floor without a sound, holding it all in as my toes curled in my thigh high leather boots. Eye turned to the microphone, women screaming out all kinds of nasty things. Do it to *me. Eat me, you sexy skinny Brothah. You got a big thang! Let me and me girls get some.* Eye winked, ignoring childish pleas of desire and licked my nut from my fingers with a smack, winking at a fat woman at the fifth table from the right of the stage. Eye walked seductively to the microphone and paused, looking it over, popping my ass to the floor. Jodeci sang, *"Eye wanna get you swea-tay!"*

The women went nuts. A few women jumped on the table, swinging their bras in the air like a helicopter. All Eye saw were women alerting me, telling me wordlessly to cum get that money. *That* could wait. When you made money wait that was called investing in time, seeing what their money would do for you. Some bitches upped dollars to seduce you to their table, so the stock in my mental frame of mind took a much needed leap towards future earnings to put in my bank account.

Rule number one of business: never let a bitch with money know you're desperate. Look at their dollars like shit, wink and go get another bitch's money.

Eye popped my romp on the floor and slowly did the snake back up to my feet, my tongue sliding along the microphone stand, my forehead lowered and my eyes staring at the ceiling.

Gyrating, as Eye used both hands to jack the stand like my dick. Wanting that nut from the base. Utilize me, beat.

Eye looked to the left, winked, popped my romp, thrust myself forward, the trunk of the elephant thongs bouncing with a purpose. A skinny woman ran towards the stage with a hundred dollar bill and begged to slide it in my thongs. Eye held up a finger, tilting my head. No, no, no, no. That's not enough. Eye got cock strong dick. Eye'm not those Brothahs you won over waving a hundred dollar bill Eye may not get.

She pulled out another hundred and Eye fingered her to the stage. She ran up the stairs, tripping over clumsy footing. Eye wrapped my arms around her, lowered her to the floor, kissed her vinyl-clad coochie and stood up, taking both bills into my hands. Eye thrust my pelvis forward, bumping the bitch off the stage. The crowd stood, laughing and cheering. My nipples erect, Eye stroked myself, narrowing my eyes and a Barry White song came on. *Eye wanna do it Good to ya.*

Eye worked the room, lowering towards the floor, putting a boot clad foot up on a chair, balls in a Hoe's face, and rubbed her head as she started licking the sweat from my asshole. She skipped my exposed anatomy, and Eye realized with a jolt she was actually a tranny bitch. Chick with a dick. Eye got $20 out of her and some smoking head. She sucked my booty till my toes curled, and that's when Eye bumped my ass cheeks in her/his face and danced a few tables over, and climbed on top of it with he/she's spit drying on my hole. Doing my little dance, taking the hat and popping down Doo Doo Brown style *YEE HA!* and putting the sombrero on another thick woman's head. Eye targeted all big girls. Because the light skinned Hoes thought they were all that; bitch my dick and coochie better than yours, Hoe act like you know.

They were steaming, too, because Eye knew bitches hated to be ignored and talked so much they'd rather be heard and Eye wasn't a patient ass Brothah today and Eye could care less about coochie right now when money ruled me and my mind and all Eye wanted for compensation was my goddamn money and see ya' later, Honey! So a few of them waved their cash in the air, half-assed snapping and really wasn't feeling the beat and Eye danced right past their asses and didn't as much as fart on the bitches.

They're ducking behind their cash, lowering their heads and asses back in their seats. Eye turned to face the stage and Eye saw cash all over it. Glistening under neon lights. Money looked different with this kinda lighting, seeing shit Eye never thought eyed see. Hypnotized, Eye danced up to the stage, wanting more money. Now Eye'm being greedy. Instead of getting in and getting out, Eye wanted to rule…so Eye danced like Eye was giving a free concert. Janet Jackson music playing and Eye realized Andy put on Janet's *Throb* and Eye did the entire routine she did on Saturday Night Live, and got not only a standing ovation when Eye was done. But Eye turned and lay on my back, sweaty body clinging to the stage's money. Ain't mine yet till Eye pick it up. Eye closed my eyes and inhale as deeply as Eye can. Then Eye exhaled. Phew!

*By the time the club cleared,* Eye was in one of the back rooms, laying down on the huge black and green sofa. Having showered, my body was still drained and Eye counted $1,765 dollars in cash. For a thirty minute strip/dance show. Andy was looking at me, looking flawless in his suit. He always looked flawless. Blow dried his hair like a female and even awakened in the mornings refreshed. Hair always in place, even when he slept. But he was far from a bitch. Oh, no. Nothing about Andy spelled B-I-T-C-H…It wasn't in his walk, sex skills, head game nor his talk. He was one of the strongest, toughest, most troubled men Eye would ever know.

When a man puts the fear of God in your heart then he has you. He has you mentally, physically and spiritually because Eye dissed church, fell out of the church and made him my entire universe. In my heart was a shrine for him, and he became the very breath that kept me alive.

Only Eye didn't realize this. Eye told people Eye loved God, yet never told them that at the time Andy was my God. Eye worshipped the very grounds he walked on, and Jehovah wasn't pleased. He showed me many troubled signs of bad things to come in my life through my dreams, but Eye would never write them down, never really cared about the revelation and still had Andy's breakfast, lunch and dinner piping hot. He fucked who he wanted when he wanted and Eye didn't care. Eye was the young 19 year old fascinated with an older man that had it all. Money, clothes, dick, hoes, houses, cars, and a host of strip clubs. He was my Messiah

And that's when my world started to plummet. At the seams. When he brutally *beat* me after telling him Eye fell in love with him. He screwed and beat me so badly sometimes Eye couldn't move. And Eye thought it was love. Eye thought Eye had to stay with him to prove that loyalty, take him as he was, never trying to change a man who couldn't even save or change himself; so Eye became his savior.

Anything Eye wanted Eye had. Access to everything, but he monitored it closely. Anything appeared out of synch within his limitations he beat me like a hooker at the Special Olympics. He looked at me lying comfortably on the huge sofa and he lit a cigarillo, clapping. He smiled that boyish grin that set me ablaze with trepidation and pleasure. Eye felt its pulse in the base of my asshole set off by the pundits of my throbbing member labeled "Dick."

"Eye really enjoyed your performance, baby."

Eye was glowing. "Thank you."

"You got all the strippers mad."

"Why?"

"Their regular patrons have switched to Pharoah. They have lost money."

"Eye didn't want to do that."

"You're the baddest Niggah on the *roster.* Who knew you could dance with such elegance. You were nasty, raunchy yet classy and one of a kind. The way your body moves hypnotizes me and all Eye could think about while you made 60 types of pussies wet was my ten inch cut Puerto Rican/ Jamaican *stick* deep inside you."

He got on one knee and Eye gasped from the sincerity of his eyes. Yet Eye knew well enough to brace myself because the sincerity of the eyes betrayed the tone of a shaken, angry voice. He did his best to dress Shaken Angry Voice in winter clothes when Halloween had yet to debut. But Eye played it off, and smiled anyway, counting my money.

"You love money, Pharoah?"

"No. Eye don't."

"Then why do you count it over and over?" He was stroking my booty hole, looking deeply into my eyes and Eye still didn't look away from the money Eye earned through appropriate entertainment. Remember this was a strip club. What Eye did was appropriate for the horny just-discovering-their-pussies divorcees that, hours ago, occupied every possible seat, even the seats and stools at the bar.

"Eye love what it could do for me. But Eye'm certainly not attached to it, Andy."

He rubbed my scalp with carefully executed fingers through my high top fade. Felt so good.

"How much did you make?"

"Well over a thousand. Again!"

"Well over?"

"Yes."

"No one has made that much money his opening day or trial run!"

"Eye'm not everyone else. Certainly not Cederick."

"Most *certainly* Cederick. He had the highest opening trial run and debut. You doubled that. He's extremely pissed."

"And you're telling me because?"

"Eye thought you should know. All the strippers support you. Except Cederick, he's your arch nemesis and he wants your head. He already attacked you once."

"Eye barely know him."

"But he was the one that introduced you to this Club. Hell he introduced you to me. When he brought you, before Eye found out we go to the same college, he told me to give you a chance."

"Eye don't owe him anything. Just because he introduced me into the game doesn't mean he dictate my rules. Eye set rules to govern myself following my own authority. Not yours." He snatched my money and grabbed me by the throat, shoving it deep inside my mouth. His eyes fire engine red, Eye shook with fear.

"You watch how you talk to me. You're my bitch. Eye run you!" He spit in my face and Eye frowned.

"You do what Eye say? Listen. You can't just come in here, claiming *anything*; taking over like you put in all the hard work to make this place what it's retained in profits. Cederick is a major asset to this club."

Eye spit the money out of my mouth and looked him deeply in the eyes. "And now Eye'm gonna take it further than that. Nobody wants his washed up ass. And why are you defending Cederick. Don't tell me you used to bone him."

"As a matter of fact yes Eye did. He's still one of my bitches. Does what the hell Eye want."

"What?" Eye was in shock at his bluntness.

"You heard me. You better do as Eye say. Your Mama already wants to throw you out and you have no life. You'll die without her support."

Eye was quiet because he was right.

"Eye'm keeping your money," he said.

"Eye earned that money! Eye have to pay off college loans."

"FUCK COLLEGE!" he screamed.

Eye grew quiet.

"Eye don't even want to go there. But Eye have to. My parents are very controlling. Well, my mother is at least. My father…"

"Your father what?" Eye asked.

He released my neck. "Can rot in hell."

# DOME$TIC VI☯LENCE

Eight months of domestic violence Eye had to endure. The man Eye was in love with has flipped the script and controlled everything about me. Eye had to cut off family *and* friends. So instead of turning my back on them (Eye loved them too much) Eye just stopped calling, hanging out with them and going around. Eye could hardly spend time with family. He was jealous of them all. So Eye stopped being home as much and spent all my time with Andy and he was always at the club so Eye had to be with him. Couldn't even go to the bathroom by myself or the store. One of his goons had to be with me. And they told him everything and Eye hated them for it.

Andy believed anything they said. So since Eye was at the club early he worked me more than the other strippers. Eye made them a lot of money and Eye hardly got $600. Andy would eat cocaine off my ass after beating my ass if Eye didn't cook right or if his house was half assed cleaned or if Eye didn't iron his clothes, have his books out for college *or* if Eye sassed him.

One night he beat my ass because Eye wouldn't suck and fuck his friends. He smacked me and beat me with the belt with metal clumps…And, laughing, each one of them took turns raping me and left me on the floor till Eye fell asleep. Eye had never screamed for Mama to help me so loud in my life. Only thing was…she didn't hear me.

Weeks of stripping would go by and Andy had better ideas. Seemed a few on the low brothahs came to see me strip bringing their sisters or female friends. Mutual acquaintances, business associates. Andy set it all up and he told me Eye didn't have a choice. So Eye did what he said.

Escorting. Making top dollar doing sexual services for thirty and forty year olds and Andy got the money and Eye never saw a dime. For over a month Eye loved em long time, me so horny. Lost within the incarceration of my flesh. Lost who Eye was gradually becoming another part of myself that was…born. After a few more weeks of escorting Eye decided Eye'd had enough of Andy. There was an annual award show coming up where clubs across the state sent in their best strippers for Best Body, Best Dancer and Biggest Money Maker for Awards. Andy told me all the Boys had to be there. It was going to be held at a very expensive hotel.

And it was. A hotel on South Beach. On a hot, humid Friday night. 8 p.m. Eye was clad in a white suit and fresh hair cut, miserably sitting by Andy. If Eye wanted something to drink Eye couldn't even get up and walk across the room. So Andy made Cederick get it and his ugly ass laughed under his breath, enjoying every moment. When was he going to get it? He was serving me! I didn't have to move to get a drink, Lurch! All Eye had to do was sit here and be the cute Niggah Eye was. Umm Cederick…Eye'm done, Eye want another drink. What? Andy, Cederick said he isn't…oh, okay—thought so. When he brought me the red wine…he handed it to me…when my enclosing fingers grasped the stem of the flute glass Cederick released it, saying "Oh, shit, *dawg*. Eye'm so sorry," and red wine spilt in my white suit coat and Eye didn't jump back or flinch. Eye smiled, laughed and said, "This white suit was tired anyway. It needed some color."

And everyone started laughing, and Eye was clapping and laughing too. Stood my sexy ass up in a ruined white five hundred dollar suit and raised my hand towards Cederick, who was clearly embarrassed his plan failed. "And Cederick, the wonderful director!" Eye said sarcastically, and people cheering and applauding and Eye sat down, crossed my legs in a masculine way of course and looked at Andy and said, "Eye'm getting tired of your groupie bitches."

And fell into a bitter silence.

***The awards ceremony*** started and the room was jam-packed. About 600 guests were there dressed nicely in a suit. Strippers from all over Florida (Tampa, Jacksonville,

Orlando...) were in the place and Eye was stunned that this kinda stuff went on. Some buff Brothah won for Sexiest Body and some in the closet looking five foot midget-ass-goon-wanna-be-Brothah won for Best Dancer. A tall, scrawny, buff white boy won for Rookie of the Year and a Jamaican man with long dreads and a huge penis won for Overall Entertainer. The Biggest Money Maker category was being announced, and they didn't call out any names as nominees. Then it dawned on me they didn't call out nominees in the first place. They announced the category and called out the winner.

The emcee, as handsome and hot as he was, grinned at the podium and said, "And The Biggest Money Maker goes to Pharoah Wilson."

*What* the...? Some folks clapped and others whistled. Cederick's mouth was wide open in shock, and as Eye walked to the podium to get a gift wrapped box Cederick pushed me into the podium, and jumped on top of me.

"You *muthafuckah*! That was supposed to be my award."

He punched me repeatedly in the face and Eye was growing weaker.

Andy threw Cederick off me and helped me to my feet.

The room was silenced. "You know what, dawg. Keep that award you want it that bad," Eye said, taking the box and opening it. "Let's see what you won, bitch."

Eye pulled out a huge black dildo, filled with jelly and Eye slapped him with it and he fell on his back. "What the fuck? Is this some kinda joke? Who gave me a dildo as the prize? Eye thought it was supposed to be an award."

"It was," said the emcee. "It was supposed to be $1,000 and a trophy. Looks like the trophy was broken and stuffed in the box with the dildo, bruh."

He pointed at the trophy on the ground, in the box.

And the $1,000. Gone.

*When Eye got to Andy's* house Eye stormed in the room and opened drawers...taking my shit out. Eye'd had enough. This has gone on long enough. It was time to wake up. Eye knew Eye was 20 years old now and Eye know its going on two years Eye've stripped for Andy and did this dumb bull crap.

"And what are you doing?"

Eye put my clothes on the bed, walked to his closet and grabbed my suit case.

"Eye'm gone."

"You're not leaving."

Eye glared at him. "Mess with me tonight, put your hands on me, *Andy* Eye swear Eye will gut your Hoe ass. Fuck with it," Eye said dangerously, meaning every single solitary word. He held up his hands. Strangely accommodating. "Let's talk about it, baby. Eye don't like to see you hurt."

"What?" Eye said, walking up to him. "What? You beat me! You abuse me all the time and Eye let you Because Eye'm used to the beatings. Eye went through four years of rape when Eye was little…do you *really* think you're hurting me?"

He was stunned. Don't act so stunned now, Brothah. "Oh my God, Pharaoh. Tell me you're lying?"

"*Forget* you!"

"Eye see it in your eyes that you're fed up. And for that Eye will never raise my hands to you again. Pharoah, damn man! Damn! My father raped me when Eye was seventeen years old. Because Eye quit football and turned my back on an all paid scholarship to Texas State."

Eye didn't give a fuck. But he kept talking. "Eye realized my family was clinging to me because Eye was going to be famous. So Eye quit. My daddy called me a bitch and fucked me like one in front of my Mama and she turned her back, rolling her eyes saying, 'You turn your back on possibly going to the Pros, we don't know you! Fuck you!' and she closed the door on my father stealing my joy and innocence."

Damn! "My God."

"So Eye know what that's like."

"Why are you telling me this?"

"Because Eye want to learn to heal."

"Do it without me. Cederick has embarrassed me for the last time. Something's going on that's deeper than me stepping on his cash cow's toes. There's something going on Eye'm not seeing, but Eye know its there."

"It's nothing, man. You're paranoid. Look, Eye love you baby. You complete me. Eye know Eye can act crazy sometimes, but Eye'm so afraid of losing you, Pharoah. You're my fantasy, don't you get it. Eye look at you and see perfection. You're gorgeous and Eye am in love; Eye am infatuated; and Eye am in lust. Eye can't keep my hands off you."

And he took me into his arms and tongue kissed me like it's the last time and he pulled off my pants and ate me out through my fruit of a looms and he massaged my cheeks while pulling my *drawers* to the left and he slowly, cautiously, lovingly slid up inside me—deep—till Eye felt the sting of passion. Eye tried to contain it but couldn't. Eye burst open…the river of ecstasy drowning, suffocating, vanishing, fumigating mu soul…we row with his Ore, deep stroking my colon. My prostate going mad.

He engulfed me, showering my face with gentle kisses. Releasing his being to make me stay.

"Please baby don't leave me baby. You gonna give another Brothah my ass, dawg? You said that's mine? You gonna break my heart like that?"

"Hell no, baby."

"You promise?"

"Eye promise, Daddy."

"Oh, you feel so good, *Brothah*! Eye'm going in deeper."

He pushed forward and his Temple filled me up and Eye paused, wide eyed, mouth wide open. "Don't run from it. Take it baby. Tell me you gonna stay while you take this ten inch pipe."

By the time he was done, Eye was in the laundry room glowing, throwing his dirty clothes in the wash.

Then Eye put him a TV dinner in the microwave.

And took him a beer.

*Being with my manager*/boyfriend was an abusive time for me. This man was everything Eye ever wanted in a lover. In the beginning, he did everything by the book a lover should do in a relationship. He got to know me inside and out, learned my favorite color, how Eye liked my eggs, what size underwear Eye wore, my shoe size. In return Eye learned everything about him. His upbringing and where he came from. His life and passion. His failures and successes. We didn't have sex a lot the first few months we were together. We used to lay holding each other, talking into the night about life, our goals and dreams and our fears.

Everything was perfect. Picture perfect without flaws spells T-O-O- P-E-R-F-E-C-T. He never saw a flaw in anything Eye did, always agreed with me, cooked for me, cleaned behind me and wouldn't let me lift a finger to do anything for myself. When Eye was on stage stripping he cheered me on, bought me food, took me out and started ignoring the other dancers and they had it out for me. Before Eye came Andy and the stripper boys had sex with women together (for a pricey fee—there was even a booking fee…), hung out around town every weekend and ate out together. Since Eye been in the picture Andy was totally engrossed in me, and Eye loved it. Eye never asked him to cut off his friends and when Eye told him he should hang out with them he accused me of trying to talk to another Brothah so Eye dismissed the request and forgot about it.

Everything was kosher. Till the day Eye fell in love.

*Our fifth month in a heavy* relationship Eye awakened one morning and *realized* Eye was madly in love with Andy and that there wasn't anything Eye wouldn't do for him. Stripping brought me in some major cash and Eye gave it to my baby and he put it up for me because Eye was terrible saving money. Eye smiled, brushing my teeth, my dick hard. Eye turned on the stereo, and Patti Labelle was singing *The Right Kinda Lover*…so Eye jammed a little bit, because Eye loved Miss Patsy and Eye washed my face, took a piss and flushed.

Eye danced all the way to the house phone and called Andy. He answered on the first ring.

"Hey, baby."

"Hey, Pharoah. What you doing up so early?"

"School, remember?"

"Oh, yea. College."

"Ha. Don't sound so convincing."

"What are you up to, baby?"

"...*Stroking* Spot with the naked eye. It misses you."

"Is that right?"

"Eye love making love to you. The way you moan in bed sets me on fire."

Eye was tingling all over. "So come pick me up."

"Eye'm on the way."

*He got to Mom's house* around 10 a.m. He called me and told me he was outside. Eye rushed out the door, telling everyone goodbye. When Eye got in the car he engulfed me, then gave me some tongue. Kissing him made me feel like floating on clouds. A possessive hand on my upper thigh, he backed onto SW 1**th Avenue, and made a left at the light onto Moody Drive. "How are you, baby?" he asked, winking at me with a boyish smile.

Eye blushed. "Eye'm still try'na wake up."

"How did you sleep?"

"Eye slept good."

"Did you dream about me?"

"Yea, Eye did."

"What did you dream about?" He asked, speeding past the small blinking light on the corner of Moody Drive and Allapattah, SW 112th Avenue.

"You."

Eye wasn't surprised. "Oh, yea?"

He winked at me. "Yea."

He turned into a clearing in the bushes, and drove up the dirt road towards a small bend.

He braked, turned off the car, pulled me to his lips and said, "Eye bet you didn't dream about this."

And we did the do for the next two hours.

Eye would get lost in this relationship, whatever it was. Eye took what Eye could get because of the self hatred Eye had for myself. Moving about God's green earth without guidance or acceptance. Daddy paid for my life with a bounced check because he wrote me off like a broad with wasted coochie and a flat chest. Nobody invested in wasted coochie so you banged a new bitch to see f you still "Got it." As long as the dick was good you still "Got it!" You could be the ugliest mofo in the world, learn to slang King Kong even Tarzan's tight little tushy gonna want some Donkey Kong. Eye needed that male companion for one reason: to have a *father* figure. Someone to be an aggressor, taking charge and telling me how to steer this ship called a Fuked Up Life.

Andy became my new drug of choice. What he said went. When he gave an order Eye carried it out to the hilt. He hated feisty Brothahs, and Eye was spicy. So to tame me he wrestled around with me, took my body and went up so deep inside me my eyes rolled to the back of my head as if in a trance, letting his nervous, anxious hands guide my spine.

We were together nearly two years. Eye stripped my life and clothes and self respect away like snake skin for nearly two years. Then Eye fell in love, or Eye thought Eye did. Eye realized Eye loved him when he was so deep inside me with his left hand gripping my neck tightly, but lovingly, and his right hand pushed down on the small of my back while he was digging tombs inside my Nefertiti.

When Eye said "Eye love you," he banged me harder, kissing the sweat from trembling lips. Lips smelling of male Nookie. We always ate coochie and screwed females before he screwed me, without washing the coochie from his lower body. So why wash my lips. Both sets of my lips smelled of good coochie. He was grinning, with tears forming in his eyes. "Really, baby? You love me?"

The slapping sounds hypnotized me and the power of his dick made his submissive lover. Yes, Eye'm in love with you, Daddy."

"Eye'm Daddy?" he asked breathlessly, grinding inside me; he pushed inside my flesh deeper, using both hands to bring the bottom of his totem pole to the bottom of my booty hole.

"Yesssss." He pressed my head to the pillow and raised my ass up a little higher and he thrust inside me long, hard and deep and when Eye had to nut he pulled out of me and beat my ass. He pushed me on the floor amidst my gentle orgasm, and he jumped on top of me, slapping me repeatedly in the face. The evil side of him rendered me speechless.

"If you love me you will do what Eye say, bitch! You will cater to me, cook my food, do what Eye say and the money you make stripping you aren't allowed to look at, smell or touch!" He jumped up, grabbed me by the high top fade and took off his belt and beat my ass so badly Eye was reverted back to that 6 year old kid, the one who was torn apart and raped, and all Eye saw was him, the Thing from my past, beating and conditioning me inside something only he understood.

Eye was paralyzed with fear and overcome with emotion as the tears fell. Eye raised my arms above my head, screaming out *please* and he gradually stopped, taking a look at me.

"Face me!"

Eye walked up to his face, trembling.

"Will you do what Eye say?"

"Yes, Daddy."

He smiled. "Good. Get on your knees and suck my _____. When you're done get ready for your stripping number tonight. Eye got just the thing Eye want you to do."

Eye obeyed.

## MAMA DEARE$T

*Out of the thousand plus* dollars Eye generated each night Eye stripped, he only gave me three hundred dollars. Kept the rest. Eye felt pimped, but Eye was madly in love with him. So in love Eye was willing to look past all his indifferences and love him for the realest he was. Eye was the submissive one and it was my job (as a Bottom) to make sure he was comfortable in our relationship. If he wanted to be the Man and run things (*spoiled* ass!)...then by all means, do so. He beats my ass to a pulp sometimes, and despite the blood loss my love for him shined strong as ever. Eye keep forgiving him because of what he suffered as a kid, and that enables the loyalty Eye have for him. He buys me things and takes me out on the town in matching suits and wines and dines me in public with so much sex appeal and masculinity people actually think we're brothers instead of lovers. Eye became so dependent on Andy Eye thought he was my heaven. Everything Eye did was a direct reflection of him. But then Eye woke the up when my perception of him shattered during an outing? We were together for almost two years when, one particular place we went to, unraveled the scheme. The restaurant had the heart of Italy in the main assembly. Beautiful tables with silk cloth, lacquered chairs and chandeliers so overwhelmingly breathtaking Eye nearly vomited from the climate change.

His mother was a political woman. She knew all sorts of people. Eye heard she was about to become a senator or *something* like that. Judging from the clientele eating from plates more expensive than my mother's house, this had to be true. Eye saw the purest, cleanest bottle of Hennessy Eye had ever saw in my life. Eye never knew vodka shined so expensively from the solitude of a clientele's flute glass.

Her diamonds glistened brighter than any star Eye ever saw in the sky and Eye got a chill every time she looked at me dine with her son.

Eye remembered how he looked at me. Like an unstable man trapped in a snow storm. Clearly lost within a realm notwithstanding his current ideology.

His eyes bulged out of his head. "Pharoah. My mother is here."

Eye rolled my eyes like, "Oh *no*, man. Eye don't know where to go." Eye was being very sarcastic.

"She spotted us. She's over there by the entrance."

"Eye gotta get out of here," Eye went on, stifling a yawn.

"Quick, get under the table."

Now my eyes bulged outta my head. "What? Do Eye look like a *freaking* carpet?"

"No, you look like shit. Get under the table."

"But people will see."

"Look around, dummy! Half of these people are drunk. Dressed in expensive garb and the gab fest of bullshit trickling into my ears was nothing short of lame. Get under the table, Brothah." Eye got under the table, and rests my head in his lap. Eye was *Mad! Mad! Mad!* Why are we pretending in front of his Mama? Eye held my breath when Eye heard the chair slide from the table. Oh, no. She saw me. What do Eye do?

*"Where is he?"* she asked viciously.

"Where is who, Mom?"

"Don't play games, Andy. Eye always knew you were gay."

"Eye'm not gay."

"Bull!" she sounded, looking around discreetly with a killer smile. Hair pulled into a tight bun with huge curls framing her face. "Yes you are. Eye never seen you with a woman, as fine as you are."

"Don't remind me, Mama."

"Where is he? Eye know Eye saw a man at this table."

"It was one of the waiters, mother. Eye told him Eye wasn't satisfied with my drink and he sat down and asked me what he could do to erase my slight unease."

"Well, the waiters here are very accommodating. Very polite. As they well should be. Our taxes employ these sonsofbitches. Never talk to the hired help. Your drink isn't to par you shout Eye want to see the manager, and you let your unease unfold on the one in charge. He orders waiters to serve the drinks. The waiter Eye'm sure had to…sneak you a free drink to pacify your…slight unease, Son."

That teed him off. Aw. He *teed* off. Poor thing. "Go to hell, ok. Bad enough you messed up my life."

"Eye messed up your life?"

Eye rolled my eyes, squeezing his upper thighs, trying to get him to calm down. They are in the middle of an expensive Italian restaurant, where none of the food and drinks has prices or pictures, talking about family stuff. Two blacks. Who gave two *damns* about their problems? With or without money blacks manage to cum up short.

"Yes, you did. Where's my *father*, mother?"

"Oh, God. And how old are you? He…fell off the face of the earth. And good ridden. He barely lasted ten minutes in the sack. Eye think we created you in a matter of minutes. When you screwed up that scholarship he…"

"Eye hate you."

"Eye'm your mother. Eye had you. You respect me."

Eye unzipped his pants and pulled out his huge pole in an expensive Italian restaurant. Living on the edge, move over Aerosmith! The muscles in his thighs and legs jerked. Eye know it hurt…"You don't respect me so why should Eye respect you?" he asked.

"Because you're the black sheep of the family."

"You walk, look and talk like a crackah and Eye'm the Black Sheep?"

"Eye resent that!"

His penis hung low like a vine. Eye started tonguing the swollen mushroom head, taking it deep into my salivating mouth, gripping his inches like the sternness of steel, holding my breath and taking it deep to the throat.

Oh, he calmed all the way down. He was twirling his hips slightly, yet keeping his composure. "Mom. Eye would like to be alone."

"You still haven't answered my question."

Eye was sucking as loud as Eye could, taking it from my mouth and spitting on it. Eye wasn't scared of the trick. And quite frankly Eye was getting tired of being under this table. Eye didn't even take this shit over the phone. He tapped my head, yet his other hand was pushing my mouth up and down on him. Oh he felt it all right. The tops of his toes seemed to mobilize. Eye realized then he was curling his toes in his shiny loafers. "What is that noise?" she asked.

He looked disgruntled. "What noise?" He held up his hands. "Eye don't hear anything."

"What is that on your hand?"

"What?"

"Looks like saliva. Oh my God!"

She stood up and looked under the table.

"Oh my God! *Sissy!* Sucking my son's dick under the table?"

Eye used the back of my arm to wipe spit from my mouth. Glad Eye was wearing a black suit. Hid all my business. Eye got from under the table. Eye didn't give a shit. What were they gonna do? Beat my skinny ass. Eye wish a bitch would today. Eye said, "Eye dropped my earring on the floor." Eye held it up. "See, you nasty bitch."

"Pharoah! That's my mother!" Andy sounded and actually sounded dumb as hell. Didn't stand up to your mother but trying to publicly stand up for her against the strength of my tongue? Chile. *General Hospital* is down the street, on Channel 10.

Eye looked at him. "She's talks to you like you're the bitch yet Eye gotta respect the bitch? Eye heard everything she said to you." Eye faced her. "You need your ugly ass whipped."

"Are you going to do it?"

"Eye would. But Eye let women handle my light weight. Eye don't hit women, but Eye damn sure do curse them the out, bitch. What kinda mother are you?"

"*You're* the faggot!"

"*Eye'm* the faggot? That ain't what Eye heard, you dickless trick."

Andy's mouth fell open. "Pharoah! Shut up! Bitch SHUT UP!"

"Eye'ma bitch and your Mama snatching your wig in a restaurant? Didn't she walk out on your daddy raping you over a goddamn football scholarship?" Both of them turned white in the face. "Fuck you, Andy. We're so over and through. Eye'm not committing to a man who lets his mother pull his cock ring. Are you crazy? Eye actually let you beat me?"

"You can't leave me!" he said, his mother looking on in shame.

"And you said you were displeased with a goddamn drink!" she boasted. "*You* said a waiter was sitting at the table with your slight uneasy ass. And you were lying! All to cover up this bull. Eye denounce you as a son!"

"Mama!"

"Eye heard his daddy was a punk!" Eye said, crossing my arms across my chest. Now what, bitch. Explain it. Eye'm listening. As well as everyone else in the establishment serving lukewarm food. Everyone fell silent. She covered her mouth, stunned. Tears formed in her eyes and Eye picked up a glass of water and dumped it on her ass.

"Cool off, bitch. Eye heard he was gay. You walked in on him *banging* your brother, you know…the one you moved away from and abandoned. The one you left to die in the ghetto while you lunch with moneyed muthafuckahs. Yet your son is the black sheep. God or bad he's your goddamn brother. And everything you achieved outside of him his ass came into your bed behind your back and destroyed. Andy told me your husband, his daddy banged your brother better than he ever stroked *you.*"

"GO TO HELL! What is this nonsense, Andy? Are you going to allow this?"

"Andy doesn't have a choice." Eye looked at him. "We're done with. Forever. Hear me. Go fuck your *Mama.* She's been butt-poking you for years, didn't you tell me that, Andy?"

"What?"

"Eye'm gone. Eye'm outta here. Eye quit all that stripping bullshit, too. Eye made the money, *keep* the change."

And Eye spun on my heel and walked towards the EXIT. "Your penis tasted like shit!" And the doors closed behind me. And *complete* pandemonium.

*Eye took a cab to his house.* When Eye got there Eye pulled out my suit cases and started packing my things once and for all. Fuck that Boy that Cried Wolf crap. This Niggah name Pharoah (ya'll know him, he cool as fuck) was getting outta dodge and wasn't gonna look back. Eye was devastated. Because Eye loved a man who emotionally embarrassed me. Eye was in love with an image. Eye was in love with the seeds of his success. Eye wanted to be his so Eye could show off and he was beating me for showing off.

Eye was reflecting another man's picture of perseverance, neglecting my own blemishing soul, overlooking my own blessings. Huge tears burned the epidermis of my face. Opening and closing drawers, packing my clothes. Eye didn't know how Eye was going to get all this shit to Mama's house. If she lets me come back.

Andy bought me all this stuff, letting me keep the bags. Now the baggage was suffocating me and Eye was too weak to carry simply just one. Andy's phone rang endlessly, but Eye didn't answer it. For what? Reflections couldn't talk so Eye'll just keep quiet and quietly pack my items. Eye had over $5,000 in cash in a small wooden box with a lock. Eye pocketed the key and put the box in my book bag.

Eye went into the bathroom and stared myself in the mirror. Looking flawless, yet my heart looked terrible. Eye didn't know who that Brothah was looking at me from the reflection, when Eye'm still reflecting Andy's failures and passing them off as my own.

What kind of man was Eye? Eye was the man Daddy wanted me to be. A failed mutha-shut-yo'-mouff. That's why his ass abandoned me. Didn't show or teach me a thing. Now Eye couldn't stand up and be a man.

Eye didn't know how to. No one ever showed me how. Eye ran cold water over my face, crying so hard Eye lowered myself to my knees, covering my face. Shaken. Destroyed. Devastated, Eye looked up and leaned against the wall. Less energetic, and properly silenced. Eye managed to stand up and turn off the cold and hot water knobs. They twisted silently. Eye walked out into the bedroom, staring at my feet. A zombie of my own design, the design influenced by Andy. We all draw tings into, yet others influence the outcome. Eye looked up and came face to face with Andy. Holding a Beretta.

Aimed at my chest.

# THE ANGER OF THE BEA$T

♋

*He was distraught. The look becomes* him really well. My breath caught in my throat, Eye stood firm and still. Guns scared me half to death. Eye tired to hide that fear from my face but my cheekbones were weak sonsofbitches and weren't built to hold a single tear. No matter how you squint when you force one. "Eye can't believe you pulled me and my father out of the closet in a restaurant Eye've dined for nearly 15 years."

"And you blame me?"

"*Yea* Eye blame you, Pharaoh. Eye blame you for everything that has gone wrong. Eye told you to hide under the table, not suck me up."

"Yet you didn't stop it."

"Eye wasn't supposed to."

"So you have to take part of the blame for what occurred with your overbearing mother."

"She's not overbearing! She loves hard. She loves her family."

"Any woman calling her son a faggot is one stupid bitch. Where do you think she learned it from?"

"Eye have a gun, bitch."

Eye held up my hands. "Eye can see that. But you can't blame me for your mother's accusation. She said she always knew you were gay. That means she clocked the flavor of your tea before you realized you drank tea, and that's my fault?"

"The things you repeated to my mother were things Eye told you in confidence."

"And Eye held you at that regard. Until you withered in public from her icy words."

"Eye always wanted to tell her just how Eye felt, yet Eye didn't have the courage."

"Because she loves hard? Because she loves her family, Andy?"

"Shut up!"

"Eye told your mother what you wanted to say. It nearly crippled her. She could hardly breathe through those dick sucking lips. Eye spoke your truth with my voice. It clearly opened her eyes. What happened when Eye left?"

"She said she disowned me. Yet when Eye walked past her and out of her life she grabbed my arm and told me we could go back to the family house and talk about it. That she already lost her husband to her brother, so she wasn't equipped to lose her son."

"A son made through a flawed union."

"Pharoah…"

"Your daddy was always gay, Andy. You told me that one day when you were drunk. You said your father told you he married your mother because his father, a Pastor, suspected him of being homosexual in the congregation. So that was a cover-up marriage, and you were the misled seed. Your only job in this life was to make him feel his manhood through his stern discipline, and nothing more. You're a Mascot for the Your Daddy is Gay Academy. He still chased dick, Andy. YOU TOLD ME THAT! He even raped you."

He shot a huge hole in the wall behind me, and Eye shut up.

"That's your problem. You don't know when to shut the fuck up. You went on and on, Pharaoh, telling my business. Making me face something Eye wasn't prepared to face. Eye don't want to lose my mother so Eye hid my lifestyle."

"Why are you protecting a woman who loves her status in government more than the welfare of her own adult son? Are you serious?"

"My father was an incredible man."

"Eye never said he was. And if he was Mr. Incredible, why did he treat you like shit, Andy?"

"He's a man. He was supposed to be hard on me."

"Andy. You once told me your Daddy beat you for saying a boy was cute when you were in the third grade. You said he stripped you naked, beat you with an extension cord, poured salt all over your body then pissed all over you. You told me that was the worst pain of your life."

"Pharaoh! Shut up!"

He put the gun in my face, pressing the barrel direct center of my forehead. Eye puked up so badly it got all over him and he didn't flinch.

"Eye'm gonna kill you, bitch. Eye've heard enough. Eye can't take you and that mouth any longer. You stepped all over my manhood."

"Oh, yea? Your Mama tap dancing on it, too. Shoot me bruh Eye don't care."

"You do care. You threw up all over me, bitch. Oh you care."

"You gonna kill me anyway, so Eye'ma say what the fuck Eye wanna say."

He slapped me across the face with the weapon, blood all over my teeth and lips. The pain gave me a dizzying head ache.

"Eye love you, Pharaoh. Eye'm not letting you leave. Eye just gotta beat your ass back in line. Eye told you. Eye rule you. You worship me. You do what ever the fuck Eye say." Eye shook my head. "Eye denounce you. Eye love no one. Eye don't even love myself. How can Eye be in love with you when Eye don't even love myself? Eye don't know what love is or what it looks like. Eye never have seen love. All Eye ever seen in my life is pain and pain disguised beautifully as love. Tricking me. My father left me. Mama picked a Brothah over me. Eye had a rough goddamn life, and you bitching over your daddy being gay?"

"Pharoah. Eye don't want you hurt. Eye gotta protect you, baby. Eye already lost my Daddy. Your remind me so much of him. You look just like him, Pharaoh. That's why Eye fell in love with you and Eye gotta control you. Eye am the man for you. Do what Eye say and we *won't* have any problems, Daddy. Eye wouldn't have to beat you and make you sell your ass."

"What?"

# DADDY, THE ILLU$ION

"*You hurt my mother. Marrying* her knowing you could never truly love her because you're gay. You love dick, just like *she* do. Why did Mama have to walk in on you screwing my uncle? Her own brother, Pharoah?"

"What are you talking about? Eye never even met your Daddy."

"Daddy stop lying. You always told me you were my King, you were the Pharoah of the house. Remember telling me that?"

"Andy? Eye'm not your father!"

"SHUT UP!" He rammed the back of my head into the wall.

Eye blinked rapidly, trying to hold my forehead. But Eye fell deeper into the blackness of his paranoia. Eye didn't know who Eye was at the moment.

"You will pay for what you did to us, Dad. You are a weak excuse of a man. You raped me, bum!"

He pressed the gun into my bloody mouth.

"Eye should shoot you right here." His eyes balls of hate. "Now Mama blames me for her flaws. She calls me what she called you. She blames me for everything that you did. Eye lost my mother because of you."

"Andy…"

"SHUT UP!"

"Eye thought you said you'd never intentionally hurt me, Andy."

He blinked twice and held his breath, taking the gun from my mouth. He started taking a few steps back, avoiding my eyes.

"Eye did say that."

"So you lied."

"Eye didn't lie.

"Yes you did! You beat me, cause me discomfort in my life. Make me do what you say. You don't do that to those you love."

"My Daddy did it to my Mother, Pharoah. Beat her ass and made her stay in the marriage. Made her represent the image of family. They were both in politics. She feared him so badly she did exactly what he wanted. Even watched him get fucked by other men in their bed duct taped to the chair."

"Andy, Eye hear you…"

"No you don't."

"Eye'm leaving you, Andy. Right now Eye don't care if you beat me or not. You're gonna be beating me all the way to the grave. Eye hate you. Eye don't want to be here. Eye'm not taking none of this shit with me. Just give me my book bag and let me go!"

"Eye'm not letting you go! Eye possess you. You are my possession, bitch!"

Eye started to walk past him, the gun fearing me no more and he pushed me on the bed and raped me on his sheets. No matter how Eye fought he beat me with the butt of his weapon and overpowered me. He came inside me so many times Eye lost count. Eye kept falling in and out of consciousness. He rode me like a wave rides the sea. Eye couldn't contain myself nor did Eye ever try. Eye was so weak inside Eye forgot what strength was. When he was done with my body he whipped me. My body jerked, yet Eye could hardly open my eyes nor move. Eye felt my skin tear. Eye felt the blood. He threw salt all over my body. The stinging made me scream. He stood in the bed and began to piss all over me, the wetness dissolved the salt into my open wounds and Eye yelled. *Nobody* heard me.

Nobody but Andy.

Eye blacked out. Eye don't know how long Eye've been unconscious, but Eye did know Eye was alive. Eye knew who Eye was. Eye was still here, but everything was so dark, Lord. What Eye've decided for my life has hindered me beyond understanding. Eye roam around the blackness, flinging my arms and connecting with nothing. Eye felt nothing. Eye was breathing, but Eye couldn't see a thing.

Eye started turn, tripping over myself yet nothing lines my darkened path. But Eye ran faster, sometimes falling flat on my face and Eye got up and kept running. Didn't bother to dust myself off. For what? Eye couldn't see a thing.

As Eye blinked against the darkness the bottom of my Eye lids pulled up brief pictures of light and objects. So Eye blinked faster and everything came into focus.

Andy was asleep next to me. An empty Vodka bottle and a small empty bottle of sleeping pills. He tried to sit up, but it was so hard. But Eye kept trying. Each time Eye moved my arms Eye got a little stronger than Eye was before so Eye moved my feet and my toes and Eye used my hands to sit up. My arms trembled with my legs.

My body felt like it was on fire. Eye stood up and grabbed my pants and put them on. Eye fell on my ass doing so, but Eye sucked up the pain and kept putting them on.

Eye found my shirt by the bathroom door. Eye snatched it up and put it on. Eye took one of his fancy baseball caps and pulled it low over my eyes. Eye took his car keys and made my way out into the living room. Gripping my book bag, Eye had to get out of here. His abuse has gone on long enough. Eye am being beaten for what his father had done to his family. Eye was being beaten because Eye reminded Andy of his father, so he said. Eye know enough to know that that ain't love. That's obsession. Obsessed with changing a past you couldn't change. What's done was done. Written in the Book and documented with an index and page numbers. Maybe it's catalogued in libraries and shelved next to amazing books like Hitler, Swastikas and the untold stories of battered souls. Eye opened the front door and made my way to his car.

Eye was two hours away from home.

*Eye drove myself to my Mitsubishi* Gallant Mama helped me get. It was parked at a friend's house in South Miami. Shit, Eye still had to pay her back the $3,000 she gave me to put down on it. Once Eye got to my car Eye wiped Andy's car of my prints, wiped down the keys, tossed them on the seat with rag-clad hands and closed the door. Just in case he called the police and reported his car stolen. Eye jumped in my car, and blasted Tupac's *Picture me Rolling*, fleeing the past. Leaving Andy and his emotional, sexual and physical abuse, hi deranged Senator mother and his crazed family history behind.

Forever!

*Eye drove to the Cutler Ridge* Mall. It was around Christmas time, and Eye grabbed my book bag and parked by the Main entrance. Cloudy day. Not so sunny, but that's ok. It was a little chilly. Making my way into the mall, Eye was approaching a shoe store and Kay Bee toy Store. Eye looked at all the holiday decorations hanging everywhere.

Everyone was in their versions of a Festive Mood. Rubbed off on me in a positive way. Eye was walking past the shoe store when Eye heard, "Shut up, Boy! Eye can't afford that expensive video game for you. Mama pays bills!"

"Not fair! You said if Eye made straight A's on my report card you will get me the game!"

The level of frustration that befell her haggard, yet subtle face unnerved me. "*No*, Brian…"

"Eye hate you" No he didn't. Eye saw the strong love for his mother and siblings flashing dangerously in his eyes. He's acting out, trying to get her attention more than a game. He used the game as a muse between linking the two together to get what he felt he deserved. "Eye'ma tell Daddy!" She smacked him and several adults noticed, but they turned a blind eye because of how rude the child was being to the parent. "*Forget* your no good Daddy. He is doing life without in prison! He will *never* get out." She crippled him emotionally, hit him where he felt it the most. Feelings control our thoughts…He lost steam. "So *tell* his dumb ass! TELL HIM!"

He wasn't as confident as before. He was embarrassed and wanted to run away. "Eye want the game!"

Eye walked up to her just as she broke down on a nearby bench. Eye could tell she didn't fight with her childen regularly, this happened to be one of those rare occasions she had to smack him in public. The way her hands shook and the apologetic gleam in her eyes told me she's never smacked him before in his life. This was the first time, and it was eating away at her. Her son's back was turned to her, and his arms folded across his puffed-out chest, anger raging in his dark eyes. She covered her forehead, sobbing. Three other small kids were crying with her, climbing in her lap, trying to stroke her hair or kiss her face.

Brian, had to be about 16 years old, put his hands on his hips, showcasing rebellion. Yet the sight of his mother crying did a number on him. "Eye'm sorry, Mama," he said and Eye interrupted.

"Excuse me, ma'am."

She looked up at me with red eyes. "What do you want, boy?" The vibrations oozing off this family sent a sense of duty through my veins, and it thumped along the vessels of a dark heart that was slowly turning blue again. One of my best-friends told me the blood is blue inside the body and once it hits oxygen outside the body it turned red. Red and blue. Like police sirens and bloods and Cripps. Interesting.

Eye was energy, smiling at her. "Eye overheard what you said to your son." The angel in her eyes diminished, and in its place was a defensive vulture. "You stay outta my business!" She jumped up to her feet. "Eye'm a God fearing woman. Eye beat my kids, so what! What? You gonna call the law on me? At least Eye'm trying to raise my kids! Why are you trying to get the crackahs to take my children from me? They are all Eye have."

Eye wasn't here to cause her discord. So Eye didn't feed into it. Eye just got out of a rough situation, Eye could have died tonight. Eye appreciated having life at that moment, and to make up for the wrong doing and bad decisions Eye made over the past year or so with Andy, Eye to rewrite a wrong and do something positive. Eye had a thought. "Are you *really* that God fearing?"

She rolled her eyes. "Yes!"

Eye narrowed my own. "So that means you believe in him?"

"Yes Eye do, muthafuckah."

"If you believe in him, why are you cursing me? Eye'm nearly 21 years old."

"So what? You shouldn't be butting in my goddamn business."

Eye challenged her. "Pray to him to get your son that game, if you believe in him."

"Eye will *not.*"

Brian said, "She needs to do something. Because Eye want my game. Eye stay home and look after my siblings. Eye'm not a bad kid. Eye do good in school. Eye am the model son. And she still doesn't keep her word." Eye didn't notice it before but he called her out as well. Threatening to take himself out of the equation, and she would have to look after her kids herself, which meant she couldn't work nor go out on Fridays anymore. Things were getting ugly and fast.

My thought became my feelings. Eye felt good about what eye thought, and it manifested, ten fold pushing the rest of the black and the darkness from my heart. "Pray to him if you believe in God."

"Leave me alone."

"Pray to him. You can't even pray to the one you claim to believe in. And you show your oldest child this. No wonder he doesn't believe in prayer.'

"How did you know that?" Brian asked, looking me over.

"By the way you talk down to your mother. That's how Eye know."

She closed her eyes tightly. "God please help me get my son that game! Amen." She glared at me.

"See. Eye did it. He doesn't answer. As always."

"Do you always pray to him?"

She got in my face. "Yes. Every damn day and night. Eye pray for the big and small things, yet he doesn't answer. He ignores me." Eye opened my book bag and handed her the wooden box. "What is this?" She looked it over suspiciously. Her kids were looking, too. Eye handed Brian the key. "Respect your mother, or you lose it all."

"Lose all of what?" he asked.

"Unlock it."

"Is this a bomb?" she asked.

"No. Open it. You said you believe in God."

"Eye do."

Brian unlocked $5,000 in cash, Money Eye made from stripping. Well the residuals were going to help this mother of four with a rebellious son. The sight of the cash made her slap her forehead. "Oh, God! Oh, God, thank you!"

"Don't thank me, continue thanking God. Jesus died for us all, and Eye know how rough it can get for a single mother. My mom is a single mother. Eye used to be Brain when Eye was his age. Full of hate and anger for the things Eye didn't understand."

Brian hugged me tightly. "Thank you, Mr.! Eye can get my game!"

"Thank you, Son!" She hugged me too, kissing my cheek.

"Make your life and your kid's life better. Ya'll need that money more than Eye do. Eye stripped to make that money. Eye don't deserve that." She took a hundred dollar bill and stuffed it in my pocket. "Eye appreciate this. Eye don't know who you are or where you come from, but your mother raised a mighty fine son. Thank you so much. Eye almost don't want to take the money." Eye pushed the box towards her. "Take it," Eye said. "…It's *yours.*" And Eye took the money from my pocket and handed it to Brian. "Eye want to see straight A's on that report card again. That's my down payment. My investment is there."

"Thank you. What's your name?"

Eye held my head high. "Pharoah." Eye will NEVER put man before Jehovah ever again. Not after the Hell Eye just went through. Not after the misery Eye suffered, and survived. With y sanity.

Damn…Eye want to write…

# HOME GOING SERVICE FOR:

Sunrise:
January 2009

Sunset:
January 2009

THE FINAL CHAPTER

THE FINAL OBITUARY

PHAROAH C. WILSON

VS

SATAN

January 2009
12:00 a.m.
Sweet Home Baptist Church
56 N.W. DOWNTOWN MIAMI
Pharoah vs. Satan

## Luke 22:3-6

*Then Satan entered into Judas called Iscariot, who was of the number of the twelve. He went away and conferred with the chief priests and officers how he might betray him to them. And they were glad, and agreed to give him money. So he consented and sought an opportunity to betray him to them in the absence of a crowd.*

## Ephesians 6:10-18

*Finally, be strong in the Lord and in the strength of his might. Put on the whole armor of God, that you may be able to stand against the schemes of the devil. For we do not wrestle against flesh and blood, but against the rulers, against the authorities, against the cosmic powers over this present darkness, against the spiritual forces of evil in the heavenly places. Therefore take up the whole armor of God, that you may be able to withstand in the evil day, and having done all, to stand firm. Stand therefore, having fastened on the belt of truth, and having put on the breastplate of righteousness…*

**A Time to be Born:** Pharoah Wilson, Jr.…

…When your neighbor trespasses against you, you must not trespass against them…

**A Time to Grow:** …Meeting up with a therapist to deal with his past was supposed to be a new beginning…

**A Time to Reflect:** …would it *be* the end of Pharoah Wilson, Jr…?

**A Time to Die and be mourned:** A part of him *died* when those therapy sessions ended. Mr. Jennings said they were free, but as Pharoah should have figured out…

They came at a price…

# Day 7

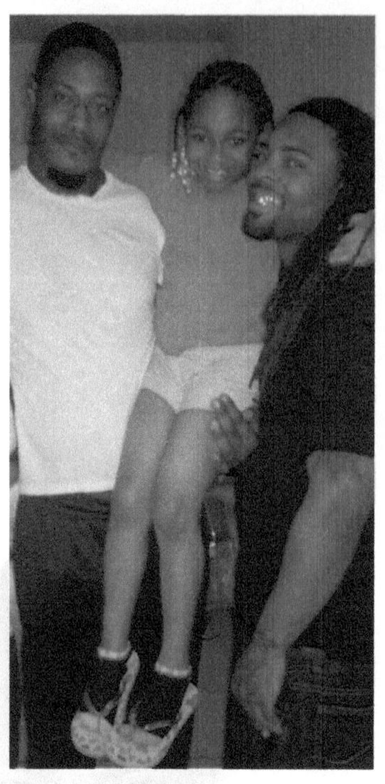

Pharoah and his brother Tyrone Payne, his niece amara Payne with her cute self, John and Shauntiya. Below: Pharoah with his siblings.

**Pushing folders, yellow tablets and** notes aside, Lord Jennings stood up in a zombie state, stretching. Eye smiled, feeling good about doing these therapy sessions. Allowed me to look at my life and see myself through the reflection of memory. Eye have been through a lot, survived a lot and even Eye didn't realize just how much Eye've endured. Survived every brutal and subtle plight that came my way. Eye was a lot stronger than Eye thought, and looking at my pictures in frames all over his house and realizing Eye cared about Lord as a friend did a number on me. Yes, we had sex and Eye still didn't understand *how* that happened being Eye was in a committed relationship with my significant other. And no matter how Eye tried to analyze it, no matter how Eye kept telling myself that Lord keeping me locked in his condo was *harmless*, Eye knew that deep down something was there, whatever it was, and it beckoned for attention. Something wasn't right.

"Lord. What's wrong?" Eye asked him. He seemed different.

He smiled, his eyes glossy. Shirtless, his jeans barely stayed on his amazing ass, but Eye tried not to look. Eye kept looking in his eyes.

"Eye'm happy right now," he said, but the tone of his voice betrayed his words.

Eye smiled. "You are? Why?"

"You've *successfully* admitted to me all your faults, truths, lies and endurance. Eye am so proud. And to think when you first came here seven days ago you were afraid to ride the elevator."

*Eye know, right!* "Eye conquered that fear."

"Eye know you have. You've covered a lot in seven days. And Eye know it's a start. Eye know you still have work to do on yourself, but Eye commend you for your strength and for remaining humble."

"And God fearing!"

He looked at me without blinking, handing me a drink. Hypnotiq. Straight. "This drink is for you. To *celebrate*."

"Celebrate what?" Eye asked

"Conquering your life in seven days," he said. *Damn* he was happy, or was he?

Eye studied him. "Ok, sounds good." Eye wasn't a huge drinker. In fact liquor was nasty as shit, but Eye guess in this instance Eye could oblige. Reluctantly, Eye sipped, smacking my lips, barely swallowing it. It tasted nasty, but Eye didn't want to appear amateurish in front of him so Eye sat up straight. Turning on classical music, he sat next to me, looking deeply into my eyes, his right hand resting on my left knee cap. He sipped, and said, "Taste good."

*Ugh!* "Yes, it does," Eye lied.

"We should play a game."

*Eye'm not in the mood.* "Eye like games. You got Scrabble?"

"Yes, Eye do. But Eye'm not talking about board games. You're much too sophisticated for that," he said, setting his drink down. "We should play Wolf."

"Wolf?" Eye sipped the drink once more, frowning in confusion. "What the bleep is a god-bleep Wolf?"

"Wolf is a simple game. It has only one rule. Whoever can wolf down the drink first win a prize."

*Sounds harmless. Why not.* "Ok, Eye can swing with that."

He smiled coyly, leaning over, kissing my cheek, his nipples and dick hardening. Eye pretended not to notice. Something seemed different with Lord. His eyes didn't seem or feel the same. In fact, looking deeply into his heavenly eyes Eye didn't see heaven at all. The Law of Cause and Effect came to mind. Eye saw the darkness.

**Eye held my glass midair** and we made a toast.

"To the future of Dapharoah69."

*Dude, Eye don't even know if Eye have a future. These books may never touch a single person or see the light of day.* "To a new and burgeoning friendship," Eye said, clanking my glass against his and Eye wolfed down my drink, slamming the glass on the expensive low table. A few of his yellow pads containing my life fell on the floor.

"Eye won!" Eye stammered, smiling, jumping up to my feet in victory, my fists raised in the air.

Eye was laughing and Lord hadn't even touched his drink. Instead he pulled out a small package of cocaine from the arm rest, a small glass topped mirror and sipped his drink. *Had that been in there the entire time?* Eye was perplexed. "Eye thought you didn't smoke weed or do drugs," Eye said, yawning. Eye was getting tired, and Eye should be. Eye have been staying up for hours and hours telling a shrink my life and my demons. And telling him my Jehovahs and Lucifers did a number on me because Eye was in a position to examine myself and see what needed an oil change, tune up or what needed to be donated to the Good Will and given to the less fortunate. Eye yawned again, and when Eye tried to walk towards the kitchen Eye tripped over my foot and fell over the low table, hitting my head on the floor. That shit hurt. Moaning, Eye rolled over on my back and Lord picked up the cocaine and dumped it all over my face, pressing his bare foot on my chest, leaning into my face.

"So easily one can get into your life and become a permanent fixture."

The room was spinning. "What…what the…hell is going on?"

"Helpless little bitch aren't you? Eye don't understand you. Eye really don't."

*Oh my God!* "What…what are you…doing to me?"

"Eye put a lil' something in your drink. Pharoah, haven't you learned a thing from your life? You sat in this condo for seven days pouring your soul out to a therapist that isn't even a therapist at all!"

"What?" Eye was in shock, my energy draining from my body. Eye could hardly move my fingers and Lord knows Eye tried to sit up or stand up but my head was spinning me deeper into a vortex.

"Eye am infatuated and obsessed with you. Eye always have been. Eye think you are the most beautiful man in the world. Eye always wanted to *bang* you. Eye have your porn videos and Eye been an admirer of yours for five plus years. Eye never spoke to you or sent you a message."

He stood up, kicking the side of my face. Blood spurted on the white tiled floor and Eye turned on my side and he kicked me so hard in the back Eye winced from the pain, and felt helpless because Eye was too drugged up to react let alone breathe properly. He laughed the most evil laugh Eye have ever heard. This sexy man Eye thought was a new friend, a man Eye thought wanted to help me deal with my past has turned out to be a crazed fan—or maybe he wasn't a fan, just crazy! "Helpless, 'ey Pharoah? You are a dream come true. Eye have always been madly in love with you. You are so sexy, you're very handsome and you have an incredible body. You suck and take dick well," he went on, unzipping his pants, appearing manic. It was hard to focus on him, my heart pounding through my chest. He got on his knees and helped me to my knees. Eye nearly fell back on the floor.

"Come on, Pharoah. Eye'll help you," he said, his eyes dark red. He put cocaine in my mouth, pulled me to his nose and he held the left side of it, snorting it. His head yanked back, his face flushing beet red.

"Ahhh shit I love it!"

"Please…" The coke tasted bitter…dissolved on my tongue. He studied me, his head tilting side to side cautiously, guardedly and slowly. He gave me some tongue, my lips unmoving. He bit my bottom lip and Eye screamed.

"Kiss me bitch!"

"Please!"

"Eye wanna love you. Eye want you to be my *slave.* You will never leave this condo, Pharoah."

"Oh my God...*Please.*"

"You are not allowed to go outside, which is why Eye changed the locks on my door. Eye will feed you only bread and water. Oh, and you won't be needing these," he said, snatching up the blue plastic bag with my Meds and throwing them towards the sliding glass door. The ocean thunderously roared from 56 stories below.

Eye shook in my skin. "Eye need my Meds, Lord. Eye will perish without them."

"That's the plan…Eye will get deep inside you as you slowly perish."

Eye closed my eyes. "God, please help me."

"THERE IS NO GOD! Are you stupid, bitch? Your

GOD sat by and let a man rape you as a child. He sat by and watched you suffer when Chantell aborted your child! He watched. WATCHED! Probably eating the best popcorn he could muster. And you still pledge allegiance to him?"

"*Yes*…why is my head pounding?" Eye asked, attempting to rub my temples and he slapped me so hard my head snapped back. He spit in my face.

"God watches you now. If he truly exist. He doesn't, Pharoah. He doesn't."

"God is not doing this to me. You are."

He pushed me backward, my back slamming hard against the tile. It hurt so badly Eye puked, nearly *choking* from my own vomit. He slowly walked up to me, one foot over the other, the sky filled with stars Eye could hardly see. Everything seemed to turn into blurs, then ghosts, then the most demonic ghouls Eye have ever encountered. Eye had problems thinking or breathing and Eye thought Eye was going to die. "Miamilicious. Mr King of *Erotica.* The one who writes books that got fans *praising* you. Do you realize you are GOD to some of your fans?"

Eye couldn't form the words. My body felt like it was shutting down. "Are you ignoring me?" he asked dangerously, straddling my neck, trying to shove his dick in my mouth. He started pissing and Eye tried with all my might to push him off but Eye was so weak. Eye was gagging, then choking. Hot piss filled my mouth. Then he leaned forward on his elbows and started banging me in the mouth and Eye puked again and he kept pumping my throat, moaning and laughing and Eye puked again as his huge dick filled my esophagus.

"Eye love when your sexy ass choke on my pipe."

My body shook on the floor, my hands finding his sides, weakly, and Eye dug my nails into him and he screamed so loud he rolled off the top of me and slapped me repeatedly.

"Time for the revelation, The King of Erotica. Pharoah. This isn't a book. You won't live past tonight to write another one. You took something from me, Pharoah, something you didn't realize you took and you must pay the price."

"What…what…price, price what…."

He laughed again, this time even more sinister than the last. He was getting off on my grief and fear. He walked over to one of the tall bookshelves, took every book of mine and dropped them in a pile on the floor. "You are an amazing talent. A very talented man." He was butt naked, his huge penis swinging freely. "It is almost an honor to fuck you. Thousands of men masturbate to your pictures. Eye love the picture of you on South Beach with that pretty boy pussy tooted slightly towards the waves." He opened a small counter in the pricey kitchen and pulled out a small leather pouch. He unzipped it, approaching me. He pulled out a needle. My eyes widened with fear. Eye tried to roll on my stomach and push up but he got on his knees, spread my cheeks and he began to feast. Loosening me up. It felt good, but Eye made myself go numb. He kept eating more effectively, running his tongue all over my opened hole, then sliding his fingers and tongue deep inside.

"Give in to me, Pharoah."

"Nooooo.....please...."

"When Eye am done eating, Eye am going to fuck you till the sun rise. Raw. Eye have herpes, Pharoah. Oh yes Eye do. And Eye will give it to you." He turned me on my back and injected a needle into my arm.

Smiling evilly. His glassy eyes devoid of life. Eye shook so hard Eye couldn't breathe.

"This my friend, my dear Pharoah, is heroine Eye am pumping into your body. Eye will pump more and more into you as the night dawns into the break of day. Eye will then fuck you while you slowly die. Eye will watch you suffer."

"Why are you...doing this to me? WHY WHY?"

"Pharoah. Look deeply into my eyes and tell me where you remember them from."

"Eye never met you...before." My throat burned and my stomach felt like it was on fire. Eye had to moan, but Eye refused to cry.

"Yes you have. Think long and fucking hard, Pharaoh. WHERE DO YOU REMEMBER ME FROM?"

"Eye DON'T KNOW!"

"WE HAD A ONE NIGHT STAND, BITCH!"

"NO WE DIDN'T!"

"My father used to be one of your…Pastor$ when you were a whorish little teenager."

Eye grew painfully silent. Looking deep into abysmal eyes.

"Eye don't know your father."

"Sure you do. You know my mother, too. You had a threesome with both of them. You destroyed their church with your revelation to the congregation and that broke up my family."

Eye was rendered speechless."Oh my God!"

"Yes, your God is a fraud. Church isn't real, Pharoah. God isn't real. My father was a faithful follower of your God as long as the people gave their hard earned money to his faggot ass. Do you know how it feels to have a gay father and to walk in on him and your mother *sexing* a teenage punk? They *banged* you so well you hadn't realized Eye also fucked you, Pharoah. In the darkness. All the lights off. Eye had to have you, Pharoah. You thought Eye was my father. You took the pipe real good! *You* were my first."

Eye grew silent, listening to this. "Can't talk? And watching you on this couch opening up to me, listening to how you explained my mother and father touching and sexing you angered me but Eye hid it from my face. Eye knew who you were. Eye just wanted to hear you say it. Because of you my family was destroyed. The congregation ripped my family apart and my mother divorced my father and he committed suicide in his bathroom."

"Oh my God!"

"THERE IS NO GOD!" He jumped up and kicked me in the side over and over. Eye crawled into the fetal position.

"YOU HEAR THAT ALLAH. JEHOVAH. BUDDAH, WHATEVER YOUR NAME IS. YOU'RE NOT REAL, ARE YOU? YOU ARE DESIGNED. CREATED BY CAUCASSIONS INSIDE THOSE FICTIONAL BESTSELLING BOOKS CALLED THE HOLY BIBLE! JESUS NEVER EXISTED!"

He was spinning in circles, with his arms outstretched, committing blasphemy. Eye cringed inside, because nothing Eye go through tonight would turn me away from God.

It was then Eye realized why Eye didn't sign the book

deal with that publisher. It was then Eye realized why they laughed at me for coming to New York without legal representation. They were going to give me a million dollar payment if Eye denounced God. They probably would have given me the world. But then again that's the world today. Entertainment figures selling their souls to the devil for fame. Did Eye want to do that? Did Eye want to go that route just to make enough money to feed my mother, brothers, friends and my nieces? Did Eye want fame that badly?

My heart swelled with thoughts of the love of y life, John, and never seeing him again, never touching his lips when he smiled, and never kissing his salty tears away. The thought of never touching him, and making love and exploding together brought huge tears to my eyes. *Jennings* has been drugging my drinks, weed and food since day one. And now Eye was going to die. And Eye was ready for it. Eye was scared of the way Eye may be checking out, but Eye never feared death itself because it was inevitable. It was going to happen whether Eye wanted it to happen or not. He grabbed my feet and started pulling me towards the ceiling glass door. Eye was weak Eye couldn't even grab the low table legs to give some form of resistance.

"You took my family."

"Your mother and father took your family. Eye was a goddamn minor!"

"SO WHAT!"

"Go to hell, Lord."

"Wrong choice of words." He turned me on my stomach and slid his dick up inside me. "You talk a lot of shit, Pharoah. Is this how Thugzilla fucked you on camera for the world to see?"

"Please!"

"Eye got a better idea!" He pulled out of me, and vanished into the bedroom. Eye tried my best to crawl towards the front door, but then Eye realized he locked it and the key was on his person. Wildly Eye looked around, and decided to get a knife from the kitchen. But before Eye could crawl towards it he appeared with a white Jason mask over his face. He set up a digital camera on a small tripod before me, then opened some lighter fluid and squirted it all over my books. He struck a match and dropped it, my books going up in flames.

"Please, Lord."

"Beg me. Eye am your Lord. Eye am more real than your God."

"You are not God!"

"WRONG!" He pressed record on the camera and he raped me, repeatedly for the next couple hours. Eye passed out a few times, and didn't know how long Eye was unconscious. When Eye came to he was still fucking me like Eye wasn't worth anything.

When he had to cum he pulled out of me, yanked my face to his dick and came on my cheek, wiping nut all over my mouth and eyes and Eye spit on the floor.

"You're on camera, Pharoah. My face is covered. Yours is exposed. Eye am going to upload this video on every social network that Eye could possibly think of. Eye am going to destroy you from the inside out. Eye may even send your mother the video with your heart as a Christmas gift with a Happy Thanksgiving card attached."

"Please, man. If you're gonna kill me…just do it, man. JUST DO IT!"

"No, that's too easy. Eye want you to feel exactly what Eye felt when Eye cried over my father's casket."

"Man give it to God."

"GOD ISN'T REAL!"

"HE IS!"

"Pharoah. Your mother forced religion on you and forced you to go to church when you were a child. You didn't have a say in the matter. My mother and father forced me and their parents forced them. See the vicious cycle. The human race gotta be forced into serving a God they can't question, let alone see. And even when my mother grew up and away from church my Pastor father married her and beat her ass back into the church. My father used to beat me till Eye saw blood. Told me Eye better not wince or show any sign of weakness so Eye endured the shit with a poker face. Eye prayed to a God that had forsaken me. Eye lost faith then. Then the state took me from my parents because they barely fed me. Eventually my parents won me back, but they had to prove they could take care of me and they did. My father got worse. My dad screwed me the way he screwed Mama. He had to control his household and banging Mom and Eye relinquished our control over our lives. Eye hated myself for it, Pharoah because, like you, Eye grew to love it."

"Lord…God heals."

"No he doesn't. My father screwed me then beat me and my mother's asses and made us go to church and serve God. Eye used to vomit from his public display of humbleness to his neighbor yet destroyed me as his son."

"Oh my…Eye'm sorry…you went through that."

"And you think you had a rough life. There is always someone going through something worse than you. You don't appreciate your life. You are selfish. You are arrogant. You think its all about you!"

"God heals angry hearts, man."

Hate colored his face. He was about to snap and there wasn't a thing Eye could do about it.

"GOD IS A HOAX! MY OWN FATHER SAID THIS TO ME! CHURCH IS A HOAX, DESIGNED TO KEEP US AS A PEOPLE CONDITIONED." Eye was silent, listening to him.

"Don't you get it? Can you claim your church donations on your taxes? You eat the flesh of Jesus and drink the wine, his blood during communion with a room filled with sinners."

"Lord, listen…you don't have to do this, bruh. You are not your parents."

"Yes Eye am. Eye am just like my father. You have feelings for me and Eye am not your father."

"Eye care as a friend."

"This condo belongs to me. When my father died Eye

collected insurance. When my mother died Eye collected insurance. My father was also a shrink. When he killed himself Eye kept up his certificates and doctorates. Those aren't my accomplishments, Pharoah. Eye used them to get to you. Eye wanted to understand the man who not only write good books, but Eye wanted to understand why you allowed my parents to use your minor body for their sick perverted pleasure."

Eye tried to sit up, and shockingly he didn't attack me. He appeared sleepy, almost tired. "Eye was 14, man! A *kid*!"

"YOU COULDA STOPPED IT!"

"No Eye couldn't! My mind tried to save my flesh, flesh that loved and lived for your father's tender touch. He paid attention to me. He listened to me. My own mother never listened to me."

Blood stained my face. He was calming down, but danger was *still* in his dead eyes. Eye was still dizzy.

Then it happened. He snapped, attacking me, taking me completely off guard. He snatched me up and punched me in the face, and Eye slammed into the book shelf. Eye tried to raise my fists, but he ran into me, the book shelf rocking and books fell to the floor.

He pressed the side of my face on the cold tile.

"You see the book on Pharoahs under the shelf, like you found in the first grade?"

"Nooo, man! No!"

"Niggahs can't even stick together, so why do you call yourself Pharoah? You aren't royalty. Niggahs don't want shit in life. They just wanna smoke pot, sell drugs, screw people or get some head. That's it."

He pulled me to my feet and Eye swung at him, hitting him in the face; and he pushed me, and Eye ram backward, falling into the bathroom. Toilet filled with feces and piss. He shoved my head in the commode and Eye held my breath, grossed out, flinging my arms and he pressed my head further in the toilet, my forehead resting on the bottom of the commode and bubbles rose to the top of the water. Eye used everything inside me, everything that comprised my heart, mind, body and soul to breathe yet Eye couldn't.

Eye was suffocating, my life flashing before my eyes.

Eye know what that *meant* now. And it wasn't a good feeling at all. Eye tried to press up with my hands but he slid his back inside me and started thrusting…pressing my head down harder on the porcelain. My body began to fail me. Everything started gradually shutting down. But Eye wouldn't give up just yet. Eye wasn't gonna go out without a fight. No matter how unrealistic it seemed.

Pulling me up, he bounced inside me, choking me. When he said he had to nut Eye threw my head back into his face and he yelled so loud Eye damn near went deaf.

He punched me, over and over and grabbed my feet and started dragging me to the balcony. Eye was trying to grab hold of anything that Eye could, but couldn't grab a thing. He opened the ceiling to floor glass door and pulled me out onto the balcony. The cool breeze blew across my body. Half moon up, the smell of surf below. Fifty six stories up into the heavens, 56 stories above Hell below. Eye was going to die. He snatched me up, this cock strong bitch, and he pushed me against the railing.

"Eye'm done playing with you. Check out time. Since God is so real, let's see him save you." He wrapped his hands around my neck and slowly pushed me over the edge of the railing. My feet were no longer touching the floor. And Eye died right there inside. Eye completely gave up, let it all go. My body shook so badly Eye couldn't breathe, my hands trembled profusely. My heart beat so fast Eye was surprised Eye didn't have a heart attack. Eye refused to look down. Eye couldn't because if Eye did Eye would die from traumatic shock alone. Suddenly Eye wanted to ride the elevator.

"On the seventh day of therapy you realized Eye was a fraud. A fake. Eye wasn't who Eye told you Eye was. You need to be careful who you let in your circle. Everyone doesn't like you. Everyone don't like your books. Some people hate you just because you're successful. Those who failed at what you do so well envy you. Closeted gay men wanna screw your books and your talent, not you. They hate you. They wanna screw your resources; then once they obtain the keys to your kingdom they try to destroy you. And you make it easy."

The darkness was consuming me. It snapped throughout my body, my heart and my mind and Eye said, "Eye hate..." And Eye caught myself.

"You what? Say it. You hate me. SAY IT! You hate me!"

Eye stalled. Hate was such a strong word. "You know what? Eye don't hate you. Hating you is easy. Eye love you, man. Despite it, Eye love even my enemies. Eye pray for you. Eye really pray to God to save your soul."

He squeezed my neck with so much hatred on his face. "*How* do you do it? How did you survive all the shit you have and still have faith in a God you never lain eyes on? Eye could never be that strong."

Eye was weakening. Losing consciousness, giving up the fight. Living life was too much for me. Too many rules. Too many things Eye had to obey. Laws and sanctions. Tired of changing for others to be what they wanted me to be. Tired of being talked about, scandalized and battered. Tired of it all. Eye was exhausted. Maybe taking my life would be a good thing. Eye wouldn't have to pay rent or taxes. Creditors could get off my back. Eye could be free. Eye dangle 56 stories above the ocean, or whatever body of water that was—the Atlantic Ocean. Bayside behind me. Eye felt light as a feather and as timid as a ghost. The wind was picking up, gently and inviting. He leaned into my face. "Eye'm gonna make you pay for taking my family."

This is it, Lord. This is where my decision making has led me. To chaos and destruction. When will it ever stop? Or will it stop right now? Fuck books. Fuck a literary career. To be successful comes with too many people holding you down out of envy and jealousy. Because they couldn't do it they won't allow you. The Law of Allowance was a powerful law! Eye looked into the face of evil and felt myself letting go. The tears fell. "Tell God to save you now..." he whispered, my eyes fluttering closed. "Better yet denounce him. Eye want to hear you say the words. Tell me he isn't real. Tell me you are your own individual God. Tell me you are the maker and creator of your destiny. And Eye will let you live. Tell me, Pharoah."

Eye closed my eyes...and gave it all to God. *Everything.*

Life, love, books, pain, misery, things Eye could and couldn't control, this scenario, the pain and torture. Eye gave it to God. Eye had complete faith in God. Whatever happened would be his Will. If Lord pushed me over the balcony and Eye fell 56 stories towards the water it would be God's Will. Eye wouldn't question it, because God wasn't evil. He was love. Purity. Eye didn't deserve any of the blessings he bestowed on me.

He was the true living God and it didn't matter if Eye never saw him. What mattered was that my praying and believing has gotten me through HIV, suicide, rape, prison, deceptive lovers, crooked county officials, backstabbing family. God has delivered me through it all, and if Eye die tonight my life will be immortalized through my books and that will be a testimony. *God, forgive me for all those Eye have hurt. When Eye was much younger, God, yes Eye didn't truly love you because Eye was forced to, so Eye rebelled and questioned it and denounced it and thought Eye could do it alone. But God Eye can't do it alone.*

"Pharoah, denounce him."

*Eye need help, God. If Eye die tonight Eye pray you give Mama strength to carry my family, rid her heart of the bitterness she denies. Protect my nieces, God, because Eye won't be here to be their protector. Enter my brother Laron's heart to move back down to Miami and raise his daughters and leave that girlfriend of his alone in Michigan. Touch Darshawn's heart and rid it of the anger and hatred he may or may not have towards the things he's gone through in life.*

"PHAROAH DENOUNCE HIM! AND EYE WILL LET YOU LIVE!"

*Protect my family, God please.*

*Eye believe in you, God and Eye know Jesus died for all sins, even my sins, even my bisexual sins Jesus paid for with his life, Eye am not worthy, Lord.*

"SHUT UP, PHAROAH! God is not real! SHUT UP!"

Eye spoke aloud, yet calmly. Eye love and believe in God and would not denounce him for nobody and whoever wanted me to could suck a raw fart out my ass.

*"As a man Eye love you God and Eye am thankful to you for helping me endure my trials and tribulations. Eye know you're*

*real, God. Eye feel it in my heart and soul; Eye even feel it in my bones. Eye am NOT my OWN GOD!"*

"YES YOU ARE!" He spat in my face and Eye felt nothing. Eye didn't even feel his saliva touch my face.

*"Eye was only made in God's image. Satan's greatest trick is to show the world that he doesn't exist, when he does. Eye don't wanna be my own God. Being your own GOD comes with mansions and episodes of MTV Cribs with you as the narrator and tour guides before an envious world and pricey cars and millions of dollars in endorsements and the world praising you for your talent instead of thanking Jehovah for the blessings. Being your own God comes with #1 New York Times bestseller status and #1 Pop and R&B hits and multiplatinum albums and publicly bragging about the charities you donate your tax write-off money to and it feeds egotistical souls embedded with the wrong type of spirits and money hungry cash cows that represent false idol worship.*

*"God help me, please. Whatever happens to me it is your Will.*

*"Amen.*

*"So be it."*

Complete silence. Eye could hear the surf below; feel the wind on my body. Eye slowly opened my eyes, albeit being drained and exhausted. Lord still held me by the neck. Eye smiled at him, and the tears stopped falling.

"You felt alone when and after your father abused you. Eye know the feeling, but your pain is all your own."

He didn't blink. He stared at me.

Eye went on. "There were nights you couldn't sleep because it played over and over in your head what your father demanded and what your mother allowed to happen. She failed to protect you and your protector was screwing you and your mother. You can't count the tears you shed. Eye can feel you right now, feel the times you wanted to end it all. You contemplated suicide numerous times yet couldn't bring yourself to do it because you wanted to find out the purpose for your life. This is not your purpose. You sought vengeance against me for the distorted thoughts of your parents.

"Your father stripped you of your human traits and disguised you as another form of society's lie. Eye understand Mr. Jennings. Eye will no longer call you Lord, because you are not the King of Kings or Lord of Lords and you will never be. But you can be a reflection of his image, for you were made in it, bruh."

"Pharoah." His tears flowed. For the first time he showed emotion. "Eye don't believe in God…"

"Your father abused you and as a man you think you can go back and protect the little boy or the confused teenager he used to dismantle with his aggression, confusion and penis. You know my life, Mr. Jennings. Eye poured my soul out to you, a complete stranger that had the motive of killing me the entire time. Was my pouring my life to you as meaningless as you made it out to be? Is your misguided vengeance that important you will support black on black crime, as if enough systems aren't against the African American race *already*?"

"Yes…yes," he stuttered, confused. Trapped. "Eye mean, um, no, shit. No, Pharoah. Eye do have a heart."

"Eye forgave myself for the abuse Eye suffered. Eye forgave myself for those Eye hurt after Eye asked for their forgiveness. Eye sleep with a free conscious nightly. Blame your father for what he went through and acknowledge your part in it all. Victim or not, reclaim your life by forgiving yourself. Let it go, and it's hard…Eye *know*, bruh. But *Eye* did it. And so can you. If you don't forgive the perpetrator he still has control over you from his grave. He's resting in peace, you're living in Hell."

He loosened his hands around my neck, his eyes clouding over. His body losing the tension, his muscles relaxing. Eye had him. Right where Eye wanted him.

"Eye understand your situation, but Eye don't feel your pain. Its all your own. You're the only one who can feel and deal with your pain."

"SHUT UP!"

"God is real. As real as snow. He's the rays of the sun that energizes life to aid productivity amongst the human race. He's the form of procreation. We are the best evidence that God exist. We are living proof of his existence, bruh. Were we not once a sperm cell/Mama's egg? Look at us now!"

He took his hands from behind my neck and he was like

a little boy shaking in the cold and Eye didn't have the urge to kill him or push him over the edge. His soul needed saving and it didn't know how to ask for it so the answer was destruction and vengeance.

"How do you remain so strong, Pharoah? Eye literally deceived you, beat you, raped you, drugged you and tried to kill you. Yet you stand here like nothing happened. Eye don't get it. You still love God?"

A flash of anger beckoned me to do his ass in, but Eye fought it. Eye refrained. He wasn't worth my freedom. Eye already lost my freedom once, 12 years ago. "Yes, bruh. Eye do. If you put a gun to my head Eye will still love and honor God. If you put a gun to my nieces head or my mother's head Eye will never denounce God. Eye have his full armor. Eye love God. And then Eye love not people next but myself. Eye am learning to love me. Eye am learning to love *everything* about me. Eye embrace me, bruh. You can't break me. Eye wouldn't change a thing about myself." He attempted to hug me, yet he withdrew his arms as if Eye was on fire and he was gun powder. He cleared his throat, wiped his face and leaned against the wall. He stared blankly into the sky. "If you had to do it all over again, living the life you lived, knowing what you know now—would you have broken up my family?"

Eye said, "Yes," without hesitation.

"Why?"

"Because it would lead me to this exact moment, this instance. To tell you it's never too late to turn to God, and let him work in your life, bruh. Prayer, effective prayer Eye should say, changes things. If you allow it. Prayer takes practice. The more you pray the easier it gets. He's patient. He understands. That doesn't mean you won't sin, bruh. You'll live in sin till the day you die. Eye, too, resorted to vengeance, bruh, in my life, trying to correct a past Eye didn't understand nor create. Eye thought anger was an answer. Lashing out got me nowhere. Eye felt worse than Eye did before Eye attacked. Eye met a new type of devil every time. Urging me on. Giving me the tools to destroy myself and everything Eye hold dear in my heart. Aren't you tired of losing yourself to another's plan of destruction?"

He was quiet for a long drawn out moment and Eye was so tired Eye just wanted to go to sleep. But Eye was seemingly getting through to Mr. Jennings so Eye kept silently praying in my heart and mind and kept talking and calming him down.

"Pharoah." It was a whisper as it dawned on him exactly what he did to me. He seemed to withdraw into himself.

"God is love, bruh. Eye like me. Everything! From the color and shape of my eyes to my slight buck teeth. My bisexuality resulted from experience and curiosity and circumstance. It was not predetermined from Mom's thoughts during painful child birth. Eye was not born with nuts on the brain. Embrace you, bruh. Eye don't believe the entire Bible. Eye question a lot of it. Eye don't trust what Caucasians rewrote and edited. But Eye do believe in God, the *Son* and the Holy Spirit. And Eye believe in myself."

"Pharoah." He reached out to touch me and Eye took his hand and squeezed it. "Eye don't know what to believe."

My eyes fluttered. "Eye'm so tired, Jennings. So tired of this. Eye'm exhausted, bruh. Eye'm high. Eye'm scared. Eye'm tired of arguing and fighting with people." Eye felt weak. Eye sunk to my knees and lowered my head because my head was about to spin.

"Pharoah, what's wrong?"

As if he had to ask. "Eye don't wanna write anymore books. Eye don't want this gift anymore. This is just too much."

"Pharoah." He tried to help me stand up but Eye wouldn't budge. My body was gradually shutting down from shock.

"Do you think Eye enjoy being bisexual or gay, whatever you wanna call it? No! Eye hate it. There's a time Eye wanted a wife and 12 kids because Eye have a huge family. Eye used to dream. Wanted the baddest bitch as my mate. But that's all it was. A dream. A fantasy. Imagery. Make believe." Deliberate creation…

Eye stared at my hands on my lap, about to fall on my face.

Eye continued, my voice weakening. "…Eye've been writing ever since Eye was a small child. Fourteen hours a day, right now of my life, goes into Creation. Eye've done this for the past three years! Eye'm done. Eye'm drained. Eye'm tired. Eye just need to rest." He got on his knees in front of me, cupping my hands and kissing them.

"Pharoah. Eye'm sorry, man. For all of this. For deceiving you. For abusing you. Eye'm so sorry, man." He seemed genuinely sorry, but how do you just forgive and let go of something that nearly killed you? Ultimately, Eye had to forgive him, and that's the bitter truth. He attacked me, brutally did shit to me and now what was Eye supposed to do? *Eye WANNA KILL HIM! Eye WANNA BASH HIS FACE IN!* But Eye didn't, because Eye matured in a lot of ways.

"Let me tell you about Job," Eye went on, looking up into his eyes. "He lost his health, land, animals, kids, money and family. But not once did he lose his faith in God.

"Eye know the story. My daddy used to be a Pa$tor, remember?" Eye struggled to stand up. He tried to help and Eye denounced it. Eye then stumbled past him. Growing weary of life and family and the art of war and the bickering and the arguing. My life ain't worth the handle Oprah flushed her piss with.

"Eye just want to be Pharoah again," Eye said cautiously. "Eye lost myself."

Eye started snatching books off his book shelves, throwing them on the floor. "Eye hate this shit! Eye hate writing. Free me of this shit! Eye AM STARTING TO HATE WIRITNG OH MY GOD! Eye give this shit up, Lord! Why did you choose me?"

Eye pushed over book shelves, watching them break apart. Books falling all over the place. Eye was kicking them, picking them up and ripping them in half. Eye was screaming, ripping out the pages and tossing the loose leaf pages over my head like they had minds of their own.

"PHAROAH! STOPPP!"

"Eye will NEVER write another book. Eye just want the voices in my head to stop talking to me. But Eye'm too obsessed with writing books!"

"Pharoah, man." He wrapped his arms around me. This time full of love and acceptance and understanding. Eye wasn't receptive to his touch. Eye was getting even sleepier. Drained. If he was gonna kill me then do it while Eye'm sleep. Eye have been through enough pain. Please, God.

"Pharoah," said Lord, holding on to me. "You are a strong man. Gifted. Talented. You help so many and give them your all. Eye'm sorry, again, man."

*Didn't you just try to kill me?* "Eye just wanna go to sleep. Mama hates me. Daddy didn't want me. People use me. But God loves me. Eye wanna go where God is."

He laid me on the floor.

"God protect me while Eye sleep. Just for a little while."

Eye closed my eyes.

*It took a while to convince* myself Eye was awake let alone still alive. But Eye had a migraine headache and warmth engulfed my face. My eyes weigh more than documented weight loss. Eye inhale deeply and slowly, with great resistance, open my eyes. They were itchy. Took awhile for the room to come into focus. Eye lay there, still and quiet. Taking the room in. My photos gone from the frames. The place was cleaned to a shine. Floors were mopped, bathroom cleaned and all the statuettes and books were put on the shelves. The ones Eye destroyed were in the trash. Standing up, Eye was naked. Where were my clothes? Eye kept hearing beeping noises. Eye looked over in the kitchen and Eye heard it again. The dryer had stopped.

Eye checked it and it was my clothes he washed. Eye smiled for some reason. "*Jennings…*" Then it all came back to me. The heroine. The cocaine he dumped on me. Drugging Hypnotiq and tricking me into playing a game called *Wolf*. Pushing my head into a pissy toilet. Dangling me over the balcony. Eye was nauseated. Holding my stomach, Eye walked throughout the condo.. There was no sign of him.

"Damn it! He locked me in this prison again!"

Eye approached the front door and tried to knob.

It turned, but Eye didn't get excited because the bolt was locked. Eye pulled on the door. It opened.

It was unlocked.

Sigh. Eye took one last look at a place, paradise, Eye was nearly urdered, and no one knew where Eye was. Eye gripped my bag, fighting tears. Eye survived. Eye smiled. Eye smiled big, showing all my teeth as y eyes glittered in the sunlight pouring over the breathtaking million dollar condo. Shaking my head the smile died from my face. "Goodbye. Eye turn my back on you, forever."

Eye closed the door and made my way to the elevator. Eye smiled when Eye pressed the Down button. Eye was looking forward to the fast swoosh downward, making my heart pitter patter in anticipation. Once the shiny silver doors snapped open, Eye gripped my bag again and walked on the magnificent ceramic flooring. Mirrors all around me, whispering something to me and Eye istenend, smiling even bigger as the doors closed. The ride was smooth. Eye closed my eyes and prayed. Thank you Jesus for saving my life. Amen. Suddenly, the lights went out and the elevator jerked. Eye didn't even scream. Eye smiled, and covered my heart. The mirrors whispered again, eight different darkened reflections telling me things eye already know. Eye love Jesus with all my heart, Eye believe in Him because of what he pulled me through nd the fact that the Big Bang Theory didn't ccreate 9 planets that orbits the sun.

Eye felt myself floating, and Eye smiled, my closed eyes keeping e safe. Eye heard a bell, and then a cool breeze cupped my face. Eye felt it in my toes as Eye walked off the elevator, for once in my life calling on God first when a potential problem arose on the elevator. And he was right on time. Hallelujah!

**Eye didn't know what the** future held for me, or if Eye would continue to write and create books or not. Eye left Jennings condo and took nothing with me. Eye left all the memo pads, the recordings and the photographs. Left it all behind like a pissy mattress on a street corner. Eye never heard from him again nor do Eye know what ever happened to him. Eye don't know if he believes in God or if he's still losing sleep over his thirst for vengeance. Eye never pressed charges nor did Eye call the police. The heroine he pumped into my body has been eradicated and everything Eye endured in that condo Eye wrote out of my mind and told myself Eye would never talk about. Yet sitting here typing this and reliving those candidly sinister moments, Eye have to admit that Eye cruise the Internet giving people the benefit of the doubt rather than being cautious about who Eye talk to. Jennings taught me something. He told me Eye'm too trusting. He told me everyone doesn't like me or my books, and this was confirmed when my cousin Y'vonia Payne sat me down and told me the same thing, back in July of 2010.

So it took a few months of practice, but Eye changed it. Eye don't allow everyone in my circle and Eye don't try to get in everyone's circle. Eye didn't know if my books will ever make the New York Times Bestseller's list. It used to be a goal of mine; you know we all should have goals. But going through and surviving the latest chapter in my life, battling Satan himself, my goal has changed.

Eye may never sit on *Oprah's* couch nor shoot a movie with Tyler Perry. No one may be interested in my life story. But one thing was for *sure*...Eye pray and then carve my own way. God guides and protects me. Eye am his instrument and he plays the Sax incredibly well. With Jehovah watching me, Eye will travel this road whether it twists onto the wrong path and have me doing Yields on One Way streets—or if it'll diverge in a yellow wood while Eye remain One Traveler…learning from mistakes as Eye make them. As Eye continue to write and release books, Eye will live by one code. **May no weapon formed against me prosper.**

**Haters and false idols, wizardry**, Astrology, voodoo and witch craft, the weakness of my flesh and my ass, mind and dick are weapons of Mass Destruction Satan uses artfully. After all…It's his Free Will. ..Eye will look to Jesus when faced with obstacles, and Eye will tank him even for the little things. After all, its my Free Will…. Vanity.

LORD JENNINGS
SELF DESTRUCT.
DUST...

GRAND HYATT, BUCK HEAD ATL

www.ingramcontent.com/pod-product-compliance
Lightning Source LLC
Chambersburg PA
CBHW020944310726
48980CB00001B/50

*9780578103686*